T0288608

BABYLON & SUMER

MYTHS & TALES

ANTHOLOGY OF CLASSIC TALES

Foreword by Fiona Collins

Associate Editor: Jason Emerson

FLAME TREE PUBLISHING

This is a FLAME TREE Book

Publisher & Creative Director: Nick Wells
Editorial Director: Catherine Taylor
Special thanks to: Jason Emerson and the ETCSL

Publisher's Note: Due to the historical nature of the classic text, we're aware that there may be some language used which has the potential to cause offence to the modern reader. However, wishing overall to preserve the integrity of the text, rather than imposing contemporary sensibilities, we have left it unaltered.

FLAME TREE PUBLISHING
6 Melbray Mews, Fulham,
London SW6 3NS, United Kingdom
www.flametreepublishing.com

First published 2024

24 26 28 27 25
1 3 5 7 9 10 8 6 4 2

ISBN: 978-1-80417-802-7
Special ISBN: 978-1-80417-947-5

The cover image is created by Flame Tree Studio based on artwork by Slava Gerj, Gabor Ruszkai and Dima Moroz. Internal decorations are courtesy Shutterstock.com and the following artists: Zvereva Yana and Karlionau (story headers).

A copy of the CIP data for this book is available from the British Library.

Printed and bound in China

BABYLON & SUMER MYTHS & TALES

ANTHOLOGY OF CLASSIC TALES

Foreword by Fiona Collins
Associate Editor: Jason Emerson

FLAME TREE PUBLISHING

Contents

Foreword

THIS BOOK contains ancient tales from two great cultures. Both were already long lost before Alexander the Great conquered the region, known to him and his fellow Greeks as Mesopotamia, in 332 BCE. How have these relics of a lost civilization survived since ancient times? Word of mouth can keep stories alive for hundreds of years, but only writing them down preserves them for thousands of years.

When Nineveh, Assyria's capital city, was sacked in 612 BCE, King Ashurbanipal's library was burnt down. A library of books would have been lost for ever. But the desert land between the Tigris and the Euphrates was too arid for trees, so paper was unknown, and thus this was a library of intricately marked clay tablets. The conflagration baked and preserved them. Though not destroyed, they became lost in the shifting sands of what is now modern Iraq. It was almost two thousand years before scholars found what was left, and even longer until they could decipher the cuneiform script and read what they had found. Once they could, they uncovered a treasure trove of stories.

One of these scholars was George Smith, a self-taught Assyriologist who worked in the British Museum in the 1860s, translating clay tablets. When he realized that a tablet he was reading contained a version of the Legend of the Flood, which predated the Old Testament by centuries, he was so excited that he ran around the room, tearing off his clothes.

That flood legend is to be found in this book. It's quite different from the story of the flood which Smith knew from his bible. It recounts a very different version of human relations with the gods. Though you may well prefer to keep your clothes on, I nonetheless hope that you will be as thrilled and intrigued by this, and the many other strange tales herein, as George Smith was then, as I am now.

My involvement, as a storyteller, with Sumerian myths and tales began in the early 1990s, when I began to tell the myths of the goddess Inanna. I have immersed myself in the stories and culture from which these legends come. I have found much that touches me in the stories: Inanna's Descent to the Nether World explores the experience of death and loss in a way that still resonates today. The Epic of Gilgamesh is a tale of friendship and commitment. The 'dialogues' offer glimpses into the everyday life of the Sumerian people, as they debate which is better: grain or sheep, summer or winter, the hoe or the plough?

In 1997, I attended a storytelling performance of The Epic of Gilgamesh, the oldest written story in existence, at the Iraqi Cultural Centre in London. As the storytelling ended, an audience member stood up. With tears in his eyes, he said: 'I was born 80 years ago, on Christmas Day, in Babylon. Listening to you tell this story has taken me back to my home and my childhood. I liked these stories then. And I like them now.'

A link was made that night between the scribes who had recorded the story in Sumerian, more than 4000 years ago, the twentieth-century storytellers who were telling it in English, and the exile, far from home, who was reminded of the stories he heard told in Arabic in his childhood home, not far from both modern Baghdad and the site of ancient Babylon.

The urge to tell stories is part of what it is to be human. These stories, from a culture utterly different from anything existing now, still have something to say to us, across hundreds of miles and thousands of years. This tells me that what we human beings have in common with each other outweighs the differences of time, culture, geography and language that divide us. I believe this is one of the most important understandings we can glean from these stories, first told by people long ago and far away.

Fiona Collins, PhD, MA
Traditional storyteller

Publisher's Note

WE OFFER THIS COLLECTION as a starting point for the general reader in your journey of discovery of ancient Mesopotamian mythology and civilization, a topic that may be new to many of you but which stretches back to one of the true cradles of civilization. Please note that, aside from the foreword and introduction, the main body of the book (including much of the introductory material) is a curated selection of mostly late-nineteenth- and early–mid-twentieth-century texts from noted Assyriologists and folklorists, along with extracts from an interesting historical novel by Margaret Potter Horton (1881–1911) offered as a complementary counterpoint. More about these scholars and writers can be found at the back of this book.

It should be thus remembered that these texts are of the era during which they were translated, interpreted and written. This means that contemporary mores are sometimes in effect, as well as conclusions and assumptions that have since been disproved or corrected through further discoveries and study. Nonetheless, these works provide interesting historiographical insight, and fascinating descriptions and narratives that will enthrall and encourage further reading.

EPIC
BABYLON
& SUMER
MYTHS & TALES
ANTHOLOGY OF CLASSIC TALES
Foreword by Fiona Collins
Associate Editor: Jason Emerson
FLAME TREE PUBLISHING
TALES

History, Religion & Myth

Introduction

FOR A LONG TIME Babylon was no more than a mighty name – a gigantic skeleton whose ribs protruded here and there from the sands of Syria in colossal ruin of tower and temple. But through the labours of a band of scholars and explorers whose lives and work must be classed as among the most romantic passages in the history of human effort we have been enabled to view the wondrous panorama of human civilization as it evolved in the valleys of the Tigris and Euphrates.

We are dealing with a race austere and stern, a race of rigorous religious devotees and conquerors, the Romans of the East – but not an unimaginative race, for the Babylonians and Assyrians came of that stock which gave to the world its greatest religions, Judaism, Christianity and Islam, a race not without the sense of mystery and science, for Babylon was the mother of astrology and magic, and established the beginnings of the study of the stars; and, lastly, of commerce, for the first true financial operations and the first houses of exchange were founded in the shadows of her temples and palaces.

The Akkadians

THE BOUNDARIES OF THE LAND where the races of Babylonia and Assyria evolved one of the most remarkable and original civilizations in the world's history are the two mighty rivers of Western Asia, the Tigris and Euphrates, Assyria being identical with the more northerly and mountainous portion, and Babylonia with the southerly part, which inclined to be flat and marshy. Both tracts of country were inhabited by people of the same race, save that the Assyrians had acquired the characteristics of a population dwelling in a hilly country and had become to some extent intermingled with Hittite and Amorite elements. But both were branches of an ancient Semitic stock, the epoch of whose entrance into the land it is impossible to fix. In the oldest inscriptions discovered we find those Semitic immigrants at strife with the indigenous people of the country, the Akkadians, with whom they were subsequently to mingle and whose beliefs and magical and occult conceptions especially they were afterward to incorporate with their own.

Who, then, were the Akkadians whom the Babylonian Semites came to displace but with whom they finally mingled? Great and bitter has been the controversy which has raged around the racial affinities of this people. Some have held that they were themselves of Semitic stock, others that they were of a race more nearly approaching the Mongol, the Lapp and the Basque. In such a book as this, the object of which is to present an account of the Babylonian mythology, it is unnecessary to follow the protagonists of either theory into the dark recesses where the conflict has led them. But the probability is that the Akkadians, who are usually represented upon their monuments as a beardless people with oblique eyes, were connected with that great Mongolian family which has thrown out tentacles from its original home in central Asia to the frozen regions of the Arctic, the north of Europe, the Turkish Empire, aye, and perhaps to America itself! Akkadian in its linguistic features and especially in its grammatical structure shows a resemblance to the Ural-Altaic group of languages which embraces Turkish and Finnish, and this is in itself good evidence that the people who spoke it belonged to that ethnic division. But the question is a thorny one, and pages, nay, volumes might be occupied in presenting the arguments for and against such a belief.

It was from the Akkadians, however, that the Babylonian Semites received the germs of their culture; indeed it may be avowed that this aboriginal people carried them well on the way toward civilization. Not only did they instruct the Semitic newcomers in the arts of writing and reading, but they strongly biased their religious beliefs, and so inspired them with the idea of the sanctity of their own faith that the later Babylonian priesthood preserved the old Akkadian tongue among them as a sacred language, just as the Roman priesthood has retained the use of the dead Latin speech. Indeed, the proper pronunciation of Akkadian was an absolute necessity to the successful performance of religious ritual, and it is passing strange to observe that the Babylonian priests composed new religious texts in a species of dog-Akkadian, just as the monks of the Middle Ages composed their writings in dog-Latin! – with such zeal have the religious in all ages clung to the cult of the ancient, the mystic and half-forgotten thing unknown to the vulgar.

When we first encounter Babylonian civilization we find it grouped round about two nuclei, Nippur in the North and Eridu in the South. The first had grown up around a sanctuary of the god En-lil, who held sway over the ghostly animistic spirits which at his bidding might pose as the friends or enemies of men. A more 'civilized' deity held sway at Eridu, which was the home of Ea, or Oannes, the god of light and wisdom, who exercised his knowledge of the healing art for the benefit of his votaries. From the waters of the Persian Gulf, whence he rose each morning, he brought knowledge of all manner of crafts and trades, arts and industries, for the behoof of his infant city, even the mystic and difficult art of impressing written characters on clay. It is a beautiful picture which we have from the old legend of this sea-born wisdom daily enlightening the life of the little white city near the waters. The Semites possessed a deep and almost instinctive love of wisdom. In the writings attributed to Solomon and in the rich and wondrous Psalms of David – those deep mines of song and sagacity – we find the glories of wisdom again and again extolled. Even yet there are few peoples among whom the love of scholarship, erudition and religious wisdom is more cultivated for its own sake than with the Jews.

These rather different cultures of the North and South, working toward a common centre, met and fused at a period prior to the commencement of history, and we even find the city of Ur, whence Abram came, a near neighbour of Eridu, colonized by Nippur! The culture of Eridu prevailed nevertheless, and its mightiest offshoot was the ultimate centre of Euphratean civilization – Babylon itself. The first founders of the city were undoubtedly of Sumerian stock – the expression 'Sumerian' being that in vogue among modern scholars for the older 'Akkadian', and therefore interchangeable with it.

The Semite Conquerors

IT WAS PROBABLY ABOUT THE TIME of the juncture of the civilizations of Eridu and Nippur that the Semites entered the country.

There are indications which lead to the belief that, as in the case of the Semitic immigrants in Egypt, they came originally from Arabia. The Semite readily accepted the Sumerian civilization which he found flourishing in the valley of the Euphrates, and adapted the Sumerian system of writing to his own language, in what manner will be indicated later. But the Sumerians themselves were not above borrowing from the rich Semitic tongue, and many of the earliest Sumerian texts we encounter are strongly Semitized. But although the Semites appear to have filtered into Sumerian territory by way of Eridu and Ur, the first definite notices we have of their presence within it are in the monuments of the more northern portion of that territory, in what is known as Akkad, in the neighbourhood of Bagdad, where they founded a small kingdom in much the same manner as the Jutes founded the kingdom of Kent. The earliest monuments, however, come from Lagash, the modern Tel-lo, some thirty miles north of Ur, and recount the dealings of the high-priest of that place with other neighbouring dignitaries. The priests of Lagash became kings, and their conquests extended beyond the confines of Babylonia to Elam on the east, and southward to the Persian Gulf.

Sargon, A Babylonian Conqueror

BUT THE FIRST GREAT SEMITIC EMPIRE in Babylonia was that founded by the famous Sargon of Akkad. As is the case with many popular heroes and monarchs whose deeds are remembered in song and story – for example, Perseus, OEdipus, Cyrus, Romulus and our own King Arthur – the early years of Sargon were passed in obscurity.

Sargon is, in fact, one of the 'fatal children'. He was, legend stated, born in concealment and sent adrift, like Moses, in an ark of bulrushes on the waters of the Euphrates, whence he was rescued and brought up by one Akki, a husbandman. But the time of his recognition at length arrived, and he received the crown of Babylonia. His foreign conquests were extensive. On four successive occasions he invaded Syria and Palestine, which he succeeded in welding into a single empire with Babylonia. Pressing his victories to the margin of the Mediterranean, he erected upon its shores statues of himself as an earnest of his conquests. He also overcame Elam and northern Mesopotamia and quelled a rebellion of some magnitude in his own dominions. His son, Naram-Sin, claimed for himself the title of 'King of the Four Zones', and enlarged the empire left him by his father, penetrating even into Arabia. A monument unearthed by J. de Morgan at Susa depicts him triumphing over the conquered Elamites. He is seen passing his spear through the prostrate body of a warrior whose hands are upraised as if pleading for quarter. His head-dress is ornamented with the horns emblematic of divinity, for the early Babylonian kings were the direct vicegerents of the gods on earth.

Even at this comparatively early time (*c.* 3800 BCE) the resources of the country had been well exploited by its Semitic conquerors, and their absorption of the Sumerian civilization had permitted them to make very considerable progress in the enlightened arts. Some of their work in bas-relief, and even in the lesser if equally difficult craft of gem-cutting, is among the finest efforts of Babylonian art. Nor were they deficient in more utilitarian fields. They constructed roads through the most important portions of the empire, along which a service of posts carried messages at stated intervals, the letters conveyed by these being stamped or franked by clay seals, bearing the name of Sargon.

The First Library in Babylonia

Sargon is also famous as the first founder of a Babylonian library. This library appears to have contained works of a most surprising nature, having regard to the period at which it was instituted. One of these was entitled *The Observations of Bel*, and consisted of no less than seventy-two books dealing with astronomical matters of considerable complexity; it registered and described the appearances of comets, conjunctions of the sun and moon, and the phases of the planet Venus, besides recording many eclipses. This wonderful book was long afterward translated into Greek by the Babylonian historian Berossus, and it demonstrates the great antiquity of Babylonian astronomical science even at this very early epoch. Another famous work contained in the library of Sargon dealt with omens, the manner of casting them, and their interpretation – a very important side-issue of Babylonian magico-religious practice.

Among the conquests of this great monarch, whose splendour shines through the shadows of antiquity like the distant flash of arms on a misty day, was the fair island of Cyprus. Even imagination reels at the well-authenticated assertion that 5,700 years ago the keels of a Babylonian conqueror cut the waves of the Mediterranean and landed upon the shores of flowery Cyprus stern Semitic warriors, who, loading themselves with loot, erected statues of their royal leader and returned with their booty. In a Cyprian temple Luigi Palma di Cesnola (1832–1904), the soldier, diplomat and amateur archaeologist, discovered, down in the lowest vaults, a haematite cylinder which described its owner as a servant of Naram-Sin, the son of Sargon, so that a certain degree of communication must have been kept up between Babylonia and the distant island, just as early Egypt and Crete were bound to each other by ties of culture and commerce.

The High-Priest Gudea

BUT THE EMPIRE which Sargon had founded was doomed to precipitate ruin. The seat of power was diverted southward to Ur. In the reign of Dungi, one of the monarchs who ruled from this southern sphere, a great vassal of the throne, Gudea, stands out as one of the most remarkable characters in early Babylonian antiquity.

This Gudea (*c.* 2700 BCE) was high-priest of Lagash, a city perhaps thirty miles north of Ur, and was famous as a patron of the architectural and allied arts. He ransacked western Asia for building materials. Arabia supplied him with copper for ornamentation, the Amames mountains with cedar-wood, the quarries of Lebanon with stone, while the deserts adjacent to Palestine furnished him with rich stones of all kinds for use in decorative work, and districts on the shores of the Persian Gulf with timber for ordinary building purposes. His architectural ability is vouched for by a plan of his palace, measured to scale, which is carved upon the lap of one of his statues in the Louvre.

Hammurabi the Great

LIKE THAT WHICH PRECEDED IT, the dynasty of Ur fell, and Arabian or Canaanite invaders usurped the royal power in much the same manner as the Shepherd Kings seized the sovereignty of Egypt. A subsequent foreign yoke, that of Elam, was thrown off by Hammurabi (also known as 'Khammurabi'), perhaps the most celebrated and most popularly famous name in Babylonian history.

This brilliant, wise and politic monarch did not content himself with merely expelling the hated Elamites, but advanced to further conquest with such success that in the thirty-second year of his reign (2338 BCE) he had formed Babylonia into a single monarchy with the capital at Babylon itself. Under the fostering care of Hammurabi, Babylonian art and literature unfolded and blossomed with a luxuriance surprising to contemplate at this distance of time. It is astonishing, too, to note how completely he succeeded in welding into one homogeneous whole the various elements of the empire he carved out for himself. So surely did he unify his conquests that the Babylonian power as he left it survived undivided for nearly 1,500 years. The welfare of his subjects of all races was constantly his care. No one satisfied of the justice of his cause feared to approach him. The legal code which he formulated and which remains as his greatest claim to the applause of posterity is a monument of wisdom and equity. If Sargon is to be regarded as the Arthur of Babylonian history surely Hammurabi is its Alfred. The circumstances of the lives of the two monarchs present a decidedly similar picture. Both had in their early years to free their country from a foreign yoke, both instituted a legal code, were patrons of letters and assiduous in their attention to the wants of their subjects.

If a great people has frequently evolved a legal code of sterling merit there are cases on record where such an institution has served to make a people great, and it is probably no injustice to the Semites of Babylonia to say of them that the code of Hammurabi made them what they were. A copy of this world-famous code was found at Susa by J. de Morgan, and is now in the Louvre.

A Court Murder

WHAT THE BABYLONIAN CHRONOLOGISTS called 'the First Dynasty of Babylon' fell in its turn, and it is claimed that a Sumerian line of eleven kings took its place. Their sway lasted for 368 years – a statement which is obviously open to question. These were themselves overthrown and a Kassite dynasty from the mountains of Elam was founded by Kandis (*c.* 1780 BCE) which lasted for nearly six centuries. These alien monarchs failed to retain their hold on much of the Asiatic and Syrian territory which had paid tribute to Babylon and the suzerainty of Palestine was likewise lost to them. It was at this epoch, too, that the high-priests of Asshur in the north took the title of king, but they appear to have been subservient to Babylon in some degree. Assyria grew gradually in power. Its people were hardier and more warlike than the art-loving and religious folk of Babylon, and little by little they encroached upon the weakness of the southern kingdom until at length an affair of tragic proportions entitled them to direct interference in Babylonian politics.

The circumstances which necessitated this intervention are not unlike those of the assassination of King Alexander of Serbia and Draga, his Queen, that happened 3,000 years later. The Kassite king of Babylonia had married the daughter of Assur-yuballidh of Assyria. But the match did not meet with the approval of the Kassite faction at court, which murdered the bridegroom-king. This atrocious act met with swift vengeance at the hands of Assur-yuballidh of Assyria, the bride's father, a monarch of active and statesmanlike qualities, the author of the celebrated series of letters to Amen-hetep IV of Egypt, unearthed at Tel-el-Amarna. He led a punitive army into Babylonia, hurled from the throne the pretender placed there by the Kassite faction, and replaced him with a scion of the legitimate royal stock. This king, Burna-buryas, reigned for over twenty years, and upon his decease the Assyrians, still nominally the vassals of the Babylonian Crown, declared themselves independent of it. Not content with such a revolutionary measure, under Shalmaneser I (1300 BCE) they laid claim to the suzerainty of the Tigris-Euphrates region, and extended their conquests even to the boundaries of far Cappadocia, the Hittites and numerous other confederacies submitting to their yoke. Shalmaneser's son, Tukulti-in-Aristi, took the city of Babylon, slew its king, Bitilyasu, and thus completely shattered the claim of the older state to supremacy. He had reigned in Babylon for some seven years when he was faced by a popular revolt, which seems to have been headed by his own son, Assur-nazir-pal, who slew him and placed Hadad-nadin-akhi on the throne. This king conquered and killed the Assyrian monarch of his time, Bel-kudur-uzur, the last of the old Assyrian royal line, whose death necessitated the institution of a new dynasty, the fifth monarch of which was the famous Tiglath-pileser I.

Tiglath-Pileser

TIGLATH-PILESER, or Tukulti-pal-E-sana, to confer on him his full Assyrian title, came to the throne about 1120 BCE, and soon commenced the career of active conquest which was to render his name one of the most famous in the warlike annals of Assyria.

Campaigns in the Upper Euphrates against alien immigrants who had settled there were followed by the conquest of the Hittites of Subarti, in Assyrian territory. Pressing northward toward Lake Van in the Kurdish country he subsequently turned his arms westward and overran Malatia. Cappadocia and the Aramaeans of Northern Syria next felt the force of his arms, and he penetrated on this occasion even to the sources of the Tigris. He left behind him the character of a great warrior, a great hunter and a great builder, restoring the semi-ruinous temples of Asshur and Hadad or Rimmon in the city of Asshur.

It is not until the reign of Assur-nazir-pal III (*c.* 883 BCE) that we are once more enabled to take up the thread of Assyrian history with any degree of certainty. In this reign artistic development appears to have proceeded apace; but it cannot be said of Assur-nazir-pal that in him culture went hand in hand with humanity, the records of his cruelties being long and revolting. His successor, Shalmaneser II, possessed an insatiable thirst for military glory, and during his reign of thirty-five years overthrew a great confederacy of Syrian chiefs which included Ahab, King of Israel. He was disturbed during the latter part of his reign by the rebellion of his eldest son. But his second son, Samsi-Rammon, came to his father's assistance, and his faithful adherence secured him the succession to the throne in 824 BCE.

Semiramis the Great

IT WAS PROBABLY IN THE REIGN of Tiglath-pileser that the queen known in legend as Semiramis lived. It would have been wonderful indeed had the magic of her name not been connected with romance by the Oriental imagination. Semiramis! The name sparkles and scintillates with gems of legend and song. Myth, magic and music encircle it and sweep round it as fairy seas surround some island paradise. It is a central rose in the chaplet of legend, it has been enshrined in music perhaps the most divine and melodious which the songful soul of Italy has ever conceived – yet not more beauteous than itself.

Let us introduce into the iron chain of Assyrian history the golden link of the legend of this Helen of the East, and having heard the fictions of her greatness let us attempt to remove the veils which hide her real personality from view and look upon her as she was – Sammuramat the Babylonian, queen and favourite of Samsi-Rammon, who crushed the assembled armies of Media and Chaldea, and whose glories are engraved upon a column which, setting forth the tale of her conquests, describes her in all simplicity as "A woman of the palace of Samsi-Rammon, King of the World".

Legend says that Ninus, King of Assyria, having conquered the Babylonians, proceeded toward Armenia with the object of reducing the people of that country. But its politic king, Barsanes, unable to meet him by armed force, made a voluntary submission, accompanied by presents of such magnificence that Ninus was placated. But, insatiable in his desire for conquest, he turned his eyes to Media, which he speedily subdued. His next ambition was to bring under his rule the territory between the Tanais and the Nile. This great task occupied him for no less than seventeen years, by which time all Asia had submitted to him, with the single exception of Bactria, which still maintained its independence. Having laid the foundations of the city of Nineveh, he resolved to proceed against the Bactrians. His army was of dimensions truly mythical, for he was said to be accompanied by 7,000,000 of infantrymen, 2,000,000 of horse-soldiers, with the addition of 200,000 chariots equipped with scythes.

It was during this campaign, says Diodorus Siculus, that Ninus first beheld Semiramis. Her precise legendary or mythical origin is obscure. Some writers aver that she was the daughter of the fish-goddess Ataryatis, or Derketo, and Oannes, the Babylonian god of wisdom, who has already been alluded to. Ataryatis was a goddess of Ascalon in Syria, and after birth her daughter Semiramis was miraculously fed by doves until she was found by one Simmas, the royal shepherd, who brought her up and married her to Onnes, or Menon, one of Ninus's generals. He fell by his own hand, and Ninus thereupon took Semiramis to wife, having profoundly admired her ever since her conduct at the capture of Bactria, where she had greatly distinguished herself. Not long afterward Ninus died, leaving a son called Ninyas.

During her son's minority Semiramis assumed the regency, and the first great work she undertook was the interment of her husband, whom she buried with great splendour, and raised over him a mound of earth no less than a mile and a quarter high and proportionally wide, after which she built Babylon. This city being finished, she made an expedition into Media; and wherever she went left memorials of her power and munificence. She erected vast structures, forming lakes and laying out gardens of great extent, particularly in Chaonia and

Ecbatana. In short, she levelled hills, and raised mounds of an immense height, which retained her name for ages. After this she invaded Egypt and conquered Ethiopia, with the greater part of Libya; and having accomplished her wish, and there being no enemy to cope with her, excepting the kingdom of India, she resolved to direct her forces toward that quarter. She had an army of 3,000,000 foot, 500,000 horse and 100,000 chariots. For the passing of rivers and engaging the enemy by water she had procured 2000 ships, to be so constructed as to be taken to pieces for the advantage of carriage: which ships were built in Bactria by men from Phoenicia, Syria and Cyprus. With these she fought a naval engagement with Strabrobates, King of India, and at the first encounter sunk 1,000 of his ships. After this she built a bridge over the river Indus, and penetrated into the heart of the country. Here Strabrobates engaged her. Being deceived by the numerous appearance of her elephants, he at first gave way, for being deficient in those animals she had procured the hides of 3,000 black oxen, which, being properly sewn and stuffed with straw, presented the appearance of so many elephants. All this was done so naturally that even the real elephants of the Indian king were deceived. But the stratagem was at last discovered, and Semiramis was obliged to retreat, after having lost a great part of her army. Soon after this she resigned the government to her son Ninyas, and died. According to some writers, she was slain by his hand.

It was through the researches of Professor Lehmann-Haupt of Berlin that the true personal significance of Semiramis was recovered. Until the year 1910 the legends of Diodorus and others were held to have been completely disproved and Semiramis was regarded as a purely mythical figure. Jacob Bryant (1715–1804) in his *Ancient Mythology*, published at the beginning of the nineteenth century, proves the legendary status of Semiramis to his own satisfaction. He says: "It must be confessed that the generality of historians have represented Semiramis as a woman, and they describe her as a great princess who reigned in Babylon; but there are writers who from their situation had opportunities of better intelligence, and by those she is mentioned as a deity. The Syrians, says Athenagoras, worshipped Semiramis, and adds that she was esteemed the daughter of Dercatus and the same as the Suria Dea.... Semiramis was said to have been born at Ascalon because Atargatus was there worshipped under the name of Dagon, and the same memorials were preserved there as at Hierapolis and Babylon. These memorials related to a history of which the dove was the principal type. It was upon the same account that she was said to have been changed to a dove because they found her always depicted and worshipped under that form.... From the above I think it is plain that Semiramis was an emblem and that the name was a compound of Sama-ramas, or ramis, and it signified 'the divine token', a type of providence, and as a military ensign, (for as such it was used) it may with some latitude be interpreted 'the standard of the most High'. It consisted of the figure of a dove, which was probably encircled with the iris, as those two emblems were often represented together. All who went under that standard, or who paid any deference to that emblem, were styled Semarim or Samorim. It was a title conferred upon all who had this device for their national insigne".

There is much more of this sort of thing, typical of the mythic science of the eighteenth and early nineteenth centuries. It is easy to see how myth became busy with the name of the Assyrian Queen, whose exploits undoubtedly aroused the enthusiasm not only of the Assyrians themselves but of the peoples surrounding them. Just as any great work in ancient Britain was ascribed to the agency of Merlin or Arthur, so such monuments as could not otherwise be accounted for were attributed to Semiramis. Western Asia is monumentally eloquent of her name, and even the Behistun inscriptions of Darius have been placed to her credit. Herodotus states that one of the gates of Babylon was called after her, and that she raised the artificial banks that confined the river Euphrates. Her fame lasted until well into the Middle Ages, and the Armenians called the district round Lake Van, Shamiramagerd.

There is very little doubt that her fame became mingled with that of the goddess Ishtar: she possesses the same Venus-like attributes, the dove is her emblem, and her story became so inextricably intertwined with that of the Babylonian goddess that she ultimately became a variant of her. The story of Semiramis is a triumphant vindication of the manner in which by certain mythical processes a human being can attain the rank of a god or goddess, for Semiramis was originally very real indeed. A column discovered in 1909 describes her as "a woman of the palace of Samsi-rammon, King of the World, King of Assyria, King of the Four Quarters of the World". This dedication indicates that Semiramis, or, to give her her Assyrian title, Sammuramat, evidently possessed an immense influence over her husband, Samsi-rammon, and that perhaps as queen-mother that influence lasted for more than one reign, so that the legend that after a regency of forty-two years she delivered up the kingdom to her son, Ninyas, may have some foundation in fact. She seems to have made war against the Medes and Chaldeans. The story that on relinquishing her power she turned into a dove and disappeared may mean that her name, Sammuramat, was easily connected with the Assyrian *summat*, the word for 'dove'; and for a person of her subsequent legendary fame the mythical connection with Ishtar is easily accounted for.

The Second Assyrian Empire

WHAT IS KNOWN AS the Second Assyrian Empire commenced with the reign of Tiglath-pileser III, who organized a great scheme of provincial government. This plan appears to have been the first forecast of the feudal system, for each province paid a fixed tribute and provided a military contingent.

Great efforts were made to render the army as irresistible as possible with the object of imposing an Assyrian supremacy upon the entire known world. Tiglath overran Armenia, defeated the Medes and Hittites, seized the seaports of Phoenicia and the trade routes connecting them with the centres of Assyrian commerce, and finally conquered Babylon, where in 729 BCE he was invested with the sovereignty of 'Asia'. Two years later he died, but his successor, Shalmaneser IV, carried on the policy he had initiated. He had, however, only five years of life in which to do so, for at the end of that period the usurping general Sargon, who laid claim to be a descendant of Sargon the Great of Akkad, seized the royal power of Babylon. He was murdered in 705 BCE, and his son Sennacherib, of Biblical fame, appears to have been unable to carry on affairs with the prudence or ability of his father. He outraged the religious feelings of the people by razing to the ground the city of Babylon, because of the revolt of the citizens. The campaign he made against Hezekiah, King of Judah, was marked by a complete failure. Hezekiah had allied himself with the Philistine princes of Ascalon and Ekron, but when he saw his Egyptian allies beaten at the battle of Eltekeh he endeavoured to buy off the invaders by numerous presents, though without success.

The wonderful deliverance of Jerusalem from the forces of Sennacherib, recorded in Scripture, and sung by Byron in his *Hebrew Melodies*, appears to have a good foundation in fact. It seems that the Assyrian army was attacked and almost decimated by plague, which obliged Sennacherib to return to Nineveh, but it is not likely that the phenomenon occurred in the watch of a night. Sennacherib was eventually murdered by his two sons, who, the deed accomplished, fled to Armenia. Of all the Assyrian monarchs he was perhaps the most pompous and the least fitted to rule. The great palace at Nineveh and the great wall of that city, eight miles in circumference, were built at his command.

His son and successor, Esar-haddon, initiated his reign by sending back the sacred image of Merodach to its shrine at Babylon, which city he restored. He was solemnly declared king in the restored temple of Merodach, and during his reign both Babylonia and Assyria enjoyed quiet and contentment. War with Egypt broke out in 670 BCE, and the Egyptians were thrice defeated with heavy loss. The Assyrians entered Memphis and instituted a protectorate over part of the country. Two years later Egypt revolted, and while marching to quell the outbreak Esar-haddon died on the road – his fate resembling that of Edward I, who died while on his way to overcome the Scottish people, then in rebellion against his usurpation.

Assur-bani-pal: Sardanapalus the Splendid?

ESAR-HADDON WAS SUCCEEDED by Assur-bani-pal, known to Greek legend as Sardanapalus. How far the legendary description of him squares with the historical it is difficult to say. The former states that he was the last king of Assyria, and the thirtieth in succession from Ninyas. Effeminate and corrupt, he seems to have been a perfect example of the *roi fainéant*. The populace of the conquered provinces, disgusted with his extravagances, revolted, and an army led by Arbaces, satrap of Medea, and Belesys, a Babylonian priest, surrounded him in Nineveh and threatened his life. Sardanapalus, however, throwing off his sloth, made such a vigorous defence that for two years the issue was in doubt. The river Tigris at this juncture overflowed and undermined part of the city wall, thus permitting ingress to the hostile army. Sardanapalus, seeing that resistance was hopeless, collected his wives and treasures in his palace and then set it on fire, so that all perished.

It is a strange coincidence that the fate which legend ascribes to Sardanapalus was probably that which really overtook the brother of Assur-bani-pal, Samas-sum-yukin. It is likely that the self-immolation of Sardanapalus is merely a legendary statement of a rite well known to Semitic religion, which was practised at Tarsus down to the time of Dio Chrysostom, and the memory of which survives in other Greek legends, especially those of Heracles-Melcarth and Queen Dido. At Tarsus an annual festival was held and a pyre erected upon which the local Heracles or Baal was burned in effigy. This annual commemoration of the death of the god in fire probably had its origin in the older rite in which an actual man or sacred animal was burned as representing the deity.

The Golden Bough contains an instructive passage concerning the myth of Sardanapalus. Sir James Frazer writes: "There seems to be no doubt that the name Sardanapalus is only the Greek way of representing Ashurbanapal, the name of the greatest and nearly the last King of Assyria. But the records of the real monarch which have come to light within recent years give little support to the fables that attached to his name in classical tradition. For they prove that, far from being the effeminate weakling he seemed to the Greeks of a later age, he was a warlike and enlightened monarch, who carried the arms of Assyria to distant lands and fostered at home the growth of science and letters. Still, though the historical reality of King Ashurbanapal is as well attested as that of Alexander or Charlemagne, it would be no wonder if myths gathered, like clouds, around the great figure that loomed large in the stormy sunset of Assyrian glory. Now the two features that stand out most prominently in the legends of Sardanapalus are his extravagant debauchery and his violent death in the flames of a great pyre, on which he burned himself and his concubines to save them from falling into the hands of his victorious enemies. It is said that the womanish king, with painted face and arrayed in female attire, passed his days in the seclusion of the harem, spinning purple wool among his concubines and wallowing in sensual delights; and that in the epitaph which he caused to be carved on his tomb he recorded that all the days of his life he ate and drank and toyed, remembering that life is short and full of trouble, that fortune is uncertain, and that others would soon enjoy the good things which he must leave behind. These traits bear little resemblance to the portrait of Ashurbanapal either in life or death; for after a brilliant career of conquest the Assyrian king died in old age, at the height of human ambition, with peace at home and triumph abroad, the admiration of his subjects and the terror of his foes. But if the traditional characteristics of Sardanapalus harmonize but ill with what we know of the real monarch of that name, they fit well enough with all that we know or can conjecture of the mock kings who led a short life and a merry during the revelry of the Sacaea, the Asiatic equivalent of the Saturnalia. We can hardly doubt that for the most part such men, with death staring them in the face at the end of a few days, sought to drown care and deaden fear by plunging madly into all the fleeting joys that still offered themselves under the sun. When their brief pleasures and sharp sufferings were over, and their bones or ashes mingled with the dust, what more natural that on their tomb – those mounds in which the people saw, not untruly, the graves of the lovers of Semiramis – there should be carved some such lines as those which tradition placed in the mouth of the great Assyrian king, to remind the heedless passer-by of the shortness and vanity of life?"

According to Sir James Frazer, then, the real Sardanapalus may have been one of those mock kings who led a short but merry existence before a sacrifice ended their convivial career. We have analogous instances in the sacrifice of Sandan at Tarsus and that of the representative of the Mexican god, Tezcatlipoca. The legend of Sardanapalus is thus a distorted reminiscence of the death of a magnificent king sacrificed in name of a god.

When the real Assur-bani-pal succeeded Esar-haddon as King of Assyria, his brother Samas-sum-yukin was created Viceroy of Babylonia, but shortly after he claimed the kingship itself, revived the old Sumerian language as the official tongue of the Babylonian court, and initiated a revolt which shook the Assyrian empire from one end to the other. A great struggle ensued between the northern and southern powers, and at last Babylon was forced to surrender through starvation, and Samas-sum-yukin was put to death.

Assur-bani-pal, like Sardanapalus, his legendary counterpart, found himself surrounded by enemies. Having conquered Elam as well as Babylonia, he had to face the inroads of hordes of

Scythians, who poured over his frontiers. He succeeded in defeating and slaying one of their chiefs, Dugdamme, whom in an inscription he calls a "limb of Satan", but shortly after this he died himself. His empire was already in a state of decay, and had not long to stand.

The First Great Library

BUT IF ASSUR-BANI-PAL WAS EFFEMINATE and lax in government, he was the first great patron of literature. It is to his magnificent library at Nineveh that we owe practically all that we have preserved of the literature that was produced in Babylonia. He saw that the southern part of his empire was far more intellectual and cultured than Assyria, and he despatched numerous scribes to the temple schools of the south, where they copied extensively from their archives every description of literary curiosity – hymns, legends, medical prescriptions, myths and rituals were all included in the great library at Nineveh. These have been restored to us through the labours of the archaeologists Sir Austen Henry Layard (1817–94) and Hormuzd Rassam (1826–1910). It is a most extraordinary instance of antiquarian zeal in an epoch which we regard as not far distant from the beginnings of verifiable history.

Nearly 20,000 fragments of brick, bearing the results of Assur-bani-pal's researches, are housed in the British Museum, and this probably represents only a portion of his entire collection. Political motives have been attributed to Assur-bani-pal in thus bringing together such a great library. It has been argued that he desired to make Assyria the centre of the religious influence of the empire. This woulddderogate greatly from the view that sees in him a king solely fired with the idea of preserving and retaining all that was best in ancient Babylonian literature in the north as well as in the south, and having beside him for his own personal use those records which many circumstances prove he was extremely desirous of obtaining. Thus we find him sending officials on special missions to obtain copies of certain works. It is also significant that Assur-bani-pal placed his collection in a library and not in a temple – a fact which discounts the theory that his collection of literature had a religious-political basis.

The Last Kings of Assyria

AFTER THE DEATH of Assur-bani-pal, the Scythians succeeded in penetrating into Assyria, through which they pushed their way as far as the borders of Egypt, and the remains of the Assyrian army took refuge in Nineveh.

The end was now near at hand. The last King of Assyria was probably Sin-sar-iskin, the Sarakos of the Greeks, who reigned for some years and who even tells us through the medium of inscriptions that he intended to restore the ruined temples of his land. War broke out with Babylonia, however, and Cyaxares, the Scythian King of Ecbatana, came to the assistance of the Babylonians. Nineveh was captured by the Scythians, sacked and destroyed, and the Assyrian empire was at an end.

Nebuchadnezzar

BUT STRANGELY ENOUGH the older seat of power, Babylon, still flourished to some extent. By superhuman exertions, Nebuchadnezzar II (or Nebuchadrezzar), who reigned for forty-three years, sent the standard of Babylonia far and wide through the known world. In 567 BCE he invaded Egypt. In one of his campaigns he marched against Jerusalem and put its king, Jehoiakim, to death, but the king whom the Babylonian monarch set up in his place was deposed and the royal power vested in Zedekiah. Zedekiah revolted in 558 BCE and once more Jerusalem was taken and destroyed, the principal inhabitants were carried captive to Babylon, and the city was reduced to a condition of insignificance.

This, the first exile of the Jews, lasted for seventy years. The story of this captivity and of Nebuchadnezzar's treatment of the Jewish exiles is graphically told in the Book of Daniel, whom the Babylonians called Belteshazzar. Daniel refused to eat the meat of the Babylonians, probably because it was not prepared according to Jewish rite. He and his companions ate pulse and drank water, and fared upon it better than the Babylonians on strong meats and wines. The King, hearing of this circumstance, sent for them and found them much better informed than all his magicians and astrologers. Nebuchadnezzar dreamed dreams, and informed the Babylonian astrologers that if they were unable to interpret them they would be cut to pieces and their houses destroyed, whereas did they interpret the visions they would be held in high esteem. They answered that if the King would tell them his dream they would show the interpretation thereof; but the King said that if they were wise men in truth they would know the dream without requiring to be told it, and upon some of the astrologers of the court replying that the request was unreasonable, he was greatly incensed and ordered all of them to be slain. But in a vision of the night the secret was revealed to Daniel, who begged that the wise men of Babylon be not destroyed, and going to a court official he offered to interpret the dream. He told the King that in his dream he had beheld a great image, whose brightness and form were terrible. The head of this image was of fine gold, the breast and arms of silver, and the other parts of brass, excepting the legs which were of iron, and the feet which were partly of that metal and partly of clay. But a stone was cast at it which smote the image upon its feet and it brake into pieces and the wind swept away the remnants. The stone that had smitten it became a great mountain and filled the whole earth.

Then Daniel proceeded to the interpretation. The King, he said, represented the golden head of the image; the silver an inferior kingdom which would rise after Nebuchadnezzar's death; and a third of brass which should bear rule over all the earth. The fourth dynasty from Nebuchadnezzar would be as strong as iron, but since the toes of the image's feet were partly of iron and partly of clay, so should that kingdom be partly strong and partly broken. Nebuchadnezzar was so awed with the interpretation that he fell upon his face and worshipped Daniel, telling him how greatly he honoured the God who could have revealed such secrets to him; and he set him as ruler over the whole province of Babylon, and made him chief of the governors over all the wise men of that kingdom.

But Daniel's three companions – Shadrach, Meshach and Abednego – refused to worship a golden image which the King had set up, and he commanded that they should be cast into a fiery furnace, through which they passed unharmed.

This circumstance still more turned the heart of Nebuchadnezzar in the direction of the God of Israel. A second dream which he had, he begged Daniel to interpret. He said he had seen a tree in the midst of the earth of more than natural height, which flourished and was exceedingly strong, so that it reached to heaven. So abundant was the fruit of this tree that it provided meat for the whole earth, and so ample its foliage that the beasts of the field had shadow under it, and the fowls of the air dwelt in its midst. A spirit descended from heaven and called aloud, demanding that the tree should be cut down and its leaves and fruit scattered, but that its roots should be left in the earth surrounded by a band of iron and brass. Then, ordering that the tree should be treated as if it were a man, the voice of the spirit continued to ask that it should be wet with the dew of heaven, and that its portion should be with the beasts in the grass of the earth. "Let his heart be changed from a man's", said the voice, "and let a beast's heart be given him; and let seven times pass over him".

Then was Daniel greatly troubled. He kept silence for a space until the King begged him to take heart and speak. The tree, he announced, represented Nebuchadnezzar himself, and what had happened to it in the vision would come to pass regarding the great King of Babylon. He would be driven from among men and his dwelling would be with the beasts of the field. He would be made to eat grass as oxen and be wet with the dew of heaven, and seven times would pass over him, till he knew and recognized that the Most High ruled in the kingdom of man and gave it to whomsoever he desired.

Twelve months after this Nebuchadnezzar was in the midst of his palace at Babylon, boasting of what he had accomplished during his reign, when a voice from heaven spoke, saying: "O King Nebuchadnezzar, to thee it is spoken, the kingdom is departed from thee", and straightway was Nebuchadnezzar driven from man and he did eat grass as an ox and his body was wet with the dew of heaven, till his hair was grown like eagle's feathers and his nails like bird's claws.

At the termination of his time of trial Nebuchadnezzar lifted his eyes to heaven, and praising the Most High admitted his domination over the whole earth. Thus was the punishment of the boaster completed.

It has been stated with some show of probability that the judgment upon Nebuchadnezzar was connected with that weird disease known as lycanthropy, from the Greek words *lukos*, a wolf, and *anthropos*, a man. It develops as a kind of hysteria and is characterized by a belief on the part of the victim that he has become an animal. There are, too, cravings for strange food, and the afflicted person runs about on all fours. Among primitive peoples such a seizure is ascribed to supernatural agency, and garlic or onion – the common scourge of vampires – is held to the nostrils.

The Last of the Babylonian Kings

NABONIDUS (555–539 BC) was the last of the Babylonian kings – a man of a very religious disposition and of antiquarian tastes. He desired to restore the temple of the moon-god at Harran and to restore such of the images of the gods as had been removed to the ancient shrines. But first he desired to find out whether this procedure would meet with the approval of the god Merodach.

To this end he consulted the augurs, who opened the liver of a sheep from which they drew favourable omens. But on another occasion he aroused the hostility of the god and incidentally of the priests of E-Sagila by preferring the sun-god to the great Bel of Babylon. He tells us in an inscription that when restoring the temple of Shamash at Sippar he had great difficulty in unearthing the old foundation-stone, and that, when at last it was unearthed, he trembled with awe as he read thereon the name of Naram-sin, who, he says, ruled 3,200 years before him. But destiny lay in wait for him, for Cyrus the Persian invaded Babylonia in 538 BCE, and after defeating the native army at Opis he pressed on to Babylon, which he entered without striking a blow. Nabonidus was in hiding, but his place of concealment was discovered. Cyrus, pretending to be the avenger of Bel-Merodach for the slights the unhappy Nabonidus had put upon the god, had won over the people, who were exceedingly angry with their monarch for attempting to remove many images of the gods from the provinces to the capital. Cyrus placed himself upon the throne of Babylon and about a year before his death (529 BCE) transferred the regal power to his son, Cambyses. Assyrian-Babylonian history here ceases and is merged into Persian. Babylonia recovered its independence after the death of Darius. A king styling himself Nebuchadnezzar III arose, who reigned for about a year (521–520 BCE), at the end of which time the Persians once more returned as conquerors. A second revolt in 514 BCE caused the partial destruction of the walls, and finally the great city of Babylon became little better than a quarry out of which the newer city of Seleucia and other towns were built.

The History of Berossus

IT WILL BE OF INTEREST to examine at least one of the ancient authorities upon Babylonian history. Berossus, a priest of Bel at Babylon, who lived about 250 BCE, compiled from native documents a history of his country, which he published in Greek. His writings have perished, but extracts from them have been preserved by Josephus and Eusebius.

There is a good deal of myth in Berossus' work, especially when he deals with the question of cosmology, the story of the deluge, and so forth; also the 'facts' which he places before us as history cannot be reconciled with those inscribed on the monuments. He seems indeed to have arranged his history so that it should exactly fill the assumed period of 36,000 years, beginning with the creation of man and ending with the conquest of Babylon by Alexander the Great. Berossus tells of a certain Sisuthrus (Ut-Napishtim), whose history will be recounted in full in another chapter. He then relates a legend of the advent of the fish-man or fish-god, Oannes, from the waters of the Persian Gulf. Indeed he alludes to three beings of this type, who, one after another, appeared to instruct the Babylonians in arts and letters.

Berossus' Account of the Deluge

MORE IMPORTANT is his account of the deluge. There is more than one Babylonian version of the deluge: that which is to be found in the *Gilgamesh Epic*, and Berossus' account. As the latter is quite as important, we shall give it in his own words:

"After the death of Ardates, his son (Sisuthrus) succeeded and reigned eighteen sari. In his time happened the great deluge; the history of which is given in this manner. The Deity, Cronus, appeared to him in a vision; and gave him notice, that upon the fifteenth day of the month Daesius there would be a flood, by which mankind would be destroyed. He therefore enjoined him to commit to writing a history of the beginning, procedure and final conclusion of all things, down to the present term; and to bury these accounts securely in the City of the Sun at Sippara. He then ordered Sisuthrus to build a vessel, and to take with him into it his friends and relations; and trust himself to the deep. The latter implicitly obeyed: and having conveyed on board everything necessary to sustain life, he took in also all species of animals, that either fly, or rove upon the surface of the earth. Having asked the Deity where he was to go, he was answered, To the gods: upon which he offered up a prayer for the good of mankind. Thus he obeyed the divine admonition: and the vessel, which he built, was five stadia in length, and in breadth two. Into this he put everything which he had got ready; and last of all conveyed into it his wife, children and friends.

"After the flood had been upon the earth, and was in time abated, Sisuthrus sent out some birds from the vessel; which not finding any food, nor any place to rest their feet, returned to him again. After an interval of some days; he sent them forth a second time: and they now returned with their feet tinged with mud. He made trial a third time with these birds: but they returned to him no more: from whence he formed a judgment, that the surface of the earth was now above the waters. Having therefore made an opening in the vessel, and finding upon looking out, that the vessel was driven to the side of a mountain, he immediately quitted it, being attended with his wife, children and the pilot. Sisuthrus immediately paid his adoration to the earth: and having constructed an altar, offered sacrifices to the gods. These things being duly performed, both Sisuthrus, and those who came out of the vessel with him, disappeared. They, who remained in the vessel, finding that the others did not return, came out with many lamentations and called continually on the name of Sisuthrus. Him they saw no more; but they could distinguish his voice in the air, and could hear him admonish them to pay due regard to the gods; and likewise inform them, that it was upon account of his piety that he was translated to live with the gods; that his wife and children, with the pilot, had obtained the same honour. To this he added, that he would have them make the best of their way to Babylonia, and search for the writings at Sippara, which were to be made known to all mankind. The place where these things happened was in Armenia. The remainder having heard these words, offered sacrifices to the gods; and, taking a circuit, journeyed towards Babylonia".

Berossus adds that the remains of the vessel were to be seen in his time upon one of the Corcyrean mountains in Armenia; and that people used to scrape off the bitumen, with which it had been outwardly coated, and made use of it by way of an antidote for poison or amulet. In this manner they returned to Babylon; and having found the writings at Sippara, they set about building cities and erecting temples; and Babylon was thus inhabited again.

The Tower of Babel

MANY ATTEMPTS HAVE BEEN MADE to attach the legend of the confusion of tongues to certain ruined towers in Babylonia, especially to that of E-Sagila, the great temple of Merodach, and some remarks upon this most interesting tale may not be out of place at this point.

The myth is not found in Babylonia itself, and in its best form may be discovered in Scripture. In the Bible story we are told that every region was of one tongue and mode of speech. As men journeyed westward from their original home in the East, they encountered a plain in the land of Shinar where they settled. In this region they commenced building operations, constructed a city and laid the foundations of a tower, the summit of which they hoped would reach to heaven itself. It would appear that this edifice was constructed with the object of serving as a great landmark to the people so that they should not be scattered over the face of the earth, and the Lord came down to view the city and the tower, and he considered that as they were all of one language this gave them undue power, and that what they imagined to themselves under such conditions they would be able to achieve. So the Lord scattered them abroad over the face of every region, and the building of the tower ceased and the name of it was called 'Babel', because at that place the single language of the people was confounded. Of course it is merely the native name of Babylon, which translated means 'gate of the god', and has no such etymology as the Scriptures pretend, – the Hebrews confusing their verb *balal* 'to confuse or confound', with the word *babel*.

Nimrod, the Mighty Hunter

IT IS STRANGE that the dispersion of tribes at Babel should be connected with the name of Nimrod, who figures in Biblical as well as Babylonian tradition as a mighty hunter. Epiphanius states that from the very foundation of this city (Babylon) there commenced an immediate scene of conspiracy, sedition and tyranny, which was carried on by Nimrod, the son of Chus the AEthiop.

Around this dim legendary figure a great deal of learned controversy has raged. Before we examine his legendary and mythological significance, let us see what legend and Scripture say of him. In the Book of Genesis (chap. x, 8, *ff.*) he is mentioned as "a mighty hunter before Yahweh: wherefore it is said, Even as Nimrod the mighty hunter before the Lord". He was also the ruler of a great kingdom. "The beginning of his kingdom was Babel, and Erech, and Accad and Calneh in the land of Shinar. Out of that land went forth Asshur" (that is, by compulsion of Nimrod) "and built Nineveh", and other great cities. In the Scriptures Nimrod is mentioned as a descendant of Ham, but this may arise from the reading of his father's name as *Cush*, which in the Scriptures indicates a coloured race. The name may possibly be *Cash* and should relate to the Cassites.

It appears then that the sons of Cush or Chus, the Cassites, according to legend, did not partake of the general division of the human race after the fall of Babel, but under the leadership of Nimrod himself remained where they were. After the dispersion, Nimrod built Babylon and fortified the territory around it. It is also said that he built Nineveh and trespassed upon the land of Asshur, so that at last he forced Asshur to quit that territory. The Greeks gave him the name of Nebrod or Nebros, and preserved or invented many tales concerning him and his apostasy, and concerning the tower which he is supposed to have erected. He is described as a gigantic person of mighty bearing, and a contemner of everything divine; his followers are represented as being equally presumptuous and overbearing. In fact he seems to have appeared to the Greeks very much like one of their own Titans.

Nimrod has been identified both with Merodach, the tutelar god of Babylon, and with Gilgamesh, the hero of the epic of that name, with Orion, and with others. The name, according to Petrie, has even been found in Egyptian documents of the XXII Dynasty as 'Nemart'.

Nimrod seems to be one of those giants who rage against the gods, as do the Titans of Greek myth and the Jotunn of Scandinavian story. All are in fact earth-gods, the disorderly forces of nature, who were defeated by the deities who stood for law and order. The derivation of the name Nimrod may mean 'rebel'. In all his later legends, for instance, those of them that are related by Philo in his *De Gigantibus* (a title which proves that Nimrod was connected with the giant race by tradition), he appears as treacherous and untrustworthy. The theory that he is Merodach has no real foundation either in scholarship or probability. As a matter of fact the Nimrod legend seems to be very much more archaic than any piece of tradition connected with Merodach, who indeed is a god of no very great antiquity.

Abram and Nimrod

Many Jewish legends bring Abram into relationship with Nimrod, the mythical King of Babylon. According to legend Abram was originally an idolater, and many stories are preserved respecting his conversion. Jewish legend states that the Father of the Faithful originally followed his father Terah's occupation, which was that of making and selling images of clay; and that, when very young, he advised his father "to leave his pernicious trade of idolatry by which he imposed on the world".

The Jewish Rabbins relate that on one occasion, his father Terah having undertaken a considerable journey, the sale of the images devolved on him, and it happened that a man who pretended to be a purchaser asked him how old he was. "Fifty years", answered the Patriarch. "Wretch that thou art", said the man, "for adoring at that age a thing which is only one day old!" Abram was astonished; and the exclamation of the old man had such an effect upon him, that when a woman soon after brought some flour, as an offering to one of the idols, he took an axe and broke them to pieces, preserving only the largest one, into the hand of which he put the axe. Terah returned home and inquired what this havoc meant. Abram replied that the deities had quarrelled about an offering which a woman had brought, upon which the larger one had seized an axe and destroyed the others. Terah replied that he must be in jest, as it was impossible that inanimate statues could so act; and Abram immediately retorted on his father his own words, showing him the absurdity of worshipping false deities. But Terah, who does not appear to have been convinced, delivered Abram to Nimrod, who then dwelt in the Plain of Shinar, where Babylon was built. Nimrod, having in vain exhorted Abram to worship fire, ordered him to be thrown into a burning furnace, exclaiming – "Let your God come and take you out". As soon as Haran, Abram's youngest brother, saw the fate of the Patriarch, he resolved to conform to Nimrod's religion; but when he saw his brother come out of the fire unhurt, he declared for the "God of Abram", which caused him to be thrown in turn into the furnace, and he was consumed. A certain writer, however, narrates a different version of Haran's death. He says that he endeavoured to snatch Terah's idols from the flames, into which they had been thrown by Abram, and was burnt to death in consequence.

The 'Babylonica' and the Tale of Sinonis and Rhodanes

FRAGMENTS OF BABYLONIAN HISTORY, or rather historical romance, occur in the writings of early authors other than Berossus. One of these is to be found in the *Babylonica* of Iamblichus, a work embracing no less than sixteen books, by a native of Chalchis in Coele-Syria, who was much enamoured of the mysterious ancient life of Babylonia and Assyria, and who died about 333 CE. All that remains of what is palpably a romance, which may have been founded upon historical probability, is an epitome of the *Babylonica* by Photius, which, still further condensed, is as follows:

Attracted by her beauty and relying on his own great power, Garmus, King of Babylon, decided to marry Sinonis, a maiden of surpassing beauty. She, however, was already in love with another, Rhodanes, and discouraged Garmus' every advance. Her attachment became known to the King, but did not alter his determination, and to prevent the possibility of any attempt at flight on the part of the lovers, he appointed two eunuchs, Damas and Saca, to watch their movements. The penalty for negligence was loss of ears and nose, and that penalty the eunuchs suffered. In spite of their close vigilance the lovers escaped. Damas and Saca were, however, placed at the head of troops and despatched to recapture the fugitives. Their relentless search was not the lovers' only anxiety, for in seeking refuge with some shepherds in a meadow, they encountered a demon – a satyr, which in the shape of a goat haunted that part of the country. This demon, to Sinonis' horror, began to pay her all sorts of weird, fantastic attentions, and finally compelled her and Rhodanes to abandon the protection of the shepherds for the concealment offered by a cavern. Here they were discovered by Damas and his forces, and must have been captured but for the opportune arrival and attack of a swarm of poisonous bees which routed the eunuchs. When the runaways were alone again they tasted and ate some of the bees' honey, and almost immediately lost consciousness. Later Damas again attacked the cavern, but finding the lovers still unconscious he and his troops left them there for dead.

In time, however, they recovered and continued their flight into the country. A man, who afterward poisoned his brother and accused them of the crime, offered them sanctuary. Only the suicide of this man saved them from serious trouble and probably recapture, and from his house they wandered into the company of a robber. Here again the troops of Damas came upon them and burned their dwelling to the ground. In desperation the fugitives masqueraded as the ghosts of the people the robber had murdered in his house. Their ruse succeeded and once again their pursuers were thrown off the scent. They next encountered the funeral of a young girl, and witnessed her apparent return to life almost at the door of the sepulchre. In this sepulchre Sinonis and Rhodanes slept that night, and once more were believed to be dead by Damas and his soldiers. Later, however, Sinonis tried to dispose of their grave clothes and was arrested in the act. Soracchus, the magistrate of the district, decided to send her to Babylon. In despair she and Rhodanes took some poison with which they had provided themselves against such an emergency. This had been anticipated by their guards, however, with the result that a sleeping draught had been substituted for the poison, and sometime later the lovers to their amazement awoke to find themselves in the vicinity of Babylon. Overcome by such a succession of misfortunes, Sinonis stabbed herself, though not fatally. Soracchus, on learning this, was moved to compassion, and consented to the escape of his prisoners.

After this the lovers embarked on a new series of adventures even more thrilling than those which had gone before. The Temple of Venus (Ishtar), situated on an island of the Euphrates, was their first destination after escaping from the captivity of Soracchus. Here Sinonis' wound was healed, and afterward they sought refuge with a cottager, whose daughter consented to dispose of some trinkets belonging to Sinonis. In doing so the girl was mistaken for Sinonis, and news that Sinonis had been seen in the neighbourhood was sent at once to Garmus. While selling the trinkets the cottage girl had become so alarmed by the suspicious questions and manner of the purchasers that she hurried home with all possible speed. On her way back her curiosity was excited by sounds of a great disturbance issuing from a house hard by, and on entering she was appalled to discover a man in the very act of taking his life after murdering his mistress. Terrified and sprinkled with blood she sped back to her father's house. On hearing the girl's story, Sinonis realised that the safety of herself and Rhodanes lay only in flight. They prepared at once to go, but before starting Rhodanes kissed the peasant girl. Sinonis, discovering what he had done by the blood on his lips, became furious with jealousy. In a transport of rage she tried to stab the girl, and on being prevented rushed to the house of Setapo, a wealthy Babylonian of evil repute. Setapo welcomed her only too cordially. At first Sinonis pretended to meet his mood, but as time went by she relented of her treatment of Rhodanes and began to cast about for some means of escape. As the evening wore on she plied Setapo with wine until he was intoxicated, then during the night she murdered him, and in the first early dawn left the house. The slaves of Setapo pursued and overtook her, however, and committed her to custody to answer for her crime.

All Babylon rejoiced with its king over the news of Sinonis' discovery. So great was Garmus' delight that he commanded that all the prisoners throughout his dominions should be released, and in this general boon Sinonis shared. Meanwhile the dog of Rhodanes had scented out the house in which the peasant girl had witnessed the suicide of the lover who had murdered his mistress, and while the animal was devouring the remains of the woman the father of Sinonis arrived at the same house. Thinking the mutilated body was that of his daughter he buried it, and on the tomb he placed the inscription: "Here lies the beautiful Sinonis". Some days later Rhodanes passed that way, and on reading the inscription added to it, "And also the beautiful Rhodanes". In his grief he would have stabbed himself had not the peasant girl who had been the cause of Sinonis' jealousy prevented him by telling him who in reality was buried there.

During these adventures Soracchus had been imprisoned for allowing the lovers to escape, and this, added to the threat of further punishment, induced him to help the Babylonian officers to trace Rhodanes. So in a short time Rhodanes was prisoner once again, and by the command of Garmus was nailed to a cross. In sight of him the King danced delirious with revengeful joy, and while he was so engaged a messenger arrived with the news that Sinonis was about to be espoused by the King of Syria, into whose dominions she had escaped. Rhodanes was taken down from the cross and put in command of the Babylonian army. This seeming change of fortune was really dictated by the treachery of Garmus, as certain inferior officers were commanded by Garmus to slay Rhodanes should he defeat the Syrians, and to bring Sinonis alive to Babylon. Rhodanes won a sweeping victory and also regained the affection and trust of Sinonis. The officers of Garmus, instead of obeying his command, proclaimed the victor king, and all ended auspiciously for the lovers.

The Sacred Literature of Babylonia

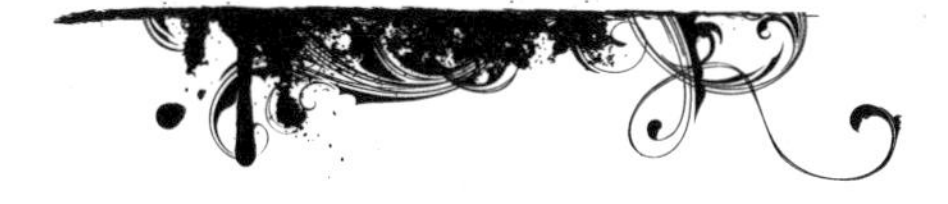

THE LITERATURE which the peculiar and individual script of cuneiform has brought down to us is chiefly religious, magical, epical and legendary. The last three categories are dealt with elsewhere, so that it only falls here to consider the first class, the religious writings.

These are usually composed in Semitic Babylonian without any trace of Akkadian influence, and it cannot be said that they display any especial natural eloquence or literary distinction. In an address to the sun-god, which begins nobly enough with a high apostrophe to the golden luminary of day, we find ourselves descending gradually into an atmosphere of almost ludicrous dullness. The person praying desires the sun-god to free him from the commonplace cares of family and domestic annoyances, enumerating spells against all of his relatives in order that they may not place their 'ban' upon him.

In another, written in Akkadian, the penitent addresses Gubarra, Merodach and other gods, desiring that they direct their eyes kindly upon him and that his supplication may reach them. Strangely enough the prayer fervently pleads that its utterance may *do good to the gods!* that it may let their hearts rest, their livers be quieted, and gladden them like a father and a mother who have begotten children. This is not so strange when we come to consider the nature of these hymns, many of which come perilously near the borderline of pure magic – that is, they closely resemble spells. We find, too, that those which invoke the older deities such as Gibi the fire-god, are more magical in their trend than those addressed to the later gods when a higher sense of religious feeling had probably been evolved. Indeed, it does not seem too much to say that some of these early hymns may have served the purpose of later incantations.

Most of those 'magical' hymns appear to have emanated from that extremely ancient seat of religion, Eridu, and are probably relics of the time when as yet magic and religion were scarcely differentiated in the priestly or the popular mind.

Hymn to Adar

A fine hymn to Adar describes the rumbling of the storm in the abyss, the 'voice' of the god:

The terror of the splendour of Anu in the midst of heaven.

The gods, it is said, urge Adar on, he descends like the deluge, the champion of the gods swoops down upon the hostile land. Nusku, the messenger of Mul-lil, receives Adar in the temple and addresses words of praise to him:

Thy chariot is as a voice of thunder.
To the lifting of thy hands is the shadow turned.
The spirits of the earth, the great gods, return to the winds.

Many of the hymns assist us to a better understanding of the precise nature of the gods, defining as they do their duties and offices and even occasionally describing their appearance. Thus in a hymn to Nebo we note that he is alluded to as "the supreme messenger who binds all things together", "the scribe of all that has a name", "the lifter up of the stylus supreme", "director of the world", "possessor of the reed of augury", "traverser of strange lands", "opener of wells", "fructifier of the corn" and "the god without whom the irrigated land and the canal are unwatered". It is from such texts that the mythologist is enabled to piece together the true significance of many of the deities of ancient peoples.

A hymn to Nusku in his character of fire-god is also descriptive and picturesque. He is alluded to as "wise prince, the flame of heaven", "he who hurls down terror, whose clothing is splendour", "the forceful fire-god", "the exalter of the mountain peaks" and "the uplifter of the torch, the enlightener of darkness".

Gods & Deities

Introduction

ANCIENT BABYLONIA was for over 4,000 years the garden of Western Asia. In the days of Hezekiah and Isaiah, when it had come under the sway of the younger civilization of Assyria on the north, it was "a land of corn and wine, a land of bread and vineyards, a land of oil olive and of honey". Herodotus found it still flourishing and extremely fertile. "This territory", he wrote, "is of all that we know the best by far for producing grain; it is so good that it returns as much as two hundredfold for the average, and, when it bears at its best, it produces three hundredfold. The blades of the wheat and barley there grow to be full four fingers broad; and from millet and sesame seed, how large a tree grows, I know myself, but shall not record, being well aware that even what has already been said relating to the crops produced has been enough to cause disbelief in those who have not visited Babylonia".

The topography of the land is important because it not only generated and sustained the multiple deities worshipped by the ancient Babylonians, it also invited immigrants from other lands to settle there, bringing with them their own gods, intermingling – and sometimes conflicting – with Babylonian pantheons, and generally advancing generations of belief and culture.

In this section, writings from Donald A. Mackenzie explain the importance of water, weather, sun and moon to the gods of Babylon; who these gods were, good and bad, how they created life, affected the lives of their worshippers, and what were the Babylonian myths about these deities. Particularly, we will read about Ea, the god of water, Enlil, the god of war, and Ashur, the sun deity and national god of Assyria.

The Land of Rivers and the God of the Deep

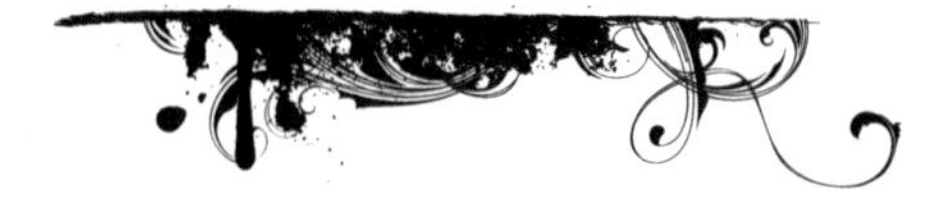

Rivers, Canals, Seasons and Climate

THIS HISTORIC COUNTRY is bounded on the east by Persia and on the west by the Arabian desert. In shape somewhat resembling a fish, it lies between the two great rivers, the Tigris and the Euphrates, two miles wide at its broadest part, and narrowing to thirty-five miles towards the "tail" in the latitude of Baghdad; the "head" converges to a point above Basra, where the rivers meet and form the Shatt-el-Arab, which pours into the Persian Gulf after meeting the Karun and drawing away the main volume of that double-mouthed river.

The distance from Baghdad to Basra is about 300 miles, and the area traversed by the Shatt-el-Arab is slowly extending at the rate of a mile every thirty years or so, as a result of the steady accumulation of silt and mud carried down by the Tigris and Euphrates. When Sumeria was beginning to flourish, these two rivers had separate outlets, and Eridu, the seat of the cult of the sea god Ea, which now lies 125 miles inland, was a seaport at the head of the Persian Gulf. A day's journey separated the river mouths when Alexander the Great broke the power of the Persian Empire.

In the days of Babylonia's prosperity the Euphrates was hailed as "the soul of the land" and the Tigris as "the bestower of blessings". Skilful engineers had solved the problem of water distribution by irrigating sun-parched areas and preventing the excessive flooding of those districts which are now rendered impassable swamps when the rivers overflow. A network of canals was constructed throughout the country, which restricted the destructive tendencies of the Tigris and Euphrates and developed to a high degree their potentialities as fertilizing agencies. The greatest of these canals appear to have been anciently riverbeds. One, which is called Shatt en Nil to the north, and Shatt el Kar to the south, curved eastward from Babylon, and sweeping past Nippur, flowed like the letter S towards Larsa and then rejoined the river. It is believed to mark the course followed in the early Sumerian period by the Euphrates river, which has moved steadily westward many miles beyond the sites of ancient cities that were erected on its banks.

Another important canal, the Shatt el Hai, crossed the plain from the Tigris to its sister river, which lies lower at this point, and does not run so fast. Where the artificial canals were constructed on higher levels than the streams which fed them, the water was raised by contrivances known as "shaddufs"; the buckets or skin bags were roped to a weighted beam, with the aid of which they were swung up by workmen and emptied into the canals. It is possible that this toilsome mode of irrigation was substituted in favourable parts by the primitive water wheels which are used in our own day by the inhabitants of the country who cultivate strips of land along the riverbanks.

In Babylonia there are two seasons – the rainy and the dry. Rain falls from November till March, and the plain is carpeted in spring by patches of vivid green verdure and brilliant wildflowers. Then the period of drought ensues; the sun rapidly burns up all vegetation, and everywhere the eye is wearied by long stretches of brown and yellow desert. Occasional sandstorms darken the heavens, sweeping over sterile wastes and piling up the shapeless mounds which mark the sites of ancient cities. Meanwhile the rivers are increasing in volume, being fed by the melting snows at their mountain sources far to the north. The swift Tigris, which is 1,146 miles long, begins to rise early in March and reaches its highest level in May; before the end of June it again subsides. More sluggish in movement, the Euphrates, which is 1,780 miles long, shows signs of rising a fortnight later than the Tigris, and is in flood for a more extended period; it does not shrink to its lowest level until early in September.

By controlling the flow of these mighty rivers, preventing disastrous floods, and storing and distributing surplus water, the ancient Babylonians developed to the full the natural resources of their country, and made it – what it may once again become – one of the fairest and most habitable areas in the world. Nature conferred upon them bountiful rewards for their labour; trade and industries flourished, and the cities increased in splendour and strength. Then as now the heat was great during the long summer, but remarkably dry and unvarying, while the air was ever wonderfully transparent under cloudless skies of vivid blue. The nights were cool and of great beauty, whether in brilliant moonlight or when ponds and canals were jewelled by the lustrous displays of clear and numerous stars which glorified that homeland of the earliest astronomers.

Early Trade and Foreign Influences

Babylonia is a treeless country, and timber had to be imported from the earliest times. The date palm was probably introduced by man, as were certainly the vine and the fig tree, which were widely cultivated, especially in the north. Stone, suitable for building, was very scarce, and limestone, alabaster, marble and basalt had to be taken from northern Mesopotamia, where the mountains also yield copper and lead and iron. Except Eridu, where ancient workers quarried sandstone from its sea-shaped ridge, all the cities were built of brick, an excellent clay being found in abundance. When brick walls were cemented with bitumen they were given great stability. This resinous substance is found in the north and south. It bubbles up through crevices of rocks on river banks and forms small ponds. Two famous springs at modern Hit, on the Euphrates, have been drawn upon from time immemorial. "From one", writes a traveller, "flows hot water black with bitumen, while the other discharges intermittently bitumen, or, after a rainstorm, bitumen and cold water.... Where rocks crop out in the plain above Hit, they are full of seams of bitumen". Present-day Arabs call it "kiyara", and export it for coating boats and roofs; they also use it as an antiseptic, and apply it to cure the skin diseases from which camels suffer.

Sumeria had many surplus products, including corn and figs, pottery, fine wool and woven garments, to offer in exchange for what it most required from other countries. It must, therefore, have had a brisk and flourishing foreign trade at an exceedingly remote period. No doubt numerous alien merchants were attracted to its cities, and it may be that they induced or encouraged Semitic and other raiders to overthrow governments and form military aristocracies, so that they themselves might obtain necessary concessions and achieve a degree of political ascendancy. It does not follow, however, that the peasant class was greatly affected by periodic revolutions of this kind, which brought little more to them than a change of rulers. The needs of the country necessitated the continuance of agricultural methods and the rigid observance of existing land laws; indeed, these constituted the basis of Sumerian prosperity.

Conquerors have ever sought reward not merely in spoil, but also the services of the conquered. In northern Babylonia the invaders apparently found it necessary to conciliate and secure the continued allegiance of the tillers of the soil. Law and religion being closely associated, they had to adapt their gods to suit the requirements of existing social and political organizations. A deity of pastoral nomads had to receive attributes which would give him an agricultural significance; one of rural character had to be changed to respond to the various calls of city life. Besides, local gods could not be ignored on account of their popularity. As a result, imported beliefs and religious customs must have been fused and absorbed according to their bearing on modes of life in various localities. It is probable that the complex character of certain deities was due to the process of adjustment to which they were subjected in new environments.

Local Religious Cults

The petty kingdoms of Sumeria appear to have been tribal in origin. Each city was presided over by a deity who was the nominal owner of the surrounding arable land, farms were rented or purchased from the priesthood, and pasture was held in common. As in Egypt, where we find, for instance, the artisan god Ptah supreme at Memphis, the sun god Ra at Heliopolis, and the cat goddess Bast at Bubastis, the various local Sumerian and Akkadian deities had distinctive characteristics, and similarly showed a tendency to absorb the attributes of their rivals. The chief deity of a state was the central figure in a pantheon, which had its political aspect and influenced the growth of local theology. Cities, however, did not, as a rule, bear the names of deities, which suggests that several were founded when Sumerian religion was in its early animistic stages, and gods and goddesses were not sharply defined from the various spirit groups.

Ea, God of the Deep, Identical with Oannes of Berosus

A distinctive and characteristic Sumerian god was Ea, who was supreme at the ancient sea-deserted port of Eridu. He is identified with the Oannes of Berosus, who referred to the deity as "a creature endowed with reason, with a body like that of a fish, with feet below like those of a man, with a fish's tail". This description recalls the familiar figures of Egyptian gods and priests attired in the skins of the sacred animals from whom their powers were derived, and the fairy lore about swan maids and men, and the seals and other animals who could divest themselves of their "skin coverings" and appear in human shape. Originally Ea may have been a sacred fish.

The Indian creative gods Brahma and Vishnu had fish forms. In Sanskrit literature Manu, the eponymous "first man", is instructed by the fish to build a ship in which to save himself when the world would be purged by the rising waters. Ea befriended in similar manner the Babylonian Noah, called Pir-napishtim, advising him to build a vessel so as to be prepared for the approaching Deluge. Indeed the Indian legend appears to throw light on the original Sumerian conception of Ea. It relates that when the fish was small and in danger of being swallowed by other fish in a stream it appealed to Manu for protection. The sage at once lifted up the fish and placed it in a jar of water. It gradually increased in bulk, and he transferred it next to a tank and then to the river Ganges. In time the fish complained to Manu that the river was too small for it, so he carried it to the sea. For these services the god in fish form instructed Manu regarding the approaching flood, and afterwards piloted his ship through the weltering waters until it rested on a mountain top.

Origin as a Sacred Fish

If this Indian myth is of Babylonian origin, as appears probable, it may be that the spirit of the river Euphrates, "the soul of the land", was identified with a migrating fish. The growth of the fish suggests the growth of the river rising in flood. In Celtic folk tales high tides and valley floods are accounted for by the presence of a "great beast" in sea, loch, or river. In a class of legends, "specially connected with the worship of Atargatis", wrote Professor Robertson Smith, "the divine life of the waters resides in the sacred fish that inhabit them. Atargatis and her son, according to a legend common to Hierapolis and Ascalon, plunged into the waters – in the first case the Euphrates, in the second the sacred pool at the temple near the town – and were changed into fishes". The idea is that "where a god dies, that is, ceases to exist in human form, his life passes into the waters where he is buried; and this again is merely a theory to bring the divine water or the divine fish into harmony with anthropomorphic ideas. The same thing was sometimes effected in another way by saying that the anthropomorphic deity was born from the water, as Aphrodite sprang from sea foam, or as Atargatis, in another form of the Euphrates legend, … was born of an egg which the sacred fishes found in the Euphrates and pushed ashore".

Fish Deities in Babylonia and Egypt

As "Shar Apsi", Ea was the "King of the Watery Deep". The reference, however, according to Jastrow, "is not to the salt ocean, but the sweet waters flowing under the earth which feed the streams, and through streams and canals irrigate the fields". As Babylonia was fertilized by its rivers, Ea, the fish god, was a fertilizing deity. In Egypt the "Mother of Mendes" is depicted carrying a fish upon her head; she links with Isis and Hathor; her husband is Ba-neb-Tettu, a form of Ptah, Osiris and Ra, and as a god of fertility he is symbolized by the ram. Another Egyptian fish deity was the god Rem, whose name signifies "to weep"; he wept fertilizing tears, and corn was sown and reaped amidst lamentations. He may be identical with Remi, who was a phase of Sebek, the crocodile god, a developed attribute of Nu, the vague primitive Egyptian deity who symbolized the primordial deep. The connection between a fish god and a corn god is not necessarily remote when we consider that in Babylonia and Egypt the harvest was the gift of the rivers.

The Euphrates, indeed, was hailed as a creator of all that grew on its banks.

O thou River who didst create all things,
When the great gods dug thee out,
They set prosperity upon thy banks,
Within thee Ea, the King of the Deep, created his dwelling …
Thou judgest the cause of mankind!
O River, thou art mighty! O River, thou art supreme!
O River, thou art righteous!

In serving Ea, the embodiment or the water spirit, by leading him, as the Indian Manu led the Creator and "Preserver" in fish form, from river to water pot, water pot to pond or canal, and then again to river and ocean, the Babylonians became expert engineers and experienced agriculturists, the makers of bricks, the builders of cities, the framers of laws. Indeed, their civilization was a growth of Ea worship. Ea was their instructor. Berosus states that, as Oannes, he lived in the Persian Gulf, and every day came ashore to instruct the inhabitants of Eridu how to make canals, to grow crops, to work metals, to make pottery and bricks, and to build temples; he was the artisan god – Nun-ura, "god of the potter"; Kuski-banda, "god of goldsmiths", etc. – the divine patron of the arts and crafts. "Ea knoweth everything", chanted the hymn maker. He taught the people how to form and use alphabetic signs and instructed them in mathematics: he gave them their code of laws. Like the Egyptian artisan god Ptah, and the linking deity Khnumu, Ea was the "potter or moulder of gods and man". Ptah moulded the first man on his potter's wheel: he also moulded the sun and moon; he shaped the universe and hammered out the copper sky. Ea built the world "as an architect builds a house". Similarly, the Vedic Indra, who wielded a hammer like Ptah, fashioned the universe after the simple manner in which the Aryans made their wooden dwellings.

Ea an Artisan God, and Links with Egypt and India

Like Ptah, Ea also developed from an artisan god into a sublime Creator in the highest sense, not merely as a producer of crops. His word became the creative force; he named those things he desired to be, and they came into existence. "Who but Ea creates things", exclaimed a priestly poet. This change from artisan god to creator (Nudimmud) may have been due to the tendency of early religious cults to attach to their chief god the attributes of rivals exalted at other centres. Ea, whose name is also rendered Aa, was identified with Ya, Ya'u, or Au, the Jah of the Hebrews. "In Ya-Daganu, 'Jah is Dagon'", writes Professor Pinches, "we have the elements reversed, showing a wish to identify Jah with Dagon, rather than Dagon with Jah; whilst another interesting name, Au-Aa, shows an identification of Jah with Aa, two names which have every appearance of being etymologically connected". Jah's name "is one of the words for 'god' in the Assyro-Babylonian language".

Ea was "Enki", "lord of the world", or "lord of what is beneath"; Amma-ana-ki, "lord of heaven and earth"; Sa-kalama, "ruler of the land", as well as Engur, "god of the abyss", Naqbu, "the deep" and Lugal-ida, "king of the river". As rain fell from "the waters above the firmament", the god of waters was also a sky and earth god.

The Indian Varuna was similarly a sky as well as an ocean god before the theorizing and systematizing Brahmanic teachers relegated him to a permanent abode at the bottom of the sea. It may be that Ea-Oannes and Varuna were of common origin.

The Babylonian Dagan and Dagon of the Philistines

Another Babylonian deity, named Dagan, is believed to be identical with Ea. His worship was certainly of great antiquity. "Hammurabi", writes Professor Pinches, "seems to speak of the Euphrates as being 'the boundary of Dagan', whom he calls his creator. In later inscriptions the form Daguna, which approaches nearer to the West Semitic form (Dagon of the Philistines), is found in a few personal names.

It is possible that the Philistine deity Dagon was a specialized form of ancient Ea, who was either imported from Babylonia or was a sea god of more than one branch of the Mediterranean race. The authorities are at variance regarding the form and attributes of Dagan. Our know-ledge regarding him is derived mainly from the Bible. He was a national rather than a city god. There are references to a Beth-dagon, "house or city of Dagon"; he had also a temple at Gaza, and Samson destroyed it by pulling down the two middle pillars which were its main support. A third temple was situated in Ashdod. When the captured ark of the Israelites was placed in it the image of Dagon "fell on his face", with the result that "the head of Dagon and both the palms of his hands were cut off upon the threshold; only the stump of Dagon was left". A further reference to "the threshold of Dagon" suggests that the god had feet like Ea-Oannes.

Those who hold that Dagon had a fish form derive his name from the Semitic "dag = a fish", and suggest that after the idol fell only the fishy part (dago) was left. On the other hand, it was argued that Dagon was a corn god, and that the resemblance between the words Dagan and Dagon are accidental. Professor Sayce makes reference in this connection to a crystal seal from Phoenicia in the Ashmolean Museum, Oxford, bearing an inscription which he reads as Baal-dagon. Near the name is an ear of corn, and other symbols, such as the winged solar disc, a gazelle and several stars, but there is no fish. It may be, of course, that Baal-dagon represents a fusion of deities.

As we have seen in the case of Ea-Oannes and the deities of Mendes, a fish god may also be a corn god, a land animal god and a god of ocean and the sky. The offering of golden mice representing "your mice that mar the land", made by the Philistines, suggests that Dagon was the fertilizing harvest god, among other things, whose usefulness had been impaired, as they believed, by the mistake committed of placing the ark of Israel in the temple at Ashdod. The Philistines came from Crete, and if their Dagon was imported from that island, he may have had some connection with Poseidon, whose worship extended throughout Greece. This god of the sea, who is somewhat like the Roman Neptune, carried a lightning trident and caused earthquakes. He was a brother of Zeus, the sky and atmosphere deity, and had bull and horse forms. As a horse he pursued Demeter, the earth and corn goddess, and, like Ea, he instructed mankind, but especially in the art of training horses. In his train were the Tritons, half men, half fishes, and the water fairies, the Nereids. Bulls, boars and rams were offered to this sea god of fertility. Amphitrite was his spouse.

Deities of Water and Harvest in Other Cultures

An obscure god Shony, the Oannes of the Scottish Hebrides, received oblations from those who depended for their agricultural prosperity on his gifts of fertilizing seaweed. He is referred to in Martin's Western Isles, and is not yet forgotten. The Eddie sea god Njord of Noatun was the father of Frey, the harvest god. Dagda, the Irish corn god, had for wife Boann, the goddess of the river Boyne. Osiris and Isis of Egypt were associated with the Nile. The connection between agriculture and the water supply was too obvious to escape the early symbolists, and many other proofs of this than those referred to could be given.

Ea's Spouse Damkina

Ea's "faithful spouse" was the goddess Damkina, who was also called Nin-ki, "lady of the earth". "May Ea make thee glad", chanted the priests. "May Damkina, queen of the deep, illumine thee with her countenance; may Merodach (Marduk), the mighty overseer of the Igigi (heavenly spirits), exalt thy head". Merodach was their son: in time he became the Bel, or "Lord", of the Babylonian pantheon.

Demons of Ocean in Babylonia and India

Like the Indian Varuna, the sea god, Ea-Oannes had control over the spirits and demons of the deep. The "ferryman" who kept watch over the river of death was called Arad-Ea, "servant of Ea". There are also references to sea maidens, the Babylonian mermaids, or Nereids. We have a glimpse of sea giants, which resemble the Indian Danavas and Daityas of ocean, in the chant:

Seven are they, seven are they,
In the ocean deep seven are they,
Battening in heaven seven are they,
Bred in the depths of ocean....
Of these seven the first is the south wind,
The second a dragon with mouth agape....

A suggestion of the Vedic Vritra and his horde of monsters.

These seven demons were also "the messengers of Anu", who, although specialized as a sky god in more than one pantheon, appears to have been closely associated with Ea in the earliest Sumerian period. His name, signifying "the high one", is derived from "ana", "heaven"; he was the city god of Erech (Uruk). It is possible that he was developed as an atmospheric god with solar and lunar attributes. The seven demons, who were his messengers, recall the stormy Maruts, the followers of Indra. They are referred to as

Forcing their way with baneful windstorms,
Mighty destroyers, the deluge of the storm god,
Stalking at the right hand of the storm god.

When we deal with a deity in his most archaic form it is difficult to distinguish him from a demon. Even the beneficent Ea is associated with monsters and furies. "Evil spirits", according to a Babylonian chant, were "the bitter venom of the gods". Those attached to a deity as "attendants" appear to represent the original animistic group from which he evolved. In each district the character of the deity was shaped to accord with local conditions.

Enlil, Storm and War God of Nippur

At Nippur, which was situated on the vague and shifting boundary line between Sumer and Akkad, the chief god was Enlil, whose name is translated "lord of mist", "lord of might", and "lord of demons" by various authorities. He was a storm god and a war god, and "lord of heaven and earth", like Ea and Anu. An atmospheric deity, he shares the attributes of the Indian Indra, the thunder and rain god, and Vayu, the wind god; he also resembles the Semitic Adad or Rim-man, who links with the Hittite Tarku. All these are deities of tempest and the mountains – Wild Huntsmen in the Raging Host. The name of Enlil's temple at Nippur has been translated as "mountain house", or "like a mountain", and the theory obtained for a time that the god must therefore have been imported by a people from the hills. But as the ideogram for "mountain" and "land" was used in the earliest times, as King shows, with reference to foreign countries, it is more probable that Enlil was exalted as a world god who had dominion over not only Sumer and Akkad, but also the territories occupied by the rivals and enemies of the early Babylonians.

Enlil is known as the "older Bel" (lord), to distinguish him from Bel Merodach of Babylon. He was the chief figure in a triad in which he figured as earth god, with Anu as god of the sky and Ea as god of the deep. This classification suggests that Nippur had either risen in political importance and dominated the cities of Erech and Eridu, or that its priests were influential at the court of a ruler who was the overlord of several city states.

Associated with Bel Enlil was Beltis, later known as "Beltu – the lady". She appears to be identical with the other great goddesses, Ishtar, Nana, Zer-panitum, etc., a "Great Mother", or consort of an early god with whom she was equal in power and dignity.

Early Gods of Babylonia and Egypt of Common Origin

In the later systematized theology of the Babylonians we seem to trace the fragments of a primitive mythology which was vague in outline, for the deities were not sharply defined, and existed in groups. Enneads were formed in Egypt by placing a local god at the head of a group of eight elder deities. The sun god Ra was the chief figure of the earliest pantheon of this character at Heliopolis, while at Hermopolis the leader was the lunar god Thoth. Professor Budge is of opinion that "both the Sumerians and the early Egyptians derived their primeval gods from some common but exceedingly ancient source", for he finds in the Babylonian and Nile valleys that there is a resemblance between two early groups which "seems to be too close to be accidental".

The Egyptian group comprises four pairs of vague gods and goddesses – Nu and his consort Nut, Hehu and his consort Hehut, Kekui and his consort Kekuit, and Kerh and his consort Kerhet. "Man always has fashioned", he says, "and probably always will fashion, his god or gods in his own image, and he has always, having reached a certain stage in development, given to his gods wives and offspring; but the nature of the position taken by the wives of the gods depends upon the nature of the position of women in the households of those who write the legends and the traditions of the gods. The gods of the oldest company in Egypt were, the writer believes, invented by people in whose households women held a high position, and among whom they possessed more power than is usually the case with Oriental peoples".

We cannot say definitely what these various deities represent. Nu was the spirit of the primordial deep, and Nut of the waters above the heavens, the mother of moon and sun and the stars. The others were phases of light and darkness and the forces of nature in activity and repose.

Nu is represented in Babylonian mythology by Apsu-Rishtu, and Nut by Mummu-Tiamat or Tiawath; the next pair is Lachmu and Lachamu, and the third, Anshar and Kishar. The fourth pair is missing, but the names of Anu and Ea (as Nudimmud) are mentioned in the first tablet of the Creation series, and the name of a third is lost. Professor Budge thinks that the Assyrian editors substituted the ancient triad of Anu, Ea, and Enlil for the pair which would correspond to those found in Egypt. Originally the wives of Anu and Ea may have made up the group of eight primitive deities.

There can be little doubt but that Ea, as he survives to us, is of later characterization than the first pair of primitive deities who symbolized the deep. The attributes of this beneficent god reflect the progress, and the social and moral ideals of a people well advanced in civilization. He rewarded mankind for the services they rendered to him; he was their leader and instructor; he achieved for them the victories over the destructive forces of nature. In brief, he was the dragon slayer, a distinction, by the way, which was attached in later times to his son Merodach, the Babylonian god, although Ea was still credited with the victory over the dragon's husband.

When Ea was one of the pre-Babylonian group – the triad of Bel-Enlil, Anu and Ea – he resembled the Indian Vishnu, the Preserver, while Bel-Enlil resembled Shiva, the Destroyer, and Anu, the father, supreme Brahma, the Creator and Father of All, the difference in exact adjustment being due, perhaps, to Sumerian political conditions.

Ea, as we have seen, symbolized the beneficence of the waters; their destructive force was represented by Tiamat or Tiawath, the dragon, and Apsu, her husband, the archenemy of the gods. We shall find these elder demons figuring in the Babylonian Creation myth, which receives treatment in a later chapter.

Ea's City as Cradle of Sumerian Civilization

The ancient Sumerian city of Eridu, which means "on the seashore", was invested with great sanctity from the earliest times, and Ea, the "great magician of the gods", was invoked by workers of spells, the priestly magicians of historic Babylonia. Excavations have shown that Eridu was protected by a retaining wall of sandstone, of which material many of its houses were made. In its temple tower, built of brick, was a marble stairway, and evidences have been forthcoming that in the later Sumerian period the structure was lavishly adorned. It is referred to in the fragments of early literature which have survived as "the splendid house, shady as the forest", that "none may enter". The mythological spell exercised by Eridu in later times suggests that the civilization of Sumeria owed much to the worshippers of Ea. At the sacred city the first man was created: there the souls of the dead passed towards the great Deep. Its proximity to the sea – Ea was Nin-bubu, "god of the sailor" – may have brought it into contact with other peoples and other early civilizations. Like the early Egyptians, the early Sumerians may have been in touch with Punt (Somali-land), which some regard as the cradle of the Mediterranean race. The Egyptians obtained from that sacred land incense-bearing trees which had magical potency. In a fragmentary Babylonian charm there is a reference to a sacred tree or bush at Eridu. Professor Sayce has suggested that it is the Biblical "Tree of Life" in the Garden of Eden. His translations of certain vital words, however, is sharply questioned by Mr. R. Campbell Thompson of the British Museum, who does not accept the theory. It may be that Ea's sacred bush or tree is a survival of tree and water worship.

If Eridu was not the "cradle" of the Sumerian race, it was possibly the cradle of Sumerian civilization. Here, amidst the shifting rivers in early times, the agriculturists may have learned to control and distribute the water supply by utilizing dried-up beds of streams to irrigate the land. Whatever successes they achieved were credited to Ea, their instructor and patron; he was Nadimmud, "god of everything".

Rival Pantheons and Representative Deities

IN DEALING WITH THE CITY cults of Sumer and Akkad, consideration must be given to the problems involved by the rival mythological systems. Pantheons not only varied in detail, but were presided over by different supreme gods. One city's chief deity might be regarded as a secondary deity at another centre. Although Ea, for instance, was given first place at Eridu, and was so pronouncedly Sumerian in character, the moon god Nannar remained supreme at Ur, while the sun god, whose Semitic name was Shamash, presided at Larsa and Sippar. Other deities were similarly exalted in other states.

As has been indicated, a mythological system must have been strongly influenced by city politics. To hold a community in sway, it was necessary to recognize officially the various gods worshipped by different sections, so as to secure the constant allegiance of all classes to their rulers. Alien deities were therefore associated with local and tribal deities, those of the nomads with those of the agriculturists, those of the unlettered folks with those of the learned people. Reference has been made to the introduction of strange deities by conquerors. But these were not always imposed upon a community by violent means. Indications are not awanting that the worshippers of alien gods were sometimes welcomed and encouraged to settle in certain states. When they came as military allies to assist a city folk against a fierce enemy, they were naturally much admired and praised, honoured by the women and the bards, and rewarded by the rulers.

In the epic of Gilgamesh, the Babylonian Hercules, we meet with Ea-bani, a Goliath of the wilds, who is entreated to come to the aid of the besieged city of Erech when it seemed that its deities were unable to help the people against their enemies.

The gods of walled-round Erech
To flies had turned and buzzed in the streets;
The winged bulls of walled-round Erech
Were turned to mice and departed through the holes.

Ea-bani was attracted to Erech by the gift of a fair woman for wife. The poet who lauded him no doubt mirrored public opinion. We can see the slim, shaven Sumerians gazing with wonder and admiration on their rough heroic ally.

All his body was covered with hair,
His locks were like a woman's,
Thick as corn grew his abundant hair.
He was a stranger to the people and in that land.
Clad in a garment like Gira, the god,
He had eaten grass with the gazelles,
He had drunk water with savage beasts.
His delight was to be among water dwellers.

Theories Regarding Origin of Life

Like the giant Alban, the eponymous ancestor of a people who invaded prehistoric Britain, Ea-bani appears to have represented in Babylonian folk legends a certain type of foreign settlers in the land. No doubt the city dwellers, who were impressed by the prowess of the hairy and powerful warriors, were also ready to acknowledge the greatness of their war gods, and to admit them into the pantheon. The fusion of beliefs which followed must have stimulated thought and been productive of speculative ideas. "Nowhere", remarks Professor Jastrow, "does a high form of culture arise without the commingling of diverse ethnic elements".

We must also take into account the influence exercised by leaders of thought like En-we-dur-an-ki, the famous high priest of Sippar, whose piety did much to increase the reputation of the cult of Shamesh, the sun god. The teachings and example of Buddha, for instance, revolutionized Brahmanic religion in India.

A mythology was an attempt to solve the riddle of the Universe, and to adjust the relations of mankind with the various forces represented by the deities. The priests systematized existing folk beliefs and established an official religion. To secure the prosperity of the State, it was considered necessary to render homage unto whom homage was due at various seasons and under various circumstances.

The religious attitude of a particular community, therefore, must have been largely dependent on its needs and experiences. The food supply was a first consideration. At Eridu, as we have seen, it was assured by devotion to Ea and obedience to his commands as an instructor. Elsewhere it might happen, however, that Ea's gifts were restricted or withheld by an obstructing force – the raging storm god, or the parching, pestilence-bringing deity of the sun. It was necessary, therefore, for the people to win the favour of the god or goddess who seemed most powerful, and was accordingly considered to be the greatest in a. particular district. A rain god presided over the destinies of one community, and a god of disease and death over another; a third exalted the war god, no doubt because raids were frequent and the city owed its strength and prosperity to its battles and conquests. The reputation won by a particular god throughout Babylonia would depend greatly on the achievements of his worshippers and the progress of the city civilization over which he presided. Bel-Enlil's fame as a war deity was probably due to the political supremacy of his city of Nippur; and there was probably good reason for attributing to the sun god a pronounced administrative and legal character; he may have controlled the destinies of exceedingly well-organized communities in which law and order and authority were held in high esteem.

In accounting for the rise of distinctive and rival city deities, we should also consider the influence of divergent conceptions regarding the origin of life in mingled communities. Each foreign element in a community had its own intellectual life and immemorial tribal traditions, which reflected ancient habits of life and perpetuated the doctrines of eponymous ancestors. Among the agricultural classes, the folk religion which entered so intimately into their customs and labours must have remained essentially Babylonish in character. In cities, however, where official religions were formulated, foreign ideas were more apt to be imposed, especially when embraced by influential teachers. It is not surprising, therefore, to find that in Babylonia, as in Egypt, there were differences of opinion regarding the origin of life and the particular natural element which represented the vital principle.

Vital Principle in Water

One section of the people, who were represented by the worshippers of Ea, appear to have believed that the essence of life was contained in water. The god of Eridu was the source of the "water of life". He fertilized parched and sunburnt wastes through rivers and irrigating canals, and conferred upon man the sustaining "food of life". When life came to an end –

Food of death will be offered thee ...
Water of death will be offered thee ...

Offerings of water and food were made to the dead so that the ghosts might be nourished and prevented from troubling the living. Even the gods required water and food; they were immortal because they had drunk ambrosia and eaten from the plant of life. When the goddess Ishtar was in the Underworld, the land of the dead, the servant of Ea exclaimed:

"Hail! lady, may the well give me of its waters, so that I may drink".

The goddess of the dead commanded her servant to "sprinkle the lady Ishtar with the water of life and bid her depart". The sacred water might also be found at a confluence of rivers. Ea bade his son, Merodach, to "draw water from the mouth of two streams", and "on this water to put his pure spell".

The worship of rivers and wells which prevailed in many countries was connected with the belief that the principle of life was in moisture. In India, water was vitalized by the intoxicating juice of the Soma plant, which inspired priests to utter prophecies and filled their hearts with religious fervour. Drinking customs had originally a religious significance. It was believed in India that the sap of plants was influenced by the moon, the source of vitalizing moisture and the hiding-place of the mead of the gods. The Teutonic gods also drank this mead, and poets were inspired by it. Similar beliefs obtained among various peoples. Moon and water worship were therefore closely associated; the blood of animals and the sap of plants were vitalized by the water of life and under control of the moon.

Creative Tears of Weeping Deities

The body moisture of gods and demons had vitalizing properties. When the Indian creator, Prajapati, wept at the beginning, "that (the tears) which fell into the water became the air. That which he wiped away, upwards, became the sky". The ancient Egyptians believed that all men were born from the eyes of Horus except negroes, who came from other parts of his body. The creative tears of Ra, the sun god, fell as shining rays upon the earth. When this god grew old saliva dripped from his mouth, and Isis mixed the vitalizing moisture with dust, and thus made the serpent which bit and paralyzed the great solar deity.

Other Egyptian deities, including Osiris and Isis, wept creative tears. Those which fell from the eyes of the evil gods produced poisonous plants and various baneful animals. Orion, the Greek giant, sprang from the body moisture of deities. The weeping ceremonies in connection with agricultural rites were no doubt believed to be of magical potency; they encouraged the god to weep creative tears.

Ea, the god of the deep, was also "lord of life" (Enti), "king of the river" (Lugal-ida) and god of creation (Nudimmud). His aid was invoked by means or magical formulae. As the "great magician of the gods" he uttered charms himself, and was the patron of all magicians. One spell runs as follows:

I am the sorcerer priest of Ea …
To revive the … sick man
The great lord Ea hath sent me;
He hath added his pure spell to mine,
He hath added his pure voice to mine,
He hath added his pure spittle to mine.
– R. C. Thompson's translation

Significance of Widespread Spitting Customs

Saliva, like tears, had creative and therefore curative qualities; it also expelled and injured demons and brought good luck. Spitting ceremonies are referred to in the religious literature of Ancient Egypt. When the Eye of Ra was blinded by Set, Thoth spat in it to restore vision. The sun god Turn, who was linked with Ra as Ra-Tum, spat on the ground, and his saliva became the gods Shu and Tefnut. In the Underworld the devil serpent Apep was spat upon to curse it, as was also its waxen image which the priests fashioned.

Several African tribes spit to make compacts, declare friendship and to curse.

Park, the explorer, refers in his Travels to his carriers spitting on a flat stone to ensure a good journey. Arabian holy men and descendants of Mohammed spit to cure diseases. Mohammed spat in the mouth of his grandson Hasen soon after birth. Theocritus, Sophocles and Plutarch testify to the ancient Grecian customs of spitting to cure and to curse, and also to bless when children were named. Pliny has expressed belief in the efficacy of the fasting spittle for curing disease, and referred to the custom of spitting to avert witchcraft. In England, Scotland and Ireland spitting customs are not yet obsolete. North of England boys used to talk of "spitting their sauls" (souls). When the Newcastle colliers held their earliest strikes they made compacts by spitting on a stone. There are still "spitting stones" in the north of Scotland. When bargains are made in rural districts, hands are spat upon before they are shaken. The first money taken each day by fishwives and other dealers is spat upon to ensure increased drawings. Brand, who refers to various spitting customs, quotes Scot's Discovery of Witchcraft regarding the saliva cure for king's evil, which is still, by the way, practised in the Hebrides. Like Pliny, Scot recommended ceremonial spitting as a charm against witchcraft. In China spitting to expel demons is a common practice. We still call a hasty person a "spitfire", and a calumniator a "spit-poison".

Divine Water in Blood and Divine Blood in Water

The life principle in trees, etc., as we have seen, was believed to have been derived from the tears of deities. In India sap was called the "blood of trees", and references to "bleeding trees" are still widespread and common. "Among the ancients", wrote Professor Robertson Smith, "blood is generally conceived as the principle or vehicle of life, and so the account often given of sacred waters is that the blood of the deity flows in them. Thus as Milton writes:

Smooth Adonis from his native rock
Ran purple to the sea, supposed with blood
Of Thammuz yearly wounded.
– Paradise Lost, i, 450.

The ruddy colour which the swollen river derived from the soil at a certain season was ascribed to the blood of the god, who received his death wound in Lebanon at that time of the year, and lay buried beside the sacred source".

In Babylonia the river was regarded as the source of the life blood and the seat of the soul. No doubt this theory was based on the fact that the human liver contains about a sixth of the blood in the body, the largest proportion required by any single organ. Jeremiah makes "Mother Jerusalem" exclaim: "My liver is poured upon the earth for the destruction of the daughter of my people", meaning that her life is spent with grief.

Inspiration was derived by drinking blood as well as by drinking intoxicating liquors – the mead of the gods. Indian magicians who drink the blood of the goat sacrificed to the goddess Kali, are believed to be temporarily possessed by her spirit, and thus enabled to prophesy. Malayan exorcists still expel demons while they suck the blood from a decapitated fowl.

Similar customs were prevalent in Ancient Greece. A woman who drank the blood of a sacrificed lamb or bull uttered prophetic sayings.

Life Principle in Breath

But while most Babylonians appear to have believed that the life principle was in blood, some were apparently of opinion that it was in breath – the air of life. A man died when he ceased to breathe; his spirit, therefore, it was argued, was identical with the atmosphere – the moving wind – and was accordingly derived from the atmospheric or wind god. When, in the Gilgamesh epic, the hero invokes the dead Ea-bani, the ghost rises up like a "breath of wind". A Babylonian charm runs:

The gods which seize on men
Came forth from the grave;
The evil wind gusts
Have come forth from the grave,
To demand payment of rites and the pouring out of libations
They have come forth from the grave;
All that is evil in their hosts, like a whirlwind,
Hath come forth from the grave.

The Hebrew "nephesh ruach" and "neshamah" (in Arabic "ruh" and "nefs") pass from meaning "breath" to "spirit" In Egypt the god Khnumu was "Kneph" in his character as an atmospheric deity. The ascendancy of storm and wind gods in some Babylonian cities may have been due to the belief that they were the source of the "air of life". It is possible that this conception was popularized by the Semites. Inspiration was perhaps derived from these deities by burning incense, which, if we follow evidence obtained elsewhere, induced a prophetic trance. The gods were also invoked by incense. In the Flood legend the Babylonian Noah burned incense. "The gods smelled a sweet savour and gathered like flies over the sacrificer". In Egypt devotees who inhaled the breath of the Apis bull were enabled to prophesy.

Fire Deities

In addition to water and atmospheric deities Babylonia had also its fire gods, Girru, Gish Bar, Gibil, and Nusku. Their origin is obscure. It is doubtful if their worshippers, like those of the Indian Agni, believed that fire, the "vital spark", was the principle of life which was manifested by bodily heat. The Aryan fire worshippers cremated their dead so that the spirits might be transferred by fire to Paradise. This practice, however, did not obtain among the fire worshippers of Persia, nor, as was once believed, in Sumer or Akkad either. Fire was, however, used in Babylonia for magical purposes. It destroyed demons, and put to flight the spirits of disease. Possibly the fire-purification ceremonies resembled those which were practised by the Canaanites, and are referred to in the Bible. Ahaz "made his son to pass through the fire, according to the abominations of the heathen". Ezekiel declared that "when ye offer your gifts, when ye make your sons to pass through the fire, ye pollute yourselves with all your idols". In Leviticus it is laid down: "Thou shalt not let any of thy seed pass through the fire to Moloch".

It may be that in Babylonia the fire-cleansing ceremony resembled that which obtained at Beltane (May Day) in Scotland, Germany and other countries. Human sacrifices might also have been offered up as burnt offerings. Abraham, who came from the Sumerian city of Ur, was prepared to sacrifice Isaac, Sarah's first born. The fire gods of Babylonia never achieved the ascendancy of the Indian Agni; they appear to have resembled him mainly in so far as he was connected with the sun. Nusku, like Agni, was also the "messenger of the gods". When Merodach or Babylon was exalted as chief god of the pantheon his messages were carried to Ea by Nusku. He may have therefore symbolized the sun rays, for Merodach had solar attributes.

It is possible that the belief obtained among even the water worshippers of Eridu that the sun and moon, which rose from the primordial deep, had their origin in the everlasting fire in Ea's domain at the bottom of the sea. In the Indian god Varuna's ocean home an "Asura fire" (demon fire) burned constantly; it was "bound and confined", but could not be extinguished. Fed by water, this fire, it was believed, would burst forth at the last day and consume the universe. A similar belief can be traced in Teutonic mythology. The Babylonian incantation cult appealed to many gods, but "the most important share in the rites", says Jastrow, "are taken by fire and water – suggesting, therefore, that the god of water – more particularly Ea – and the god of fire … are the chief deities on which the ritual itself hinges". In some temples there was a bit rimki, a "house of washing", and a bit nuri, a "house of light".

It is possible, of course, that fire was regarded as the vital principle by some city cults, which were influenced by imported ideas. If so, the belief never became prevalent. The most enduring influence in Babylonian religion was the early Sumerian; and as Sumerian modes of thought were the outcome of habits of life necessitated by the character of the country, they were bound, sooner or later, to leave a deep impress on the minds of foreign peoples who settled in the Garden of Western Asia. It is not surprising, therefore, to find that imported deities assumed Babylonian characteristics, and were identified or associated with Babylonian gods in the later imperial pantheon.

Moon Gods of Ur and Harran

Moon worship appears to have been as ancient as water worship, with which, as we have seen, it was closely associated. It was widely prevalent throughout Babylonia. The chief seat of the lunar deity, Nannar or Sin, was the ancient city of Ur, from which Abraham migrated to Harran, where the "Baal" (the lord) was also a moon god. Ur was situated in Sumer, in the south, between the west bank of the Euphrates and the low hills bordering the Arabian desert, and not far distant from sea, washed Eridu. No doubt, like that city, it had its origin at an exceedingly remote period. At any rate, the excavations conducted there have afforded proof that it flourished in the prehistoric period.

As in Arabia, Egypt and throughout ancient Europe and elsewhere, the moon god of Sumeria was regarded as the "friend of man". He controlled nature as a fertilizing agency; he caused grass, trees and crops to grow; he increased flocks and herds, and gave human offspring. At Ur he was exalted above Ea as "the lord and prince of the gods, supreme in heaven, the Father of all"; he was also called "great Anu", an indication that Anu, the sky god, had at one time a lunar character. The moon god was believed to be the father of the sun god: he was the "great steer with mighty horns and perfect limbs".

His name Sin is believed to be a corruption of "Zu-ena", which signifies "knowledge lord". Like the lunar Osiris of Egypt, he was apparently an instructor of mankind; the moon measured time and controlled the seasons; seeds were sown at a certain phase of the moon, and crops were ripened by the harvest moon. The mountains of Sinai and the desert of Sin are called after this deity.

As Nannar, which Jastrow considers to be a variation of "Nannar", the "light producer", the moon god scattered darkness and reduced the terrors of night. His spirit inhabited the lunar stone, so that moon and stone worship were closely associated; it also entered trees and crops, so that moon worship linked with earth worship, as both linked with water worship.

The consort of Nannar was Nin-Uruwa, "the lady of Ur", who was also called Nin-gala. She links with Ishtar as Nin, as Isis of Egypt linked with other mother deities. The twin children of the moon were Mashu and Mashtu, a brother and sister, like the lunar girl and boy of Teutonic mythology immortalized in nursery rhymes as Jack and Jill.

Antiquity of Sun Worship

Sun worship was of great antiquity in Babylonia, but appears to have been seasonal in its earliest phases. No doubt the sky god Anu had his solar as well as his lunar attributes, which he shared with Ea. The spring sun was personified as Tammuz, the youthful shepherd, who was loved by the earth goddess Ishtar and her rival Eresh-ki-gal, goddess of death, the Babylonian Persephone. During the winter Tammuz dwelt in Hades, and at the beginning of spring Ishtar descended to search for him among the shades. But the burning summer sun was symbolized as a destroyer, a slayer of men, and therefore a war god. As Ninip or Nirig, the son of Enlil, who was made in the likeness of Anu, he waged war against the earth spirits, and was furiously hostile towards the deities of alien peoples, as befitted a god of battle. Even his father feared him, and when he was advancing towards Nippur, sent out Nusku, messenger of the gods, to soothe the raging deity with soft words. Ninip was symbolized as a wild bull, was connected with stone worship, like the Indian destroying god Shiva, and was similarly a deity of Fate. He had much in common with Nin-Girsu, a god of Lagash, who was in turn regarded as a form of Tammuz.

Nergal, another solar deity, brought disease and pestilence, and, according to Jensen, all misfortunes due to excessive heat. He was the king of death, husband of Eresh-ki-gal, queen of Hades. As a war god he thirsted for human blood, and was depicted as a mighty lion, He was the chief deity of the city of Cuthah, which, Jastrow suggests, was situated beside a burial place of great repute, like the Egyptian Abydos.

Shamash as the "Great Judge"

The two great cities of the sun in ancient Babylonia were the Akkadian Sippar and the Sumerian Larsa. In these the sun god, Shamash or Babbar, was the patron deity. He was a god of Destiny, the lord of the living and the dead, and was exalted as the great Judge, the lawgiver, who upheld justice; he was the enemy of wrong, he loved righteousness and hated sin, he inspired his worshippers with rectitude and punished evildoers. The sun god also illumined the world, and his rays penetrated every quarter: he saw all things, and read the thoughts of men; nothing could be concealed from Shamash. One of his names was Mitra, like the god who was linked with Varuna in the Indian Rigveda. These twin deities, Mitra and Varuna, measured out the span of human life. They were the source of all heavenly gifts: they regulated sun and moon, the winds and waters, and the seasons.

These did the gods establish in royal power over themselves,
because they were wise and the children of wisdom,
and because they excelled in power.
– Prof. Arnold's trans. of Rigvedic Hymn

Mitra and Varuna were protectors of hearth and home, and they chastised sinners. "In a striking passage of the Mahabharata", says Professor Moulton, "one in which Indian thought comes nearest to the conception of conscience, a kingly wrongdoer is reminded that the sun sees secret sin".

Aryan Mitra or Mithra and Linking Babylonian Deities

In Persian mythology Mitra, as Mithra, is the patron of Truth, and "the Mediator" between heaven and earth. This god was also worshipped by the military aristocracy of Mitanni, which held sway for a period over Assyria. In Roman times the worship of Mithra spread into Europe from Persia. Mithraic sculptures depict the deity as a corn god slaying the harvest bull; on one of the monuments "cornstalks instead of blood are seen issuing from the wound inflicted with the knife". The Assyrian word "metru" signifies rain. As a sky god Mitra may have been associated, like Varuna, with the waters above the firmament. Rain would therefore be gifted by him as a fertilizing deity. In the Babylonian Flood legend it is the sun god Shamash who "appointed the time" when the heavens were to "rain destruction" in the night, and commanded Pir-napishtim, "Enter into the midst of thy ship and shut thy door". The solar deity thus appears as a form of Anu, god of the sky and upper atmosphere, who controls the seasons and the various forces of nature. Other rival chiefs of city pantheons, whether lunar, atmospheric, earth, or water deities, were similarly regarded as the supreme deities who ruled the Universe, and decreed when man should receive benefits or suffer from their acts of vengeance.

Varuna and Shamash Hymns Compared

It is possible that the close resemblances between Mithra and Mitra of the Aryan-speaking peoples of India and the Iranian plateau, and the sun god of the Babylonians – the Semitic Shamash, the Sumerian Utu – were due to early contact and cultural influence through the medium of Elam. As a solar and corn god, the Persian Mithra links with Tammuz, as a sky and atmospheric deity with Anu, and as a god of truth, righteousness and law with Shamash. We seem to trace in the sublime Vedic hymns addressed by the Indian Aryans to Mitra and Varuna the impress of Babylonian religious thought:

Whate'er exists within this earth, and all within the sky,
Yea, all that is beyond, King Varuna perceives....
– Rigveda, iv, 16

O Varuna, whatever the offence may be
That we as men commit against the heavenly folk,
When through our want of thought we violate thy laws,

Chastise us not, O god, for that iniquity.
– Rigveda, vii, 89.

Shamash was similarly exalted in Babylonian hymns:

The progeny of those who deal unjustly will not prosper.
What their mouth utters in thy presence
Thou wilt destroy, what issues from their mouth thou wilt dissipate.
Thou knowest their transgressions, the plan of the wicked thou rejectest.
All, whoever they be, are in thy care....
He who takes no bribe, who cares for the oppressed,
Is favoured by Shamash, – his life shall be prolonged.

The worshippers of Varuna and Mitra in the Punjab did not cremate their dead like those who exalted the rival fire god Agni. The grave was the "house of clay", as in Babylonia. Mitra, who was identical with Yama, ruled over departed souls in the "Land of the Pitris" (Fathers), which was reached by crossing the mountains and the rushing stream of death. As we have seen, the Babylonian solar god Nergal was also the lord of the dead.

As Ma-banda-anna, "the boat of the sky", Shamash links with the Egyptian sun god Ra, whose barque sailed over the heavens by day and through the underworld of darkness and death during the night. The consort of Shamash was Aa, and his attendants were Kittu and Mesharu, "Truth" and "Righteousness".

Like the Hittites, the Babylonians had also a sun goddess: her name was Nin-sun, which Jastrow renders "the annihilating lady". At Erech she had a shrine in the temple of the sky god Anu.

The Female Origin of Life

We can trace in Babylonia, as in Egypt, the early belief that life in the Universe had a female origin. Nin-sun links with Ishtar, whose Sumerian name is Nana. Ishtar appears to be identical with the Egyptian Hathor, who, as Sekhet, slaughtered the enemies of the sun god Ra. She was similarly the goddess of maternity, and is depicted in this character, like Isis and other goddesses of similar character, suckling a babe. Another Babylonian lady of the gods was Ama, Mama or Mami, "the creatress of the seed of mankind", and was "probably so called as the 'mother' of all things".

A characteristic atmospheric deity was Ramman, the Rimmon of the Bible, the Semitic Addu, Adad, Hadad, or Dadu. He was not a presiding deity in any pantheon, but was identified with Enlil at Nippur. As a hammer god, he was imported by the Semites from the hills. He was a wind and thunder deity, a rain bringer, a corn god and a god of battle like Thor, Jupiter, Tarku, Indra and others, who were all sons of the sky.

In this brief review of the representative deities of early Babylonia, it will be seen that most gods link with Anu, Ea and Enlil, whose attributes they symbolized in various forms. The prominence accorded to an individual deity depended on local conditions, experiences and influences. Ceremonial practices no doubt varied here and there, but although one section might exalt Ea and another Shamash, the religious faith of the people as a whole did not differ to any marked extent; they served the gods according to their lights, so that life might be prolonged and made prosperous, for the land of death and "no return" was regarded as a place of gloom and misery.

Deities of Good and Evil

When the Babylonians appear before us in the early stages of the historical period they had reached that stage of development set forth so vividly in the Orations of Isocrates: "Those of the gods who are the source to us of good things have the title of Olympians; those whose department is that of calamities and punishments have harsher titles: to the first class both private persons and states erect altars and temples; the second is not worshipped either with prayers or burnt sacrifices, but in their case we perform ceremonies of riddance".

The Sumerians, like the Ancient Egyptians, developed their deities, who reflected the growth of culture, from vague spirit groups, which, like ghosts, were hostile to mankind. Those spirits who could be propitiated were exalted as benevolent deities; those who could not be bargained with were regarded as evil gods and goddesses. A better understanding of the character of Babylonian deities will therefore be obtained by passing the demons and evil spirits under review.

Ashur the National God of Assyria

THE RISE OF ASSYRIA brings into prominence the national god Ashur, who had been the city god of Asshur, the ancient capital. When first met with, he is found to be a complex and mystical deity, and the problem of his origin is consequently rendered exceedingly difficult. Philologists are not agreed as to the derivation of his name, and present as varied views as they do when dealing with the name of Osiris. Some give Ashur a geographical significance, urging that its original form was Aushar, "water field"; others prefer the renderings "Holy", "the Beneficent One", or "the Merciful One"; while not a few regard Ashur as simply a dialectic form of the name of Anshar, the god who, in the Assyrian version, or copy, of the Babylonian Creation myth, is chief of the "host of heaven", and the father of Anu, Ea and Enlil.

If Ashur is to be regarded as an abstract solar deity, who was developed from a descriptive place name, it follows that he had a history, like Anu or Ea, rooted in Naturalism or Animism. We cannot assume that his strictly local character was produced by modes of thought which did not obtain elsewhere. The colonists who settled at Asshur no doubt imported beliefs from some cultural area; they must have either given recognition to a god, or group of gods, or regarded the trees, hills, rivers, sun, moon, stars and the animals as manifestations of the "self-power" of the Universe, before they undertook the work of draining and cultivating the "water field" and erecting permanent homes. Those who settled at Nineveh, for instance, believed that they were protected by the goddess Nina, the patron deity of the Sumerian city of Nina. As this goddess was also worshipped at Lagash, and was one of the many forms of the Great Mother, it would appear that in ancient times deities had a tribal rather than a geographical significance.

Ashur as Anshar and Anu

If the view is accepted that Ashur is Anshar, it can be urged that he was imported from Sumeria. "Out of that land (Shinar)", according to the Biblical reference, "went forth Asshur, and builded Nineveh". Asshur, or Ashur (identical, Delitzsch and Jastrow believe, with Ashir), may have been an eponymous hero – a deified king like Etana, or Gilgamesh, who was regarded as an incarnation of an ancient god. As Anshar was an astral or early form of Anu, the Sumerian city of origin may have been Erech, where the worship of the mother goddess was also given prominence.

Damascius rendered Anshar's name as "Assoros", a fact usually cited to establish Ashur's connection with that deity. This writer stated that the Babylonians passed over "Sige, the mother, that has begotten heaven and earth", and made two – Apason (Apsu), the husband, and Tauthe (Tiawath or Tiamat), whose son was Moymis (Mummu). From these another progeny came forth – Lache and Lachos (Lachmu and Lachamu). These were followed by the progeny Kissare and Assoros (Kishar and Anshar), "from which were produced Anos (Anu), Illillos (Enlil) and Aos (Ea). And of Aos and Dauke (Dawkina or Damkina) was born Belos (Bel Merodach), whom they say is the Demiurge" (the world artisan who carried out the decrees of a higher being).

Lachmu and Lachamu, like the second pair of the ancient group of Egyptian deities, probably symbolized darkness as a reproducing and sustaining power. Anshar was apparently an impersonation of the night sky, as his son Anu was of the day sky. It may have been believed that the soul of Anshar was in the moon as Nannar (Sin), or in a star, or that the moon and the stars were manifestations of him, and that the soul of Anu was in the sun or the firmament, or that the sun, firmament and the wind were forms of this "self-power".

If Ashur combined the attributes of Anshar and Anu, his early mystical character may be accounted for. Like the Indian Brahma, he may have been in his highest form an impersonation, or symbol, of the "self-power" or "world soul" of developed Naturalism – the "creator", "preserver" and "destroyer" in one, a god of water, earth, air and sky, of sun, moon and stars, fire and lightning, a god of the grove, whose essence was in the fig, or the fir cone, as it was in all animals. The Egyptian god Amon of Thebes, who was associated with water, earth, air, sky, sun and moon, had a ram form, and was "the hidden one", was developed from one of the elder eight gods; in the Pyramid Texts he and his consort are the fourth pair. When Amon was fused with the specialized sun god Ra, he was placed at the head of the Ennead as the Creator. "We have traces", says Jastrow, "of an Assyrian myth of Creation in which the sphere of creator is given to Ashur".

Animal Forms of Sky God

Before a single act of creation was conceived of, however, the early peoples recognized the eternity of matter, which was permeated by the "self-power" of which the elder deities were vague phases. These were too vague, indeed, to be worshipped individually. The forms of the "self-power" which were propitiated were trees, rivers, hills or animals. As indicated in the previous chapter, a tribe worshipped an animal or natural object which dominated its environment. The animal might be the source of the food supply, or might have to be propitiated to ensure the food supply. Consequently they identified the self-power of the Universe with the particular animal with which they were most concerned. One section identified the spirit of the heavens with the bull and another with the goat. In India Dyaus was a bull, and his spouse, the earth mother, Prithivi, was a cow.

The Egyptian sky goddess Hathor was a cow, and other goddesses were identified with the hippopotamus, the serpent, the cat, or the vulture. Ra, the sun god, was identified in turn with the cat, the ass, the bull, the ram and the crocodile, the various animal forms of the local deities he had absorbed. The eagle in Babylonia and India, and the vulture, falcon and mysterious Phoenix in Egypt, were identified with the sun, fire, wind and lightning. The animals associated with the god Ashur were the bull, the eagle and the lion. He either absorbed the attributes of other gods, or symbolized the "Self-Power" of which the animals were manifestations.

Anshar as Star God on the Celestial Mount

The earliest germ of the Creation myth was the idea that night was the parent of day, and water of the earth. Out of darkness and death came light and life. Life was also motion. When the primordial waters became troubled, life began to be. Out of the confusion came order and organization. This process involved the idea of a stable and controlling power, and the succession of a group of deities – passive deities and active deities. When the Babylonian astrologers assisted in developing the Creation myth, they appear to have identified with the stable and controlling spirit of the night heaven that steadfast orb the Polar Star. Anshar, like Shakespeare's Caesar, seemed to say:

I am constant as the northern star,
Of whose true-fixed and resting quality
There is no fellow in the firmament.
The skies are painted with unnumbered sparks;
They are all fire, and every one doth shine;
But there's but one in all doth hold his place.

Associated with the Polar Star was the constellation Ursa Minor, "the Little Bear", called by the Babylonian astronomers, "the Lesser Chariot". There were chariots before horses were introduced. A patesi of Lagash had a chariot which was drawn by asses.

The seemingly steadfast Polar Star was called "Ilu Sar", "the god Shar", or Anshar, "star of the height ", or "Shar the most high". It seemed to be situated at the summit of the vault of heaven. The god Shar, therefore, stood upon the Celestial mountain, the Babylonian Olympus. He was the ghost of the elder god, who in Babylonia was displaced by the younger god, Merodach, as Mercury, the morning star, or as the sun, the planet of day; and in Assyria by Ashur, as the sun, or Regulus, or Arcturus, or Orion. Yet father and son were identical. They were phases of the One, the "self-power".

A deified reigning king was an incarnation of the god; after death he merged in the god, as did the Egyptian Unas. The eponymous hero Asshur may have similarly merged in the universal Ashur, who, like Horus, an incarnation of Osiris, had many phases or forms.

Isaiah's Parable

Isaiah appears to have been familiar with the Tigro-Euphratean myths about the divinity of kings and the displacement of the elder god by the younger god, of whom the ruling monarch was an incarnation, and with the idea that the summit of the Celestial mountain was crowned by the "north star", the symbol of Anshar. "Thou shalt take up this parable", he exclaimed, making use of Babylonian symbolism, "against the king of Babylon and say, How hath the oppressor ceased! the golden city ceased! ... How art thou fallen from heaven, O Lucifer, son of the morning! how art thou cut down to the ground, which didst weaken the nations! For thou hast said in thine heart, I will ascend unto heaven, I will exalt my throne above the stars of God; I will sit also upon the mount of the congregation, in the sides of the north; I will ascend above the heights of the clouds; I will be like the most High". The king is identified with Lucifer as the deity of fire and the morning star; he is the younger god who aspired to occupy the mountain throne of his father, the god Shar – the Polar or North Star.

Symbols of World God and World Hill

It is possible that the Babylonian idea of a Celestial mountain gave origin to the belief that the earth was a mountain surrounded by the outer ocean, beheld by Etana when he flew towards heaven on the eagle's back. In India this hill is Mount Meru, the "world spine", which "sustains the earth"; it is surmounted by Indra's Valhal, or "the great city of Brahma". In Teutonic mythology the heavens revolve round the Polar Star, which is called "Veraldar nagli", the "world spike"; while the earth is sustained by the "world tree". The "ded" amulet of Egypt symbolized the backbone of Osiris as a world god: "ded" means "firm", "established"; while at burial ceremonies the coffin was set up on end, inside the tomb, "on a small sandhill intended to represent the Mountain of the West – the realm of the dead". The Babylonian temple towers were apparently symbols of the "world hill". At Babylon, the Du-azaga, "holy mound", was Merodach's temple E-sagila, "the Temple of the High Head". E-kur, rendered "the house or temple of the Mountain", was the temple of Bel Enlil at Nippur. At Erech, the temple of the goddess Ishtar was E-anna, which connects her, as Nina or Ninni, with Anu, derived from "ana", "heaven". Ishtar was "Queen of heaven".

Goat Gods and Bull Gods

Now Polaris, situated at the summit of the celestial mountain, was identified with the sacred goat, "the highest of the flock of night". Ursa Minor (the "Little Bear" constellation) may have been "the goat with six heads", referred to by Professor Sayce. The six astral goats or goat-men were supposed to be dancing round the chief goat-man or Satyr (Anshar). Even in the dialogues of Plato the immemorial belief was perpetuated that the constellations were "moving as in a dance". Dancing began as a magical or religious practice, and the earliest astronomers saw their dancing customs reflected in the heavens by the constellations, whose movements were rhythmical. No doubt, Isaiah had in mind the belief of the Babylonians regarding the dance of their goat-gods when he foretold: "Their houses shall be full of doleful creatures; and owls (ghosts) shall dwell there, and satyrs shall dance there". In other words, there would be no people left to perform religious dances beside the "desolate houses"; the stars only would be seen dancing round Polaris.

Tammuz, like Anshar, as sentinel of the night heaven, was a goat, as was also Nin-Girsu of Lagash. A Sumerian reference to "a white kid of En Mersi (Nin-Girsu)" was translated into Semitic, "a white kid of Tammuz". The goat was also associated with Merodach. Babylonians, having prayed to that god to take away their diseases or their sins, released a goat, which was driven into the desert. The present Polar Star, which was not, of course, the Polar star of the earliest astronomers, the world having rocked westward, is called in Arabic Al-Jedy, "the kid". In India, the goat was connected with Agni and Varuna; it was slain at funeral ceremonies to inform the gods that a soul was about to enter heaven. Ea, the Sumerian lord of water, earth and heaven, was symbolized as a "goat fish". Thor, the Teutonic fertility and thunder god, had a chariot drawn by goats. It is of interest to note that the sacred Sumerian goat bore on its forehead the same triangular symbol as the Apis bull of Egypt.

Ashur was not a "goat of heaven", but a "bull of heaven", like the Sumerian Nannar (Sin), the moon god of Ur, Ninip of Saturn, and Bel Enlil. As the bull, however, he was, like Anshar, the ruling animal of the heavens; and like Anshar he had associated with him "six divinities of council".

Symbols of Gods as "High Heads"

Other deities who were similarly exalted as "high heads" at various centres and at various periods, included Anu, Bel Enlil and Ea, Merodach, Nergal and Shamash. A symbol of the first three was a turban on a seat, or altar, which may have represented the "world mountain". Ea, as "the world spine", was symbolized as a column, with ram's head, standing on a throne, beside which crouched a "goat fish". Merodach's column terminated in a lance head, and the head of a lion crowned that of Nergal. These columns were probably connected with pillar worship, and therefore with tree worship, the pillar being the trunk of the "world tree". The symbol of the sun god Shamash was a disc, from which flowed streams of water; his rays apparently were "fertilizing tears", like the rays of the Egyptian sun god Ra. Horus, the Egyptian falcon god, was symbolized as the winged solar disc.

The Winged Disc

It is necessary to accumulate these details regarding other deities and their symbols before dealing with Ashur. The symbols of Ashur must be studied, because they are one of the sources of our knowledge regarding the god's origin and character. These include (1) a winged disc with horns, enclosing four circles revolving round a middle circle; rippling rays fall down from either side of the disc; (2) a circle or wheel, suspended from wings, and enclosing a warrior drawing his bow to discharge an arrow; and (3) the same circle; the warrior's bow, however, is carried in his left hand, while the right hand is uplifted as if to bless his worshippers. These symbols are taken from seal cylinders.

An Assyrian standard, which probably represented the "world column", has the disc mounted on a bull's head with horns. The upper part of the disc is occupied by a warrior, whose head, part of his bow and the point of his arrow protrude from the circle. The rippling water rays are V-shaped, and two bulls, treading river-like rays, occupy the divisions thus formed. There are also two heads – a lion's and a man's – with gaping mouths, which may symbolize tempests, the destroying power of the sun, or the sources of the Tigris and Euphrates.

Jastrow regards the winged disc as "the purer and more genuine symbol of Ashur as a solar deity". He calls it "a sun disc with protruding rays", and says: "To this symbol the warrior with the bow and arrow was added – a despiritualization that reflects the martial spirit of the Assyrian empire".

Human Figure as Soul of the Sun

The sun symbol on the sun boat of Ra encloses similarly a human figure, which was apparently regarded as the soul of the sun: the life of the god was in the "sun egg". In an Indian prose treatise it is set forth: "Now that man in yonder orb (the sun) and that man in the right eye truly are no other than Death (the soul). His feet have stuck fast in the heart, and having pulled them out he comes forth; and when he comes forth then that man dies; whence they say of him who has passed away, 'he has been cut off (his life or life string has been severed)'". The human figure did not indicate a process of "despiritualization" either in Egypt or in India. The Horus "winged disc" was besides a symbol of destruction and battle, as well as of light and fertility. Horus assumed that form in one legend to destroy Set and his followers. But, of course, the same symbols may not have conveyed the same ideas to all peoples. As Blake put it:

What to others a trifle appears
Fills me full of smiles and tears....
With my inward Eye, 't is an old Man grey,
With my outward, a Thistle across my way.

Indeed, it is possible that the winged disc meant one thing to an Assyrian priest, and another thing to a man not gifted with what Blake called "double vision".

Ashur as Hercules and Gilgamesh

What seems certain, however, is that the archer was as truly solar as the "wings" or "rays". In Babylonia and Assyria the sun was, among other things, a destroyer from the earliest times. It is not surprising, therefore, to find that Ashur, like Merodach, resembled, in one of his phases, Hercules, or rather his prototype Gilgamesh. One of Gilgamesh's mythical feats was the slaying of three demon birds. These may be identical with the birds of prey which Hercules, in performing his sixth labour, hunted out of Stymphalus. In the Greek Hipparcho-Ptolemy star list Hercules was the constellation of the "Kneeler", and in Babylonian-Assyrian astronomy he was (as Gilgamesh or Merodach) "Sarru", "the king". The astral "Arrow" (constellation of Sagitta) was pointed against the constellations of the "Eagle", "Vulture" and "Swan". In Phoenician astronomy the Vulture was "Zither" (Lyra), a weapon with which Hercules (identified with Melkarth) slew Linos, the musician. Hercules used a solar arrow, which he received from Apollo. In various mythologies the arrow is associated with the sun, the moon and the atmospheric deities, and is a symbol of lightning, rain and fertility, as well as of famine, disease, war and death.

The green-faced goddess Neith of Libya, compared by the Greeks to Minerva, carries in one hand two arrows and a bow. If we knew as little of Athena (Minerva), who was armed with a lance, a breastplate made of the skin of a goat, a shield and helmet, as we do of Ashur, it might be held that she was simply a goddess of war. The archer in the sun disc of the Assyrian standard probably represented Ashur as the god of the people – a deity closely akin to Merodach, with pronounced Tammuz traits, and therefore linking with other local deities like Ninip, Nergal and Shamash, and partaking also like these of the attributes of the elder gods Anu, Bel Enlil and Ea.

Gods Differentiated by Cults

All the other deities worshipped by the Assyrians were of Babylonian origin. Ashur appears to have differed from them just as one local Babylonian deity differed from another. He reflected Assyrian experiences and aspirations, but it is difficult to decide whether the sublime spiritual aspect of his character was due to the beliefs of alien peoples, by whom the early Assyrians were influenced, or to the teachings of advanced Babylonian thinkers, whose doctrines found readier acceptance in a "new country" than among the conservative ritualists of ancient Sumerian and Akkadian cities. New cults were formed from time to time in Babylonia, and when they achieved political power they gave a distinctive character to the religion of their city states. Others which did not find political support and remained in obscurity at home, may have yet extended their influence far and wide.

Buddhism, for instance, originated in India, but now flourishes in other countries, to which it was introduced by missionaries. In the homeland it was submerged by the revival of Brahmanism, from which it sprung, and which it was intended permanently to displace. An instance of an advanced cult suddenly achieving prominence as a result of political influence is afforded by Egypt, where the fully developed Aton religion was embraced and established as a national religion by Akhenaton, the so-called "dreamer". That migrations were sometimes propelled by cults, which sought new areas in which to exercise religious freedom and propagate their beliefs, is suggested by the invasion of India at the close of the Vedic period by the "later comers", who laid the foundations of Brahmanism. They established themselves in Madhyadesa, "the Middle Country", "the land where the Brahmanas and the later Samhitas were produced". From this centre went forth missionaries, who accomplished the Brahmanization of the rest of India.

Fertility Gods as War Gods

It may be, therefore, that the cult of Ashur was influenced in its development by the doctrines of advanced teachers from Babylonia, and that Persian Mithraism was also the product of missionary efforts extended from that great and ancient cultural area. Mitra, as has been stated, was one of the names of the Babylonian sun god, who was also a god of fertility. But Ashur could not have been to begin with merely a battle and solar deity. As the god of a city state he must have been worshipped by agriculturists, artisans and traders; he must have been recognized as a deity of fertility, culture, commerce and law. Even as a national god he must have made wider appeal than to the cultured and ruling classes. Bel Enlil of Nippur was a "world god" and war god, but still remained a local corn god.

Assyria's greatness was reflected by Ashur, but he also reflected the origin and growth of that greatness. The civilization of which he was a product had an agricultural basis. It began with the development of the natural resources of Assyria, as was recognized by the Hebrew prophet, who said: "Behold, the Assyrian was a cedar in Lebanon with fair branches.... The waters made him great, the deep set him up on high with her rivers running round about his plants, and sent out her little rivers unto all the trees of the field. Therefore his height was exalted above all the trees of the field, and his boughs were multiplied, and his branches became long because of the multitude of waters when he shot forth. All the fowls of heaven made their nests in his boughs, and under his branches did all the beasts of the field bring forth their young, and under his shadow dwelt all great nations. Thus was he fair in his greatness, in the length of his branches; for his root was by great waters. The cedars in the garden of God could not hide him: the fir trees were not like his boughs, and the chestnut trees were not like his branches; nor any tree in the garden of God was like unto him in his beauty".

Asshur, the ancient capital, was famous for its merchants. It is referred to in the Bible as one of the cities which traded with Tyre "in all sorts of things, in blue clothes, and broidered work, and in chests of rich apparel, bound with cords, and made of cedar".

As a military power, Assyria's name was dreaded. "Behold", Isaiah said, addressing King Hezekiah, "thou hast heard what the kings of Assyria have done to all lands by destroying them utterly". The same prophet, when foretelling how Israel would suffer, exclaimed: "O Assyrian, the rod of mine anger, and the staff in their hand is mine indignation. I will send him against an hypocritical nation, and against the people of my wrath will I give him a charge, to take the spoil, and to take the prey, and to tread them down like the mire of the streets".

We expect to find Ashur reflected in these three phases of Assyrian civilization. If we recognize him in the first place as a god of fertility, his other attributes are at once included. A god of fertility is a corn god and a water god. The river as a river was a "creator", and Ashur was therefore closely associated with the "watery place", with the canals or "rivers running round about his plants". The rippling water-rays, or fertilizing tears, appear on the solar discs. As a corn god, he was a god of war. Tammuz's first act was to slay the demons of winter and storm, as Indra's in India was to slay the demons of drought, and Thor's in Scandinavia was to exterminate the frost giants. The corn god had to be fed with human sacrifices, and the people therefore waged war against foreigners to obtain victims. As the god made a contract with his people, he was a deity of commerce; he provided them with food and they in turn fed him with offerings.

Ashur's Tree and Animal forms

In Ezekiel's comparison of Assyria to a mighty tree, there is no doubt a mythological reference. The Hebrew prophets invariably utilized for their poetic imagery the characteristic beliefs of the peoples to whom they made direct reference. The "owls", "satyrs" and "dragons" of Babylon, mentioned by Isaiah, were taken from Babylonian mythology, as has been indicated. When, therefore, Assyria is compared to a cedar, which is greater than fir or chestnut, and it is stated that there are nesting birds in the branches, and under them reproducing beasts of the field, and that the greatness of the tree is due to "the multitude of waters", the conclusion is suggested that Assyrian religion, which Ashur's symbols reflect, included the worship of trees, birds, beasts and water. The symbol of the Assyrian tree – probably the "world tree" of its religion – appears to be "the rod of mine anger ... the staff in their hand"; that is, the battle standard which was a symbol of Ashur. Tammuz and Osiris were tree gods as well as corn gods.

Now, as Ashur was evidently a complex deity, it is futile to attempt to read his symbols without giving consideration to the remnants of Assyrian mythology which are found in the ruins of the ancient cities. These either reflect the attributes of Ashur, or constitute the material from which he evolved.

As Layard pointed out many years ago, the Assyrians had a sacred tree which became conventionalized. It was "an elegant device, in which curved branches, springing from a kind of scroll work, terminated in flowers of graceful form. As one of the figures last described was turned, as if in act of adoration, towards this device, it was evidently a sacred emblem; and I recognized in it the holy tree, or tree of life, so universally adored at the remotest period in the East, and which was preserved in the religious systems of the Persians to the final overthrow of their Empire ... The flowers were formed by seven petals".

This tree looks like a pillar, and is thrice crossed by conventionalized bull's horns tipped with ring symbols which may be stars, the highest pair of horns having a larger ring between them, but only partly shown as if it were a crescent. The tree with its many "sevenfold" designs may have been a symbol of the "Sevenfold-one-are-ye" deity. This is evidently the Assyrian tree which was called "the rod" or "staff".

What mythical animals did this tree shelter? Layard found that "the four creatures continually introduced on the sculptured walls", were "a man, a lion, an ox and an eagle".

In Sumeria the gods were given human form, but before this stage was reached the bull symbolized Nannar (Sin), the moon god, Ninip (Saturn, the old sun), and Enlil, while Nergal was a lion, as a tribal sun god. The eagle is represented by the Zu bird, which symbolized the storm and a phase of the sun, and was also a deity of fertility. On the silver vase of Lagash the lion and eagle were combined as the lion-headed eagle, a form of Nin-Girsu (Tammuz), and it was associated with wild goats, stags, lions and bulls. On a mace head dedicated to Nin-Girsu, a lion slays a bull as the Zu bird slays serpents in the folk tale, suggesting the wars of totemic deities, according to one "school", and the battle of the sun with the storm clouds according to another. Whatever the explanation may be of one animal deity of fertility slaying another, it seems certain that the conflict was associated with the idea of sacrifice to procure the food supply.

Ashur as Nisroch

In Assyria the various primitive gods were combined as a winged bull, a winged bull with human head (the king's), a winged lion with human head, a winged man, a deity with lion's head, human body and eagle's legs with claws, and also as a deity with eagle's head and feather headdress, a human body, wings and feather-fringed robe, carrying in one hand a metal basket on which two winged men adored the holy tree, and in the other a fir cone.

Layard suggested that the latter deity, with eagle's head, was Nisroch, "the word Nisr signifying, in all Semitic languages, an eagle". This deity is referred to in the Bible: "Sennacherib, king of Assyria, ... was worshipping in the house of Nisroch, his god". Professor Pinches is certain that Nisroch is Ashur, but considers that the "ni" was attached to "Ashur" (Ashuraku or Ashurachu), as it was to "Marad" (Merodach) to give the reading Ni-Marad = Nimrod. The names of heathen deities were thus made "unrecognizable, and in all probability ridiculous as well.... Pious and orthodox lips could pronounce them without fear of defilement". At the same time the "Nisr" theory is probable: it may represent another phase of this process. The names of heathen gods were not all treated in like manner by the Hebrew teachers. Abed-nebo, for instance, became Abed-nego (Daniel, i, 7), as Professor Pinches shows.

Lightning Symbol in Disc

Seeing that the eagle received prominence in the mythologies of Sumeria and Assyria, as a deity of fertility with solar and atmospheric attributes, it is highly probable that the Ashur symbol, like the Egyptian Horus solar disk, is a winged symbol of life, fertility and destruction. The idea that it represents the sun in eclipse, with protruding rays, seems rather far-fetched, because eclipses were disasters and indications of divine wrath; it certainly does not explain why the "rays" should only stretch out sideways, like wings, and downward like a tail, why the "rays" should be double, like the double wings of cherubs, bulls, etc., and divided into sections suggesting feathers, or why the disk is surmounted by conventionalized horns, tipped with star-like ring symbols, identical with those depicted in the holy tree. What particular connection the five small rings within the disk were supposed to have with the eclipse of the sun is difficult to discover.

In one of the other symbols in which appears a feather-robed archer, it is significant to find that the arrow he is about to discharge has a head shaped like a trident; it is evidently a lightning symbol.

Ezekiel's Reference to Life Wheel

When Ezekiel prophesied to the Israelitish captives at Tel-abib, "by the river of Chebar" in Chaldea (Kheber, near Nippur), he appears to have utilized Assyrian symbolism. Probably he came into contact in Babylonia with fugitive priests from Assyrian cities.

This great prophet makes interesting references to "four living creatures", with "four faces" – the face of a man, the face of a lion, the face of an ox, and the face of an eagle; "they had the hands of a man under their wings, ... their wings were joined one to another; ... their wings were stretched upward: two wings of every one were joined one to another.... Their appearance was like burning coals of fire and like the appearance of lamps.... The living creatures ran and returned as the appearance of a flash of lightning".

Elsewhere, referring to the sisters, Aholah and Aholibah, who had been in Egypt and had adopted unmoral ways of life, Ezekiel tells that when Aholibah "doted upon the Assyrians" she "saw men pourtrayed upon the wall, the images of the Chaldeans pourtrayed with vermilion, girded with girdles upon their loins". Traces of the red colour on the walls of Assyrian temples and palaces have been observed by excavators. The winged gods "like burning coals" were probably painted in vermilion.

Ezekiel makes reference to "ring" and "wheel" symbols. In his vision he saw "one wheel upon the earth by the living creatures, with his four faces. The appearance of the wheels and their work was like unto the colour of beryl; and they four had one likeness; and their appearance and their work was as it were a wheel in the middle of a wheel.... As for their rings, they were so high that they were dreadful; and their rings were full of eyes round about them four. And when the living creatures went, the wheels went by them; and when the living creatures were lifted up from the earth, the wheels were lifted up. Whithersoever the spirit was to go, they went, thither was their spirit to go; and the wheels were lifted up over against them; for the spirit of the living creature was in the wheels.... And the likeness of the firmament upon the heads of the living creature was as the colour of terrible crystal, stretched forth over their heads above.... And when they went I heard the noise of their wings, like the noise of great waters, as the voice of the Almighty, the voice of speech, as the noise of an host; when they stood they let down their wings...".

Another description of the cherubs states: "Their whole body, and their backs, and their hands, and their wings and the wheels, were full of eyes (? stars) round about, even the wheels that they four had. As for the wheels, it was cried unto them in my hearing, O wheel!" – or, according to a marginal rendering, "they were called in my hearing, wheel, or Gilgal", i.e. move round.... "And the cherubims were lifted up".

It would appear that the wheel (or hoop, a variant rendering) was a symbol of life, and that the Assyrian feather-robed figure which it enclosed was a god, not of war only, but also of fertility. His trident-headed arrow resembles, as has been suggested, a lightning symbol. Ezekiel's references are suggestive in this connection. When the cherubs "ran and returned" they had "the appearance of a flash of lightning", and "the noise of their wings" resembled "the noise of great waters". Their bodies were "like burning coals of fire". Fertility gods were associated with fire, lightning and water. Agni of India, Sandan of Asia Minor, and Melkarth of Phoenicia were highly developed fire gods of fertility. The fire cult was also represented in Sumeria.

Indian Wheel and Discus

In the Indian epic, the Mahabharata, the revolving ring or wheel protects the Soma (ambrosia) of the gods, on which their existence depends. The eagle giant Garuda sets forth to steal it. The gods, fully armed, gather round to protect the life-giving drink. Garuda approaches "darkening the worlds by the dust raised by the hurricane of his wings". The celestials, "overwhelmed by that dust", swoon away. Garuda afterwards assumes a fiery shape, then looks "like masses of black clouds", and in the end its body becomes golden and bright "as the rays of the sun". The Soma is protected by fire, which the bird quenches after "drinking in many rivers" with the numerous mouths it has assumed. Then Garuda finds that right above the Soma is "a wheel of steel, keen edged, and sharp as a razor, revolving incessantly. That fierce instrument, of the lustre of the blazing sun and of terrible form, was devised by the gods for cutting to pieces all robbers of the Soma". Garuda passes "through the spokes of the wheel", and has then to contend against "two great snakes of the lustre of blazing fire, of tongues bright as the lightning flash, of great energy, of mouth emitting fire, of blazing eyes". He slays the snakes.... The gods afterwards recover the stolen Soma.

Garuda becomes the vehicle of the god Vishnu, who carries the discus, another fiery wheel which revolves and returns to the thrower like lightning. "And he (Vishnu) made the bird sit on the flagstaff of his car, saying: 'Even thus thou shalt stay above me'".

The Persian god Ahura Mazda hovers above the king in sculptured representations of that high dignitary, enclosed in a winged wheel, or disk, like Ashur, grasping a ring in one hand, the other being lifted up as if blessing those who adore him.

Shamash, the Babylonian sun god; Ishtar, the goddess of heaven; and other Babylonian deities carried rings as the Egyptian gods carried the ankh, the symbol of life. Shamash was also depicted sitting on his throne in a pillar-supported pavilion, in front of which is a sun wheel. The spokes of the wheel are formed by a star symbol and threefold rippling "water rays".

Hittite Winged Disc

In Hittite inscriptions there are interesting winged emblems; "the central portion" of one "seems to be composed of two crescents underneath a disk (which is also divided like a crescent). Above the emblem there appear the symbol of sanctity (the divided oval) and the hieroglyph which Professor Sayce interprets as the name of the god Sandes". In another instance "the centre of the winged emblem may be seen to be a rosette, with a curious spreading object below. Above, two dots follow the name of Sandes, and a human arm bent 'in adoration' is by the side...". Professor Garstang is here dealing with sacred places "on rocky points or hilltops, bearing out the suggestion of the sculptures near Boghaz-Keui, in which there may be reasonably suspected the surviving traces of mountain cults, or cults of mountain deities, underlying the newer religious symbolism". Who the deity is it is impossible to say, but "he was identified at some time or other with Sandes". It would appear, too, that the god may have been "called by a name which was that used also by the priest". Perhaps the priest king was believed to be an incarnation of the deity.

Sandes or Sandan was identical with Sandon of Tarsus, "the prototype of Attis", who links with the Babylonian Tammuz. Sandon's animal symbol was the lion, and he carried the "double axe" symbol of the god of fertility and thunder. As Professor Frazer has shown in The Golden Bough, he links with Hercules and Melkarth.

Solar Wheel Causes Seasonal Changes

All the younger gods, who displaced the elder gods as one year displaces another, were deities of fertility, battle, lightning, fire and the sun; it is possible, therefore, that Ashur was like Merodach, son of Ea, god of the deep, a form of Tammuz in origin. His spirit was in the solar wheel which revolved at times of seasonal change. In Scotland it was believed that on the morning of May Day (Beltaine) the rising sun revolved three times. The younger god was a spring sun god and fire god. Great bonfires were lit to strengthen him, or as a ceremony of riddance; the old year was burned out. Indeed the god himself might be burned (that is, the old god), so that he might renew his youth. Melkarth was burned at Tyre. Hercules burned himself on a mountain top, and his soul ascended to heaven as an eagle.

Bonfires to Stimulate Solar Deity

These fiery rites were evidently not unknown in Babylonia and Assyria. When, according to Biblical narrative, Nebuchadnezzar "made an image of gold" which he set up "in the plain of Dura, in the province of Babylon", he commanded: "O people, nations, and languages ... at the time ye hear the sound of the cornet, flute, harp, sackbut, psaltery, dulcimer and all kinds of musick ... fall down and worship the golden image". Certain Jews who had been "set over the affairs of the province of Babylonia", namely, "Shadrach, Meshach and Abed-nego", refused to adore the idol. They were punished by being thrown into "a burning fiery furnace", which was heated "seven times more than it was wont to be heated". They came forth uninjured.

In the Koran it is related that Abraham destroyed the images of Chaldean gods; he "brake them all in pieces except the biggest of them; that they might lay the blame on that". According to the commentators the Chaldaeans were at the time "abroad in the fields, celebrating a great festival". To punish the offender Nimrod had a great pyre erected at Cuthah. "Then they bound Abraham, and putting him into an engine, shot him into the midst of the fire, from which he was preserved by the angel Gabriel, who was sent to his assistance". Eastern Christians were wont to set apart in the Syrian calendar the 25th of January to commemorate Abraham's escape from Nimrod's pyre.

It is evident that the Babylonian fire ceremony was observed in the spring season, and that human beings were sacrificed to the sun god. A mock king may have been burned to perpetuate the ancient sacrifice of real kings, who were incarnations of the god.

Burning of Gods and Kings

Isaiah makes reference to the sacrificial burning of kings in Assyria: "For through the voice of the Lord shall the Assyrian be beaten down, which smote with a rod. And in every place where the grounded staff shall pass, which the Lord shall lay upon him, it shall be with tabrets and harps: and in battles of shaking will he fight with it. For Tophet is ordained of old; yea, for the king it is prepared: he hath made it deep and large: the pile thereof is fire and much wood: the breath of the Lord, like a stream of brimstone, doth kindle it". When Nineveh was about to fall, and with it the Assyrian Empire, the legendary king, Sardanapalus, who was reputed to have founded Tarsus, burned himself, with his wives, concubines and eunuchs, on a pyre in his palace. Zimri, who reigned over Israel for seven days, "burnt the king's house over him with fire". Saul, another fallen king, was burned after death, and his bones were buried "under the oak in Jabesh".

In Europe the oak was associated with gods of fertility and lightning, including Jupiter and Thor. The ceremony of burning Saul is of special interest. Asa, the orthodox king of Judah, was, after death, "laid in the bed which was filled with sweet odours and divers kinds of spices prepared by the apothecaries' art: and they made a very great burning for him". Jehoram, the heretic king of Judah, who "walked in the way of the kings of Israel", died of "an incurable disease. And his people made no burning for him, like the burning of his fathers".

The conclusion suggested by the comparative study of the beliefs of neighbouring peoples, and the evidence afforded by Assyrian sculptures, is that Ashur was a highly developed form of the god of fertility, who was sustained, or aided in his conflicts with demons, by the fires and sacrifices of his worshippers.

Magical Ring and Other Symbols of Scotland

It is possible to read too much into his symbols. These are not more complicated and vague than are the symbols on the standing stones of Scotland – the crescent with the "broken" arrow; the trident with the double rings, or wheels, connected by two crescents; the circle with the dot in its centre; the triangle with the dot; the large disk with two small rings on either side crossed by double straight lines; the so-called "mirror", and so on. Highly developed symbolism may not indicate a process of spiritualization so much, perhaps, as the persistence of magical beliefs and practices. There is really no direct evidence to support the theory that the Assyrian winged disk, or disk "with protruding rays", was of more spiritual character than the wheel which encloses the feather-robed archer with his trident-shaped arrow.

Ashur's Wheel of Life and Eagle Wings

The various symbols may have represented phases of the god. When the spring fires were lit, and the god "renewed his life like the eagle", his symbol was possibly the solar wheel or disk with eagle's wings, which became regarded as a symbol of life. The god brought life and light to the world; he caused the crops to grow; he gave increase; he sustained his worshippers. But he was also the god who slew the demons of darkness and storm. The Hittite winged disk was Sandes or Sandon, the god of lightning, who stood on the back of a bull. As the lightning god was a war god, it was in keeping with his character to find him represented in Assyria as "Ashur the archer" with the bow and lightning arrow. On the disk of the Assyrian standard the lion and the bull appear with "the archer" as symbols of the war god Ashur, but they were also symbols of Ashur the god of fertility.

The life or spirit of the god was in the ring or wheel, as the life of the Egyptian and Indian gods, and of the giants of folk tales, was in "the egg". The "dot within the circle", a widespread symbol, may have represented the seed within "the egg" of more than one mythology, or the thorn within the egg of more than one legendary story. It may be that in Assyria, as in India, the crude beliefs and symbols of the masses were spiritualized by the speculative thinkers in the priesthood, but no literary evidence has survived to justify us in placing the Assyrian teachers on the same level as the Brahmans who composed the Upanishads.

King and Ashur

Temples were erected to Ashur, but he might be worshipped anywhere, like the Queen of Heaven, who received offerings in the streets of Jerusalem, for "he needed no temple", as Professor Pinches says. Whether this was because he was a highly developed deity or a product of folk religion it is difficult to decide. One important fact is that the ruling king of Assyria was more closely connected with the worship of Ashur than the king of Babylonia was with the worship of Merodach. This may be because the Assyrian king was regarded as an incarnation of his god, like the Egyptian Pharaoh. Ashur accompanied the monarch on his campaigns: he was their conquering war god. Where the king was, there was Ashur also. No images were made of him, but his symbols were carried aloft, as were the symbols of Indian gods in the great war of the Mahabharata epic.

Ashur Associated with Lunar, Fire, and Star Gods

It would appear that Ashur was sometimes worshipped in the temples of other gods. In an interesting inscription he is associated with the moon god Nannar (Sin) of Haran. Esarhaddon, the Assyrian king, is believed to have been crowned in that city. "The writer", says Professor Pinches, "is apparently addressing Assur-bani-apli, 'the great and noble Asnapper':

"When the father of my king my lord went to Egypt, he was crowned (?) in the ganni of Harrah, the temple (lit. 'Bethel') of cedar. The god Sin remained over the (sacred) standard, two crowns upon his head, (and) the god Nusku stood beside him. The father of the king my lord entered, (and) he (the priest of Sin) placed (the crown?) upon his head, (saying) thus: 'Thou shalt go and capture the lands in the midst'. (He we)nt, he captured the land of Egypt. The rest of the lands not submitting (?) to Assur (Ashur) and Sin, the king, the lord of kings, shall capture (them)".

Ashur and Sin are here linked as equals. Associated with them is Nusku, the messenger of the gods, who was given prominence in Assyria. The kings frequently invoked him. As the son of Ea he acted as the messenger between Merodach and the god of the deep. He was also a son of Bel Enlil, and like Anu was guardian or chief of the Igigi, the "host of heaven". Professor Pinches suggests that he may have been either identical with the Sumerian fire god Gibil, or a brother of the fire god, and an impersonation of the light of fire and sun. In Haran he accompanied the moon god, and may, therefore, have symbolized the light of the moon also. Professor Pinches adds that in one inscription "he is identified with Nirig or En-reshtu" (Nin-Girsu = Tammuz). The Babylonians and Assyrians associated fire and light with moisture and fertility.

The Osirian Clue

The astral phase of the character of Ashur is highly probable. As has been indicated, the Greek rendering of Anshar as "Assoros", is suggestive in this connection. Jastrow, however, points out that the use of the characters Anshar for Ashur did not obtain until the eighth century BCE. "Linguistically", he says, "the change of Ashir to Ashur can be accounted for, but not the transformation of An-shar to Ashur or Ashir; so that we must assume the 'etymology' of Ashur, proposed by some learned scribe, to be the nature of a play upon the name". On the other hand, it is possible that what appears arbitrary to us may have been justified in ancient Assyria on perfectly reasonable, or at any rate traditional, grounds. Professor Pinches points out that as a sun god, and "at the same time not Shamash", Ashur resembled Merodach. "His identification with Merodach, if that was ever accepted, may have been due to the likeness of the word to Asari, one of the deities' names".

As Asari, Merodach has been compared to the Egyptian Osiris, who, as the Nile god, was Asar-Hapi. Osiris resembles Tammuz and was similarly a corn deity and a ruler of the living and the dead, associated with sun, moon, stars, water and vegetation. We may consistently connect Ashur with Aushar, "water field", Anshar, "god of the height", or "most high", and with the eponymous King Asshur who went out on the land of Nimrod and "builded Nineveh", if we regard him as of common origin with Tammuz, Osiris and Attis – a developed and localized form of the ancient deity of fertility and corn.

Hittite and Persian Influences

Ashur had a spouse who is referred to as Ashuritu, or Beltu, "the lady". Her name, however, is not given, but it is possible that she was identified with the Ishtar of Nineveh. In the historical texts Ashur, as the royal god, stands alone. Like the Hittite Great Father, he was perhaps regarded as the origin of life. Indeed, it may have been due to the influence of the northern hillmen in the early Assyrian period, that Ashur was developed as a father god – a Baal. When the Hittite inscriptions are read, more light may be thrown on the Ashur problem. Another possible source of cultural influence is Persia. The supreme god Ahura-Mazda (Ormuzd) was, as has been indicated, represented, like Ashur, hovering over the king's head, enclosed in a winged disk or wheel, and the sacred tree figured in Persian mythology. The early Assyrian kings had non-Semitic and non-Sumerian names. It seems reasonable to assume that the religious culture of the ethnic elements they represented must have contributed to the development of the city god of Asshur.

Myths of Origin

Introduction

THE THEORIES and concepts evolved by the Sumerians to explain the origin of the universe and the existence of gods and men come from many sources. The texts of these sources comprise this chapter, as related and translated by experts Donald A. Mackenzie, Samuel Noah Kramer and Robert William Rogers. Some of the texts are reprinted from the Electronic Text Corpus of Sumerian Literature, a project of the University of Oxford, which comprises a selection of nearly 400 literary compositions recorded on sources which come from ancient Mesopotamia (modern Iraq) and date to the late third and early second millennia BCE.

Among the texts included are, "Gilgamesh, Enkidu and the Nether World", various tales of Enki, Enlil, Inana, Merodach the Dragon Slayer and multiple dragon myths, and Myths of Kur, specifically, "Innana's Descent to the Nether World". Other myths related in this chapter include the Babylonian version of the Deluge, or the great flood of the Bible, and "Adapa and the Food of Life", which, like the Biblical story of the apple in the Garden of Eden, shows how poor decisions can make immortals mortal.

Whether these myths relate to the creation of man, the creation of the gods, man's battles against demons and evil spirits, or how humans found food and water, all of these tales involve the importance of humanity's need to explain and understand where we came from and where we fit in the world.

The Creation of the Universe

THE MAJOR SOURCE for the Sumerian conception of the creation of the universe is the introductory passage to a Sumerian poem ... entitled "Gilgamesh, Enkidu and the Nether World". The history of its decipherment is illuminating and not uninteresting. In 1934, [it was discovered] that eight pieces belonging to the poem – seven excavated in Nippur and one in Ur – had already been copied and published, thus: Hugo Radau, once of the University Museum, published two from Philadelphia in 1910; Stephen Langdon published two from Istanbul in 1914; Edward Chiera published one from Istanbul in 1924 and two more from Philadelphia in 1934; C. J. Gadd, of the British Museum, published an excellently preserved tablet from Ur in 1930. But an intelligent reconstruction and translation of the myth were still impossible, largely because the tablets and fragments, some of which seemed to duplicate each other without rhyme or reason and with but little variation in their wording, could not be properly arranged. In 1936, ... a serious effort [was made] to reconstruct the contents of the poem ["Inana's Descent to the Otherworld"], which obviously seemed to contain a charming and significant story. And it was then that [a] clue [was found] which enabled [an arrangement of] the pieces in their proper order.

This clue crystallized from an effective utilization of two stylistic features which characterize Sumerian poetry. The first is one which ranks very low in the scale of artistic technique but which from the point of view of the decipherer is truly a boon. It may be described as follows. When the poet finds it advisable to repeat a given description or incident, he makes this repeated passage coincide with the original to the very last detail. Thus when a god or hero orders his messenger to deliver a message, this message, no matter how long and detailed, is given twice in the text, first when the messenger is instructed by his master, and a second time when the message is actually delivered. The two versions are thus practically identical, and the breaks in the one passage may be restored from the other.

As for the second stylistic feature, it may be thus sketched. The Sumerian poet uses *two* dialects in his epic and mythic compositions, the *main* dialect, and another known as the *Emesal* dialect. The latter resembles the main dialect very closely and differs only in showing several regular and characteristic phonetic variations. What is more interesting, however, is the fact that the poet uses this Emesal dialect in rendering the direct speech of a *female*, not male, deity; thus the speeches of Inanna, queen of heaven, are regularly rendered in the Emesal dialect. And so, on examining carefully the texts, [it was] realized that what in the case of several passages had been taken to be a mere meaningless and unmotivated duplication, actually contained a speech of the goddess Inanna in which she repeats in the *Emesal* dialect all that the poet had previously described in narrative form in the *main* dialect. With this clue as a guide ... piecing together the first part of this poem [was successful]; this was published in 1938. The latter half of the poem still remained largely unintelligible, and even the first and published part had several serious breaks in the text. In 1939 ... in Istanbul a broken prism inscribed with the poem [was discovered]. And in the course of the past year [was] identified and copied seven additional pieces in the University Museum at Philadelphia. As a result we now have sixteen pieces inscribed with the poem; over 250 lines of its text can now be intelligently reconstructed and, barring a passage here and there, be correctly translated.

The story of our poem, briefly sketched, runs as follows: Once upon a time there was a *huluppu*-tree, perhaps a willow; it was planted on the banks of the Euphrates; it was nurtured by the waters of the Euphrates. But the South Wind tore at it, root and crown, while the Euphrates flooded it with its waters. Inanna, queen of heaven, walking by, took the tree in her hand and brought it to Erech, the seat of her main sanctuary, and planted it in her holy garden. There she tended it most carefully. For when the tree grew big, she planned to make of its wood a chair for herself and a couch.

Years passed, the tree matured and grew big. But Inanna found herself unable to cut down the tree. For at its base the snake "who knows no charm" had built its nest. In its crown, the Zu-bird – a mythological creature which at times wrought mischief – had placed its young. In the middle Lilith, the maid of desolation, had built her house. And so poor Inanna, the light-hearted and ever joyful maid, shed bitter tears. And as the dawn broke and her brother, the sun-god Utu, arose from his sleeping chamber, she repeated to him tearfully all that had befallen her *huluppu*-tree.

Now Gilgamesh, the great Sumerian hero, the forerunner of the Greek Heracles, who lived in Erech, overheard Inanna's weeping complaint and chivalrously came to her rescue. He donned his armour weighing fifty minas – about fifty pounds – and with his "ax of the road", seven talents and seven minas in weight – over 400 pounds – he slew the snake "who knows no charm" at the base of the tree. Seeing which, the Zu-Bird fled with his young to the mountain, and Lilith tore down her house and fled to the desolate places which she was accustomed to haunt. The men of Erech who had accompanied Gilgamesh now cut down the tree and presented it to Inanna for her chair and couch.

What did Inanna do? Of the base of the *huluppu*-tree she made an object called the *pukku* (probably a drum), and of its crown she made another related object called the *mikku* (probably a drumstick), and gave them both to Gilgamesh, evidently as a reward for his gallantry. Follows a passage of twelve lines describing Gilgamesh's activity with these two objects whose meaning I am still unable to penetrate, although it is in perfect shape. When our story becomes intelligible again, it continues with the statement that "because of the cry of the young maidens" the *pukku* and the *mikku* fell into the nether world, evidently through a hole in the ground. Gilgamesh put in his hand to retrieve them but was unable to reach them; he put in his foot but was quite as unsuccessful. And so he seated himself at the gate of the nether world and cried with fallen face:

My pukku, who will bring it up from the nether world?
My mikku, who will bring it up from the "face" of the nether world?

His servant, Enkidu, his constant follower and companion, heard his master's cries, and said to him:

My master, why dost thou cry, why is thy heart sick?
Thy pukku, I will bring it up from the nether world,
Thy mikku, I will bring it up from the "face" of the nether world.

Thereupon Gilgamesh warned him of the dangers involved in his plan to descend to the nether world – a splendid passage, brief and concise in describing the taboos of the lower regions. Said Gilgamesh to Enkidu:

If now thou wilt descend to the nether world,
A word I speak to thee, take my word,
Advice I offer thee, take my advice.

Do not put on clean clothes,
Lest the (dead) heroes will come forth like enemies;
Do not anoint thyself with the good oil of the vessel,
Lest at its smell they will crowd about thee.

Do not throw the throw-stick in the nether world,
Lest they who were struck down by the throw-stick will surround thee;
Do not carry a staff in thy hand,
Lest the shades will flutter all about thee.

Do not put sandals on thy feet,
In the nether world make no cry;
Kiss not thy beloved wife,
Kiss not thy beloved son,
Strike not thy hated wife,
Strike not thy hated son,
Lest thy "cry" of the nether world will seize thee;
(The cry) for her who is lying, for her who is lying,
The mother of the god Ninazu who is lying,
Whose holy body no garment covers,
Whose holy breast no cloth wraps.

But Enkidu heeded not the advice of his master and he did the very things against which Gilgamesh had warned him. And so he was seized by the nether world and was unable to reascend to the earth. Thereupon Gilgamesh, greatly troubled, proceeded to the city of Nippur and wept before the great air-god Enlil, the god who in the third millennium BCE was the leading deity of the Sumerian pantheon:

O Father Enlil, my pukku fell into the nether world,
My mikku fell into the nether world;
I sent Enkidu to bring them up to me, the nether world has seized him.
Namtar (a demon) has not seized him, Ashak (a demon) has not seized him,
The nether world has seized him.
Nergal, the ambusher, who spares no one, has not seized him,
The nether world has seized him.
In battles where heroism is displayed he has not fallen,
The nether world has seized him.

But Enlil refused to stand by Gilgamesh, who then proceeded to Eridu and repeated his plea before the water-god Enki, the "god of wisdom". Enki ordered the sun-god Utu to open a hole in the nether world and to allow the shade of Enkidu to ascend to earth. The sun-god Utu did as bidden and the shade of Enkidu appeared to Gilgamesh. Master and servant embraced and Gilgamesh questioned Enkidu about what he saw in the nether world. The passage from here to the end of the poem is badly broken, but the following partly extant colloquy will serve as an illustration:

Gilgamesh: "Him who has one son hast thou seen!"
Enkidu: "I have seen".
Gilgamesh: "How is he treated?"
Enkidu: (Answer broken)

Gilgamesh: "Him who has two sons hast thou seen?"
Enkidu: "I have seen".
Gilgamesh: "How is he treated?"
Enkidu: (Answer broken)

Gilgamesh: "Him who has three sons hast thou seen?"
Enkidu: "I have seen".
Gilgamesh: "How is he treated?"
Enkidu: "... much water he drinks".

Gilgamesh: "Him who has four sons hast thou seen!"
Enkidu: "I have seen".
Gilgamesh: "How is he treated?"
Enkidu: "Like ... his heart rejoices".

Gilgamesh: "Him who has five sons hast thou seen!"
Enkidu: "I have seen".
Gilgamesh: "How is he treated?"
Enkidu: "Like a good scribe, his arm has been
opened, He brings justice to the palace".

Gilgamesh: "Him who has six sons hast thou seen?"
Enkidu: "I have seen".
Gilgamesh: "How is he treated?"
Enkidu: "Like him who guides the plow his heart rejoices".

Gilgamesh: "Him who has seven sons hast thou seen!"
Enkidu: "I have seen".
Gilgamesh: "How is he treated?"
Enkidu: "As one close to the gods, he . . ".

Another of the questions runs thus:

Gilgamesh: "Him whose dead body lies (unburied) in the plain hast thou seen?"
Enkidu: "I have seen".
Gilgamesh: "How is he treated?"
Enkidu: "His shade finds no rest in the nether world".

And so our poem ends. It is the *introduction* to this composition which furnishes the most significant material for the Sumerian concepts of the creation of the universe. The intelligible part of the introduction reads as follows:

After heaven had been moved away from earth,
After earth had been separated from heaven,
After the name of man had been fixed;

After An had carried off heaven,
After Enlil had carried off earth,
After Ereshkigal had been carried off into Kur as its prize;

After he had set sail, after he had set sail,
After the father for Kur had set sail,
After Enki for Kur had set sail;

Against the king the small ones it (Kur) hurled,
Against Enki, the large ones it hurled;
Its small ones, stones of the hand,
Its large ones, stones of … reeds,
The keel of the boat of Enki,
In battle, like the attacking storm, overwhelm;

Against the king, the water at the head of the boat,
Like a wolf devours,
Against Enki, the water at the rear of the boat,
Like a lion strikes down.

If we paraphrase and analyze the contents of this passage, it may be worded as follows: Heaven and earth, originally united, were separated and moved away from each other, and thereupon the creation of man was ordained. An, the heaven-god, then carried off heaven, while Enlil, the air-god, carried off earth. All this seems to be according to plan. Then, however, occurred something disruptive. For the goddess Ereshkigal, the counterpart of the Greek Persephone, whom we know as queen of the nether world, but who originally was probably a sky-goddess, was carried off into the nether world, perhaps by Kur. No doubt to avenge this deed, the water-god Enki set sail to attack Kur. The latter, evidently to be conceived as a monster or dragon, did not stand idly by, but hurled stones, large and small, against the keel of Enki's boat, while the primeval waters attacked Enki's boat front and rear. Our poem does not give the result of this struggle between Enki and Kur, since the entire cosmogonic or creation introduction has nothing to do with the basic contents of our Gilgamesh composition; it was placed at the head of the poem only because the Sumerian scribes were accustomed to begin their stories with several introductory lines dealing with creation.

It is from the first half of this introduction that we obtain therefore the following cosmogonic concepts:

1. At one time heaven and earth were united.
2. Some of the gods existed before the separation of heaven and earth.

3. Upon the separation of heaven and earth, it was, as might have been expected, the heaven-god An who carried off heaven, but it was the air-god Enlil who carried off the earth.

Among the crucial points *not stated* or *implied* in this passage are the following:

1. Were heaven and earth conceived as created, and if so, by whom?
2. What was the shape of heaven and earth as conceived by the Sumerians?
3. Who separated heaven from earth?

Fortunately, the answers to these three questions can be gleaned from several other Sumerian texts dating from our period. Thus:

1. In a tablet which gives a list of the Sumerian gods, the goddess Nammu, written with the ideogram for "sea", is described as "the mother, who gave birth to heaven and earth". Heaven and earth were therefore conceived by the Sumerians as the created products of the primeval sea.

2. The myth "Cattle and Grain", which describes the birth in heaven of the spirits of cattle and grain, who were then sent down to earth to bring prosperity to mankind, begins with the following two lines:

After on the mountain of heaven and earth,
An had caused the Anunnaki (his followers) to be born....

It is not unreasonable to assume, therefore, that heaven and earth united were conceived as a mountain whose base was the bottom of the earth and whose peak was the top of the heaven.

3. The myth "The Creation of the Pickax", which describes the fashioning and dedication of this valuable agricultural implement, is introduced with the following passage:

The lord, that which is appropriate verily he caused to appear,
The lord whose decisions are unalterable,
Enlil, who brings up the seed of the land from the earth,
Took care to move away heaven from earth,
Took care to move away earth from heaven.

And so we have the answer to our third question; it was the air-god Enlil, who separated and removed heaven from earth.

If now we sum up the cosmogonic or creation concepts of the Sumerians, evolved to explain the origin of the universe, they may be stated as follows:

1. First was the *primeval sea*. Nothing is said of its origin or birth, and it is not unlikely that the Sumerians conceived it as having existed eternally.
2. The *primeval sea* begot the cosmic *mountain* consisting of heaven and earth united.
3. Conceived as gods in human form, An (heaven) was the male and Ki (earth) was the female. From their union was begotten the air-god Enlil.
4. Enlil, the air-god, separated heaven from earth, and while his father An carried off heaven, Enlil himself carried off his mother Ki, the earth. The union of Enlil and his mother Ki-in historical times she is perhaps to be identified with the goddess called

variously Ninmah, "great queen"; Ninhursag, "queen of the (cosmic) mountain"; Nintu, "queen who gives birth" – set the stage for the organization of the universe, the creation of man and the establishment of civilization".

The Organization of the Universe

THE SUMERIAN EXPRESSION for "universe" is *an-ki*, literally "heaven-earth". The organization of the universe may therefore be subdivided into that of heaven and that of earth. Heaven consists of the sky and the space above the sky which is called the "great above"; here dwell the sky-gods. Earth consists of the surface of the earth and the space below which is called the "great below"; here dwell the underworld or chthonic deities. For the organization of heaven the relatively little mythological material which is available to date may be sketched as follows: Nanna, the moon-god, the major astral deity of the Sumerians, is born of Enlil, the air-god, and his wife Ninlil, the air-goddess. Nanna, the moon-god, is conceived as travelling in a gufa across the heavens, thus bringing light to the pitch-dark lapis lazuli sky. The "little ones", the stars, are scattered about him like grain while the "big ones", perhaps the planets, walk about him like wild oxen".

Nanna, the moon-god, and his wife Ningal are the parents of Utu, the sun-god, who rises in the "mountain of the east" and sets in the "mountain of the west". As yet we find no mention of any boat or chariot used by the sun-god Utu to traverse the sky. Nor is it clear just what he does at night. The not unnatural assumption that upon reaching the "mountain of the west" at the end of the day he continues his journey at night through the nether world, arriving at the "mountain of the east" at dawn, is not borne out by the extant data. Indeed to judge from a prayer to the sun-god which reads:

O Utu, shepherd of the land, father of the black-headed people,
When thou liest down, the people, too, lie down,
O hero Utu, when thou risest, the people, too, rise.

or from a description of the break of dawn which reads:

As light broke forth, as the horizon grew bright....
As Utu came forth from his ganunu,

or from a description of the setting of the sun which reads:

Utu has gone forth with lifted head to the bosom of his mother Ningal;

the Sumerians seemed to have conceived of Utu as sleeping through the night.

Turning to the organization of the earth, we learn that it was Enlil, the air-god, who "caused the good day to come forth"; who set his mind to "bring forth seed from the earth" and to establish the *hegal*, that is, plenty, abundance and prosperity in the land. It was this same Enlil who fashioned the pickax and probably the plow as prototypes of the agricultural implements to be used by man; who appointed Enten, the farmer-god, as his steadfast and trustworthy field-worker. On the other hand it was the water-god Enki who begot Uttu, the goddess of plants. It is Enki, moreover, who actually organizes the earth, and especially that part of it which includes Sumer and its surrounding neighbors, into a going concern. He decrees the fates of Sumer, Ur and Meluhha, and appoints the various minor deities to their specific duties. And it is both Enlil and Enki, that is, both the air-god and the water-god, who send Labar, the cattle-god, and Ashnan, the grain-goddess, from heaven to earth in order to make abundant its cattle and grain.

The above outline of the organization of the universe is based upon nine Sumerian myths whose contents we now have wholly or in large part. Two of these involve the moon-god Nanna; they are: *Enlil and Ninlil. the Begetting of Nanna; The Journey of Nanna to Nippur.* The remaining seven are of prime importance for the Sumerian concepts of the origin and establishment of culture and civilization on earth. These are *Emesh and Enten: Enlil Chooses the Farmer-god; The Creation of the Pickax; Cattle and Grain; Enki and Ninhursag: the Affairs of the Water-god; Enki and Sumer: the Organization of the Earth and its Cultural Processes; Enki and Eridu: the Journey of the Water-god to Nippur; Inanna and Enki: the Transfer of the Arts of Civilization from Eridu to Erech.* We shall now proceed to sketch briefly the contents of each of these myths; their wealth and variety, it is hoped, will enable the reader to evaluate the Sumerian mythological concepts together with their spiritual and religious implications.

Enlil and Ninlil: The Begetting of Nanna

THIS DELIGHTFUL MYTH, consisting of 152 lines of text, is almost complete. It seems to have been evolved to explain the begetting of the moon-god Nanna as well as that of the three underworld deities, Nergal, Ninazu and a third whose name is illegible. If rightly interpreted this poem furnishes us with the first known example of the metamorphosis of a god; Enlil assumes the form of three different individuals in impregnating his wife Ninlil with the three nether world deities.

The poem begins with an introductory passage descriptive of the city of Nippur, a Nippur that seems to be conceived as having existed before the creation of man:

Behold the "bond of heaven and earth", the city, . . .
Behold Nippur, the city, . . .
Behold the "kindly wall", the city, . . .

Behold the Idsalla, its pure river,
Behold the Karkurunna, its quay,
Behold the Karasarra, its quay where the boats stand,
Behold the Pulal, its well of good water,
Behold the Idnunbirdu, its pure canal,
Behold Enlil, its young man,
Behold Ninlil, its young maid,
Behold Nunbarshegunu, its old woman.

After this brief background sketch the actual story begins. Nunbarshegunu, the "old woman" of Nippur, Ninlil's mother, instructs her daughter how to obtain the love of Enlil:

In those days the mother, her begetter, gave advice to the maid,
Nunbarshegunu gave advice to Ninlil:
"At the pure river, O maid, at the pure river wash thyself,
O Ninlil, walk along the bank of the Idnunbirdu,
The bright-eyed, the lord, the bright-eyed,
The 'great mountain', father Enlil, the bright-eyed, will see thee,
The shepherd ... who decrees the fates, the bright-eyed, will see thee,
He will .... he will kiss thee".

Ninlil follows her mother's instructions and as a consequence is impregnated by "the water" of Enlil and conceives the moon-god Nanna. Enlil then departs from Nippur in the direction of the nether world, but is followed by Ninlil. As he leaves the gate he instructs the "man of the gate" to give the inquisitive Ninlil no information of his whereabouts. Ninlil comes up to the "man of the gate" and demands to know whither Enlil has gone. Enlil then *seems to take the form of the "man of the gate" and answers for him.* The passage involved is as yet unintelligible; it seems to contain a refusal to divulge Enlil's whereabouts. Ninlil thereupon reminds him that while, true enough, Enlil is his king, she is his queen. Thereupon Enlil, still impersonating "the man of the gate", cohabits with her and impregnates her. As a result Ninlil conceives Meslamtaea, more commonly known as Nergal, the king of the nether world. In spite of the unintelligible parts, the flavor of this remarkable passage will be readily apparent from the following quotations:

Enlil ... departed from the city,
Nunamnir (a name of Enlil) ... departed from the city.
Enlil walked, Ninlil followed,
Nunamnir walked, the maid followed,
Enlil says to the man of the gate:

"O man of the gate, man of the lock,
O man of the bolt, man of the pure lock,
Thy queen Ninlil is coming;
If she asks thee about me,
Tell her not where I am".

Ninlil approached the man of the gate:
"O man of the gate, man of the lock,

O man of the bolt, man of the pure lock,
Enlil, thy king, where is he going?"
Enlil answers her for the man of the gate:
"Enlil, the king of all the lands, has commanded me":

Four lines follow containing the substance of this command but their meaning is obscure. Then comes the following dialogue between Ninlil and Enlil, the latter impersonating the "man of the gate":

Ninlil: "True, Enlil is thy king, but I am thy queen".
Enlil: "If now thou art my queen, let my hand touch thy . . ".
Ninlil: "The 'water' of thy king, the bright 'water' is in my heart,
The 'water' of Nanna, the bright 'water' is in my heart".
Enlil: "The 'water' of my king, let it go toward heaven, let it go toward earth,
Let my 'water', like the 'water' of my king, go toward earth".
Enlil, as the man of the gate, lay down in the
He kissed her, he cohabited with her,
Having kissed her, having cohabited with her,
The "water" of ... Meslamtaea he caused to flow over (her) heart.

The poem then continues with the begetting of the nether world deity Ninazu; this time it is the "man of the river of the nether world, the man-devouring river" whom Enlil impersonates. In all other respects, the passage is a repetition of that describing the begetting of Meslamtaea; thus:

Enlil walked, Ninlil followed,
Nunamnir walked, the maid followed,
Enlil says to the man of the river of the nether world, the man-devouring river:

"O man of the river of the nether world, the man-devouring river,
Thy queen Ninlil is coming;
If she asks thee about me,
Tell her not where I am".

Ninlil approached the man of the river of the nether world, the man-devouring river:
"O man of the river of the nether world, the man-devouring river,
Enlil, thy king, where is he going?"

Enlil answers her for the man of the river of the
nether world, the man-devouring river:
"Enlil, the king of all the lands, has commanded me".

The substance of the command is unintelligible. Follows the dialogue between Ninlil and Enlil, the latter impersonating the "man of the river of the nether world, the man-devouring river":

Ninlil: "True, Enlil is thy king, but I am thy queen".
Enlil: "If now thou art my queen, let my hand touch thy . . ".

Ninlil: "The 'water' of thy king, the bright 'water' is in my heart,
The 'water' of Nanna, the bright 'water' is in my heart".
Enlil: "The 'water' of my king, let it go toward heaven, let it go toward earth,
Let my 'water', like the 'water' of my king, go toward earth".
Enlil, as the man of the river of the nether world, the
man-devouring river, lay down in the ....
He kissed her, he cohabited with her,
Having kissed her, having cohabited with her,
The "water" of Ninazu, the king of ..., he caused to flow over (her) heart.

The poem then continues with the begetting of the third underworld deity whose name is illegible; this time it is the "man of the boat" whom Enlil impersonates. Our myth then comes to a close with a brief hymnal passage in which Enlil is exalted as the lord of abundance and the king whose decrees are unalterable.

The Journey of Nanna to Nippur

TO THE SUMERIANS of the third millennium BCE, Nippur was the spiritual center of their country. Its tutelary deity, Enlil, was the leading god of the Sumerian pantheon; his temple, Ekur, was the most important temple in Sumer. And so, the blessing of Enlil was a prime essential for the establishment of prosperity and abundance in the other important cities of Sumer, such as Eridu and Ur. To obtain this blessing, the tutelary deities of these cities were conceived as travelling to Nippur laden with gifts for its god and temple. Our myth describes just such a journey from Ur to Nippur of the moon-god Nanna (also known as Sin and Ashgirbabbar), the tutelary deity of Ur. In this myth, as in the preceding Enlil-Ninlil composition, the cities such as Nippur and Ur seem to be fully built and rich in animal and plant life, although man seems to be still nonexistent.

Beginning with a description of the glory of Nippur, our poem continues a passage describing Nanna's decision to visit his father's city:

To go to his city, to stand before his father,
Ashgirbabbar set his mind:
"I, the hero, to my city I would go, before my father I would stand;
I, Sin, to my city I would go, before my father I would stand,
Before my father Enlil I would stand;
I, to my city I would go, before my mother Ninlil I would stand,
Before my father I would stand".

And so he loads up his gufa with a rich assortment of trees, plants and animals. On his journey from Ur to Nippur, Nanna and his boat make stop at five cities: Im (?), Larsa, Erech and two cities whose names are illegible; in each of these Nanna is met and greeted by the respective tutelary deity. Finally he arrives at Nippur:

At the lapis lazuli quay, the quay of Enlil, Nanna-Sin drew up his boat, At the white quay, the quay of Enlil, Ashgirbabbar drew up his boat, On the ... of the father, his begetter, he stationed himself,

To the gatekeeper of Enlil he says:

At the lapis lazuli quay, the quay of Enlil,
Nanna-Sin drew up his boat,
At the white quay, the quay of Enlil,
Ashgirbabbar drew up his boat,
On the ... of the father, his begetter, he stationed himself,
To the gatekeeper of Enlil he says:
"Open the house, gatekeeper, open the house,
Open the house, O protecting genie, open the house,
Open the house, thou who makest the trees come forth, open the house,
O . . ., who makest the trees come forth, open the house,
Gatekeeper, open the house, O protecting genie, open the house".

The gatekeeper opens the door for Nanna:

Joyfully, the gatekeeper joyfully opened the door;
The protecting genie who makes the trees come forth, joyfully,
The gatekeeper joyfully opened the door;
He who makes the trees come forth, joyfully,
The gatekeeper joyfully opened the door;
With Sin, Enlil rejoiced.

The two gods feast; then Nanna addresses Enlil his father as follows:

"In the river give me overflow,
In the field give me much grain,
In the swampland give me grass and reeds,
In the forests give me ...
In the plain give me ...
In the palm-grove and vineyard give me honey and wine,
In the palace give me long life,
To Ur I shall go".

And Enlil accedes to his son's request:

He gave him, Enlil gave him,
To Ur he went.
In the river he gave him overflow,
In the field he gave him much grain,

In the swampland he gave him grass and reeds,
In the forests he gave him . . .,
In the plain he gave him . . . .
In the palm-grove and vineyard he gave him honey and wine,
In the palace he gave him long life.

Emesh and Enten: Enlil Chooses the Farmer-God

THIS MYTH IS the closest extant Sumerian parallel to the Biblical Cain-Abel story, although it ends with a reconciliation rather than a murder. It consists of over 300 lines, only about half of which are complete; because of the numerous breaks, the meaning of the text is therefore often difficult to penetrate. Tentatively the contents of the poem may be reconstructed as follows:

Enlil, the air-god, has set his mind to bring forth trees and grain and to establish abundance and prosperity in the land. For this purpose two cultural beings, the brothers Emesh and Enten, are created, and Enlil assigns to each specific duties. The text is so badly damaged at this point that it is impossible to make out the exact nature of these duties; the following very brief intelligible passages will at least indicate their general direction:

Enten caused the ewe to give birth to the lamb, the goat to give birth to the kid,
Cow and calf he caused to multiply, much fat and milk he caused to be produced,
In the plain, the heart of the wild goat, the sheep and the donkey he made to rejoice,
The birds of the heaven, in the wide earth he had them set up their nests
The fish of the sea, in the swampland he had them lay their eggs,
In the palm-grove and vineyard he made to abound honey and wine,
The trees, wherever planted, he caused to bear fruit,
The furrows . . .,
Grain and crops he caused to multiply,
Like Ashnan (the grain goddess), the kindly maid, he caused strength to appear.
Emesh brought into existence the trees and the fields,
he made wide the stables and sheepfolds,
In the farms he multiplied the produce,
The . . . he caused to cover the earth,
The abundant harvest he caused to be brought into the
houses, he caused the granaries to be heaped high.

But whatever the nature of their original duties, a violent quarrel breaks out between the two brothers. Several arguments ensue, and finally Emesh challenges Enten's claim to the position of "farmer of the gods". And so they betake themselves to Nippur where each states his case before Enlil. Thus Enten complains to Enlil:

"O father Enlil, knowledge thou hast given me, I brought the water of abundance,
Farm I made touch farm, I heaped high the granaries,
Like Ashnan, the kindly maid, I caused strength to appear;
Now Emesh, the .... the irreverent, who knows not the heart of the fields,
On my first strength, on my first power, is encroaching;
At the palace of the king ..."

Emesh's version of the quarrel, which begins with several flattering phrases cunningly directed to win Enlil's favor, is brief but as yet unintelligible. Then:

Enlil answers Emesh and Enten:
"The life-producing water of all the lands, Enten is its 'knower',
As farmer of the gods he has produced everything,
Emesh, my son, how dost thou compare thyself with Eaten, thy brother?"
The exalted word of Enlil whose meaning is profound,
The decision taken, is unalterable, who dares transgress it!
Emesh bent the knees before Enten,
Into his house he brought ..., the wine of the grape and the date,
Emesh presents Enten with gold, silver and lapis lazuli,
In brotherhood and friendship, happily, they pour out libations,
Together to act wisely and well they determined.
In the struggle between Emesh and Enten,
Enten, the steadfast farmer of the gods, having proved greater than Emesh,
... O father Enlil, praise!

The Creation of the Pickax

THIS POEM consisting of 108 lines is practically complete, although not a few of the passages still remain obscure and unintelligible. It begins with a long introductory passage which is of prime significance for the Sumerian conception of the creation and organization of the universe.

If the following translation of this important passage seems sodden, stilted and obscure, the reader is asked to remember that although the meanings of most of the Sumerian words and phrases are known, we still have little insight into their overtones, into their connotations and implications. For the background and situation which these words and phrases imply and assume, still elude us; and it is this background and situation, part and parcel of the Sumerian mythological and religious pattern and well known to the Sumerian poet and his "reader", which are so vital to a full understanding of the text. It is only with the gradual accumulation of living contexts from Sumerian literature that we may hope to overcome this difficulty; as yet it is best to hew close to the literal word. The introductory passage reads:

The lord, that which is appropriate verily he caused to appear,
The lord whose decisions are unalterable,
Enlil, who brings up the seed of the land from the earth,
Took care to move away heaven from earth,
Took care to move away earth from heaven.
In order to make grow the creature which came forth,
In the "bond of heaven and earth" (Nippur) he stretched out the . . .

He brought the pickax into existence, the "day" came forth,
He introduced labor, decreed the fate,
Upon the pickax and basket he directs the "power".
Enlil made his pickax exalted,
His pickax of gold, whose head is of lapis lazuli,
The pickax of his house, of ... silver and gold,
His pickax whose ... is of lapis lazuli,
Whose tooth is a one-horned ox ascending a large wall.

The lord called up the pickax, decrees its fate,
He set the kindu, the holy crown, upon his head,
The head of man he placed in the mould,
Before Enlil he (man?) covers his land,
Upon his black-headed people he looked steadfastly.
The Anunnaki who stood about him,
He placed it (the pickax?) as a gift in their hands,
They soothe Enlil with prayer,
They give the pickax to the black-headed people to hold.

After Enlil had created the pickax and decreed its exalted fate, the other important deities add to its powers and utility. The poem concludes with a long passage in which the usefulness of the pickax is described in glowing terms; the last lines read:

The pickax and the basket build cities,
The steadfast house the pickax builds, the steadfast house the pickax establishes,
The steadfast house it causes to prosper.

The house which rebels against the king,
The house which is not submissive to its king,
The pickax makes it submissive to the king.

Of the bad ... plants it crushes the head,
Plucks at the roots, tears at the crown,
The pickax spares the ... plants;
The pickax, its fate decreed by father Enlil,
The pickax is exalted.

Cattle and Grain

THE MYTH INVOLVING LAHAR, the cattle-god, and his sister Ashnan, the grain-goddess, represents another variation of the Cain-Abel motif in Near East mythology. Labar and Ashnan, according to our myth, were created in the creation chamber of the gods in order that the Annunnaki, the children and followers of the heaven-god An, might have food to eat and clothes to wear. But the Anunnaki were unable to make effective use of the products of these deities; it was to remedy this situation that man was created. All this is told in an introductory passage ….

The passage following the introduction is another poetic gem; it describes the descent of Lahar and Ashnan from heaven to earth and the cultural benefits which they bestow on mankind:

In those days Enki says to Enlil:
"Father Enlil, Lahar and Ashnan,
They who have been created in the Dulkug,
Let us cause them to descend from the Dulkug".

At the pure word of Enki and Enlil,
Lahar and Ashnan descended from the Dulkug.
For Lahar they (Enlil and Enki) set up the sheepfold,
Plants, herbs and … they present to him;

For Ashnan they establish a house,
Plow and yoke they present to her.
Lahar standing in his sheepfold,
A shepherd increasing the bounty of the sheepfold is he;
Ashnan standing among the crops,
A maid kindly and bountiful is she.

Abundance of heaven …
Lahar and Ashnan caused to appear,
In the assembly they brought abundance,
In the land they brought the breath of life,
The decrees of the god they direct,
The contents of the warehouses they multiply,
The storehouses they fill full.

In the house of the poor, hugging the dust,
Entering they bring abundance;
The pair of them, wherever they stand,
Bring heavy increase into the house;
The place where they stand they sate, the place where they sit they supply,
They made good the heart of An and Enlil.

But then Labar and Ashnan drank much wine and so they began to quarrel in the *farms* and fields. In the arguments which ensued, each deity extolled its achievements and belittled those of its opponent. Finally, Enlil and Enki intervened, but the end of the poem which contains their decision is still wanting.

Enki and Ninhursag: The Affairs of the Water-God

BOTH FOR INTRICACY of story and for simplicity of style, this myth is one of the most remarkable compositions in our entire group. The hero is Enki, the great water-god of the Sumerians, one of the four creating deities of Sumer; his closest Greek counterpart is Poseidon. The place of our story is Dilmun, a district which is perhaps to be identified with eastern shores of the Persian Gulf and which in historical times, therefore, actually lay outside of Sumer proper.

Our poem begins with a description of Dilmun as a land of innocence and bliss:

The land Dilmun is a pure place, the land Dilmun is a clean place,
The land Dilmun is a clean place, the land Dilmun is a bright place;
He who is all alone laid himself down in Dilmun,
The place, after Enki had laid himself by his wife,
That place is clean, that place is bright;
He who is all alone laid himself down in Dilmun,
The place, after Enki had laid himself by Ninsikil,
That place is clean, that place is bright.

In Dilmun the raven uttered no cries,
The kite uttered not the cry of the kite,
The lion killed not,
The wolf snatched not the lamb,
Unknown was the kid-killing dog,
Unknown was the grain-devouring boar,
The bird on high … not its young,
The dove … not the head,
The sick-eyed says not "I am sick-eyed",
The sick-headed says not "I am sick-headed",
Its (Dilmun's) old woman says not "I am an old woman",
Its old man says not "I am an old man",
Its unwashed maid is not … in the city,
He who crosses the river utters no …,
The overseer does not …,

The singer utters no wail,
By the side of the city he utters no lament.

What is wanting in this paradise land, however, is sweet water. And so the goddess of Dilmun, Ninsikil, pleads with Enki for fresh water. Enki heeds her plea and orders the sun-god Utu to bring forth fresh water from the earth for Dilmun. As a result:

Her city drinks the water of abundance,
Dilmun drinks the water of abundance,
Her wells of bitter water, behold they are become wells of good water,
Her fields and farms produced crops and grain,
Her city, behold it is become the house of the banks and quays of the land,
Dilmun, behold it is become the house of the banks and quays of the land.

Dilmun supplied with water, our poem next describes the birth of Uttu, the goddess of plants, a birth which results from the following rather intricate process. Enki first impregnates the goddess Ninhursag, or, to give her one of her other names, Nintu, the Sumerian goddess who in an earlier day may have been identical with Ki, the mother earth. Follows a period of gestation lasting nine days, the poet being careful to note that each day corresponds to a month in the human period of gestation; of this union is begotten the goddess Ninsar. This interesting passage runs as follows:

Upon Ninhursag he caused to flow the "water of the heart",
She received the "water of the heart", the water of Enki.
One day being her one month,
Two days being her two months,
Three days being her three months,
Four days being her four months,
Five days (being her five months,)
Six days (being her six months,)
Seven days (being her seven months,)
Eight days (being her eight months,)
Nine days being her nine months, the months of "womanhood",
Like ... fat, like ... fat, like good butter,
Nintu, the mother of the land, like ... fat, (like ... fat, like good butter,)
Gave birth to Ninsar.

Ninsar in turn is impregnated by her father Enki and after nine days of gestation she gives birth to the goddess Ninkur. Ninkur, too, is then impregnated by Enki and so finally is born Uttu, the goddess of plants. To this plant-goddess now appears her great-grandmother Ninhursag, who offers her advice pertinent to her future relationship with Enki. Part of the passage is broken, and much of what is not broken I fail as yet to comprehend. But whatever the advice, Uttu follows it in all detail. As a result, she is in turn impregnated by Enki and eight different plants sprout forth. But Enki eats up the plants; thus:

Enki, in the swampland, in the swampland, lies stretched out,
He says to his messenger Isimud:
"What is this (plant), what is this (plant)?"

His messenger, Isimud, answers him;
"My king, this is the 'tree-plant'", he says to him.
He cuts it off for him and he (Enki) eats it.

Enki: "What is this, what is this?"
Isimud: "My king, this is the 'honey-plant'".
He tears it off for him and he eats it.

And so on until Enki has eaten all the eight plants. Thereupon Ninhursag, who, it will be recalled, is actually responsible for the creation of these plants, curses Enki. The curse reads:

"Until thou art dead, I shall not look upon thee with the 'eye of life'".

Having uttered the curse, Ninhursag disappears. The gods are chagrined; they "sit in the dust". Up speaks the fox to Enlil:

"If I bring Ninhursag before thee, what shall be my reward?"

Enlil promises the fox a due reward and the latter succeeds in bringing her back; how he goes about this task is not clear, however, since part of the text is broken and much of the preserved part is as yet unintelligible. And so Ninhursag proceeds to remove the effects of her curse from the rapidly sinking Enki. This she achieves by giving birth to a special deity for each of Enki's pains. This passage which closes our poem runs as follows:

Ninhursag: "My brother, what hurts thee?"
Enki: "My … hurts me".
Ninhursag: "To the god Abu I gave birth for thee".

Ninhursag: "My brother, what hurts thee?"
Enki: "My hip hurts me".
Ninhursag: "To the god Nintul I gave birth for thee".

Ninhursag: "My brother, what hurts thee?"
Enki: "My tooth hurts me".
Ninhursag: "To the goddess Ninsutu I gave birth for thee".

Ninhursag: "My brother, what hurts thee?"
Enki: "My mouth hurts me".
Ninhursag: "To the goddess Ninkasi I gave birth for thee".

Ninhursag: "My brother, what hurts thee?"
Enki: "My … hurts me".
Ninhursag: "To the god Nazi I gave birth for thee".
Ninhursag: "My brother, what hurts thee?"
Enki: "My side hurts me".
Ninhursag: "To the goddess Dazimua I gave birth for thee".

Ninhursag: "My brother, what hurts thee?"
Enki: "My rib hurts me".
Ninhursag: "To the goddess Ninti I gave birth for thee".

Ninhursag: "My brother, what hurts thee?"
Enki: "My ... hurts me".
Ninhursag: "To the god Enshagag I gave birth for thee".

Ninhursag: "For the little ones to which I gave birth
Enki: "Let Abu be the king of the plants,
Let Nintul be the lord of Magan,
Let Ninsutu marry Ninazu,
Let Ninkasi be (the goddess who) sates the heart,
Let Nazi marry Nindar,
Let Dazimua marry Ningishzida,
Let Ninti be the queen of the month,
Let Enshagag be the lord of Dilmun".

O Father Enki, praise!

And so, as the reader will note, the eight aches and pains which had come upon Enki as punishment for his eating the eight plants, were healed by the eight deities born of Ninhursag for that purpose. Moreover, the superficiality and barren artificiality of the concepts implied in this closing passage of our myth, although not apparent from the English translation, are brought out quite clearly by the Sumerian original. For the fact is that the actual relationship between each of the "healing" deities and the sickness which it is supposed to cure, is verbal and nominal only; this relationship manifests itself in the fact that the name of the deity contains in it part or all of the word signifying the corresponding aching part of Enki's body. In brief, it is only because the name of the deity *sounded* like the sick body-member that the makers of this myth were induced to associate the two; actually there is no organic relationship between them.

Enki and Sumer: The Organization of the Earth and Its Cultural Processes

THIS COMPOSITION furnishes us with a detailed account of the activities of the water-god Enki, the Sumerian god of wisdom, in organizing the earth and establishing what might be termed law and order upon it. The first part of our poem, approximately 100 lines, is too fragmentary for a reconstruction of its contents.

When the poem becomes intelligible, Enki is decreeing the fate of Sumer:

O Sumer, great land, of the lands of the universe,
Filled with steadfast brightness, the people from sunrise
to sunset obedient to the divine decrees,
Thy decrees are exalted decrees, unreachable,
Thy heart is profound, unfathomable,
Thy ... is like heaven, untouchable.

"The king, begotten, adorns himself with lasting jewel,
The lord, begotten, sets crown on head,
Thy lord is an honored lord; with An, the king, he sits in
the shrine of heaven,
Thy king is the great mountain, the father Enlil,
Like ... the father of all the lands.

"The Anunnaki, the great gods,
In thy midst have taken up their dwelling place,
In thy large groves they consume (their) food.

"O house of Sumer, may thy stables be many, may thy cows multiply,
May thy sheepfolds be many, may thy sheep be myriad,
May thy ... stand,
May thy steadfast ... lift hand to heaven,
May the Anunnaki decree the fates in thy midst".

Enki then goes to Ur, no doubt the capital of Sumer at the time our poem was composed, and decrees its fate:

To Ur he came,
Enki, king of the abyss, decrees the fate:
"O city, well-supplied, washed by much water, firm standing ox,
Shrine of abundance of the land, knees opened, green like the 'mountain',
Hashur-forest, wide shade .... heroic, Thy perfected decrees he has directed,
The great mountain, Enlil, in the universe has uttered thy exalted name;
O thou city whose fates have been decreed by Enki,
O thou shrine Ur, neck to heaven mayest thou rise".

Enki then comes to Meluhha, the "black mountain", perhaps to be identified with the eastern coast of Africa. Remarkably enough, Enki is almost as favorably disposed to this land as to Sumer itself. He blesses its trees and reeds, its oxen and birds, its silver and gold, its bronze and copper, its human beings. From Meluhha, Enki goes to the Tigris and Euphrates Rivers. He fills them with sparkling water and appoints the god Enbilulu, the "*knower*" of rivers, in charge. Enki then fills the rivers with fishes and makes a deity described as the "son of Kesh" responsible for them. He next turns to the sea (Persian Gulf), sets up its rules, and appoints the goddess Sirara in charge.

Enki now calls to the winds and appoints over them the god Ishkur, who has charge of the "silver lock of the 'heart' of heaven". The plow and yoke, fields and vegetation, are next on the list:

The plow and the yoke he directed,
The great prince Enki caused the ... ox to ...
To the pure crops he roared,
In the steadfast field he made grain grow;
The lord, the jewel and ornament of the plain,
The ... farmer of Enlil,
Enkimdu, him of the canals and ditches,
Enki placed in their charge.

The lord called to the steadfast field, he caused it to produce much grain,
Enki made it bring forth its small and large beans ....
The ... grains he heaped up for the granary,
Enki added granary to granary,
With Enlil he increases abundance in the land;
Her whose head is .... whose face is ....
The lady who .... the might of the land, the steadfast support of the black-headed people,
Ashnan, strength of all things,
Enki placed in charge.

Enki now turns to the pickax and the brickmold, and appoints the brick-god Kabta in charge. He then directs the building implement *gugun*, lays foundations and builds houses, and places them under the charge of Mushdamma, the "great builder of Enlil". He then fills the plain with plant and animal life and places Sumugan, "king of the 'mountain'", in control. Finally Enki builds stables and sheepfolds, fills them with milk and fat, and puts them in the care of the shepherd-god Dumuzi. The rest of our text is destroyed and we do not know how the poem ends.

Enki and Eridu: The Journey of the Water-God to Nippur

ONE OF THE OLDEST and most venerated cities in Sumer was Eridu, which lies buried today under the mound Abu-Shahrain; a thorough excavation of this significant site would in all probability immensely enrich our knowledge of Sumerian culture and civilization, especially in their more spiritual aspects.

According to one Sumerian tradition, it was the oldest city in Sumer, the first of the five cities founded before the flood; our myth, on the other hand, implies that the city Nippur preceded it in age. In this city, which in ancient times must have been situated on the Persian Gulf, the water-god Enki, also known as Nudimmud, builds his "sea-house":

After the water of creation had been decreed,
After the name hegal (abundance), born in heaven,
Like plant and herb had clothed the land,
The lord of the abyss, the king Enki,
Enki, the lord who decrees the fates,
Built his house of silver and lapis lazuli;
Its silver and lapis lazuli, like sparkling light,
The father fashioned fittingly in the abyss.

The (creatures of) bright countenance and wise,
coming forth from the abyss,
Stood all about the lord Nudimmud;
The pure house be built, he adorned it with lapis lazuli,
He ornamented it greatly with gold,
In Eridu he built the house of the water-bank,
Its brickwork, word-uttering, advice-giving,
Its ... like an ox roaring,
The house of Enki, the oracles uttering.

Follows a long passage in which Isimud, the messenger of Enki, sings the praises of the "sea-house". Then Enki *raises* the city Eridu *from the abyss* and makes it *float* over the water like a lofty mountain. Its green fruit-bearing gardens he fills with birds; fishes, too, be makes abundant. Enki is now ready to proceed by boat to Nippur to obtain Enlil's blessing for his newly built city and temple. He therefore rises from the abyss:

When Enki rises, the fish ... rise,
The abyss stands in wonder,
In the sea joy enters,
Fear comes over the deep,
Terror holds the exalted river,
The Euphrates, the South Wind lifts it in waves.

And so Enki seats himself in his boat and first arrives in Eridu itself; here he slaughters many oxen and sheep. He then proceeds to Nippur where immediately upon his arrival he prepares all kinds of drinks for the gods and especially for Enlil. Then:

Enki in the shrine Nippur,
Gives his father Enlil bread to eat,
In the first place he seated An (the heaven-god),
Next to An he seated Enlil,
Nintu he seated at the "big side",
The Anunnaki seated themselves one after the other.

And so the gods feast and banquet until their hearts become "good" and Enlil is ready to pronounce his blessing:

Enlil says to the Anunnaki:

Enlil says to the Anunnaki:
"Ye great gods who are standing about,
My son has built a house, the king Enki;
Eridu, like a mountain, he has raised up from the earth,
In a good place he has built it.

Eridu, the clean place, where none may enter,
The house built of silver, adorned with lapis lazuli,
The house directed by the seven "lyre-songs", given over to incantation,
With pure songs ....
The abyss, the shrine of the goodness of Enki, befitting the divine decrees,
Eridu, the pure house having been built,
O Enki, praise!"

Inanna and Enki: The Transfer of the Arts of Civilization from Eridu to Erech

THIS MAGNIFICENT MYTH with its particularly charming story involves Inanna, the queen of heaven, and Enki, the lord of wisdom. Its contents are of profound significance for the study of the history and progress of civilization, since it contains a list of over 100 divine decrees governing all those cultural achievements which, according to the more or less superficial analysis of the Sumerian scribes and thinkers, made up the warp and woof of Sumerian civilization.

As early as 1911 a fragment belonging to this myth and located in the University Museum at Philadelphia was published by David W. Myhrman. Three years later, Arno Poebel published another Philadelphia tablet inscribed with part of the composition; this is a large, well-preserved six-column tablet whose upper left corner was broken off. This broken corner piece [was discovered] in 1937, twenty-three years later, in the Museum of the Ancient Orient at Istanbul. As early as 1914, therefore, a large part of the myth had been copied and published. However, no translation was attempted in all these years since the story seemed to make no connected sense; and what could be made out, seemed to lack intelligent motivation. In 1937 ... a small piece [was discovered] which supplied the missing clue, and as a result, this tale of the all too human Sumerian gods can now be told.

Inanna, queen of heaven, and tutelary goddess of Erech, is anxious to increase the welfare and prosperity of her city, to make it the center of Sumerian civilization, and thus to exalt her own name and fame. She therefore decides to go to Eridu, the ancient and hoary seat of Sumerian culture where Enki, the Lord of Wisdom, who "knows the very heart of the gods", dwells in his watery abyss, the Abzu. For Enki has under his charge all the divine decrees that are fundamental to civilization. And if she can obtain them, by fair means or foul, and bring them to her beloved city Erech, its glory and her own will indeed be unsurpassed. As she approaches the Abzu of Eridu, Enki, no doubt taken in by her charms, calls his messenger Isimud and thus addresses him:

"Come, my messenger, Isimud, give ear to my instructions,
A word I will say to thee, take my word.
The maid, all alone, has directed her step to the Abzu,
Inanna, all alone, has directed her step to the Abzu,
Have the maid enter the Abzu of Eridu,
Have Inanna enter the Abzu of Eridu,
Give her to eat barley cake with butter,
Pour for her cold water that freshens the heart,
Give her to drink date-wine in the 'face of the lion',
... for her .... make for her ...,
At the pure table, the table of heaven,
Speak to Inanna words of greeting".

Isimud does exactly as bidden by his master, and Inanna and Enki sit down to feast and banquet. After their hearts had become happy with drink, Enki exclaims:

"O name of My power, O name of my power,
To the pure Inanna, my daughter, I shall present . . ..
Lordship, ... -ship, godship, the tiara exalted and enduring, the throne of kingship".

Pure Inanna took them.
"O name of my power, O name of my power,
To the pure Inanna, my daughter, I shall present ....
The exalted scepter, staffs, the exalted shrine, shepherdship, kingship".
Pure Inanna took them.

He thus presents, several at a time, over 100 divine decrees which are the basis of the culture pattern of Sumerian civilization. And when it is realized that this myth was inscribed as early as 2000 BCE. and that the concepts involved were no doubt current centuries earlier, it is no exaggeration to state that no other civilization, outside of the Egyptian, can at all compare in age and quality with that developed by the Sumerians. Among these divine decrees presented by Enki to Inanna are those referring to lordship, godship, the exalted and enduring crown, the throne of kingship, the exalted scepter, the exalted shrine, shepherdship, kingship, the numerous priestly offices, truth, descent into the nether world and ascent from it, the "standard", the flood, sexual intercourse and prostitution, the *legal* tongue and the *libellous* tongue, art, the holy cult chambers, the "hierodule of heaven", music, eldership, heroship and power, enmity, straightforwardness, the destruction of cities and lamentation, rejoicing of the heart, falsehood, the rebel land, goodness and justice, the craft of the carpenter, metal worker, scribe, smith, leather worker, mason and basket weaver, wisdom and understanding, purification, fear and *outcry*, the kindling flame and the *consuming* flame, weariness, the shout of victory, counsel, the troubled heart, judgment and decision, exuberance, musical instruments.

Inanna is only too happy to accept the gifts offered her by the drunken Enki. She takes them, loads them on her "boat of heaven", and makes off for Erech with her precious cargo. But after the effects of the banquet had worn off, Enki noticed that the divine decrees were gone from their usual place. He turns to Isimud and the latter informs him that he, Enki himself, had presented them to his daughter Inanna. The upset Enki greatly rues his munificence and decides to prevent the "boat of heaven" from reaching Erech at all costs. He therefore dispatches his messenger Isimud together with a group of sea monsters to follow Inanna and her boat to the first of the seven stopping stations that are situated between the Abzu of Eridu and Erech. Here the sea monsters are to seize the "boat of heaven" from Inanna; Inanna, herself, however, must be permitted to continue her journey to Erech afoot. The passage covering Enki's instructions to Isimud and Isimud's conversation with Inanna, who reproaches her father Enki as an "Indian-giver", will undoubtedly go down as a classic poetic gem. It runs as follows:

The prince calls his messenger Isimud,

The prince calls his messenger Isimud,
Enki gives the word to the "good name of heaven":
"Oh my messenger Isimud, 'my good name of heaven'".

"Oh my king Enki, here I stand, forever is praise".

"The 'boat of heaven', where now has it arrived?"

"At the quay Idal it has arrived".

"Go, and let the sea monsters seize it from her".

Isimud does as bidden, overtakes the "boat of heaven", and says to Inanna:

"Oh my queen, thy father has sent me to thee,
Oh Inanna, thy father has sent me to thee,
Thy father, exalted is his speech,
Enki, exalted is his utterance,
His great words are not to go unheeded".

Holy Inanna answers him:
"My father, what has he spoken to thee, what has he said to thee?
His great words that are not to go unheeded, what pray are they?"

"My king has spoken to me,
Enki has said to me:
'Let Inanna go to Erech,
But thou, bring me back the "boat of heaven" to Eridu'".

Holy Inanna says to the messenger Isimud:
"My father, why pray has he changed his word to me,
Why has he broken his righteous word to me,
Why has he defiled his great words to me?
My father has spoken to me falsehood, has spoken to me falsehood,
Falsely has he uttered the name of his power, the name of the Abzu".

Barely had she uttered these words,
The sea monsters seized the "boat of heaven".
Inanna says to her messenger Ninshubur:
"Come, my true messenger of Eanna,
My messenger of favorable words,
My carrier of true words,
Whose hand never falters, whose foot never falters,
Save the 'boat of heaven', and Inanna's presented decrees".

This Ninshubur does. But Enki is persistent. He sends Isimud accompanied by various sea monsters to seize the "boat of heaven" at each of the seven stopping points between Eridu and Erech. And each time Ninshubur comes to Inanna's rescue. Finally, Inanna and her boat arrive safe and sound at Erech, where amidst jubilation and feasting on the part of its delighted inhabitants, she unloads the divine decrees one at a time. The poem ends with a speech addressed by Enki to Inanna, but the text is seriously damaged and it is not clear whether it is reconciliatory or retaliatory in character.

The Creation of Man

THE COMPOSITION NARRATING the creation of man has been found inscribed on two duplicating tablets: one is a Nippur tablet in our University Museum; the other is in the Louvre, which acquired it from an antique dealer. In spite of the fact that by 1934 the Louvre tablet and the greater part of the University Museum tablet had already been copied and published, the contents remained unintelligible. Primarily responsible for this unfortunate situation is the fact that our University Museum tablet, which is better preserved than the Louvre fragment, arrived in Philadelphia some four or five decades ago, broken into four parts. By 1919 two of the pieces had already been recognized and joined; these were copied and published by Stephen Langdon. In 1934 Edward Chiera published the third piece but failed to recognize that it joined the two pieces published by Langdon in 1919. It was the discovery of this fact, together with the identifying of the fourth and still unpublished piece which *joins* the three published pieces, that enabled [scholars] to arrange the contents in the proper order.

It should be emphasized here that the approximately 150 lines which make up the text of our poem still present numerous crucial breaks; many of the lines are poorly preserved.

Moreover, the linguistic difficulties in this composition are particularly burdensome; not a few of the crucial words are met here for the first time in Sumerian literature. The translation is therefore full of gaps and its tentative character must be underlined. Nevertheless it does present the fullest picture thus far available of the concepts concerned with the creation of man as current in Sumer during the third millennium BCE.

Among the oldest known conceptions of the creation of man are those of the Hebrews and the Babylonians; the former is narrated in the book of Genesis, the latter forms part of the Babylonian "Epic of Creation". According to the Biblical story, or at least according to one of its versions, man was fashioned from clay for the purpose of ruling over all the animals. In the Babylonian myth, man was made of the blood of one of the more troublesome of the gods who was killed for that purpose; he was created primarily in order to serve the gods and free them from the need of working for their bread. According to our Sumerian poem, which antedates both the Hebrew and the Babylonian versions by more than a millennium, man was fashioned of clay as in the Biblical version. The purpose for which he was created, however, was to free the gods from laboring for their sustenance, as in the Babylonian version.

The poem begins with what may be a description of the difficulties of the gods in procuring their bread, especially, as might have been expected, after the female deities had come into being. The gods complain, but Enki, the water-god, who, as the Sumerian god of wisdom, might have been expected to come to their aid, is lying asleep in the deep and fails to hear them. Thereupon his mother, the primeval sea, "the mother who gave birth to all the gods", brings the tears of the gods before Enki, saying:

"O my son, rise from thy bed, from thy ... work what is wise,
Fashion servants of the gods, may they produce their ...",

Enki gives the matter thought, leads forth 'the host of "good and princely *fashioners*" and says to his mother, Nammu, the primeval sea:

O my mother, the creature whose name thou hoist uttered, it exists,
Bind upon it the ... of the gods;
Mix the heart of the clay that is over the abyss,
The good and princely fashioners will thicken the clay,
Thou, do thou bring the limbs into existence;
Ninmah (the earth-mother goddess) will work above thee,
... (goddesses of birth) will stand by thee at thy fashioning;
O my mother, decree thou its (the newborn's) fate,
Ninmah will bind upon it the ... of the gods,
... as man ...

After a break of several lines, whose contents, if ever recovered, should prove most illuminating, the poem describes a feast arranged by Enki for the gods, no doubt to commemorate man's creation. At this feast Enki and Ninmah drink much wine and become somewhat exuberant. Thereupon Ninmah takes some of the clay which is over the abyss and fashions six different types of individuals, while Enki decrees their fate and gives them bread to eat. The character of only the last two types is intelligible; these are the barren woman and the sexless or eunuch type. The lines read:

The ... she (Ninmah) made into a woman who cannot give birth.
Enki upon seeing the woman who cannot give birth,
Decreed her fate, destined her to be stationed in the "woman house".

The ... she (Ninmah) made into one who has no
male organ, who has no female organ.
Enki, upon seeing him who has no male organ, who has no female organ,
To stand before the king, decreed as his fate.

After Ninmah had created these six types of man, Enki decides to do some creating of his own. The manner in which he goes about it is not clear, but whatever it is that he does, the resulting creature is a failure; it is weak and feeble in body and spirit. Enki is now anxious that Ninmah help this forlorn creature; he therefore addresses her as follows:

"Of him whom thy hand has fashioned, I have decreed the fate,
Have given him bread to eat;
Do thou decree the fate of him whom my hand has fashioned,
Do thou give him bread to eat".

Ninmah tries to be good to the creature but to no avail. She talks to him but he fails to answer. She gives him bread to eat but he does not reach out for it. He can neither sit nor stand, nor bend the knees. A long conversation between Enki and Ninmah then follows, but the tablets are so badly broken at this point that it is impossible to make out the sense of the contents. Finally, Ninmah seems to utter a curse against Enki because of the sick, lifeless creature which he produced, a curse which Enki seems to accept as his due.

In addition to the creation poem outlined above, a detailed description of the purpose for which mankind was created is given in the introduction to the myth "Cattle and Grain"; it runs as follows. After the Anunnaki, the heaven-gods, had been born, but before the creation of Lahar, the cattle-god, and Ashnan, the grain-goddess, there existed neither cattle nor grain. The gods therefore "knew not" the eating of bread nor the dressing of garments. The cattle-god Lahar and the grain-goddess Ashnan were then created in the creation chamber of heaven, but still the gods remained unsated. It was then that man "was given breath", for the sake of the welfare of the sheepfolds and "good things" of the gods. This introduction reads as follows:

After on the mountain of heaven and earth,
An (the heaven-god) had caused the Anunnaki (his followers) to be born
Because the name Ashnan (the grain-goddess) had
not been born, had not been fashioned,
Because Uttu (the goddess of plants) had not been fashioned,
Because to Uttu no temenos had been set up,
There was no ewe, no lamb was dropped,
There was no goat, no kid was dropped,
The ewe did not give birth to its two lambs,
The goat did not give birth to its three kids.

Because the name of Ashnan, the wise, and Lahar (the cattle-god),
The Anunnaki, the great gods, did not know,

The ... grain of thirty days did not exist,
The ... grain of forty days did not exist,
The small grains, the grain of the mountain, the grain of the pure living creatures did not exist.

Because Uttu had not been born, because the crown (of vegetation?) had not been raised,
Because the lord ... had not been born,
Because Sumugan, the god of the plain, had not come forth,
Like mankind when first created,
They (the Anunnaki knew not the eating of bread,
Knew not the dressing of garments,
Ate plants with their mouth like sheep,
Drank water from the ditch.

In those days, in the creation chamber of the gods,
In their house Dulkug, Lahar and Ashnan were fashioned;
The produce of Lahar and Ashnan,
The Anunnaki of the Dulkug eat, but remain unsated;
In their pure sheepfolds milk, . . ., and good things,
The Anunnaki of the Dulkug drink, but remain unsated;
For the sake of the good things in their pure sheepfolds,
Man was given breath.

The creation of man concludes our study of Sumerian cosmogony, of the theories and concepts evolved by the Sumerians to explain the origin of the universe and the existence of gods and men. It cannot be sufficiently stressed that the Sumerian cosmogonic concepts, early as they are, are by no means *primitive*. They reflect the mature thought and reason of the thinking Sumerian as he contemplated the forces of nature and the character of his own existence. When these concepts are analyzed; when the theological cloak and polytheistic trappings are removed *(although this is by no means always possible at present because of the limited character of our material as well as of our understanding and interpretation of its contents*), the Sumerian creation concepts indicate a keenly observing mentality as well as an ability to draw and formulate pertinent conclusions from the data observed. Thus, rationally expressed, the Sumerian cosmogonic concepts may be summarized as follows:

1. First was the primeval *sea*; it is not unlikely that it was conceived by the Sumerian as *eternal* and *uncreated*.
2. The primeval sea engendered a *united heaven and earth*.
3. Heaven and earth were conceived as *solid* elements. Between them, however, and *from them*, came the gaseous element *air*, whose main characteristic is that of expansion. Heaven and earth were thus separated by the expanding element *air*.
4. Air, being lighter and far less dense than either heaven or earth, succeeded in producing the *moon*, which may have been conceived by the Sumerians as made of the same stuff as air. The *sun* was conceived as born of the *moon*; that is, it emanated and developed from the moon just as the latter emanated and developed from air.

5. After heaven and earth had been separated, *plant*, *animal* and *human* life became possible on earth; all life seems to have been conceived as resulting from a union of air, earth and water; the sun, too, was probably involved. Unfortunately, in this matter of production and reproduction of plant and animal life on earth, our extant material is very difficult to penetrate.

Transferred into theological language, these rationalistic Sumerian concepts may be described as follows:

1. First was the goddess *Nammu*, the primeval sea personified.
2. The goddess *Nammu* gave birth to *An*, the male heaven-god, and *Ki*, the earth-goddess.
3. The union of *An* and *Ki* produced the air-god *Enlil*, who proceeded to separate the heaven-father *An* from the earth-mother *Ki*.
4. *Enlil*, the air-god, now found himself living in utter darkness, with the sky, which may have been conceived by the Sumerians as made of pitch-dark lapis lazuli, forming the ceiling and walls of his house, and the surface of the earth, its floor. He therefore begot the moon-god Nanna to brighten the darkness of his house. The moon-god *Nanna* in turn begot the sun-god *Utu*, who became brighter than his father. It is not without interest to note here that the idea that the son, the begotten one, becomes stronger than the father, the begetter – in a deeper sense this is actually what happens in the development which we term *progress* – is native to the philosophy and psychology of the Near East. *Enlil*, the air-god, for example, becomes in historical times more powerful than his father *An*, the heaven-god. At a later date *Marduk*, the god of the Semitic Babylonians, becomes more powerful than his father *Enki*, the water-god. In the Christian dogma, Christ, the son, becomes in many ways more significant and pertinent for man and his salvation than God, the father.
5. *Enlil*, the air-god, now unites with his mother *Ki*, the earth-goddess. It is from this union but with considerable help from *Enki*, the water-god, that the vegetable and animal life is produced on earth. Man, on the other hand, seems to be the product of the combined efforts of the goddess *Nammu*, the primeval sea; of the goddess *Ninmah*, who may perhaps be identified with *Ki*, the mother earth; and finally of the water-god *Enki*. Just what is involved in this particular combination-and there is every reason to believe that in view of the more or less superficial data of the times there was good logic behind it and not mere playful fantasy – it is difficult to gather from our present material and limited understanding.

Creation Legend: Merodach the Dragon Slayer

IN THE BEGINNING the whole universe was a sea. Heaven on high had not been named, nor the earth beneath. Their begetter was Apsu, the father of the primordial Deep, and their mother was Tiamat, the spirit of Chaos. No plain was yet formed, no marsh could be seen; the gods had no existence, nor had their fates been determined. Then there was a movement in the waters, and the deities issued forth. The first who had being were the god Lachmu and the goddess Lachamu. Long ages went past. Then were created the god Anshar and the goddess Kishar. When the days of these deities had increased and extended, they were followed by Anu, god of the sky, whose consort was Anatu; and Ea, most wise and all-powerful, who was without an equal. Now Ea, god of the deep, was also Enki, "lord of earth", and his eternal spouse, Damkina, was Gashan-ki, "lady of earth". The son of Ea and Damkina was Bel, the lord, who in time created mankind. Thus were the high gods established in power and in glory.

Apsu and the Tiamat Dragon

Now Apsu and Tiamat remained amidst confusion in the deeps of chaos. They were troubled because their offspring, the high gods, aspired to control the universe and set it in order. Apsu was still powerful and fierce, and Tiamat snarled and raised tempests, smiting herself. Their purpose was to work evil amidst eternal confusion.

Then Apsu called upon Mummu, his counsellor, the son who shared his desires, and said, "O Mummu, thou who art pleasing unto me, let us go forth together unto Tiamat and speak with her".

So the two went forth and prostrated themselves before the Chaos Mother to consult with her as to what should be done to prevent the accomplishment of the purpose of the high gods.

Plot to Destroy the Beneficent Gods

Apsu opened his mouth and spake, saying, "O Tiamat, thou gleaming one, the purpose of the gods troubles me. I cannot rest by day nor can I repose by night. I will thwart them and destroy their purpose. I will bring sorrow and mourning so that we may lie down undisturbed by them".

Tiamat heard these words and snarled. She raised angry and roaring tempests; in her furious grief she uttered a curse, and then spake to Apsu, saying, "What shall we do so that their purpose may be thwarted and we may lie down undisturbed again?"

Mummu, the counsellor, addressing Apsu, made answer, and said, "Although the gods are powerful, thou canst overcome them; although their purpose is strong, thou canst thwart it. Then thou shalt have rest by day and peace by night to lie down".

Ea overcomes Apsu and Mummu

The face of Apsu grew bright when he heard these words spoken by Mummu, yet he trembled to think of the purpose of the high gods, to whom he was hostile. With Tiamat he lamented because the gods had changed all things; the plans of the gods filled their hearts with dread; they sorrowed and spake with Mummu, plotting evil.

Then Ea, who knoweth all, drew near; he beheld the evil ones conspiring and muttering together. He uttered a pure incantation and accomplished the downfall of Apsu and Mummu, who were taken captive.

Kingu, who shared the desires of Tiamat, spake unto her words of counsel, saying, "Apsu and Mummu have been overcome and we cannot repose. Thou shalt be their Avenger, O Tempestuous One".

The Vengeful Preparations of the Dragon

Tiamat heard the words of this bright and evil god, and made answer, saying, "On my strength thou canst trust. So let war be waged".

Then were the hosts of chaos and the deep gathered together. By day and by night they plotted against the high gods, raging furiously, making ready for battle, fuming and storming and taking no rest.

Mother Chuber, the creator of all, provided irresistible weapons. She also brought into being eleven kinds of fierce monsters – giant serpents, sharp of tooth with unsparing fangs, whose bodies were filled with poison instead of blood; snarling dragons, clad with terror, and of such lofty stature that whoever saw them was overwhelmed with fear, nor could any escape their attack when they lifted themselves up; vipers and pythons, and the Lachamu, hurricane monsters, raging hounds, scorpion men, tempest furies, fish men and mountain rams. These she armed with fierce weapons and they had no fear of war.

Then Tiamat, whose commands are unchangeable and mighty, exalted Kingu, who had come to her aid, above all the evil gods; she made him the leader to direct the army in battle, to go in front, to open the attack. Robing Kingu in splendour, she seated him on high and spoke, saying:

"I have established thy command over all the gods. Thou shalt rule over them. Be mighty, thou my chosen husband, and let thy name be exalted over all the spirits of heaven and spirits of earth".

Unto Kingu did Tiamat deliver the tablets of fate; she laid them in his bosom, and said, "Thy commands cannot be changed; thy words shall remain firm".

Thus was Kingu exalted; he was vested with the divine power of Anu to decree the fate of the gods, saying, "Let thy mouth open to thwart the fire god; be mighty in battle nor brook resistance".

Then had Ea knowledge of Tiamat's doings, how she had gathered her forces together, and how she had prepared to work evil against the high gods with purpose to avenge Apsu. The wise god was stricken with grief, and he moaned for many days. Thereafter he went and stood before his father, Anshar, and spake, saying, "Our mother, Tiamat, hath turned against us in her wrath. She hath gathered the gods about her, and those thou didst create are with her also".

When Anshar heard all that Ea revealed regarding the preparations made by Tiamat, he smote his loins and clenched his teeth, and was ill at ease. In sorrow and anger he spoke and said, "Thou didst go forth aforetime to battle; thou didst bind Mummu and smite Apsu. Now Kingu is exalted, and there is none who can oppose Tiamat".

Anshar called his son, Anu, before him, and spoke, saying: "O mighty one without fear, whose attack is irresistible, go now before Tiamat and speak so that her anger may subside and her heart be made merciful. But if she will not hearken unto thee, speak thou for me, so that she may be reconciled".

Anu was obedient to the commands of Anshar. He departed, and descended by the path of Tiamat until he beheld her fuming and snarling, but he feared to approach her, and turned back.

Then Ea was sent forth, but he was stricken with terror and turned back also.

Anshar's Appeal to Merodach

Anshar then called upon Merodach, son of Ea, and addressed him, saying, "My son, who softeneth my heart, thou shalt go forth to battle and none shall stand against thee".

The heart of Merodach was made glad at these words. He stood before Anshar, who kissed him, because that he banished fear. Merodach spake, saying: "O lord of the gods, withdraw not thy words; let me go forth to do as is thy desire. What man hath challenged thee to battle?"

Anshar made answer and said: "No man hath challenged me. It is Tiamat, the woman, who hath resolved to wage war against us. But fear not and make merry, for thou shalt bruise the head of Tiamat. O wise god, thou shalt overcome her with thy pure incantation. Tarry not but hasten forth; she cannot wound thee; thou shalt come back again".

The words of Anshar delighted the heart of Merodach, who spake, saying: "O lord of the gods, O fate of the high gods, if I, the avenger, am to subdue Tiamat and save all, then proclaim my greatness among the gods. Let all the high gods gather together joyfully in Upshukinaku (the Council Hall), so that my words like thine may remain unchanged, and what I do may never be altered. Instead of thee I will decree the fates of the gods".

Then Anshar called unto his counsellor, Gaga, and addressing him, said: "O thou who dost share my desires, thou who dost understand the purpose of my heart, go unto Lachmu and Lachamu and summon all the high gods to come before me to eat bread and drink wine. Repeat to them all I tell you of Tiamat's preparations for war, of my commands to Anu and Ea, who turned back, fearing the dragon, of my choice of Merodach to be our avenger, and his desire to be equipped with my power to decree fate, so that he may be made strong to combat against our enemy".

The Festival of the High Gods

As Anshar commanded so did Gaga do. He went unto Lachmu and Lachamu and prostrated himself humbly before them. Then he rose and delivered the message of Anshar, their son, adding: "Hasten and speedily decide for Merodach your fate. Permit him to depart to meet your powerful foe".

When Lachmu and Lachamu heard all that Gaga revealed unto them they uttered lamentations, while the Igigi (heavenly spirits) sorrowed bitterly, and said: "What change hath happened that Tiamat hath become hostile to her own offspring? We cannot understand her deeds".

All the high gods then arose and went unto Anshar. They filled his council chamber and kissed one another. Then they sat down to eat bread and drink sesame wine. And when they were made drunk and were merry and at their ease, they decreed the fate for Merodach.

Merodach Exalted as Ruler of the Universe

In the chamber of Anshar they honoured the Avenger. He was exalted as a prince over them all, and they said: "Among the high gods thou art the highest; thy command is the command of Anu. Henceforth thou wilt have power to raise up and to cast down. None of the gods will dispute thy authority. O Merodach, our avenger, we give thee sovereignty over the entire Universe. Thy weapon will ever be irresistible. Smite down the gods who have raised revolt, but spare the lives of those who repose their trust in thee".

Then the gods laid down a garment before Merodach, saying: "Open thy mouth and speak words of command, so that the garment may be destroyed; speak again and it will be brought back".

Merodach spake with his mouth and the garment vanished; he spake again and the garment was reproduced.

All the gods rejoiced, and they prostrated themselves and cried out, "Merodach is King!"

Thereafter they gave him the sceptre and the throne and the insignia of royalty, and also an irresistible weapon with which to overcome his enemies, saying: "Now, O Merodach, hasten and slay Tiamat. Let the winds carry her blood to hidden places".

So was the fate of Merodach decreed by the gods; so was a path of prosperity and peace prepared for him. He made ready for battle; he strung his bow and hung his quiver; he slung a dart over his shoulder, and he grasped a club in his right hand; before him he set lightning, and with flaming fire he filled his body. Anu gave unto him a great net with which to snare his enemies and prevent their escape. Then Merodach created seven winds – the wind of evil, the uncontrollable wind, the sandstorm, and the whirlwind, the fourfold wind, the sevenfold wind, and the wind that has no equal – and they went after him. Next he seized his mighty weapon, the thunderstone, and leapt into his storm chariot, to which were yoked four rushing and destructive steeds of rapid flight, with foam-flecked mouths and teeth full of venom, trained for battle, to overthrow enemies and trample them underfoot. A light burned on the head of Merodach, and he was clad in a robe of terror. He drove forth, and the gods, his fathers, followed after him: the high gods clustered around and followed him, hastening to battle.

Merodach drove on, and at length he drew nigh to the secret lair of Tiamat, and he beheld her muttering with Kingu, her consort. For a moment he faltered, and when the gods who followed him beheld this, their eyes were troubled.

Tiamat snarled nor turned her head. She uttered curses, and said: "O Merodach, I fear not thy advance as chief of the gods. My allies are assembled here, and are more powerful than thou art".

Merodach uplifted his arm, grasping the dreaded thunderstone, and spake unto Tiamat, the rebellious one, saying: "Thou hast exalted thyself, and with wrathful heart hath prepared for war against the high gods and their fathers, whom thou dost hate in thy heart of evil. Unto Kingu thou hast given the power of Anu to decree fate, because thou art hostile to what is good and loveth what is sinful. Gather thy forces together, and arm thyself and come forth to battle".

When Tiamat heard these mighty words she raved and cried aloud like one who is possessed; all her limbs shook, and she muttered a spell. The gods seized their weapons.

Dragon Slain and Host Taken Captive

Tiamat and Merodach advanced to combat against one another. They made ready for battle. The lord of the high gods spread out the net which Anu had given him. He snared the dragon and she could not escape. Tiamat opened her mouth which was seven miles wide, and Merodach called upon the evil wind to smite her; he caused the wind to keep her mouth agape so that she could not close it. All the tempests and the hurricanes entered in, filling her body, and her heart grew weak; she gasped, overpowered. Then the lord of the high gods seized his dart and cast it through the lower part of her body; it tore her inward parts and severed her heart. So was Tiamat slain.

Merodach overturned the body of the dead dragon and stood upon it. All the evil gods who had followed her were stricken with terror and broke into flight. But they were unable to escape. Merodach caught them in his great net, and they stumbled and fell uttering cries of distress, and the whole world resounded with their wailing and lamentations. The lord of the high gods broke the weapons of the evil gods and put them in bondage. Then he fell upon the monsters which Tiamat had created; he subdued them, divested them of their powers, and trampled them under his feet. Kingu he seized with the others. From this god great Merodach took the tablets of fate, and impressing upon them his own seal, placed them in his bosom.

So were the enemies of the high gods overthrown by the Avenger. Ansar's commands were fulfilled and the desires of Ea fully accomplished.

Merodach Rearranges the Pantheon

Merodach strengthened the bonds which he had laid upon the evil gods and then returned to Tiamat. He leapt upon the dragon's body; he clove her skull with his great club; he opened the channels of her blood which streamed forth, and caused the north to carry her blood to hidden places. The high gods, his fathers, clustered around; they raised shouts of triumph and made merry. Then they brought gifts and offerings to the great Avenger.

Merodach rested a while, gazing upon the dead body of the dragon. He divided the flesh of Ku-pu, and devised a cunning plan.

Then the lord of the high gods split the body of the dragon like that of a mashde fish into two halves. With one half he enveloped the firmament; he fixed it there and set a watchman to prevent the waters falling down. With the other half he made the earth. Then he made the abode of Ea in the deep, and the abode of Anu in high heaven. The abode of Enlil was in the air.

Merodach set all the great gods in their several stations. He also created their images, the stars of the Zodiac, and fixed them all. He measured the year and divided it into months; for twelve months he made three stars each. After he had given starry images of the gods separate control of each day of the year, he founded the station of Nibiru (Jupiter), his own star, to determine the limits of all stars, so that none might err or go astray. He placed beside his own the stations of Enlil and Ea, and on each side he opened mighty gates, fixing bolts on the left and on the right. He set the zenith in the centre.

Merodach decreed that the moon god should rule the night and measure the days, and each month he was given a crown. Its various phases the great lord determined, and he commanded that on the evening of its fullest brilliancy it should stand opposite the sun.

He placed his bow in heaven (as a constellation) and his net also.

Creation of Man

We have now reached the sixth tablet, which begins with a reference to words spoken to Merodach by the gods. Apparently Ea had conceived in his heart that mankind should be created. The lord of the gods read his thoughts and said: "I will shed my blood and fashion bone … I will create man to dwell on the earth so that the gods may be worshipped and shrines erected for them. I will change the pathways of the gods…".

The rest of the text is fragmentary, and many lines are missing. Berosus states, however, that Belus (Bel Merodach) severed his head from his shoulders. His blood flowed forth, and the gods mixed it with earth and formed the first man and various animals.

In another version of the creation of man, it is related that Merodach "laid a reed upon the face of the waters; he formed dust, and poured it out beside the reed.... That he might cause the gods to dwell in the habitation of their heart's desire, he formed mankind". The goddess Aruru, a deity of Sippar, and one of the forms of "the lady of the gods", is associated with Merodach as the creatrix of the seed of mankind. "The beasts of the field and living creatures in the field he formed". He also created the Tigris and Euphrates rivers, grass, reeds, herbs and trees, lands, marshes and swamps, cows, goats, etc.

In the seventh tablet Merodach is praised by the gods – the Igigi (spirits of heaven). As he has absorbed all their attributes, he is addressed by his fifty-one names; henceforth each deity is a form of Merodach. Bel Enlil, for instance, is Merodach of lordship and domination; Sin, the moon god, is Merodach as ruler of night; Shamash is Merodach as god of law and holiness; Nergal is Merodach of war; and so on. The tendency to monotheism appears to have been most marked among the priestly theorists of Babylon.

Merodach as Asari

Merodach is hailed to begin with as Asari, the introducer of agriculture and horticulture, the creator of grain and plants. He also directs the decrees of Anu, Bel and Ea; but having rescued the gods from destruction at the hands of Kingu and Tiamat, he was greater than his "fathers", the elder gods. He set the Universe in order, and created all things anew. He is therefore Tutu, "the creator", a merciful and beneficent god. The following are renderings of lines 25 to 32:

Tutu: Aga-azaga (the glorious crown) may he make the crowns glorious –
The lord of the glorious incantation bringing the dead to life;
He who had mercy on the gods who had been overpowered;
Made heavy the yoke which he had laid on the gods who were his enemies,
(And) to redeem(?) them created mankind.
"The merciful one", "he with whom is salvation",
May his word be established, and not forgotten,
In the mouth of the black-headed ones whom his hands have made.
– Pinches' translation

Tutu as Aga-azag may mankind fourthly magnify!
"The Lord of the Pure Incantation", "the Quickener of the Dead",
"Who had mercy upon the captive gods",
"Who removed the yoke from upon the gods his enemies",
"For their forgiveness did he create mankind",
"The Merciful One, with whom it is to bestow life!"
May his deeds endure, may they never be forgotten
In the mouth of mankind whom his hands have made.
– King's translation

Apparently the Babylonian doctrine set forth that mankind was created not only to worship the gods, but also to bring about the redemption of the fallen gods who followed Tiamat.

Those rebel angels (ili, gods) He prohibited return;
He stopped their service; He removed them unto the gods (ili) who were His enemies.
In their room he created mankind.

Tiamat as Source of Good and Evil

Tiamat, the chaos dragon, is the Great Mother. She has a dual character. As the origin of good she is the creatrix of the gods. Her beneficent form survived as the Sumerian goddess Bau, who was obviously identical with the Phoenician Baau, mother of the first man. Another name of Bau was Ma, and Nintu, "a form of the goddess Ma", was half a woman and half a serpent, and was depicted with "a babe suckling her breast". The Egyptian goddesses Nehebkau and Uazit were serpents, and the goddesses Isis and Nepthys had also serpent forms. The serpent was a symbol of fertility, and as a mother was a protector. Vishnu, the Preserver of the Hindu Trinity, sleeps on the world-serpent's body. Serpent charms are protective and fertility charms.

As the origin of evil Tiamat personified the deep and tempests. In this character she was the enemy of order and good, and strove to destroy the world.

I have seen
The ambitious ocean swell and rage and foam
To be exalted with the threatening clouds.

The Dragon as the Serpent or Worm

Tiamat was the dragon of the sea, and therefore the serpent or leviathan. The word "dragon" is derived from the Greek "drakon", the serpent known as "the seeing one" or "looking one", whose glance was the lightning. The Anglo-Saxon "fire drake" ("draca", Latin "draco") is identical with the "flying dragon".

In various countries the serpent or worm is a destroyer which swallows the dead. "The worm shall eat them like wool", exclaimed Isaiah in symbolic language. It lies in the ocean which surrounds the world in Egyptian, Babylonian, Greek, Teutonic, Indian, and other mythologies. The Irish call it "moruach", and give it a mermaid form like the Babylonian Nintu. In a Scottish Gaelic poem Tiamat figures as "The Yellow Muilearteach", who is slain by Finn-mac-Coul, assisted by his warrior band.

There was seen coming on the top of the waves
The crooked, clamouring, shivering brave …
Her face was blue black of the lustre of coal,
And her bone-tufted tooth was like rusted bone.

The serpent figures in folk tales. When Alexander the Great, according to Ethiopic legend, was lowered in a glass cage to the depths of the ocean, he saw a great monster going past, and sat for two days "watching for its tail and hinder parts to appear". An Argyllshire Highlander had a similar experience. He went to fish one morning on a rock. "He was not long there when he saw the head of an eel pass. He continued fishing for an hour and the eel was still passing. He went home, worked in the field all day, and having returned to the same rock in the evening, the eel was still passing, and about dusk he saw her tail disappearing". Tiamat's sea-brood is referred to in the Anglo-Saxon epic Beowulf as "pickers". The hero "slew by night sea monsters on the waves" (line 422).

The well dragon – the French "draco" – also recalls the Babylonian water monsters. There was a "dragon well" near Jerusalem. From China to Ireland rivers are dragons, or goddesses who flee from the well dragons. The demon of the Rhone is called the "drac". Floods are also referred to as dragons, and the Hydra, or water serpent, slain by Hercules, belongs to this category. Water was the source of evil as well as good. To the Sumerians, the ocean especially was the abode of monsters. They looked upon it as did Shakespeare's Ferdinand, when, leaping into the sea, he cried: "Hell is empty and all the devils are here".

Folk Tale aspect of Creation Myth

There can be little doubt but that in this Babylonian story of Creation we have a glorified variation of the widespread Dragon myth. Unfortunately, however, no trace can be obtained of the pre-existing Sumerian oral version which the theorizing priests infused with such sublime symbolism. No doubt it enjoyed as great popularity as the immemorial legend of Perseus and Andromeda, which the sages of Greece attempted to rationalize, and parts of which the poets made use of and developed as these appealed to their imaginations.

The lost Sumerian story may be summarized as follows: There existed in the savage wilds, or the ocean, a family of monsters antagonistic to a group of warriors represented in the Creation legend by the gods. Ea, the heroic king, sets forth to combat with the enemies of man, and slays the monster father, Apsu, and his son, Mummu. But the most powerful demon remains to be dealt with. This is the mother Tiamat, who burns to avenge the deaths of her kindred. To wage war against her the hero makes elaborate preparations, and equips himself with special weapons. The queen of monsters cannot be overcome by ordinary means, for she has great cunning, and is less vulnerable than were her husband and son. Although Ea may work spells against her, she is able to thwart him by working counter spells. Only a hand-to-hand combat can decide the fray. Being strongly protected by her scaly hide, she must be wounded either on the under part of her body or through her mouth by a weapon which will pierce her liver, the seat of life. It will be noted in this connection that Merodach achieved success by causing the winds which followed him to distend the monster's jaws, so that he might be able to inflict the fatal blow and prevent her at the same time from uttering spells to weaken him.

British Neolithic Legends

This type of story, in which the mother monster is greater and more powerful than her husband or son, is exceedingly common in Scottish folklore. In the legend which relates the adventures of "Finn in the Kingdom of Big Men", the hero goes forth at night to protect his allies against the attacks of devastating sea monsters. Standing on the beach, "he saw the sea advancing in fiery kilns and as a darting serpent.... A huge monster came up, and looking down below where he (Finn) was, exclaimed, 'What little speck do I see here?' Finn, aided by his fairy dog, slew the water monster. On the following night a bigger monster, "the father", came ashore, and he also was slain. But the most powerful enemy had yet to be dealt with. "The next night a Big Hag came ashore, and the tooth in the front of her mouth would make a distaff. 'You killed my husband and son', she said". Finn acknowledged that he did, and they began to fight. After a prolonged struggle, in which Finn was almost overcome, the Hag fell and her head was cut off.

The story of "Finlay the Changeling" has similar features. The hero slew first a giant and then the giant's father. Thereafter the Hag came against him and exclaimed, "Although with cunning and deceitfulness you killed my husband last night and my son on the night before last, I shall certainly kill you tonight". A fierce wrestling match ensued on the bare rock. The Hag was ultimately thrown down. She then offered various treasures to ransom her life, including "a gold sword in my cave", regarding which she says, "never was it drawn to man or to beast whom it did not overcome". In other Scottish stories of like character the hero climbs a tree, and says something to induce the hag to open her mouth, so that he may plunge his weapon down her throat.

The Grendel story in Beowulf, the Anglo-Saxon epic, is of like character. A male water monster preys nightly upon the warriors who sleep in the great hall of King Hrothgar. Beowulf comes over the sea, as did Finn to the "Kingdom of Big Men", to slay Grendel. He wrestles with this man-eater and mortally wounds him. Great rejoicings ensue, but they have to be brought to an abrupt conclusion, because the mother of Grendel has meanwhile resolved "to go a sorry journey and avenge the death of her son".

The narrative sets forth that she enters the Hall in the darkness of night. "Quickly she grasped one of the nobles tight, and then she went towards the fen", towards her submarine cave. Beowulf follows in due course, and, fully armoured, dives through the waters and ultimately enters the monster's lair. In the combat the "water wife" proves to be a more terrible opponent than was her son. Indeed, Beowulf was unable to slay her until he possessed himself of a gigantic sword, "adorned with treasure", which was hanging in the cave. With this magic weapon he slays the mother monster, whose poisonous blood afterwards melts the "damasked blade". Like Finn, he subsequently returns with the head of one of the monsters.

German and Egyptian Contracts

An interesting point about this story is that it does not appear in any form in the North German cycle of Romance. Indeed, the poet who included in his epic the fiery dragon story, which links the hero Beowulf with Sigurd and Siegfried, appears to be doubtful about the mother monster's greatness, as if dealing with unfamiliar material, for he says: "The terror (caused by Grendel's mother) was less by just so much as woman's strength, woman's war terror, is (measured) by fighting men". Yet, in the narrative which follows the Amazon is proved to be the stronger monster of the two. Traces of the mother monster survive in English folklore, especially in the traditions about the mythical "Long Meg of Westminster", referred to by Ben Jonson in his masque of the "Fortunate Isles":

Westminster Meg,
With her long leg,
As long as a crane;
And feet like a plane,
With a pair of heels
As broad as two wheels.

Meg has various graves. One is supposed to be marked by a huge stone in the south side of the cloisters of Westminster Abbey; it probably marks the trench in which some plague victims – regarded, perhaps, as victims of Meg – were interred. Meg was also reputed to have been petrified, like certain Greek and Irish giants and giantesses. At Little Salkeld, near Penrith, a stone circle is referred to as "Long Meg and her Daughters". Like "Long Tom", the famous giant, "Mons Meg" gave her name to big guns in early times, all hags and giants having been famous in floating folk tales as throwers of granite boulders, balls of hard clay, quoits and other gigantic missiles.

The stories about Grendel's mother and Long Meg are similar to those still repeated in the Scottish Highlands. These contrast sharply with characteristic Germanic legends, in which the giant is greater than the giantess, and the dragon is a male, like Fafner, who is slain by Sigurd, and Regin whom Siegfried overcomes. It is probable, therefore, that the British stories of female monsters who were more powerful than their husbands and sons, are of Neolithic and Iberian origin – immemorial relics of the intellectual life of the western branch of the Mediterranean race.

In Egypt the dragon survives in the highly developed mythology of the sun cult of Heliopolis, and, as sun worship is believed to have been imported, and the sun deity is a male, it is not surprising to find that the night demon, Apep, was a personification of Set. This god, who is identical with Sutekh, a Syrian and Asia Minor deity, was apparently worshipped by a tribe which was overcome in the course of early tribal struggles in pre-dynastic times. Being an old and discredited god, he became by a familiar process the demon of the conquerors. In the eighteenth dynasty, however, his ancient glory was revived, for the Sutekh of Rameses II figures as the "dragon slayer". It is in accordance with Mediterranean modes of thought, however, to find that in Egypt there is a great celestial battle heroine. This is the goddess Hathor-Sekhet, the "Eye of Ra". Similarly in India, the post-Vedic goddess Kali is a destroyer, while as Durga she is a guardian of heroes. Kali, Durga and Hathor-Sekhet link with the classical goddesses of war, and also with the Babylonian Ishtar, who, as has been shown, retained the outstanding characteristics of Tiamat, the fierce old "Great Mother" of primitive Sumerian folk religion.

Biblical References to Dragons

It is possible that in the Babylonian dragon myth the original hero was Ea. As much may be inferred from the symbolic references in the Bible to Jah's victory over the monster of the deep: "Art thou not it that hath cut Rahab and wounded the dragon?" "Thou brakest the heads of the dragons in the waters; thou brakest the heads of leviathan in pieces, and gayest him to be meat to the people inhabiting the wilderness"; "He divideth the sea with his power, and by his understanding he smiteth through the proud (Rahab). By his spirit he hath garnished the heavens: his hand hath formed (or pierced) the crooked serpent"; "Thou hast broken Rahab in pieces as one that is slain: thou hast scattered thine enemies with thy strong arm"; "In that day the Lord with his sore and great and strong sword shall punish leviathan the piercing (or stiff) serpent, even leviathan that crooked serpent; and he shall slay the dragon that is in the sea".

The Father and Son Theme

In the Babylonian Creation legend Ea is supplanted as dragon slayer by his son Merodach. Similarly, Ninip took the place of his father, Enlil, as the champion of the gods. "In other words", writes Dr. Langdon, "later theology evolved the notion of the son of the earth god, who acquires the attributes of the father, and becomes the god of war. It is he who stood forth against the rebellious monsters of darkness, who would wrest the dominion of the world from the gods who held their conclave on the mountain. The gods offer him the Tablets of Fate; the right to utter decrees is given unto him". This development is "of extreme importance for studying the growth of the idea of father and son, as creative and active principles of the world". In Indian mythology Indra similarly takes the place of his bolt-throwing father Dyaus, the sky god, who so closely resembles Zeus. Andrew Lang has shown that this myth is of widespread character. Were the Babylonian theorists guided by the folklore clue?

Merodach and Tammuz

Now Merodach, as the son of Ea whom he consulted and received spells from, was a brother of "Tammuz of the Abyss". It seems that in the great god of Babylon we should recognize one of the many forms of the primeval corn spirit and patriarch – the shepherd youth who was beloved by Ishtar. As the deity of the spring sun, Tammuz slew the winter demons of rain and tempest, so that he was an appropriate spouse for the goddess of harvest and war. Merodach may have been a development of Tammuz in his character as a demon slayer.

When he was raised to the position of Bel, "the Lord", by the Babylonian conquerors, Merodach supplanted the older Bel – Enlil of Nippur. Now Enlil, who had absorbed all the attributes of rival deities, and become a world god, was the

Lord of the harvest lands … lord of the grain fields,

being "lord of the anunnaki", or "earth spirits". As agriculturists in early times went to war so as to secure prisoners who could be sacrificed to feed the corn spirit, Enlil was a god of war and was adored as such:

The haughty, the hostile land thou dost humiliate ….
With thee who ventureth to make war?

He was also "the bull of goring horns … Enlil the bull", the god of fertility as well as of battle.

Asari, one of Merodach's names, links him with Osiris, the Egyptian Tammuz, who was supplanted by his son Horus. As the dragon slayer, he recalls, among others, Perseus, the Grecian hero, of whom it was prophesied that he would slay his grandfather. Perseus, like Tammuz and Osiris, was enclosed in a chest which was cast into the sea, to be rescued, however, by a fisherman on the island of Seriphos. This hero afterwards slew Medusa, one of the three terrible sisters, the Gorgons – a demon group which links with Tiamat. In time, Perseus returned home, and while an athletic contest was in progress, he killed his grandfather with a quoit. There is no evidence, however, to show that the displacement of Enlil by Merodach had any legendary sanction of like character.

The god of Babylon absorbed all other deities, apparently for political purposes, and in accordance with the tendency of the thought of the times, when raised to supreme rank in the national pantheon; and he was depicted fighting the winged dragon, flapping his own storm wings, and carrying the thunder weapon associated with Ramman.

Merodach's spouse Zer-panitum was significantly called "the lady of the Abyss", a title which connects her with Damkina, the mother, and Belit-sheri, the sister of Tammuz. Damkina was also a sky goddess like Ishtar.

Zer-panitum was no pale reflection of her Celestial husband, but a goddess of sharply defined character with independent powers. Apparently, she was identical with Aruru, creatrix of the seed of mankind, who was associated with Merodach when the first man and the first woman were brought into being. Originally, she was one of the mothers in the primitive spirit group, and so identical with Ishtar and the other prominent goddesses.

Monotheistic Tendency

As all goddesses became forms of Ishtar, so did all gods become forms of Merodach. Sin was "Merodach as illuminator of night", Nergal was Merodach of war", Addu (Ramman) was "Merodach of rain" and so on. A colophon which contains a text in which these identifications are detailed, appears to be "a copy", says Professor Pinches, "of an old inscription", which, he thinks, "may go back as far as 2000 BCE. This is the period at which the name Yaum-ilu, 'Jah is god', is found, together with references to ilu as the name for the one great god, and is also, roughly, the date of Abraham, who, it may be noted, was a Babylonian of Ur of the Chaldees".

In one of the hymns Merodach is addressed as follows:

Who shall escape from before thy power?
Thy will is an eternal mystery!
Thou makest it plain in heaven
And in the earth.
Command the sea
And the sea obeyeth thee.
Command the tempest
And the tempest becometh a calm.
Command the winding course
Of the Euphrates,
And the will of Merodach
Shall arrest the floods.
Lord, thou art holy!
Who is like unto thee?
Merodach thou art honoured
Among the gods that bear a name.

The monotheistic tendency, which was a marked feature of Merodach worship, had previously become pronounced in the worship of Bel Enlil of Nippur. Although it did not affect the religion of the masses, it serves to show that among the ancient scholars and thinkers of Babylonia religious thought had, at an early period, risen far above the crude polytheism of those who bargained with their deities and propitiated them with offerings and extravagant flattery, or exercised over them a magical influence by the performance of seasonal ceremonies, like the backsliders in Jerusalem, censured so severely by Jeremiah, who baked cakes to reward the Queen of Heaven for an abundant harvest, and wept with her for the slain Tammuz when he departed to Hades.

Perhaps it was due to the monotheistic tendency, if not to the fusion of father-worshipping and mother-worshipping peoples, that bi-sexual deities were conceived of. Nannar, the moon god, was sometimes addressed as father and mother in one, and Ishtar as a god as well as a goddess. In Egypt Isis is referred to in a temple chant as "the woman who was made a male by her father Osiris", and the Nile god Hapi was depicted as a man with female breasts.

Myths of Kur

ONE OF THE MOST DIFFICULT groups of concepts to identify and interpret is that represented by the Sumerian word *kur*. That one of its primary meanings is "mountain" is attested by the fact that the sign used for it is actually a pictograph representing a mountain. From the meaning "mountain" developed that of "foreign land", since the mountainous countries bordering Sumer were a constant menace to its people. *Kur* also came to mean "land" in general; Sumer itself is described as *kur-gal*, "great land".

But in addition the Sumerian word *kur* represented a cosmic concept. Thus it seems to be identical to a certain extent with the Sumerian *ki-gal*, "great below". Like *ki-gal*, therefore, it has the meaning "nether world"; indeed in such poems as "Inanna's Descent to the Nether World" and "Gilgamesh, Enkidu and the Nether World", the word regularly used for "nether world" is *kur*. *Kur* thus cosmically conceived is the empty space between the earth's crust and the primeval sea. Moreover, it is not improbable that the monstrous creature that lived at the bottom of the "great below" immediately over the primeval waters is also called Kur; if so, this monster Kur would correspond to a certain extent to the Babylonian Tiamat. In three of four "Myths of Kur", it is one or the other of these cosmic aspects of the word *kur* which is involved.

The Destruction of Kur: The Slaying of the Dragon

It is now more than half a century since the Babylonian "Epic of Creation", which centres largely about the slaying of the goddess Tiamat and her host of dragons, has been available to scholar and layman. Inscribed in Accadian, a Semitic language, on tablets dating from the first millennium BCE – tablets that are therefore later by more than a millennium than our Sumerian literary inscriptions – it is quoted and cited in the major works concerned with mythology and religion as an example of Semitic mythmaking. But even a surface examination of its contents clearly reveals Sumerian origin and influence. The very names of its protagonists are in large part Sumerian. What prevented scholars from making any effective comparisons, is the fact that so little was known of any original Sumerian tales involving the slaying of a dragon. It is therefore deeply gratifying to be in a position to present the contents of what are probably three distinct Sumerian versions of the dragon-slaying myth. Two of these are almost entirely unknown; their contents have been reconstructed and deciphered by me in the course of the past several years. The third has been known to a certain extent for a number of decades, but the new material in Istanbul and Philadelphia adds considerably to its contents and clarity.

Obviously enough the dragon-slaying motif is not confined to the myths of Mesopotamia. Almost all peoples and all ages have had their dragon stories. In Greece, especially, these tales, involving both gods and heroes, were legion. There was hardly a Greek hero who did not slay his dragon, although Heracles and Perseus are perhaps the best known dragon-killers. With the rise of Christianity, the heroic feat was transferred to the saints; witness the story of "St. George and the Dragon" and its numerous and ubiquitous parallels. The names are different and the details vary from story to story and from place to place. But that at least some of the incidents go back to a more original and central source, is more than likely. And since the dragon-slaying theme was an important motif in the Sumerian mythology of the third millennium BCE, it is not unreasonable to assume that many a thread in the texture of the Greek and early Christian dragon tales winds back to Sumerian sources.

As stated above, we may have three versions of the slaying-of-the-dragon myth as current in Sumer in the third millennium BCE. The first involves the Sumerian water-god Enki, whose closest parallel among the Greek gods is Poseidon. The hero of the second is Ninurta, prototype of the Babylonian god Marduk when playing the role of the "hero of the gods" in the Babylonian "Epic of Creation". In the third it is Inanna, counterpart of the Semitic Ishtar, who plays the leading role. In all three versions, however, the monster to be destroyed is termed

Kur. Its exact form and shape are still uncertain, but there are indications that in the first two versions it is conceived as a large serpent which lived in the bottom of the "great below" where the latter came in contact with the primeval waters. For at least according to one of the versions, when Kur is destroyed, these waters rise to the surface of the earth and all cultivation with its resulting vegetation becomes impossible.

It is the first of the three versions of the slaying of the dragon which seems to be the more original; the details of the story, few as they are, are significant and instructive. For in the first place, the battle between the god and Kur seems to take place not long after the separation of heaven and earth. Moreover, the crime involved is probably that of abducting a goddess; it therefore brings to mind the Greek story of the rape of Persephone. Finally, it is the water-god Enki, the "god of wisdom", one of the ruling and creating deities of Sumer, who is the hero of the story. Unfortunately, we have only a very brief laconic passage from which to reconstruct our story; the tablets on which the details of the myth are inscribed are still lying no doubt in the ruins of Sumer. What we do have is part of the introductory prologue to the epic tale "Gilgamesh, Enkidu and the Nether World"…. Briefly sketched, this version of our story runs as follows:

After heaven and earth had been separated, An, the heaven-god, carried off the heaven, while Enlil, the air-god, carried off the earth. It was then that the foul deed was committed. The goddess Ereshkigal was carried off violently into the nether world, perhaps by Kur itself. Thereupon Enki, the water-god, whose Sumerian origin is uncertain, but who toward the end of the third millennium BCE. gradually became one of the most important deities of the Sumerian pantheon, set out in a boat, in all probability to attack Kur and avenge the abduction of the goddess Ereshkigal. Kur fought back savagely with all kinds of stones, large and small. Moreover, it attacked Enki's boat, front and rear, with the primeval waters which it no doubt controlled. Here our brief prologue passage ends, since the author of "Gilgamesh, Enkidu and the Nether World" is not interested in the dragon story primarily but is anxious to proceed with the Gilgamesh tale. And so we are left in the dark as to the outcome of the battle. There is little doubt, however, that Enki was victorious. Indeed, it is not at all unlikely that the myth was evolved in large part for the purpose of explaining why, in historical times, Enki, like the Greek Poseidon, was conceived as a sea-god; why he is described as "lord of the abyss"; and why his temple in Eridu was designated as the "sea-house".

The second version of the slaying-of-the-dragon myth is particularly significant since this is the version which must have been utilized in large part by the Semitic redactors of the Babylonian "Epic of Creation". The story is part of a large epic tale of over 600 lines, best entitled "The Feats and Exploits of Ninurta". The contents can now be reconstructed in large part from at least forty-nine tablets and fragments, thirty of which have been copied and published by various scholars in the course of the past several decades; a large part of the text has therefore been known for some time. Nevertheless, because of the numerous breaks and gaps, several of the more important pieces could not be properly arranged. This situation was eased to a considerable extent when I located in Istanbul and Philadelphia more than a score of additional pieces belonging to the poem. And so, while the text is still badly broken at numerous crucial points, the contents as a whole can now be reconstructed with a fair degree of certainty.

Hero of the tale is Ninurta, the warrior-god, who was conceived by the Sumerians as the son of Enlil, the air-god. After a hymnal introduction the story begins with an address to Ninurta by Sharur, his personified weapon. For some reason not stated in the text as yet available, Sharur has set its mind against Kur. In its speech, therefore, which is full of phrases extolling the heroic qualities and deeds of Ninurta, it urges Ninurta to attack and destroy Kur. Ninurta sets out to do as bidden. At first, however, be seems to have met more than his match and he "flees like a bird". Once again, however, Sharur addresses him with reassuring and encouraging words. Ninurta now attacks Kur fiercely with all the weapons at his command, and Kur is completely destroyed.

With the destruction of Kur, however, a serious calamity overtakes the land. The primeval waters which Kur had held in check rise to the surface and as a result of their violence no fresh water can reach the fields and gardens. The gods of the land who "carried the pickax and the basket", that is, who had charge of irrigating the land and preparing it for cultivation, are desperate. The Tigris waters do not rise, the river carries no good water.

Famine was severe, nothing was produced,
The small rivers were not cleaned, the dirt was not carried off,
On the steadfast fields no water was sprinkled, there was no digging of ditches,
In all the lands there were no crops, only weeds grew.
Thereupon the lord sets his lofty mind,
Ninurta, the son of Enlil, brings great things into being.

He sets up a heap of stones over the dead Kur and heaps it up like a great wall in front of the land. These stones hold back the "mighty waters" and as a result the waters of the lower regions rise no longer to the surface of the earth. As for the waters which had already flooded the land, Ninurta gathers them and leads them into the Tigris, which is now in a position to water the fields with its overflow. To quote the poet:

What had been scattered, he gathered,
What by Kur had been dissipated,
He guided and hurled into the Tigris,
The high waters it pours over the farmland.

Behold now everything on earth
Rejoiced afar at Ninurta, the king of the land;
The fields produced much grain,
The harvest of palm-grove and vineyard was fruitful,
It was heaped up in granaries and hills;
The lord made mourning disappear from the land,
He made good the liver of the gods.

Hearing of her son's great and heroic deeds, his mother Ninmah – also known as Ninhursag and Nintu, and more originally perhaps as Ki, the mother earth – is taken with love for him; she becomes so restless that she is unable to sleep in her bedchamber. She therefore addresses Ninurta from afar with a prayer for permission to visit him and feast her eyes upon him. Ninurta looks at her with the "eye of life", saying:

"O thou lady, because thou wouldst come to a foreign land,
O Ninmah, because for my sake thou wouldst enter an inimical land,
Because thou hast no fear of the terror of the battle surrounding me,
Therefore, of the hill which I, the hero, have heaped up,
Let its name be Hursag (mountain), and thou be its queen".

Ninurta then blesses the Hursag that it may produce all kinds of herbs, wine and honey, various kinds of trees, gold, silver and bronze, cattle, sheep and all "four-legged creatures". After this blessing of the Hursag, he turns to the stones, cursing those which have been his enemies in his battle with Kur and blessing those which have been his friends; this entire passage, in style and tone, *not in content*, is very reminiscent of the blessing and cursing of Jacob's sons in the forty-ninth chapter of Genesis. The poem closes with a long hymnal passage exalting Ninurta.

The third version of the slaying-of-the-dragon myth is a poem consisting of 190 lines of text which may be best entitled "Inanna and Ebih". Although by 1934 eight pieces belonging to the story had already been copied and published by the late Edward Chiera and Stephen Langdon, so little was understood of the myth that several of the pieces were not even recognized as belonging to it. A thorough re-examination of the material, including four hitherto unknown pieces, two from Istanbul and two from Philadelphia, enabled me to reconstruct the major part of the text in the course of the past two years.

The dragon-slayer in this version of the story is not a god but a goddess, none other than Inanna, the counterpart of the Semitic Ishtar. For curious as it may seem, Inanna, to judge from our literary material, was conceived not only as the goddess of love but also as the goddess of battle and strife. And the reason for one of the puzzling and enigmatic epithets regularly ascribed to Inanna in the hymns, namely, "destroyer of Kur", is now clear. In our myth, it must be noted, Kur is also called "mountain Ebih", a district northeast of Sumer. This Kur represents, therefore, an inimical land, and is not to be identified with the cosmic Kur of the Ninurta and Enki versions.

The poem begins with a long hymnal passage extolling the virtues of Inanna. Follows a long address by Inanna to An, the heaven-deity, nominally, at least, the leading deity of the Sumerian pantheon (actually by the third millennium BCE, Enlil, the air-god, had already usurped his place). While the meaning of her speech is at times difficult to penetrate, Inanna's demand is clear; unless Kur, which seems quite unaware of, or at least oblivious to, her might and power, becomes duly submissive and is ready to glorify her virtues, she will do violence to the monster. To quote but part of her threat:

"The long spear I shall hurl upon it,
The throw-stick, the weapon, I shall direct against it,
At its neighboring forests I shall strike up fire,
At its ... I shall set up the bronze ax,
All its waters like Gibil (the fire-god) the purifier I shall dry up,
Like the mountain Aratta, I shall remove its dread,
Like a city cursed by An, it will not be restored,
Like (a city) on which Enlil frowns, it shall not rise up".

An answers her with a detailed account of the mischief which Kur has wrought against the gods:

"Against the standing place of the gods it has directed its terror,
In the sitting place of the Anunnaki it has led forth fearfulness,
Its dreadful fear it has hurled upon the land,
The 'mountain', its dreadful rays of fire it has directed
against all the lands".

Continuing with a description of the power and wealth of Kur, An warns Inanna against attacking it. But Inanna is not taken aback by An's discouraging speech. Full of anger and wrath she opens the "house of battle" and leads out all her weapons and aids. She attacks and destroys Kur, and stationing herself upon it, she utters a paean of self-glorification.

Inanna's Descent to the Nether World

The text of this myth, ... designated as "Inanna's Descent to the Nether World", has been reconstructed and deciphered by me in the course of the past six years. Its influence on literature and mythology has been universal and profound. Moreover, the story of its decipherment furnishes a most illuminating illustration of the not uninteresting process involved in the reconstruction of the texts of the Sumerian literary compositions.

For many years, for almost three-quarters of a century, a myth usually designated as "Ishtar's Descent to the Nether World" has been known to scholar and layman. Like the Babylonian "Epic of Creation", this poem was found inscribed in the Accadian language on tablets dating from the first millennium BCE; these, therefore, postdate our Sumerian literary tablets by more than a millennium. Like the "Epic of Creation", "Ishtar's Descent to the Nether World", too, was therefore generally assumed to be of Semitic origin; it is cited and quoted in the major works concerned with mythology and religion as a remarkable example of Babylonian mythmaking. With the appearance of the publications devoted to the Nippur material, however, it became gradually obvious that this "Semitic" myth goes back to a Sumerian original in which Ishtar is replaced by Inanna, her Sumerian counterpart. Arno Poebel, now of the Oriental Institute of the University of Chicago, was the first to locate three small pieces belonging to this myth in the University Museum at Philadelphia; these were published as early as 1914. In the very same year, the late Stephen Langdon, of Oxford, published two pieces which he had uncovered in the Museum of the Ancient Orient at Istanbul. One of these was the upper half of a large four-column tablet which, as will soon become evident, proved to be of major importance for the reconstruction of the text of the myth. The late Edward Chiera uncovered three additional pieces in the University Museum. These were published in his two posthumous volumes....

By this time, therefore, we had eight pieces, all more or less fragmentary, dealing with the myth. Nevertheless the contents remained obscure, for the breaks in the tablets were so numerous and came at such crucial points in the story that an intelligent reconstruction of the extant parts of the myth remained impossible. It was a fortunate and remarkable discovery of Chiera which saved the situation. He discovered in the University Museum at Philadelphia, the *lower* half of the very same four-column tablet whose *upper* half had been found and copied by Langdon years before in the Museum of the Ancient Orient at Istanbul. The tablet had evidently been broken before or during the excavation, and the two halves had become separated; the one had been retained in Istanbul, and the other had come to Philadelphia. Unfortunately, Chiera, who fully realized the significance of his discovery, died before he was in a position to utilize it.

It was by making use of this lower half of the four-column tablet, despite the fact that it, too, is very poorly preserved, that [scholars could] reconstruct the contents of the myth. For when the two halves of the tablet were joined, the combined text furnished an excellent framework in which and about which all the other extant fragments could be properly arranged. Needless to say, there were still numerous gaps and breaks in the text which made the translation and interpretation of the text no easy matter, and the meaning of several of the more significant passages in the story remained obscure. In 1937 [it was discovered] in Istanbul three additional pieces belonging to the myth, and upon returning to the United States in 1939 [were] located another large piece in the University Museum at Philadelphia, and yet another in 1940. These three fragments helped to fill in the most serious lacunae in my first reconstruction and translation, and as a result, the myth, as far as it goes, is now almost complete; the scientific edition, including the original text, and its transliteration and translation, has just been published".

Inanna, queen of heaven, the goddess of light and love and life, has set her heart upon visiting the nether world, perhaps in order to free her lover Tammuz. She gathers together all the appropriate divine decrees, adorns herself with her queenly robes and jewels, and is ready to enter the "land of no return". Queen of the nether world is her elder sister and bitter enemy Ereshkigal, the goddess of darkness and gloom and death. Fearing lest her sister put her to death in the nether world, Inanna instructs her messenger, Ninshubur, who is always at her beck and call, that if after three days she shall have failed to return, he is to go to heaven and set up a hue and cry for her in the assembly hall of the gods. Moreover, he is to go to Nippur, the very city where our tablets have been excavated, and there weep and plead before the god Enlil to save Inanna from Ereshkigal's clutches. If Enlil should refuse, he is to go to Ur, Ur of the Chaldees, whence according to Biblical tradition Abraham migrated to Palestine, and there repeat his plea before Nanna, the great Sumerian moon-god. If Nanna, too, refuses, he is to go to Eridu, the city in which Sumerian civilization is said to have originated, and weep and plead before Enki, the "god of wisdom". And the latter, "who knows the food of life, who knows the water of life", will restore Inanna to life.

Having taken these precautions, Inanna descends to the nether world and approaches Ereshkigal's temple of lapis lazuli. At the gate she is met by the chief gatekeeper, who demands to know who she is and why she came. Inanna concocts a false excuse for her visit, and the gatekeeper, upon instructions from his mistress Ereshkigal, leads her through the seven gates of the nether world. As she passes through each of the gates part of her robes and jewels are removed in spite of her protest. Finally after entering the last gate she is brought stark naked and on bended knees before Ereshkigal and the seven Anunnaki, the dreaded judges of the nether world. These latter fasten upon Inanna their "look of death", whereupon she is turned into a corpse and hung from a stake.

So pass three days and three nights. On the fourth day, Ninshubur, seeing that his mistress has not returned, proceeds to make the rounds of the gods in accordance with his instructions. As Inanna had foreseen, both Enlil of Nippur and Nanna of Ur refuse all help. Enki, however, devises a plan to restore her to life. He fashions the *kurgarru* and *kalaturru*, two sexless creatures, and entrusts to them the "food of life" and the "water of life", with instructions to proceed to the nether world and to sprinkle this food and this water sixty times upon Inanna's suspended corpse. This they do and Inanna revives. As she leaves the nether world, however, to reascend to the earth, she is accompanied by the shades of the dead and by the bogies and harpies who have their home there. Surrounded by this ghostly, ghastly crowd, she wanders through Sumer from city to city.

Here all extant source material for "Inanna's Descent to the Nether World" unfortunately breaks off, but this is not the end of the myth. It is not too much to hope, however, that someday in the not-too-distant future the pieces on which the conclusion of the story is inscribed will be discovered and deciphered. Following is a literal translation of the composition; even in its present incomplete state it provides an excellent illustration of the mood and temper, the swing and rhythm of Sumerian poetry:

From the "great above" she set her mind toward the "great below",
The goddess, from the "great above" she set her mind toward the "great below",
Inanna, from the "great above" she set her mind toward the "great below".

My lady abandoned heaven, abandoned earth,
To the nether world she descended,
Inanna abandoned heaven, abandoned earth,
To the nether world she descended,
Abandoned lordship, abandoned ladyship,
To the nether world she descended.

In Erech she abandoned Eanna,
To the nether world she descended,
In Badtibira she abandoned Emushkalamma,
To the nether world she descended,
In Zabalam she abandoned Giguna,
To the nether world she descended,
In Adab she abandoned Esharra,
To the nether world she descended,
In Nippur she abandoned Baratushgarra,
To the nether world she descended,
In Kish she abandoned Hursagkalamma,
To the nether world she descended,
In Agade she abandoned Eulmash,
To the nether world she descended.

The seven divine decrees she fastened at the side,
She sought out the divine decrees, placed them at her hand,
All the decrees she set up at (her) waiting foot,
The shugurra, the crown of the plain, she put upon her head,
Radiance she placed upon her countenance,
The … rod of lapis lazuli she gripped in (her) hand,
Small lapis lazuli stones she tied about her neck,
Sparkling … stones she fastened to her breast,
A gold ring she gripped in her hand,
A … breastplate she bound about her breast,
All the garments of ladyship she arranged about her body,
… ointment she put on her face.

Inanna walked toward the nether world,
Her messenger Ninshubur walked at her side,
The pare Inanna says to Ninshubur:
"O (thou who art) my constant support,
My messenger of favorable words,
My carrier of supporting words,
I am now descending to the nether world.

"When I shall have come to the nether world,
Fill heaven with complaints for me,
In the assembly shrine cry out for me,
In the house of the gods rush about for me,
Lower thy eye for me,, lower thy mouth for me,
With … lower thy great … for me,
Like a pauper in a single garment dress for me,
To the Ekur, the house of Enlil, all alone direct thy step.

"Upon thy entering the Ekur, the house of Enlil,
Weep before Enlil:
'O father Enlil, let not thy daughter be put to death in the nether world,
Let not thy good metal be ground up into the dust of the nether world,
Let not thy good lapis lazuli be broken up into the stone of the stone-worker,
Let not thy boxwood be cut up into the wood of the wood-worker,
Let not the maid Inanna be put to death in the nether world'.

"If Enlil stands not by thee in this matter, go to Ur.

"In Ur upon thy entering the house of the … of the land,
The Ekishshirgal, the house of Nanna,
Weep before Nanna:
'O Father Nanna, let not thy daughter be put to death in the nether world,
Let not thy good metal be ground up into the dust of the nether world,
Let not thy good lapis lazuli be broken up into the stone of the stone-worker,
Let not thy boxwood be cut up into the wood of the wood-worker,
Let not the maid Inanna be put to death in the nether world'.

"If Nanna stands not by thee in this matter, go to Eridu.

"In Eridu upon thy entering the house of Enki,
Weep before Enki:
'O father Enki, let not thy daughter be put to death in the nether world,
Let not thy good metal be ground up into the dust of the nether world,
Let not thy good lapis lazuli be broken up into the stone of the stone-worker,
Let not thy boxwood be cut up into the wood of the wood-worker,
Let not the maid Inanna be put to death in the nether world'.

"Father Enki, the lord of wisdom,
Who knows the food of life, who knows the water of life,
He will surely bring me to life".

Inanna walked toward the nether world,
To her messenger Ninshubur she says:
"Go, Ninshubur,
The word which I have commanded thee …"

When Inanna had arrived at the lapis lazuli palace of the nether world,
At the door of the nether world she acted evilly,
In the palace of the nether world she spoke evilly:
"Open the house, gatekeeper, open the house,
Open the house, Neti, open the house, all alone I would enter".

Neti, the chief gatekeeper of the nether world,
Answers the pure Inanna:
"Who pray art thou?"

"I am the queen of heaven, the place where the sun rises".

"If thou art the queen of heaven, the place where the sun rises,
Why pray hast thou come to the land of no return?
On the road whose traveller returns not how has thy heart led thee?"

The pure Inanna answers him:
"My elder sister Ereshkigal,
Because her husband, the lord Gugalanna, had been killed,
To witness the funeral rites,
...; so be it".

Neti, the chief gatekeeper of the nether world,
Answers the pure Inanna:
"Stay, Inanna, to my queen let me speak,
To my queen Ereshkigal let me speak ... let me speak".

Neti, the chief gatekeeper of the nether world,
Enters the house of his queen Ereshkigal and says to her:
"O my queen, a maid,
Like a god ...,
The door ...,
...,
In Eanna ...,
The seven divine decrees she has fastened at the side,
She has sought out the divine decrees, has placed them at her hand,
All the decrees she has set up at (her) waiting foot,
The shugurra, the crown of the plain, she has put upon her head,
Radiance she has placed upon her countenance,
The ... rod of lapis lazuli she has gripped in (her) hand,
Small lapis lazuli stones she has tied about her neck,
Sparkling ... stones she has fastened to her breast,
A gold ring she has gripped in her hand,
A ... breastplate she has bound about her breast,
All her garments of ladyship she has arranged about her body,
... ointment she has put on her face".

Then Ereshkigal . . .,
Answers Neti, her chief gatekeeper:
"Come, Neti, chief gatekeeper of the nether world,
Unto the word which I command thee, give ear.
Of the seven gates of the nether world, open their locks,
Of the gate Ganzir, the 'face' of the nether world, define its rules;
Upon her (Inanna's) entering,
Bowed low … let her …"

Neti, the chief gatekeeper of the nether world,
Honored the word of his queen.
Of the seven gates of the nether world, he opened their locks,
Of the gate Ganzir, the 'face' of the nether world, he defined its rules.
To the pure Inanna he says:
"Come, Inanna, enter".

Upon her entering the first gate,
The shugurra, the "crown of the plain" of her head, was removed.
"What, pray, is this?"
"Extraordinarily, O Inanna, have the decrees of the nether world been perfected,
O Inanna, do not question the rites of the nether world".

Upon her entering the second gate,
The … rod of lapis lazuli was removed.
"What, pray, is this?"
"Extraordinarily, O Inanna, have the decrees of the nether world been perfected,
O Inanna, do not question the rites of the nether world".

Upon her entering the third gate,
The small lapis lazuli stones of her neck were removed.
"What, pray, is this?"
"Extraordinarily, O Inanna, have the decrees of the nether world been perfected,
O Inanna, do not question the rites of the nether world".

Upon her entering the fourth gate,
The sparkling … stones of her breast were removed.
"What, pray, is this?"
"Extraordinarily, O Inanna, have the decrees of the nether world been perfected,
O Inanna, do not question the rites of the nether world".

Upon her entering the fifth gate,
The gold ring of her hand was removed.
"What, pray, is this?"
"Extraordinarily, O Inanna, have the decrees of the nether world been perfected,
O Inanna, do not question the rites of the nether world".

Upon her entering the sixth gate,
The … breastplate of her breast was removed.
"What, pray, is this?"
"Extraordinarily, O Inanna, have the decrees of the nether world been perfected,
O Inanna, do not question the rites of the nether world".

Upon her entering the seventh gate,
All the garments of ladyship of her body were removed.
"What, pray, is this?"
"Extraordinarily, O Inanna, have the decrees of the nether world been perfected,
O Inanna, do not question the rites of the nether world".

Bowed low …

The pure Ereshkigal seated herself upon her throne,
The Anunnaki, the seven judges, pronounced judgment before her,
They fastened (their) eyes upon her, the eyes of death,
At their word, the word which tortures the spirit,
…,
The sick woman was turned into a corpse,
The corpse was hung from a stake.

After three days and three nights had passed,
Her messenger Ninshubur,
Her messenger of favorable words,
Her carrier of supporting words,
Fills the heaven with complaints for her,
Cried for her in the assembly shrine,
Rushed about for her in the house of the gods,
Lowered his eye for her, lowered his mouth for her,
With … he lowered his great … for her,
Like a pauper in a single garment he dressed for her,
To the Ekur, the house of Enlil, all alone he directed his step.

Upon his entering the Ekur, the house of Enlil,
Before Enlil he weeps:
"O father Enlil, let not thy daughter be put to death in the nether world,
Let not thy good metal be ground up into the dust of the nether world,
Let not thy good lapis lazuli be broken up into the stone of the stone-worker,
Let not thy boxwood be cut up into the wood of the wood-worker,
Let not the maid Inanna be put to death in the nether world".

Father Enlil answers Ninshubur:
"My daughter, in the 'great above' …, in the 'great below' …,
Inanna, in the 'great above' …, in the 'great below'. . .,
The decrees of the nether world, the … decrees, to their place …,
Who, pray, to their place …?"

Father Enlil stood not by him in this matter, he went to Ur.

In Ur upon his entering the house of the … of the land,
The Ekishshirgal, the house of Nanna,
Before Nanna he weeps:
"O father Nanna, let not thy daughter be put to death in the nether world,
Let not thy good metal be ground up into the dust of the nether world,
Let not thy good lapis lazuli be broken up into the stone of the stone-worker,
Let not thy boxwood be cut up into the wood of the wood-worker,
Let not the maid Inanna be put to death in the nether world".

Father Nanna answers Ninshubur:
"My daughter in the 'great above' …, in the 'great below' …,
Inanna, in the 'great above' …, in the 'great below' . . .,
The decrees of the nether world, the … decrees, to their place …,
Who, pray, to their place …?"

Father Nanna stood not by him in this matter, he went to Eridu.
In Eridu upon his entering the house of Enki,
Before Enki he weeps:
"O father Enki, let not thy daughter be put to death in the nether world,
Let not thy good metal be ground up into the dust of the nether world,
Let not thy good lapis lazuli be broken up into the stone of the stone-worker,
Let not thy boxwood be cut up into the wood of the wood-worker,
Let not the maid Inanna be put to death in the nether world".

Father Enki answers Ninshubur:
"What now has my daughter done! I am troubled,
What now has Inanna done! I am troubled,
What now has the queen of all the lands done! I am troubled,
What now has the hierodule of heaven done! I am troubled".

… he brought forth dirt (and) fashioned the kurgarru,
… he brought forth dirt (and) fashioned the kalaturru,
To the kurgarru he gave the food of life,
To the kalaturru he gave the water of life,
Father Enki says to the kalaturru and kurgarru:
… (nineteen lines destroyed)
"Upon the corpse hung from a stake direct the fear of the rays of fire,
Sixty times the food of life, sixty times the water of life, sprinkle upon it,
Verily Inanna will arise".

… (twenty-four(?) lines destroyed)
Upon the corpse hung from a stake they directed the fear of the rays of fire,
Sixty times the food of life, sixty times the water of life, they sprinkled upon it,
Inanna arose.

Inanna ascends from the nether world,
The Anunnaki fled,
(And) whoever of the nether world that had descended peacefully to the nether world;
When Inanna ascends from the nether world,
Verily the dead hasten ahead of her.

Inanna ascends from the nether world,
The small demons like … reeds,
The large demons like tablet styluses,
Walked at her side.
Who walked in front of her, being without …, held a staff in the hand,
Who walked at her side, being without …, carried a weapon on the loin.
They who preceded her,
They who preceded Inanna,
(Were beings who) know not food, who know not water,
Who eat not sprinkled flour,
Who drink not libated wine,
Who take away the wife from the loins of man,
Who take away the child from the breast of the nursing mother.

Inanna ascends from the nether world;
Upon Inanna's ascending from the nether world,
Her messenger Ninshubur threw himself at her feet,
Sat in the dust, dressed in dirt.
The demons say to the pure Inanna:
"O Inanna, wait before thy city, we would bring him to thee".

The pure Inanna answers the demons:
"(He is) my messenger of favorable words,
My carrier of supporting words,
He fails not my directions,
He delays not my commanded word,
He fills heaven with complaints for me,
In the assembly shrine he cried out for me,
In the house of the gods he rushed about for me,
He lowered his eye for me, he lowered his mouth for me,
With … he lowered his great … for me,
Like a pauper in a single garment he dressed for me,
To the Ekur, the house of Enlil,
In Ur, to the house of Nanna,
In Eridu, to the house of Enki (he directed his step),
He brought me to life".
"Let us precede her, in Umma to the Sigkurshagga let us precede her".

In Umma, from the Sigkurshagga,
Shara threw himself at her feet,
Sat in the dust, dressed in dirt.

The demons say to the pure Inanna:
"O Inanna, wait before thy city, we would bring him to thee".

The pure Inanna answers the demons:
(Inanna's answer is destroyed)

"Let us precede her, in Badtibira to the Emushkalamma let us precede her".

In Badtibira from the Emushkalamma,
… threw themselves at her feet,
Sat in the dust, dressed in dirt.
The demons say to the pure Inanna:
"O Inanna, wait before thy city, we would bring them to thee".

The pure Inanna answers the demons:
(Inanna's answer destroyed; the end of the poem is wanting)

Miscellaneous Myths

The Deluge

THAT THE BIBLICAL DELUGE STORY is not original with the Hebrew redactors of the Bible has been known now for more than half a century – from the time of the discovery and decipherment of the eleventh tablet of the Semitic Babylonian "Epic of Gilgamesh". The Babylonian deluge myth itself, however, is of Sumerian origin. For in 1914 Arno Poebel published and carefully translated a fragment consisting of the lower third of a six-column Sumerian tablet in the Nippur collection of the University Museum, the larger part of whose contents is devoted to the deluge myth. Unfortunately, this fragment still remains unique and unduplicated….

The first part of the poem deals with the creation of man and animals and with the founding of the five antediluvian cities: Eridu, Badtibira, Larak, Sippar and Shuruppak. For some reason – the passage involved is completely destroyed – the flood was decreed to wipe out man. But at least some of the gods seemed to regret this decision. It was probably the water-god Enki, however, who contrived to save mankind. He informed Ziusudra, the Sumerian counterpart of the Biblical Noah, a pious, god-fearing and humble king, of the dreadful decision of the gods and advised him to save himself by building a very large boat. The long passage giving the details of the construction of the boat is destroyed; when our text begins again it is in the midst of describing the flood:

All the windstorms, exceedingly powerful, attacked as one,
The deluge raged over the surface of the earth.
After, for seven days and seven nights,

The deluge had raged in the land,
And the huge boat had been tossed about on the great waters,
Utu came forth, who sheds light on heaven and earth.
Ziusudra opened a window of the huge boat,
Ziusudra, the king,
Before Utu prostrated himself,
The king kills an ox, slaughters a sheep.

Again a long break follows; when our text becomes Intelligible once more, it is describing the immortalizing of Ziusudra:

Ziusudra, the king,
Before An and Enlil prostrated himself;
Life like a god they give him,
Breath eternal like a god they bring down for him.

In those days, Ziusudra, the king,
The preserver of the name of … and man,
In the mountain of crossing, the mountain of Dilmun, the place where the sun rises,
They (An and Enlil) caused to dwell.

The remainder of the poem is destroyed.

The Marriage of Martu

As yet we have but one tablet inscribed with the text of this poem; it is in the Nippur collection of the University Museum and has been copied and translated in part by Edward Chiera some twenty years ago. The action of the story takes place in the city of Ninab, "the city of cities, the land of princeship", a still unidentified locality in Mesopotamia. Its tutelary deity seems to have been Martu, a west-Semitic god adopted by the Sumerians into their pantheon. The relative time when the events took place is described in laconic, antithetical phrases at the beginning of the poem, phrases whose exact meaning is as yet obscure:

Ninab existed, Shittab did not exist,
The pure crown existed, the pure tiara did not exist,
The pure herbs existed, the pure cedar trees did not exist,
Pure salt existed, pure nitrum did not exist,
Cohabitation … existed,
In the meadows there was birth-giving.

For some reason not altogether clear in the text, the god Martu decides to get married. He therefore goes to his mother and asks her to take him a wife:

Martu to his mother,
Into the house enters, says:
"In my city my friends have taken wives unto themselves,
My neighbors have taken wives unto themselves,

In my city I (alone) of my friends have no wife,
Have no wife, have no child".

The remainder of the speech is obscure; it ends with:

"O my mother, take for me a wife,
My gifts I shall bring to thee".

His mother advises him accordingly. A great feast is then prepared in Ninab, and to it comes Numushda, the tutelary deity of Kazallu, with his wife and daughter. During this feast Martu performs some heroic deed – the passage involved is partly broken and largely unintelligible – which brings joy to Numushda of Kazallu. As a reward the latter offers Martu silver and lapis lazuli. But Martu refuses; it is the hand of Numushda's daughter which he claims as his reward. Numushda gladly consents; so, too, does his daughter, although an effort is made by one of her close relatives to disparage Martu in her eyes as a crude barbarian:

"Uncooked meat he eats,
During his life he has no house,
When he dies he lies unburied,
O my .... why wouldst thou marry Martu?"

To this argument Numushda's daughter answers simply: "Martu I shall marry", and our poem ends.

Inanna Prefers the Farmer

This charming agricultural myth, which I have entitled "Inanna Prefers the Farmer", is another example of the Cain-Abel motif. The characters of our poem are four in number: the seemingly ubiquitous Inanna; her brother, the sun-god Utu; the shepherd-god Dumuzi; the farmer-god Enkimdu. The plot is as follows. Inanna is about to choose a spouse. Her brother Utu urges her to marry the shepherd-god Dumuzi, but she prefers the farmer-god Enkimdu. Thereupon Dumuzi steps up and demands to know why she prefers the farmer; he, Dumuzi, the shepherd, has everything that the farmer has and more. Inanna does not answer, but Enkimdu, the farmer, who seems to be a peaceful, cautious type, tries to appease the belligerent Dumuzi. The latter refuses to be appeased, however, until the farmer promises to bring him all kinds of gifts and – here it must be stressed the meaning of the text is not quite certain – even Inanna herself.

The intelligible part of the poem begins with an address by the sun-god Utu to his sister Inanna:

"O my sister, the much possessing shepherd,
O maid Inanna, why dost thou not favor?
His oil is good, his date-wine is good,
The shepherd, everything his hand touches is bright,
O Inanna, the much-possessing Dumuzi ...,
Full of jewels and precious stones, why dost thou not favor?
His good oil he will eat with thee,
The protector of the king, why dost thou not favor?"

But Inanna refuses:

"The much-possessing shepherd I shall not marry,
In his new ... I shall not walk,
In his new ... I shall utter no praise,
I, the maid, the farmer I shall marry,
The farmer who makes plants grow abundantly,
The farmer who makes the grain grow abundantly".

A break of about twelve lines follows, in which Inanna continues to give the reasons for her preference. Then the shepherd-god Dumuzi steps up to Inanna, protesting her choice – a passage that is particularly remarkable for its intricately effective phrase-pattern:

"The farmer more than I, the farmer more than I,
The farmer what has he more than I?
If he gives me his black garment, I give him, the farmer, my black ewe,
If he gives me his white garment, I give him, the farmer, my white ewe,
If he pours me his first date-wine, I pour him, the farmer, my yellow milk,
If he pours me his good date-wine, I pour him, the farmer, my kisim-milk
If he pours me his 'heart-turning' date-wine, I pour him, the farmer, my bubbling milk,
If he pours me his water-mixed date-wine, I pour him, the farmer, my plant-milk,
If he gives me his good portions, I give him, the farmer, my nitirda-milk,
If he gives me his good bread, I give him, the farmer, my honey-cheese,
If he gives me his small beans, I give him my small cheeses;
More than he can eat, more than he can drink,
I pour out for him much oil, I pour out for him much milk;
More than I, the farmer, what has he more than I?"

Follow four lines whose meaning is not clear; then begins Enkimdu's effort at appeasement:

"Thou, O shepherd, why dost thou start a quarrel?
O shepherd, Dumuzi, why dost thou start a quarrel?
Me with thee, O shepherd, me with thee why dost thou compare?
Let thy sheep eat the grass of the earth,
In my meadowland let thy sheep pasture,
In the fields of Zabalam let them eat grain,
Let all thy folds drink the water of my river Unun".

But the shepherd remains adamant:

"I, the shepherd, at my marriage do not enter, O farmer, as my friend,
O farmer, Enkimdu, as my friend, O farmer, as my friend, do not enter".

Thereupon the farmer offers to bring him all kinds of gifts:

"Wheat I shall bring thee, beans I shall bring thee,
Beans of ... I shall bring thee,

The maid Inanna (and) whatever is pleasing to thee,
The maid Inanna ... I shall bring thee".

And so the poem ends, with the seeming victory of the shepherd-god Dumuzi over the farmer-god Enkimdu.

Adapa and the Food of Life

[SUMMARY: ADAPA, OR PERHAPS ADAMU, son of Ea, had recieved from his father, the god Ea, wisdom, but not eternal life. He was a semi-divine being and was the wise man and priest of the temple of Ea at Eridu, which he provided with the ritual bread and water. In the exercise of this duty he carried on fishing upon the Persian Gulf. When Adapa was fishing one day on a smooth sea, the south wind rose suddenly and overturned his boat, so that the was thrown into the sea. Angered by the mishap, he broke the wings of the south wind so that for seven days it could not blow the sea's coolness over the hot land. Anu calls Adapa to account for this misdeed, and his father Ea warns him as to what should befall him. He tells him how to fool Tammuz and Gishzida, who will meet him at the gate of heaven. Ea cautions him not to eat or drink anything in heaven, as Ea fears that the food and drink of death will be set before Adapa. However, the food and drink of eternal life are set before him instead, and Adapa's over-caution deprives him of immortality. He has to return to Earth instead.]

Tablet No. 1

He possessed intelligence ...,
His command like the command of Anu ...
He (Ea) granted him a wide ear to reveal the destiny of the land,
He granted him wisdom, but he did not grant him eternal life.
In those davs, in those years the wise man of Eridu,
Ea had created him as chief among men,
A wise man whose command none should oppose,
The prudent, the most wise among the Anunnaki was he,
Blameless, of clean hands, anointed, observer of the divine statutes,
With the bakers he made bread
With the bakers of Eridu, he made bread,
The food and the water for Eridu he made daily,
With his clean hands he prepared the table,
And without him the table was not cleared.
The ship he steered, fishing and hunting for Eridu he did.
Then Adapa of Eridu
While Ea, ... in the chamber, upon the bed.

Daily the closing of Eridu he attended to.
Upon the pure dam, the new moon dam) he embarked upon the ship,
The wind blew and his ship departed, With the oar, be
steered his ship Upon the broad sea ...

Tablet No. 2

The south wind .... when
He had driven me to the house of my lord, I said,
O South wind, on the way I shall to thee ... everything that,
Thy wing, will I break". As he spoke with his mouth,
The wing of the South wind was broken, seven days
The South wind blew not upon the land. Anu
Called to his messenger Ilabrat:
Why has the South wind not blown upon the land for seven days?
His messenger Ilabrat answered him: "My lord,
Adapa, the son of Ea, the wing of the South wind
Has broken".
When Anu heard these words
He cried, Help!" He ascended his throne,
"Let someone bring him",
Likewise Ea, who knows the heaven. He roused him
... he caused him to wear. With a mourning garment
He garbed him, and gave him counsel
Saying: " Adapa, before the face of Anu the King thou art to go ... to heaven
When thou comest up, and when thou approachest the door of Anu,
At the door of Anu, Tammuz and Gishzida are standing,
"they will see thee, they will ask thee; 'Sir',
For whose sake dost thou so appear, Adapa? For whom
Art thou clad in a mourning garment?' 'In our country
two gods have vanished, therefore
Am I so'. 'Who are the two gods, who in the land
Have vanished?' 'Tammuz and Gishzida'. They will look at one another and
Be astonished. Good words
They will speak to Anu. A good countenance of Anu
They will show thee. When thou standest before Anu
Food of death they will set before thee,
Eat not. Water of death they will set before thee,
Drink not. Garments they will set before thee,
Put them on. Oil they will set before thee, anoint thyself.
The counsel that I have given thee, forget not. The words
Which I have spoken, hold fast". The messenger
Of Anu came: "Adapa has broken
The wing of the South wind. Bring him before me".
The road to Heaven he made him take, and to Heaven he ascended.
When he came to Heaven, when he approached the door of Anu,
At the door of Ann, Tammuz and Gisbzida are standing.

When they saw him, Adapa, they cried: "Help,
Sir, for whom dost thou so appear? Adapa,
For whom art thou clad in a mourning garment?"
In the country two gods have vanished; therefore am I clad
In mourning garments". "Who are the two gods, who
have vanished from the land?"
"Tammuz and Gishzida". They looked at one another and
Were astonished. When Adapa before Anu, the King,
Drew near, and Anu saw him, he cried:
"Come hither, Adapa. Why hast thou broken the wings
Of the South wind? "Adapa answered Ann: "My lord,
For the house of my lord in the midst of the sea,
I was catching fish. The sea was like a mirror,
The South wind blew, and capsized me.
To the house of my lord was I driven. In the anger
of my heart,
I took heed". Tammuz and Gishzida
Answered ... "art thou". To Anu
They speak. He calmed himself, his heart was ...
"Why has Ea revealed to impure mankind
The heart of heaven and earth? A heart
... has created within him, has made him a name?
What can we do with him? Food of life
Bring him, that be man, eat". Food of life
They brought him, but he ate not. Water of life
They brought him, but he drank not. Garments
They brought him. He clothed himself. Oil
They brought him. He anointed himself.
Anu looked at him; he wondered at him.
"Come, Adapa, why hast thou not eaten, not drunken?
Now thou shalt not live". ... men ...Ea, my lord
Said: "Eat not, drink not".
Take him and bring him back to his earth.
... looked upon him.

Tablet No. 3

"When heard that
In the anger of his heart
His messenger he sent.
He who knows the heart of the great gods ...
To King Ea to come,
To him, he caused words to be borne.
... to him, to King Ea.
He sent a messenger
With a wide ear, knowing the heart of the great gods,
... of the heavens be fixed.

A soiled garment he made him wear,
With a mourning garment he clad him,
A word he spoke to him.
"Adapa, before the King Anu thou shalt go
Fail not the order, keep my word
When thou comest up to heaven, and approachest the door of Anu,
Tammuz and Gishzida at the door of Anu are standing.

Ninĝišzida's Journey to the Netherworld

"**ARISE AND GET** on board, arise, we are about to sail, arise and get on board!" – Woe, weep for the bright daylight, as the barge is steered away! – "I am a young man! Let me not be covered against my wishes by a cabin, as if with a blanket, as if with a blanket!"

Stretching out a hand to the barge, to the young man being steered away on the barge, stretching out a hand to {my young man Damu} being taken away on the barge, stretching out a hand to Ištaran of the bright visage being taken away on the barge, stretching out a hand to Alla, master of the battle-net, being taken away on the barge, stretching out a hand to Lugal-šud-e being taken away on the barge, stretching out a hand to Ninĝišzida being taken away on the barge – his younger sister was crying in lament to him in {the boat's cabin}.

His older sister removed the cover (?) from {the boat's cabin}: "Let me sail away with you, let me sail away with you, {brother}, let me sail away with you.

She was crying a lament to him at the boat's bow: "{Brother}, let me sail away with you".

"My young man Damu, let me sail away with you, {brother}, let me sail away with you. Ištaran of the bright visage, let me sail away with you, {brother}, let me sail away with you. Alla, master of the battle-net, let me sail away with you, {brother}, let me sail away with you. Lugal-šud-e, let me sail away with you, {brother}, let me sail away with you. Ninĝišzida, let me sail away with you, {brother}, let me sail away with you".

The evil demon who was in their midst called out to {Lugal-ki-suna}: " {Lugal-ki-suna}, look at your sister!" Having looked at his sister, {Lugal-ki-suna} said to her: "He sails with me, he sails with me. Why should you sail? Lady, the demon sails with me. Why should you sail? The thresher sails with me. Why should you sail? The man who has bound my hands sails with me. Why should you sail? The man who has tied my arms sails with me. Why should you sail?"

"The river of the nether world produces no water, no water is drunk from it. The fields of the Nether World produce no grain, no flour is eaten from it. The sheep of the nether world produce no wool, no cloth is woven from it. As for me, even if my mother digs as if for a canal, I shall not be able to drink the water meant for me. The waters of springtime will not be poured for me as they are for the tamarisks; I shall not sit in the shade intended for me. The dates I should bear like a date palm will not reveal (?) their beauty for me. I am a field threshed by my demon – you would scream at it. He has put manacles on my hands – you would scream at it. He has put a neck-stock on my neck – you would scream at it".

Ama-šilama (Ninĝišzida's sister) said to Ninĝišzida: "The ill-intentioned demon may accept something – there should be a limit to it for you. My brother, your demon may accept something, there should be a limit to it for you. For him let me ...... from my hand the ......, there should be a limit to it for you. For him let me ...... from my hand the ......, there should be a limit to it for you. For him let me ...... from my hips the dainty lapis lazuli beads, there should be a limit to it for you. For him let me ...... from my hips the ...... my lapis lazuli beads, there should be a limit to it for you".

"You are a beloved ..., there should be a limit to it for you. How they treat you, how they treat you! – there should be a limit to it for you. My brother, how they treat you, how haughtily they treat you! – there should be a limit to it for you. "I am hungry, but the bread has slipped away from me!" – there should be a limit to it for you. "I am thirsty, but the water has slipped away from me!" – there should be a limit to it for you".

The evil demon who was in their midst, the clever demon, that great demon who was in their midst, called out to the man at the boat's bow and to the man at the boat's stern: "Don't let the mooring stake be pulled out, don't let the mooring stake be pulled out, so that she may come on board to her brother, that this lady may come on board the barge".

When Ama-šilama had gone on board the barge, a cry approached the heavens, a cry approached the earth, that great demon set up an enveloping cry before him on the river: "Urim, at my cry to the heavens lock your houses, lock your houses, city, lock your houses! Shrine Urim, lock your houses, city, lock your houses! Against your lord who has left the *ĝipar*, city, lock your houses!"

1 line fragmentary

approx. 1 line missing

2 lines fragmentary ...... a holy sceptre. ...... a holy robe of office. ...... a holy crown. ...... a lapis-lazuli sceptre.

He ...... to the empty river, the rejoicing (?) river: "You (addressing Ama-šilima) shall not draw near to this house, ... to the place of Ereškigala. My mother ...... out of her love. As for you (addressing the demon), you may be a great demon ......, ... your hand against the nether world's office of throne-bearer".

"My king will no longer shed tears in his eyes. The drum will ...... his joy in tears. Come! May the fowler utter a lament for you in his well-stocked house, lord, may he utter a lament for you. How he has been humiliated! May the young fisherman utter a lament for you in his well-stocked house, lord, may he utter a lament for you. How he has been humiliated! May the mother of the dead *gudug* priest {utter a lament for you in her empty *ĝipar*}, utter a lament for you, lord, may she utter a lament for you. How he has been humiliated! May the mother high priestess utter a lament {for you who have left the *ĝipar*}, lord, may she utter a lament for you. How he has been humiliated!"

"My king, bathe with water your head that has rolled in the dust. ...... in sandals your feet defiled from the defiled place". The king bathed with water his head that had rolled in the dust. ...... in sandals his feet defiled from the defiled place. "Not drawing near to this house, ... your throne ...... to you "Sit down". May your bed ...... to you "Lie down"". He ate food in his mouth, he drank choice wine.

Great holy one, Ereškigala, praising you is sweet.

How Grain Came to Sumer

MEN USED TO EAT GRASS with their mouths like sheep. In those times, they did not know grain, barley or flax. An brought these down from the interior of heaven. Enlil lifted his gaze around as a stag lifts its horns when climbing the terraced ... hills. He looked southwards and saw the wide sea; he looked northwards and saw the mountain of aromatic cedars. Enlil piled up the barley, gave it to the mountain. He piled up the bounty of the Land, gave the *innuḫa* barley to the mountain. He closed off access to the wide-open hill. He ... its lock, which heaven and earth shut fast (?), its bolt, which ...

Then Ninazu ......, and said to his brother Ninmada: "Let us go to the mountain, to the mountain where barley and flax grow; ...... the rolling river, where the water wells up from the earth. Let us fetch the barley down from its mountain, let us introduce the innuḫa barley into Sumer. Let us make barley known in Sumer, which knows no barley".

Ninmada, the worshipper of An, replied to him: "Since our father has not given the command, since Enlil has not given the command, how can we go there to the mountain? How can we bring down the barley from its mountain? How can we introduce the innuḫa grain into Sumer? How can we make barley known in Sumer, which knows no barley?"

"Come, let us go to Utu of heaven, who as he lies there, as he lies there, sleeps a sound sleep, to the hero, the son of Ningal, who as he lies there sleeps a sound sleep". He raised his hands towards Utu of the seventy doors (?).

Utu ...... table (?) ....

The Šumunda Grass

THE ABBA instructed, the abba instructed:

When the rain rained, when walls were demolished, when it rained potsherds and fireballs, when one person confronted another defiantly, when there was copulation – he also copulated, when there was kissing – he also kissed. When the rain said: "I will rain", when the wall said: "I will rain (scribal error for 'demolish'?)", when the flood said: "I will sweep everything away" – Heaven impregnated (?), Earth gave birth, she gave birth also to the šumunda grass. Earth gave birth, Heaven impregnated (?), she gave birth also to the šumunda grass.

His luxuriant reeds carry fire. They who defied it, who defied it, the umma who had survived that day, the abba who had survived that day, the chief gala priest who had survived that year, whoever had survived the Flood – the šumunda grass crushed them with labour, crushed them with labour, made them crouch in the dust.

The šumunda grass is a fire carrier, he cannot be tied into bundles, the grass cannot be shifted, the grass cannot be loosened, the grass cannot be loosened. When built into a booth, one moment he stands up, one moment he lies down. Having kindled a fire, he spreads it wide. The šumunda grass's habitat is among his bitter waters. He butts about (saying): "I will start, I will start a fire".

He set fire to the base of the E-ana; there he was bound, there he was fettered. When he protested, Inana seized a raven there and set it on top of him. The shepherd abandoned his sheep in their enclosure. Inana seized the raven there.

When the rain had rained, when walls had been demolished, when it rained potsherds and fireballs, when Dumuzid was defied – the rain rained, walls were demolished, the cowpen was demolished, the sheepfold was ripped out, wild floodwaters were hurled against the rivers, wild rains were hurled against the marshes. By (?) the … of the Tigris and the Euphrates, of the Tigris and the Euphrates, long grass grew, long grass …

5 lines missing

He tied him into bundles, he shifted him, he … šumunda grass, the fire-carrier. He bundled up the šumunda grass, the fire carrier, bundled up the fire carrier. The launderer who made her garments clean asks her, Inana – the carpenter who gave her the spindle to hold in her hand (asks her), Inana – the potter who fashioned pots and jugs (asks her), Inana. The potter gave her holy drinking vessels, the shepherd brought her his sheep, the shepherd brought her his sheep – he asks her. He brought her all kinds of luxuriant plants, as if it were the harvest.

Her voice reached Heaven, her voice reached Earth, her resounding cry covered the horizon like a garment, was spread over it like a cloth, she hurled fierce winds at the head of the šumunda grass (saying): "Šumunda grass, your name … You shall be a plant … You shall be a hateful plant … Your name …".

approx. 23 lines missing

Tales of Heroes

Introduction

IN BABYLONIAN MYTH and literature, the three greatest heroes are Gilgamesh, Lugalbanda and Enmerkar, and their stories are included in this chapter.

The story of Gilgamesh, king of Uru who reigned around 2700 BCE, is the oldest epic in literature. The tale, retold and rewritten by Babylonian, Assyrian and Hittite scribes, survives on twelve incomplete tablets, each containing about three hundred lines. In the story, Gilgamesh, who is part divine and part human, goes on a quest for immortality when he realizes that even semi-divine beings must die. The text presented here, translated and published in 1928 by R. Campbell Thompson, is one of the first essentially complete academic translations of the epic of Gilgamesh. It includes all of the principal episodes of the epic: the wild man Enkidu; the battle with Humbaba, the cedar forest demon; the death of Enkidu, the journey of Gilgamesh to find the secret of eternal life, in the course of which he encounters the Babylonian Noah, Uta-Napishtim, and hears the story of the great flood.

Next we have the story of "Lugalbanda and Enmerkar", courtesy of the Electronic Text Corpus of Sumerian Literature. The story tells of the heroic journey to Aratta made by Lugalbanda in the service of Enmerkar, king of Uruk, a city-state in southern Mesopotamia, who is thought to have lived at the end of the fourth or beginning of the third millennium BCE. According to the epic, Uruk was under attack by Semitic nomads. In order to save his domain, Enmerkar required the aid of Inanna, who was in Aratta. The epic concerns the events of Lugalbanda's journey and the message given him from Inanna for Enmerkar. Although obscure, Inanna's reply seems to indicate that Enmerkar was to make special water vessels and was also to catch strange fish from a certain river.

The Epic of Gilgamesh

The First Tablet
Of The Tyranny of Gilgamesh, and the Creation of Enkidu

Column I
The Argument

HE WHO (the heart of) all matters hath proven let him [teach] the nation,
[He who all] knowledge possesseth, therein shall he [school] all the people,
[He shall his wisdom impart (?)] and (so) shall they] share it] together.
[Gilgamesh(?)] – he was the [Master] of wisdom, with [knowledge of all things,
He 'twas discovered the secret concealed …
(Aye), handed down the tradition relating to (things) prediluvian,
Went on a journey afar, (all) aweary and [worn with his toiling(?)],
[Graved] on a table of stone all the travail.
Of Erech, the high-wall'd,
He (it was) built up the ramparts; (and) he (it was) clamp'd the foundation,
Like unto brass, of [E]-Anna, the sacred, the treasury hallow'd,
[Strengthen'd] its base to grant wayleave to no [one] …
… the threshold which from [of old (?)] …
… [E]-Anna …
… to grant wayleave [to no one (?)] …

(About thirty lines wanting. The description of Gilgamesh runs on to the beginning of the next Column)

Column II

Two-thirds of him are divine, and [one-third of him human,] …
The form of his body …
He hath forced to take …
(Gap of about three lines)
(The Plaint of Erech(?) to the gods against the tyrant Gilgamesh)
… of Erech 'tis he who hath [taken],
… (while) tow'reth [his] crest like an aurochs,
Ne'er hath the shock of [his] weapons (its) [peer]; are driven [his] fellows
Into the toils, while cow'd are the heroes of Erech un- …
Gilgamesh leaveth no son to [his] father, [his] arrogance swelling
(Each) day and [night]; [aye, he] is the shepherd of Erech, the high-[wall'd],
He is [our(?)] shepherd … [masterful, dominant, subtle] …

[Gilgamesh] leaveth no [maid to her mother, nor] daughter to [hero],
[(Nay), nor a spouse to a husband]"
(And so), to (th' appeal of) their wailing
[Gave ear th' Immortals]: the gods of high heaven address'd the god Anu],
(Him who was) Seigneur of Erech: "'Tis thou a son hast begotten,
(Aye, in sooth, all) tyrannous, [while tow'reth his crest like an aurochs],
Ne'er hath [the shock of his weapons] (its) peer; are driven [his fellows]
Into the toils, awhile cow'd are the heroes of Erech un- ....]
Gilgamesh leaveth no son to his father, [his arrogance swelling]
(Each) day and night; aye, he is the shepherd of Erech, [the high-wall'd],
He is their shepherd ... masterful, dominant, subtle ...
Gilgamesh leaveth no maid to [her mother], nor daughter to hero,
(Nay), nor a spouse to a [husband]".
(And so), to (th' appeal of) their wailing
[Anu] gave ear, call'd the lady Aruru: "'Twas thou, O Aruru,
Madest [(primeval seed of) mankind(?)]: do now make its fellow,
So that he [happen on Gilgamesh], yea, on the day of his pleasure,
So that they strive with each other, and he unto Erech give [surcease]".

The Creation of Enkidu

So when the goddess Aruru heard this, in her mind she imagined
(Straightway, this) Concept of Anu, and, washing her hands, (then) Aruru
Finger'd some clay, on the desert she moulded (it): [(thus) on the desert]
Enkidu made she, a warrior, (as he were) born (and) begotten,
(Yea), of Ninurta the double, [and put forth] the whole of his body
Hair: in the way of a woman he snooded his locks (in a fillet);
Sprouted luxuriant growth of his hair-like (the awns of) the barley,
Nor knew he people nor land; he was clad in a garb like Sumuqan.
E'en with gazelles did he pasture on herbage, along with the cattle
Drank he his fill, with the beasts did his heart delight at the water.

The Encounter of Enkidu with the Hunter

(Then) did a hunter, a trapper, come face to face with this (fellow),
Came on him [one], two, three days, at the place where (the beasts) drank (their) water;
(Sooth), when the hunter espied him, his face o'ermantled with terror,
He and his cattle went unto his steading, [dismay'd] (and) affrighted,

Crying aloud, [distress'd in, his heart, and) his face overclouded,
... woe in his belly ... (Aye, and) his face was the same
as of one [who hath gone] a far [journey].

Column III

Open'd [his mouth (then)] the hunter, and spake, addressing [his father]:
"Father, there is [a] great fellow come [forth from out of the mountains],

(O, but) [his] strength is the greatest [(the length and breadth) of the country],
[Like to a double] of Anu's own self [his strength] is enormous,
Ever (?) [he rangeth at large] o'er the mountains, [(and) ever] with cattle
[Grazeth on herbage (and) ever he setteth] his foot to the water,
[So that I fear] to approach him. The pits which I [myself] hollow'd
[(With mine own hands) hath he fill'd in (again)], (and) the traps of my [setting]
[Torn up, (and) out of my clutches hath holpen escape] (all) the cattle,
Beasts of the desert: to work at my fieldcraft [he will not allow] me".
[Open'd his mouth (then) his father, and spake], addressing the hunter:
"Gilgamesh [dwelleth] in Erech, [my son, whom no one] hath vanquish'd,
[(Nay, but) 'tis his strength is greatest (the length and breadth) of the country]
[Like to a double of Anu's own self], his strength is [enormous],
[Go, set] thy face [towards Erech: and when he hears of] a monster,
[He will say 'Go, O hunter, a courtesan-girl, a hetaera]
Take [with thee] ... like a strong one;
[When he the cattle shall gather again] to the place of (their) drinking,
[So shall she put off] her [mantle] (the charm of) her beauty [revealing];
[(Then) shall he spy her, and (sooth) will embrace her, (and thenceforth) his cattle,
[Which in] his very own deserts [were rear'd], will (straightway) deny him'."

How Gilgamesh First Heard of Enkidu

Unto the rede of his father the hunter [hath hearken'd, (and straightway)]
He will away [unto Gilgamesh].
Taking the road towards Erech
Turn'd he [his steps, and to] Gilgamesh [came, his speech thus addressing]:
(Saying): "There is a great fellow [come forth from out of the mountains],
[(O, but) his strength] is the greatest, (the length and breadth) of the country,
Like to a double of Anu's own self [his strength] is enormous,
[Ever (?)] he rangeth at large o'er the mountains, (and) ever with cattle
[Grazeth on herbage, (and)] ever [he setteth] his foot to the water,
So that I fear to approach [him]. The pits which I [myself] hollow'd
(With mine own hands) hath he fill'd in (again, and) the traps of my [setting]
Torn up, (and) out of my clutches hath holpen escape (all) the cattle,
Beasts [of the desert]: to work at my fieldcraft he will not allow me".
Gilgamesh unto him, unto the hunter made answer (in this wise):
"Go, (good) my hunter, take with thee a courtesan-girl, a hetaera,
When he the cattle shall [gather] again to the place of (their) drinking,
So shall she put off her mantle, (the charm of her) beauty [revealing],
(Then) shall he spy her, and (sooth) will embrace her, (and thenceforth) his cattle
Which in his very own deserts were rear'd will (straightway) deny him".

The Seduction of Enkidu

Forth went the hunter, took with him a courtesan-girl, a hetaera,
(So) did they start on their travels, went forth on their journey (together),

(Aye), at the term of three days arrived at the pleasance appointed.
Sate they down in their ambush (?), the hunter and the hetaera,
One day, two days they sat by the place where (the beasts) drank (their) water.
(Then) at last came the cattle to take their fill in their drinking.

Column IV

Thither the animals came that their hearts might delight in the water,
(Aye), there was Enkidu also, he whom the mountains had gender'd,
E'en with gazelles did he pasture on herbage, along with the cattle
Drank he his fill, with the beasts did his heart delight at the water,
So beheld him the courtesan-girl, the lusty great fellow,
(O but) a monster (all) savage from out of the depths of the desert!
"'Tis he, O girl! O, discover thy beauty, thy comeliness shew (him),
So that thy loveliness he may possess – (O), in no wise be bashful,
Ravish the soul of him – (certes), as soon as his eye on thee falleth,
He, forsooth, will approach thee, and thou – O, loosen thy mantle,
So that he clasp thee, and (then) with the wiles of a woman shalt ply him;
(Wherefore) his animals, bred in his desert, will (straightway) deny him,
(Since) to his breast he hath held thee.
The girl, displaying her bosom,
Shew'd him her comeliness, (yea) so that he of her beauty possess'd him,
Bashful she was not, (but) ravish'd the soul of him, loosing her mantle,
So that he clasp'd her, (and then) with the wiles of a woman she plied him,
Holding her unto his breast.
('Twas thus that) Enkidu dallied
Six days, (aye) seven nights, with the courtesan-girl in his mating.

How Enkidu Was Inveigled into Erech to Fight with Gilgamesh

Sated at length with her charms, he turn'd his face to his cattle,
O the gazelles, (how) they scamper'd away, as soon as they saw him!
Him, yea, Enkidu, – fled from his presence the beasts of the desert!
Enkidu losing his innocence – so, when the cattle fled from him,
Failed his knees, and he slack'd in his running, (not) as aforetime:
Natheless he (thus) hath attain'd his full growth and hath broaden'd (his) wisdom.
Sat he again at the feet of the woman, the woman his features
Scanning, and, while she was speaking, his ears heard (the words) she was saying:
"Comely thou art, e'en like to a god, O Enkidu, shalt be,
Why with the beasts (of the field) dost thou (ever) range over the desert?
Up! for I'll lead thee to Erech, the high-wall'd – (in sooth), to the Temple
Sacred, the dwelling of Anu and Ishtar, where, highest in power,
Gilgamesh is, and prevaileth o'er men like an aurochs".
Her counsel
E'en as she spake it found favour, (for) conscious he was of his longing
Some companion to seek; so unto the courtesan spake he:

"Up, then, O girl, to the Temple, the holy (and) sacred, invite me,
Me, to the dwelling of Anu and Ishtar, where, highest in power,
Gilgamesh is, and prevaileth o'er men like an aurochs – for I, too,

Column V

I, I will summon him, challenging boldly (and) crying through Erech,
'I too, am mighty!' Nay, I, forsooth [I], will (e'en) destiny alter –
(Truly), 'tis he who is born in the desert whose vigour [is greatest!]
... I will [please] thee,
... [whatever] there be, that would I know".
"Enkidu, come (then) to [Erech], the high-wall'd, [where] people [array] them
[Gorgeous] in festal attire, (and) each day the day is a revel,
[Eunuch]-priests [clashing] (their) cymbals, and [dancing]-girls ...
... flown with their wantoning, gleeful, and keeping the nobles
Out of their beds! (Nay), Enkidu, [joy] in thy life (to its fullest)
[Thou shalt] taste – (forsooth) will I shew thee a man who is happy,
Gilgamesh! View him, O look on his face, (how) comely his manhood!
Dower'd with lustiness is he, the whole of his body with power
Brimming, [his] vigour is stronger than thine, (all) day and night restless!
Enkidu, temper thine arrogance – Gilgamesh, loveth him Shamash,
Anu, (and) Enlil and Ea have dower'd his wisdom with largesse.

How Gilgamesh Dreamt of Enkidu

(Sooth), or ever from out of thy mountains thou camest, in Erech
Gilgamesh thee had beheld in a dream; so, Gilgamesh coming
Spake to his mother, the dream to reveal.
'O my mother, a vision
Which I beheld in my night-time. (Behold), there were stars of the heavens,
When something like unto Anu's own self fell down on my shoulders,
(Ah, though) I heaved him, he was o'erstrong for me, (and though) his grapple
Loosed I, I was unable to shake him (from off me): (and now, all the meanwhile),
People from Erech were standing about [him, the] artisans [pressing].
On [him behind], (while) throng'd him [the heroes]; my (very) companions
Kissing [his] feet; [I, I to my breast] like a woman did hold him,
(Then) [I] presented him low at [thy] feet, [that] as mine own equal.
[Thou] might'st account him'.
[She] who knoweth all wisdom (thus) to her Seigneur she answer'd,
[She] who knoweth all wisdom, to Gilgamesh (thus) did she answer:
'(Lo), by the stars of the heavens are represented thy [comrades],
[That which was like unto] Anu's [own self], which fell on thy shoulders,
[Which thou didst heave, but he was, o'erstrong for thee, [(aye),
though his grapple
Thou didst unloose], but to shake him from off thee thou wert [un] able,
[So didst present] him low at my feet, [that] as thine own equal
[I might] account him – [and thou to thy breast like a woman] didst hold him:

Column VI

[This is a stoutheart, a] friend, one ready to stand by [a comrade],
One whose strength [is the greatest, (the length and breadth) of the country],
[Like to a double of Anu's own self his] strength is enormous.
[(Now), since thou] to thy breast didst hold him [the way of a woman],
[This is a sign that] thou art the one he will [never] abandon:
[This] of thy dream is the [meaning]'.
[Again he spake] to his mother,
'[Mother], a second dream [did I] see: [Into Erech, the high-wall'd],
Hurtled an axe, and they gather'd about it: [the meanwhile, from Erech]
[People] were standing about it, [the people] (all) thronging before it,
[Artisans pressing] behind it, [while] I at thy feet did present it,
[I], like a woman I held it to me [that] thou might'st account it,
As mine own equal'.
[She the [all]-wise, who knoweth all wisdom, (thus) answer'd her offspring,
[She the all-wise] who knoweth all wisdom, to Gilgamesh answer'd:
'(Lo, that) [Axe] thou didst see (is) a Man; like a woman didst hold him,
Unto thy breast, [that] as thine own equal I might account him,
[This] is a stoutheart, a friend, one ready to stand by a comrade,
One whose strength is the [greatest (the length and breadth) of the country],
(Like to a double of] Anu's [own self], his strength is enormous'.
[Gilgamesh open'd his mouth, and] addressing his mother, (thus spake he):
'[Though] great [danger (?)] befall, [a friend (?)] shall I have ...'"

(The Assyrian Edition of the seventh century has three more lines on the First Tablet, which correspond with Column II, l. 3 of the Second Tablet of the Old Babylonian Edition. This latter has already begun with the episode of the two dreams, approximately Column V, l. 24 of the Assyrian First Tablet, and the text is so similar in both that I have not repeated it here. The Old Babylonian Edition here takes up the story, repeating one or two details).

The Second Tablet of the Meeting of Gilgamesh and Enkidu

Column II

While Gilgamesh (thus) is the vision revealing
Enkidu sitteth before the hetaera, and she [displaying her] bosom,
Shewing [her beauty (?)], the place of his birth he forgetteth.
(So) Enkidu dallied
(Thus) for six days, seven nights, with the courtesan-girl in his mating.
Broke into [speech] then, the nymph, and (thus) unto Enkidu spake she:
"(Yea, as) I view thee, (e'en) like a god, O Enkidu, shalt be,
Why with the beasts (of the field) dost thou (ever) range over the desert?
Up, for I'll lead thee to [Erech] broad-marketed, (aye), to the Temple
Sacred, the dwelling of Anu – O Enkidu, come, that I guide thee,
Unto E-Anna, the dwelling of Anu, where [Gilgamesh] (liveth),

(He), the supreme of creation; and thou, aye, thou wilt [embrace him]
Like [to a woman], (and e'en) [as] thyself thou shalt [love him].
O, rouse thee
Up from the ground – 'tis a shepherd's bed (only)".
Her utterance heard he,
Welcomed her rede: the advice of the woman struck home in his bosom.
She one garment took off wherewith she might clothe him: the other
She herself wore, (and so) taking her hand like a brother she led him
(Thus) to the booths(?) of the shepherds, the place of the sheepfolds. The shepherds
Gather'd at sight of him
(*Gap of four or five lines*)

Column III
How the Hetaera Schooled Enkidu

He (in the past) of the milk of the wild things to suck was accustom'd!
Bread which she set before him he broke, but he gazed and he stared:
Enkidu bread did not know how to eat, nor had he the knowledge
Mead how to quaff!
(Then) the woman made answer, to Enkidu speaking,
"Enkidu, taste of the bread, (for) of life 'tis; (forsooth), the essential,
Drink thou, (too), of the mead, 'tis the wonted use of the country".
Enkidu ate of the bread, (aye, ate) until he was gorged,
Drank of the mead seven bumpers; his spirits rose, (and), exultant,
Glad was his heart, and cheerful his face: [himself(?)] was he rubbing,
Oil on the hair of his body anointed: and (thus) became human.
Donn'd he a garment to be like a man, (and) taking his weapon,
Hunted the lions, which harried the shepherds o' nights: and the jackals
Caught he. (So) he, having mastered the lions, the shepherds slept soundly.
Enkidu – (he) was their warden – (becometh) a man of full vigour.
(Now) is one of the heroes speaking to [Gilgamesh(?)]....

(*About thirteen lines are missing, a gap in which a sinister figure has evidently appeared, sent evidently by Gilgamesh to learn the meaning of the arrival of the strangers in Erech. Enkidu sees him and speaks*)

Column IV

(Then while) he pleasured, he lifted his eyes, (and), observing the fellow,
Spake he unto the woman: "O doxy, bring me (this) fellow,
Why hath he come? I would know his intention".
The woman the fellow
Call'd that he come to him, that he might see him: "O, why art thou seeking,
Sir? (Pray), which is the way to thy rest-house?"
The man spake, addressing
Enkidu: "You to the House of Community [Gilgamesh calleth],
(This is) the custom of men, and a homage (too) to the great ones:
Come, then, and heap up the offerings such as are due to the city,

Come, on behalf of the common weal bring in the food of the city.
('Tis) for the king of broad-marketed Erech to look on thy greeting,
Gilgamesh, king of broad-marketed Erech to look on thy greeting;
First doth he mate with the woman allotted by fate, and then after
Speak by the counsel of god, and so from the shape of the omens
(Utter the rede of) his destiny".
(So) at the words of the fellow
Went they before him.
(Gap of about nine lines)

Column V
The Entry of Enkidu into Erech

[Enkidu] going [in front], with the courtesan coming behind him,
Enter'd broad-marketed Erech; the populace gather'd behind him,
(Then), as he stopp'd in the street of broad-marketed Erech, the people
Thronging, behind him exclaim'd "Of a truth, like to Gilgamesh is he,
Shorter in stature a trifle, [his] composition is stronger.
... [(once)] like a [weakling] baby he *suck'd* the milk of the wild things!
Ever the breadcakes in Erech give glorious (climax) to manhood!
He a (mere) savage becometh a hero of proper appearance,
(Now) unto Gilgamesh, god-like, his composition is equal".

How Enkidu fought with Gilgamesh for the Hetaera

Strewn is the couch for the love-rites, and Gilgamesh (now) in the night-time
Cometh to sleep, to delight in the woman: (but) [Enkidu], coming
(There) in the highway, doth block up the passage to Gilgamesh, [threat'ning]
He with his strength ...
(Gap of seven or eight lines)

Column VI

Gilgamesh ... behind him ...
Burgeon'd [his rage], (and) he rush'd to [attack] him: they met in the highway.
Enkidu barr'd up the door with his foot, (and) to Gilgamesh entry –
Would not concede: they grappled and snorted(?) like bulls, (and) the threshold
Shatter'd: the (very) wall quiver'd as Gilgamesh, Enkidu grappled,
Snorting(?) like bulls, (and) the threshold they shatter'd, the (very) wall quiver'd.

The Birth of Friendship

Gilgamesh bent his leg to the ground: (so) his fury abated,
(Aye, and) his ardour was quell'd: so soon as was quelled his ardour,
Enkidu (thus) unto Gilgamesh spake: "(Of a truth), did thy mother
Bear thee as one, and one only: (that choicest) cow of the steer-folds,

Nin-sun exalted thy head above heroes, and Enlil hath dower'd
Thee with the kingship o'er men".

The Third Tablet
The Expedition to the Forest of Cedars Against Humbaba

(About a column and a half of the beginning of the Old Babylonian version on the Yale tablet are so broken that almost all the text is lost. Gilgamesh and Enkidu have now become devoted friends, thus strangely stultifying the purpose for which Enkidu was created, and now is set afoot the great expedition against the famous Cedar Forest guarded by the Ogre Humbaba. The courtesan has now for a brief space left the scene, having deserted Enkidu, much to his sorrow. The mutilated Assyrian Version gives a hint that the mother of Gilgamesh is now describing the fight to one of her ladies(?) Rishat-Nin … and where her recital becomes connected the story runs thus)

Column II
(The Tale of the Fight)

"He lifted up [his foot, to the door …
(?) They raged furiously …
Enkidu hath not [his equal] … unkempt is the hair …
(Aye) he was born in the desert, and [no] one [his presence can equal]".

Enkidu's sorrow at the loss of his Love

Enkidu (there) as he stood gave ear [to his utterance (?)], grieving
Sitting [in sorrow]: his eyes fill'd [with tears], and his arms lost their power,
[Slack'd was his bodily vigour]. Each clasp'd [the hand of] the other.
[Holding] like [brothers] their grip … [(and) to Gilgamesh] Enkidu answer'd:
"Friend, 'tis my darling hath circled (her arms) round my neck (to farewell me),
(Wherefore) my arms lose their power, my bodily vigour is slacken'd".

The Ambition of Gilgamesh

Gilgamesh open'd his mouth, and to Enkidu spake he (in this wise):

Column III

(Gap of about two lines)
"[I, O my friend, am determined to go to the Forest of Cedars],
[(Aye) and] Humbaba the Fierce [will] o'ercome and destroy [what is evil]
[(Then) will I cut down] the Cedar…".
Enkidu open'd his mouth, and to Gilgamesh spake he (in this wise),
"Know, then, my friend, what time I was roaming with kine in the mountains
I for a distance of two hours' march from the skirts of the Forest

Into its depths would go down. Humbaba – his roar was a whirlwind,
Flame (in) his jaws, and his very breath Death! O, why hast desired
This to accomplish? To meet(?) with Humbaba were conflict unequall'd".
Gilgamesh open'd his mouth and to Enkidu spake he (in this wise):
"[Tis that I need] the rich yield of its mountains [I go to the Forest]" ...
(Seven mutilated lines continuing the speech of Gilgamesh, and mentioning "the dwelling [of the gods?]" (of the beginning of the Fifth Tablet), and "the axe", for cutting down the Cedars).
Enkidu open'd his mouth [and] to Gilgamesh spake he (in this wise):
"(But) when we go to the Forest [of Cedars] ... its guard is a [Fighter],
Strong, never [sleeping], O Gilgamesh....
(Three mutilated lines, apparently explaining the powers which Shamash (?), the Sun-god, and Adad, the Storm-god, have bestow'd on Humbaba).

Column IV

So that he safeguard the Forest of Cedars a terror to mortals
Him hath Enlil appointed – Humbaba, his roar is a whirlwind,
Flame (in) his jaws, and his very breath Death! (Aye), if he in the Forest.
Hear (but) a tread(?) on the road – 'Who is this come down to his Forest?'
So that he safeguard the Forest of Cedars, a terror to mortals,
Him hath Enlil appointed, and fell hap will seize him who cometh
Down to his Forest".
Gilgamesh open'd his mouth and to Enkidu spake he (in this wise):
"Who, O my friend, is unconquer'd by [death]? A divinity, certes,
Liveth for aye in the daylight, but mortals – their days are (all) number'd,
All that they do is (but) wind – But to thee, now death thou art dreading,
Proffereth nothing of substance thy courage – I, I'll be thy ward!
'Tis thine own mouth shall tell thou didst fear the onslaught (of battle),
(I, forsooth) if I should fall, my name will have stablish'd (forever).
Gilgamesh 'twas, who fought with Humbaba, the Fierce!
(In the future),
After my children are born to my house, and climb up thee, (saying):
'Tell to us all that thou knowest'....
(Four lines mutilated)
[(Yea), when thou] speakest [in this wise], thou grievest my heart (for) the Cedar
[I am] determined [to fell], that I may gain [fame] everlasting.

The Weapons are Cast for the Expedition

(Now), O my friend, [my charge] to the craftsmen I fain would deliver,
So that they cast in our presence [our weapons]".
[The charge] they deliver'd
Unto the craftsmen: the mould (?) did the workmen prepare, and the axes
Monstrous they cast: (yea), the celts did they cast, each (weighing) three talents;
Glaives, (too,) monstrous they cast, with hilts each (weighing) two talents,
Blades, thirty manas to each, corresponding to fit them: [the inlay(?)],

Gold thirty manas (each) sword: (so) were Gilgamesh, Enkidu laden
Each with ten talents.

Gilgamesh Takes Counsel with the Elders

(And now) [in] the Seven Bolt [Portal of Erech]
Hearing [the bruit(?)] did the artisans gather, [assembled the people(?)],
(There) in the streets of broad-marketed Erech, [in] Gilgamesh' honour(?)],
[So did the Elders of Erech] broad-marketed take seat before him.
[Gilgamesh] spake [thus: "O Elders of Erech] broad-marketed, [hear me!]
[I go against Humbaba, the Fierce, who shall say, when he heareth],

Column V

'(Ah), let me look on (this) Gilgamesh, he of whom (people) are speaking,
He with whose fame the countries are fill'd' – 'Tis I will o'erwhelm him,
(There) in the Forest of Cedars – I'll make the land hear (it)
(How) like a giant the Scion of Erech is – (yea, for) the Cedars
I am determined to fell, that I may gain fame everlasting".
Gilgamesh (thus) did the Elders of Erech broad-marketed answer:
"Gilgamesh, 'tis thou art young, that thy valour (o'ermuch) doth uplift thee,
Nor dost thou know to the full what thou dost seek to accomplish.
Unto our ears hath it come of Humbaba, his likeness is twofold.
Who (of free will) then would [seek to] oppose [in encounter] his weapons?
Who for a distance of two hours' march from the skirts of the Forest
Unto its depths would [go] down? Humbaba, his roar is a whirlwind,
Flame (in) his jaws, and his very breath Death! (O), why hast desired.
This to accomplish? To meet(?) with Humbaba were conflict unequall'd".
Gilgamesh unto the rede of his counsellors hearken'd and ponder'd,
Cried to [his] friend: "Now, indeed, O [my] fried, [will I] thus [voice opinion].
I (forsooth) dread him, and (yet) to [(the depths of the) Forest] I'll take [me] ..."
(*About seven lines mutilated or missing in which the Elders bless Gilgamesh in farewell*)
"... may thy god (so) [protect] thee,
Bringing thee back [(safe and)] sound to the walls of [broad-marketed] Erech".
Gilgamesh knelt [before Shamash] a word [in his presence] to utter:
"Here I present myself, Shamash, [to lift up] my hands (in entreaty),
O that hereafter my life may be spared, to the ramparts of [Erech]
Bring me again: spread thine aegis [upon me]".
And Shamash made answer,
[Speaking] his oracle....
(*About six lines mutilated or missing*)

Column VI

Tears adown Gilgamesh' [cheeks were (now)] streaming: "A road I have never
Traversed [I go, on a passage(?)] I know not, (but if) I be spared
(So) in content [will I] come [and will pay thee(?)] due meed (?) of thy homage".

(Two mutilated lines with the words "on seats" and "his equipment".)
Monstrous [the axes they brought(?)], they deliver'd [the bow] and the quiver
[Into] (his) hand; (so) taking a celt, [he slung on (?)] his quiver,
[Grasping] another [celt(?) he fasten'd his glaive] to his baldrick.
[But, or ever the twain] had set forth on their journey, they offer'd
[Gifts] to the Sun-god, that home he might bring them to Erech (in safety).

The Departure of the Two Heroes

(Now) do the [Elders] farewell him with blessings, to Gilgamesh giving
Counsel [concerning] the road: "O Gilgamesh, to thine own power
Trust not (alone); (but at least) let thy [road] be traversed [before] thee,
Guard thou thy person; let Enkidu go before thee (as vaward).
(Aye, for) 'twas he hath discover'd the [way], the road he hath travell'd.
(Sooth), of the Forest the passes are all under sway (?) [of] Humbaba,
[(Yea), he who goeth] as vaward is (able) to safeguard a comrade,
O that the Sun-god [may grant] thee [success to attain] thine [ambition],
O that he grant that thine eyes see (consummate) the words of thy utt'rance
O that he level the path that is block'd, cleave a road for thy treading,
Cleave, too, the berg for thy foot! May the god Lugal-banda
Bring in thy night-time a message to thee, with which shalt be gladden'd,
So that it help thine ambition, (for), like a boy thine ambition
On the o'erthrow of Humbaba thou fixest, as thou hast settled.

Wash, (then), thy feet: when thou haltest, shalt hollow a pool, so that ever
Pure be the water within thy skin-bottle, (aye), cool be the water
Unto the Sun-god thou pourest, (and thus) shalt remind Lugal-banda".
Enkidu open'd his mouth, and spake unto Gilgamesh, (saying):
"[Gilgamesh], art (?) thou (in truth) full equal to making (this) foray?
Let [not] thy heart be afraid; trust me".
On (his) shoulder his mantle
[Drew] he, (and now) [on the road] to Humbaba they set forth (together).
(Five lines mutilated; the two heroes meet a man who sets them on their way)
"... they went with me ... [tell] you ... in joy of heart".
[So when he heard this his word, the man on his way did [direct him]:
"Gilgamesh, go, ... let thy brother (?) precede [thee] ... [(and) in thine ambition].
[O that the Sun-god (?)] may shew [thee] success!"

(The Old Babylonian Version breaks off after three more fragmentary lines. The following is the Assyrian Version of Column VI, l. 21, and onwards of the preceding text. It marks the beginning of the Third Tablet in the Assyrian Version, opening with the episode of the conclave of the Elders)

"Gilgamesh, put not thy faith in the strength of thine own person (solely),
Quench'd be thy wishes to trusting(?) (o'ermuch) in thy (shrewdness in) smiting.
(Sooth), he who goeth as vaward is able to safeguard a comrade,
He who doth know how to guide hath guarded his friend; (so) before thee,

Do thou let Enkidu go, (for 'tis) he to the Forest of Cedars
Knoweth the road: 'tis he lusteth for battle, and threateneth combat.
Enkidu – he would watch over a friend, would safeguard a comrade,
(Aye, such a one) would deliver his person from out of the pitfalls.
We, O King, in our conclave have paid deep heed to thy welfare,
Thou, O King, in return with an (equal) heed shalt requite us".
Gilgamesh open'd his mouth, and spake unto Enkidu, saying:
"Unto the Palace of Splendour, O friend, come, let us betake us,
Unto the presence of Nin-sun, the glorious Queen, (aye) to Nin-sun,
Wisest of (all) clever women, all-knowing; a well-devised pathway
She will prescribe for our feet".

Clasp'd they their hands, each to each, and went to the Palace of Splendour,
Gilgamesh, Enkidu. Unto the glorious Queen, (aye) to Nin-sun
Gilgamesh came, and he enter'd in unto [the presence of Nin-sun]:
"Nin-sun, O fain would I tell thee [how] I a far journey [am going],
(Unto) the home [of Humbaba to counter a] warfare I know not,
[Follow a road] which I [know] not, [(aye) from the time of my starting],
[Till my return, until I arrive at the Forest of Cedars,]
[Till I o'erthrow Humbaba, the Fierce, and destroy from the country.]
[All that the Sun-god abhorreth of evil]"....

(The rest of the speech of Gilgamesh is lost until the end of the Column, where we find him still addressing his mother, and apparently asking that she shall garb herself in festal attire to beg a favour of the Sun-god)

" ... garb thyself; ... in thy presence.
(So) to her offspring, to Gilgamesh [Nin-sun] gave ear ... -ly,

Column II

Enter'd [her chamber] ... [and deck'd herself] with the flowers of *Tulal*(?),
[Put on] the festal garb of her body....
[Put on] the festal garb of her bosom ..., her head [with a circlet]
Crown'd, and ... the ground *ipirani*.
Climb'd [she the stairway], ascended the roof, and [the parapet(?)] mounted,
Offer'd her incense to Shamash, (her) sacrifice offer'd [to Shamash],
(Then) towards Shamash her hands she uplifted (in orison saying):
"Why didst thou give (this) restlessness of spirit
With which didst dower Gilgamesh, [my] son?
That now thou touchest him, and (straight) he starteth
A journey far to where Humbaba (dwelleth),
To counter warfare which he knoweth not,
Follow a pathway which he knoweth not,
(Aye), from the very day on which he starteth,
Till he return, till to the Cedar Forest
He reach; till he o'erthrow the fierce Humbaba,

And from the land destroy all evil things
Which thou abhor'st; the day which [thou hast set]
As term, of (that) strong man (who) feareth thee,
May Aa, (thy) bride, be [thy] remembrancer.
He the night-watches…".

(Columns III, IV, and V are much mutilated. There is the remnant of a passage in Assyrian, corresponding to the Third Tablet of the Old Babylonian Version, Column III, 15, which gives Enkidu's speech about "the mountains", "the cattle of the field" and how "he waited": then follows another fragment with a mention of the "corpse" [of Humbaba] and of the Anunnaki (the Spirits of Heaven), and a repetition of the line "that strong man (who) feareth [thee]". Then a reference to "the journey" until [Gilgamesh shall have overthrown the fierce Humbaba], be it after an interval of days, months, or years; and another fragment probably part of the previous text, where someone "heaps up incense" [to a god], and Enkidu again speaks with someone, but the mutilated text does not allow us much light on its connection, and although there is another fragment, the connection again is not obvious. The last column is a repetition of what the Elders said to Gilgamesh):

"(Aye, such an one) [would deliver his person] from out of the pitfalls.
[We, O King], in our conclave [have paid deep heed to thy welfare],
(Now), O King, in thy turn with an (equal) heed] shalt requite us".
Enkidu [open'd] his mouth [and spake unto Gilgamesh, saying]:
"Turn, O my friend … a road not…".

The Fourth Tablet
The Arrival at the Gate of the Forest

(**OF COLUMN I** *about ll. 1-36 are mutilated or missing, there being actually the beginnings of only sixteen lines. When the text becomes connected the heroes have reached the Gate of the Forest*)

Column I
Enkidu addresses the Gate

Enkidu lifted [his eyes] … and spake with the Gate as ['t were human(?)]:
"O thou Gate of the Forest without understanding (? …
Sentience which thou hast not, …

I for (full) forty leagues have admired thy [wonderful] timber,
(Aye), till I sighted the towering Cedar …
(O but) thy wood hath no peer (in the country) …
Six *gar* thy height, and two *gar* thy breadth …
(Sooth, but) thy stanchion (?), thy socket (?), thy pivot
(?), thy lock (?), and thy shutter (?),
[(All of them) must have been fashion'd for thee] in the City of Nippur!
O, if I had but known, O Gate, that this was [thy grandeur],
This, too, the grace [of thy structure], then either an axe had I lifted
Or I had … or bound together…".

(Of the next Column remains a fragment, and that only presumed to belong to one of the above fragments from its appearance, which speaks of terror, a dream and sorrow: "let me pray the gods.... may thy? god be ... the father of the gods". Again, of the third Column there is only a small portion left of the right half (this fragment, too, being also presumed to belong to the same tablet as that above-mentioned), speaking of Gilgamesh, the Forest, and Enkidu. The fourth Column is entirely lost. Of Column V the latter part survives, in this case without any uncertainty. After a few broken lines it runs as follows, the first speaker being probably Enkidu, and the scene the Gate of the Forest):

"... [O, haste] thee, withstand him, he will not [pursue(?) thee],
[We will] go on down into the wood not daunted, together (?)].
... Thou shall put on seven garments ...
... putting on, and six ... (?) ..."
He like a mighty wild bull . . .
Flung he the Portal afar, and [his] mouth was fill'd (with his challenge),
Cried to the Guard of the Forest: "Up (?) ...!
['Tis I will challenge] Humbaba like to a ..."
(*A small gap*)

Column VI
Enkidu is speaking

"Trouble (?) [I foresee(?)] wherever I go .
O my friend, I have [seen] a dream which un- ".
The day of the dream he had seen fulfilled...

(Enkidu is stricken with fear at thought of the combat).
Enkidu lay for a day, [yea, a second] – for Enkidu [lying]
(Prone) on his couch, was a third and a fourth day . . ., a fifth, sixth and seventh,
Eighth, ninth, [and tenth]. While Enkidu [lay in his] sickness ..., th' eleventh,
(Aye, till) the twelfth ... on [his] couch was Enkidu [lying].
Call'd he to Gilgamesh, ...
"(O but), my comrade, ... hateth me ... because within Erech
I was afraid of the combat, and ... My friend, who in battle ..".
(*A small gap in which Gilgamesh has answered. Enkidu replies*):

[Enkidu open'd] his [mouth] and spake [unto Gilgamesh, saying]:
("Nay, but), [my friend, let us no wise] go down [to the depths of the Forest],
(For) 'tis my hands [have grown weak], and [my arms] are stricken with palsy".

* * *

Gilgamesh open'd his mouth and spake [unto Enkidu], saying:
"Shall we, O friend, [play] the coward? ...
... thou shalt surpass them all(?) ...
[Thou, O] my friend, art cunning in warfare, art [shrewd(?)] in the battle,
(So) shalt thou touch the ... and of [death] have no terror,

(Two difficult and mutilated lines)
[So that] the palsy (now striking) thine arms [may] depart, and the weakness
Pass [from thy hands]! [Be brave(?)] and resist! O my comrade, together
We will go down – let the combat [in no wise diminish(?)] thy courage!
O forget death, and be fearful(?) of nothing(?) …(for he who is) [valiant(?)],
Cautious (and) careful, by leading [the way] hath his own body guarded,
(He 'tis) will safeguard a comrade".
A name by their [valour(?)] …
They will establish. (And now) they together arrive at the barrier(?),
[Still'd into silence(?)] their speech, and they themselves (suddenly) stopping.

The Fifth Tablet
Of the Fight with Humbaba

Column I
The Wonders of the Forest

STOOD THEY and stared at the Forest, they gazed at the height of the Cedars,
Scanning the avenue into the Forest: (and there) where Humbaba
Stalk'd, was a path, (and) straight were his tracks, and good was the passage.
(Eke) they beheld the Mount of the Cedar, the home of th' Immortals,
Shrine [of Irnini, the Cedar uplifting its pride 'gainst the mountain,
Fair was its shade, (all) full of delight, with bushes (there) spreading,
Spread, too, the … the Cedar the incense …

(After a few mutilated lines the Column breaks: the upper part of Column II contains about twenty lines badly mutilated; then the lower part is more complete, beginning with visions granted to the hero).

Column II
Gilgamesh Relates His Dreams

"[Then came another dream to me, comrade, and this second] vision
[Pleasant, indeed], which I saw, (for) we (?) [twain were standing together]
[High on (?) a] peak of the mountains, [and then did the mountain peak] topple,
[Leaving us twain (?)] to be like … (?) which are born in the desert".
Enkidu spake to his comrade the dream (?) [to interpret], (thus saying):
"Comrade, (in sooth, this) vision [of thine unto us] good fortune (forbodeth),
(Aye), 'tis a dream of great gain [thou didst see], (for, bethink you), O comrade,
(Surely) the mountain which thou hast beholden [must needs be Humbaba(?)].
(Thus doth it mean) we shall capture Humbaba, (and) [throw down his] carcass,
[Leaving] his corpse in abasement – tomorrow's (outcome) will I [shew thee]".

* * *

(Now) at the fortieth league did they break their fast [with a morsel],
(Now) at the sixtieth rested, and hollow'd a pit in the sunshine …

Gilgamesh mounted above [it] … (and) pour'd out his meal [for the mountain]:
"Mountain, a dream do thou grant … breathe on him ..".

Column III

Granted [the mountain] a dream … it breathed on him …
Then a chill windblast [up]-sprang (and) [a gust] passing over …
[Made] him to cower, and … [thereat he sway'd] like the corn of the mountains …
Gilgamesh, [squatting] bent-kneed, supported his haunches, (and straightway)
Sleep (such as) floweth on man descended upon him: [at] midnight
Ending his slumber (all sudden), he hied him to speak to his comrade:
"Didst thou not call me, O friend? (O), why am I waken'd (from slumber)?
Didst thou not touch me – (for), why am I fearful(?), (or) hath not some spirit
Pass'd (me)? (Or,) why is my flesh (all) a-quiver?

The Dream of the Volcano, Which Probably Represents Humbaba

A third dream, O comrade,
I have beheld: but all awesome (this) dream which I have beholden:
(Loud) did the firmament roar, (and) earth (with the echo) resounded,
Sombre the day, with darkness uprising, (and) levin bolts flashing,
Kindled were flames, [and there, too, was Pestilence (?)] fill'd to o'erflowing,
Gorgéd was Death! (Then) [faded] the glare, (then) faded the fires,
Falling, [the brands] turn'd to ashes – [Come, let us go] down to the desert,
That we may counsel together".
Enkidu (now) to interpret his dream unto Gilgamesh speaketh:
(Remainder of Column III broken away)

(A variant version is found on one of the Semitic tablets from Boghaz Keui. Where the sense becomes connected it briefly describes how the heroes halt for the night and at midnight sleep departs from the hero who tells his dream to Enkidu, after asking much in the same way why he is frightened at waking from his dream. "Besides my first dream a second … In my dream, O friend, a mountain … he cast me down, seized my feet … The brilliance increased: a man …, most comely of all the land was his beauty … Beneath the mountain he drew me, and … water he gave me to drink, and my desire [was assuaged]; to earth he set [my] feet … Enkidu unto this god … unto Gilgamesh spake: "My friend, we will go ... whatever is hostile ... Not the mountain … Come, lay aside fear ... "The rest after about mutilated seven lines is lost).

(Column IV is all lost, and hardly anything of Column V remains. Column VI once contained the story of the great fight, but except for a few broken lines at the end it is all lost. But we can fortunately replace it from the Hittite version from Boghaz Keui)

Column VI
The Fight with Humbaba

In the following manner … the Sun-god in heaven … the trees:
He saw [Gilgamesh]: of the Sun-god in heaven in …

And [shew'd him] the dam on the ditches.
Gilgamesh [spake] then [in orison] unto the Sun-god in heaven;
"Lo, on that day to the city … which is in the city:
I in sooth [pray] to the Sun-god in heaven: I on a road have now started, ..".
Unto th' entreaty of Gilgamesh hearken'd the Sun-god in heaven,
Wherefore against Humbaba he raised mighty winds: (yea), a great wind,
Wind from the North, (aye), [a wind from the South], yea [a tempest] (and) storm wind,
Chill wind, (and) whirlwind, a wind of (all) evil: 'twas eight winds he raiséd,
Seizing [Humbaba] before and behind, so that nor to go forwards,
Nor to go back was he able: and then Humbaba surrender'd.
Wherefore to Gilgamesh spake (thus) Humbaba: "O Gilgamesh, (pr'y thee),
Stay, (now, thy hand): be [thou] now my [master], and I'll be thy henchman:
[O disregard] (all) [the words which I spake [(so) boastfull against thee,
Weighty … I would lay me down … and the Palace.
Thereat to [Gilgamesh] Enkidu [spake]: "[Of the rede which] Humbaba
[Maketh to thee] thou darest in nowise offer acceptance.
(Aye, for) Humbaba [must] not [remain alive] ..".

(The Hittite Version here breaks off. The Assyrian Version ends with six badly mutilated lines of which the last tells the successful issue of the expedition).

. . . . [they cut off] the head of Humbaba.

The Sixth Tablet
of the Goddess Ishtar, Who Fell in Love with the Hero After His Exploit Against Humbaba

Column I
Gilgamesh is Removing the Stains of Combat

(NOW) IS HE washing his stains, (and) is cleansing his garments in tatters,
Braiding (?) (the locks of) his hair (to descend loose) over his shoulders,
Laying aside his garments besmirchen, (and) donning his clean ones,
Putting on armlets (?), and girding his body about with a baldric,
Gilgamesh bindeth his fillet, and girdeth himself with a baldric.

Ishtar Sees Him and Seeks to Wed Him

(Now) Lady Ishtar espieth the beauty of Gilgamesh: (saith she),
"Gilgamesh, come, be a bridegroom, to me of the fruit (of thy body)
Grant me largesse: (for) my husband shalt be and I'll be thy consort.
O, but I'll furnish a chariot for thee, (all) azure and golden,
Golden its wheel, and its yoke precious stones, each day to be harness'd
Unto great mules: (O), enter our house with the fragrance of cedar.
(So) when thou enterest into our house shall threshold and dais
Kiss thy feet, (and) beneath thee do homage kings, princes and rulers,
Bringing thee yield of the mountains and plains as a tribute: thy she-goats

Bring forth in plenty, thy ewes shall bear twins, thy asses attaining
(Each) to the size of a mule, (and) thy steeds in thy chariot winning
Fame for their gallop: [thy mules] in the yoke shall ne'er have a rival".

* * *

[Gilgamesh] open'd his mouth in reply, Lady Ishtar [to answer]:
"Aye, but what must I give] thee, (if (?)) I should take thee in marriage?
[I must provide thee with oil] for (thy) body, and clothing: (aye, also)
[Give thee (thy)] bread and (thy) victual: (sooth), must be sustenance
[ample]
Meet for divinity – [I, (too), must give thee (thy) drink] fit for royalty.
... I shall be bound, ... let us amass (?), ... clothe with a garment.
[What, then, will be my advantage, supposing) I take thee in marriage?
[Thou'rt but a ruin which giveth no shelter (?) to man] from the weather,
Thou'rt but a back door [not] giving resistance to blast or to windstorm,

Thou'rt but a palace which dasheth the heroes [within it to pieces],
Thou'rt but a pitfall (which letteth) its covering [give way (all treach'rous)],
Thou art but pitch which [defileth] the man who doth carry it with him,
Thou'rt but a bottle which [leaketh] on him who doth carry it with him,
Thou art but limestone which [letteth] stone ramparts [fall crumbling in ruin].
Thou'rt but chalcedony [failing to guard (?)] in an enemy's country,
Thou'rt but a sandal which causeth its owner [to trip (by the wayside)].
Who was ever [thy] husband [thou faithfully lovedst] for all time?
Who hath been ever thy lord who hath gain'd [over thee the advantage?
Come, and I will unfold thee [the endless tale] of thy husbands.

* * *

(Sooth), thou shalt vouch (?) for the truth (?) of (this) list – Thy maidenhood's consort,
Tammuz, each year dost make him the cause of Wailing, (then cometh
Next) the bird Roller gay-feather'd thou lovedst, and (yet) thou didst smite him
Breaking his wing: in the grove doth he stand, crying *kappi* 'my wing!'
Lovedst thou also a Lion, in (all) the full strength of (his) vigour,
(Yet) thou didst dig for him seven and seven (deep) pits (to entrap him).
Lovedst thou also a Stallion, magnificent he in the battle,
Thou wert the cause of a bridle, a spur and a whip to him: (also)
Thou wert the cause of his fifty miles galloping; thou wert the cause, too,
(Eke), of exhaustion and sweating (?); (thereafter), 'twas thou who didst (also)
Unto his mother Silili give cause for (her deep) lamentation.
Lovedst thou also a Shepherd, a neatherd, for thee without ceasing
Each day to sacrifice yeanlings for thee would heap thee his charcoal,
(Yet) thou didst smite him, transforming him into a jackal: his herd boy
Yea, his own herd boy drove him away, and his dogs tore his buttocks.
Lovedst thou, too, Ishullanu, the gardener he of thy sire,
Bringing delights (?) to thee ceaseless, while daily he garnish'd thy platter;

'Twas for thee only to cast thine eyes on him, and with him be smitten.
'O Ishullanu of mine, come, let me taste of thy vigour,
Put forth thy hand, too, ...'
But he, Ishullanu,
Said to thee 'What dost thou ask me? Save only my mother hath baked (it),
Nought have I eaten – (and) what I should eat would be bread of transgression,
(Aye) and iniquity! (Further), the reeds are a cloak against winter'.
Thou this [his answer] didst hear, didst smite him and make him a spider(?),
Making him lodge midway up a [dwelling(?)] – not to move upwards
Lest there be drainage; nor down, lest a crushing [o'erwhelm him].
So, too, me in my turn thou wouldst love and (then) [reckon] me like them".

* * *

[Heard] this (then) Ishtar: she burst into rage and [went up] to Heaven,
Hied her (thus) Ishtar to Anu, [her father], to Antu, her mother,
Came she [to tell (them)]: "O father, doth Gilgamesh load me with insult,
Gilgamesh tale of my sins, my sins and iniquities telleth".

* * *

Anu made answer, (thus) speaking, and said unto Ishtar the Lady:
"Nay, thou didst ask him [to grant thee largesse of the fruit of his body],
(Hence) he the tale of thy sins, thy sins and iniquities telleth".

The Creation of the Divine Bull which is to Destroy the Heroes

Ishtar made answer (thus) speaking, and said unto [Anu, her father]:
"Father, O make (me) a Heavenly Bull, which shall Gilgamesh [vanquish],
Filling [its body] with flame ...
But if thou'lt [not] make [this Bull], then ...
I'll smite ..., I'll put ..., I'll ...
More than the ... will be the ...

* * *

Anu [made answer, (thus) speaking, and said unto] Ishtar, the Lady:
"[If I the Heavenly Bull shall create, for which] thou dost ask me,
(Then) seven years of (leer) husks [must needs follow after his onslaught (?)].
Wilt thou [for man] gather [corn (?)], and increase [for the cattle(?)] the fodder (?)".

[Ishtar made answer, (thus) speaking [and said unto] Anu, her father:
"[Corn for mankind] have I hoarded, have grown [for the cattle the fodder],
[If seven] years of (leer) husks [must needs follow after his onslaught (?)]
[I will for man] gather [corn and increase for the cattle] the fodder".

(Perhaps a small gap)

(About seven lines are so badly mutilated that little can be gleaned from them except that the fight with the Heavenly Bull is about to take place in Erech. After these [100 men] descend [upon the Bull], but with his (fiery) breath [he annihilates them]. Then come 200 with the same result, and then 300 more, again to be overcome).

Enkidu girded (?) his middle; (and straightway) Enkidu, leaping,
Seized on the Heavenly Bull by [his] horns, and (headlong) before him
Cast down the Heavenly Bull his full length, …
(Aye), by the thick of his tail.

(Gap of thirteen mutilated lines)

Chased him did Enkidu, … the Heavenly Bull …
Seized him and by [the thick] of his tail …
(Gap of about fourteen mutilated lines in which the Bull is slain.)
(So), what time they the Bull of the Heavens had kill'd, its heart they r
emovéd,
Unto the Sun-god they offer'd in sacrifice; when the libation
Unto the Sun they had voided, they sate them down, the two brothers.

* * *

The Frenzy of Ishtar

(Then) mounted Ishtar (the crest of) the ramparts of Erech, the high-wall'd,
(So) to the roof-top ascended, (and there) gave voice to her wailing;
"Woe unto Gilgamesh – he who by killing the Bull of the Heavens,
Made me lament". When Enkidu heard this, the shrieking of Ishtar,
Wrenching the member from out of the Bull, he toss'd (it) before her;
"If I could only have reach'd thee, i'faith, I'd ha' served thee the same way,
I'd ha' let dangle his guts on thy flanks (as a girdle about thee)".
Ishtar assembled the girl-devotees, the hetaerae and harlots,
Over the member (torn out) from the Bull she led the lamenting.

The Triumph of Gilgamesh

Gilgamesh call'd to the masters of craft, the artists, (yea), all of them,
That at the size of its horns (all) the guilds of the crafts speak their praises
Each had of azure in weight thirty minas to be as their setting,
Two fingers their….
Both of them held six measures of oil; to his god Lugal-banda
He for (his) unguent devoting, brought in, and (thus) let them hang (there),
(There) in the shrine of his forbears.
(And now) in the River Euphrates
Washing their hands, they start (on their progress) and come (to the city);

(Now) are they striding the highway of Erech, the heroes of Erech
Thronging (about them) to see them. (Then) Gilgamesh utter'd a riddle
Unto the notables (?):
Who, pr'ythee, is most splendid of heroes,
Who, pr'ythee, is most famous of giants?
Gilgamesh – he is most splendid of heroes,
[Enkidu – he is most] famous of giants.

(Three mutilated lines follow)

* * *

So in his palace did Gilgamesh hold high revel: (thereafter),
(While all) the heroes asleep, on their nightly couches were lying
Enkidu, too, was asleep, and a vision beheld, and (so) coming
Enkidu (now) his dream to reveal: (thus) spake he unto his comrade.

The Seventh Tablet
The Death of Enkidu

Column I
Enkidu's Dream

"**WHY, O MY FRIEND**, do the great gods (now) take counsel together?"

(The remainder of the Column is lost in the Assyrian, but it can be partially supplied from the Hittite Version: "... Then came the day ... [Enkidu] answered Gilgamesh: '[Gilgamesh, hear the] dream which I [saw] in the night: [Now Enlil], Ea, and the Sun-god of heaven ...[the Sun-god (?)] Enlil spake in return: "[These who the heavenly] Bull have kill'd [and Humbaba have smitten]: ... which help'd at the cedar . . . [Enlil hath said (?)] 'Enkidu shall die: [but Gilgamesh] shall not die'." Then answer'd Enlil boldly '[O Sun-god], at thy behest did they slay the Heavenly Bull and Humbaba. But now shall Enkidu die'. But Enlil turn'd angrily to the Sun-god: 'What dost thou them as befitting . . .? With his comrade thou settest out daily. '"But Enkidu laid himself down to rest before Gilgamesh, and by the dam . . . him the ditch: 'My brother, of (great) worth is my [dream]'." (It breaks off after a few mutilated lines more).

(Column II entirely lost. From the Hittite it is clear that Enkidu has dreamt that the gods have taken counsel together, that Enkidu is to die, but Gilgamesh remain alive. It would appear from the succeeding material that Enkidu, stricken presumably by fever, attributes all his misfortunes to the hetaera whom he loads with curses. The first part of the next fragment begins "destroy his power, weaken his strength", probably referring to Enkidu. Then says Enkidu, after three broken lines: "... the hetaera ... who has brought (?) a curse, 'O hetaera, I will decree (thy) [fate(?)] for thee – thy woes(?)] . . . shall never end for all eternity. [Come], I will curse thee with a bitter curse, ... with desolation shall its curse come on thee: [may there never be] satisfaction of thy desire' – and then follow the broken ends of six lines and then – "'[May ...] fall on thy house, may the

... of the street be thy dwelling, [may the shade of the wall be thy] abode, ... for thy feet, [may scorching heat and thirsty smite thy strength'" The rest of the curse is badly broken, but it is exceeding probable that the following are the fragments which should be assigned here).

(*The End of Enkidu's curse on the Hetaera*).

"Of want ... since me it is that ... hath ...
And me the fever [hath laid] on my back".

* * *

The Answer of Shamash

Heard him the Sun-god, and open'd his mouth, and from out of the heavens
(Straightway) he call'd him: "O Enkidu, why dost thou curse the hetaera?

She 'twas who made thee eat bread, for divinity proper: (aye), wine (too),
She made thee drink, ('twas) for royalty proper: a generous mantle
Put on thee, (aye), and for comrade did give to thee Gilgamesh splendid.
Now on a couch of great size will he, (thy) friend (and) thy brother
Gilgamesh, grant thee to lie, on a handsome couch will he grant thee
Rest, and to sit on a throne of great ease, a throne at (his) left hand,
So that the princes of Hades may kiss thy feet (in their homage);
He, too, will make (all) the people of Erech lament in thy (honour),
Making them mourn thee, (and) damsels (and) heroes constrain to thy service,
[While he himself for thy sake will cause his body to carry
Stains, [(and) will put on] the skin of a lion, and range o'er the desert".

* * *

Enkidu [(then) giving ear] to the words of the valiant Shamash
Speaking ... his wrath was appeased.

(*One or two lines missing*)

Column IV
Enkidu, Relenting, Regrets His Curse, and Blesses the Hetaera

" ... may ... restore to thy place!
[(So, too), may monarchs and princes] and chiefs be with love [for thee] smitten;
[None smite (?)] his breech [in disgust (?); against thee; and for thee may
the hero]
Comb out his locks; ... who would embrace [thee],
Let him his girdle unloose . . . and thy [bed] be azure and golden;
May ... entreat thee kindly (?), ... are heap'd his *ishshikku*

May the gods make thee enter ...
[Mayst thou] be left as the mother of seven brides ..".

Enkidu, Sorrowful at His Approaching End, Sleeps Alone and Dreams

[Enkidu] ... woe in his belly ... sleeping alone,
[Came] in the night [to discover] his heaviness unto his comrade:
"[Friend], (O) a dream I have seen in my nighttime: the firmament [roaring],
Echo'd the earth, and I [by myself was standing(?) ...
[When perceived I a man (?)], (all) dark was his face, [and] was liken 'd
[Unto] ... his face, ... [and] his nails like claws of a lion.
Me did he overcome ... climbing up ... press'd me down,
Upon me ... my (?) body ...

(Here follows a gap of perhaps three lines, until what is still presumably the dream is again taken up by the other half of the Column at l. 31 (?) with a description of the Underworld which is being shewn to Enkidu in premonition of his death).

. . . . like birds my hands: (and) he seized (?) me,
Me did he lead to the Dwelling of Darkness, the home of Irkalla,
Unto the Dwelling from which he who entereth cometh forth never!
(Aye), by the road on the passage whereof there can be no returning,
Unto the Dwelling whose tenants are (ever) bereft of the daylight,
Where for their food is the dust, and the mud is their sustenance: bird-like
Wear they a garment of feathers: and, sitting (there) in the darkness,
Never the light will they see. On the Gate ... when I enter'd
On the house (?) ... was humbled the crown,
For ... those who (wore) crowns, who of old ruled over the country,
... of Anu and Enlil 'twas they set the bakemeats,
Set . . . ., cool was the water they served from the skins. When I enter'd
Into (this) House of the Dust, were High Priest and acolyte sitting,
Seer and magician, the priest who the Sea of the great gods anointed,
(Here) sat Etana, Sumuqan; the Queen of the Underworld (also),
Ereshkigal, in whose presence doth bow the Recorder of Hades,
[Belit]-seri, and readeth before her; [she lifted] her head (and) beheld me,
... and took this ...

(The text here breaks off)

The Eighth Tablet
Of the Mourning of Gilgamesh, and What Came of It

(**THE FIRST COLUMN** *is badly mutilated, and all we can glean from it is that "as soon as something of morning has dawned", Gilgamesh addressing Enkidu, compares him to a gazelle, and promises to glorify him. Then follows apparently a recital by Gilgamesh of their exploits together, "mountains [we ascended, we reach'd] the Forest of Cedars, [travelling]* *night and day . . . [with wild beasts (?)] drawing nigh after us". Enkidu is lying dying or dead, and Column II begins with Gilgamesh keening over his dead friend before the Elders of Erech*):

"Unto me hearken, O Elders, to me, aye, me [shall ye listen],
'Tis that I weep for my [comrade] Enkidu, bitterly crying
Like to a wailing woman: my grip is [slack'd] on the curtleaxe
(Slung at) my thigh, (and) the brand at my belt from my sight [is removed].
(Aye, and) my festal attire [lends nought of its aid for] my pleasure,
Me, me hath [sorrow] assailed, and [cast] me [down in affliction].

* * *

Comrade (and) henchman, who chased the wild ass, the pard of the desert,
Comrade (and) henchman, who chased the wild ass, the pard of the desert,
Enkidu – we who all [haps] overcame, ascending [the mountains].
Captured the Heavenly Bull, and [destroy'd (him)]: we o'erthrew Humbaba,
He who [abode] in the Forest [of Cedars – O, what is this slumber
Now hath o'ercome [thee], (for now) art thou dark, nor art able to hear [me]?"
Natheless he raised not [his eyes, and] his heart, (when Gilgamesh) felt (it),
Made no beat.
Then he veil'd (his) friend like a bride ...
Lifted his voice like a lion ...
[Roar'd] like a lioness robb'd of [her] whelps. In front of his [comrade]
Paced he backwards and forwards, tearing and casting his ringlets(?),
Plucking and casting away (all) the grace of his ...

* * *

Then when something of morning had dawn'd, did Gilgamesh ...

(*Column II here breaks off. Column III begins with Gilgamesh still mourning, telling his dead friend all he will do for him in the words of Shamash in the preceding tablet, so that we may supply the last two (?) lines of Column II as follow*):

Column II
The Lament of Gilgamesh

"[O, on a couch of great size will I, thy friend and thy brother,

Column III

[Gilgamesh, grant thee to lie], on [a handsome] couch [will I grant thee
Rest, and] to sit on [a throne of great size, a throne at (my) left hand],
So that the princes of Hades [may kiss thy feet (in their homage)];
I, too, will make (all) [the people of Erech] lament in thy (honour),
[Making them mourn thee], (and) damsels (and) heroes [constrain to thy service],

While I myself for thy sake [will cause my body to carry]
[Stains], (and) will put on the skin of a [lion, and range o'er the desert]".

* * *

Then when something of morning had dawn'd did [Gilgamesh] ...
Loosing his girdle ...

(Column IV has only five fragmentary lines at the end, mentioning "to my friend", "thy sword", "likeness", and "to the god Bibbu", i.e., a planet or Mercury. Column V has only a bare dozen fragmentary lines at the end):

Column V

"... Judge of the Anunnaki ..."
(Then), when Gilgamesh heard this, he form'd of the slaying a concept.

* * *

(Then), with the dawn of the morning did Gilgamesh fashion a ...
Brought out also a mighty platter of wood from the highlands.
Fill'd he with honey a bowl of (bright) ruby, a bowl (too) of azure,
Fill'd he with cream; (and) adorn'd he the ..., and Shamash instructed ...

(One line lost at end of Column. Column VI is all lost)

The Ninth Tablet
Gilgamesh in Terror of Death
Seeks Eternal Life

Column I
Gilgamesh Determines to
Seek Eternal Life

GILGAMESH BITTERLY WEPT for his comrade, (for) Enkidu, ranging
Over the desert: "I, too – shall I not die like Enkidu also?
Sorrow hath enter'd my heart; I fear death as I range o'er the desert,
I will get hence on the road to the presence of Uta-Napishtim,

– Offspring of Ubara-Tutu is he – and with speed will I travel.
(If) 'tis in darkness that I shall arrive at the Gates of the Mountains,
Meeting with lions, then terror fall on me, I'll lift my head (skywards),
Offer my prayer to the Moon-god, (or else) to ... the gods let my orison
Come ... 'O deliver me!'" ... He slept ... (and) a dream ...
[Saw he] ... which were rejoicing in life,
Poised he [his] axe ... in his hand, (and) drew [his glaive from] his baldric,

Lance-like leapt he amongst them … smiting, … (and) crushing.
(*The rest of the Column is mutilated*)

Column II
The Hero Reaches the Mountains of Mashu

Mashu the name of the hills; as he reach'd the Mountains of Mashu,
Where ev'ry day they keep watch o'er [the Sun-god's] rising [and setting],
Unto the Zenith of Heaven [uprear'd are] their summits, (and) downwards
(Deep) unto Hell reach their breasts: (and there) at their portals stand sentry
Scorpion-men, awful in terror, their (very) glance Death: (and) tremendous,
Shaking the hills, their magnificence; they are the Wardens of Shamash,
Both at his rising and setting. (No sooner) did Gilgamesh see them"
(Than) from alarm and dismay was his countenance stricken with pallor,
Senseless, he grovell'd before them.
(Then) unto his wife spake the Scorpion:
"Lo, he that cometh to us – 'tis the flesh of the gods is his body".
(Then) to the Scorpion-man answered his wife: "Two parts of him god-(like),
(Only) a third of him human".

(*Eight broken lines remain, in which the Scorpion-man addresses presumably Gilgamesh, asking him [why he has goner a far journey, and telling him how hard the traverse is. Column III begins with the third line in which Gilgamesh is evidently telling the Scorpion-man that he proposes to cask(?)] Uta-Napishtim about death and life. But the Scorpion-man says that [the journey has never before been made, that none [has crossed] the mountains. The traverse is by the Road of the Sun by a journey of twenty-four hours, beginning with deep darkness. The last half of this Column and the first half of Column IV are lost, but it would appear that the Scorpion-man describes the journey hour by hour, and that Gilgamesh accepts the trial of his strength "[even though it be] in pain …, [though my face be weather]d] with cold [and heat] (and) in grief [I go] …" Then the Scorpion-man, with a final word about the mountains of Mashu, farewells him, wishing him success.*

"[(Then) when] Gilgamesh [heard this], [he set off] at the word of the Scorpion-man, taking] the Road of the Sun . . ". The first two hours are in deep darkness, without light, which did not allow [him to see ... behind him] ..". Each succeeding period of two hours is the same until the eighth is reached and passed, and by the ninth he apparently comes to the first glimmer of light. Finally, with the twelfth double hour, he reaches the full blaze of the sun, and there he beholds the Tree of the Gods, the description of which is given in the only four complete lines, 48-51, of Column V. It is conceivable that this is the Vine, the Tree of Life, whence Siduri, the Maker of Wine, plucks the fruit for her trade).

Bearing its fruit (all) ruby, and hung about with (its) tendrils.
Fair for beholding, and azure the boskage it bore; (aye), 'twas bearing
Fruits (all) desirable unto the eye.

(*Column VI in the Assyrian is nearly all lost, and it is uncertain what part the Tree plays: but at this point a third Old Babylonian tablet helps us out. At this point, according to this early version the Sun-god takes pity on the hero*).

"[He of the wild things hath dresséd] their pelts and the flesh of them eateth.
Gilgamesh, [never] a crossing [shall be (?)] where none hath been ever,
(No), [so long] as the gale driveth water".
Shamash was touch'd, that he summon'd him, (thus) unto Gilgamesh speaking:
"Gilgamesh, why dost thou run, (forasmuch as) the life which thou sleekest
Thou shalt not find?" (Whereat) Gilgamesh answer'd the warrior Shamash:
"Shall I, after I roam up and down o'er the waste as a wand'rer,
Lay my head in the bowels of earth, and throughout the years slumber
Ever and aye? Let mine eyes see the Sun and be sated with brightness,
(Yea, for) the darkness is (banish'd) afar, if wide be the brightness.
When will the man who is dead (ever) look on the light of the Sunshine?"

(*With this ends all our connected text of Column VI, the Assyrian Version ending with about a dozen mutilated lines containing a mention of numerous minerals and stones, and evidently Gilgamesh has now come to the girl Siduri the sabitu, which last word is generally taken to mean a provider of strong waters*).

The Tenth Tablet
How Gilgamesh Reached Uta-Napishtim

Column I
Gilgamesh Meets Siduri

DWELT SIDURI, the maker of wine …
Wine(?) was her trade, her trade was …
Cover'd she was with a veil and …
Gilgamesh wander'd [towards her] …
Pelts was he wearing …
Flesh of the gods in [his body] possessing, but woe in [his belly],
(Aye), and his countenance like to a (man) who hath gone a far journey.
Look'd in the distance the maker of wine, (and) a word in her bosom
Quoth she, in thought with herself: "This is one who would ravish (?) [a woman],
Whither doth he advance in … ?" As soon as the Wine-maker saw him,
Barr'd she [her postern], barr'd she her inner door, barr'd she [her chamber(?)].
Straightway did Gilgamesh, too, in his turn catch the sound [of her shutting(?)],
Lifted his chin, and so did he let [his attention fall on her].

* * *

Unto her (therefore) did Gilgamesh speak, to the Wine-maker saying]:
"Winemaker, what didst thou see, that [thy postern (now)] thou hast barréd,
Barréd thine inner door, [barréd thy chamber(?)]? O, I'll smite [thy] portal,
[Breaking the bolt] …

(*About nine lines mutilated, after which it is possible to restore l.* 32 – *Column II*, 8).

[Unto him (answer 'd) the Winemaker, speaking to Gilgamesh, (saying):
"Why is thy vigour (so) wasted, (or why) is thy countenance sunken,
(Why) hath thy spirit a sorrow (?), (or why) hath thy cheerfulness surcease?
(O, but) there's woe in thy belly! Like one who hath gone a far journey
(So) is thy face – (O,) with cold and with heat is thy countenance weather'd,
… that thou shouldst range over the desert".
Gilgamesh unto her (answer'd and) spake to the Winemaker, saying:
"Winemaker, 'tis not my vigour is wasted, nor countenance sunken,
Nor hath my spirit a sorrow (?), (forsooth), nor my cheerfulness surcease,

No, 'tis not woe in my belly: nor doth my visage resemble
One who hath gone a far journey – nor is my countenance weather'd
Either by cold or by heat … that (thus) I range over the desert.
Comrade (and) henchman, who chased the wild ass, the pard of the desert,
Comrade (and) henchman, who chased the wild ass, the pard of the desert,
Enkidu – we who all haps overcame, ascending the mountains,
Captured the Heavenly Bull, and destroy'd him]: we [o'erthrew Humbaba,
He who abode in the Forest of Cedars; we slaughter'd the lions

Column II

There in the Gates (?) of the mountains (?); with me enduring all hardships,
Enkidu, (he was) my comrade – the lions we slaughter'd (together),
(Aye), enduring all hardships – and him his fate hath o'ertaken.
(So) did I mourn him six days, (yea), a se'nnight, until unto burial
I could consign (?) him … (then) did I fear …
Death did I dread, that I range o'er the desert]: the hap of my comrade
[Lay on me heavy(?) – O 'tis a long road that I range o'er] the desert!
Enkidu, (yea), [of my comrade the hap lay heavy (?) upon me] –
['Tis a long road] that I range o'er the desert – O, how to be silent],
(Aye, or) how to give voice? [(For) the comrade I ha' (so) lovéd]
Like to the dust [hath become]; O Enkidu, (he was) my comrade,
He whom I loved hath become alike the dust] – [I,] shall I not, also,
Lay me down [like him], throughout all eternity [never returning]?"

* * *

(Here may be interpolated, for convenience, the Old Babylonian Version of this episode in the Berlin tablet of 2000 BCE. *Column II, 1; III, 14)*:

Column II

"He who enduréd all hardships with me, whom I lovéd dearly,
Enkidu, – he who enduréd all hardships with me (is now perish'd),
Gone to the common lot of mankind! (And) I have bewail'd him
Day and night long: (and) unto the tomb I have not consign'd him.
(O but) my friend cometh not (?) to my call – six days, (yea), a se'nnight

He like a worm hath lain on his face – (and) I for this reason
Find no life, (but must needs) roam the desert like to a hunter,
(Wherefore), O Winemaker, now that (at last) I look on thy visage,
Death which I dread I will see not!"

The Philosophy of the Winemaker
The Winemaker Gilgamesh answer'd:

Column III

"Gilgamesh, why runnest thou, (inasmuch as) the life which thou seekest,
Thou canst not find? (For) the gods, in their (first) creation of mortals,
Death allotted to man, (but) life they retain'd in their keeping.
Gilgamesh, full be thy belly,
Each day and night be thou merry, (and) daily keep holiday revel,
Each day and night do thou dance and rejoice; (and) fresh be thy raiment,
(Aye), let thy head be clean washen, (and) bathe thyself in the water,
Cherish the little one holding thy hand; be thy spouse in thy bosom
Happy – (for) this is the dower [of man] …

(Here the Old Babylonian Version breaks off and we must return to the Assyrian).

Gilgamesh, Dissatisfied with a Winemaker's Philosophy, Would Seek Further Afield

[Gilgamesh] (thus) continued his speech to the Winemaker, (saying),
"[Pr'ythee, then], Winemaker, which is the way unto Uta-Napishtim?
[What (is)] its token, I pr'ythee, vouchsafe me, vouchsafe me its token.
If it be possible (even) the Ocean (itself) will I traverse,
(But) if it should be impossible, (then) will I range o'er the desert".

* * *

The Winemaker, in Accordance with Tradition, Attempts to Dissuade Him

(Thus) did the Wine-maker answer to him, unto Gilgamesh (saying),
"There hath been never a crossing, O Gilgamesh: never aforetime
Anyone, coming thus far, hath been able to traverse the Ocean:
Warrior Shamash doth cross it, 'tis true, but who besides Shamash
Maketh the traverse? (Yea), rough is the ferry, (and) rougher its passage,
(Aye), too, 'tis deep are the Waters of Death, which bar its approaches.
Gilgamesh, if perchance thou succeed in traversing the Ocean,
What wilt thou do, when unto the Waters of Death thou arrivest?
Gilgamesh, there is Ur-Shanabi, boatman to Uta-Napishtim,
He with whom sails (?) are, the *urnu* of which in the forest he plucketh,
(Now) let him look on thy presence, (and) [if it be] possible with him
Cross – (but) if it be not, (then) do thou retrace thy steps (homewards)".

Gilgamesh, hearing this, [taketh] (his) axe in his [hand],
awhile he draweth Glaive from his baldric (?)].

(The remainder of this Column in the Assyrian Version is so much mutilated that little can be made out, but what is obviously essential is that Gilgamesh meets Ur-Shanabi, but destroys the sails (?) of the boat for some reason. Before going on with the restoration of the Assyrian Version, we can interpolate Column IV from the Old Babylonian Version of the Berlin Tablet)

(Then) did Ur-Shanabi speak to him (yea), unto Gilgamesh, (saying):
"Tell to me what is thy name, (for) I am Ur-Shanabi, (henchman),
(Aye), of far Uta-Napishtim". To him did Gilgamesh answer:
"Gilgamesh, (that) is my name, come hither from Erech(?), E-Anni (?),
(One) who hath traversed the Mountains, a wearisome journey of Sunrise,
Now that I look on thy face, Ur-Shanabi – Uta-Napishtim
Let me see also – the Distant one!" Him did Ur-Shanabi [answer],
Gilgamesh: ..."

(In the Assyrian Version Ur-Shanabi presently addresses Gilgamesh in exactly the same words as Siduri, the Winemaker, with the same astonishment at his weather-beaten appearance):

Column III

(Thus) did Ur-Shanabi speak to him, (yea), unto Gilgamesh, (saying)
"Why is thy vigour all wasted ..."

(It continues thus, to be supplied for ll. 2-31 *from Columns I,* 33-*II,* 14 *with due bracketing for the last words, and then the text goes on)*:

Gilgamesh (thus) continued his speech to Ur-Shanabi, (saying)
"Pr'ythee, Ur-Shanabi, which is [the way unto Uta-Napishtim?
What is its token, I pr'ythee, vouchsafe me, vouchsafe me nits token].
If it be possible (even) the Ocean (itself) will I traverse,
But if it should be impossible, [(then) will I range o'er the desert]".

* * *

(Thus) did Ur-Shanabi speak to him, (yea), unto Gilgamesh, (saying):
"Gilgamesh, 'tis thine own hand hath hinder'd [thy crossing the Ocean],
Thou hast destroyéd the sails(?), (and) hast piercéd (?) the ...
(Now) destroy'd are the sails(?), and the *urnu* not ...

Gilgamesh, take thee thy axe in [thy] hand; O, descend to the forest,
[Fashion thee] poles each of five gar in length; make (knops of) bitumen,
Sockets, (too), add (to them): bring [them me]". (Thereat), when Gilgamesh [heard this],
Took he the axe in his hand, (and) [the glaive] drew forth [from his baldric],
Went to the forest, and poles each of five gar in length [did he fashion],

(Knops of) bitumen he made, and he added (their) sockets: and brought them ...,
Gilgamesh (then), and Ur-Shanabi fared them forth [in their vessel],
Launch'd they the boat on the billow, and they themselves [in her embarking].
After the course of a month and a half he saw on the third day
How that Ur-Shanabi (now) at the Waters of Death had arrivéd.

Column IV

(Thus) did Ur-Shanabi [answer] him, [(yea), unto Gilgamesh, (saying)]:
"Gilgamesh, take the ... away ...
Let not the Waters of Death touch thy hand....
Gilgamesh, take thou a second, a third and a fourth pole (for thrusting),
Gilgamesh, take thou a fifth, (and) a sixth and a seventh (for thrusting),
Gilgamesh, take thou an eighth, (and) a ninth and a tenth pole (for thrusting),
Gilgamesh, take an eleventh, a twelfth pole!" He ceased from (his) poling,
(Aye) with twice-sixty (thrusts); (then) ungirded his loins....
Gilgamesh.... (?), and set up the mast in its socket.

He Reaches Uta-Napishtim

Uta-Napishtim look'd into the distance and, inwardly musing,
Said to himself: "(Now), why are [the sails(?)] of the vessel destroyéd,
Aye, and one who is not of my ... (?) doth ride on the vessel?
(This) is no mortal who cometh: nor....
I look, but (this) is no [mortal]....
I look, but.... I look but....

(Remainder of Column lost, but about l. 42 it becomes apparent that Uta-Napishtim is asking Gilgamesh in exactly the same words as Siduri, the Winemaker, and Ur-Shanabi "Why is thy vigour (all) wasted?" and so on, down to Column V, l. 22 "[I], shall I not also lay me down like him, throughout all eternity never returning?"):

Gilgamesh (thus) continued his speech unto Uta-Napishtim,
"Then [I bethought me], I'll get hence and see what far Uta-Napishtim

Saith (on the matter). (And so), again (?) I came through all countries,
Travell'd o'er difficult mountains, (aye), [and] all seas have I traversed,
Nor hath (ever) my face had its fill of gentle sleep (?): (but) with hardship
Have I exhausted myself, (and) my flesh have I laden with sorrow.
Ere I had come to the [House(?)] of the Wine-Maker, spent were my garments,
... Owl, bat, lion, pard, wild cat, deer, ibex and....
[Flesh] of them (all) have I eaten, (and eke) their pelts have I dress'd (?) [me]".

(The remainder of the Column is mutilated: there is some mention of "let them bolt her gate ...; with pitch and bitumen...". in l. 33, and then nothing which gives connected sense until Column VI, ll. 26-39):

Column VI

"Shall we forever build house(s), for ever set signet (to contract),
Brothers continue to share, or among [foes (?)] always be hatred?
(Or) will forever the stream (that hath risen) in spate bring a torrent,
Kulilu-bird [to] *Kirippu*-bird ... ?
Face which doth look on the sunlight . . . presently (?) shall not be . . .
Sleeping and dead [are]r alike, from Death they mark no distinction
Servant and master, when once thy have reach'd [their full span allotted],
Then do the Anunnaki, great gods, . . .
Mammetum, Maker of Destiny with them, doth destiny settle,
Death, (aye), and Life they determine; of Death is the day not revealéd".

The Eleventh Tablet
The Flood

Column I
The Cause of the Flood

GILGAMESH UNTO HIM spake, to Uta-Napishtim the Distant:
"Uta-Napishtim, upon thee I gaze, (yet) in no wise thy presence
Strange is, (for) thou art like me, and in no wise different art thou;
Thou art like me; (yea) a stomach for fighting doth make thee consummate,
[Aye, and to rest (?)] on thy back thou dost lie. [O tell me (?)], how couldst thou
Stand in th' Assemblage of Gods to petition for life (everlasting)?"

Uta-Napishtim (addressing him thus) unto Gilgamesh answer'd:
"Gilgamesh, I unto thee will discover the (whole) hidden story,
Aye, and the rede of the Gods will I tell thee.
The City Shurippak –
(O 'tis) a city thou knowest! – is set [on the marge] of Euphrates,
Old is this city, with gods in its midst. (Now), the great gods a deluge
Purposed to bring: . . . there was Anu, their sire; their adviser
Warrior Enlil; Ninurta, their herald; their leader(?) Ennugi;
Nin-igi-azag – 'tis Ea – , (albeit) conspirator with them,
Unto a reed-hut their counsel betray'd he: "O Reed-hut, O Reed-hut!
Wall, wall! Hearken, O Reed-hut, consider, O Wall! O thou Mortal,
Thou of Shurippak, thou scion of Ubara-Tutu, a dwelling
Pull down, (and) fashion a vessel (therewith); abandon possessions,
Life do thou seek, (and) thy hoard disregard, and save life; every creature
Make to embark in the vessel. The vessel, which thou art to fashion,
Apt be its measure; its beam and its length be in due correspondence,
(Then) [on] the deep do thou launch it". And I – sooth, I apprehending,
(This wise) to Ea, my lord, did I speak: '[See], Lord, what thou sayest
Thus, do I honour, I'll do – (but) to city, to people and elders
Am I, forsooth, to explain?' (Then) Ea made answer in speaking,
Saying to me – me, his henchman! – 'Thou mortal, shalt speak to them this wise:

"'Tis me alone (?) whom Enlil so hateth that I in your city
No (more) may dwell, nor turn my face unto the land which is Enlil's.
[I will go] down to the Deep, (there) dwelling with Ea, my [liege] lord,
(Wherefore) [on] you will he shower down plenty, yea, fowl [in great number(?)],
Booty of fish … [and big] the harvest.
… causing a plentiful rainfall (?) to come down upon you".

* * *

[(Then) when something] of morning had dawn'd….

(Five lines mutilated)

Pitch did the children provide, (while) the strong brought [all] that was needful.
(Then) on the fifth day (after) I laid out the shape (of my vessel),
Ten *gar* each was the height of her sides, in accord with her planning(?),
Ten *gar* to match was the size of her deck (?), and the shape of the forepart (?)

Did I lay down, (and) the same did I fashion; (aye), six times cross-pinn'd her,
Sevenfold did I divide her …, divided her inwards
Ninefold: hammer'd the caulking within her, (and) found me a quant-pole,
(All) that was needful I added; the hull with six *shar* of bitumen
Smear'd I, (and) three *shar* of pitch [did I smear] on the inside; some people,
Bearing a vessel of grease, three *shar* of it brought (me); (and) one *shar*
(Out of this) grease did I leave, which the tackling (?) consumed; (and) the
boatman
Two *shar* of grease stow'd away; (yea), beeves for the … I slaughter'd,
Each day lambs did I slay: mead, beer, oil, wine, too, the workmen
[Drank] as though they were water, and made a great feast like the New Year,

(Five mutilated lines "I added salve for the hand(s)", "the vessel was finish'd . . . Shamash the great". "was difficult", "…? I caused to bring above and below", "two-thirds of it"):

* * *

[All I possess'd I] laded aboard her; the silver I laded
All I possess'd; gold, all I possess'd I laded aboard her,
All I possess'd of the seed of all living [I laded aboard] her.
Into the ship I embark'd all my kindred and family (with me),
Cattle (and) beasts of the field (and) all handicraftsmen embarking.
(Then) decreed Shamash the hour: " … (?)
Shall in the night let a plentiful rainfall(?) pour down….
(Then) do thou enter the vessel, and (straightway) shut down thy hatchway".
Came (then) that hour (appointed), …(?)
Did in the night let a plentiful rainfall(?) pour down…. (?)
View'd I the aspect of day: to look on the day bore a horror,
(Wherefore) I enter'd the vessel, and (straightway) shut down my hatchway,

(So, too) to shut down the vessel to Puzur-Amurri (?), the boatman,
Did I deliver the poop (of the ship), besides its equipment.

* * *

(Then), when something of dawn had appear'd, from out the horizon
Rose a cloud darkling; (lo), Adad (the storm-god) was rumbling within it,
Nabu and Sharru were leading the vanguard, and coming as heralds
Over the hills and the levels: (then) Irragal wrench'd out the bollards;
Havoc Ninurta let loose as he came, th' Anunnaki their torches
Brandish'd, and shrivell'd the land with their flames; desolation from Adad
Stretch'd to (high) Heaven, (and) all that was bright was turn'd into darkness.

(Four lines mutilated "the land like ..", "for one day the st[orm] ..", "fiercely blew...". "like a battle ...").

Nor could a brother distinguish his brother; from heaven were mortals
Not to be spied. O, were stricken with terror the gods at the Deluge,
Fleeing, they rose to the Heaven of Anu, and crouch'd in the outskirts,
Cow'ring like curs were the gods (while) like to a woman in travail
Ishtar did cry, she shrieking aloud, (e'en) the sweet-spoken Lady
(She of the gods): 'May that day turn to dust, because I spake evil
(There) in th' Assemblage of Gods! O, how could I utter (such) evil
(There) in the Assemblage of Gods, (so) to blot out my people, ordaining
Havoc! Sooth, then, am I to give birth, unto (these) mine own people
Only to glut (with their bodies) the Sea as though they were fish-spawn?'
Gods – Anunnaki – wept with her, the gods were sitting (all) humbled,
(Aye), in (their) weeping, (and) closed were their lips amid(?)] the Assemblage.
Six days, a se'nnight the hurricane, deluge, (and) tempest continued
Sweeping the land: when the seventh day came, were quellèd the warfare,
Tempest (and) deluge which like to an army embattail'd were fighting.
Lull'd was the sea, (all) spent was the gale, assuaged was the deluge,
(So) did I look on the day; (lo), sound was (all) still'd; and all human
Back to (its) clay was return'd, and fen was level with roof-tree.
(Then) I open'd a hatchway, and down on my cheek stream'd the sunlight,
Bowing myself, I sat weeping, my tears o'er my cheek(s) overflowing,
Into the distance I gazed, to the furthest bounds of the Ocean,
Land was uprear'd at twelve (points), and the Ark on the Mountain of Nisir
Grounded; the Mountain of Nisir held fast, nor gave lease to her shifting.
One day, (nay,) two, did Nisir hold fast, nor give lease to her shifting.
Three days, (nay), four, did Nisir hold fast, nor give lease to her shifting,
Five days, (nay,) six, did Nisir hold fast, nor give lease to her shifting.
(Then), when the seventh day dawn'd, I put forth a dove, and released (her),
(But) to and fro went the dove, and return'd (for) a resting-place was not.
(Then) I a swallow put forth and released; to and fro went the swallow,
She (too) return'd, (for) a resting-place was not; I put forth a raven,
Her, (too,) releasing; the raven went, too, and th' abating of waters

Saw; and she ate as she waded (and) splash'd, (unto me) not returning.
Unto the four winds (of heaven) I freed (all the beasts), and an off'ring
Sacrificed, and a libation I pour'd on the peak of the mountain,
Twice seven flagons devoting, (and) sweet cane, (and) cedar and myrtle,

Heap'd up beneath them; the gods smelt the savour, the gods the sweet savour
Smelt; (aye,) the gods did assemble like flies o'er him making the off'ring.
Then, on arriving, the Queen (of the gods) the magnificent jewels
Lifted on high, which Anu had made in accord with her wishes;
'O ye Gods! I will (rather) forget (this) my necklet of sapphires,
Than not maintain these days in remembrance, nor ever forget them.
(So), though (the rest of) the gods may present themselves at the off'ring,
Enlil (alone of the gods) may (himself) not come to the off'ring,
Because he, unreasoning, brought on a deluge, and therefore my people
Unto destruction consign'd'.

Then Enlil, on his arrival,
Spied out the vessel, and (straightway) did Enlil burst into anger,
Swollen with wrath 'gainst the gods, the Igigi: 'Hath any of mortals
'Scaped? Sooth, never a man could have lived through (the welter of) ruin'.
(Then) did Ninurta make answer and speak unto warrior Enlil,
Saying: 'O, who can there be to devise such a plan, except Ea?
Surely, 'tis Ea is privy to ev'ry design'. Whereat Ea
Answer'd and spake unto Enlil, the warrior, saying: 'O chieftain
Thou of the gods, thou warrior! How, forsooth, how (all) uncounsell'd
Couldst thou a deluge bring on? (Aye,) visit his sin on the sinner
Visit his guilt on the guilty, (but) O, have mercy, that (thereby)
He shall not be cut off; be clement, that he may not [perish].
O, instead of thy making a flood, let a lion come, man to diminish;
O, instead of thy making a flood, let a jackal come, man to diminish;
O, instead of thy making a flood, let a famine occur, that the country
May be [devour'd(?)]; instead of thy making a flood, let the Plague-god
Come and the people [o'erwhelm];

Sooth, indeed 'twas not I of the Great Gods the secret revealéd,
(But) to th' Abounding in Wisdom vouchsafed I a dream, and (in this wise)
He of the gods heard the secret. Deliberate, now, on his counsel'.
(Then) to the Ark came up Enlil; my hand did he grasp, and uplifted
Me, even me, and my wife, too, he raised, and, bent-kneed beside me,
Made her to kneel; our foreheads he touch'd as he stood there between us,
Blessing us; 'Uta-Napishtim hath hitherto only been mortal,
Now, indeed, Uta-Napishtim and (also) his wife shall be equal
Like to us gods; in the distance afar at the mouth of the rivers
Uta-Napishtim shall dwell'. (So) they took me and (there) in the distance

Caused me to dwell at the mouth of the rivers.

But thee, as for thee, pray,
Who will assemble the gods for thy (need), that the life which thou sleekest
Thou mayst discover? Come, fall not asleep for six days, aye, a se'nnight!"

But Gilgamesh is Too Mortal to Resist Even Sleep

(Then), while he sat on his haunches a sleep like a breeze breathed upon him.
Spake to her, Uta-Napishtim, yea, unto his wife: "O, behold him,
E'en the strong fellow who asketh for life, (how) hath breathéd upon him
Sleep like a breeze!" (Then) his wife unto Uta-Napishtim the Distant
Answer'd: "O, touch him, and let the man wake, that the road he hath traversed
He may betake himself homeward in peace, that he by the portal
Whence he fared forth may return to his land". Spake Uta-Napishtim,
(Yea), to his wife: "(How) the troubles of mortals do trouble thee also!
Bake then his flour (and) put at his head, but the time he is sleeping
On the house-wall do thou mark it". (So straightway) she (did so), his flour
Baked she (and) set at his head, but the time he was sleeping she noted
On the house-wall. (So), *first* was collected his flour, (then) *secondly* sifted,
Thirdly, 'twas moisten'd, and *fourthly* she kneaded his dough, and so *fifthly*
Leaven she added, and sixthly 'twas baked; (then) *seventh* – he touch'd him,
All on a sudden, and (so from his slumber) awoke the (great) fellow!

* * *

Gilgamesh unto him spake, (yea) to Uta-Napishtim the Distant:
"(Tell me), I pr'ythee (?), was 't thou, who when sleep was shower'd upon me
All on a sudden didst touch me, and (straightway) rouse me (from slumber)?"
Uta-Napishtim to Gilgamesh [spake, (yea), unto him spake he]:
"Gilgamesh, told was the tale of thy meal . . . and (then) did I wake thee:
['*One*' – was collected] thy flour: [(then) '*two*'] – it was sifted; (and) '*thirdly*' –
Moisten'd: (and) '*fourthly*' – she kneaded thy dough [(and) '*fifthly*'] the leaven
Added: (and) '*sixthly*' – 'twas baked: [(and) '*seventh*'] – 'twas I on a sudden
Touch'd thee and thou didst awake". To Uta-Napishtim, the Distant,
Gilgamesh answer'd: "O, [how] shall I act, (or) where shall I hie me,

Uta-Napishtim? A Robber (from me) hath ravish'd my [courage,]
Death [in] my bedchamber broodeth, and Death is wherever I [listen]".

* * *

[Spake] to [him, (yea),] to the boatman Ur-Shanabi Uta-Napishtim:

"'Tis thou, Ur-Shanabi ... the crossing, will hate thee,
(Sooth), to all those who come to its marge, doth its marge set a limit:
(This) man for whom thou wert guide – are stains to cover his body,
Or shall a skin hide the grace of his limbs? Ur-Shanabi, take him,
Lead him to where he may bathe, that he wash off his stains in the water
(White) as the snow: let him cast off his pelt(s) that the sea may remove (them);
Fair let his body appear: of his head be the fillet renewéd,
Let him, as clothes for his nakedness, garb himself in a mantle,

Such that, or ever he come to his city, and finish his journey,
No (sign of) age shall the mantle betray, but preserve (all) its freshness".
Wherefore Ur-Shanabi took him, and where he might bathe did he lead him,
Washing his stains in the [water] like snow, his pelt(s), [too], discarding,
So that the sea might bear them away; (and) his body appeared
Fair; [of] his head he [the fillet] renewed, and himself in a mantle
Garb'd, as the clothes for his nakedness, [such that or ever his city
Reach he], or ever he finish his journey, [the mantle betray not
Age, but] preserve [(all) its freshness].
(So) into their vessel embarked
Gilgamesh, (aye), and Ur-Shanabi, launching (their) craft [on the billow],
They themselves riding aboard (her).

The Magic Gift of Restored Youth

To Uta-Napishtim, the Distant,
Spake (then) his wife: "Came Gilgamesh (hither) aweary with rowing,
What wilt thou give wherewith he return to his land?" and the meanwhile
Gilgamesh, lifting his pole, was pushing the boat at the seashore.
(Then answer'd) Uta-Napishtim to him, (yea), [to] Gilgamesh [spake he]:
"Gilgamesh, (hither) didst come (all) aweary with rowing; (O, tell me),
What shall I give thee (as gift) wherewith to return to thy country?
Gilgamesh, I will reveal thee a hidden matter … I'll tell thee:
There is a plant like a thorn with its root (?) [deep down in the ocean],
Like unto those of the briar (in sooth) its prickles will scratch [thee],
(Yet) if thy hand reach this plant, [thou'lt surely find life (everlasting)]".
(Then), when Gilgamesh heard this, he loosen'd) [his girdle about him],
Bound heavy stones [on his feet], which dragg'd him down to the sea-deeps,
[Found he the plant]; as he seized on the plant, (lo), [its prickles did scratch him].

Cut he the heavy stones [from his feet] that again it restore him
Unto its shore.

* * *

Gilgamesh spake to him, (yea), to the boatman Ur-Shanabi (this wise):
"(Nay, but) this plant is a plant of great wonder(?), Ur-Shanabi", said he,
"Whereby a man may attain his desire – I'll take it to Erech,
(Erech), the high-wall'd, and give it to eat [unto …].
'Greybeard-who-turneth-to-man-in-his-prime' is its name and I'll eat it
I myself, that again I may come to my youthful condition".

The Quest Ends in Tragedy

Broke they their fast at the fortieth hour: at the sixtieth rested.
Gilgamesh spied out a pool of cool water, (and) therein descending
Bathed in the water. (But here was) a serpent who snuff'd the plant's fragrance,

Darted he up [from the water (?)], and snatch'd the plant, uttering malison
As he drew back. Then Gilgamesh sate him, (and) burst into weeping.
Over his cheeks flow'd his tears: to the boatman Ur -Shanabi [spake he(?)]
"(Pr'ythee), [for] whom have toiléd mine arms, O Ur-Shanabi, (tell me),
(Pr'ythee), for whom hath my heart's blood been spent? (yea), not for mine own self,
Have I the guerdon achieved; (no), 'tis for an earth-lion (only)
Have I the guerdon secured – (and) now at the fortieth hour
(Such an) one reiveth (it) – O, when I open'd the sluice and . . .ed the attachment,
(Aye), I noted the sign (?) which to me was vouchsafed as a warning,
Would I had turn'd and abandon'd the boat at the marge (of the ocean)!"
Broke they their fast at the fortieth hour: at the sixtieth rested,
(So in the end) to the middle of Erech, the high-wall'd, arrivéd.

The Pride of the Architect

Gilgamesh spake to him, (yea), to the boatman Ur-Shanabi (this wise):
"Do thou, Ur-Shanabi, go up and walk on the ramparts of Erech,
Look on its base, and take heed of its bricks, if its bricks be not kiln-burnt,
(Aye), and its groundwork be not bitumen, e'en seven courses,
One *shar* the city, (and) one *shar* the gardens, and one *shar* the (2)
... the Temple of Ishtar, amass'd I three *shar* and ... (?) of Erech.

The Twelfth Tablet
Gilgamesh, in Despair, Enquires of the Dead

Column I
How the Dead Haunt the Living

(THEN), WHAT TIME that the seine had pass'd through the Architect's dwelling,
(Aye, and) the net [had taken its toll] ... [said he]:
"Lord, what [is't I may do] ...
(Now, what time that) the seine hath [pass'd through the Architect's dwelling],
(Aye and) the net [hath taken its toll] ..."
Gilgamesh [unto him spake] ...
"If unto ...
(About two lines wanting, in which Gilgamesh presumably asks how the dead may be made to haunt the mourner).
"Gilgamesh, . . ".

The Mourner's Duty

"If to the . . . [thou drawest], unto the temple . . .
Raiment clean [shalt not don], (but) like to a townsman shalt....
Nor with sweet oil from the cruse be anointed, (lest) at its fragrance

Round thee they gather: nor mayst thou set bow to the earth, (lest) around thee
Circle those shot by the bow; nor a stick in thy hand mayst thou carry,
(Lest) (stricken) ghosts should gibber against thee: nor shoe to thy footsole
Put on, nor make on the ground a (loud) echo: thy wife, whom thou lovest,
Kiss (her) thou mayst not, thy wife whom thou hatest – thou mayst not
chastise (her),
(Aye, and) thy child whom thou lovest not kiss, nor thy child whom thou hatest
Mayst not chastise, (for) the mourning of earth doth hold thee enthralléd.

"She who dead lieth,
She who dead lieth,
Mother of Ninazu,
She who dead lieth,
No more with mantle are
Veil'd her fair shoulders,
No more her bosom
Drawn, like the lard cruse!"

Gilgamesh by Contravening These Customs Attempts to Raise Enkidu

(So) did he draw [the … to …, and came to the temples,
[Put on clean raiment] … (and) like to a townsman …
(Aye), with [sweet] oil from the cruse [was] anointed: (then) at [its] fragrance
Round him they gather 'd: the bow did he set (?) [to the earth], and around him
Circled the spirits, (yea,) those who were [shot] by the bow at him gibber'd,
[Carried] a stick in his hand [and the (stricken) ghosts at him gibber'd(?)].
[Put on] a shoe to [his foot-sole, and made on the ground a (loud)] echo.
[Kiss'd he] his wife [whom he lovéd, chastiséd his] wife whom he hated,
[Kiss'd he his child] whom he lovéd, chastiséd [his] child whom he hated.
(Aye, in good sooth, 'twas) the mourning of earth which did hold him enthralled

"She who (dead) lieth,
[She who] (dead) lieth,
Mother of Ninazu,
She who (dead) lieth,
No (more) with mantle are
Veil'd [her] fair shoulders,
No (more) her bosom
Drawn, like the lard cruse".

Cried(?) [he] (for) Enkidu out of the earth to ascend: "[Not] (the Plague-god),
Namtar, hath [seized] him, nor fever, (but only) the earth: nor the Croucher,
[Nergal], the ruthless, hath seized him, (but only) the earth: neither fell he
There where was [battle] of mortals; 'twas only the earth [which hath
seized him.] "
(So) . . . for his servitor Enkidu sorrow'd the offspring of Nin-sun,

(Aye), as he went all alone unto [Ekur], the temple of Enlil:
"[Enlil], (my) Father, ('tis now) that the seine hath stricken me also,
Down to the earth – the net to the earth hath stricken me also.
Enkidu 'tis – whom [I pray thee] to raise [from the earth] – not (the Plague-god),
Namtar, hath seized him, nor fever, [but only the earth]: nor the Croucher,
Nergal, the ruthless, hath seized shim, but only the earth]: [neither fell he]
There where was battle of mortals: ['twas only the earth which hath seized him]".
(But) no answer did Enlil, the father vouchsafe.
[To the Moon-god he hied him (?)]:
"Moon-god, (my) Father, ('tis now) that the seine [hath stricken me also,
Down to the earth] – the net [to the earth hath stricken me also].
Enkidu 'tis – whom [I pray thee] to raise [from the earths – not (the Plague-god),
Namtar, hath seized him, [nor] fever, [but only the earth: nor] the Croucher,
Nergal, [the ruthless, hath seized him, but only the earth]: [neither fell he]
There where [was battle of mortals: 'twas only the earth which hath seized him".
[(But) no answer the Moon-god vouchsafed:
(Then) to Ea he hied him:]
["Ea, (my) Father, 'tis now that the seine hath stricken me also,]
[Down to the earth – the net to the earth hath stricken me also.]
[Enkidu 'tis, – whom I pray thee to raise from the earth – not (the Plague-god),]
Nam[tar, hath seized him, nor fever, but only the earth: nor] the Croucher,
Nergal, the ruthless, [hath seized him, but only the earth: neither fell he]
There where was battle of mortals: ['twas only the earth which hath seized him]".
Ea, the father, [gave ear (and) to Nergal], the warrior-hero,
[Spake he]: "O Nergal, O warrior-hero, [give ear to my speaking(?)]!
[Ope now,] a hole [in the earth], that the spirit of [Enkidu, (rising)],
[May from the earth issue forth, and so have speech] with [his] brother".
Nergal, the warrior-hero, [gave ear to the speaking of Ea],
Oped, then, a hole in the earth, and the spirit of Enkidu issued
Forth from the earth like a wind. They embraced and....
Communed together, mourning.
"Tell, O my friend, O tell, O my friend, (O) tell (me, I pr'y thee),
What thou hast seen of the laws of the Underworld?" "(Nay, then,) O comrade;

I will not tell thee, (yea,) I will not tell thee – (for), were I to tell thee,
What I have seen of the laws of the Underworld, – sit thee down weeping!"
"(Then) let me sit me down weeping".
(The wretched lot of all who must die).

"(So be it): [the friend(?)] thou didst fondle
(Thereby) rejoicing thee – [into his body(?), as though 'twere a] mantle
Old, hath the worm made its entry: (in sooth, then) [the bride(?)] thou
didst fondle,
(Thereby) rejoicing thee – fill'd with the dust [is her body]....
... he hath spoken and [into the ground (?) is he sunken,
... he hath spoken and [into the ground (?) is he sunken".
"[He who fell in ....]

[Didst thou see him?]". "(Aye), I saw...".
(About seventeen lines missing).
"As a pillar beautiful
[Props?] an inner por[tico (?)] ...
(About twenty-five lines missing).
"He who falleth from a pole
Didst thou see him? "(Aye), I saw]:
Straightway for ....
By removal of a plug ... "
"He whom death ...
"Didst thou see him?" "[(Aye) I saw]:
He's at rest upon a couch,
Limpid water doth he drink".
"(Then, the hero) slain in fight,
Didst thou see him?" "(Aye) I saw:
Father, mother raise his head,
O'er him wife [in bitter woe]".
"He whose corpse in desert lieth,
Hast thou seen him?" "(Aye), I saw;
Not in earth doth rest his spirit".
"He whose ghost hath none to tend,
Didst thou see him?" "(Aye), I saw,
Lees of cup, and broken bread
Thrown into the street he eateth".

Lugalbanda and Enmerkar

Lugalbanda in the Mountain Cave

WHEN IN ANCIENT DAYS heaven was separated from earth, when in ancient days that which was fitting ..., when after the ancient harvests ... barley was eaten (?), when boundaries were laid out and borders were fixed, when boundary-stones were placed and inscribed with names, when dykes and canals were purified, when ... wells were dug straight down; when the bed of the Euphrates, the plenteous river of Unug, was opened up, when ..., when ..., when holy An removed ..., when the offices of en and king were famously exercised at Unug, when the sceptre and staff of Kulaba were held high in battle – in battle, Inana's game; when the black-headed were blessed with long life, in their settled ways and in their ..., when they presented the mountain goats with pounding hooves and the mountain stags beautiful with their antlers to Enmerkar son of Utu –

– now at that time the king set his mace towards the city, Enmerkar son of Utu prepared an ... expedition against Aratta, the mountain of the holy divine powers. He was going to set off to destroy the rebel land; the lord began a mobilization of his city. The herald made the horn signal sound in all the lands. Now levied Unug took the field with the wise king, indeed levied Kulaba followed Enmerkar. Unug's levy was a flood, Kulaba's levy was a clouded sky. As they covered the ground like heavy fog, the dense dust whirled up by them reached up to heaven. As if to rooks on the best seed, rising up, he called to the people. Each one gave his fellow the sign.

Their king went at their head, to go at the … of the army. Enmerkar went at their head, to go at the … of the army.

2 lines unclear

… gu-nida emmer-grain to grow abundantly. When the righteous one who takes counsel with Enlil (i.e. Enmerkar) took away the whole of Kulaba, like sheep they bent over at the slope of the mountains, … at the edge of the hills they ran forward like wild bulls. He sought … at the side – they recognised the way. He sought …

Five days passed. On the sixth day they bathed. … on the seventh day they entered the mountains. When they had crossed over on the paths – an enormous flood billowing upstream into a lagoon … Their ruler (i.e. Enmerkar), riding on a storm, Utu's son, the good bright metal, stepped down from heaven to the great earth. His head shines with brilliance, the barbed arrows flash past him like lightning; at his side the bronze pointed axe of his emblem shines for him, he strides forward keenly with the pointed axe, like a dog set on consuming a corpse.

At that time there were seven, there were seven – the young ones, born in Kulaba, were seven. The goddess Uraš had borne these seven, the Wild Cow had nourished them with milk. They were heroes, living in Sumer, they were princely in their prime. They had been brought up eating at the god An's table. These seven were the overseers for those that are subordinate to overseers, were the captains for those that are subordinate to captains were the generals for those that are subordinate to generals. They were overseers of 300 men, 300 men each; they were captains of 600 men, 600 men each; they were generals of seven šar (25,200) of soldiers, 25,200 soldiers each. They stood at the service of the lord as his élite troops.

Lugalbanda, the eighth of them, …… was washed in water. In awed silence he went forward, … he marched with the troops. When they had covered half the way, covered half the way, a sickness befell him there, 'head sickness' befell him. He jerked like a snake dragged by its head with a reed; his mouth bit the dust, like a gazelle caught in a snare. No longer could his hands return the hand grip, no longer could he lift his feet high. Neither king nor contingents could help him. In the great mountains, crowded together like a dustcloud over the ground, they said: "Let them bring him to Unug". But they did not know how they could bring him. "Let them bring him to Kulaba". But they did not know how they could bring him. As his teeth chattered (?) in the cold places of the mountains, they brought him to a warm place there.

… a storehouse, they made him an arbour like a bird's nest. … dates, figs and various sorts of cheese; they put sweetmeats suitable for the sick to eat, in baskets of dates, and they made him a home. They set out for him the various fats of the cowpen, the sheepfold's fresh cheese, butter …, as if laying a table for the holy place, the valued place (i.e. as if for a funerary offering). Directly in front of the table they arranged for him beer for drinking, mixed with date syrup and rolls … with butter. Provisions poured into leather buckets, provisions all put into leather bags – his brothers and friends, like a boat unloading from the harvest-place, placed stores by his head in the mountain cave. They

... water in their leather waterskins. Dark beer, alcoholic drink, light emmer beer, wine for drinking which is pleasant to the taste, they distributed by his head in the mountain cave as on a stand for waterskins. They prepared for him incense resin, ... resin, aromatic resin, ligidba resin and first-class resin on pot-stands in the deep hole; they suspended them by his head in the mountain cave. They pushed into place at his head his axe whose metal was tin, imported from the Zubi mountains. They wrapped up by his chest his dagger of iron imported from the Gig (Black) mountains. His eyes – irrigation ditches, because they are flooding with water – holy Lugalbanda kept open, directed towards this. The outer door of his lips – overflowing like holy Utu – he did not open to his brothers. When they lifted his neck, there was no breath there any longer. His brothers, his friends took counsel with one another:

"If our brother rises like Utu from bed, then the god who has smitten him will step aside and, when he eats this food, when he drinks (?) this, will make his feet stable. May he bring him over the high places of the mountains to brick-built Kulaba".

"But if Utu calls our brother to the holy place, the valued place (i.e. the hereafter), the health of his limbs will leave (?) him. Then it will be up to us, when we come back from Aratta, to bring our brother's body to brick-built Kulaba".

Like the dispersed holy cows of Nanna, as with a breeding bull when, in his old age, they have left him behind in the cattle pen, his brothers and friends abandoned holy Lugalbanda in the mountain cave; and with repeated tears and moaning, with tears, with lamentation, with grief and weeping, Lugalbanda's older brothers set off into the mountains.

Then two days passed during which Lugalbanda was ill; to these two days, half a day was added. As Utu turned his glance towards his home, as the animals lifted their heads toward their lairs, at the day's end in the evening cool, his body was as if anointed with oil. But he was not yet free of his sickness.

When he lifted his eyes to heaven to Utu, he wept to him as if to his own father. In the mountain cave he raised to him his fair hands:

"Utu, I greet you! Let me be ill no longer! Hero, Ningal's son, I greet you! Let me be ill no longer! Utu, you have let me come up into the mountains in the company of my brothers. In the mountain cave, the most dreadful spot on earth, let me be ill no longer! Here where there is no mother, there is no father, there is no acquaintance, no one whom I value, my mother is not here to say "Alas, my child!" My brother is not here to say "Alas, my brother!" My mother's neighbour who enters our house is not here to weep over me. If the male and female protective deities were standing by, the deity of neighbourliness would say, "A man should not perish". A lost dog is bad; a lost man is terrible. On the unknown way at the edge of the mountains, Utu, is a lost man, a man in an even more terrible situation. Don't make me flow away like water in a violent death! Don't make me eat saltpetre as if it were barley! Don't make me fall like a throw-stick somewhere in the desert unknown to me! Afflicted with a name which excites my brothers' scorn, let me be ill no longer! Afflicted with the derision of my comrades, let me be ill no longer! Let me not come to an end in the mountains like a weakling!"

Utu accepted his tears. He sent down his divine encouragement to him in the mountain cave.

She who makes ... for the poor, whose game (i.e. battle) is sweet, the prostitute who goes out to the inn, who makes the bedchamber delightful, who is food to the poor man – Inana (i.e. the evening star), the daughter of Suen, arose before him like a bull in the Land. Her brilliance, like that of holy Šara, her stellar brightness illuminated for him the mountain cave. When he lifted his eyes upwards to Inana, he wept as if before his own father. In the mountain cave he raised to her his fair hands:

"Inana, if only this were my home, if only this were my city! If only this were Kulaba, the city in which my mother bore me ...! Even if it were to me as the waste land to a snake! If it were to me as a crack in the ground to a scorpion! My mighty people ...! My great ladies ...! ... to E-ana!"

2 lines unclear

"The little stones of it, the shining stones in their glory, saĝkal stones above, ... below, from its crying out in the mountain land Zabu, from its voice ... open – may my limbs not perish in the mountains of the cypresses!"

Inana accepted his tears. With power of life she let him go to sleep just like the sleeping Utu. Inana enveloped him with heart's joy as if with a woollen garment. Then, just as if ..., she went to brick-built Kulaba.

The bull that eats up the black soup, the astral holy bull-calf (i.e. the moon), came to watch over him. He shines (?) in the heavens like the morning star, he spreads bright light in the night – Suen is greeted as the new moon; Father Nanna gives the direction for the rising Utu. The glorious lord whom the crown befits, Suen, the beloved son of Enlil, {the god} {(1 ms. has instead:) the lord} reached the zenith splendidly. His brilliance like {holy Šara}, his starry radiance illuminated for him the mountain cave. When Lugalbanda raised his eyes to heaven to Suen, he wept to him as if to his own father. In the mountain cave he raised to him his fair hands:

"King whom one cannot reach in the distant sky! Suen whom one cannot reach in the distant sky! King who loves justice, who hates evil! Suen who loves justice, who hates evil! Justice brings joy justly to your heart. A poplar, a great staff, forms a sceptre for you, you who loosen the bonds of justice, who do not loosen the bonds of evil. If you encounter evil before you, it is dragged away behind ...... When your heart becomes angry, you spit your venom at evil like a snake which drools poison".

Suen accepted his tears and gave him life. He conferred on his feet the power to stand.

A second time (i.e. at the following sunrise), as the bright bull rising up from the horizon, the bull resting among the cypresses, a shield standing on the ground, watched by the assembly, a shield coming out from the treasury, watched by the young men – the youth Utu extended his holy splendour down from heaven, he bestowed them on holy Lugalbanda in the mountain cave. His good protective god hovered ahead of him, his good protective goddess walked behind him. The god which had smitten him {stepped aside}. When he raised his eyes heavenward to Utu, he wept to him as to his own father. In the mountain cave he raised to him his fair hands:

"Utu, shepherd of the land, father of the black-headed, when you go to sleep, the people go to sleep with you; youth Utu, when you rise, the people rise with you. Utu, without you no net is stretched out for a bird, no slave is taken away captive. To him who walks alone, you are his brotherly companion; Utu, you are the third of them who travel in pairs. You are the blinkers for him who wears the neck-ring. Like a holy zulumḫi garment, your sunshine clothes the poor man and the scoundrel as well as him who has no clothes; as a garment of white wool it covers the bodies even of debt slaves. Like rich old men, the old women praise your sunshine sweetly, until their oldest days. Your sunshine is as mighty as oil. Great wild bulls run forward". (alludes to a proverb)

1 line unclear

"Hero, son of Ningal, ... to you".

2 lines unclear

"Brother … his brother. He causes his plough to stand in the …… Praise to you is so very sweet, it reaches up to heaven. Hero, son of Ningal, they laud you as you deserve".

Holy Lugalbanda came out from the mountain cave. Then the righteous one who takes counsel with Enlil (i.e. Utu?) caused life-saving plants to be born. The rolling rivers, mothers of the hills, brought life-saving water. He bit on the life-saving plants, he sipped from the life-saving water. After biting on the life-saving plants, after sipping from the life-saving water, here he on his own set a trap (?) in the ground, and from that spot he sped away like a horse of the mountains. Like a lone wild ass of Šakkan he darted over the mountains. Like a large powerful donkey he raced; a slim donkey, eager to run, he bounded along.

That night, in the evening, he set off, hurrying through the mountains, a wasteland in the moonlight. He was alone and, even to his sharp eyes, there was not a single person to be seen. With the provisions stocked in leather pails, provisions put in leather bags, his brothers and his friends had been able to bake bread on the ground, with some cold water. Holy Lugalbanda had carried the things from the mountain cave. He set them beside the embers. He filled a bucket … with water. In front of him he split what he had placed. He took hold of the … stones. Repeatedly he struck them together. He laid the glowing (?) coals on the open ground. The fine flintstone caused a spark. Its fire shone out for him over the waste land like the sun. Not knowing how to bake cakes, not knowing an oven, with just seven coals he baked giziešta dough. While the bread was baking by itself, he pulled up šulḫi reeds of the mountains, roots and all, and stripped their branches. He packed up all the cakes as a day's ration. Not knowing how to bake cakes, not knowing an oven, with just seven coals he had baked giziešta dough. He garnished it with sweet date syrup.

A brown wild bull, a fine-looking wild bull, a wild bull tossing its horns, a wild bull in hunger (?), resting, seeking with its voice the brown wild bulls of the hills, the pure place – in this way it was chewing aromatic šimgig as if it were barley, it was grinding up the wood of the cypress as if it were esparto grass, it was sniffing with its nose at the foliage of the šenu shrub as if it were grass. It was drinking the water of the rolling rivers, it was belching from ilinnuš, the pure plant of the mountains. While the brown wild bulls, the wild bulls of the mountains, were browsing about among the plants, Lugalbanda captured this one in his ambush (?). He uprooted a juniper tree of the mountains and stripped its branches. With a knife holy Lugalbanda trimmed its roots, which were like the long rushes of the field. He tethered the brown wild bull, the wild bull of the mountains, to it with a halter.

A brown goat and a buck-goat – flea-bitten goats, lousy goats, fatty (?) goats – in this way they were chewing aromatic šimgig as if it were barley, they were grinding up the wood of the cypress as if it were esparto grass, they were sniffing with their noses at the foliage of the šenu shrub as if it were grass. They were drinking the water of the rolling rivers, they were belching from ilinnuš, the pure plant of the mountains. While the brown goats and the buck-goats were browsing about among the plants, Lugalbanda captured these two in his ambush (?). He uprooted a juniper tree of the mountains and stripped its branches. With a knife holy Lugalbanda cut off its roots, which were like the long rushes of the field. With chains he fettered the brown goat and the buck-goat, both the goats.

He was alone and, even to his sharp eyes, there was not a single person to be seen. Sleep overcame the king (i.e. Lugalbanda) – sleep, the country of oppression; it is like a towering flood, like a hand demolishing a brick wall, a hand raised high, a foot raised high; covering like syrup that which is in front of it, overflowing like syrup onto that which is in front of it; it knows no overseer, knows no captain, yet it is overpowering for the hero. And by means of Ninkasi's wooden cask (i.e. with the help of beer), sleep finally overcame Lugalbanda. He laid down ilinnuš, pure herb of the mountains, as a couch, he spread out a zulumḫi garment, he unfolded there a white linen sheet. There being no … room for bathing, he made do with that place. The king lay down not to sleep, he lay down to dream – not turning back at the door of the dream, not turning back at the door-pivot. To the liar it talks in lies, to the truthful it speaks truth. It can make one man happy, it can make another man sing, but it is the closed tablet-basket of the gods. It is the beautiful bedchamber of Ninlil, it is the counsellor of Inana. The multiplier of mankind, the voice of one not alive – Zangara, the god of dreams, himself like a bull, bellowed at Lugalbanda. Like the calf of a cow he lowed:

"Who will slaughter (?) a brown wild bull for me? Who will make its fat melt for me? He shall take my axe whose metal is tin, he shall wield my dagger which is of iron. Like an athlete I shall let him bring away the brown wild bull, the wild bull of the mountains, I shall let him like a wrestler make it submit. Its strength will leave it. When he offers it before the rising sun, let him heap up like barleycorns the heads of the brown goat and the buck-goat, both the goats; when he has poured out their blood in the pit – let their smell waft out in the desert so that the alert snakes of the mountains will sniff it".

Lugalbanda awoke – it was a dream. He shivered – it was sleep. He rubbed his eyes, he was overawed. He took his axe whose metal was tin, he wielded his dagger which was of iron. Like an athlete he brought away the brown wild bull, the wild bull of the mountains, like a wrestler he made it submit. Its strength left it. He offered it before the rising sun. He heaped up like barleycorns the heads of the brown goat and the buck-goat, both of the goats. He poured out their blood in the pit so that their smell wafted out in the desert. The alert snakes of the mountains sniffed it.

As the sun was rising …, Lugalbanda, invoking the name of Enlil, made An, Enlil, Enki and Ninḫursaĝa sit down to a banquet at the pit, at the place in the mountains which he had prepared. The banquet was set, the libations were poured – dark beer, alcoholic drink, light emmer beer, wine for drinking which is pleasant to the taste. Over the plain he poured cool water as a libation. He put the knife to the flesh of the brown goats, and he roasted the dark livers there. He let their smoke rise there, like incense put on the fire. As if Dumuzid had brought in the good savours of the cattle pen,

So An, Enlil, Enki and Ninḫursaĝa consumed the best part of the food prepared by Lugalbanda. Like the shining place of pure strength, the holy altar of Suen, … On top of the altar of Utu and the altar of Suen …, he decorated the two altars with the lapis lazuli … of Inana. Suen … He bathed the a-an-kar. When he had bathed the …, he set out all the cakes properly.

(Description of the demons) They make … Enki, father of the gods; they are …, they …; like a string of figs dripping with lusciousness, they hang their arms. They are gazelles of Suen running in flight, they are the fine smooth cloths of Ninlil, they are the helpers of Iškur; they pile up flax, they pile up barley; they are wild animals on the rampage, they descend like a storm on a rebel land hated by Suen, indeed they descend like a storm. They lie up during all the long day, and during the short night they enter … houses (?); during the long day, during the short night they lie in beds …, they give … At dead of night they …, in the breeze … swallows of Utu; they enter into house after house, they peer into street after street, they are talkers, they are repliers to talkers, seeking words with a mother, replying to a great lady; they nestle at the bedside, they smite …, when the black … are stolen, they leave … the doors and tables of humans, they change …, they tie the door-pivots together. The hero who …, Utu who …, the heroic youth Utu of the good word

2 lines unclear

the incantation ... of the youth Utu, which the Anuna, the great gods, do not know, from that time ...,

3 lines unclear

The wise elders of the city ...

1 line unclear

the incantation ... of the youth Utu, which the Anuna, the great gods, do not know,

5 lines unclear

they are able to enter the presence of Utu, of Enlil, god of the ..., the bearded son of Ningal ...; they give to Suen ..., they confirm with their power the fate of the foreign lands. At dead of night they know the black wild boar, at midday to Utu ... he can ... his incantation,

3 lines unclear

They enter before An, Enlil, ..., Inana, the gods; they know ..., they watch ..., they ... at the window; the door of the shining mountain, the doorbolt of the shining mountain;

4 lines unclear

they stand ...,

1 line unclear

They pursue ... Inana ..., who are favoured by Inana's heart, who stand in the battle, they are the fourteen torches of battle ..., at midnight they ..., at dead of night they pursue like wildfire, in a band they flash together like lightning, in the urgent storm of battle, which roars loudly like a great flood rising up; they who are favoured in Inana's heart, who stand in the battle, they are the seven torches of battle ...; they stand joyfully as she wears the crown under a clear sky, with their foreheads and eyes they are a clear evening. Their ears ... a boat, with their mouths they are wild boars resting in a reed thicket; they stand in the thick of battle, with their life-force they ...,

1 line unclear

who are favoured in Inana's heart, who stand in the battle, by Nintur of heaven they are numerous, by the life of heaven they hold ...; the holy shining battle-mace reaches to the edge of heaven and earth, ... reaches.

1 line unclear

As Utu comes forth from his chamber, the holy battle-mace of An ..., the just god who lies alongside a man; they are wicked gods with evil hearts, they are ... gods. It is they, like Nanna, like Utu, like Inana of the fifty divine powers, ... in heaven and earth ...; they are the interpreters of spoken evil, the spies of righteousness,

2 lines unclear

... a clear sky and numerous stars,

1 line unclear

... fresh cedars in the mountains of the cypress, ... a battle-net from the horizon to the zenith,

unknown no. of lines missing

Lugalbanda and the Anzud Bird

Lugalbanda lies idle in the mountains, in the faraway places; he has ventured into the Zabu mountains. No mother is with him to offer advice, no father is with him to talk to him. No one is with him whom he knows, whom he values, no confidant is there to talk to him. In his heart he speaks to himself: "I shall treat the bird as befits him, I shall treat Anzud as befits him. I shall greet his wife affectionately. I shall seat Anzud's wife and Anzud's child at a banquet. An will fetch Ninguena for me from her mountain home – the expert woman who redounds to her mother's credit, Ninkasi the expert who redounds to her mother's credit. Her fermenting-vat is of green lapis lazuli, her beer cask is of refined silver and of gold. If she stands by the beer, there is joy, if she sits by the beer, there is gladness; as cupbearer she mixes the beer, never wearying as she walks back and forth, Ninkasi, the keg at her side, on her hips; may she make my beer-serving perfect. When the bird has drunk the beer and is happy, when Anzud has drunk the beer and is happy, he can help me find the place to which the troops of Unug are going, Anzud can put me on the track of my brothers."

Now the splendid 'eagle'-tree of Enki on the summit of Inana's mountain of multicoloured cornelian stood fast on the earth like a tower, all shaggy like an aru. With its shade it covered the highest eminences of the mountains like a cloak, was spread out over them like a tunic. Its roots rested like saĝkal snakes in Utu's river of the seven mouths. Nearby, in the mountains where no cypresses grow, where no snake slithers, where no scorpion stings, in the midst of the mountains the buru-az bird had put its nest and laid therein its eggs; nearby the Anzud bird had set his nest and settled therein his young. It was made with wood from the juniper and the box trees. The bird had made the bright twigs into a bower. When at daybreak the bird stretches himself, when at sunrise Anzud cries out, at his cry the ground quakes in the Lulubi mountains. He has a shark's teeth and an eagle's claws. In terror of him wild bulls run away into the foothills, stags run away into their mountains.

Lugalbanda is wise and he achieves mighty exploits. In preparation of the sweet celestial cakes he added carefulness to carefulness. He kneaded the dough with honey, he added more honey to it. He set them before the young nestling, before the Anzud chick, gave the baby fatty meat to eat. He fed it sheep's fat. He popped the cakes into its beak. He settled the Anzud chick in its nest, painted its eyes with kohl, dabbed white cedar scent onto its head, put up a twisted roll of salt meat. He withdrew from the Anzud's nest, awaited him in the mountains where no cypresses grow. At that time the bird was herding together wild bulls of the mountains, Anzud was herding together wild bulls of the mountains. He held a live bull in his talons, he carried a dead bull across his shoulders. He poured forth his bile like 10 gur of water. The bird halted (?) once, Anzud halted (?) once. When the bird called back to the nest, when Anzud called back to the nest, his fledgling did not answer him from the nest. When the bird called a second time to the nest, his fledgling did not answer from the nest. Whenever the bird had called back to the nest before, his fledgling had answered from the nest; but now when the bird called back to the nest, his fledgling did not answer him from the nest. The bird uttered a cry of grief that reached up to heaven, his wife cried out "Woe!" Her cry reached the abzu. The bird with this cry of "Woe!" and his wife with this cry of grief made the Anuna, gods of the mountains, actually crawl into crevices like ants. The bird says to his wife, Anzud says to his wife, "Foreboding weighs upon my nest, as over the great cattle-pen of Nanna. Terror lies upon it, as when wild lions start butting each other. Who has taken my child from its nest? Who has taken the Anzud from its nest?"

But it seemed to the bird, when he approached the nest, it seemed to Anzud, when he approached the nest, that it had been made like a god's dwelling-place. It was brilliantly festooned. His chick was settled in its nest, its eyes were painted with kohl, sprigs of white cedar were fixed on its head. A twisted piece of salt meat was hung up high. The bird is exultant, Anzud is exultant: "I am the prince who decides the destiny of rolling rivers. I keep on the straight and narrow path the righteous who follow Enlil's counsel. My father Enlil brought me here. He let me bar the entrance to the mountains as if with a great door.

If I fix a fate, who shall alter it? If I but say the word, who shall change it? Whoever has done this to my nest, if you are a god, I will speak with you, indeed I will befriend you. If you are a man, I will fix your fate. I shall not let you have any opponents in the mountains. You shall be 'Hero-fortified-by-Anzud'."

Lugalbanda, partly from fright, partly from delight, partly from fright, partly from deep delight, flatters the bird, flatters Anzud: "Bird with sparkling eyes, born in this district, Anzud with sparkling eyes, born in this district, you frolic as you bathe in a pool. Your grandfather, the prince of all patrimonies, placed heaven in your hand, set earth at your feet. Your wingspan extended is like a birdnet stretched out across the sky! ...... on the ground your talons are like a trap laid for the wild bulls and wild cows of the mountains! Your spine is as straight as a scribe's! Your breast as you fly is like Niraḫ parting the waters! As for your back, you are a verdant palm garden, breathtaking to look upon. Yesterday I escaped safely to you, since then I have entrusted myself to your protection. Your wife shall be my mother" (he said), "You shall be my father" (he said), "I shall treat your little ones as my brothers. Since yesterday I have been waiting for you in the mountains where no cypresses grow. Let your wife stand beside you to greet me. I offer my greeting and leave you to decide my destiny."

The bird presents himself before him, rejoices over him, Anzud presents himself before him, rejoices over him. Anzud says to holy Lugalbanda, "Come now, my Lugalbanda. Go like a boat full of precious metals, like a grain barge, like a boat going to deliver apples, like a boat piled up high with a cargo of cucumbers, casting a shade, like a boat loaded lavishly at the place of harvest, go back to brick-built Kulaba with head held high!" – Lugalbanda who loves the seed will not accept this.

"Like Šara, Inana's beloved son, shoot forth with your barbed arrows like a sunbeam, shoot forth with reed-arrows like moonlight! May the barbed arrows be a horned viper to those they hit! Like a fish killed with the cleaver, may they be magic-cut! May you bundle them up like logs hewn with the axe!" – Lugalbanda who loves the seed will not accept this.

"May Ninurta, Enlil's son, set the helmet Lion of Battle on your head, may the breastplate (?) that in the great mountains does not permit retreat be laid on your breast! May you ... the battle-net against the enemy! When you go to the city, ...!" – Lugalbanda who loves the seed will not accept this.

"The plenty of Dumuzi's holy butter churn, whose butter is the butter of all the world, shall be granted (?) to you. Its milk is the milk of all the world. It shall be granted (?) to you." – Lugalbanda who loves the seed will not accept this. As a kib bird, a freshwater kib, as it flies along a lagoon, he answered him in words.

The bird listened to him. Anzud said to holy Lugalbanda, "Now look, my Lugalbanda, just think again. It's like this: a wilful plough-ox should be put back in the track, a balking ass should be made to take the straight path. Still, I shall grant you what you put to me. I shall assign you an allotted destiny according to your wishes."

Holy Lugalbanda answers him: "Let the power of running be in my thighs, let me never grow tired! Let there be strength in my arms, let me stretch my arms wide, let my arms never become weak! Moving like the sunlight, like Inana, like the seven storms, those of Iškur, let me leap like a flame, blaze like lightning! Let me go wherever I look to, set foot wherever I cast my glance, reach wherever my heart desires and let me loosen my shoes in whatever place my heart has named to me! When Utu lets me reach Kulaba my city, let him who curses me have no joy thereof; let him who wishes to strive with me never say "Just let him come!" I shall have the woodcarvers fashion statues of you, and you will be breathtaking to look upon. Your name will be made famous thereby in Sumer and will redound to the credit of the temples of the great gods."

So Anzud says to holy Lugalbanda: "The power of running be in your thighs! Never grow tired! Strength be in your arms! Stretch your arms wide, may your arms never become weak! Moving like the sun, like Inana, like the seven storms of Iškur, leap like a flame, blaze like lightning! Go wherever you look to, set foot wherever you cast your glance, reach wherever your heart desires, loosen your shoes in whatever place your heart has named to you! When Utu lets you reach Kulaba your city, he who curses you shall have no joy thereof; he who wishes to strive with you shall never say "Just let him come!" When you have had the woodcarvers fashion statues of me, I shall be breathtaking to look upon. My name will be made famous thereby in Sumer and will redound to the credit of the temples of the great gods. May ... shake for you ... like a sandal. ... the Euphrates ... your feet ..."

He took in his hand such of his provisions as he had not eaten, and his weapons one by one. Anzud flew on high, Lugalbanda walked on the ground. The bird, looking from above, spies the troops. Lugalbanda, looking from below, spies the dust that the troops have stirred up. The bird says to Lugalbanda, "Come now, my Lugalbanda. I shall give you some advice: may my advice be heeded. I shall say words to you: bear them in mind. What I have told you, the fate I have fixed for you, do not tell it to your comrades, do not explain it to your brothers. Fair fortune may conceal foul: it is indeed so. Leave me to my nest: you keep to your troops." The bird hurried to his nest. Lugalbanda set out for the place where his brothers were.

Like a pelican emerging from the sacred reedbed, like laḫama deities going up from the abzu, like one who is stepping from heaven to earth, Lugalbanda stepped into the midst of his brothers' picked troops. His brothers chattered away, the troops chattered away. His brothers, his friends weary him with questions: "Come now, my Lugalbanda, here you are again! The troops had abandoned you as one killed in battle. Certainly, you were not eating the good fat of the herd! Certainly, you were not eating the sheepfold's fresh cheese. How is it that you have come back from the great mountains, where no one goes alone, whence no one returns to mankind?" Again his brothers, his friends weary him with questions: "The banks of the mountain rivers, mothers of plenty, are widely separated. How did you cross their waters? – as if you were drinking them?"

Holy Lugalbanda replies to them, "The banks of the mountain rivers, mothers of plenty, are widely separated. With my legs I stepped over them, I drank them like water from a waterskin; and then I snarled like a wolf, I grazed the water-meadows, I pecked at the ground like a wild pigeon, I ate the mountain acorns." Lugalbanda's brothers and friends consider the words that he has said to them. Exactly as if they were small birds flocking together all day long they embrace him and kiss him. As if he were a gamgam chick sitting in its nest, they feed him and give him drink. They drive away sickness from holy Lugalbanda.

Then the men of Unug followed them as one man; they wound their way through the hills like a snake over a grain-pile. When the city was only a double-hour distant, the armies of Unug and Kulaba encamped by the posts and ditches that surrounded Aratta. From the city it rained down javelins as if from the clouds, slingstones numerous as the raindrops falling in a whole year whizzed down loudly from Aratta's walls. The days passed, the months became long, the year turned full circle. A yellow harvest grew beneath the sky. They looked askance at the fields. Unease came over them. Slingstones numerous as the raindrops falling in a whole year landed on the road. They were hemmed in by the barrier of mountain thornbushes thronged with dragons. No one knew how to go back to the city, no was rushing to go back to Kulaba. In their midst Enmerkar son of Utu was afraid, was troubled, was disturbed by this upset. He sought someone whom he could send back to the city, he sought someone whom he could send back to Kulaba. No one said to him "I will go to the city." No one said to him "I will go to Kulaba." He went out to the foreign host. No one said to him "I will go to the city." No one said to him "I will go to Kulaba." He stood before the élite troops. No one said to him "I will go to the city." No one said to him "I will go to Kulaba." A second time he went out to the foreign host. No one said to him "I will go to the city." No one said to him "I will go to Kulaba." He stepped out before the élite troops.

Lugalbanda alone arose from the people and said to him, "My king, I will go to the city, but no one shall go with me. I will go alone to Kulaba. No one shall go with me." – "If you go to the city, no one shall go with you. You shall go alone to Kulaba, no one shall go with you." He swore by heaven and by earth: "Swear that you will not let go from your hands the great emblems of Kulaba."

After he had stood before the summoned assembly, within the palace that rests on earth like a great mountain Enmerkar son of Utu berated Inana: "Once upon a time my princely sister holy Inana summoned me in her holy heart from the bright mountains, had me enter brick-built Kulaba. Where there was a marsh then in Unug, it was full of water. Where there was any dry land, Euphrates poplars grew there. Where there were reed thickets, old reeds and young reeds grew there. Divine Enki who is king in Eridu tore up for me the old reeds, drained off the water completely. For fifty years I built, for fifty years I was successful. Then the Martu peoples, who know no agriculture, arose in all Sumer and Akkad. But the wall of Unug extended out across the desert like a bird net. Yet now, here in this place, my attractiveness to her has dwindled. My troops are bound to me as a cow is bound to its calf; but like a son who, hating his mother, leaves his city, my princely sister holy Inana has run away from me back to brick-built Kulaba. If she loves her city and hates me, why does she bind the city to me? If she hates the city and yet loves me, why does she bind me to the city? If the mistress removes herself from me to her holy chamber, and abandons me like an Anzud chick, then may she at least bring me home to brick-built Kulaba: on that day my spear shall be laid aside. On that day she may shatter my shield. Speak thus to my princely sister, holy Inana."

Thereupon holy Lugalbanda came forth from the palace. Although his brothers and his comrades barked at him as at a foreign dog trying to join a pack of dogs, he stepped proudly forward like a foreign wild ass trying to join a herd of wild asses. "Send someone else to Unug for the lord." – "For Enmerkar son of Utu I shall go alone to Kulaba. No one shall go with me" – how he spoke to them! "Why will you go alone and keep company with no one on the journey? If our beneficent spirit does not stand by you there, if our good protective deity does not go with you there, you will never again stand with us where we stand, you will never again dwell with us where we dwell, you will never again set your feet on the ground where our feet are. You will not come back from the great mountains, where no one goes alone, whence no one returns to mankind!" – "Time is passing, I know. None of you is going with me over the great earth." While the hearts of his brothers beat loudly, while the hearts of his comrades sank, Lugalbanda took in his hand such of his provisions as he had not eaten, and each of his weapons one by one. From the foot of the mountains, through the high mountains, into the flat land, from the edge of Anšan to the top of Anšan, he crossed five, six, seven mountains.

By midnight, but before they had brought the offering-table to holy Inana, he set foot joyfully in brick-built Kulaba. His lady, holy Inana, sat there on her cushion. He bowed and prostrated himself on the ground. With eyes Inana looked at holy Lugalbanda as she would look at the shepherd Ama-ušumgal-ana. In a voice, Inana spoke to holy Lugalbanda as she would speak to her son Lord Šara: "Come now, my Lugalbanda, why do you bring news from the city? How have you come here alone from Aratta?"

Holy Lugalbanda answered her: "What Enmerkar son of Utu quoth and what he says, what your brother quoth and what he says, is: "Once upon a time my princely sister holy Inana summoned me in her holy heart from the mountains, had me enter brick-built Kulaba. Where there was a marsh then in Unug, it was full of water. Where there was any dry land, Euphrates poplars grew there. Where there were reed thickets, old reeds and young reeds grew there. Divine Enki who is king in Eridu tore up for me the old reeds, drained off the water completely. For fifty years I built, for fifty years I was successful. Then the Martu peoples, who know no agriculture, arose in all Sumer and Akkad. But the wall of Unug extended out across the desert like a bird net. Yet now, here in this place, my attractiveness to her has dwindled. My troops are bound to me as a cow is bound to its calf; but like a son who, hating his mother, leaves his city, my princely sister holy Inana has run away from me back to brick-built Kulaba. If she loves her city and hates me, why does she bind the city to me? If she hates the city and yet loves me, why does she bind me to the city? If the mistress removes herself from me to her holy chamber and abandons me like an Anzud chick, then may she at least bring me home to brick-built Kulaba: on that day my spear shall be laid aside. On that day she may shatter my shield. Speak thus to my princely sister, holy Inana."

Holy Inana uttered this response: "Now, at the end, on the banks, in the water-meadows, of a clear river, of a river of clear water, of the river which is Inana's gleaming waterskin, the suḫurmaš fish eats the honey-herb; the toad eats the mountain acorns; and the … fish, which is a god of the suḫurmaš fish, plays happily there and darts about. With his scaly tail he touches the old reeds in that holy place. The tamarisks of the place, as many as there are, drink water from that pool."

"It stands alone, it stands alone! One tamarisk stands alone at the side! When Enmerkar son of Utu has cut that tamarisk and has fashioned it into a bucket, he must tear up the old reeds in that holy place roots and all, and collect them in his hands. When he has chased out from it the … fish, which is a god of the suḫurmaš fish, caught that fish, cooked it, garnished it and brought it as a sacrifice to the a-an-kar weapon, Inana's battle-strength, then his troops will have success for him; then he will have brought to an end that which in the subterranean waters provides the life-strength of Aratta."

"If he carries off from the city its worked metal and smiths, if he carries off its worked stones and its stonemasons, if he renews the city and settles it, all the moulds of Aratta will be his."

Now Aratta's battlements are of green lapis lazuli, its walls and its towering brickwork are bright red, their brick clay is made of tinstone dug out in the mountains where the cypress grows.

Praise be to holy Lugalbanda.

Enmerkar and the Lord of Aratta

City, majestic bull bearing vigour and great awesome splendour, Kulaba, …, breast of the storm, where destiny is determined; Unug, great mountain, in the midst of … There the evening meal of the great abode of An was set. In those days of yore, when the destinies were determined, the great princes allowed Unug Kulaba's E-ana to lift its head high. Plenty, and carp floods, and the rain which brings forth dappled barley were then increased in Unug Kulaba. Before the land of Dilmun yet existed, the E-ana of Unug Kulaba was well founded, and the holy ĝipar of Inana in brick-built Kulaba shone forth like the silver in the lode. Before ... carried ..., before ......, before ... carried ..., before the commerce was practised; before gold, silver, copper, tin, blocks of lapis lazuli, and mountain stones were brought down together from their mountains, before ... bathed for the festival, ..., ... time passed.

2 lines missing

... was colourfully adorned, and ..., the holy place, was ... with flawless lapis lazuli, its interior beautifully formed like a white meš tree bearing fruit. The lord of Aratta placed on his head the golden crown for Inana. But he did not please her like the lord of Kulaba. Aratta did not build for holy Inana – unlike the Shrine E-ana, the ĝipar, the holy place, unlike brick-built Kulaba.

At that time, the lord chosen by Inana in her heart, chosen by Inana in her holy heart from the bright mountain, Enmerkar, the son of Utu, made a plea to his sister, the lady who grants desires, holy Inana:

"My sister, let Aratta fashion gold and silver skilfully on my behalf for Unug. Let them cut the flawless lapis lazuli from the blocks, let them ... the translucence of the flawless lapis lazuli ... build a holy mountain in Unug. Let Aratta build a temple brought down from heaven – your place of worship, the Shrine E-ana; let Aratta skilfully fashion the interior of the holy ĝipar, your abode; may I, the radiant youth, may I be embraced there by you. Let Aratta submit beneath the yoke for Unug on my behalf. Let the people of Aratta bring down for me the mountain stones from their mountain, build the great shrine for me, erect the great abode for me, make the great abode, the abode of the gods, famous for me, make my me prosper in Kulaba, make the abzu grow for me like a holy mountain, make Eridug gleam for me like the mountain range, cause the abzu shrine to shine forth for me like the silver in the lode. When in the abzu I utter praise, when I bring the me from Eridug, when, in lordship, I am adorned with the crown like a purified shrine, when I place on my head the holy crown in Unug Kulaba, then may the ... of the great shrine bring me into the ĝipar, and may the ... of the ĝipar bring me into the great shrine. May the people marvel admiringly, and may Utu witness it in joy."

Thereupon the splendour of holy An, the lady of the mountains, the wise, the goddess whose kohl is for Ama-ušumgal-ana, Inana, the lady of all the lands, called to Enmerkar, the son of Utu:

"Come, Enmerkar! I shall offer you advice: let my counsel be heeded. I shall speak words to you; let them be heard. Choose from the troops as a messenger one who is eloquent of speech and endowed with endurance. Where and to whom shall he carry the important message of wise Inana? Let him bring it up into the Zubi mountains, let him descend with it from the Zubi mountains. Let Susa and the land of Anšan humbly salute Inana like tiny mice. In the great mountain ranges, let the teeming multitudes grovel in the dust for her. Aratta shall submit beneath the yoke to Unug. The people of Aratta shall bring down the mountain stones from their mountains, and shall build the great shrine for you, and erect the great abode for you, will cause the great abode, the abode of the gods, to shine forth for you; will make your me flourish in Kulaba, will make the abzu grow for you like a holy mountain, will make Eridug shining for you like the mountain range, will cause the abzu shrine to shine forth for you like the glitter in the lode. When in the abzu you utter praise, when you bring the me from Eridug, when, in lordship, you are adorned with the crown like a purified shrine, when you place on your head the holy crown in Unug Kulaba, then may the ... of the great shrine bring you into the ĝipar, and may the ... of the ĝipar bring you into the great shrine. May the people marvel admiringly, and may Utu witness it in joy. Because ... shall carry daily, when ... in the evening cool ..., – in the place of Dumuzid where the ewes, kids and lambs are numerous, the people of Aratta shall run around for you like the mountain sheep in the akalag fields, the fields of Dumuzid. Rise like the sun over my holy breast! You are the jewel of my throat! Praise be to you, Enmerkar, the son of Utu!"

The lord gave heed to the words of holy Inana, and chose from the troops as a messenger one who was eloquent of speech and endowed with endurance. Where and to whom will he carry the important message of wise Inana?

"You shall bring it up into the Zubi mountains, you shall descend with it from the Zubi mountains. Let Susa and the land of Anšan humbly salute Inana like tiny mice. In the great mountain ranges, let the teeming multitudes grovel in the dust for her. Messenger, speak to the lord of Aratta and say to him: "Lest I make the people fly off from that city like a wild dove from its tree, lest I make them fly around like a bird over its well-founded nest, lest I requite (?) them as if at a current market rate, lest I make it gather dust like an utterly destroyed city, lest like a settlement cursed by Enki and utterly destroyed, I too utterly destroy Aratta; lest like the devastation which swept destructively, and in whose wake Inana arose, shrieked and yelled aloud, I too wreak a sweeping devastation there – let Aratta pack nuggets of gold in leather sacks, placing alongside it the kugmea ore; package up precious metals, and load the packs on the donkeys of the mountains; and then may the Junior Enlil of Sumer have them build for me, the lord whom Nudimmud has chosen in his sacred heart, a mountain of a shining me; have them make it luxuriant for me like a boxwood tree, have them make its shining horns colourful for me as when Utu comes forth from his chamber, have them make its doorposts gleam brightly for me."

"Chant to him the holy song, the incantation sung in its chambers – the incantation of Nudimmud: "On that day when there is no snake, when there is no scorpion, when there is no hyena, when there is no lion, when there is neither dog nor wolf, when there is thus neither fear nor trembling, man has no rival! At such a time, may the lands of Šubur and Ḫamazi, the many-tongued, and Sumer, the great mountain of the me of magnificence, and Akkad, the land possessing all that is befitting, and the Martu land, resting in security – the whole universe, the well-guarded people – may they all address Enlil together in a single language! For at that time, for the ambitious lords, for the ambitious princes, for the ambitious kings, Enki, for the ambitious lords, for the ambitious princes, for the ambitious kings, for the ambitious lords, for the ambitious princes, for the ambitious kings – Enki, the lord of abundance and of steadfast decisions, the wise and knowing lord of the Land, the expert of the gods, chosen for wisdom, the lord of Eridug, shall change the speech in their mouths, as many as he had placed there, and so the speech of mankind is truly one.""

The lord added further instructions for the messenger going to the mountains, to Aratta: "Messenger, by night, drive on like the south wind! By day, be up like the dew!"

The messenger gave heed to the words of his king. He journeyed by the starry night, and by day he travelled with Utu of heaven. Where and to whom will he carry the important message of Inana with its stinging tone? He brought it up into the Zubi mountains, he descended with it from the Zubi mountains. Susa and the land of Anšan humbly saluted Inana like tiny mice. In the great mountain ranges, the teeming multitudes grovelled in the dust for her. He traversed five mountains, six mountains, seven mountains. He lifted his eyes as he approached Aratta. He stepped joyfully into the courtyard of Aratta, he made known the authority of his king. Openly he spoke out the words in his heart. The messenger transmitted the message to the lord of Aratta:

"Your father, my master, has sent me to you; the lord of Unug, the lord of Kulaba, has sent me to you." "What is it to me what your master has spoken? What is it to me what he has said?"

"This is what my master has spoken, this is what he has said. My king who from his birth has been fitted {for lordship}, the lord of Unug, the saĝkal snake living in Sumer, who pulverises {mountains} like flour, the stag of the tall mountains, endowed with princely antlers, wild cow, kid pawing the holy soapwort with its hoof, whom the good cow had given birth to in the heart of the mountains, Enmerkar, the son of Utu, has sent me to you."

"This is what my master said: "Lest I make the people fly off from that city like a wild dove from its tree, lest I make them fly around like a bird over its well-founded nest, lest I requite (?) them as if at a current market rate, lest I make it gather dust like an utterly destroyed city, lest like a settlement cursed by Enki and utterly destroyed, I too utterly destroy Aratta; lest like the devastation which swept destructively, and in whose wake Inana arose, shrieked and yelled aloud, I too wreak a sweeping devastation there – let Aratta pack nuggets of gold in leather sacks, placing alongside it the kugmea ore; package up precious metals, and load the packs on the donkeys of the mountains; and then may the Junior Enlil of Sumer have them build for me, the lord whom Nudimmud has chosen in his sacred heart, a mountain of a shining me; have them make it luxuriant for me like a boxwood tree, have them make its shining horns colourful for me as when Utu comes forth from his chamber, have them make its doorposts gleam brightly for me. Chant to him for me the holy song, the incantation sung in its chambers – the Incantation of Nudimmud."

"Say whatever you will say to me, and I shall announce that message in the shrine E-ana as glad tidings to the scion of him with the glistening beard, whom his stalwart cow gave birth to in the mountain of the shining me, who was reared on the soil of Aratta, who was given suck at the udder of the good cow, who is suited for office in Kulaba, the mountain of great me, to Enmerkar, the son of Utu; I shall repeat it in his ĝipar, fruitful as a flourishing meš tree, to my king, the lord of Kulaba."

When he had spoken thus to him, (the lord of Aratta replied): "Messenger, speak to your king, the lord of Kulaba, and say to him: "It is I, the lord suited to purification, I whom the huge heavenly neck-stock, the queen of heaven and earth, the goddess of the numerous me, holy Inana, has brought to Aratta, the mountain of the shining me, I whom she has let bar the entrance of the mountains as if with a great door. How then shall Aratta submit to Unug? Aratta's submission to Unug is out of the question! Say this to him."

When he had spoken thus to him, the messenger replied to the lord of Aratta: "The great queen of heaven, who rides upon the awesome me, dwelling on the peaks of the bright mountains, adorning the dais of the bright mountains – my lord and master, who is her servant, has had them install her as the divine queen of E-ana. Aratta shall bow, O lord, in absolute submission! She has spoken to him thus, in brick-built Kulaba."

Thereupon, the lord became depressed and deeply troubled. He had no answer; he was searching for an answer. He stared at his own feet, trying to find an answer. He found an answer and gave a cry. He bellowed the answer to the message like a bull to the messenger:

"Messenger! Speak to your king, the lord of Kulaba, and say to him: 'This great mountain range is a meš tree grown high to the sky; its roots form a net, and its branches are a snare. It may be a sparrow but it has the talons of an Anzud bird or of an eagle. The barrier of Inana is perfectly made and is impenetrable (?). Those eagle talons make the blood of the enemy run from the bright mountain. Although in Aratta there is weeping ..., water libations are offered and flour is sprinkled; on the mountain, sacrifices and prayers are offered in obeisance. With fewer than five or 10 men, how can mobilized Unug proceed against the Zubi mountains? Your king is heading in all haste against my military might, but I am equally eager for a contest. (As the proverb goes,) he who ignores a rival, does not get to eat everything up, like the bull which ignores the bull at its side. But he who acknowledges a contest can be the outright winner, like the bull which acknowledges the bull at its side – or does he reject me in this contest? Like ..., can match no one – or does he still reject me in this contest? Again, I have words to say to you, messenger: I have an artful proposal to make to you ..., may it get across to you ... Repeat this to your master, to the lord of Kulaba, a lion lying on its paws in E-ana, a bull bellowing within it, within his ĝipar, fruitful as a flourishing meš tree. The mountain range is a warrior, ... high, like Utu going to his abode at twilight, like one from whose face blood drips; or like Nanna, who is majestic in the high heavens, like him whose countenance shines with radiance, who ... is like the woods in the mountains."

"Now if Enmerkar just makes straight for the ... of Aratta, for the benevolent protective spirit of the mountain of holy powers, for Aratta, which is like a bright crown of heaven, then I shall make my pre-eminence clear, and he need not pour barley into sacks, nor have it carted, nor have that barley carried into the settlements, nor place collectors over the labourers."

"But if he were actually to have barley poured into carrying-nets, and to have it loaded on the packasses at whose sides reserve donkeys have been placed, and were to have it heaped up in a pile in the courtyard of Aratta – were he really to heap it up in such a manner; and were Inana, the luxuriance of the grain pile, who is the 'illuminator of the lands', the 'ornament of the settlements', who adorns the seven walls, who is the heroic lady, fit for battle, who, as the heroine of the battleground, makes the troops dance the dance of Inana – were she actually to cast off Aratta as if to a carrion-pursuing dog, then in that case I should submit to him; he would indeed have made me know his preeminence; like the city, I in my smallness would submit to him.' So say to him."

After he had spoken thus to him, the lord of Aratta made the messenger repeat the message just as he himself had said it. The messenger turned on his thigh like a wild cow; like a sand fly he went on his way in the morning calm. He set foot joyfully in brick-built Kulaba. The messenger rushed to the great courtyard, the courtyard of the throne room. He repeated it word perfect to his master, the lord of Kulaba; he even bellowed at him like a bull, and Enmerkar listened to him like an ox driver. The king had him sit ... at his right side. As he turned his left side to him, he said: "Does Aratta really understand the implications of his own stratagem?"

After day had broken and Utu had risen, the sun god of the Land lifted his head high. The king combined the Tigris with the Euphrates. He combined the Euphrates with the Tigris. Large vessels were placed in the open air, and he stood small vessels beside them, like lambs lying on the grass. ... vessels were placed in the open air adjacent to them. Then the king, Enmerkar, the son of Utu, placed wide apart the ešda vessels, which were of gold. Thereupon, the ... clay tablet, the pointed stylus of the assembly, the golden statue fashioned on a propitious day, beautiful Nanibgal, grown with a fair luxuriance, Nisaba, the lady of broad wisdom, opened for him her holy house of wisdom. He entered the palace of heaven, and became attentive. Then the lord opened his mighty storehouse, and firmly set his great lidga measure on the ground. The king removed his old barley from the other barley; he soaked the greenmalt all through with water; its lip ... the ḫirin plant. He narrowed the meshes of the carrying nets. He measured out in full (?) the barley for the granary, adding for the teeth of locusts. He had it loaded on the packasses at whose sides reserve donkeys were placed. The king, the lord of broad wisdom, the lord of Unug, the lord of Kulaba, despatched them directly to Aratta. He made the people go on to Aratta on their own, like ants out of crevices. Again the lord added instructions for the messenger going to the mountains, to Aratta:

"Messenger, speak to the lord of Aratta and say to him: 'The base of my sceptre is the divine power of magnificence. Its crown provides a protective shade over Kulaba; under its spreading branches holy Inana refreshes herself in the shrine E-ana. Let him snap off a splinter from it and hold that in his hand; let him hold it in his hand like a string of cornelian beads, a string of lapis lazuli beads. Let the lord of Aratta bring that before me.' So say to him."

After he had thus spoken to him, the messenger went on his way to Aratta; his feet raised the dust of the road, and made the little pebbles of the hills thud; like a dragon prowling the desert, he was unopposed. After the messenger reached Aratta, the people of Aratta stepped forward to admire the packasses. In the courtyard of Aratta, the messenger measured out in full (?) the barley for the granary, adding for the teeth of locusts. As if from the rains of heaven and the sunshine, Aratta was filled with abundance. As when the gods return to their seats (?), Aratta's hunger was sated. The people of Aratta covered their fields with the water-soaked greenmalt. Afterwards, couriers and šatam officials ...

2 lines unclear

The citizens of Aratta were mindful; he revealed the matter to Aratta. Consequently, in Aratta, from the hand ... his hand ... to the lord of Unug.

"As for us, in the direst hunger, in our direst famine, let us prostrate ourselves before the lord of Kulaba!"

The eloquent elders wrung their hands in despair, leaning against the wall; indeed, they were even placing their treasuries (?) at the disposal of the lord. His sceptre ... in the palace ... Openly he spoke out the words in his heart:

"Your father, my master, sent me to you. Enmerkar, the son of Utu, sent me to you."

"What is it to me what your master has spoken? What is it to me what he has said?" "This is what my master has spoken, this is what he has said: "The base of my sceptre is the divine power of magnificence. Its crown provides a protective shade over Kulaba; under its spreading branches holy Inana refreshes herself in the shrine E-ana.Let him snap off a splinter from it and hold that in his hand; let him hold it in his hand like a string of cornelian beads, a string of lapis lazuli beads. Let the lord of Aratta bring that before me. So say to him."

After he had spoken thus to him, for that reason he went inside the sanctuary ... and lay himself down in a fast. Day broke. He discussed the matter at length, he spoke unspeakable words; he circulated with this matter as if it were barley eaten by a donkey.

And what did one speak to another? What did one say to another? What one said to another, so indeed it was.

"Messenger, speak to your king, the lord of Kulaba, and say to him: "Let him put in his hand and contemplate a sceptre that is not of wood, nor designated as wood {– not ildag wood, nor šim-gig wood, not cedar wood, nor cypress wood, not ḫašur cypress, nor palm wood, not hardwood, nor zabalum wood}, not poplar as in a chariot, not reedwork as in whip handles; not gold, nor copper, not genuine kugmea metal nor silver, not cornelian, nor lapis lazuli – let him snap off a splinter from that and hold it in his hand; let him hold it in his hand like a string of cornelian beads, a string of lapis lazuli beads. Let the lord of Kulaba bring that before me." So say to him."

After he had spoken to him thus, the messenger went off like a young donkey, braying as it is cut off from the chariot tongue; he trotted like an onager running on dry land, he filled his mouth with wind; he ran in one track (?) like a long-woolled sheep butting other sheep in its fury. He set foot joyfully in brick-built Kulaba. He transmitted the message word for word to his master, the lord of Kulaba. Now Enki gave Enmerkar wisdom, and the lord gave instructions to his chief steward. In his house ..., the king received ... He wrapped it up like ..., and inspected it. He pounded ... with a pestle like herbs, he poured it like oil on the ... reed. From the sunlight it emerged into the shade, and from the shade it emerged into the sunlight. After five years, ten years had passed, he split the ... reed with an axe. The lord looked at it, pleased, and poured on ... fine oil, fine oil of the bright mountains. The lord placed the sceptre in the hands of the messenger going to the mountains. The messenger, whose journeying to Aratta was like a pelican over the hills, like a fly over the ground, who darted through the mountains as swiftly as carp swim, reached Aratta. He set foot joyfully in the courtyard of Aratta, and put the sceptre in ... He ... and ... it. The lord of Aratta, eying the sceptre, which was shining awesomely in the sanctuary, his holy dwelling – he, the lord, called to his šatam official:

"Aratta is indeed like a slaughtered sheep! Its roads are inded like those of the rebel lands! Since holy Inana has given the primacy of Aratta to the lord of Kulaba, now it seems that holy Inana is looking with favour on her man who has sent a messenger to make the severe message as clear as the light of Utu. So in Aratta where can one go in this crisis? How long before the yoke-rope becomes bearable? As for us, in the direst hunger, in our direst famine, are we to prostrate ourselves before the lord of Kulaba?"

The lord of Aratta entrusted a message to the messenger as if it were an important tablet:

"Messenger! Speak to your master, the lord of Kulaba, and say to him: "A champion who is not black-coloured, a champion who is not white-coloured, a champion who is not brown-coloured, a champion who is not red-coloured, a champion who is not yellow-coloured, a champion who is not multicoloured – let him give you such a champion. My champion will compete against his champion, and let the more able one prevail!" Say this to him."

After he had spoken to him thus, the messenger set off, ulum, alam. In brick-built Kulaba, he was speechless, like a ... He gazed like a goat on the mountain slopes, he ... as if it were a huge mir snake coming out from the brambles. In ... he lifted his head. ... of Aratta ... From his seat, he addressed him like a raging torrent:

"Messenger! Speak to the lord of Aratta and say to him: "A garment that is not black-coloured, a garment that is not white-coloured, a garment that is not brown-coloured, a garment that is not red-coloured, a garment that is not yellow-coloured, a garment that is not multicoloured – I shall give him such a garment. My champion is embraced by Enlil. I shall send him such a champion. My champion will compete against his champion, and let the more able one prevail!" Say this to him. Second, speak to him and say: "Let him immediately pass from subterfuge ... In his city, let them go before him like sheep. Let him, like their shepherd, follow behind them. As he goes, let the mountain of bright lapis lazuli humble itself before him like a crushed reed. And let them heap up its shining gold and silver in the courtyard of Aratta for Inana the lady of E-ana." Third, speak to him and say: "Lest I make the people fly off from that city like a wild dove from its tree, lest I smash them like ..., lest I requite (?) them as if at a current market rate, lest I make ... them walk in ..., when he goes, let them take the mountain stones, and rebuild for me the great shrine Eridug, the abzu, the E-nun; let them adorn its architrave for me ... Let them make its protection spread over the Land for me." His speaking ... Recite his omen to him. At that time, the lord ..., on the throne daises and on the chairs, the noble seed, ..."

His speech was substantial, and its contents extensive. The messenger, whose mouth was heavy, was not able to repeat it. Because the messenger, whose mouth was tired, was not able to repeat it, the lord of Kulaba patted some clay and wrote the message as if on a tablet. Formerly, the writing of messages on clay was not established. Now, under that sun and on that day, it was indeed so. The lord of Kulaba inscribed the message like a tablet. It was just like that. The messenger was like a bird, flapping its wings; he raged forth like a wolf following a kid. He traversed five mountains, six mountains, seven mountains. He lifted his eyes as he approached Aratta. He stepped joyfully into the courtyard of Aratta, he made known the authority of his king. Openly he spoke out the words in his heart. The messenger transmitted the message to the lord of Aratta:

"Your father, my master, has sent me to you; the lord of Unug, the lord of Kulaba, has sent me to you." "What is it to me what your master has spoken? What is it to me what he has said?"

"This is what my master has spoken, this is what he has said. My king is like a huge meš tree, ... son of Enlil; this tree has grown high, uniting heaven and earth; its crown reaches heaven, its trunk is set upon the earth. He who is made to shine forth in lordship and kingship, Enmerkar, the son of Utu, has given me a clay tablet. O lord of Aratta, after you have examined the clay tablet, after you have learned the content of the message, say whatever you will say to me, and I shall announce that message in the shrine E-ana as glad tidings to the scion of him with the glistening beard, whom his stalwart cow gave birth to in the mountains of the shining me, who was reared on the soil of Aratta, who was given suck at the udder of the good cow, who is suited for office in Kulaba, the mountain of great me, to Enmerkar, the son of Utu; I shall repeat it in his ĝipar, fruitful as a flourishing meš tree, to my king, the lord of Kulaba."

After he had spoken thus to him, the lord of Aratta received his kiln-fired tablet from the messenger. The lord of Aratta looked at the tablet. The transmitted message was just nails, and his brow expressed anger. The lord of Aratta looked at his kiln-fired tablet. At that moment, the lord worthy of the crown of lordship, the son of Enlil, the god Iškur, thundering in heaven and earth, caused a raging storm, a great lion, in ... He was making the mountains quake ..., he was convulsing the mountain range ...; the awesome radiance ... of his breast; he caused the mountain range to raise its voice in joy. On Aratta's parched flanks, in the midst of the mountains, wheat grew of its own accord, and chickpeas also grew of their own accord; they brought the wheat which grew of its own accord into the granary of ... for the lord of Aratta, and heaped it up before him in the courtyard of Aratta. The lord of Aratta looked at the wheat. The messenger's eyes looked askance ... The lord of Aratta called to the messenger:

"Inana, the lady of all the lands, has not run away from the primacy of her city, Aratta, nor has she stolen it for Unug; she has not run away from her E-zagin, nor has she stolen it for the shrine E-ana; she has not run away from the mountain of the shining me, nor has she stolen it for brick-built Kulaba; she has not run away from the adorned bed, nor has she stolen it for the shining bed; she has not run away from the purification for the lord, nor has she stolen it for the lord of Unug, the lord of Kulaba. Inana, the lady of all the lands, has surrounded Aratta, on its right and left, for her like a rising flood. They are people whom she has separated from other people, they are people whom Dumuzid has made step forth from other people, who firmly establish the holy words of Inana. Let the clever champion and the ... of Dumuzid whirl about! Quickly, come now, ... After the flood had swept over, Inana, the lady of all the lands, from her great love of Dumuzid, has sprinkled the water of life upon those who had stood in the face of the flood and made the Land subject to them."

The clever champion, when he came, had covered his head with a colourful turban, and wrapped himself in a garment of lion skins.

4 lines unclear

Inana ... Her song was pleasing to her spouse, Ama-ušumgal-ana. Since that time, she has made it perfect in the holy ear, the holy ear of Dumuzid, has sung it and has let the words be known.

When the old woman came to the mountain of the shining me, she went up to him like a maiden who in her day is perfect, painted her eyes with kohl, wrapped herself in a white garment, came forth with the good crown like the moonlight. She arranged the ... on her head. She made Enmerkar, her spouse, occupy the throne-dais with her. She raised up ..., and indeed, for Aratta, the ewes and their lambs now multiply; indeed, for Aratta, the mother goats and their kids multiply; indeed, for Aratta, the cows and their calves multiply; indeed, for Aratta, the donkey mares and their black, swift-footed foals multiply. In Aratta, they say together: "Let them heap up and pile up for the grain piles; the abundance is truly your abundance." After having made ... for the lord of Aratta, let him ... He will ... He came forth ..., he set right for her.

3 lines missing

(An unidentified person speaks:) "... befitting ..., the ilu song of the heart, ... your abundance in his ... Enlil has granted you ..., and may ... be made known. ... his father was not luxuriantly fertile, and poured forth no semen. Enlil, king of all the lands ...... In accordance with the tasks which he has now established, the people of Aratta ... their task of plying gold, silver and lapis lazuli; the men who ... golden fruit, fruit trees, with their figs and grapes, shall heap the fruit up in great mounds ...; and shall dig out the flawless lapis lazuli from the roots of the trees, and shall remove the succulent part of the reeds from the crowns of the trees, and then shall heap them up in a pile in the courtyard of E-ana for Inana, the lady of E-ana."

"Come, my king, I shall offer you advice: let my counsel be heeded. I shall speak words to you; let them be heard. Let the people choose a man ... of the foreign lands, and let the people of Aratta speak ... When I go from here, the ever-sparkling lady gives me my kingship. Ĝeštin-ana ... In that city ..., festivals were not ... Daily ..."

approx. 6 lines missing

Enmerkar and En-suḫgir-ana

Brickwork rising out {from the pristine mountain} – Kulaba, city which reaches from heaven to earth; Unug, whose fame like the rainbow reaches up to the sky, a multicoloured sheen, as the new moon standing in the heavens.

Built in magnificence with all the great powers, lustrous mount founded on a favourable day, like moonlight coming up over the land, like bright sunlight radiating over the land, the rear cow and ... cow coming forth in abundance: all this is Unug, the glory of which reaches the highland and its radiance, genuine refined silver, covers Aratta like a garment, is spread over it like linen.

At that time the day was lord, the night was sovereign, and Utu was king. Now the name of the lord of Aratta's minister was minister Ansiga-ria. The name of the minister of Enmerkar, the lord of Kulaba, was Namena-tuma. He with the ... lord, he with the ... prince; he with the ... lord, he with the ... prince; he with the ...... lord, he with the ... prince; he with the man born to be a god; he with a man manifest as a god, with the lord of Unug, the lord of Kulaba – En-suḫgir-ana, the lord of Aratta, is to make a contest with him, saying first to the messenger concerning Unug:

"Let him submit to me, let him bear my yoke. If he submits to me, indeed submits to me, then as for him and me – he may dwell with Inana within a walled enclosure (?), but I dwell with Inana in the E-zagin of Aratta; he may lie with her on the splendid bed, but I lie in sweet slumber with her on the adorned bed, he may see dreams with Inana at night, but I converse with Inana awake. He may feed the geese with barley, but I will definitely not feed the geese with barley. I will ... the geese's eggs in a basket and ... their goslings. The small ones into my pot, the large ones into my kettle, and the rulers of the land who submitted will consume, together with me, what remains from the geese". This is what he said to Enmerkar.

The messenger runs like a wild ram and flies like a falcon. He leaves in the morning and returns already at dusk, like small birds at dawn, he ...... over the open country, like small birds at midnight, he hides himself in the interior of the mountains. Like a throw-stick, he stands at the side. Like a solitary donkey of Šakkan, he {runs over} the mountains, he dashes like a large, powerful donkey. A slim donkey, eager to run, he rushes forth. A lion in the field at dawn, he lets out roars; like a wolf which has seized a lamb, he runs quickly. The small places he has reached, he fills with ... for him; the large places he has reached, he ...... boundary (?).

He entered the presence of the lord in {his holy ĝipar}. "My king has sent me to you. The lord of Aratta, En-suḫgir-ana, has sent me to you". "This is what my king says: "Let him submit to me, let him bear my yoke. If he submits to me, indeed submits to me, then as for him and me – he may dwell with Inana within a walled enclosure (?), but I dwell with Inana in the E-zagin of Aratta; he may lie with her on the splendid bed, but I lie in sweet slumber with her on the adorned bed, he may see dreams with Inana at night, but I converse with Inana awake. He may feed the geese with barley, but I will definitely not feed the geese with barley. I will ... the geese's eggs in a basket and ... their goslings. The small ones into my pot, the large ones into my kettle, and the rulers of the land who submitted will consume, together with me, what remains from the geese".

The lord of Unug ... he is their ..., he is their rudder. ... he is the neck-stock which clamps down upon them, ... to the place of its foundation. He is their falcon which flies in the sky, he is their bird-net. The brickwork of the great temple of Aratta ... in Aratta ... great ... bring (?) ...

He patted it like a lump of clay, he examined it like a clay-tablet: "He may dwell with Inana in the E-zagin of Aratta, but I dwell with her ... as her earthly companion (?). He may lie with her in sweet slumber on the adorned bed, but I lie on Inana's splendid bed strewn with pure plants. Its back is an ug lion, its front is a piriĝ lion. The ug lion chases the piriĝ lion, the piriĝ lion chases the ug lion. As the ug lion chases the piriĝ lion and the piriĝ lion chases the ug lion, the day does not dawn, the night does not pass. I accompany Inana for a journey of fifteen leagues and yet Utu the sun god cannot see my holy crown, when she enters my holy ĝipar. Enlil has given (?) me the true crown and sceptre. Ninurta, the son of Enlil, held me on his lap as the frame holds the waterskin. Aruru, the sister of Enlil, extended her right breast to me, extended her left breast to me. When I go up to the great shrine, the Mistress screeches like an Anzud chick, and other times when I go there, even though she is not a duckling, she shrieks like one. She … from the city of her birth. No city was made to be so well-built as the city of Unug (?). It is Unug where Inana dwells and as regards Aratta, what does it have to do with this? It is brick-built Kulaba where she lives, and as regards the mount of the lustrous me, what can it do about this? For five or ten years she will definitely not go to Aratta. Since the great holy lady of the E-ana took counsel with me (?) about whether to go also to Aratta, since she {let me know} about this matter, I know that she will not go to Aratta. He who has nothing shall not feed the geese with barley, but I will feed the geese with barley. I will … the geese's eggs in a basket and … their goslings. The small ones into my pot, the old ones into my kettle, and the rulers {of the Land} who submitted will consume, together with me, what remains from the geese".

The messenger of Enmerkar reached En-suḫgir-ana, reached his holy ĝipar, his most holy place, the most holy place where he was sitting, its … En-suḫgir-ana asked for instructions, he searched for an answer. He summoned the išib priests, the lumaḫ priests, the gudug priests and girsiga attendants who dwell in the ĝipar and took counsel with them. "What shall I say to him? What shall I say to him? What shall I say to the lord of Unug, the lord of Kulaba? His bull stood up to fight my bull and the bull of Unug has defeated it. His man has been struggling with my man and the man of Unug has defeated him. His warrior (?) has been struggling with my warrior (?) and the warrior (?) of Unug … him".

The convened assembly answered him straightforwardly: "It was you who first sent a boastful (?) message to Unug for Enmerkar. You cannot hold back (?) Enmerkar, you have to hold back (?) yourself. Calm down; your heart will prompt you to achieve nothing, as far as can be known (?)". "If my city becomes a ruin mound, then I will be a potsherd of it, but I will never submit to the lord of Unug, the lord of Kulaba".

A sorcerer whose skill was that of a man of Ḫamazu, Ur-ĝiri-nuna, whose skill was that of a man of Ḫamazu, who came over to Aratta after Ḫamazu had been destroyed, practised (?) sorcery in the inner chamber at the E-ĝipar. He said to minister Ansiga-ria: "My lord, why is it that the great fathers of the city, the founders in earlier times (?), do not …, do not give advice. I will make Unug dig canals. I will make Unug submit to the shrine of Aratta. After the word of Unug …, I will make the territories from below to above, from the sea to the cedar mountain, from above to the mountain of the aromatic cedars, submit to my great army. Let Unug bring its own goods by boat, let it tie up boats as a transport flotilla towards the E-zagin of Aratta". The minister Ansiga-ria rose up in his city, he …

… Ansiga-ria …, if only … "My lord, why is it that the great fathers of the city, the founders in earlier times (?), do not …, do not give advice. I will make Unug dig canals. I will make Unug submit to the shrine of Aratta. After the word of Unug …, I will make the territories from below to above, from the sea to the cedar mountain, from above to the mountain of the aromatic cedars, submit to my great army. Let Unug bring its own goods by boat, let it tie up boats as a transport flotilla towards the E-zagin of Aratta".

This made the lord extremely happy, so he gave five minas of gold to him, he gave five minas of silver to him. He promised him that he would be allotted fine food to eat, he promised him that he would be allotted fine drink to drink. "When their men are taken captive, your life … happiness (?) in your hand (?) prosperity (?)", he promised to him.

The sorcerer, farmer of the best seeds, directed his steps towards Ereš, the city of Nisaba, and reached the animal pen, the house where the cows live. The cow trembled with fear at him in the animal pen. He made the cow speak so that it conversed with him as if it were a human being: "Cow, who will eat your butter? Who will drink your milk?" "My butter will be eaten by Nisaba, my milk will be drunk by Nisaba. My cheese, skilfully produced bright crown, was made fitting for the great dining hall, the dining hall of Nisaba. Until my butter is delivered from the holy animal pen, until my milk is delivered from the holy byre, the steadfast wild cow Nisaba, the first-born of Enlil, will not impose any levy on the people". "Cow, your butter to your shining horn; your milk to your back". So the cow's butter was ... to its shining horn; its milk was ... to its back ...

He reached the holy byre, the byre of Nisaba. The goat trembled with fear at him in the byre. He made the goat speak so that it conversed with him as if it were a human being. "Goat, who will eat your butter? Who will drink your milk?" "My butter will be eaten by Nisaba, my milk will be drunk by Nisaba. My cheese, skilfully produced bright crown, was made fitting for the great dining hall, the dining hall of Nisaba. Until my butter is delivered from the holy animal pen, until my milk is delivered from the holy byre, the steadfast wild cow Nisaba, the first-born of Enlil, will not impose any levy on the people". "Goat, your butter to your shining horn, your milk to your back". So the goat's butter was ... to its shining horn; its milk was made to depart to its back.

On that day the animal pen and the byre were turned into a house of silence; they were dealt a disaster. There was no milk in the udder of the cow, the day darkened for the calf, its young calf was hungry and wept bitterly. There was no milk in the udder of the goat; the day darkened for the kid. The buck-goat lay starving, its life ... The cow spoke bitterly to its calf. The goat ... to its kid. The holy churn was empty, ... was hungry, ... lay starving.

On that day the animal pen and the byre were turned into a house of silence; they were dealt a disaster. The cowherd dropped his staff from his hand: he was shocked. The shepherd hung the crook at his side and wept bitterly. The shepherd boy did not enter (?) the byre and animal pen, but took another way; the milk carrier did not sing loudly, but took another road. The cowherd and shepherd of Nisaba, sons born of the same mother, were brought up in the animal pen and byre. The name of the first one was Maš-gula, the name of the second one was Ur-edina. At the great gate, facing sunrise, the place marvelled at by the land, both of them crouched in the debris and appealed to Utu for help: "The sorcerer from Aratta entered the animal pen. He made the milk scarce, so the young calves could not get any. {In the animal pen and the byre he caused distress; he made the butter and milk scarce}. He threw its ..., was dealt a disaster".

... approached. ... caused damage (?) ... turned toward Ereš. ... the Euphrates ... the river of the gods. She made her way to the city whose destiny was decreed by An and Enlil ... Wise Woman Saĝburu ... hand ... for him.

Both of them threw fish spawn (?) into the river. The sorcerer made a giant carp {come out} from the water. Wise Woman Saĝburu, however, made an eagle {come out} from the water. {The eagle seized the giant carp and fled to the mountains}.

A second time they threw fish spawn (?) into the river. The sorcerer made a ewe and its lamb {come out} from the water. Wise Woman Saĝburu, however, made a wolf {come out} from the water. The wolf seized the ewe and its lamb and dragged them to the wide desert.

A third time they threw fish spawn (?) into the river. The sorcerer made a cow and its calf {come out} from the water. Wise Woman Saĝburu, however, made a lion {come out} from the water. The lion seized the cow and its calf and {took} them to the reedbeds.

A fourth time they threw fish spawn (?) into the river. The sorcerer made an ibex and a wild sheep {come out} from the water. Wise Woman Saĝburu, however, made a mountain leopard {come out} from the water. The leopard seized the ibex and the wild sheep and took them to the mountains.

A fifth time they threw fish spawn (?) into the river. The sorcerer made a gazelle kid come out from the water. Wise Woman Saĝburu, however, made a tiger and a … lion come out from the water. The tiger and the … lion seized the gazelle kid and {took} them to the forest. What happened made the face of the sorcerer darken, made his mind confused.

Wise Woman Saĝburu said to him: "Sorcerer, you do have magical powers, but where is your sense? How on earth could you think of going to do sorcery at Ereš, which is the city of Nisaba, a city whose destiny was decreed by An and Enlil, the primeval city, the beloved city of Ninlil?"

The sorcerer answered her: "I went there without knowing all about this. I acknowledge your superiority – please do not be bitter". He pleaded, he prayed to her: "Set me free, my sister; set me free. Let me go in peace to my city. Let me return safely to Aratta, the mount of the lustrous me. I will {make known} your greatness in all the lands. I will sing your praise in Aratta, the mount of the lustrous me".

Wise Woman Saĝburu answered to him: "You have caused distress in the animal pen and the byre; you have made the butter and milk scarce there. You have removed the lunch-table, the morning- and evening-table. You have cut off butter and milk from the evening meal of the great dining hall, … distress …… Your sin that butter and milk … cannot be forgiven. Nanna the king … the byre … milk; … established that it was a capital offence and I am not pardoning your life". Wise Woman Saĝburu … her decision about the sorcerer in the assembly (?). She threw her prisoner from the bank of the Euphrates. She seized from him his life-force and then returned to her city, Ereš.

Having heard this matter, En-suḫgir-ana sent a man to Enmerkar: "You are the beloved lord of Inana, you alone are exalted. Inana has truly chosen you for her holy lap, you are her beloved. From the south to the highlands, you are the great lord, and I am only second to you; from the moment of conception I was not your equal, you are the older brother. I cannot match you ever".

In the contest between Enmerkar and En-suḫgir-ana, Enmerkar proved superior to En-suḫgir-ana. Nisaba, be praised!

Didactic Stories

Introduction

THE VARIOUS STORIES in this chapter come directly from translations of the original Sumerian sources. The stories are instructional, many of them as parables or poetic monologues, which instruct the people on how to live their lives as decent, honourable, and pious humans. Basically, these stories give us insight into the fundamental social mores and beliefs of the ancient Babylonians.

Among the ten texts in this chapter are "The Song of the Hoe", a praise poem celebrating the hoe for its multiple uses and linking it to the god Enlil and his creation of the world; "The Home of the Fish", a poetic monologue intended to instruct people to recognize people who are sincere or those whose invitations lead others into a trap; and "The Debate Between Bird and Fish", a poem of literary debate about difficult neighbours and how quickly problems can escalate.

A Man and His God

A PERSON SHOULD steadfastly proclaim the exaltedness of his god. A young man should devoutly praise the words of his god; the people living in the righteous Land should unravel them like a thread. May the balaĝ singer assuage the spirit of his neighbour and friend. May it soothe their (?) hearts, bring forth ..., utter ..., and measure out ... Let his mouth shaping a lament soothe the heart of his god, for a man without a god does not obtain food.

There is a young man who does not wickedly put his efforts into evil murder, yet he spends the time in grief, asag illness and bitter suffering. The fate demon has brought need and ... close to him. Bitter ... has confused his judgment (?) of it, and covered his .... Behind his back they have overpowered him like a .... Before his god the youth, the young man weeps bitterly over the malice he has suffered. He is reverent and performs obeisance.

He speaks ... of his suffering. In his total exhaustion ..., he weeps. ..., he weeps bitterly. He was able to fill the ... for him. He ... to him and addresses him:

"Grief ..., despair ..., and ... has been put in place. I am a young man, I am knowledgeable, but what I know does not come out right with me. The truth which I speak has been turned (?) into a lie. A man of deceit has overwhelmed me like the south wind and prostrated me before him. My unwitting arm has shamed me before you. You have doled out to me suffering ever anew. When I go into the house I despair. When I, a young man, go out into the street, I am depressed".

"My righteous shepherd has become angry with me, a youth, and looked upon me with hostility. My herdsman has plotted malice against me although I am not his enemy. My companion does not say a true word to me. My friend falsifies my truthfully spoken words. A man of deceit has spoken insulting words to me while you, my god, do not respond to him and you carry off my understanding. An ill-wisher has spoken insulting words to me – he angered me, was like a storm and created anguish. I am wise – why am I tied up with ignorant youths? I am discerning – why am I entangled among ignorant men?"

"Food is all about, yet my food is hunger. When shares were allotted to all the people, my allotted share was suffering. A brother ... insulted me, created anguish. He ... my ..., raised up ... and carried off ... A hostile ... without wisdom wrote on clay (?). He sought the ... of the journey. He cut down the ... of the road like a tree. He ... the supervisor and ... my steward".

"My god, ... before you. I would speak to you: my tears are excess and my words are supplication. I would tell you about it, would unravel to you like a thread the evil of my path. ... the confusion of what I have done (?). Let the wise ... in my plans; tears will not cease. I am less qualified than my friend; I am inferior to my companion".

"Now, let my mother who bore me not cease lamenting for me before you. Let my sister, truly a sweet-voiced balaĝ singer, narrate tearfully to you the deeds by which I was overpowered. Let my wife voice my suffering ... to you. Let the singer expert in chanting unravel my bitter fate to you like a thread".

"My god, the day shines bright over the Land, but for me the day is black. The bright day has become (?) a ... day. Tears, lament, anguish and despair are lodged within me. Suffering overwhelms me like a weeping child. In the hands of the fate demon my appearance has been altered, my breath of life carried away. The asag demon, the evil one, bathes in my body".

"In the overwhelming bitterness of my path I never see a good dream – but unfavourable (?) visions daily never stop for me. Anguish embraced me though I am not its wife and ... Grief spread its lap for me though I am not its small child. Lamentation sweeps over me as if it were a southerly windstorm and ... My brother cried 'Alas'".

10 lines fragmentary

5 lines missing

"I weep ... and ... My god, you who are my father who begot me, lift up my face to you. Righteous cow, god (?) of mercy and supplication, let me acquire (?) noble strength. For how long will you be uncaring for me and not look after me? Like a bull I would rise to you but you do not let me rise, you do not let me take the right course. The wise heroes say true and right words: "Never has a sinless child been born to its mother; making an effort (?) does not bring success (?); a sinless workman has never existed from of old".

"My god – the ... of forgetting which I have ... against you, the ... of releasing which I have prepared before you – may you utter words of grace on a young man who knows the holy words "May he not consume me". When the day is not bright, in my vigour, in my sleep, may I walk before you. May I ... my impurities and uncleanliness in the health of the city. May you utter words of grace on him who knows the words "When anger and the evil heart came about". Indeed he speaks joyously to him who knows the words "When fear and ... burned".

"My god, ... after you have made me know my sins, at the city's (?) gate I would declare them, ones forgotten and ones visible. I, a young man, will declare my sins before you. In the assembly may tears (?) rain like drizzle. In your house may my supplicating mother weep for me. May your holy heart (?) have mercy and compassion for me, a youth. May your heart, an awe-inspiring wave, be restored towards me, the young man".

The man's god heard his bitter weeping. After his lamentation and prolonged wailing had soothed the heart of his god towards the young man, his god accepted the righteous words, the holy words he had spoken. The words of supplication which the young man had mastered, the holy prayers, delighted his god like fine oil. His god stretched his hand away from the hostile words. He ... the anguish which had embraced him though he was not its wife and had ..., and scattered to the winds the grief which had spread its arms round him. He let the lamentation which had swept over him as if it were a southerly windstorm (?) be dissipated. He eradicated the fate demon which had been lodged in his body.

He turned the young man's suffering into joy. He set by him as guardian a benevolent protective demon that keeps guard at the mouth (?). He gave him kindly protective goddesses. The young man steadfastly proclaims the exaltedness of his god. He (?) brings forth ... and makes known ... He refreshes himself .... He trusts in you and ...

"I have set my sights on you as on the rising sun. Like Ninmaḫ ..., you have let me exert great power. My god, you looked on me from a distance with your good life-giving eyes. May I proclaim well your ... and holy strength. May your ... heart be restored towards me. May you absolve my sin. May your heart be soothed towards me".

Ĝišgiĝal.

An eršagneša for a man's god.

The Home of the Fish

Segment A

MY FISH, I have built you a home! My fish, I have built you a house, I have built you a store! I have built you a house bigger than a house, in fact a large sheepfold. Inside there is incense, and I have covered it with cloths for you; in this happy place, I ... water of joy for you; a house not bothered by cords dividing the plots, ... in the gutters. In the house, there is food, food of the best quality. In the house, there is food, food in good condition. No flies buzz around in your house where beer is poured out. Your reputation ... cannot be alienated (?). The threshold and the door-bolt, the ritual flour and the incense-burner are all in place. The scent and fragance in the house are like an aromatic cedar forest. In the house, there is beer, there is good beer. There is sweet beer, and honeyed cakes, ...

Let your acquaintances come! Let your dear ones come! Let your father and grandfather come! Let the sons of your elder brother and the sons of your younger brother come! Let your little ones come, and your big ones too! Let your wife and your children come! Let your friends and companions come! Let your brother-in-law and your father-in-law come! Let the crowd by the side of your front door come! Don't leave your friends' children outside! Don't leave your neighbours outside, whoever they may be!

Enter, my beloved son! Enter, my fine son! Don't let the day go by, don't let the night come! The moonlight should not enter that house! But if the day has gone by and the night comes, enter and I will let you relax there; I have made the grounds suitable for you! Inside, I have fixed up a seat for you. My fish, no one who sleeps there will be disturbed; no one who sits there will get involved in a quarrel.

Enter, my beloved son! Enter, my fine son! As if you were in a river with brackish water, don't go investigating any canals! As if you were in silt settled on the riverbed, may you not be able to get up! As if you were in flowing water, you should not fix your bed! The moonlight should not enter that house!

And may you not succeed in getting away: face towards me! And may you not succeed in getting away like a ... to your lair: face towards me! And may you not succeed in getting away like a dog to where you go sniffing: face towards me! And may you not succeed in getting away like a ... to where you ... face towards me! And may you not succeed in getting away like a bull to your cattle-pen, like a sheep to your sheepfold: face towards me!

Now, just ... like a bull to your cattle-pen! Enter for me, and Suen will be delighted with you! Now, just ... like a sheep to your sheepfold! Enter for me, and Dumuzid will be delighted with you! When you lift your head like a bull towards your cattle-pen, Lord Ašimbabbar Suen will be delighted with you! When you raise your head like a sheep in the sheepfold, Dumuzid the shepherd will be delighted with you!

15 lines fragmentary or missing

The fish who ... May all kinds of fish also enter with you, my fish! The one with handsome barbels who eats the honey plant, my suḫur-gal fish: may he also enter with you, my fish! The one who always eats ... reeds, ..., my suḫur-tur fish: may he also enter with you, my fish! The one with big lips, who sucks the gizi reeds,

1 line fragmentary whose food ..., my eštub fish: may he also enter with you, my fish! The black punting-pole, engendered in the fields, the farrowing sow who takes away the dough from the riverbanks, my gubi fish (probably = eel): may he also enter with you, my fish!

The one with a spiny (?) tail and a spiny (?) back, who goes ..., my še-suḫur-gal (?) fish: may he also enter with you, my fish! The fish who is like a crying child in its prayers, my še-suḫur-sig (?) fish: may he also enter with you, my fish! With a pickaxe as a head, and having a comb for teeth, the branches of a fir-tree as its bones, Dumuzid's waterskin for its stomach (?), with a dehaired skin that does not need processing, with its slender tail like the fishermen's whip, the jumping fish, with naturally smoothed skin, with no entrails in its nose, the fish that hides from its adversary, whose sting goes across like a nail, that is taboo and is not placed as an offering in the city's shrines, my mur fish (= sting-ray) : may he also enter with you, my fish!

The one whose fins (?) churn the troubled waters, a fish who seizes ...... at a glance (?), my kiĝ fish: may he also enter with you, my fish! With a head like a small millstone, ... a dog's head,

1 line unclear

the fish who does not eat the ... plants, ..., my ĝir-gid fish: may he also enter with you, my fish! With the noise of his entrails ..., my gir fish: may he also enter with you, my fish! The fish who ..., the fish who knows how to escape through a reed barrier, the fish who despite being tasty is an abomination, my ab-suḫur fish: may he also enter with you, my fish! The fish that causes breaches in dykes, with venom in its jaws, my agargar fish: may he also enter with you, my fish! The one whom the merchants ..., my kamar fish: may he also enter with you, my fish! The one whom the Martu fetch away, my nunbar-gid (?) fish: may he also enter with you, my fish!

The fish who does not eat edible plants, ..., my azagur fish: may he also enter with you, my fish! The one that ... a heavy skin, ..., my muš fish: may he also enter with you, my fish!

approx. 7 lines fragmentary or missing

Segment B

..., spotted (?) ..., my ĝiru (?) fish: may he also enter with you, my fish! The one that the children bring in ..., my salsal fish: may he also enter with you, my fish! The one with snake's eyes, a ... mouse's mouth, who ... on riverbanks,

approx. 8 lines fragmentary or missing

Segment C

The one who utters its sinister cry in the marshes and rivers, my akane bird: you would be dangling from its claws, my fish! The one who circles the nets looking for you in the waters where the nets are stretched, my ubure bird: you would be dangling from its claws, my fish! The one with long legs, that laughs, the one from faraway waters, that ..., my egret (?): you would be dangling from its claws, my fish! The one who does not adorn ..., with the ... of a bird and webbed (?) feet, my kib bird: you would be dangling from its claws, my fish! The one who seizes the quadrupeds that wander into the marshes, my kuda crocodile: you would be dangling from its claws, my fish!

But you won't be dangling from their claws, you won't be snatched up by their feet! Time is pressing, my fish! Just you come to me! Time is pressing! Just you come to me! Nanše, the queen of the fishermen, will be delighted with you.

The Heron and the Turtle

Segment A

WHAT DO THEY SAY in the reedbeds whose growth is good? In the wide reedbeds of Tutub, whose growth is good? In the marshes of Kiritaba, whose growth is good? In the adara thickets of Akšak, whose growth is good? In Enki's interconnecting (?) lagoons, whose growth is good? In the smaller lagoon, Enki's lagoon, whose growth is good? In Enki's barbar reeds, whose growth is good? In the little zi reeds of Urim, whose growth is good? In Urim, where cows and calves abound, whose growth is good?

At that time, the water was drained away from the reeds ..., and they were visible at the sheepfold. The aštaltal plant, spreading its seeds from the reedbeds, and the little kumul plants came out of the earth: they are good as little ones. The small enbar reed tighten her headdress: it is good as a young maiden. The ubzal reed goes about the city: it is good as a young man. The pela reed is covered from bottom to top: it is a good daughter-in-law. The pela reed turns from bottom to top: it is a good young son. The gašam reed digs in the ground: it is good as an old man. The zi reed ... on its own: it is good as an old woman. The reedbed lifts its head beautifully: it is a good Gudea. The ildag tree lifts its head in the irrigation ditch: it is good as a king. ... with bright branches: it is a good prince.

On that day, beside the reedbeds, someone sitting on the bank prays: "Let me snatch away the heron's eggs, let me take them away ......, so that the gift-bringing bird will not be able to make a gift, so that the gift-bringing heron will not be able make a gift!"

It catches fish; it collects eggs and crushes them. It crushes the suḫur carp in the honey plants. It crushes the eštub carp in the little zi reeds. It crushes toads in the ligiligi grass. It crushes fish spawn, its offspring, its family. It strikes heron's eggs and smashes them in the sea.

The gift-giving bird made a plea; the heron entered the house of King Enki and spoke to him: "Give me ... a wide-open place to lay my eggs in". He gave her ..., and did ... for her. ... is indeed ...

1 line fragmentary – She laid eggs in the ... She laid eggs in the wide reedbeds of Tutub. She laid eggs in the marshes of Kiritaba. She laid eggs in the adara thickets of Akšak. She laid eggs in Enki's interconnecting (?) lagoons. She laid eggs in the smaller lagoon, the lagoon of Eridug. She laid eggs in Enki's barbar reeds. She laid eggs in the little zi reeds of Urim. She laid eggs in Urim, where cows and calves abound.

Then the quarrelsome turtle, he of the troublesome way, said: "I am going to pick a quarrel with the heron, the heron! I, the turtle, am going to pick a quarrel with the heron! I, whose eyes are snake's eyes, am going to pick a quarrel! I, whose mouth is a snake's mouth, am going to pick a quarrel! I, whose tongue is a snake's tongue, am going to pick a quarrel! I, whose bite is a puppy's bite, am going to pick a quarrel! With my slender hands and slender feet, I am going to pick a quarrel! I, the turtle – an oven brick – am going to pick a quarrel! I, who live in the vegetable gardens, am going to pick a quarrel! I, who like a digging tool spend my time in the mud, am going to pick a quarrel! I, an unwashed refuse-basket, am going to pick a quarrel!"

The turtle, the trapper of birds, the setter of nets, overthrew the heron's construction of reeds for her, turned her nest upside down, and tipped her children into the water. The turtle scratched the dark-eyed bird's forehead with its claws, so that her breast was covered in blood from it.

The heron cried out, shedding tears: "If I, a bird, … my empty nest and …. Let my king judge my case, and give me verdict! Let Enki judge my case, and give me verdict! May the lord of Eridug … my claim".

"A second time, may the gift-bringing bird not be able to make a gift, may the gift-bringing heron not be able to make a gift!" It (the turtle) catches fish; it collects eggs and crushes them. It crushes the suḫur carp in the {honey plants}. It crushes the eštub carp in the little zi reeds. It crushes toads in the ligiligi grass. It crushes fish spawn, its offspring, its family.

{It dug in the ground, … its head upwards …} She (the heron) cried out to King Enki: "My king, you gave me the wide reedbeds, and I laid eggs there. I laid eggs in the wide reedbeds of Tutub. I laid eggs in the marshes of Kiritaba. I laid eggs in the adara thickets of Akšak. I laid eggs in Enki's interconnecting (?) lagoons. I laid eggs in the smaller lagoon, the lagoon of Eridug. I laid eggs in Enki's barbar reeds. I laid eggs in the little zi reeds of Urim. I laid eggs in Urim, where cows and calves abound".

"Then the quarrelsome turtle, he of the troublesome way, he whose eyes are snake's eyes, he of the troublesome way, he whose mouth is a snake's mouth, he of the troublesome way, he whose tongue is a snake's tongue, he of the troublesome way, he whose bite is a puppy's bite, he of the troublesome way, he with the slender hands and slender feet, the turtle – an oven brick – he of the troublesome way, he who lives in the vegetable gardens, he of the troublesome way, he who like a digging tool spends his time in the mud, he of the troublesome way, an unwashed refuse-basket, he of the troublesome way, the turtle, the trapper of birds, the setter of nets, overthrew my heron's construction of reeds".

"He turned my nest upside down, and tipped my children into the water. The turtle scratched my forehead – me, the dark-eyed bird – with its claws, so that my breast was covered with my blood".

The prince called to his minister, Isimud: "My minister, Isimud, my Sweet Name of Heaven!" "I stand at Enki's service! What is your wish?" "First … is filtered on the left side, then a copper box is made, so that … is covered. Then you tie …, and you tie the top with string …; then you … with a piece of dough, and you irrigate the outer enclosure (?); and you put … (?) Enki's interconnecting (?) lagoons. Then let him sit …

1 line missing

1 line fragmentary

Isimud … paid attention. First he filtered … on the left side, then he made a copper box and covered … Then he tied the top with string …; then he … with a piece of dough, and he irrigated the outer enclosure (?); and he … (?) Enki's interconnecting (?) lagoons. (Enki speaks:) "Then I, the prince, will make … stand …"

The turtle called to the prince: "You are a prince! She … from fire. I am not a god; … 1 line fragmentary – King Enki … You are a prince! She … My heart … You are a prince! She … your word. My little one destroyed a wall …; she … You are a prince! You are … brickwork.

16 lines missing

Your flax (?) is single

1 line unclear

Your … is single; … the hero … Your seed is single … a tall tree. My strong copper … good semen …"

Then, on the ziggurat ……. King Enki was …… on the ziggurat. The great brickwork of the ziggurat …… the abzu; the brickwork of the abzu ……. He took dirt from his fingernail and created the dimgi vegetable. He made the dimgi …… in the ground. Your flax came out of the earth ……. He watered the little ones with his hand; he watered the big ones with his foot. The flax grew large. After the flax had grown tall, after he had bound (?) it ……

1 line fragmentary

6 lines missing

The king …….

1 line fragmentary

1 line missing

3 lines fragmentary – They seized …… for him. They …… for him. They confronted (?) …… in the desert.

1 line unclear

……, they laid out the hunting net. …… did not catch; he caught in (?) the hunting net, …… did not catch; he spread out the hunting net.

5 lines fragmentary …… of Enki

1 line fragmentary – May you be ……; may you be ……; may you be ……; may you be ……

unknown no. of lines missing

Segment B

2 lines fragmentary …… of Enki. …… did not catch; …… the hunting net. The turtle ……. Enki …… something from his fingernail. Its inside is five ……; its exterior is ten ……. A crevice ……

unknown no. of lines missing

The Song of the Hoe

(**IN THIS COMPOSITION**, the word al 'hoe' is used as often as possible, as well as many nouns or verb forms beginning with – or merely containing – the syllable al (occasionally also ar).)

Not only did the lord make the world appear in its correct form – the lord who never changes the destinies which he determines: Enlil, who will make the human seed of the Land come {forth} from the {earth} – and not only did he hasten to separate heaven from earth, and hasten to separate earth from heaven, but, in order to make it possible for humans to grow in {'Where Flesh Came Forth'} (the name of a cosmic location), he first {suspended} the axis of the world at Dur-an-ki.

He did this with the help of the hoe (al) – and so daylight broke forth (aled). By distributing (altare) the shares of duty he established daily tasks, and for the hoe (al) and the carrying-basket wages were even established. Then Enlil praised his hoe (al), his hoe (al) wrought in gold, its top inlaid with lapis lazuli, his hoe (al) whose blade was tied on with a cord, which was adorned with silver and gold, his hoe (al), the edge of whose point (?) was a plough of lapis lazuli, whose blade was like a battering ram {standing up to a great (gal) wall}. The lord evaluated the hoe (al), determined its future destiny and placed a holy crown on its head …

Here, {in (the name of a cosmic location), he set this very hoe (al) to work;} he had it place the first model of mankind in the brick mould. His Land started to break through the soil towards Enlil. He looked with favour at his black-headed people. Now the Anuna gods stepped forward to him, and did (ĝal) obeisance to him. They calmed Enlil with a prayer, for they wanted to demand (al-dug) the black-headed people from him. Ninmena, the lady who had given birth to the ruler, who had given birth to the king, now set (alĝaĝa) human reproduction going.

The leader of heaven and earth, Lord Nunamnir, named the important persons and valued (kal) persons. He formed those persons into a row and recruited them to provide for the gods. Now Enki praised Enlil's hoe (al), and the maiden Nisaba was made responsible for keeping records of the decisions. And so people took (ĝal) the shining hoes (al), the holy hoes (al), into their hands.

The E-kur, the temple of Enlil, was founded by the hoe (al). By day it was building (aldue) it, by night it caused the temple to grow (almumu). In well-founded Nibru, the hero Ninurta entered into the presence of Enlil in the inner chamber of the Tummal – the Tummal, the {bread basket (?)} of Mother Ninlil – the innermost chamber of the Tummal, with regular food deliveries. Holy Ninisina entered into the presence of Enlil with black kids and fruit offerings for the lord.

Next comes the Abzu, with the lions before it, where the divine powers may not be requested (al-dug): the hoe wielder (?) (altar), the good man, Lord Nudimmud, was building (aldue) the Abzu, Eridug having been chosen as the construction site (altar).

The mother of the gods, Ninḫursaĝa, had the mighty (?) (altar) light of the lord live with her in Keš; she had Šul-pa-e, no less, help her with the construction work (altar).

The shrine E-ana was cleaned up by means of the hoe (al) for the lady of E-ana, the good {cow (immal)}. The hoe (al) deals with ruin mounds, the hoe (al) deals with weeds.

In the city of Zabalam, the hoe (al) is Inana's workman (?). She determined the destiny of the hoe (al), with its projecting lapis-lazuli {beard}. Utu was ready to help her with her building project (altar); it is the renowned (?) building project (altar) of youthful Utu.

The lady with broad (daĝal) intelligence, Nisaba, ordered the measuring of the E-ana for a construction project (altar), and then designed her own E-ḫamun for construction (altar).

The king who measured up the hoe (al) and who passes (zal) his time in its tracks, the hero Ninurta, has introduced working with the hoe (altar) into the rebel (bal) lands. He subdues (alĝaĝa) any city that does not obey its lord. Towards heaven he roars (algigi) like a storm, earthwards he strikes (alĝaĝa) like a dragon (ušumgal). Šara {sat down on} Enlil's knees, and Enlil gave him what he had desired (al-dug): {he had mentioned the mace, the club, arrows and quiver and the hoe (al)}. Dumuzid is the one who makes the upper land fertile (allumlum). Gibil made his hoe (al) raise its head towards the heavens – he caused the hoe (al), sacred indeed, to be refined with fire. The Anuna were rejoicing (alḫulḫuledeš).

The temple of Ĝeštin-ana resembled the drumsticks, the drumsticks of Mother Ĝeštin-ana that make a pleasant sound. The lord (Enlil) bellowed at his hoe (al) like a bull. As for the grave (irigal): the hoe (al) buries people, but dead people are also brought up from the ground by the hoe (al) (This may allude to Enkidu's ghost being put in contact with Gilgameš.). With the hoe (al), the hero honoured by An, the younger brother of Nergal, the warrior Gilgameš is as powerful as a hunting net. The son of Ninsumun is pre-eminent with oars (ĝisal) (This may allude to Gilgameš rowing across the waters of death.). With the hoe (al) he is the great barber (kindagal) of the watercourses. In the {chamber} of the shrine, with the hoe (al) he is the minister (sukkal). The wicked (ḫulĝal) ...... are sons of the hoe (al); they are born in sleep from heaven.

In the sky there is the altirigu bird, the bird of the god. On the earth there is the hoe (al): a dog in the reedbeds, a dragon (ušumgal) in the forest. On the battlefield, there is the dur-allub battle-axe. By the city wall there is the battle-net (alluḫab). On the dining-table there is the bowl (maltum). In the waggon shed, there is the sledge (mayaltum). In the donkey stable there is the cupboard (argibil). The hoe (al)! – the sound of the word is sweet: it also occurs (munĝal) on the hillsides: the tree of the hillsides is the allanum oak. The fragrance of the hillsides is the arganum balm. The precious stone of the hillsides is the algameš steatite.

The hoe (al) makes everything prosper, the hoe makes everything flourish. The hoe (al) is good barley, the hoe (al) is {a hunting net}. The hoe (al) is brick moulds, the hoe (al) has made people exist (ĝal). It is the hoe (al) that is the strength of young manhood. The hoe (al) and the basket are the tools for building cities. It builds (aldue) the right kind of house, it cultivates (alĝaĝa) the right kind of fields. It is you, hoe, that extend (daĝal) the good agricultural land! The hoe (al) subdues for its owner (lugal) any agricultural lands that have been recalcitrant (bal) against their owner (lugal), any agricultural lands that have not submitted to their owner (lugal). It chops the heads off the vile esparto grasses, yanks them out at their roots, and tears at their stalks. The hoe (al) also subdues (alĝaĝa) the ḫirin weeds.

The hoe (al), the implement whose destiny was fixed by Father Enlil – the renowned hoe (al)! Nisaba be praised!

The Instructions of Šuruppag

IN THOSE DAYS, in those far remote days, in those nights, in those faraway nights, in those years, in those far remote years, at that time the wise one who knew how to speak in elaborate words lived in the Land; Šuruppag, the wise one, who knew how to speak with elaborate words lived in the Land. Šuruppag gave instructions to his son; Šuruppag, the son of Ubara-Tutu, gave instructions to his son Zi-ud-sura: My son, let me give you instructions: you should pay attention! Zi-ud-sura, let me speak a word to you: you should pay attention! Do not neglect my instructions! Do not transgress the words I speak! The instructions of an old man are precious; you should comply with them!

You should not buy a donkey which brays; it will split (?) your midriff (?).

You should not locate a field on a road; .... You should not plough a field at a path; .... You should not make a well in your field: people will cause damage on it for you. You should not place your house next to a public square: there is always a crowd (?) there.

You should not vouch for someone: that man will have a hold on you; and you yourself, you should not let somebody vouch for you.

You should not make an inspection (?) on a man: the flood (?) will give it back (?) to you.

You should not loiter about where there is a quarrel; you should not let the quarrel make you a witness. You should not let (?) yourself ...... in a quarrel. You should not cause a quarrel; .... the gate of the palace .... Stand aside from a quarrel, ... you should not take (?) another road.

You should not steal anything; you should not ...... yourself. You should not break into a house; you should not wish for the money chest (?). A thief is a lion, but after he has been caught, he will be a slave. My son, you should not commit robbery; you should not cut yourself with an axe.

You should not make a young man best man. You should not ...... yourself. You should not play around with a married young woman: the slander could be serious. My son, you should not sit alone in a chamber with a married woman.

You should not pick a quarrel; you should not disgrace yourself. You should not ...... lies; .... You should not boast; then your words will be trusted. You should not deliberate for too long (?); you cannot bear ...... glances.

You should not eat stolen food with {anyone}. You should not sink (?) your hand into blood. After you have apportioned the bones, you will be made to restore the ox, you will be made to restore the sheep.

You should not speak improperly; later it will lay a trap for you.

You should not scatter your sheep into unknown pastures. You should not hire someone's ox for an uncertain .... A safe ...... means a safe journey.

You should not travel during the night: it can hide both good and evil.

You should not buy an onager: it lasts (?) only until the end of the day.

You should not have sex with your slave girl: she will chew you up (?).

You should not curse strongly: it rebounds on you.

You should not draw up water which you cannot {reach}: it will make you weak.

1 line unclear

You should not drive away a debtor: he will be hostile towards you.

You should not establish a home with an arrogant man: he will make your life like that of a slave girl. You will not be able to travel through any human dwelling without be being shouted at: "There you go! There you go!"

You should not undo the ...... of the garden's reed fence; "Restore it! Restore it!" they will say to you.

You should not provide a stranger (?) with food; you should not wipe out (?) a quarrel.

My son, you should not use violence (?); .... You should not commit rape on someone's daughter; the courtyard will learn of it.

You should not drive away a {powerful} man; you should not destroy the outer wall. You should not drive away a young man; you should not make him turn against the city.

The eyes of the slanderer always move around as shiftily as a spindle. You should never remain in his presence; his intentions (?) should not be allowed to have an effect (?) on you.

You should not boast in {beer halls} like a deceitful man:

Having reached the field of manhood, you should not jump (?) with your hand. The warrior is unique, he alone is the equal of many; Utu is unique, he alone is the equal of many. With your life you should always be on the side of the warrior; with your life you should always be on the side of Utu.

Šuruppag gave these instructions to his son. Šuruppag, the son of Ubara-Tutu, gave these instructions to his son Zi-ud-sura.

A second time, Šuruppag gave instructions to his son. Šuruppag, the son of Ubara-Tutu, gave instructions to his son Zi-ud-sura: My son, let me give you instructions: you should pay attention! Zi-ud-sura, let me speak a word to you: you should pay attention! Do not neglect my instructions! Do not transgress the words I speak!

The beer-drinking mouth .... My little one .... The beer-drinking mouth .... Ninkasi ....

5 lines unclear

Your own man will not repay (?) it for you. The reedbeds are ......, they can hide (?) slander.

The palace is like a mighty river: its middle is goring bulls; what flows in is never enough to fill it, and what flows out can never be stopped.

When it is about someone else's bread, it is easy to say "I will give it to you", but the time of actual giving can be as far away as the sky. If you go after the man who said "I will give it to you", he will say "I cannot give it to you – the bread has just been finished up".

Property is something to be expanded (?); but nothing can equal my little ones.

The artistic mouth recites words; the harsh mouth brings litigation documents; the sweet mouth gathers sweet herbs.

The {garrulous} fills (?) his bread bag; the haughty one brings an empty bag and can fill his empty mouth only with boasting.

Who works with leather will eventually (?) work with his own leather.

The strong one can escape (?) from anyone's hand.

The fool loses something. When sleeping, the fool loses something. "Do not tie me up!" he pleads; "Let me live!" he pleads.

The imprudent decrees fates; the shameless one piles up (?) things in another's lap: "I am such that I deserve admiration".

A weak wife is always seized (?) by fate.

If you hire a worker, he will share the bread bag with you; he eats with you from the same bag, and finishes up the bag with you. Then he will quit working with you and, saying "I have to live on something", he will serve at the palace.

You tell your son to come to your home; you tell your daughter to go to her women's quarters.

You should not pass judgment when you drink beer.

You should not worry unduly about what leaves the house.

Heaven is far, earth is most precious, but it is with heaven that you multiply your goods, and all foreign lands breathe under it.

At harvest time, at the most priceless time, collect like a slave girl, eat like a queen; my son, to collect like a slave girl, to eat like a queen, this is how it should be.

Who insults can hurt only the skin; greedy eyes (?), however, can kill. The liar, shouting, tears up his garments. Insults bring (?) advice to the wicked. To speak arrogantly is like an abscess: a herb that makes the stomach sick.

1 line unclear

My words of prayer bring abundance. Prayer is cool water that cools the heart. Only (?) insults and stupid speaking receive the attention of the Land.

Šuruppag gave these instructions to his son. Šuruppag, the son of Ubara-Tutu, gave these instructions to his son Zi-ud-sura.

A third time, Šuruppag gave instructions to his son. Šuruppag, the son of Ubara-Tutu, gave instructions to his son Zi-ud-sura: My son, let me give you instructions: you should pay attention! Zi-ud-sura, let me speak a word to you: you should pay attention! Do not neglect my instructions! Do not transgress the words I speak!

You should not beat a farmer's son: he has constructed (?) your embankments and ditches.

You should not buy a prostitute: she is a mouth that bites. You should not buy a house-born slave: he is a herb that makes the stomach sick. You should not buy a free man: he will always lean against the wall. You should not buy a palace slave girl: she will always be the bottom of the barrel (?). You should rather bring down a foreign slave from the mountains, or you should bring somebody from a place where he is an alien; my son, then he will pour water for you where the sun rises and he will walk before you. He does not belong to any family, so he does not want to go to his family; he does not belong to any city, so he does not want to go to his city. He will not ...... with you, he will not be presumptuous with you.

My son, you should not travel alone eastwards. Your acquaintance should not ....

A name placed on another one ......; you should not pile up a mountain on another one.

Fate is a wet bank; it can make one slip.

The elder brother is indeed like a father; the elder sister is indeed like a mother. Listen therefore to your elder brother, and you should be obedient to your elder sister as if she were your mother.

You should not work using only your eyes; you will not multiply your possessions using only your mouth.

The negligent one ruins (?) his family.

The need for food makes some people ascend the mountains; it also brings traitors and foreigners, since the need for food brings down other people from the mountains.

A small city provides (?) its king with a calf; a huge city digs (?) a house plot (?).

... is well equipped. The poor man inflicts all kinds of illnesses on the rich man. The married man is well equipped; the unmarried makes his bed in a haystack (?). He who wishes to destroy a house will go ahead and destroy the house; he who wishes to raise up will go ahead and raise up.

By grasping the neck of a huge ox, you can cross the river. By moving along (?) at the side of the mighty men of your city, my son, you will certainly ascend (?).

When you bring a slave girl from the hills, she brings both good and evil with her. The good is in the hands; the evil is in the heart. The heart does not let go of the good; but the heart cannot let go of the evil either. As if it were a watery place, the heart does not abandon the good. Evil is a storeroom ....

2 lines unclear

May the boat with the evil sink in the river! May his waterskin split in the desert!

A loving heart maintains a family; a hateful heart destroys a family.

To have authority, to have possessions and to be steadfast are princely divine powers. You should submit to the respected; you should be humble before the powerful. My son, you will then survive (?) against the wicked.

You should not choose a wife during a festival. Her inside is illusory (?); her outside is illusory (?). {The silver on her is borrowed; the lapis lazuli on her is borrowed} {(1 ms. has instead the line:) ......; the jewellery on her is borrowed, the jewellery on her is borrowed}. The dress on her is borrowed; the linen garment on her is borrowed. With ...... nothing (?) is comparable.

You should not buy a ...... bull. You should not buy a vicious bull; ...... a hole (?) in the cattle-pen ....

One appoints (?) a reliable woman for a good household.

You should not buy a donkey at the time of harvest. A donkey which eats …… will …… with another donkey.

A vicious donkey hangs its neck; however, a vicious man, my son, …….

A woman with her own property ruins the house.

A drunkard will drown the harvest.

A female burglar (?) …… ladder; she flies into the houses like a fly. A she-donkey …… on the street. A sow suckles its child on the street. A woman who pricked herself begins to cry and holds the spindle which pricked (?) her in her hand. She enters every house; she peers into all streets. …… she keeps saying "Get out!" She looks around (?) from all parapets. She pants (?) where there is a quarrel.

2 lines unclear

Marry (?) …… whose heart hates (?). My son, ……

4 lines unclear

A heart which overflows with joy …….

Nothing at all is to be valued, but life should be sweet. You should not serve things; things should serve you. My son, …….

You should not …… grain; its …… are numerous.

You should not abuse a ewe; otherwise you will give birth to a daughter. You should not throw a lump of earth into the money chest (?); otherwise you will give birth to a son.

You should not abduct a wife; you should not make her cry (?). The place where the wife is abducted to …….

"Let us run in circles (?), saying: "Oh my foot, oh my neck!". Let us with united forces (?) make the mighty bow!"

You should not kill a ……, he is a child born by ……. You should not kill …… like ……; you should not bind him.

The wet-nurses in the women's quarters determine the fate of their lord.

You should not speak arrogantly to your mother; that causes hatred for you. You should not question the words of your mother and your personal god. The mother, like Utu, gives birth to the man; the father, like a god, makes him bright (?). The father is like a god: his words are reliable. The instructions of the father should be complied with.

Without suburbs a city has no centre either.

My son, a field situated at the bottom of the embankments, be it wet or dry, is nevertheless a source of income.

It is inconceivable (?) that something is lost forever.

… of Dilmun …

{To get lost is bad for a dog; but terrible for a man}. On the unfamiliar way at the edge of the mountains, the gods of the mountains are man-eaters. They do not build houses there as men do; they do not build cities there as men do.
1 line unclear

For the shepherd, he stopped searching, he stopped bringing back the sheep. For the farmer (?), he stopped ploughing the field.
1 line unclear

This gift of words is something which soothes the mind ……; when it enters the palace, it soothes the mind ……. The gift of many words …… stars.

These are the instructions given by Šuruppag, the son of Ubara-Tutu.

Praise be to the lady who completed the great tablets, the maiden Nisaba, that Šuruppag, the son of Ubara-Tutu, gave his instructions!

The Debate Between Hoe and Plough

O THE HOE, the Hoe, the Hoe, tied together with thongs; the Hoe, made from poplar, with a tooth of ash; the Hoe, made from tamarisk, with a tooth of sea-thorn; the Hoe, double-toothed, four-toothed; the Hoe, child of the poor, ... bereft even of a loincloth (?) – the Hoe started a quarrel ... with the Plough.

The Hoe having engaged in a dispute with the Plough, the Hoe addressed the Plough: "Plough, you draw furrows – what does your furrowing matter to me? You break clods – what does your clod-breaking matter to me? When water overflows you cannot dam it up. You cannot fill baskets with earth. You cannot press (?) clay to make bricks. You cannot lay foundations or build a house. You cannot strengthen an old wall's base. You cannot put a roof on a good man's house. Plough, you cannot straighten the town squares. Plough, you draw furrows – what does your furrowing matter to me? You make clods – what does your clod-making matter to me?"

The Plough addressed the Hoe: "I am the Plough, fashioned by great strength, assembled by great hands, the mighty registrar of Father Enlil. I am mankind's faithful farmer. To perform my festival in the fields in the harvest month, the king slaughters cattle and sacrifices sheep, and he pours beer into a bowl. The king offers the gathered (?) libation. The ub and ala drums resound. The king takes hold of my handles, and harnesses my oxen to the yoke. All the great high-ranking persons walk at my side. All the lands gaze at me in great admiration. The people watch me in joy".

"The furrow tilled by me adorns the plain. Before the stalks erected by me in the fields, the teeming herds of Šakkan kneel down. In performing my labour amid the ripened barley, the shepherd's churn is improved. With my sheaves spread over the meadows the sheep of Dumuzid are improved".

"My threshing-floors punctuating the plain are yellow hillocks radiating beauty. I pile up stacks and mounds for Enlil. I amass emmer and wheat for him. I fill the storehouses of mankind with barley. The orphans, the widows and the destitute take their reed baskets and glean my scattered ears. People come to drag away my straw, piled up in the fields. The teeming herds of Šakkan thrive".

"Hoe, digging miserably, weeding miserably with your teeth; Hoe, burrowing in the mud; Hoe, putting its head in the mud of the fields, spending your days with the brick-moulds in mud with nobody cleaning you, digging wells, digging ditches, digging ......!"

"Wood of the poor man's hand, not fit for the hands of high-ranking persons, the hand of a man's slave is the only adornment of your head. You deliver deep insults to me. You compare yourself to me. When I go out to the plain, everyone looks on but insultingly you call me "Plough, the digger of ditches"".

Then the Hoe addressed the Plough: "Plough, what does my being small matter to me, what does my being exalted matter to me, what does my being powerful matter to me? – at Enlil's place I take precedence over you, in Enlil's temple I stand ahead of you".

"I build embankments, I dig ditches. I fill all the meadows with water. When I make water pour into all the reedbeds, my small baskets carry it away. When a canal is cut, or when a ditch is cut, when water rushes out at the swelling of a mighty river, creating lagoons on all sides (?), I, the Hoe, dam it in. Neither south nor north wind can separate it".

"The fowler gathers eggs. The fisherman catches fish. People empty bird-traps. Thus the abundance I create spreads over all the lands".

"After the water has been diverted from the meadows and the work on the wet areas is taken in hand, Plough, I come down to the fields before you. I initiate the opening up of the field for you. I clear the recesses of the embankment for you. I remove the weeds in the field for you. I heap up the stumps and the roots in the field for you. But when you work the field, there is a procession (?): your oxen are six, your people four – you yourself are the eleventh .... the preparatory work in the field. And you want to compare yourself with me?"

"When you come out to the field after me, your single furrow brings you pleasure. When you put your head to work and get entangled in roots and thorns, your tooth breaks. Once your tooth is fixed, you cannot hold onto your tooth. Your farmer calls you "This Plough is done for". Carpenters have to be hired again for you, people ...... for you. A whole workshop of artisans surrounds you. The fullers depilate a ...... fleece for you. They stretch it over the wringer for you. They toil at the straps for you – then they place the foul hide on your head".

"Your work is slight but your behaviour is grand. My time of duty is twelve months, but your effective time is four months and your time of absence is eight months – you are gone for twice as long as you are present".

"Upon your boat (?) you make a hut. When you are put on board and your 'hands' rip out the beams, your 'face' has to be pulled from the water like a wine-jar. After I have made a pile of logs (?) my smoke dries you out in the house. What happens to your seeding-funnel if it once falls? Anyone who drops you smashes it, making it a completely destroyed tool".

"I am the Hoe and I live in the city. No one is more honoured than I am. I am a servant following his master. I am one who builds a house for his master. I am one who broadens the cattle-stalls, who expands the sheepfolds".

"I press (?) clay and make bricks. I lay foundations and build a house. I strengthen an old wall's base. I put a roof on a good man's house. I am the Hoe, I straighten the town-squares".

"When I have gone through the city and built its sturdy walls, have made the temples of the great gods splendid and embellished them with brown, yellow and decorative (?) clay, I build in the city of the palace where the inspectors and overseers live".

"When the weakened clay has been built up and the fragile (?) clay buttressed, they refresh themselves when the time is cool in houses I have built. When they rest on their sides by a fire which a hoe has stirred up, you do not come to the joyous celebration (?). They feed the labourer, give him drink and pay him his wages: thus I have enabled him to support his wife and children".

"I make a kiln for the boatman and heat pitch for him. By fashioning magur and magilum boats for him, I enable the boatman to support his wife and children".

"I plant a garden for the householder. When the garden has been encircled, surrounded by mud walls and the agreements reached, people again take up a hoe. When a well has been dug, a water lift constructed and a water-hoist hung, I straighten the plots. I am the one who puts water in the plots. After I have made the apple tree grow, it is I who bring forth its fruits. These fruits adorn the temples of the great gods: thus I enable the gardener to support his wife and children".

"After I have worked on the watercourse and the sluices, put the path in order and built a tower there on its banks, those who spend the day in the fields, and the fieldworkers who match them by night, go up into that tower. These people revive themselves there just as in their well-built city. The waterskins I made they use to pour water. I put life into their hearts again".

"Insultingly you call me "Plough, the digger of ditches". But when I have dug out the fresh water for the plain and dry land where no water is, those who have thirst refresh themselves at my well-head".

"What then does one person say to another? What does one tell another in detail?: "The shepherd adorns the plain with his ewes and lambs. After the heavens had been turned upside down, after bitter lament had been imposed on Sumer, after, as houses were overwhelmed by the rivers and Enlil frowned in anger upon the land, Enlil had flooded the harvest, after Enlil had acted mightily thus, Enlil did not abandon us – the single-toothed Hoe was struck against the dry earth".

"For us you raise winter like the harvest-time. We take away the hand of summer and winter. Hoe, the binder, ties the sheaves. Binding bird-traps, it ties the reed-baskets. The solitary labourer and the destitute are supported.

Then the Storm spoke: "The mortar lies still while the pestle pounds. People fight with grinding stones. The sieve disputes with the strainer. What have you done to the one who is angry? Why are you scornful of Ezina? {Why do you swap names (?) over the ripened grain}?"

Enlil adressed the Hoe: "Hoe, do not start getting so mightily angry! Do not be so mightily scornful! Is not Nisaba the Hoe's inspector? Is not Nisaba its overseer? The scribe will register your work, he will register your work. Hoe, whether he enters five or ten giĝ in your account, Hoe – or, Hoe, whether he enters one-third or one-half mana in your account, Hoe, like a maidservant, always ready, you will fulfil your task".

The Hoe having engaged in a dispute with the Plough, the Hoe triumphed over the Plough – praise be to Nisaba!

The Debate Between Grain and Sheep

WHEN, UPON THE HILL of heaven and earth, An spawned the Anuna gods, since he neither spawned nor created grain with them, and since in the Land he neither fashioned the yarn of Uttu (the goddess of weaving) nor pegged out the loom for Uttu – with no sheep appearing, there were no numerous lambs, and with no goats, there were no numerous kids, the sheep did not give birth to her twin lambs, and the goat did not give birth to her triplet kids –, the Anuna, the great gods, did not even know the names Ezina-Kusu (Grain) or Sheep.

There was no muš grain of thirty days; there was no muš grain of forty days; there was no muš grain of fifty days; there was no small grain, grain from the mountains or grain from the holy habitations. There was no cloth to wear; Uttu had not been born – no royal turban was worn; Lord Niĝir-si, the precious lord, had not been born; Šakkan (the god of wild animals) had not gone out into the barren lands. The people of those days did not know about eating bread. They did not know about wearing clothes; they went about with naked limbs in the Land. Like sheep they ate grass with their mouths and drank water from the ditches.

At that time, at the place of the gods' formation, in their own home, on the Holy Mound, they created Sheep and Grain. Having gathered them in the divine banqueting chamber, the Anuna gods of the Holy Mound partook of the bounty of Sheep and Grain but were not sated; the Anuna gods of the Holy Mound partook of the sweet milk of their holy sheepfold but were not sated. For their own well-being in the holy sheepfold, they gave them to mankind as sustenance.

At that time Enki spoke to Enlil: "Father Enlil, now Sheep and Grain have been created on the Holy Mound, let us send them down from the Holy Mound". Enki and Enlil, having spoken their holy word, sent Sheep and Grain down from the Holy Mound.

Sheep being fenced in by her sheepfold, they gave her green plants generously. For Grain they made her field and gave her the plough, yoke and team. Sheep standing in her sheepfold was a shepherd of the sheepfolds brimming with charm. Grain standing in her furrow was a beautiful girl radiating charm; lifting her raised head up from the field she was suffused with the bounty of heaven. Sheep and Grain had a radiant appearance.

They brought wealth to the assembly. They brought sustenance to the Land. They fulfilled the ordinances of the gods. They filled the storerooms of the Land with stock. The barns of the Land were heavy with them. When they entered the homes of the poor who crouch in the dust they brought wealth. Both of them, wherever they directed their steps, added to the riches of the household with their weight. Where they stood, they were satisfying; where they settled, they were seemly. They gladdened the heart of An and the heart of Enlil.

They drank sweet wine, they enjoyed sweet beer. When they had drunk sweet wine and enjoyed sweet beer, they started a quarrel concerning the arable fields, they began a debate in the dining hall.

Grain called out to Sheep: "Sister, I am your better; I take precedence over you. I am the glory of the lights of the Land. I grant my power to the saĝursaĝ (a member of the cultic personnel of Inana) – he fills the palace with awe and people spread his fame to the borders of the Land. I am the gift of the Anuna gods. I am central to all princes. After I have conferred my power on the warrior, when he goes to war he knows no fear, he knows no faltering (?) – I make him leave … as if to the playing field".

"I foster neighbourliness and friendliness. I sort out quarrels started between neighbours. When I come upon a captive youth and give him his destiny, he forgets his despondent heart and I release his fetters and shackles. I am Ezina-Kusu (Grain); I am Enlil's daughter. In sheep shacks and milking pens scattered on the high plain, what can you put against me? Answer me what you can reply!"

Thereupon Sheep answered Grain: "My sister, whatever are you saying? An, king of the gods, made me descend from the holy place, my most precious place. All the yarns of Uttu, the splendour of kingship, belong to me. Šakkan, king of the mountain, embosses the king's emblems and puts his implements in order. He twists a giant rope against the great peaks of the rebel land. He …… the sling, the quiver and the longbows".

"The watch over the élite troops is mine. Sustenance of the workers in the field is mine: the waterskin of cool water and the sandals are mine. Sweet oil, the fragrance of the gods, mixed (?) oil, pressed oil, aromatic oil, cedar oil for offerings are mine".

"In the gown, my cloth of white wool, the king rejoices on his throne. My body glistens on the flesh of the great gods. After the purification priests, the pašeš priests and the bathed priests have dressed themselves in me for my holy lustration, I walk with them to my holy meal. But your harrow, ploughshare, binding and strap are tools that can be utterly destroyed. What can you put against me? Answer me what you can reply!"

Again Grain addressed Sheep: "When the beer dough has been carefully prepared in the oven, and the mash tended in the oven, Ninkasi (the goddess of beer) mixes them for me while your big billy-goats and rams are despatched for my banquets. On their thick legs they are made to stand separate from my produce".

"Your shepherd on the high plain eyes my produce enviously; when I am standing in stalks in the field, my farmer chases away your herdsman with his cudgel. Even when they look out for you, from the open country to the hidden places, your fears are not removed from you: fanged (?) snakes and bandits, the creatures of the desert, want your life on the high plain".

"Every night your count is made and your tally-stick put into the ground, so your herdsman can tell people how many ewes there are and how many young lambs, and how many goats and how many young kids. When gentle winds blow through the city and strong winds scatter, they build a milking pen for you; but when gentle winds blow through the city and strong winds scatter, I stand up as an equal to Iškur (the god of storms). I am Grain, I am born for the warrior – I do not give up. The churn, the vat on legs (?), the adornments of shepherding, make up your properties. What can you put against me? Answer me what you can reply!"

Again Sheep answered Grain: "You, like holy Inana of heaven, love horses. When a banished enemy, a slave from the mountains or a labourer with a poor wife and small children comes, bound with his rope of one cubit, to the threshing-floor or is taken away from (?) the threshing-floor, when his cudgel pounds your face, pounds your mouth, like crushed ... your ears (?) ..., and you are ... around by the south wind and the north wind. The mortar .... As if it were pumice (?) it makes your body into flour".

"When you fill the trough the baker's assistant mixes you and throws you on the floor, and the baker's girl flattens you out broadly. You are put into the oven and you are taken out of the oven. When you are put on the table I am before you – you are behind me. Grain, heed yourself! You too, just like me, are meant to be eaten. At the inspection of your essence, why should it be I who come second? Is the miller not evil? What can you put against me? Answer me what you can reply!"

Then Grain was hurt in her pride, and hastened for the verdict. Grain answered Sheep: "As for you, Iškur is your master, Šakkan your herdsman, and the dry land your bed. Like fire beaten down (?) in houses and in fields, like small flying birds chased from the door of a house, you are turned into the lame and the weak of the Land. Should I really bow my neck before you? You are distributed into various measuring-containers. When your innards are taken away by the people in the marketplace, and when your neck is wrapped with your very own loincloth, one man says to another: "Fill the measuring-container with Grain for my ewe!"

Then Enki spoke to Enlil: "Father Enlil, Sheep and Grain should be sisters! They should stand together! Of their threefold metal ... shall not cease. But of the two, Grain shall be the greater. Let Sheep fall on her knees before Grain. Let her kiss the feet of .... From sunrise till sunset, may the name of Grain be praised. People should submit to the yoke of Grain. Whoever has silver, whoever has jewels, whoever has cattle, whoever has sheep shall take a seat at the gate of whoever has grain, and pass his time there".

Dispute spoken between Sheep and Grain: Sheep is left behind and Grain comes forward – praise be to Father Enki!

The Debate Between Winter and Summer

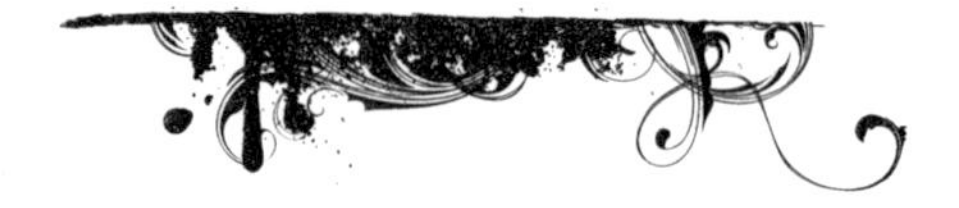

AN LIFTED HIS HEAD in pride and brought forth a good day. He laid plans for ... and spread the population wide. Enlil set his foot upon the earth like a great bull. Enlil, the king of all lands, set his mind to increasing the good day of abundance, to making the ... night resplendent in celebration, to making flax grow, to making barley proliferate, to guaranteeing the spring floods at the quay, to making ... lengthen (?) their days in abundance, to making Summer close the sluices of heaven, and to making Winter guarantee plentiful water at the quay.

He copulated with the great hills, he gave the mountain its share. He filled its womb with Summer and Winter, the plenitude and life of the Land. As Enlil copulated with the earth, there was a roar like a bull's. The hill spent the day at that place and at night she opened her loins. She bore Summer and Winter as smoothly as fine oil. He fed them pure plants on the terraces of the hills like great bulls. He nourished them in the pastures of the hills.

Enlil set about determining the destinies of Summer and Winter. For Summer founding towns and villages, bringing in harvests of plenitude for the Great Mountain Enlil, sending labourers out to the large arable tracts, and working the fields with oxen; for Winter plenitude, the spring floods, the abundance and life of the Land, placing grain in the fields and fruitful acres, and gathering in everything – Enlil determined these as the destinies of Summer and Winter.

By hand Winter guided the spring floods, the abundance and life of the Land, down from the edge of the hills. He set his foot upon the Tigris and Euphrates like a big bull and released them into the fields and fruitful acres of Enlil. He shaped lagoons in the sea. He let fish and birds together come into existence by the sea. He surrounded all the reedbeds with mature reeds, reed shoots and ... reeds.

Summer, the heroic son of Enlil, drained the large arable tracts. He ... cool water on the fields and fruitful acres like ...

2 lines unclear

5 lines fragmentary

approx. 1 line missing

1 line fragmentary

Holy Winter ... The ox ... its head in the yoke. Ninurta, Enlil's son, ... the fruitful acres. He ... grain in the large arable tracts. He fills the fields and fruitful acres of Enlil.

Winter made the ewe give birth to the lamb, he gave the kid to the goat. He made cows teem together with their calves, he provided butter and milk. On the high plain he made the deer and stag glad of heart. He made the birds of heaven set their nests in the broad spaces. The fish of the lagoons laid eggs in the reedbed. In all the orchards he made honey and wine drip (?) to the ground. He made the trees, wherever planted, bear fruit. He established gardens and provided plants. He made grain abundant in the furrows. He made Ezina appear radiant as a beautiful maiden. The harvest, the great festival of Enlil, rose heavenward.

Summer founded houses and farmsteads, he made the cattle-pens and sheepfolds wide. He brought great attractiveness to the broad arable tracts. At their edges he made ... flax ... ripen (?). He brought a plentiful harvest into the temples, he heaped up piles of grain. He founded towns and villages, he built the houses of the Land. He made the houses of the gods grow like the hills in a pure place. In E-namtila, the holy seat of kingship, fit for high daises, he established abundance for the Great Mountain Enlil.

Summer, the heroic son of Enlil, decided to bring offerings to E-namtila, the house of Enlil. He brought animals, cattle and sheep of the hill, fully grown wild rams, deer and stags, ... sheep, long-fleeced barley-fed sheep, thick-tailed sheep. Pigs grown fat in the midst of the reedbeds, porcupine, tortoise, turtle, birds brooding in their nests, taken together with their eggs, harvest crops, flour and malt for mixing, butter and milk from cattle-pen and sheepfold, wheat, hulled barley, small beans and large beans gathered in piled-high baskets, onions ... in their furrows, zaḫadin onions and shallots, seed turnips, cardamom (?), ...,

8 lines missing – Summer, the heroic son of Enlil, offered.

Winter, lordly son of Enlil, ..., released the water of life and ... opened. He gathered the ... oxen and ...... the oxen. The disputed sheep was provided, barley-fed but with a scorpion at its side. Quartz, gold and silver found in leather pouches, cedar, cypress, ..., boxwood, ..., ... tribute of the Land, figs from Mari, ..., strings of dried fruit, cool water, the tribute of the hills, ... thick honey, dida beer, ..., village ..., bibra birds, esig birds, ... birds, clipped geeese, fattened ducks, carp, ... which Winter made grow up, large pomegranates gathered from the orchards, big bunches of grapes on high, winter cucumbers, ... empty ..., brought forth ... in the early rain, large turnips, large ... cut down with the knife (?), long leeks – Winter himself brought the tribute he had collected.

Summer and Winter set about organising the animals and offerings for E-namtila, the house of Enlil. The two of them, like huge butting bulls, reared themselves triumphantly. But Winter, because his limbs had grown tired from the grain grown heavy in the furrows, and the wheat and the emmer which he had been watering by hand, turned away as from an enemy and would not draw near.

Consequently Winter was overcome by anger and he started a quarrel with Summer: "Summer, my brother, you should not praise yourself; whatever harvest produce you bring as gifts to the palace has not been made by your toil: you should not brag. As if you were the one who had done the hard work, as if you had done the farming, as if you had taken care of irrigation control during the spring floods, as if you had brought forth the ... grain in the arable tracts with the dew from heaven – how much through my toil is it that you enter the palace!"

"Whatever animals, cattle and sheep of the hill, you bring to my ....

11 lines missing

3 lines fragmentary – Your gardener ... the palace .... Honey and wine in the orchard .... Its destructive hoe .... Your gathered vegetables, the purslane, ... Whatever you ... at the gate of the palace. In the field your arm .... The straw of the grain you bring ...".

"After you have threshed it at your threshing floor, and have ... the cattle's dung, your carrying-nets are to hand, ... bearing your straw. ... the animals, the storehouses and their contents. After your houses and farmsteads ... sheep,... from your cattle, after ... their reedbeds, after ... green briars and cut ... thorns, ... storehouse ... the dung of unyoked oxen – the slave Summer, the duly-appointed labourer who will never rest from his toil, a hired man who has to return to the fields of the Land for his own sustenance!"

On that day Winter taunted Summer. Summer, the hero whom one does not challenge, searched for rude insults. He was confident in himself, considering the harvest time, and turned aside. Like a great bull eating rich grass, he raised his head.

Next, Summer replied to Winter: "Winter, you may have to stay by the side of the oven, ...; but you should not launch such serious insults against someone who does not lead a sedentary (?) life. ... for the work of tilling the Land, with its difficulties, you do not raise a cry in the gune (?) cult centre, you do not look after the house. The young scribe is neglectful, which is an abomination, and no rushes are plucked for the beds. The singer does not embellish the banquet, ... at its side".

"Winter, don't launch such insults! ... to the desert. I will make the strength of my power come forth in the house so that you recognise it. In my working term of duty, which is seven months of the year, ... does not speak softly.

2 lines missing

1 line fragmentary – Tirelessly and constantly I place abundance upon the fields".

"After they ... my seed, Winter, do not ... noise, when water is cut off from the arable tracts, when the bowls lie placed, when the fishing place has been prepared, when the fish have been piled up, I am Father Enlil's great comptroller. I harrow the fields into fruitful acres. When the oxen have stopped working the fields, when you have concentrated your efforts on the damp areas and given the sign for the field work, I do not work for you in the large arable tracts and fruitful acres early in the season. If the spring grain bends its neck in the hollow of the furrows, no one provides a fence. Whatever your farmer brings to the oxen, he will not make the oxen angry with me. Winter ... in the uplands .... The man of the bedroom ...".

Then Summer taunted Winter: "Wise ..., serious insults ..., not ...".

Thereupon Winter replied to Summer: "Summer, the donkey grazing on grass at the harvest ground and braying noisily, the mule ..., the harvest ox chafing its neck in the pegs and tossing its head in the lead rope, the innkeeper going to the harvest ground carrying a bowl in his hands, the flour ... playing ..., the bragging fieldworker who does not know the extent of the field – Summer, my brother, after you have gone out boasting about my toil, when at the turn of the year grain is brought into the houses and the granaries are packed full, when you bring the surplus, your bardul garment and your niglam garment are .... When someone gives a two mana axe to you, you go off to your steppe".

"Summer, my brother, the wet spots must not be ... when tilling the field. A man from the storehouse stands in front of you and instructs you. When on the high plain ... the ash tree ..., ... yourself ...

1 line missing

When tribute is brought in your freight boats .... When the grass has arrived in the storehouse, ... before me. What will the penned sheep eat? Your ... reeds are exhausted. The reed-cutter who sets about pruning with the sickle and splitting older reeds, the builder who places labourers in houses, never resting from his efforts, the potter who digs out clay, lights a fire and stokes it with wood ... the pot! Weaver, weave your bardul garment with the strength (?) of your aktum cloth. Brewer, bake your beer bread at the harvest ground as your assignment! Cook, produce great banquet loaves in summer! The building supervisor ... the ... of the roofs. People ... boots and shoes ...".

"Summer, my brother, as long as you go with my term of duty, great and small order you about and your string is not cut. Although you have gathered all things in the Land and filled the storehouses, in all my strength I am their owner when your limbs become tired. When the clouds have brought down the abundance of heaven, and the water of the first greening has descended from the hills, and the new grain has been put in the granary to be added to the old grain, the good farmer, having seen to his fields, shouts for joy, the carrier donkeys stand ready and he sets out confidently for the city".

"My brother, when you have put the holy plough away in the barn, the storehouse, everything you have gathered, you make a roar like fire. You sit down to plentiful food and drink. You obtain the choicest goods from the Land. For my king named by Nanna, the son of Enlil, Ibbi-Suen, when he is arrayed in the šutur garment and the ḫursaĝ garment, when you have taken care of the bardul garment and the niĝlam garment, when you have made a perfect feast for the gods, when the Anuna have placed garments on their holy bodies, in his E-namtila, the holy abode of kingship founded by An, at that place of content they prepare a choice banquet".

"When the šem and ala drums, ... and other instruments play together for him, he passes the time with your heart-gladdening tigi and zamzam instruments. But it is I who have made the wine plentiful and made much to eat and drink. I perfect the garments with fine oil. I bring up the ..., the šutur and aktum garments. As for safeguarding, the best in Sumer, in the oppressive heat (?) of Summer, where they had been put away in the bedrooms amongst the black-headed people, moths destroy the blankets and make the aktum cloth perish because of you. ... exhausts itself for you .... The wooden chest .... I am Ninkasi's help, for her I sweeten the beer, with as much cold water, the tribute of the hills, as you brought".

"After ... pots, after ... pots, after the plump grapes have been laid out in the cool breeze, I make my king's great palace ... pleasant. I am the one who cools down my king. I fill the fish hook. My comrade, grasp your leather bag, go out .... The farmer ... hardship. The farmer ... the rain. The gardener does not know how to plant purslane, your ... basket .... How can you compare yourself to me while seeking a roof under which to rest?"

For a second time Winter had taunted Summer. Summer, the heroic son of Enlil, was convinced of his own strong power and consequently trusted in himself. He acted as if in a friendly manner to the insults that Winter had spoken to him.

Then Summer replied to Winter: "Winter, you should not be so self-important about your superior strength after you have explained the grounds for your bragging. I shall speak about your abode in the city which I shall .... You seem like a man of office but you are an inept one. Your nets are for the oven-side, hearth and kiln. Like a herdsman or shepherd encumbered by sheep and lambs, helpless people run like sheep from oven-side to kiln, and from kiln to oven-side, in the face of you (?). In sunshine ...... you reach decisions, but now in the city people chomp and chew because of you".

"When the day is half done, nobody walks about in the streets. The servant, basking by the side of the oven, is in the house until sunset. The maid, not attending to the flow of the water-container, passes the day on garments. As for the fields not worked in winter, their furrows are not cut straight and their grain, having not been cast into a wholesome place, is taken away by huge flocks of rooks. The vegetable cutter ... does not ... those vegetables at the market. Carrying old reeds, the labourer is halt and lame. Don't speak with a gaping mouth of your superior strength – I will make known its shape and essence".

For a second time Summer had taunted Winter. On that day of the E-kur's festival and Sumer's plenty, the two of them stretched (?) their legs and stood combatively. Summer and Winter, like great bulls about to tear at each other's horns, bent forward like wild bulls in the main courtyard and took up their positions.

Like a great bull Winter raised his head to speak: "Father Enlil, you gave me control of irrigation; you brought plentiful water. I made one meadow adjacent to another and I heaped high the granaries. The grain became thick in the furrows. Ezina came forth in splendour like a beautiful maiden. Summer, a bragging field-administrator who does not know the extent of the field, ... my thighs grown tired from toil. ... tribute has been produced for the king's palace. Winter admires the heart of your ... in words".

Summer pondered everything in his head and calmed down. Summer spoke respectfully to Enlil: "Enlil, your verdict is highly valued, your holy word is an exalted word. The verdict you pronounce is one which cannot be altered – who can change it? There was quarrelling of brother with brother but now there is harmony. For as long as you are occupying the palace, the people will express awe. While you live there, far be it from me to mock – in fact I shall praise you".

Enlil answered Summer and Winter: "Winter is controller of the life-giving waters of all the lands – the farmer of the gods produces everything. Summer, my son, how can you compare yourself to your brother Winter?" The import of the exalted word Enlil speaks is artfully wrought, the verdict he pronounces is one which cannot be altered – who can change it?

Summer bowed to Winter and offered him a prayer. In his house he prepared emmer-beer and wine. At its side they spend the day at a succulent banquet. Summer presents Winter with gold, silver and lapis lazuli. They pour out brotherhood and friendship like best oil. By bringing sweet words to the quarrel (?) they have achieved harmony with each other.

In the dispute between Summer and Winter, Winter, the faithful farmer of Enlil, was superior to Summer – praise be to the Great Mountain, Father Enlil!

The Debate Between Bird and Fish

IN THOSE ANCIENT DAYS, when the good destinies had been decreed, and after An and Enlil had set up the divine rules of heaven and earth, then the third of them, ..., the lord of broad wisdom, Enki, the master of destinies, gathered together ... and founded dwelling places; he took in his hand waters to encourage and create good seed; he laid out side by side the Tigris and the Euphrates, and caused them to bring water from the mountains; he scoured out the smaller streams, and positioned the other watercourses.... Enki made spacious sheepfolds and cattle-pens, and provided shepherds and herdsmen; he founded cities and settlements throughout the earth, and made the black-headed multiply. He provided them with a king as shepherd, elevating him to sovereignty over them; the king rose as the daylight over the foreign countries.

...... Enki knit together the marshlands, making young and old reeds grow there; he made birds and fish live in the pools and lagoons ......; he gave ...... all kinds of living creatures as their sustenance, ... placed them in charge of this abundance of the gods. When Nudimmud, august prince, the lord of broad wisdom, had fashioned ......, he filled the reedbeds and marshes with fish and birds, indicated to them their positions and instructed them in their divine rules.

Then Fish laid its eggs in the lagoons; Bird built its nest in a gap in the reedbeds. But Bird frightened the Fish of the lagoons in its .... Fish took up a stand and cried out. Grandiosely it initiated hostilities. It roused the street by quarrelling in an overbearing manner. Fish addressed Bird murderously:

"...... Bird, ... there is no insult ......! Croaking, ... noise in the marshes ...... squawking! Forever gobbling away greedily, while your heart is dripping with evil! Standing on the plain, you can keep pecking away until they chase you off! The farmer's sons lay lines and nets for you in the furrows. The gardener sets up nets against you in gardens and orchards. He cannot rest his arm from firing his sling; he cannot sit down because of you. You cause damage in the vegetable plots; you are a nuisance. In the damp parts of fields, there are your unpleasing footprints. Bird, you are shameless: you fill the courtyard with your droppings. The courtyard sweeper-boy who cleans the house chases after you with ropes. By your noise the {house} is disturbed; your din drives people away".

"They bring you into the fattening shed. They let you moo like cattle, bleat like sheep. They pour out cool water in jugs for you. They drag you away for the daily sacrifice. The fowler brings you with bound wings. They tie up your wings and beak. Your squawking is to no profit; what are you flapping about? With your ugly voice you frighten the night; no one can sleep soundly. Bird, get out of the marshes! Get this noise of yours off my back! Go out of here into a hole on the rubbish heap: that suits you!"

Thus Fish insulted Bird on that day. But Bird, with multicoloured plumage and multicoloured face, was convinced of its own beauty, and did not take to heart the insults Fish had cast at it. As if it was a nursemaid singing a lullaby, it paid no attention to the speech, despite the ugly words that were being uttered. {Then Bird answered Fish:}

"How has your heart become so arrogant, while you yourself are so lowly? Your mouth is flabby (?), but although your mouth goes all the way round, you cannot see behind you. You are bereft of hips, as also of arms, hands and feet – try bending your neck to your feet! Your smell is awful; you make people throw up, they sneer at you! No trough would hold the kind of prepared food you eat. He who has carried you dare not let his hand touch his skin! In the great marshes and the wide lagoons, I am your persecuting demon. You cannot eat the sweet plants there, as my voice harasses you. You cannot travel with confidence in the river, as my storm-cloud covers you. As you slip through the reedbeds you are always beneath my eyes. Some of your little ones are destined to be my daily offering; you give them to me to allay my hunger. Some of your big ones are just as certainly destined for my banqueting hall ...... in the mud.

1 line unclear

"But I am the beautiful and clever Bird! Fine artistry went into my adornment. But no skill has been expended on your holy shaping! Strutting about in the royal palace is my glory; my warbling is considered a decoration in the courtyard. The sound I produce, in all its sweetness, is a delight for the person of Šulgi, son of Enlil. Fruits and produce of gardens and orchards are the enormous daily offerings due to me. Groats, flour, malt, hulled barley and emmer (?) are sweet things to my mouth. How do you not recognise my superiority from this? Bow your neck to the ground!"

Thus Bird insulted Fish on that occasion. Fish became angry, and, trusting in its heroic strength and solidness, swept across the bottom like a heavy rain cloud. It took up the quarrel. It did not take to heart the insults that Bird had cast at it. It could not bring itself to submit, but spoke unrestrainedly. Again Fish replied to Bird:

"Chopped-off beak and legs, deformed feet, cleft mouth, thin tongue! You clatter away in your ignorance, with never any reflection! Gluttonous, malformed, filling the courtyard with droppings! The little sweeper-boy sets nets in the house and chases you with ropes. The baker, the brewer, the porter, all those who live in the house are annoyed with you. Bird, you have not examined the question of my greatness; you have not taken due account of my nature. You could not understand my weakness and my strength; yet you spoke inflammatory words. Once you have really looked into my achievements, you will be greatly humbled. Your speech contains grave errors; you have not given it due consideration".

"I am Fish. I am responsibly charged with providing abundance for the pure shrines. {To the great offerings at the lustrous E-kur}, I go proudly with head raised high! Just like Ezina I am here to satisfy the hunger of the Land. I am her helper. Therefore people pay attention to me, and they keep their eyes upon me. As at the harvest festival, they rejoice over me and take care of me. Bird, whatever great deeds you may have achieved, I will teach you their pretentiousness. I shall hand back to you in your turn your haughtiness and mendacious speech".

Thereupon Fish conceived a plot against Bird. Silently, furtively, it slithered alongside. When Bird rose up from her nest to fetch food for her young, Fish searched for the most discreet of silent places. It turned her well-built nest of brushwood into a haunted house. It destroyed her well-built house, and tore down her storeroom. It smashed the eggs she had laid and threw them into the sea. Thus Fish struck at Bird, and then fled into the waters. Then Bird came, lion-faced and with an eagle's talons, flapping its wings towards its nest. It stopped in mid-flight. Like a hurricane whirling in the midst of heaven, it circled in the sky. Bird, looking about for its nest, spread wide its limbs. It trampled over the broad plain after its well-built nest of brushwood. Its voice shrieked into the interior of heaven like the Mistress's.

Bird sought for Fish, searching the marshes. Bird peered into the deep water for Fish, watching closely. Extending its claws, it just snatched from the water Fish's tiny fish-spawn, gathering them all together and piling them up in a heap. Thus Bird took its revenge and ...... its heart. Again Bird replied to Fish:

"You utter fool! Dolt, muddle-headed Fish, you are out of ......! The mouths of those who circle (?) the quay never get enough to eat, and their hunger lasts all day. Swine, rascal, gorging yourself upon your own excrement, you freak!"

"You are like a watchman living on the walls (?), ...! Fish, you kindled fire against me, you planted henbane. In your stupidity you caused devastation; you have spattered your hands with blood! Your arrogant heart will destroy itself by its own deeds! But I am Bird, flying in the heavens and walking on the earth. Wherever I travel to, I am there for the joy of its ...... named. ......, O Fish, ... bestowed by the Great Princes (a name for the Igigi) . I am of first-class seed, and my young are first-born young! ...... went with uplifted head ...... to the lustrous E-kur. ...... until distant days. ...... the numerous people say. How can you not recognise my pre-eminence? Bow your neck to the ground".

Again Bird had hurled insults at Fish. Then Fish shouted at Bird, eyeing it angrily: "Do not puff yourself up from your lying mouth! Our judge shall take this up. Let us take our case to Enki, our judge and adjudicator".

And so with the two of them jostling and continuing the evil quarrel in order to establish, the one over the other, their grandness and pre-eminence, the litigation was registered within Eridug, and they {put forward their argumentation} {(1 ms. has instead:) stood there in dispute}. ...... thrashing about (?) amid roaring like that of a bull, ... rushed forward like .... They requested a verdict ...... from King Šulgi, son of Enlil.

(Bird speaks:) "You ......, lord of true speech, pay attention to my words! I had put ...... and laid eggs there. ...... had bestowed ...... and had given as their sustenance. After ...... had started ......, ... he destroyed my house. He turned my nest of brushwood into a haunted house. He destroyed my house, and tore down my storeroom. He smashed my eggs and threw them into the sea. ...... examine what I have said. Return a verdict in my favour". ...... investigating ......, she prostrated herself to the ground.

...... announced (?) the word. ...... august, spoke from the heart: "Your words are sterling words, such as delight the heart". (Šulgi speaks:) "For how long are {they} going to persist (?) in quarrelling?" Like ...... came out supreme. Like butting ......, they jostled each other.

(Fish speaks:) "......, let it be favourable to me!" (Šulgi speaks:) "I shall instruct you in the divine rules and just ordinances of our dwelling-place. Like (?) Enki, king of the abzu, I am successful in finding solutions, and am wise in words". He answered Bird and Fish:

"To strut about in the E-kur is a glory for Bird, as its singing is sweet. At Enlil's holy table, Bird ...... precedence over you ......! It shall utter its cries in the temple of the great gods. The Anuna gods rejoice at its voice. It is suitable for banquets in the great dining hall of the gods. It provides good cheer in {the king's} {(1 ms. has instead:) Šulgi's} palace. ...... with head high, at the table of Šulgi, son of Enlil. The king ...... long life.

1 line fragmentary – Fish ...... in splendour ......".

Thereupon Fish ...... Bird.

6 lines missing or fragmentary – ...... Enki ...... bestowed.

1 line fragmentary – In the abzu of Eridug ...... Bird .... Because Bird was victorious over Fish in the dispute between Fish and Bird, Father Enki be praised!

The Debate Between Copper and Silver

(**THIS COMPOSITION** is preserved in a fragmentary state: the relationship between Segments A-C, D and I is uncertain, and the inclusion of 2 mss., preserving Segments E-F and G-H, is tentative.)

Segment A

unknown no. of lines missing

5 lines fragmentary – (Silver (?) speaks:) "Powerful with huge arms, does he have any rival? He walks carrying the precious hammer stone and anvil stone. He can create ...... and thus make it larger – ......, a brother, is your right arm; ......, a mother (?), is your left (?). He has created ......; let him show it off. Constantly digging ......, let him accumulate goods. After exalted ...... conceived (?) him, after ...... like a breast, after ...... towards the abzu, ... to the edge of the horizon, may ...... bring ...... for you. After ...... made ......".

2 lines fragmentary

31 lines missing

(Copper speaks:) "Hills and depths .... My harrow .... Levelling all the mounds ......, Strong Copper directs (?) the way. A dragon .... Strong Copper ...... the fields. Turbulent waters ...... ewes. Strong Copper ...... the mighty waters". Enlil ....

1 line fragmentary – Silver ...... Strong Copper ......

10 lines fragmentary

8 lines missing

Enlil ...... called for his minister Nuska: "My minister, Nuska!" (Nuska answered:) "Always at your service!" (Enlil replied:) "Strong Copper ...... the throne and serves – let him sit in his ......". He had barely finished speaking thus to him, when Nuska and the minister's retinue went together to ...... and said to Strong Copper "Come in!" Then Strong Copper clasped against his chest the labours of his huge arms, the abundance of heaven and earth, as an offering and a gift.

But Silver too held against his chest the goats, bulls and sheep he had slaughtered. Not planting trees in the ......, Silver ...... silver in small pieces .... After him, he ...... his famous ......, very good things, to Strong Copper on his neck. Silver ...... an old reed box. He put ...... inside it. Silver ...... silver in small pieces ....

Against Strong Copper, the strong heir of Father Enlil, he hurled vile insults, and cast vile curses: "The porters with their arms tied to their work; the potter, digging the hoe in the ground, for days on end extracting the clay with his hands; the ...... worker from daybreak in a pit unfit for washing or bathing; the shipbuilder, caulking a boat, heating up fish oil, with garments not easy to clean; the cook, heating up oil, carrying ...... water, standing by the place of testimony; the brewer, who does not untie his belt in warm weather, whose hands do not dry the clay; the maltster, never resting in winter, ...; the nest hunter (?), spreading the nets, working in hollows; the barber, cutting the growth, removing the flourishing roots; the freight wagon oxen shaking their heads; the donkeys submitting their necks to the yoke, ..., carrying firewood; ......".

7 lines fragmentary

7 lines missing

The oven ...... warm food.

2 lines fragmentary

unknown no. of lines missing

Segment B

9 lines fragmentary – (Silver speaks:) "...... one who neither ...... foundations nor erects reed fences. Get out! You wander about .... But my assigned task is in houses, in ...... and at banquets". Silver did not ...... in the ...... which he had .... He spoke this way in the matter of the ...... strength.

Then Strong Copper, the warrior of heaven (?), kept his body firm, and did not take ......; he did not show hate, but kept quiet (?). He kept his neck firm, and did not .... He ...... his rejoicing face to the gods.

Strong Copper ...... and addressed the Anuna gods: "Ninsumun, the woman of all the destinies, ... generously. The speech ......, ... wisdom, forgetting (?) ......, ..., pulling it out like a root, ..., ... my counsellor ......, ... the house's fire before Enlil, I will ...... warm water ......".

Strong Copper answered Silver: "Silver, to make lead shine (?) is not an important achievement. Restitution according to the tablets does not do the work of Copper. A hand without a wrist cannot (?) work. A weak neck carries nothing, does not ...... a thing to a load. A heart ......, mankind .... No one ...... a boat with bitumen ...... in the river".

unknown no. of lines missing

Segment C

(Copper speaks:)

1 line fragmentary ...... the oil jar, ... trap that ties someone up, ... all full of lies, ... his hand bringing taxes, ... erasing restitutions, ... people are deceived. A ...... organised by you goes to the desert, ... No one should put in a dwelling a ...... by you. A ...... by you should not make grain grow with the labours of the soil. It should not fill the silos with grain, it makes no one rejoice. It should not fill the hairy sacks with grain".

"No king should ride on a barge built by you. No one should carry things from afar on a trip in a chariot of yours. In the palace, no one should place on a table your edible .... No young man of ...... should be pleased by ...... your soil (?). No ...... of assorted woods or fine oils from you should stand on the streets. You should not work with wood, you should not work with reeds!"

3 lines fragmentary

unknown no. of lines missing

Segment D

(Copper speaks:) "...... the heavens were separated from the earth, there was no drinking water .... In order that the people should eat food ......, my father Enlil created me in a single day, and then the Tigris charged like a great wild bull".

"At that time, your feet did not move, and you did not walk around. In the ...... of Enlil, not separated from the ......, you got up, and you moved your feet toward his house. They cut you to pieces with the strength provided by me. Someone opens ...... there with the abundance I give to the population".

"Silver, consider the palace! ...... finds the time right, according to the turning starry sky, (and says:) "Come on! You will perform the work of your arms, you will help Enlil". But you stick out a long tongue like a buck-goat so that everybody can see. Indoors, the palace is your station and banquets are your assigned task (you say). – Silver, I will demonstrate to you that the palace is neither your station nor your dwelling".

"Men caulk tiny, very strong boxes for you, as they do a boat. They cover you over with their oldest rags, and someone digs a hole for you in the middle of the cattle-pen. Or they pour clay on top of you, as on a jar with a sealed mouth, and then, in the darkest place inside the house, someone buries you in the most obscure corner of a grave".

"When the time of wet ground has arrived for me, you do not supply the copper hoes that chop plants in the hard ground, so no one concerns themselves with you. When sowing time has arrived for me, you do not supply the copper adzes that make ploughs, so no one concerns themselves with you. When wintertime has arrived for me, you do not supply the copper axes that chop firewood, so no one concerns themselves with you. When harvest time has arrived for me, you do not supply the copper sickles that reap grain, so no one concerns themselves with you. For your harvest or winter, you do not supply the copper adzes and chisels which build houses, not even a female lamb, so no one concerns themselves with you".

"Silver, you are forgotten in the soil inside the house. A scared mouse in a silent house, ... – Silver, the palace is not your station! An obscure place, a grave, such is your station. Silver, banquets are not your assigned task – fasting is your assigned task. Silver, to make lead shine (?) is not an important achievement. The task of making divine statues is not likely to fall within your capabilities. Why do you keep attacking me like a dog? You snake, get back in the darkest part of the house and lie down in your grave!"

Strong Copper cast his legitimate insults against Silver, and was full of hate against him – insults of a miserable dog, like water from a brackish well. He exerted his powers against him to harass him. And at this, Silver felt thoroughly harassed; it did not befit his dignity.

Silver answered Strong Copper: "You do not give blades to the ...... wooden hoe that breaks the ...... ground. The wooden ...... tool mixes the clay (?) ......; wedges are not written by you. The wooden shovels pile up the sheaves – match your measuring devices to the measuring stick! Just approach the cargo boat that ...... the canal banks, just keep knocking on the great door of the house at night! The coppersmith wrestles with stones and with beads – they are too hard and he has to stop because of you. Work away with your tines at the dirt by the oven instead!"

"You have accumulated lies about my honourable station. Let me, the mouse, do his work – his assigned task in the ground is noble. Your teeth dig the ground, your tongue (?) moves the dirt. The copper hoe has its digging taken over by the wooden hoe in the harder ground. The copper sickles need to have the hard weeds burned. The copper axes which chop trees, stripping and pulling out tamarisks and ash shrubs, have their blades dulled. The copper saws have to lie down for a rest beside the mountain trees".

"When you keep hitting the soil, like someone falling from a roof; when they carry (?) you out from the big brambles and ...... thorns, like a dog with a ......, as if they were catching a thief at midnight; when the great, turbulent waters, regularly, yearly (?), fill the desert; when they carry the grain from the dry ground to the canal banks; when they carry the sesame from the furrows to the canal banks; when they carry to the ...... red onions, white onions, edible bulbous leeks (?) and turnips flourishing in the furrows; when they transport the salt and spice seeds lying at the edges of the fields; when they feed the various grains to cattle and sheep; when they bring ...... to the pigs born at the fattener's; when they feed dough to the porcupine's litter; when they crush coarse flour for the huge wild boars, straight-tailed fish, il (?) fish, carp, fish with bellies (?), giraba fish laying their eggs in large amounts in the shallows (?), gurgal birds, suda birds, large u birds from the middle of the sea, eggs of ducks and all kinds of birds, all the good things which thrive in the desert, at peace there.

unknown no. of lines missing

Segment E

1 line fragmentary ... Strong Copper .... I shall give small one-shekel pieces of silver; you should ...... 3 or 4 minas. If he turns his attention to the development of humanity, small 5- or 10-mina pieces of silver ......

2 lines fragmentary – The captain ...... the role of overseer.

3 lines fragmentary – small 5- or 10-mina pieces of silver ......

1 line fragmentary

unknown no. of lines missing

Segment F

2 lines fragmentary ... of Enlil .... Small ten-shekel pieces of silver ......

6 lines fragmentary

unknown no. of lines missing

Segment G

5 lines fragmentary ...... in aromatic oil of cedar .... humans, the black-headed people. Let him anoint each with my ...... aromatic oil of cedar. ...... it is an abomination to my king.

2 lines fragmentary

unknown no. of lines missing

Segment H

4 lines fragmentary ...... for my father Enlil.

2 lines fragmentary

unknown no. of lines missing

Segment I

9 lines fragmentary ... Silver and Strong Copper having carefully had a debate, Strong Copper had the lead over Silver in Enlil's house – Father Enlil be praised!

Then the days passed, the year grew long, the silos filled up and flax was beaten .... The year, the faraway days, ... The heavens ...... stars and lengthening shadows. ...... the shadows .... The stars of heaven ...... did not .... The records, to be found in the sacred tablets of the stars, ... The heavens, ..., having been separated from the earth ....

8 lines fragmentary

1 line missing

Enlil joyfully addressed Sumer. In a ...... of abundance he raised ...... to the duties of shepherd. In order to build the ...... of Enlil, to bring forth the houses of the great gods, to raise the banks of the levees and ditches, Enlil gave strength to the shepherd Ur-Namma in his majestic arms.

On Ur-Namma receiving ...... and kingship, after he ...... a good ......, Strong Copper helped him mightily. With it, the shepherd Ur-Namma ...... in great amounts. With it, he ...... the great temple of Suen in Urim. With it, he ...... the E-kur, the house of Enlil in Nibru.

He made famous the houses of the great gods, and raised high the banks of the levees and ditches.

Under him, his city .... Under him, wool .... Under him, oil .... Under him, the people eat excellent food. Ur-Namma ...... broad wisdom. Strong Copper ...... great .... When raising ......, he .... He called the one giving ...... as his ...... singer. The ...... of bright .... He investigated the ...... of Strong Copper. ...... their helpers. In order to build his .... Not neglecting ....

1 line fragmentary

*unknown no. of lines m*issing

TALES OF KINGS

Introduction

SPENCE REMINDS US that the "histories" of these ancient peoples contain fascinating narrative if the time is taken to absorb them, and thus that "The tales of the Babylonian and Assyrian kings which we present in this chapter are of value because they are taken at first hand from their own historical accounts of the great events which occurred during their several reigns. On a first examination these tablets appear dry and uninteresting, but when studied more closely and patiently they will be found to contain matter as absorbing as that in the most exciting annals of any country. Let us take first for example the wonderful inscriptions of Tiglath-pileser II (950 BCE) which refer to his various conquests, and which were discovered by George Smith at Nimrud in the temple of Nabu."

Tiglath-pileser II

TIGLATH COMMENCES WITH the usual Oriental flourish of trumpets. He styles himself the powerful warrior who, in the service of Asshur, has trampled upon his haters, swept over them like a flood, and reduced them to shadows.

He has marched, he says, from the sea to the land of the rising sun, and from the sea of the setting sun to Egypt. He enumerates the countless lands that he has conquered. The cities Sarrapanu and Malilatu among others he took by storm and captured the inhabitants to the number of 150,000 men, women and children, all of whom he sent to Assyria. Much tribute he received from the people of the conquered lands – gold, silver, precious stones, rare woods and cattle. His custom seems to have been to make his successful generals rulers of the cities he conquered, and it is noticeable that upon a victory he invariably sacrificed to the gods. His methods appear to have been drastic in the extreme. Irritated at the defiance of the people of Sarrapanu he reduced it to a heap of earth, and crucified King Nabu-Usabi in front of the gate of his city. Not content with this vengeance, Tiglath carried off his wealth, his furniture, his wife, his son, his daughters and lastly his gods, so that no trace of the wretched monarch's kingdom should remain. It is noticeable that throughout these campaigns Tiglath invariably sent the prisoners to Assyria, which shows at least that he considered human life as relatively sacred. Probably these captive people were reduced to slavery. The races of the neighbouring desert, too, came and prostrated themselves before the Assyrian hero, kissing his feet and bringing him tribute carried by sailors.

Tiglath then begins to boast about his gorgeous new residence with all the vulgarity of a *nouveau riche*. He says that his house was decorated like a Syrian palace for his glory. He built gates of ivory with planks of cedar, and seems to have had his prisoners, the conquered kings of Syria, on exhibition in the palace precincts. At the gates were gigantic lions and bulls of clever workmanship which he describes as "cunning, beautiful, valuable", and this place he called 'The Palaces of Rejoicing'.

In a fragment which relates the circumstances of his Eastern expeditions he tells how he built a city called Humur, and how he excavated the neighbouring river Patti, which had been filled up in the past, and along its bed led refreshing waters into certain of the cities he had conquered. He complains in one text that Sarduri, the King of Ararat, revolted against him along with others, but Tiglath captured his camp and Sarduri had perforce to escape upon a mare. Into the rugged mountains he rode by night and sought safety on their peaks. Later he took refuge with his warriors in the city of Turuspa. After a siege Tiglath succeeded in reducing the place. Afterwards he destroyed the land of Ararat, and made it a desert over an area of about 450 miles. Tiglath dedicated Sarduri's couch to Ishtar, and carried off his royal riding carriage, his seal, his necklace, his royal chariot, his mace and lastly a 'great ship', though we are not told how he accomplished this last feat.

Poet or Braggart?

It is strange to notice the inflated manner in which Tiglath speaks in these descriptions. He talks about people, races and rulers 'sinning' against him as if he were a god, but it must be remembered that he, like other Assyrian monarchs, regarded himself as the representative of the gods upon earth. But though his language is at times boastful and absurd, yet on other occasions it is extremely beautiful and even poetic. In speaking of the tribute he received from various monarchs he says that he obtained from them "clothing of wool and linen, violet wool, royal treasures, the skins of sheep with fleece dyed in shining purple, birds of the sky with feathers of shining violet, horses, camels and she-camels with their young ones".

He appears, too, to have been in conflict with a Queen of Sheba or Saba, one Samsi, whom he sent as a prisoner to Syria with her gods and all her possessions.

The Autobiography of Assur-bani-pal

IN A FORMER CHAPTER we outlined the mythical history of Assur-bani-pal or Sardanapalus, and in this place may briefly review the story of his life as told in his inscriptions.

He commences by stating that he is the child of Asshur and Beltis, but he evidently intends to convey that he is their son in a spiritual sense only, for he hastens to tell us that he is the "son of the great King of Riduti" (Esar-haddon). He proceeds to tell of his triumphal progress throughout Egypt, whose kings he made tributary to him. "Then", he remarks in a hurt manner, "the good I did to them they despised and their hearts devised evil. Seditious words they spoke and took evil counsel among themselves". In short, the kings of Egypt had entered into an alliance to free themselves from the yoke of Assur-bani-pal, but his generals heard of the plot and captured several of the ringleaders in the midst of their work. They seized the royal conspirators and bound them in fetters of iron. The Assyrian generals then fell upon the populations of the revolting cities and cut off their inhabitants to a man, but they brought the rulers of Egypt to Nineveh into the presence of Assur-bani-pal. To do him justice that monarch treated Necho, who is described as 'King of Memphis and Sars', with the utmost consideration, granting him a new covenant and placing upon him costly garments and ornaments of gold, bracelets of gold, a steel sword with a sheath of gold; with chariots, mules and horses.

Dream of Gyges

Continuing, Assur-bani-pal recounts how Gyges, King of Lydia, a remote place of which his fathers had not heard the name, was granted a dream concerning the kingdom of Assyria by the god Asshur. Gyges was greatly impressed by the dream and sent to Assur-bani-pal to request his friendship, but having once sent an envoy to the Assyrian court Assur-bani-pal seemed to think that he should continue to do so regularly, and when he failed in this attention the Assyrian king prayed to Asshur to compass his discomfiture. Shortly afterwards the unhappy Gyges was overthrown by the Cimmerians, against whom Assur-bani-pal had often assisted him.

Assur-bani-pal then plaintively recounts how Saulmugina, his younger brother, conspired against him. This brother he had made King of Babylon, and after occupying the throne of that country for some time he set on foot a conspiracy to throw off the Assyrian yoke. A seer told Assur-bani-pal that he had had a dream in which the god Sin spoke to him, saying that he would overthrow and destroy Saulmugina and his fellow-conspirators. Assur-bani-pal marched against his brother, whom he overthrew. The people of Babylon, overtaken by famine, were forced to devour their own children, and in their agony they attacked Saulmugina and burned him to death with his goods, his treasures and his wives. As we have before pointed out, this tale strangely enough closely resembles the legend concerning Assur-bani-pal himself. Swift was the vengeance of the Assyrian king upon those who remained. He cut out the tongues of some, while others were thrown into pits to be eaten by dogs, bears and eagles. Then after fixing a tribute and setting governors over them he returned to Assyria. It is noticeable that Assur-bani-pal distinctly states that he 'fixed upon' the Babylonians the gods of Assyria, and this seems to show that Assyrian deities existed in contradistinction to those of Babylonia.

In one expedition into the land of Elam, Assur-bani-pal had a dream sent by Ishtar to assure him that the crossing of the river Itite, which was in high flood, could be accomplished by his army in perfect safety. The warriors easily negotiated the crossing and inflicted great losses upon the enemy. Among other things they dragged the idol of Susinay from its sacred grove, and he remarks that it had never been beheld by any man in Elam. This with other idols he carried off to Assyria. He broke the winged lions which flanked the gates of the temple, dried up the drinking wells and for a month and a day swept Elam to its utmost extent, so that neither man nor oxen nor trees could be found in it – nothing but the wild ass, the serpent and the beast of the desert. The King goes on to say that the goddess Nanâ, who had dwelt in Elam for over 1600 years, had been desecrated by so doing. "That country", he declares, "was a place not suited to her. The return of her divinity she had trusted to me. 'Assur-bani-pal', she said, 'bring me out from the midst of wicked Elam and cause me to enter the temple of Anna'." The goddess then took the road to the temple of Anna at Erech, where the King raised to her an enduring sanctuary. Those chiefs who had trusted the Elamites now felt afflicted at heart and began to despair, and one of them, like Saul, begged his own armour-bearer to slay him, master and man killing each other. Assur-bani-pal refused to give his corpse burial, and cutting off its head hung it round the neck of Nabu-Quati-Zabat, one of the followers of Saulmugina, his rebellious brother. In another text Assur-bani-pal recounts in grandiloquent language how he built the temples of Asshur and Merodach.

"The great gods in their assembly my glorious renown have heard, and over the kings who dwell in palaces, the glory of my name they have raised and have exalted my kingdom.

Assur-bani-pal as Architect

"The temples of Assyria and Babylonia which Esar-haddon, King of Assyria, had begun, their foundations he had built, but had not finished their tops; anew I built them: I finished their tops.

"Sadi-rabu-matati (the great mountain of the earth), the temple of the god Assur my lord, completely I finished. Its chamber walls I adorned with gold and silver, great columns in it I fixed, and in its gate the productions of land and sea I placed. The god Assur into Sadi-rabu-matati I brought, and I raised him an everlasting sanctuary.

"Saggal, the temple of Merodach, lord of the gods, I built, I completed its decorations; Bel and Beltis, the divinities of Babylon and Ea, the divine judge from the temple of ... I brought out, and placed them in the city of Babylon. Its noble sanctuary a great ... with fifty talents of ... its brickwork I finished, and raised over it. I caused to make a ceiling of sycamore, durable wood, beautiful as the stars of heaven, adorned with beaten gold. Over Merodach the great lord I rejoiced in heart, I did his will. A noble chariot, the carriage of Merodach, ruler of the gods, lord of lords, in gold, silver and precious stones, I finished its workmanship. To Merodach, king of the whole of heaven and earth, destroyer of my enemies, as a gift I gave it.

"A couch of sycamore wood, for the sanctuary, covered with precious stones as ornaments, as the resting couch of Bel and Beltis, givers of favour, makers of friendship, skilfully I constructed. In the gate ... the seat of Zirat-banit, which adorned the wall, I placed.

"Four bulls of silver, powerful, guarding my royal threshold, in the gate of the rising sun, in the greatest gate, in the gate of the temple Sidda, which is in the midst of Borsippa, I set up".

Esar-haddon, A 'Likeable' Monarch

ESAR-HADDON, THE FATHER OF ASSUR-BANI-PAL, has been called "the most likeable" of the Assyrian kings. He did not press his military conquests for the mere sake of glory, but in general for the maintenance of his own territory. He is notable as the restorer of Babu and the reviver of its culture. He showed much clemency to political offenders, and his court was the centre of literary activity.

Assur-bani-pal, his son, speaks warmly of the sound education he received at his father's court, and to that education and its enlightening influences we now owe the priceless series of cylinders and inscriptions found in his library. He does not seem to have been able to control his rather turbulent neighbours, and he was actually weak enough (from the Assyrian point of view) to return the gods of the kingdom of Aribi after he had led them captive to Assyria. He seems to have been good-natured, enlightened and easy-going, and if he did not boast so loudly as his son he had probably greater reason to do so.

One of the descendants of Assur-bani-pal, Bel-zakir-iskun, speaks of his restoration of certain temples, especially that of Nebo, and plaintively adds: "In after days, in the time of the kings my sons ... When this house decays and becomes old who repairs its ruin and restores its decay? May he who does so see my name written on this inscription. May he enclose it in a receptacle, pour out a libation, and write my name with his own; but whoever defaces the writing of my name may the gods not establish him. May they curse and destroy his seed from the land". This is the last royal inscription of any length written in Assyria, and its almost prophetic terms seem to suggest that he who framed them must have foreseen the downfall of the civilization he represented. Does not the inscription almost foreshadow Shelley's wondrous sonnet on 'Ozymandias'?

I met a traveller from an antique land
Who said: Two vast and trunkless legs of stone
Stand in the desert. Near them, on the sand,
Half sunk, a shattered visage lies, whose frown,
And wrinkled lip, and sneer of cold command,
Tell that its sculptor well those passions read
Which yet survive, stamped on these lifeless things,
The hand that mocked them and the heart that fed;
And on the pedestal these words appear:
"My name is Ozymandias, king of kings:
Look on my works, ye mighty, and despair!"
Nothing beside remains. Round the decay
Of that colossal wreck, boundless and bare,
The lone and level sands stretch far away.

Assur-Dan III and the Fatal Eclipse

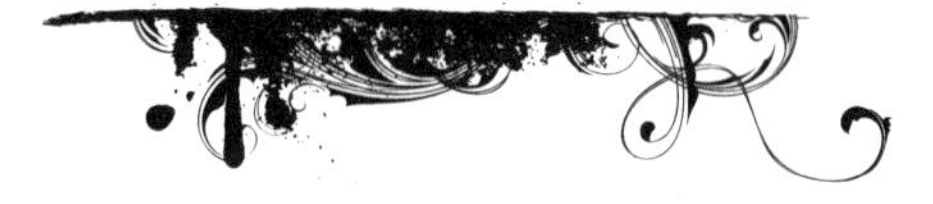

THE REIGN OF ASSUR-DAN III (773–764 BCE) supplies us with a picturesque incident. This Assyrian monarch had marched several times into Syria, and had fought the Chaldeans in Babylonia. Numerous were his tributary states and widespread his power.

But disaster crept slowly upon him, and although he made repeated efforts to stave it off, these were quite in vain. Insurrection followed insurrection, and it would seem that the priests of Babylon, considering themselves slighted, joined the malcontent party and assisted to foment discord. At the critical juncture of the fortunes of Assur-Dan there happened an eclipse of the sun, and as the black shadow crept over Nineveh and the King lay upon his couch and watched the gradual blotting out of the sunlight, he felt that his doom was upon him. After this direful portent he appears to have resisted no longer, but to have resigned himself to his fate. Within the year he was slain, and his rebel son, Adad-Narari IV, sat upon his murdered father's throne. But Nemesis followed upon the parricide's footsteps, for he in turn found a rebel in his son, and the land was smitten with a terrible pestilence.

Shalmaneser I

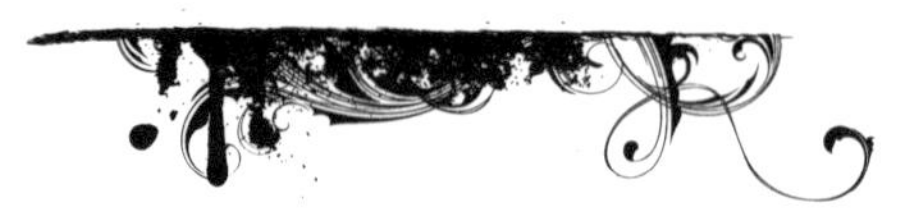

SHALMANESER I (*c.* 1270) was cast in a martial and heroic mould, and an epic might arise from the legends of his conquests and military exploits.

In his time Assyria possessed a superabundant population which required an outlet, and this the monarch deemed it his duty to supply. After conquering the provinces of Mitani to the west of the Euphrates, he attacked Babylonia, and so fiercely did he deal with his southern neighbours that we find him actually gathering the dust of their conquered cities and casting it to the four winds of heaven. Surely a more extreme manner of dealing summarily with a conquered enemy has never been recorded!

City Laments

Introduction

A CITY LAMENT is a poetic elegy for a lost or fallen city. There are five known Mesopotamian City Laments – for Urim, Sumer, Nibru, Unug and Eridug – all of which are printed in this chapter with permission from the Electronic Text Corpus of Sumerian Literature (ETCSL) .

According to Dr. Nili Samet, Assyriologist and Biblical scholar, in a 2015 article, "The City Laments are characterized by vivid, rich descriptions of the destruction of the city, the mass killing of its inhabitants, and the loss of its central temple. In addition, the laments devote special attention to the divine sphere, where the great gods order the destruction of the city, and the city patron gods beseech them to alter their decision, but to no avail. The patron gods are then forced to abandon their city prior to, or simultaneously with, the destruction. They live as deportees in foreign cites, lamenting their devastated shrine. Eventually, after the destruction, they are invited to return to their holy abode and to renew their days as of old."

The "*kirugu*" sections in the following texts are broadly equivalent to our understanding of poetic stanzas today; the word can be loosely translated as "song". Each of these *kirugu* are followed by "*ĝišgiĝal*", which acts as an "antiphon", a response to or summary of the preceding *kirugu*.

The Lament for Urim

HE HAS ABANDONED his cow-pen and has let the breezes haunt his sheepfold. The wild bull has abandoned his cow-pen and has let the breezes haunt his sheepfold. The lord of all the lands has abandoned it and has let the breezes haunt his sheepfold. Enlil has abandoned the shrine Nibru and has let the breezes haunt his sheepfold. His wife Ninlil has abandoned it and has let the breezes haunt her sheepfold. Ninlil has abandoned that house, the Ki-ur, and has let the breezes haunt her sheepfold. The queen of Keš has abandoned it and has let the breezes haunt her sheepfold. Ninmaḫ has abandoned that house Keš and has let the breezes haunt her sheepfold.

She of Isin has abandoned it and has let the breezes haunt her sheepfold. Ninisina has abandoned the shrine Egal-maḫ and has let the breezes haunt her sheepfold. The queen of Unug has abandoned it and has let the breezes haunt her sheepfold. Inana has abandoned that house Unug and has let the breezes haunt her sheepfold. Nanna has abandoned Urim and has let the breezes haunt his sheepfold. Suen has abandoned E-kiš-nu-ĝal and has let the breezes haunt his sheepfold. His wife Ningal has abandoned it and has let the breezes haunt her sheepfold. Ningal has abandoned her Agrun-kug and has let the breezes haunt her sheepfold. The wild bull of Eridug has abandoned it and has let the breezes haunt his sheepfold. Enki has abandoned that house Eridug and has let the breezes haunt his sheepfold.

Šara has abandoned E-maḫ and has let the breezes haunt his sheepfold. Ud-saḫara has abandoned that house Umma and has let the breezes haunt her sheepfold. Bau has abandoned Iri-kug and has let the breezes haunt her sheepfold. She has abandoned her flooded chamber and has let the breezes haunt her sheepfold. Her son Ab-Bau has abandoned it and has let the breezes haunt his sheepfold. Ab-Bau has abandoned Ma-gu-ena and has let the breezes haunt his sheepfold. The protective goddess of the holy house has abandoned it and has let the breezes haunt her sheepfold.

The protective goddess has abandoned E-tar-sirsir and has let the breezes haunt her sheepfold. The mother of Lagaš has abandoned it and has let the breezes haunt her sheepfold. Ĝatumdug has abandoned that house Lagaš and has let the breezes haunt her sheepfold. She of Niĝin has abandoned it and has let the breezes haunt her sheepfold. The great queen has abandoned that house Sirara and has let the breezes haunt her sheepfold. She of Kiniršа has abandoned it and has let the breezes haunt her sheepfold. Dumuzid-abzu has abandoned that house Kinirša and has let the breezes haunt her sheepfold. She of Gu-aba has abandoned it and has let the breezes haunt her sheepfold. Ninmarki has abandoned the shrine Gu-aba and has let the breezes haunt her sheepfold.
1st *kirugu*

She has let the breeze haunt her sheepfold, she groans grievously over it. O cow, your lowing no longer fills the byre, the cow-pen no longer brings joy (?) to the prince.
Its *ĝišgiĝal*.

O city, the lament is bitter, the lament made for you. Your lament is bitter, O city, the lament made for you. In his righteous destroyed city its lament is bitter. In his righteous destroyed Urim, the lament is bitter, the lament made for you. Your lament is bitter, O city, the lament made for you. In his destroyed Urim its lament is bitter. How long will your bitter lament grieve your lord who weeps? How long will your bitter lament grieve Nanna who weeps?

O brick-built Urim, the lament is bitter, the lament made for you. O E-kiš-nu-ĝal, your lament is bitter, the lament made for you. O shrine Agrun-kug, the lament is bitter, the lament made for you. O great place Ki-ur, the lament is bitter, the lament made for you. O shrine Nibru, city, the lament is bitter, the lament made for you. O brick-built E-kur, the lament is bitter, the lament made for you. O Ĝa-ĝiš-šua, the lament is bitter, the lament made for you. O Ubšu-unkena, the lament is bitter, the lament made for you. O brick-built Iri-kug, the lament is bitter, the lament made for you.

O E-tar-sirsir, the lament is bitter, the lament made for you. O Ma-gu-ena, the lament is bitter, the lament made for you. O brick-built Isin, the lament is bitter, the lament made for you. O shrine Egal-maḫ, the lament is bitter, the lament made for you. O brick-built Unug, the lament is bitter, the lament made for you. O brick-built Eridug, the lament is bitter, the lament made for you. How long will your bitter lament grieve your lord who weeps? How long will your bitter lament grieve Nanna who weeps?

O city, your name exists but you have been destroyed. O city, your wall rises high but your Land has perished. O my city, like an innocent ewe your lamb has been torn from you. O Urim, like an innocent goat your kid has perished. O city, your rites have been alienated from you, your powers have been changed into alien powers. How long will your bitter lament grieve your lord who weeps? How long will your bitter lament grieve Nanna who weeps?

2nd *kirugu*

In his righteous destroyed city its lament is bitter. In his destroyed Urim its lament is bitter.
Its *ĝišgiĝal*.

Together with the lord whose house had been devastated, his city was given over to tears. Together with Nanna whose Land had perished, Urim joined the lament. The good woman, to disquiet the lord concerning his city, Ningal, to give him no rest concerning his Land, approached him for the sake of his city – bitterly she weeps. She approached the lord for the sake of his house – bitterly she weeps. She approached him for the sake of his devastated city – bitterly she weeps. She approached him for the sake of his devastated house – before him she makes its bitter lament.

The woman, after she had composed her song (?) for the tearful balaĝ instrument, herself utters softly a lamentation for the silent house: "The storm that came to be – its lamentation hangs heavy on me. Raging about because of the storm, I am the woman for whom the storm came to be. The storm that came to be – its lamentation hangs heavy on me. The bitter storm having come to be for me during the day, I trembled on account of that day but I did not flee before the day's violence. Because of this debilitating storm I could not see a good day for my rule, not one good day for my rule".

"The bitter lament having come to be for me during the night, I trembled on account of that night but I did not flee before the night's violence. The awesomeness of this storm, destructive as the flood, truly hangs heavy on me. Because of its existence, in my nightly sleeping place, even in my nightly sleeping place truly there was no peace for me. Nor, because of this debilitating storm, was the quiet of my sleeping place, not even the quiet of my sleeping place, allowed to me".

"Because there was bitterness in my Land, I trudged the earth like a cow for its calf. My Land was not granted succcess. Because there was bitter distress in my city, I beat my wings like a bird of heaven and flew to my city; and my city was destroyed in its foundations; and Urim perished where it lay. Because the hand of the storm appeared above, I screamed and cried to it "Return, O storm, to the plain". The storm's breast did not rise".

"To me, the woman, in the Agrun-kug, my house of queenship, they did not grant a reign of distant days. Indeed they established weeping and lamentation for me. As for the house which used to be where the spirit of the black-headed people was soothed, instead of its festivals wrath and terror indeed multiply. Because of this debilitating storm, depression, and lament and bitterness, lament and bitterness have been brought into my house, the favourable place, my devastated righteous house upon which no eye had been cast. My house founded by the righteous was pushed over on its side like a garden fence".

"For E-kiš-nu-ĝal, my house of royalty, the good house, my house which has been given over to tears, they granted to me as its lot and share: its building, falsely, and its perishing, truly. Wind and rain have been made to fall on it, as onto a tent, a shelter on the denuded harvest ground, as onto a shelter on the denuded harvest ground. Urim, my all-surpassing chamber, the house and the smitten city, all have been uprooted. Like a shepherd's sheepfold it has been uprooted. The swamp has swallowed my possessions accumulated in the city".

3rd *kirugu*

Urim has been given over to tears.
Its *ĝišgiĝal*.

"On that day, when such a storm had pounded, when in the presence of the queen her city had been destroyed, on that day, when such a storm had been created, when they had pronounced the utter destruction of my city, when they had pronounced the utter destruction of Urim, when they had directed that its people be killed, on that day I did not abandon my city, I did not forsake my land".

"Truly I shed my tears before An. Truly I myself made supplication to Enlil. "Let not my city be destroyed", I implored them. "Let not Urim be destroyed", I implored them. "Let not its people perish", I implored them. But An did not change that word. Enlil did not soothe my heart with an "It is good – so be it"".

"A second time, when the council had settled itself in the pre-eminent place, and the Anuna had seated themselves to ratify decisions, I prostrated (?) myself and stretched out my arms. Truly I shed my tears before An. Truly I myself made supplication to Enlil. "Let not my city be destroyed", I implored them. "Let not Urim be destroyed", I implored them. "Let not its people perish", I implored them. But An did not change that word. Enlil did not soothe my heart with an "It is good – so be it"".

"They gave instructions that my city should be utterly destroyed. They gave instructions that Urim should be utterly destroyed. They decreed its destiny that its people should be killed. In return for the speech (?) which I had given them, they both bound me together with my city and also bound my Urim together with me. An is not one to change his command, and Enlil does not alter what he has uttered".

4th *kirugu*

Her city has been destroyed in her presence, her powers have been alienated from her.
Its *ĝišgiĝal*.

Enlil called the storm – the people groan. He brought the storm of abundance away from the Land – the people groan. He brought the good storm away from Sumer – the people groan. He issued directions to the evil storm – the people groan. He entrusted it to Kin-gal-uda, the keeper of the storm. He called upon the storm that annihilates the Land – the people groan. He called upon the evil gales – the people groan.

Enlil brought Gibil as his aid. He called the great storm of heaven – the people groan. The great storm howls above – the people groan. The storm that annihilates the Land roars below – the people groan. The evil wind, like a rushing torrent, cannot be restrained. The weapons in the city smash heads and consume indiscriminately. The storm whirled gloom around the base of the horizon – the people groan. In front of the storm, heat blazes – the people groan. A fiery glow burns with the raging storm.

After the haze had lifted at noon, he made fires blaze. He locked up the day and the rising of the bright sun together with the good storm. In the Land he did not let the bright sun rise; it shone like the evening star. In the delightful night, the time when coolness sets in, he redoubled the south wind.

The scorching potsherds made the dust glow (?) – the people groan. He swept the winds over the black-headed people – the people groan. Sumer was overturned by a snare – the people groan. It attacked (?) the Land and devoured it completely. Tears cannot influence the bitter storm – the people groan.

The reaping storm dragged across the Land. Like a flood storm it completely destroyed the city. The storm that annihilates the Land silenced the city. The storm that will make anything vanish came doing evil. The storm blazing like fire performed its task upon the people. The storm ordered by Enlil in hate, the storm which wears away the Land, covered Urim like a garment, was spread out over it like linen.

5th *kirugu*

The storm, like a lion, has attacked unceasingly – the people groan.
Its *ĝišgiĝal*.

Then the storm was removed from the city, that city reduced to ruin mounds. It was removed from Father Nanna's city reduced to ruin mounds – the people groan. Then, the storm was taken from the Land – the people groan. Its people littered its outskirts just as if they might have been broken potsherds. Breaches had been made in its walls – the people groan. On its lofty city-gates where walks had been taken, corpses were piled. On its boulevards where festivals had been held, heads lay scattered (?). In all its streets where walks had been taken, corpses were piled. In its places where the dances of the Land had taken place, people were stacked in heaps. They made the blood of the Land flow down the wadis like copper or tin. Its corpses, like fat left in the sun, melted away of themselves.

The heads of its men slain by the axe were not covered with a cloth. Like a gazelle caught in a trap, their mouths bit the dust. Men struck down by the spear were not bound with bandages. As if in the place where their mothers had laboured, they lay in their own blood. Its men who were finished off by the battle-mace were not bandaged with new (?) cloth. Although they were not drunk with strong drink, their necks drooped on their shoulders. He who stood up to the weapon was crushed by the weapon – the people groan. He who ran away from it was overwhelmed (?) by the storm – the people groan. The weak and the strong of Urim perished from hunger. Mothers and fathers who did not leave their houses were consumed by fire. The little ones lying in their mothers' arms were carried off like fish by the waters. Among the nursemaids with their strong embrace, the embrace was pried open.

The Land's judgment disappeared – the people groan. The Land's counsel was swallowed by a swamp – the people groan. The mother absconded before her child's eyes – the people groan. The father turned away from his child – the people groan. In the city the wife was abandoned, the child was abandoned, possessions were scattered about. The black-headed people were carried off from their strongholds. Its queen like a bird in fright departed from her city. Ningal like a bird in fright departed from her city. All the treasures accumulated in the Land were defiled. In all the storehouses abounding in the Land fires were kindled. In its ponds Gibil, the purifier, relentlessly did his work.

The good house of the lofty untouchable mountain, E-kiš-nu-ĝal, was entirely devoured by large axes. The people of Šimaški and Elam, the destroyers, counted its worth as only thirty shekels. They broke up the good house with pickaxes. They reduced the city to ruin mounds. Its queen cried, "Alas, my city", cried, "Alas, my house". Ningal cried, "Alas, my city", cried, "Alas, my house. As for me, the woman, both my city has been destroyed and my house has been destroyed. O Nanna, the shrine Urim has been destroyed and its people have been killed".

6th *kirugu*

In her cow-pen, in her sheepfold the woman utters bitter words: "The city has been destroyed by the storm".
Its *ĝišgiĝal*.

Mother Ningal, like an enemy, stands outside her city. The woman laments bitterly over her devastated house. Over her devastated shrine Urim, the princess bitterly declares: "An has indeed cursed my city, my city has been destroyed before me. Enlil has indeed transformed my house, it has been smitten by pickaxes. On my ones coming from the south he hurled fire. Alas, my city has indeed been destroyed before me. On my ones coming from the highlands Enlil hurled flames. Outside the city, the outer city was destroyed before me – I shall cry "Alas, my city". Inside the city, the inner city was destroyed before me – I shall cry "Alas, my city". My houses of the outer city were destroyed – I shall cry "Alas, my houses". My houses of the inner city were destroyed – I shall cry "Alas, my houses"".

"My city no longer multiplies for me like good ewes, its good shepherd is gone. Urim no longer multiplies for me like good ewes, its shepherd boy is gone. My bull no longer crouches in its cow-pen, its herdsman is gone. My sheep no longer crouch in their fold, their herdsman is gone. In the river of my city dust has gathered, and the holes of foxes have been dug there. In its midst no flowing water is carried, its tax-collector is gone. In the fields of my city there is no grain, their farmer is gone. My fields, like fields from which the hoe has been kept away (?), have grown tangled (?) weeds. My orchards and gardens that produced abundant syrup and wine have grown mountain thornbushes. My plain that used to be covered in its luxurious verdure has become cracked (?) like a kiln".

"My possessions, like a flock of rooks rising up, have risen in flight – I shall cry "O my possessions". He who came from the south has carried my possessions off to the south – I shall cry "O my possessions". He who came from the highlands has carried my possessions off to the highlands – I shall cry "O my possessions". My silver, gems and lapis lazuli have been scattered about – I shall cry "O my possessions". The swamp has swallowed my treasures – I shall cry "O my possessions". Men ignorant of silver have filled their hands with my silver. Men ignorant of gems have fastened my gems around their necks. My small birds and fowl have flown away – I shall say "Alas, my city". My slave-girls and children have been carried off by boat – I shall say

"Alas, my city". Woe is me, my slave-girls bear strange emblems in a strange city. My young men mourn in a desert they do not know".

"Woe is me, my city which no longer exists – I am not its queen. Nanna, Urim which no longer exists – I am not its owner. I am the good woman whose house has been made into ruins, whose city has been destroyed, in place of whose city a strange city has been built. I am Ningal whose city has been made into ruins, whose house has been destroyed, in place of whose house a strange house has been built".

"Woe is me, the city has been destroyed, my house too has been destroyed. Nanna, the shrine Urim has been destroyed, its people killed. Woe is me, where can I sit, where can I stand? Woe is me, in place of my city a strange house is being erected. I am the good woman in place of whose house a strange city is being built. Upon its removal from its place, from the plain, I shall say "Alas, my people". Upon my city's removal from Urim, I shall say "Alas, my house"".

The woman tears at her hair as if it were rushes. She beats the holy ub drum at her chest, she cries "Alas, my city". Her eyes well with tears, she weeps bitterly: "Woe is me, my city which no longer exists – I am not its queen. Nanna, the shrine Urim which no longer exists – I am not its owner. Woe is me, I am one whose cow-pen has been torn down, I am one whose cows have been scattered. I am Ningal on whose ewes the weapon has fallen, as in the case of an unworthy herdsman. Woe is me, I have been exiled from the city, I can find no rest. I am Ningal, I have been exiled from the house, I can find no dwelling place. I am sitting as if a stranger with head high in a strange city. Debt-slaves … bitterness …"

"I am one who, sitting in a debtors prison among its inmates, can make no extravagant claims. In that place I approached him for the sake of his city – I weep bitterly. I approached the lord for the sake of his house – I weep bitterly. I approached him for the sake of his destroyed house – I weep bitterly. I approached him for the sake of his destroyed city – I weep bitterly. Woe is me, I shall say "Fate of my city, bitter is the fate of my city". I the queen shall say "O my destroyed house, bitter is the fate of my house". O my brick-built Urim which has been flooded, which has been washed away, O my good house, my city which has been reduced to ruin mounds, in the debris of your destroyed righteous house, I shall lie down alongside you. Like a fallen bull, I will never rise up from your wall (?)".

"Woe is me, untrustworthy was your building, and bitter your destruction. I am the woman at whose shrine Urim the food offerings have been terminated. O my Agrun-kug, the all-new house whose charms never sated me, O my city no longer regarded as having been built – devastated for what reason? O my house both destroyed and devastated – devastated for what reason? Nobody at all escaped the force of the storm ordered in hate. O my house of Suen in Urim, bitter was its destruction".

7th *kirugu*

"Alas, my city, alas, my house".
Its *ĝišgiĝal*.

O queen, how is your heart …! How you have become! O Ningal, how is your heart …! How you have become! O good woman whose city has been destroyed, now how do you exist? O Ningal whose Land has perished, how is your heart …! After your city has been destroyed, now how do you exist? After your house has been destroyed, how is your heart ……! Your city has become a strange city, now how do you exist? Your house has turned to tears, how is your heart …! You are not a bird of your city which has been reduced to ruin mounds. You cannot live there as a resident in your good house given over to the pickaxe. You cannot act as queen of a people led off to slaughter.

Your tears have become strange tears, your Land no longer weeps. With no lamentation prayers, it dwells in foreign lands. Your Land like … Your city has been made into ruins; now how do you exist? Your house has been laid bare, how is your heart …! Urim, the shrine, is haunted by the breezes, now how do you exist?

Its gudug priest no longer walks in his wig, how is your heart …! Its en priestess no longer lives in the ĝipar, now how do you exist? In the uzga shrine the priest who cherishes purification rites makes no purification rites for you. Father Nanna, your išib priest does not make perfect holy supplications to you. Your lumaḫ priest does not dress in linen in your holy giguna shrine. Your righteous en priestess chosen in your ardent heart, she of the E-kiš-nu-ĝal, does not proceed joyously from the shrine to the ĝipar. The aua priests do not celebrate the festivals in your house of festivals. They do not play for you the šem and ala instruments which gladden the heart, nor the tigi. The black-headed people do not bathe during your festivals. Like … mourning has been decreed for them; their appearance has indeed changed.

Your song has been turned into weeping before you – how long will this last? Your tigi music has been turned into lamentation before you – how long will this last? Your bull is not brought into its pen, its fat is not prepared for you. Your sheep does not live in its fold, its milk is not made abundant for you. Your fat carrier does not come to you from the cow-pen – how long will this last? Your milk carrier does not come to you from the sheepfold – how long will this last? An evildoer has seized your fisherman who was carrying fish – how long will this last? Lightning carried off your fowler who was carrying birds – how long will this last? The teme plants grow in the middle of your watercourses which were once suitable for barges, and mountain thornbushes grow on your roads which had been constructed for wagons.

My queen, your city weeps before you as its mother. Urim, like a child lost in a street, seeks a place before you. Your house, like a man who has lost everything, stretches out (?) its hands to you. Your brick-built righteous house, like a human being, cries "Where are you?". My queen, you have indeed left the house, you have left the city. How long will you stand aside from your city like an enemy? Mother Ningal, you confronted your city like an enemy. Although you are a queen who loves her city, you abandoned your sheepfold. Although you are one who cares for her Land, you set it on fire.

Mother Ningal, return like a bull to your cattle-pen, like a sheep to your fold, like a bull to your cattle-pen of former days, like a sheep to your fold. My queen, like a young child to your room, return to your house. May An, king of the gods, declare "Enough!" to you. May Enlil, king of all the lands, decree your fate. May he restore your city for you – exercise its queenship! May he restore Nibru for you – exercise its queenship! May he restore Urim for you – exercise its queenship! May he restore Isin for you – exercise its queenship!

8th *kirugu*

"My powers have been alienated from me".
Its *ĝišgiĝal*.

Alas, storm after storm swept the Land together: the great storm of heaven, the ever-roaring storm, the malicious storm which swept over the Land, the storm which destroyed cities, the storm which destroyed houses, the storm which destroyed cow-pens, the storm which burned sheepfolds, which laid hands on the holy rites, which defiled the weighty counsel, the storm which cut off all that is good from the Land, the storm which pinioned the arms of the black-headed people.

9th *kirugu*

The storm which does not respect …
Its *ĝišgiĝal.*

The storm which knows no mother, the storm which knows no father, the storm which knows no wife, the storm which knows no child, the storm which knows no sister, the storm which knows no brother, the storm which knows no neighbour, the storm which knows no female companion, the storm which caused the wife to be abandoned, which caused the child to be abandoned, the storm which caused the light in the Land to disappear, the storm which swept through, ordered in hate by Enlil – Father Nanna, may that storm swoop down no more on your city. May your black-headed people see it no more.

May that storm, like rain pouring down from heaven, never recur. May that storm, which struck down all the black-headed living beings of heaven and earth, be entirely destroyed. May the door be closed on it, like the great city-gate at night-time. May that storm not be given a place in the reckoning, may its record be hung from a nail outside the house of Enlil.
10th *kirugu*

Until distant days, other days, future days.
Its *ĝišgiĝal.*

From distant days when the Land was founded, O Nanna, the humble people who lay hold of your feet have brought to you their tears for the silent house, playing music before you. May the black-headed people, cast away from you, make obeisance to you. In your city reduced to ruin mounds may a lament be made to you. O Nanna, may your restored city be resplendent before you. Like a bright heavenly star may it not be destroyed, may it pass before you.

The personal deity of a man brings you a greeting gift; a supplicant utters prayers to you. Nanna, you who have mercy on the Land, Lord Ašimbabbar – as concerns him who speaks your heart's desire, Nanna, after you have absolved that man's sin, may your heart relent towards him who utters prayers to you. He looks favourably on the man who stands there with his offering. Nanna, you whose penetrating gaze searches hearts, may its people who suffered that evil storm be pure before you. May the hearts of your people who dwell in the Land be pure before you. Nanna, in your restored city may you be fittingly praised.
11th *kirugu*

The Lament for Sumer and Urim

TO OVERTURN the appointed times, to obliterate the divine plans, the storms gather to strike like a flood.

An, Enlil, Enki and {Ninḫursaĝa} have decided its fate – to overturn the divine powers of Sumer, to lock up the favourable reign in its home, to destroy the city, to destroy the house, to destroy the cattle-pen, to level the sheepfold; that the cattle should not stand in the pen, that the sheep should not multiply in the fold, that watercourses should carry brackish water, that weeds should grow in the fertile fields, that mourning plants should grow in the open country,

that the mother should not seek out her child, that the father should not say "O my dear wife!", that the junior wife should take no joy in his embrace, that the young child should not grow vigorous on his knee, that the wet-nurse should not sing lullabies; to change the location of kingship, to defile the seeking of oracles, to take kingship away from the Land, to cast the eye of the storm on all the land, to obliterate the divine plans by the order of An and Enlil;

after An had frowned upon all the lands, after Enlil had looked favourably on an enemy land, after Nintur had scattered the creatures that she had created, after Enki had altered the course of the Tigris and Euphrates, after Utu had cast his curse on the roads and highways;

so as to obliterate the divine powers of Sumer, to change its preordained plans, to alienate the divine powers of the reign of kingship of Urim, to humiliate the princely son in his house E-kiš-nu-ĝal, to break up the unity of the people of Nanna, numerous as ewes; to change the food offerings of Urim, the shrine of magnificent food offerings; that its people should no longer dwell in their quarters, that they should be given over to live in an inimical place; that Šimaški and Elam, the enemy, should dwell in their place; that its shepherd, in his own palace, should be captured by the enemy, that Ibbi-Suen should be taken to the land Elam in fetters, that from Mount Zabu on the edge of the sea to the borders of Anšan, like a swallow that has flown from its house, he should never return to his city;

that on the two parallel banks of the Tigris and of the Euphrates bad weeds should grow, that no one should set out on the road, that no one should seek out the highway, that the city and its settled surroundings should be razed to ruin-mounds; that its numerous black-headed people should be slaughtered; that the hoe should not attack the fertile fields, that seed should not be planted in the ground, that the melody of the cowherds' songs should not resound in the open country, that butter and cheese should not be made in the cattle-pen, that dung should not be stacked on the ground, that the shepherd should not enclose the sacred sheepfold with a fence, that the song of the churning should not resound in the sheepfold;

to decimate the animals of the open country, to finish off all living things, that the four-legged creatures of Šakkan should lay no more dung on the ground, that the marshes should be so dry as to be full of cracks and have no new seed, that sickly-headed reeds should grow in the reedbeds and come to an end in a stinking morass, that there should be no new growth in the orchards, that it should all collapse by itself – so as quickly to subdue Urim like a roped ox, to bow its neck to the ground: the great charging wild bull, confident in its own strength, the primeval city of lordship and kingship, built on sacred ground.

Its fate cannot be changed. Who can overturn it? It is the command of An and Enlil. Who can oppose it?

An frightened the very dwellings of Sumer, the people were afraid. Enlil blew an evil storm, silence lay upon the city. Nintur bolted the door of the storehouses of the Land. Enki blocked the water in the Tigris and the Euphrates. Utu took away the pronouncement of equity and justice. Inana handed over victory in strife and battle to a rebellious land. Ninĝirsu poured Sumer away like milk to the dogs. Turmoil descended upon the Land, something that no one had ever known, something unseen, which had no name, something that could not be fathomed. The lands were confused in their fear. The god of the city turned away, its shepherd vanished.

The people, in their fear, breathed only with difficulty. The storm immobilized them, the storm did not let them return. There was no return for them, the storm did not retreat. This is what Enlil, the shepherd of the black-headed people, did: Enlil, to destroy the loyal households, to decimate the loyal men, to put the evil eye on the sons of the loyal men, on the first-born,

Enlil then sent down Gutium from the mountains. Their advance was as the flood of Enlil that cannot be withstood. The great wind of the countryside filled the countryside, it advanced before them. The extensive countryside was destroyed, no one moved about there.

The dark time was roasted by hailstones and flames. The bright time was wiped out by a shadow. On that day, heaven rumbled, the earth trembled, the storm worked without respite. Heaven was darkened, it was covered by a shadow; the mountains roared. Utu lay down at the horizon, dust passed over the mountains. Nanna lay at the zenith, the people were afraid. The city's god left his dwelling and stood aside. The foreigners in the city even chased away its dead. Large trees were uprooted, the forest growth was ripped out. The orchards were stripped of their fruit, they were cleaned of their offshoots. The crop drowned while it was still on the stalk, the yield of the grain diminished.

3 lines fragmentary

They piled … up in heaps, they spread … out like sheaves. There were corpses floating in the Euphrates, weapons smashed heads. The father turned away from his wife saying "This is not my wife!" The mother turned away from her child saying "This is not my child!" He who had a productive estate neglected his estate saying "This is not my estate!" The rich man took an unfamiliar path away from his possessions. In those days the kingship of the Land was defiled. The tiara and crown that had been on the king's head were both spoiled. The lands that had followed the same path were split into disunity. The food offerings of Urim, the shrine of magnificent food offerings, were changed for the worse. Nanna traded away his people, numerous as ewes.

Its king sat immobilised in his own palace. Ibbi-Suen was sitting in anguish in his own palace. In E-namtila, his place of delight, he wept bitterly. The flood dashing a hoe on the ground was levelling everything. Like a great storm it roared over the earth – who could escape it? – to destroy the city, to destroy the house, so that traitors would lie on top of loyal men and the blood of traitors flow upon loyal men.

1st *kirugu*

The storms gather to strike like a flood.
Ĝišgiĝal to the *kirugu*.

The house of Kiš, Ḫursaĝ-kalama, was destroyed. Zababa took an unfamiliar path away from his beloved dwelling. Mother Bau was lamenting bitterly in her E-Iri-kug. "Alas, the destroyed city, my destroyed house", she cried bitterly.

1 line fragmentary

2 lines missing

"Alas, the destroyed city, my destroyed house", she cried bitterly.

Kazallu, the city of teeming multitudes, was cast into confusion. Numušda took an unfamiliar path away from the city, his beloved dwelling. His wife Namrat, the beautiful lady, was lamenting bitterly. "Alas, the destroyed city, my destroyed house", she cried bitterly. Its riverbed was empty, no water flowed. Like a river cursed by Enki its opening channel was dammed up. On the fields fine grains grew no more, people had nothing to eat. The orchards were scorched like an oven, its open country was scattered. The four-legged wild animals did not run about. The four-legged creatures of Šakkan could find no rest.

Lugal-Marda stepped outside his city. Ninzuana took an unfamiliar path away from her beloved dwelling. "Alas, the destroyed city, my destroyed house", she cried bitterly. Isin, the shrine that was not a quay, was split by onrushing waters. Ninisina, the mother of the Land, wept bitter tears. "Alas, the destroyed city, my destroyed house", she cried bitterly. Enlil smote Dur-an-ki with a mace. Enlil made lamentation in his city, the shrine Nibru. Mother Ninlil, the lady of the Ki-ur shrine, wept bitter tears. "Alas, the destroyed city, my destroyed house", she cried bitterly.

Keš, built all alone on the high open country, was haunted. Adab, the settlement which stretches out along the river, {was treated as a rebellious land.} The snake of the mountains made his lair there, it became a rebellious land. The Gutians bred there, issued their seed. Nintur wept bitter tears over her creatures. "Alas, the destroyed city, my destroyed house", she cried bitterly. In Zabalam the sacred Giguna was haunted. Inana abandoned Unug and went off to enemy territory. In the E-ana the enemy set eyes upon the sacred Ĝipar shrine. The sacred Ĝipar of en priesthood was defiled. Its en priest was snatched from the Ĝipar and carried off to enemy territory. "Alas, the destroyed city, my destroyed house", she cried bitterly.

A violent storm blew over Umma and the Šeg-kuršaga. Šara took an unfamiliar path away from the E-maḫ, his beloved dwelling. Ninmul cried bitter tears over her destroyed city. "Oh my city, whose charms can no longer satisfy me", she cried bitterly. Ĝirsu, the city of heroes, was afflicted with a lightning storm. Ninĝirsu took an unfamiliar path away from the E-ninnu. Mother Bau wept bitter tears in her E-Iri-kug. "Alas, the destroyed city, my destroyed house", she cried bitterly.

On that day the word of Enlil was an attacking storm. Who could fathom it? The word of Enlil was destruction on the right, was ... on the left. This is what Enlil, the one who determines destinies, did: Enlil brought down the Elamites, the enemy, from the highlands. Nanše, the noble daughter, was settled outside the city. Fire approached Ninmarki in the shrine Gu-aba. Large boats were carrying off its silver and lapis lazuli. The lady, sacred Ninmarki, was despondent because of her perished goods. On that day he decreed a storm blazing like the mouth of a fire. The province of Lagaš was handed over to Elam. And then the queen also reached the end of her time.

Bau, as if she were human, also reached the end of her time: "Woe is me! Enlil has handed over the city to the storm. He has handed it over to the storm that destroys cities. He has handed it over to the storm that destroys houses". Dumuzid-abzu was full of fear in the house of Kinirša. Kinirša, the city to which she belongs, was ordered to be plundered. The city of Nanše, Niĝin, was delivered to the foreigners. Sirara, her beloved dwelling, was handed over to the evil ones. "Alas, the destroyed city, my destroyed house", she cried bitterly. Its sacred Ĝipar of en priesthood was defiled. Its en priest was snatched from the Ĝipar and carried off to enemy territory.

Mighty strength was set against the banks of the Id-nuna-Nanna canal. The settlements of the E-danna of Nanna, like substantial cattle-pens, were destroyed. Their refugees, like stampeding goats, were chased (?) by dogs. They destroyed Gaeš like milk poured out to dogs, and shattered its finely fashioned statues. "Alas, the destroyed city, my destroyed house", she cried bitterly. Its sacred Ĝipar of en priesthood was defiled. Its en priestess was snatched from the Ĝipar and carried off to enemy territory.

A lament was raised at the dais that stretches out toward heaven. Its heavenly throne was not set up, was not fit to be crowned (?). It was cut down as if it were a date palm and tied together. Aššu, the settlement that stretches out along the river, was deprived of water. At the place of Nanna where evil had never walked, the enemy walked. How was the house treated thus? The E-puḫruma was emptied. Ki-abrig, which used to be filled with numerous cows and numerous calves, was destroyed like a mighty cattle-pen. Ningublaga took an unfamiliar path away from the Ĝa-bura. Ninigara wept bitter tears all alone. "Alas, the destroyed city, my destroyed house", she cried bitterly. Its sacred Ĝipar of en priesthood was defiled. Its en priestess was snatched from the Ĝipar and carried off to enemy territory.

Ninazu deposited his weapon in a corner in the E-gida. An evil storm swept over Ninḫursaĝa at the E-nutura. Like a pigeon she flew from the window, she stood apart in the open country. "Alas, the destroyed city, my destroyed house", she cried bitterly. As for Ĝišbanda, the house filled with lamentation was destroyed among the weeping reeds. Ninĝišzida took an unfamiliar path away from Ĝišbanda. Azimua, the queen of the city, wept bitter tears. "Alas, the destroyed city, my destroyed house", she cried bitterly.

On that day, the storm forced people to live in darkness. In order to destroy Kuara, it forced people to live in darkness. Ninehama in her fear wept bitter tears. "Alas the destroyed city, my destroyed house", she cried bitterly. Asarluḫi put his robes on with haste and ... Lugalbanda took an unfamiliar path away from his beloved dwelling. "Alas the destroyed city, my destroyed house", she cried bitterly.

Eridug, floating on great waters, was deprived (?) of drinking water. In its outer environs, which had turned into haunted plains, ... The loyal man in a place of treachery ... Ka-ḫeĝala and Igi-ḫeĝala ...

"I, a young man whom the storm has not destroyed, ... I, not destroyed by the storm, my attractiveness not brought to an end, ... We have been struck down like beautiful boxwood trees. We have been struck down like ... with coloured eyes. We have been struck down like statues being cast in moulds. The Gutians, the vandals, are wiping us out. We turned to Father Enki in the abzu of Eridug.... whatever we shall say, whatever we shall add, ... whatever we shall say, whatever we shall add, we came out from the ... of Eridug".

"While were in charge of ... during the day, the shadows .... While we were in charge of ... during the night, the storm ... What do we receive trembling on duty during the day? What do we lose not sleeping on duty during the night? Enki, your city has been cursed, it has been given to an enemy land. Why do they reckon us among those who have been displaced from Eridug? Why do they destroy us like palm trees which we have not tended? Why do they break us up like new boats we have not caulked?"

After Enki had cast his eyes on a foreign land,

1 line unclear

... have risen up, have called on their cohorts. Enki took an unfamiliar path away from Eridug. Damgalnuna, the mother of the E-maḫ, wept bitter tears. "Alas the destroyed city, my destroyed house", she cried bitterly. Its sacred Ĝipar of en priesthood was defiled. Its en priestess was snatched from the Ĝipar and carried off to enemy territory.

In Urim no one went to fetch food, no one went to fetch water. Those who went to fetch food, went away from the food and will not return. Those who went to fetch water, went away from the water and will not return. To the south, the Elamites stepped in, slaughtering ... In the uplands, the vandals, the enemy, ... The Tidnum daily strapped the mace to their loins. To the south, the Elamites, like an onrushing wave, were .... In the uplands, like chaff blowing in the wind, they ... over the open country. Urim, like a great charging wild bull, bowed its neck to the ground.

This is what Enlil, who decides the fates, did: Again he sent down the Elamites, the enemy, from the mountains. The foremost house, firmly founded, ... In order to destroy Kisiga, ten men, even five men .... Three days and three nights did not pass, ... the city was raked by a hoe. Dumuzid left Kisiga like a prisoner of war, his hands were fettered.

5 lines fragmentary

She rode away from her possessions, she went to the mountains. She loudly sang out a lament over those untravelled mountains: "I am queen, but I shall have to ride away from my possessions, and now I shall be a slave in those parts. I shall have to ride away from my silver and lapis lazuli, and now I shall be a slave in those parts. There, slavery, ... people, who can ... it? There, slavery, Elam ..., who can ... it? Alas, the destroyed city, my destroyed house", she cried bitterly. My queen, though not the enemy, went to enemy land. Ama-ušumgal-ana ... Kisiga. Like a city ....

2nd *kirugu*

1 line fragmentary

1 line missing

Ĝišgiĝal to the *kirugu*.

7 lines missing or fragmentary

Enlil threw open the door of the grand gate to the wind. In Urim no one went to fetch food, no one went to fetch water. Its people rushed around like water being poured from a well. Their strength ebbed away, they could not even go on their way. Enlil afflicted the city with an evil famine. He afflicted the city with that which destroys cities, that which destroys houses. He afflicted the city with that which cannot be withstood with weapons. He afflicted the city with dissatisfaction and treachery. In Urim, which was like a solitary reed, there was not even fear. Its people, like fish being grabbed in a pond, sought to escape. Its young and old lay spread about, no one could rise.

At the royal station (?) there was no food on top of the platform (?). The king who used to eat marvellous food grabbed at a mere ration. As the day grew dark, the eye of the sun was eclipsing, the people experienced hunger. There was no beer in the beerhall, there was no more malt for it. There was no food for him in his palace, it was unsuitable to live in. Grain did not fill his lofty storehouse, he could not save his life. The grain-piles and granaries of Nanna held no grain. The evening meal in the great dining hall of the gods was defiled. Wine and syrup ceased to flow in the great dining hall. The butcher's knife that used to slay oxen and sheep lay hungry. Its mighty oven no longer cooked oxen and sheep, it no longer emitted the aroma of roasting meat. The sounds of the bursaĝ building, the pure ... of Nanna, were stilled. The house which used to bellow like a bull was silenced. Its holy deliveries were no longer fulfilled, its ... were alienated. The mortar, pestle and grinding stone lay idle; no one bent down over them.

The Shining Quay of Nanna was silted up. The sound of water against the boat's prow ceased, there was no rejoicing. Dust piled up in the unuribanda of Nanna. The rushes grew, the rushes grew, the mourning reeds grew. Boats and barges ceased docking at the Shining Quay. Nothing moved on your watercourse which was fit for barges. The plans of the festivals at the place of the divine rituals were altered. The boat with first-fruit offerings of the father who begot Nanna no longer brought first-fruit offerings. Its food offerings could not be taken to Enlil in Nibru. Its watercourse was empty, barges could not travel.

There were no paths on either of its banks, long grass grew there. The reed fence of the well-stocked cattle-pen of Nanna was split open. The garden's fence was vioilated and breached. The cows and their young were captured and carried off to enemy territory. The munzer-fed cows took an unfamiliar path in an open country that they did not know. Gayau, who loves cows, dropped his weapon in the dung. Šuni-dug, who stores butter and cheese, did not store butter and cheese. Those who are unfamiliar with butter were churning the butter. Those who are unfamiliar with milk were curdling (?) the milk. The sound of the churning vat did not resound in the cattle-pen. Like mighty coals that once burnt, its smoke is extinguished. The great dining hall of Nanna ...

Suen wept to his father Enlil: "O father who begot me, why have you turned away from my city which was built (?) for you? O Enlil, why have you turned away from my Urim which was built (?) for you? The boat with first-fruit offerings no longer brings first-fruit offerings to the father who begot him. Your food offerings can no longer be brought to Enlil in Nibru. The en priests of the countryside and city have been carried off by phantoms. Urim, like a city raked by a hoe, is to be counted as a ruin-mound. The Du-ur, Enlil's resting-place, has become a haunted shrine. O Enlil, gaze upon your city, an empty wasteland. Gaze upon your city Nibru, an empty wasteland".

"The dogs of Urim no longer sniff at the base of the city wall. The man who used to drill large wells scratches the ground in the marketplace. My father who begot me, enclose in your embrace my city which is all alone. Enlil, return to your embrace my Urim which is all alone. Enclose in your embrace my E-kiš-nu-ĝal which is all alone. May you bring forth offspring in Urim, may you multiply its people. May you restore the divine powers of Sumer that have been forgotten".

3rd *kirugu*

O good house, good house! O its people, its people!
Ĝišgiĝal.

Enlil then answered his son Suen: "There is lamentation in the haunted city, reeds of mourning grow there. In its midst the people pass their days in sighing. Oh Nanna, the noble son …, why do you concern yourself with crying? The judgment uttered by the assembly cannot be reversed. The word of An and Enlil knows no overturning. Urim was indeed given kingship but it was not given an eternal reign. From time immemorial, since the Land was founded, until people multiplied, who has ever seen a reign of kingship that would take precedence forever? The reign of its kingship had been long indeed but had to exhaust itself. O my Nanna, do not exert yourself in vain, abandon your city".

Then my king, the noble son, became distraught. Lord Ašimbabbar, the noble son, grieved. Nanna who loves his city left his city. Suen took an unfamiliar path away from his beloved Urim. In order to go as an exile from her city to foreign territory, Ningal quickly clothed herself and left the city. The Anuna stepped outside of Urim.

… approached Urim. The trees of Urim were sick, its reeds were sick. Laments sounded all along its city wall. Daily there was slaughter before it. Large axes were sharpened in front of Urim. The spears, the arms of battle, were prepared. The large bows, throw-sticks and shields gathered together to strike. The barbed arrows covered its outer side like a raining cloud. Large stones fell together with great thuds. Urim, confident in its own strength, stood ready for the murderers. Its people, oppressed by the enemy, could not withstand their weapons.

In the city, those who had not been felled by weapons succumbed to hunger. Hunger filled the city like water, it would not cease. This hunger contorted people's faces, twisted their muscles. Its people were as if drowning in a pond, they gasped for breath. Its king breathed heavily in his own palace. Its people dropped their weapons, their weapons hit the ground. They struck their necks with their hands and cried. They sought counsel with each other, they searched for clarification: "Alas, what can we say about it? What more can we add to it? How long until we are finished off by this catastrophe? Inside Urim there is death, outside it there is death. Inside it we are to be finished off by famine. Outside it we are to be finished off by Elamite weapons. In Urim the enemy oppresses us, oh, we are finished".

The people took refuge (?) behind the city walls. They were united in fear. {The palace that was destroyed by onrushing water was defiled, its doorbolts were torn out. Elam, like a swelling flood wave, left (?) only the ghosts. In Urim weapons smashed heads like clay pots. Its refugees were unable to flee, they were trapped inside the walls. The statues that were in the shrine were cut down.

The great stewardess Ninigara ran away from the storehouse. Its throne was cast down before it, she threw herself down into the dust.

Its mighty cows with shining horns were captured, their horns were cut off. Its unblemished oxen and grass-fed sheep were slaughtered. The palm-trees, strong as mighty copper, the heroic strength, were torn out like rushes, were plucked like rushes, their trunks were turned sideways. Their tops lay in the dust, there was no one to raise them. The midribs of their palm fronds were cut off and their tops were burnt off. Their date spadices that used to fall (?) on the well were torn out. The fertile reeds, which grew in the sacred …, were defiled. The great tribute that they had collected was hauled off to the mountains.

The house's great door ornament fell down, its parapet was destroyed. The wild animals that were intertwined on its left and right lay before it like heroes smitten by heroes. Its gaping-mouthed dragons and its awe-inspiring lions were pulled down with ropes like captured wild bulls and carried off to enemy territory. The fragrance of the sacred seat of Nanna, formerly like a fragrant cedar grove, was destroyed. The glory of the house, whose glory was once so lovely, was extinguished. Like a storm that fills all the lands, it was built there like twilight in the heavens; its doors adorned with the heavenly stars, its … Great bronze latches … were torn out. Its hinges … Together with its door fittings it (?) wept bitterly like a fugitive. The bolt, the holy lock and the great door were not fastened for it. The noise of the door being fastened had ceased; there was no one to fasten it. The … and was put out in the square.

The food offerings … of his royal dining place were altered. In its sacred place (?) the tigi, šem and ala instruments did not sound. Its mighty tigi … did not perform its sacred song. There was no eloquence in the Dubla-maḫ, the place where oaths used to be taken. The throne was not set up at its place of judgment, justice was not administered. Alamuš threw down his sceptre, his hands trembling. In the sacred bedchamber of Nanna musicians no longer played the balaĝ drum. The sacred box that no one had set eyes upon was seen by the enemy. The divine bed was not set up, it was not spread with clean hay. The statues that were in the shrine were cut down. The cook, the dream interpreter, and the seal keeper did not perform the ceremonies properly. They stood by submissively and were carried off by the foreigners. The priests of the holy uzga shrine and the sacred lustrations, the linen-clad priests, forsook the divine plans and sacred divine powers, they went off to a foreign city.

In his grief Suen approached his father. He went down on his knee in front of Enlil, the father who begot him: "O father who begot me, how long will the enemy eye be cast upon my account, how long …? The lordship and the kingship that you bestowed …, Father Enlil, the one who advises with just words, the wise words of the Land …, your inimical judgment …, look into your darkened heart, terrifying like waves. O Father Enlil, the fate that you have decreed cannot be explained, as for my hairstyle (?) of lordship and the diadem with which I was crowned". … he put on a garment of mourning.

Enlil then provided a favourable response to his son Suen: "My son, the city built for you in joy and prosperity was given to you as your reign. Destroying the city, overthrowing its great wall and battlements: all this too is part of that reign. …… the black, black days of the reign that has been your lot. As for dwelling in your home, the E-temen-ni-guru, that was properly built – indeed Urim shall be rebuilt in splendour, the people shall bow down to you. There is to be bounty at its base, there is to be grain. There is to be splendour at its top, the sun shall rejoice there. Let an abundance of grain embrace its table. May Urim, the city whose fate was pronounced by An, be restored for you". Having pronounced his blessing, Enlil raised his head toward the heavens: "May the land, south and highland, be organised for Nanna. May the roads of the mountains be set in order for Suen. Like a cloud hugging the earth, they shall submit to him. By order of An and Enlil it shall be conferred".

Father Nanna came into his city of Urim with head raised high. The youth Suen could enter again into the E-kiš-nu-ĝal. Ningal refreshed herself in her sacred living quarters.
4th *kirugu*

There is lamentation in the haunted city, mourning reeds grew there. In its midst there is lamentation, mourning reeds grew there. Its people spend their days in moaning.
Ĝišgiĝal.

O bitter storm, retreat, O storm, storm return to your home. O storm that destroys cities, retreat, O storm, storm return to your home. O storm that destroys houses, retreat, O storm, storm return to your home. Indeed the storm that blew on Sumer, blew also on the foreign lands. Indeed the storm that blew on the land, blew on the foreign lands. It has blown on Tidnum, it has blown on the foreign lands. It has blown on Gutium, it has blown on the foreign lands. It has blown on Anšan, it has blown on the foreign lands. It levelled Anšan like a blowing evil wind. Famine has overwhelmed the evildoer; those people will have to submit.

May An not change the divine powers of heaven, the divine plans for treating the people with justice. May An not change the decisions and judgments to lead the people properly. To travel on the roads of the Land: may An not change it. May An and Enlil not change it, may An not change it. May Enki and Ninmaḫ not change it, may An not change it. That the Tigris and Euphrates should again carry water: may An not change it. That there should be rain in the skies and on the ground speckled barley: may An not change it. That there should be watercourses with water and fields with grain: may An not change it. That the marshes should support fish and fowl: may An not change it. That old reeds and fresh reeds should grow in the reedbeds: may An not change it. May An and Enlil not change it. May Enki and Ninmaḫ not change it.

That the orchards should bear syrup and grapes, that the high plain should bear the mašgurum tree, that there should be long life in the palace, that the sea should bring forth every abundance: may An not change it. The land densely populated from south to uplands: may An not change it. May An and Enlil not change it, may An not change it. May Enki and Ninmaḫ not change it, may An not change it. That cities should be rebuilt, that people should be numerous, that in the whole universe the people should be cared for; O Nanna, your kingship is sweet, return to your place. May a good abundant reign be long-lasting in Urim. Let its people lie down in safe pastures, let them reproduce. O mankind …, princess overcome by lamentation and crying! O Nanna! O your city! O your house! O your people!
5th *kirugu*

The Lament for Nibru

AFTER THE CATTLE PEN had been built for the foremost divine powers – how did it become a haunted place? When will it be restored? Where once the brick of fate had been laid – who scattered its divine powers? The lamentation is reprised: how did the storeroom of Nibru, the shrine Dur-an-ki, become a haunted place? When will it be restored? After Ki-ur, the great place, had been built, after the brickwork of E-kur had been built, after Ubšu-unkena had been built, after the shrine Egal-maḫ had been built – how did they become haunted? When will they be restored?

How did the true city become empty? Its precious designs have been defiled! How were the city's festivals neglected? Its magnificent rites have been thrown into disorder! In the heart of Nibru, where the divine powers were allotted and the black-headed people prolificly multiplied, the city's heart no longer revealed any sign of intelligence – there where the Anuna used to give advice! In Ubšu-unkena, the place for making great judgments, they no longer impart decisions or justice!

Where its gods had established their dwellings, where their daily rations were offered, their daises erected, where the sacred royal offering (?) and the evening meal in their great banquet hall were destined for the pouring out of choice beer and syrup – Nibru, the city where the black-headed people used to cool themselves in its spreading shade – in their dwellings Enlil fell upon them as if they were criminals. It was he who sent them scattering, like a scattered herd of cattle. How long until its lady, the goddess Ninlil, would ask after the inner city, whose bitter tears were overwhelming?

As though it were empty wasteland, no one enters that great temple whose bustle of activity was famous. As for all the great rulers who increased the wealth of the city of Nibru – why did they disappear? For how long would Enlil neglect the Land, where the black-headed {people} ate rich grass like sheep? Tears, lamentation, depression and despair! How long would his spirit burn and his heart not be placated? Why were those who once played the šem and ala drums spending their time in bitter lamenting? Why were the lamenters sitting in its brick buildings? They were bewailing the hardship which beset them.

The men whose wives had fallen, whose children had fallen, were singing "Oh our destroyed city!". Their city gone, their homes abandoned – as those who were singing for the brick buildings of the good city, as the lamenters of wailing, like the foster-children of an ecstatic no longer knowing their own intelligence, the people were smitten, their minds thrown into disorder. The true temple wails bitterly.

1st *kirugu*

… built the temple, Ninlil ….
Its *ĝišgiĝal*

The true temple gave you only tears and lamentation – it sings a bitter song of the proper cleansing-rites that are forgotten! The brickwork of E-kur gave you only tears and lamentation – it sings a bitter song of the proper cleansing-rites that are forgotten! It weeps bitter tears over the splendid rites and most precious plans which are desecrated – its most sacred food rations neglected and …… into funeral offerings, it cries "Alas!". The temple despairs of its divine powers, utterly cleansed, pure, hallowed, which are now defiled! The true temple, which it is bitter to enter on one's own, passes the time renewing its tears.

Because the sealings of the abundant materials stored in the temple have been broken open, they have placed the loads on the ground. Because the property in its well-tended storehouses has been sent back, it says "What will they weigh out for me now?"; because the enemies who do not know good from evil have cut off all good things, it sings a bitter dirge; because they have finished off its populace there like animals, it cries "Oh my Land!". Because they have piled up the young women, young men and their little children like heaps of grain, it cries "Woe!" for them. Because they have splashed their blood on the ground like a rainstorm, there is no restraint to its crying.

The temple, like a cow whose calf is cut off, groans bitterly to itself; it is grief-stricken, and the sweet-voiced lamenters, like nursemaids singing a lullaby, respond tearfully with its name. In anguish they bewail the fact that the city's lord has smashed heads there, that he has looked away from it and toward a foreign land instead. The true temple of all the countries, which had come before him – what have the black-headed people, who had taken a true path, done regarding what have they forsaken, that their lord has become enraged with them and walks in anger?

2nd *kirugu*

It voices bitter cries because he has removed the great divine powers from within it.

Its *ĝišgiĝal*

How long will the city's lord who became angry with it not turn to it, not say "Alas!" for it? Why did he cut off the road to its brickwork? He made the noisy pigeons fly away from their windows. Why did he transform the appearance of the temple which knew voices, where they used to while away the days in sweet playing of tigi drums in the brick buildings? The temple, once a place to offer salutations in humility, is now as deathly silent as a temple which no one reveres!

As though its purification priest's equipment were not utterly sacred, as though its cleansing-rites did not bring calm in all countries, he has abandoned it, turned his breast away from it, among dejection and lamentation he has made it a sacrilege. After its fate, how long till his face would be streaked with teardrops? He rejected it thus as though it were a blasphemy! Why has joy left its brickwork? Night and day he has filled its heart with tears! Even now, he has made it foreign and a sacrilege!

Its lord, who has despoiled it like an evil wind, has destroyed that city and its temples! He has ripped out their foundations, struck them with the adze, killed wives and their children within it, he has turned that city into a deserted city – when would he restore its ancient property? Its possessions have been carried off by the wind! Enlil turned the city which used to be there into a city no longer!

He made its mind wander! He threw its intelligence into disorder and made it haunted! He took away its food and its water! He brought to an end its days of familiarity with milk and with beer! The temple which he has made a sacrilege utters bitter lamentations; he has made its eyes blurred with tears. The lamenters who perform the dirges respond to it sorrowfully. No one touches the arm of the city's lord who has removed its divine powers! No one intercedes!

3rd *kirugu*

How did Enlil make all his greatest divine powers fly away! No one ever touches his arm! No one ever intercedes!

Its *ĝišgiĝal*

I am going down to my dirge singer of bitter fates and I shall weep tearfully to him. Even now the lamenters who are expert in song make ululating wails over me! Now my people who are overcome by hardship voice laments for me one by one! Even now the places of refuge of my people whose hearts are burning in dark distress have been made known to me! My people whose hearts have been broken on the bitter way perform the lullabies of my young ones for me in tears!

The well-built houses, ladies' dwellings, were falsely founded, and they have been eroded by the winds! They are making a lament for me of how the foe has finished off my Land! They are addressing the cries of my heart, overwhelmed with bitterness, in order to soothe it! They are beginning their laments about my lord Enlil! He will have mercy and compassion on me – Enlil, father of the black-headed people, he who will give the order to restore me!

4th *kirugu*

My heart is dark, I am destroyed, I am in chaos, I have been devastated!
Its *ĝišgiĝal*

In the foremost brick buildings they sing that your fate is bitter! Even now, to Enlil who will accept your tears for you, weeping bitter tears of your own accord, speak supplications to your lord himself concerning what he did to you, concerning that fate! Say to him "My lord, how long? Look upon me with favour, my lord!" Say "Why ...?" Say "May your heart be soothed for me – overturn this sacrilege for your own good! The day is ...!" Say "Re-enter for me your dwelling in my darkened shrines!" Say "Like a bright, cleansed, sacred day, give ... for your own good!" Say "...!" Say "Your misfortunes ... will rebuild it!"

Perhaps by this means I can make him have compassion and mercy for you. Depression has weakened your heart, but I am the one who has established good cheer for you. He will fix it forever as your lot that you shall lift your head high, he will make good again the hostilities he is directing against you.

5th *kirugu*

In the city which does not know freedom he struck them down thus.
Its *ĝišgiĝal*

Even now your lord has smitten the enemy fury for you! He has had mercy on you and decreed your fate! He has said "Enough", so that he has removed lamentation from your brick buildings! In good mood and with a joyful heart he has entered in there again for you! Ninurta, the mighty commissioner, has looked after things! He stood there before the hero, his provider Išme-Dagan, and issued the command to him to completely rebuild the E-kur, the most precious shrine! He has restored its ancient property! Enlil has ordered Išme-Dagan to restore its ziggurat temple, to make it shine like the day, to make fitting the dais upon its platform!

He has put back in their place the rites which the enemy disordered and desecrated, along with the scattered divine powers! He has given him his sacred unchangeable decision that they should sanctify and purify again the cleansing-rites which the enemy had put a stop to! He has told Išme-Dagan, his beloved shepherd, that faultless bulls and faultless bucks should be slaughtered! When decrees the fate of the sacred royal offering place (?), he will offer salutations and stand there daily in supplication and prayer.

2 lines fragmentary

6th *kirugu*

How long before you will rest at ease?
Its *ĝišgiĝal*
How long will the brickwork strain its eyes upwards in tears and lamentations? Even now your lord, the Great Mountain Enlil, supreme in the universe, has removed lamentation from your brick buildings and made favourable your humour!

Now, city, your lord who has had compassion and mercy for you, Father Enlil, lord of all countries, who has commanded that you be restored, and the great mother Ninlil, who entreated him in prayer there, and the brickwork itself which said to him "Steady the trembling of Nibru!" and said to him "Rebuild my women's quarters for me! Re-establish my temples for me!" – he who mulled things over so that he came to a decision about them, Enlil, who found agreeable his command of true words, who beneficently entered the true temple which had suffered destruction – he himself is removing what he turned upon you in distress.

Just as he silenced you, when he made joy enter again he decreed as your fate the sound of choice beer and syrup being poured out to overflowing. "Enough! It is time to stifle the lament" he said to you himself. Because you have been living in a state of neglect, Enlil who has decreed your fate has said "My city, you have placated my sacred heart towards you". He has returned to you! "Nibru, you have placated my sacred heart towards you". He has returned to you! True city, he has decreed your great fate and made your reign long! Nibru, he has decreed your great fate and made your reign long!

Enlil himself has commanded Išme-Dagan that the E-kur should shine like the day! Steady sunlight shines into the Ki-ur; he has brought daylight in there again for you! Ninlil has decreed your fate in the Ĝaĝiššua! Enlil and Ninlil together founded daises in the E-kur! They dined there and enjoyed choice beer! They deliberated how to make the black-headed people secure in their dwellings! They have brought back to you the people who had been completely devastated! They have gathered back together the children whom they turned away from their mothers! The populace goes with you in their strongholds! Shrine Nibru, the Great Mountain Enlil has returned to you!

7th *kirugu*

How you suffer! How depression exhausts you!
Its *ĝišgiĝal*

Even now, they command Išme-Dagan that Sumer and Akkad should be restored at your feet, that their scattered people should be returned to their nests! They have brought the news that the magnificent rites of Eridug would not be forgotten, its heart sending forth wisdom, so that good sense should be allotted! The Anuna, the lords who decree fates, order that Adab should be rebuilt, the city whose lady fashions living things, who promotes birthing!

An and Enlil have advised that Urim should be restored, founded in a pasture, its divine powers distinct from the rest! They command the prince of the city Larsam, the herald of the universe, the judge of the numerous people, to secure its foundations, to follow the proper path! They have taken a decision concerning Unug-Kulaba, the sacred city, the handiwork of the gods, and restored it. They have brought news of the removal of all foes and enemies from the region of Zabalam, the city where the mistress of heaven concentrated her forces.

An and Enlil have looked with their beneficent gaze on Lagaš, the mooring-pole of heaven, and the shrine Ĝirsu, established long ago. They have removed the treacherous Tidnum from that temple in Umma, Šeg-kuršaga, which had been ill-treated! It is the great gods who have commanded that the foundations of Kiš should be secured, at the edge of Sumer and Akkad, its dominion superlative! Marda, the city in whose river water flows, in whose fields is fine grain – the Anuna who took those things away from it returned them to it again!

Isin, the provisioner of the Anuna, rising high since times of old – An, Enlil, Enki and Ninmaḫ have made its reign long! By their command they have handed it over and expressed their approval! They have entrusted it to Ninurta, the champion, the strong hero! They have told Ninisina, the exalted child of An, the incantation priest of the Land, to rest calmly in her sacred dwelling, Egal-maḫ! They have told Damu, the chief barber of Nunamnir, healer of the living, to make the foreign countries bow at the feet of his father and mother!

8th *kirugu*

An, Enlil, Enki and Ninmaḫ have given their orders!
Its *ĝišgiĝal*

Now see! Enlil has fixed a good day in the land! He has even now ordered the day for Nibru to raise its neck to heaven! He himself has provided a good day for the E-kur to shine! He himself has raised up the day for the Ki-ur's magnificent manifestation! He himself has restored the day for Sumer and Akkad to expand! He himself has set aside the day for houses to be built and storerooms to be enclosed! He himself has brought out the day for seeds to sprout and living things to be born! He has brought out the day for building cattle pens and founding sheepfolds!

{The ewes which bore lambs have filled the pens!} The goats which bore kids have filled the folds! The ewes which flocked with their lambs have swelled the sheepfold! The goats which flocked with their kids have caused the pens to be widened! He himself has set the day for turning destruction to the good! He has ... the day ... evil! He has brought in Išme-Dagan as assistance for the day for establishing justice in the land!

9th *kirugu*

Although Sumer and Akkad had been desecrated by the foe, afterwards hearts were appeased, spirits soothed! All the great gods thus had compassion! They looked upon those sunk in exhaustion and brought them up out of it! They restored your city which had been razed to ruins! Enlil, king of all countries, restored its shining property which had been scattered, which had been devastated! There where the populace rested in the cool after building their nests, in Nibru, the mountain of the greatest divine powers, from where they had taken an unfamiliar path – at Enlil's word the Anuna, those very lords who determine the fates, ordered that the temples which they had forsaken and the jewels, put there long ago, which had been carried off by the wind, should all be restored!

He has established there dining in joy within! Enlil has given the command to Išme-Dagan, his joyous, reverent sacral officiant, who daily serves, to sanctify its food, to purify its water! He has commanded him to purify its defiled divine powers! He has put in order its disordered and scattered rites, he has put back in their place the most sacred things, neglected and defiled. He decrees as a fate the offering of daily rations and the grinding up of fine meal and flour. He has decided to make bread plentiful on the table, to make loaves numerous!

10th *kirugu*

Father Enlil, the lord whose command cannot be altered, prince of all countries, has fixed among the black-headed people, and commanded for their benefit, a time when no one is to speak hostile words to another, when a son is to respect his father, a time to establish humility in the Land, for the inferior to be as important as the mighty, a time when the younger brother, fearing his big brother, is to show humility, a time when the elder child is to treat the younger child reasonably and to pay heed to his words, a time to take neither weak nor strong away into captivity, but to serve with great acts of good, a time to travel the disordered roadways, to extirpate evil growths, {a time when anyone is to go where they will, to hurl no insults at one's fellow,} {a time no one is to speak hostile words to another, to perform no sacrilege,} a time to remove bitterness from the Land, to establish light therein, a time when darkness is to be lifted in the Land, so that living things should rejoice.

11th *kirugu*

Now, see! After that time, Enlil, the prince who is full of pity, has been beneficent to his hero who had laid the … brick! He put in order again for him the divine powers which had been desecrated by the enemy! He sanctified again the defiled rites for him! He purified its ziggurat temple and made it resplendent for him! Within he made abundance plentiful, he filled it with choice beer and syrup! He established there at that time the pleasing of hearts, the appeasing of spirits, the ameliorating of moods!

Išme-Dagan himself stood in prayer to Enlil and offered salutations! When he had begun the lament and spoken the supplication, the prince of all countries treated his body with oil of abundance as if it were the sweetest syrup! And his prayer was heard – Enlil looked upon him with favour, Išme-Dagan whose words bring Enlil pleasure! Enlil's constant attendant, with whose thoughts he agrees! Because the humble one prostrated himself in his devotions and served there, because he will entreat him in supplication and will do obeisance, because he will complete and honour the royal offering and will return, because he will keep watch over everything and will not be negligent, Enlil has promised to Išme-Dagan his dominion of extended years!

He promised him that he will be a man of pre-eminent kingship! He promised him that he will be a king whose reign is good! He promised him that he shall have the people inhabit safe dwellings! Enlil found agreement in what he had said to the numerous people! On the day for decreeing fates, every part of Sumer and Akkad, among the black-headed people flocking like sheep, among their well-tended people, will praise forever the majesty of the Great Mountain Nunamnir, enkar weapon of the universe! It is his awe-inspiring way!

12th *kirugu*

The Lament for Unug

Segment A

(BEGINNING of 1st *kirugu*)

The … which had developed – its wiping clean (?) was to be accomplished (?). The … of heaven and earth put their divine powers … to sleep (?).

1 line fragmentary

… mortal man multiplied to become as numerous as the gods. When together … had achieved a momentous decision, the … of the gods … Enki and Ninki determined the consensus – deemed worthless. Enul and Ninul assigned the fate, …

When together An and Enlil had created it, that one resembled … When Ninlil had given it features, that one was fit for … When together Aruru, Suen and Enki had fashioned its limbs, that one turned pitch black, as at night, halfway through the watch, … All the great gods paled at its immensity and … was brought about. Like a great wild bull which bellows mightily, that one filled the world with its roar.

As its gigantic horns reached up to heaven, who trembled in his very core? As it was piled up over the mountains like a battle-net, who turned away? Who caused wailing and lamenting in those streets and …? Unug, like a loyal citizen in terror, set up an alarm (and exclaimed) "Rise up!" Why did its hand seize Unug? Why did the benevolent eye look away? Who brought about such worry and lamenting and …?

That one drew nearer. That one settled upon the ground. Why would he withdraw? Who distorted Unug's good sense and deranged its good counsel? Who smashed its good udug deity? Who struck its good lamma deity too? Who desecrated the fearsome radiance which crowned it? Who brought about mob panic in Unug? Who … sickness too? Along with the city, the foreign lands …, who … in the temple of Unug? That one …

small no. of lines missing

Segment B

(continuation of 1st *kirugu*)

1 line fragmentary – Who made …? Why was … expanded? Who made the black-headed people become so numerous? Who overthrew …? … was destroyed – who restored …? Who confronted …? That one crushed …. That one ….

small no. of lines missing

Segment C

(probable beginning of 2nd *kirugu*)

1 line fragmentary – … and Utu, who in human form renders judgment at the law court of heaven, set and did not rise again. … bore a heavy burden of sin … the altered verdicts of Lord Nunamnir.… who can smite …? and they approach (?). … he brings … forth … of Enlil … He … and puts an end to …

small no. of lines missing

Segment D

(continuation of 2nd *kirugu*)

1 line fragmentary – … each and every one … … its ways were …. … its destruction and demolition, ……. The … of the gods … attention …, who neglected …, … the city watched as the evil ghost approached … breathed painfully, he wept bitterly … there was no nodding of the head.

He consoled himself with tears and laments – the city trembled. A defiled hand smote him and flattened his skull – the city collapsed. The fearsome radiance overwhelmed like … The proud city of all the lands became like one who spreads havoc. The faithful cowherds themselves overturned every single cattle pen. The chief shepherds themselves burned (?) every sheepfold. They built them up like grain heaps, they spread them out like grain piles, they were convulsed.… they drenched the fields with water, they turned the city into a swamp. They did all that. Like reeds in a wasteland, life could not be revived. They brought ruination. Evil things menaced (?) the city. A hush settled over the awed hearts of its people like a cloak.

Its good udug deities went away, its lamma deities ran off. Its lamma deity (said) "Hide in the open country" and they took foreign paths. The city's patron god turned against it and its shepherd abandoned it. Its guardian spirit, though not an enemy, was exiled (?) to a foreign place. Thus all its most important gods evacuated Unug, they kept away from it. They hid out in the hills and wandered (?) about in the haunted plains. In the city built upon peace, food and drink were overturned like a saman vessel. In the pasture lands a tumultuous noise arose, the asses and sheep were driven away. Elderly people and babies, taking their rest, ... in front ... They saw ... and slaughtered (?) ...

3 lines fragmentary

small no. of lines missing

Segment E

(continuation of 2nd *kirugu*)

He ... and opened his clenched fist. He ... and reached out his hand. The ... of Sumer, the city whose king crossed over to an enemy land, to ... – he smote it with the might of his weapon. He ... and turned the place into dust. He ... and piled the people up in heaps. ...:, how long until its charms are restored?

2nd *kirugu*

The ... of heaven ... and the people ... to the limits of heaven.
Its *ĝišgiĝal*.

He ..., stretched forth his hand and induced terror in the land. Enlil struck out with great ferocity. He announced: "A deluge dashing the hoe on the ground shall be invoked. At its front war shall be a ...... axe, at its rear it shall be a .... Its overgrown hair shall be a harrow, its back shall be flames. Its countenance shall be a malevolent storm that enshrouds heaven and earth. The glint of its eyes shall be lightning that flashes far like the Anzud bird. Its mouth shall rage – a blazing fire that extends as far as the nether world. Its tongue shall be an inferno, raining embers, that sunders the Land. Its arms shall be the majestic Anzud bird that nothing can escape when it spreads wide its talons".

"Its ribs shall be crowbars that let light pass inside like the sun's rays. Knotted at both its hips shall be city-destroying slingstones. Its great haunches shall be dripping knives, covered with gore, that make blood flow. Its muscles shall be saws that slash, its feet those of an eagle. It shall make the Tigris and Euphrates quaver, it shall make the mountains rumble. At its reverberation the hills shall be uprooted, the people shall be pitched about like sheaves, Sumer and Akkad shall shiver, they shall be flooded like a harvest crop. The foolish shall rejoice, they shall exclaim (?): "Let it come – we shall be seeing war and battle in the city, how the sacred precinct (?) is destroyed, how the walls are battered down, how the city's peace is disrupted, how among the loyal families honest men are transformed into traitors".

"But the sensible shall beat their breasts and droop (?) their heads. At midnight they shall be afraid and tearful, and suffer insomnia. In bed, under the covers, they shall be unable to sleep soundly, they shall wander about the city. They shall be immobilised, their courage shall run out: "May our allies serving in times of war raise their forces for peace. May the word of Enlil be sent back, may it turn tail. May the venom of Nunamnir's anger become exhausted. May those vicious men who have seized the E-kur be punished. May those who have set their sight upon Nibru be swept away".

3rd *kirugu*

My heart is filled with sorrow, I am tear-stricken.
Its *ĝišgiĝal*.

Oh, Sumer! Alas – your spirit! Alas – your structure! Alas – your people! The word of An, having been assigned its place, has destroyed the sacred precinct (?). The pronouncement of Enlil, having been set in motion, ... The deluge dashing the hoe to the ground ... The great and fierce ..., Lord Nergal ... ... like Gibil, Nergal ...

1 line fragmentary

War ...... enemy lands ...... echoed. Like arrows in a quiver .... Evildoers in Sumer .... Gutium, the enemy, overturned .... Sumer, caught in a trap, ... Its people were thrown into turmoil ... The mighty heroes of Sumer ... ... the heart of a hurricane ... They advanced like the front rank of troops, ... Like ... they were crushed, every one of them ... Their war veterans gave up, their brains were muddled. The troop leaders, the most outstanding of the men, were viciously hewn down. Gutium, the enemy, ... weapons ... Not looking at each other ... Like a swelling flood, like ..., Subir poured into Sumer.

They ... like stampeding goats, they tore apart the corpses of the population. They mutilated Sumer and Akkad, they pulverised it as with a pestle. They destroyed its settlements and habitations, they razed them to ruin mounds. The best of Sumer they scattered like dust, they heaped up ... They massacred its populace, they finished off young and old alike. They destroyed the city of the Anuna gods, they set it aflame. They put out both Unug's eyes, they uprooted its young shoots. They wandered all through the libation places of the Anuna gods. And even Kulaba, which is the primeval city, they turned into a place of murder.

4th *kirugu*

Alas – Sumer! Alas – its people!
Its *ĝišgiĝal*.

Unug! They seized your wharf and your borders and ... At Unug shouts rang out, screams reverberated, its captured men .... The noise reached to the south. The south was destroyed and ... The impact forced its way to the uplands. The uplands were struck and ... To the right and left no people moved about, no habitations were built. There was no ... and the mobilisation of troops did not ... ... rose up to heaven. Heaven perished and its strength did not ... ... upon the earth. The earth was scattered, and it did not ... All the settlements were dispersed – Unug stood all alone. It was a bull, it was a champion, it was immense with pride, but it ... to the weapons. All night and even until midday battle was waged, and afterwards it did not ...

Battering rams and shields were set up, they rent its walls. They breached its buttresses, they hewed the city with axes. They set fire to its stations, they ... the city's dwellings. They destroyed it, they demolished it. Unug, the good place, was ... with dust. Like a great wild bull wounded with an arrow, ... Like a wild cow pierced with a spear, ... The mighty one rushed with his weapons and ... implements of war. Subir, rising up like a swelling floodwave, ... They trampled (?) through the streets and ... They let the blood of the people flow like that of a sacrificial cow, they tore out everything that had been built.

The citizens of Unug ... They ... and threw down ... They ... and put an end to ... They seized ... They struck ... They destroyed ... They ... They demolished ... They set up ... They heaped up ... They put an end to and did not leave behind ... ... Subir entered ...

5th *kirugu*

... cried out "... has been created" and he smeared dust ...
Its *ĝišgiĝal*.

... reached ...
19 fragmentary lines
unknown no. of lines missing

Segment F

(probable beginning of another *kirugu*)
The enemy land ... Zabalam ... In Urim, the E-kiš-nu-ĝal ... Cattlepen and sheepfold ..., evil ... The land of Subir ...
200–300 lines missing

Segment G

(part of 11th *kirugu*)
All the great gods ... The Anuna gods ...
1 line fragmentary – Sovereigns ...
1 line fragmentary
unknown no. of lines missing

Segment H

(beginning of 12th *kirugu*)
Lady Inana whose greatness is vaster than the mountains, hovering like An, vested with grandeur like Enlil, like her father, perfect by night and in the heat of the day, like Utu, surpassing in vigour, singularly exalted in all the four regions – let Išme-Dagan take pleasure in relaxing in your temple, let him murmer to you in your temple, let him raise his head to you in your E-ana.

Let Išme-Dagan serve you as your steward. Let him prepare great bulls for you. Let him dedicate great offerings to you. Let him make the beer, fat and oil plentiful for you. Let him make syrup and wine flow for you as from stone jars. Let Išme-Dagan, son of Enlil on the king's pedestal, bow in homage to you. May he make the ub and ala drums resound grandly for you. May the tigi sound sweetly for you, and may the zamzam play for you. May they play ... on the tigi for you, expressing your prayers and supplications before you.

In bringing forth ..., all that there are, at your E-ĝipar in Unug, as a humble man who has grasped your feet, as a reverent man who has experienced your exaltedness, he has brought a lament as offering to you and will ... As for everything that happened to Sumer and Akkad, which he has witnessed in Unug, the aggrieved place, may the best singers perform songs there.

If the Anuna gods emerge tearfully, let them promise to us that as it was when heaven and earth came about, nothing of that time shall be changed. If An looks kindly upon that man and at the well-built city, the place of determining fate, proclaim "Man and city! Life and well-being!" for him. Let praise ring out. Let him be made surpassing above all, to his right or left. Tireless lamma deity, take hold of his head, pronounce his fate in charitable words – by the command of An and Enlil it will remain unaltered for a long time.

12th kirugu

The Lament for Eridug

A Composite Version from Nibru

Segment A

(BEGINNING of 1st *kirugu*)

4 lines missing

The roaring storm covered it like a cloak, was spread over it like a sheet. It covered Eridug like a cloak, was spread over it like a sheet. In the city, the furious storm resounded … In Eridug, the furious storm resounded …. Its voice was smothered with silence as by a gale. Its people … Eridug was smothered with silence as by a gale. Its people …

Its king stayed outside his city as if it were an alien city. He wept bitter tears. Father Enki stayed outside his city as if it were an alien city. He wept bitter tears. For the sake of his harmed city, he wept bitter tears. Its lady, like a flying bird, left her city. The mother of E-maḫ, holy Damgalnuna, left her city. The divine powers of the city of holiest divine powers were overturned. The divine powers of the rites of the greatest divine powers were altered. In Eridug everything was reduced to ruin, was wrought with confusion.

The evil-bearing storm went out from the city. It swept across the Land – a storm which possesses neither kindness nor malice, does not distinguish between good and evil. Subir came down like rain. It struck hard. In the city where bright daylight used to shine forth, the day darkened. In Eridug where bright daylight used to shine forth, the day darkened. As if the sun had set below the horizon, it turned into twilight. As if An had cursed the city, alone he destroyed it. As if Enlil had frowned upon it, Eridug, the shrine Abzu, bowed low.

1st *kirugu*

It cried out bitterly: "O the destruction of the city! The destruction of the house!"

Its *ĝišgiĝal*.

A second time the storm destroyed the city – its song was plaintive.... was trampled (?).... intensified the lament. It cut the lock from its main gate. The storm dislodged its door.... It stacked the people up in heaps.... on its own destroyed it. It turned ...... into tears.... defiled ...

1 line missing

... It distorted its appearance.... It distorted its appearance. It circled its ... wall. It overturned its foundations. Throughout his city, the pure, radiant (?) place, the foundations were filled with dust. It cast down its ziggurat, the shrine which reaches up to heaven, into a heap of debris. The loftiness of its elevated door-ornament, befitting a house, was stripped down (?). It cut down the gate, its Great-Ziggurat-of-Heaven-and-Earth-Covered-with-Terrible-Awesomeness, its shining door, and it broke through its bolt. It ripped out its doorframe. The house was defaced.

2nd *kirugu*

The destruction of Eridug! Its destruction was grievous.
Its *ĝišgiĝal*.

At its lion-faced gate, the place where fates are determined, it mutilated the copse (?) forming the ornament of the house … Ka-ḫeĝala and Igi-ḫeĝala, the doorkeepers of the house, … Prematurely they destroyed it utterly. They completely altered … At the gate of the uzga precinct, the animal-fattener … the great offerings. Its birds and fish were neglected there. Destruction … Throughout his house, radiant (?) in silver and lapis lazuli, tears …

The hired man and the governor … The festivals … grandly … Holy songs, songs of all kinds … The šem drum and ala drum … The great divine powers, all the divine powers … The place of the gods of heaven and earth … The judgment by the king, the holy sceptre at his right side, … The en priestess, lumaḫ priest and nindiĝir priestess …,

The minister Isimud … Strangers to the house … its side. Eridug, the shrine Abzu, …… silently. The enemy …… cleansed in a magnificent robe. … a man … the people … Along with the fluids spilled from his guts, his blood spilled forth. The …, which like the azure sky was embellished forever, … grasped …

3rd *kirugu*

2 lines fragmentary
Its *ĝišgiĝal*.

… distressed and anxious … like a pigeon …

1 line fragmentary – The birds of the destroyed city … a nest. The ukuku bird, bird of heart's sorrow, … the place. Pain … The area became entangled in wild thornbushes. It … wild thornbushes. The Šimaškians and Elamites, the destroyers, looked at the holy kettles which no one may look at. In the House of Nisaba's Wisdom, the house of understanding, … covered over … The divine powers which embellish the Abzu … When the holy treasures stored in the treasury were put …, when, like a mist lying heavily on the earth, …, they went like small birds shooed from their hiding places.

7 lines fragmentary
unknown no. of lines missing

Segment B

(continuation of 4th *kirugu*)

Father Enki uttered a lament for himself …

4th *kirugu*

Bitterly Father Enki uttered a lament for himself.
Its *ĝišgiĝal*.

Because of this, Enki, king of the abzu, stayed outside his city as if it were an alien city. It bowed its neck down to the ground. Eridu's lady, holy Damgalnuna, the faithful cow, the compassionate one, clawed at her breast, clawed at her eyes. She uttered a frenzied cry. She held a dagger and a sword in her two hands – they clashed together.

She tore out her hair like rushes, uttering a bitter lament: "You, my city whose woman does not dwell there, whose charms do not satisfy her – where is a lament uttered bitterly for you?

Eridug! You, my city whose woman does not dwell there, whose charms do not satisfy her – where are tears wept for you? I fall like a bull in your lofty … falls . I am … My heart … queen …" (incorporating end of 5th *kirugu*)

Segment C

(continuation of 6th *kirugu*)

1 line fragmentary … far away … the great gods. Lord Enlil, king of the lands, looked maliciously at Sumer. He demolished it. He destroyed the Ki-ur, the great place. He razed with the pickaxe all of the shining E-kur. He destroyed it but did not abandon it – at the lunches, in his great dining hall, they call his name.

Aruru, the sister of Enlil, destroyed her city Iri-saĝ-rig. In Keš, the creation place of the Land, the people saw inside its holy sanctuary where daylight had been unknown. She destroyed it but did not abandon it – at the lunches, in her great dining hall, they call her name. Lord Nanna, Lord Ašimbabbar, destroyed his city Urim. He decimated the Land with famine. He committed a sacrilege against the E-kiš-nu-ĝal. He struck at its heart. He destroyed it but did not abandon it – at the lunches, in his great dining hall, they call his name.

Inana, the queen of heaven and earth, destroyed her city Unug. Fleeing from the E-ana, the house of seven corners and seven fires …, she destroyed it but did not abandon it – at the lunches, in her great dining hall, they call her name.

(Damgalnuna speaks:) "My beloved, who has ever seen such a destruction as that of your city Eridug!"

6th *kirugu*

"My beloved, for how long was it built? For how long is it destroyed? … adornment of the Abzu". Its *ĝišgiĝal*.

"Lord Enki, who has ever seen such a destruction as that of your city Eridug? Who has ever seen such a misfortune as that of the shrine Abzu, your house?" No one goes up to his offering terrace. At the lunches, in his great dining hall, they do not call his name. Enki, king of the abzu, felt distressed, felt anxious. At the words of his spouse, he himself began to wail. He lay down and fasted.

My king, you must not be distressed, you must not be anxious. Father Enki, you must not be distressed, you must not be anxious. Son of An, return your heart to your Ki-ur and your attention to your city. Living in an alien city is miserable – return your attention to your city. Living in an alien house is miserable – return your attention to your house. What can anyone compare with this city? – Return your attention to your city. What can anyone compare with this house? – Return your attention to your house. Eridug's day is long. Its night is over.

May your throne say to you "Sit down". May your bed say to you "Lie down". May your house say to you "Be rested". May your holy dais also say joyfully to you "Sit down". May your father An, the king of the gods, satisfy your heart. A person, a humble man, brings you a lament over your wife's faithful house. When he sings it before you, may that person soothe your heart. When he recites a prayer, look kindly upon him.

7th *kirugu*

It destroyed your … and struck against your house.
Its *ĝišgiĝal*.

… and may he restore it for you.

2 lines fragmentary – Do not hide like a criminal …

A Version from Urim

Segment A

House of princely powers, standing in mighty water – the waters have receded from it … One can walk on its wide swamp. Within it grow wild thornbushes. The delightful boat Wild goat of the abzu – the waters have receded from it; … its sheepfold … the wharf. They were Sirsir, the tutelary deity, and the man who rides the boat. At the prow … was hurled down in front of them. Evildoers destroyed the house, and its rites were disturbed.

At the giguna shrine, the sacred house, evildoers … The E-unir – the shrine raises its head as high as heaven. Its shadow …….

At the great gate, the lion-faced gate, the place where fates are determined, evildoers ……. They set fire to its door. Ka-ḫeĝala and Igi-ḫeĝala, the doorkeepers of the house, … … Enki, at the … place, … its people.… the destroyed place, the Abzu … the powers of the Anuna gods.

3 lines fragmentary (continuation of 3rd kirugu)

Segment B

Eridug … City in the reedbeds … In Eridug, young bulls … Without being a marsh boar … Eridug, like a bull … The lady of the city cried, "My city …!"

3rd *kirugu*

Father Enki! O your house, O your city, O your people … the mountains.

Its *ĝišgiĝal*.

Astrology & Astronomy

Introduction

AS DONALD A. MACKENZIE points out: The empire builders of old who enriched themselves with the spoils of war and the tribute of subject States, not only satisfied personal ambition and afforded protection for industrious traders and workers, but also incidentally promoted culture and endowed research. When a conqueror returned to his capital laden with treasure, he made generous gifts to the temples. He believed that his successes were rewards for his piety, that his battles were won for him by his god or goddess of war. It was necessary, therefore, that he should continue to find favour in the eyes of the deity who had been proved to be more powerful than the god of his enemies. Besides, he had to make provision during his absence for the constant performance of religious rites. Consequently an endowed priesthood became a necessity in all powerful and well-organized states.

Thus came into existence in Babylonia, as elsewhere, as a result of the accumulation of wealth, a leisured official class, whose duties tended to promote intellectual activity. Culture was really a by-product of temple activities. And thus the permanent triumphs of Babylonian civilization were achieved either by the priests, or in consequence of the influence they exercised. They were the grammarians and the scribes, the mathematicians and the philosophers, the teachers of the young, and the patrons of the arts and crafts. It was because the temples were centres of intellectual activity that the Sumerian language remained the language of culture for long centuries after it ceased to be the everyday speech of the people.

It remains with us to deal now with priestly contributions to the more abstruse sciences. The Babylonian priests who elaborated the study of astrology became great astronomers because they found it necessary to observe and record accurately the movements of the heavenly bodies.

The Mystery of the Stars and Planets

Primitive Star Myths

FROM THE EARLIEST TIMES of which we have knowledge, the religious beliefs of the Sumerians had vague stellar associations. But it does not follow that their myths were star myths to begin with. A people who called constellations "the ram", "the bull", "the lion", or "the scorpion", did not do so because astral groups suggested the forms of animals, but rather because the animals had an earlier connection with their religious life.

At the same time it should be recognized that the mystery of the stars must ever have haunted the minds of primitive men. Night with all its terrors appealed more strongly to their imaginations than refulgent day when they felt more secure; they were concerned most regarding what they feared most. Brooding in darkness regarding their fate, they evidently associated the stars with the forces which influenced their lives–the ghosts of ancestors, of totems, the spirits that brought food or famine and controlled the seasons. As children see images in a fire, so they saw human life reflected in the starry sky. To the simple minds of early folks the great moon seemed to be the parent of the numerous twinkling and moving orbs. In Babylon, indeed, the moon was regarded as the father not only of the stars but of the sun also; there, as elsewhere, lunar worship was older than solar worship.

Primitive beliefs regarding the stars were of similar character in various parts of the world. But the importance which they assumed in local mythologies depended in the first place on local phenomena. On the northern Eur-Asian steppes, for instance, where stars vanished during summer's blue nights, and were often obscured by clouds in winter, they did not impress men's minds so persistently and deeply as in Babylonia, where for the greater part of the year they gleamed in darkness through a dry transparent atmosphere with awesome intensity. The development of an elaborate system of astral myths, besides, was only possible in a country where the people had attained to a high degree of civilization, and men enjoyed leisure and security to make observations and compile records. It is not surprising, therefore, to find that Babylonia was the cradle of astronomy. But before this science had destroyed the theory which it was fostered to prove, it lay smothered for long ages in the debris of immemorial beliefs. It is necessary, therefore, in dealing with Babylonian astral myths to endeavour to approach within reasonable distance of the point of view, or points of view, of the people who framed them.

Babylonian religious thought was of highly complex character. Its progress was ever hampered by blended traditions. The earliest settlers in the Tigro-Euphrates valley no doubt imported many crude beliefs which they had inherited from their Palaeolithic ancestors – the modes of thought which were the moulds of new theories arising from new experiences. When consideration is given to the existing religious beliefs of various peoples throughout the world, in low stages of culture, it is found that the highly developed creeds of Babylonia, Egypt and other countries where civilization flourished were never divested wholly of their primitive traits.

Naturalism, Totemism and Animism

Among ancient peoples two grades of religious ideas have been identified, and classified as Naturalism and Animism. In the plane of Naturalism the belief obtains that a vague impersonal force, which may have more than one manifestation and is yet manifested in everything, controls the world and the lives of human beings. An illustration of this stage of religious consciousness is afforded by Mr. Risley, who, in dealing with the religion of the jungle dwellers of Chota Nagpur, India, says that "in most cases the indefinite something which they fear and attempt to propitiate is not a person at all in any sense of the word; if one must state the case in positive terms, I should say that the idea which lies at the root of their religion is that of a power rather than many powers".

Traces of Naturalism appear to have survived in Sumeria in the belief that "the spiritual, the Zi, was that which manifested life.... The test of the manifestation of life was movement". All things that moved, it was conceived in the plane of Naturalism, possessed "self-power"; the river was a living thing, as was also the fountain; a stone that fell from a hill fell of its own accord; a tree groaned because the wind caused it to suffer pain. This idea that inanimate objects had conscious existence survived in the religion of the Aryo-Indians. In the Nala story of the Indian epic, the Mahabharata, the disconsolate wife Damayanti addresses a mountain when searching for her lost husband:

This, the monarch of all mountains, ask I of the king of men;
"O all-honoured Prince of Mountains, with thy heavenward soaring peaks ...
Hast thou seen the kingly Nala in this dark and awful wood?...
Why repliest thou not, O Mountain?"

She similarly addresses the Asoka tree:

"Hast thou seen Nishadha's monarch, hast thou seen my only love? ...
That I may depart ungrieving, fair Asoka, answer me...".
Many a tree she stood and gazed on....

It will be recognized that when primitive men gave names to mountains, rivers or the ocean, these possessed for them a deeper significance than they do for us at the present day. The earliest peoples of Indo-European speech who called the sky "dyeus", and those of Sumerian speech who called it "ana", regarded it not as the sky "and nothing more", but as something which had conscious existence and "self-power". Our remote ancestors resembled, in this respect, those imaginative children who hold conversations with articles of furniture, and administer punishment to stones which, they believe, have tripped them up voluntarily and with desire to commit an offence.

In this early stage of development, the widespread totemic beliefs appear to have had origin. Families or tribes believed that they were descended from mountains, trees, or wild animals.

Aesop's fable about the mountain which gave birth to a mouse may be a relic of Totemism; so also may be the mountain symbols on the standards of Egyptian ships which appear on pre-dynastic pottery; the black dwarfs of Teutonic mythology were earth children. Adonis sprang from a tree; his mother may have, according to primitive belief, been simply a tree; Dagda, the patriarchal Irish corn god, was an oak; indeed, the idea of a "world tree", which occurs in Sumerian, Vedic-Indian, Teutonic and other mythologies, was probably a product of Totemism.

Wild animals were considered to be other forms of human beings who could marry princes and princesses as they do in so many fairy tales. Damayanti addressed the tiger, as well as the mountain and tree, saying:

I approach him without fear.
"Of the beasts art thou the monarch, all this forest thy domain; …
Thou, O king of beasts, console me, if my Nala thou hast seen".

A tribal totem exercised sway over a tribal district. In Egypt, as Herodotus recorded, the crocodile was worshipped in one district and hunted down in another. Tribes fought against tribes when totemic animals were slain. The Babylonian and Indian myths about the conflicts between eagles and serpents may have originated as records of battles between eagle clans and serpent clans. Totemic animals were tabooed. The Set pig of Egypt and the devil pig of Ireland, Scotland and Wales were not eaten except sacrificially. Families were supposed to be descended from swans and were named Swans, or from seals and were named Seals, like the Gaelic "Mac Codrums", whose surname signifies "son of the seal"; the nickname of the Campbells, "sons of the pig", may refer to their totemic boar's head crest, which commemorated the slaying, perhaps the sacrificial slaying, of the boar by their ancestor Diarmid. Mr. Garstang, in The Syrian Goddess, thinks it possible that the boar which killed Adonis was of totemic origin. So may have been the fish form of the Sumerian god Ea. When an animal totem was sacrificed once a year, and eaten sacrificially so that the strength of the clan might be maintained, the priest who wrapped himself in its skin was supposed to have transmitted to him certain magical powers; he became identified with the totem and prophesied and gave instruction as the totem. Ea was depicted clad in the fish's skin.

Animism, the other early stage of human development, also produced distinctive modes of thought. Men conceived that the world swarmed with spirits, that a spirit groaned in the wind-shaken tree, that the howling wind was an invisible spirit, that there were spirits in fountains, rivers, valleys, hills and in ocean, and in all animals; and that a hostile spirit might possess an individual and change his nature. The sun and the moon were the abodes of spirits, or the vessels in which great spirits sailed over the sea of the sky; the stars were all spirits, the "host of heaven". These spirits existed in groups of seven, or groups of three, and the multiple of three, or in pairs, or operated as single individuals.

Although certain spirits might confer gifts upon mankind, they were at certain seasons and in certain localities hostile and vengeful, like the grass-green fairies in winter, or the earth-black elves when their gold was sought for in forbidden and secret places. These spirits were the artisans of creation and vegetation, like the Egyptian Khnumu and the Indian Rhibus; they fashioned the grass blades and the stalks of corn, but at times of seasonal change they might ride on their tempest steeds, or issue forth from flooding rivers and lakes. Man was greatly concerned about striking bargains with them to secure their services, and about propitiating them, or warding off their attacks with protective charms, and by performing "ceremonies of riddance". The ghosts of the dead, being spirits, were similarly propitious or harmful on occasion; as emissaries of Fate they could injure the living.

Stars as Ghosts of Men, Giants and Wild Animals

Ancestor worship, the worship of ghosts, had origin in the stage of Animism. But ancestor worship was not developed in Babylonia as in China, for instance, although traces of it survived in the worship of stars as ghosts, in the deification of kings, and the worship of patriarchs, who might be exalted as gods or identified with a supreme god. The Egyptian Pharaoh Unas became the sun god and the constellation of Orion by devouring his predecessors. He ate his god as a tribe ate its animal totem; he became the "bull of heaven".

There were star totems as well as mountain totems. A St. Andrew's cross sign, on one of the Egyptian ship standards referred to, may represent a star. The Babylonian goddess Ishtar was symbolized as a star, and she was the "world mother". Many primitive currents of thought shaped the fretted rocks of ancient mythologies.

In various countries all round the globe the belief prevailed that the stars were ghosts of the mighty dead – of giants, kings, or princes, or princesses, or of pious people whom the gods loved, or of animals which were worshipped. A few instances may be selected at random. When the Teutonic gods slew the giant Thjasse, he appeared in the heavens as Sirius. In India the ghosts of the "seven Rishis", who were semi-divine Patriarchs, formed the constellation of the Great Bear, which in Vedic times was called the "seven bears". The wives of the seven Rishis were the stars of the Pleiades. In Greece the Pleiades were the ghosts of the seven daughters of Atlas and Pleione, and in Australia they were and are a queen and six handmaidens.

In these countries, as elsewhere, stories were told to account for the "lost Pleiad", a fact which suggests that primitive men were more constant observers of the heavenly bodies than might otherwise be supposed. The Arcadians believed that they were descended, as Hesiod recorded, from a princess who was transformed by Zeus into a bear; in this form Artemis slew her and she became the "Great Bear" of the sky. The Egyptian Isis was the star Sirius, whose rising coincided with the beginning of the Nile inundation. Her first tear for the dead Osiris fell into the river on "the night of the drop". The flood which ensued brought the food supply. Thus the star was not only the Great Mother of all, but the sustainer of all.

The brightest stars were regarded as being the greatest and most influential. In Babylonia all the planets were identified with great deities. Jupiter, for instance, was Merodach, and one of the astral forms of Ishtar was Venus. Merodach was also connected with "the fish of Ea" (Pisces), so that it is not improbable that Ea worship had stellar associations. Constellations were given recognition before the planets were identified.

Gods as Constellations and Planets

A strange blending of primitive beliefs occurred when the deities were given astral forms. As has been shown, gods were supposed to die annually. The Egyptian priests pointed out to Herodotus the grave of Osiris and also his star. There are "giants' graves" also in those countries in which the gods were simply ferocious giants. A god might assume various forms; he might take the form of an insect, like Indra, and hide in a plant, or become a mouse, or a serpent, like the gods of Erech in the Gilgamesh epic. The further theory that a god could exist in various forms at one and the same time suggests that it had its origin among a people who accepted the idea of a personal god while yet in the stage of Naturalism.

In Egypt Osiris, for instance, was the moon, which came as a beautiful child each month and was devoured as the wasting "old moon" by the demon Set; he was the young god who was slain in his prime each year; he was at once the father, husband and son of Isis; he was the Patriarch who reigned over men and became the Judge of the Dead; he was the earth spirit, he was the bisexual Nile spirit, he was the spring sun; he was the Apis bull of Memphis, and the ram of Mendes; he was the reigning Pharaoh. In his fusion with Ra, who was threefold – Khepera, Ra and Tum – he died each day as an old man; he appeared in heaven at night as the constellation Orion, which was his ghost, or was, perhaps, rather the Sumerian Zi, the spiritual essence of life. Osiris, who resembled Tammuz, a god of many forms also, was addressed as follows in one of the Isis chants:

There proceedeth from thee the strong Orion in heaven
at evening, at the resting of every day!
Lo it is I (Isis), at the approach of the Sothis (Sirius) period,
who doth watch for him (the child Osiris),
Nor will I leave off watching for him; for that which
proceedeth from thee (the living Osiris) is revered.
An emanation from thee causeth life to gods and men, reptiles
and animals, and they live by means thereof.
Come thou to us from thy chamber, in the day when thy soul begetteth emanations, –
The day when offerings upon offerings are made to thy spirit,
which causeth the gods and men likewise to live.

This extract emphasizes how unsafe it is to confine certain deities within narrow limits by terming them simply "solar gods", "lunar gods", "astral gods", or "earth gods". One deity may have been simultaneously a sun god and moon god, an air god and an earth god, one who was dead and also alive, unborn and also old. The priests of Babylonia and Egypt were less accustomed to concrete and logical definitions than their critics and expositors of the twentieth century.

Simple explanations of ancient beliefs are often by reason of their very simplicity highly improbable. Recognition must ever be given to the puzzling complexity of religious thought in Babylonia and Egypt, and to the possibility that even to the priests the doctrines of a particular cult, which embraced the accumulated ideas of centuries, were invariably confusing and vague, and full of inconsistencies; they were mystical in the sense that the understanding could not grasp them although it permitted their acceptance. A god, for instance, might be addressed at once in the singular and plural, perhaps because he had developed from an animistic group of spirits, or, perhaps, for reasons we cannot discover. This is shown clearly by the following pregnant extract from a Babylonian tablet: "Powerful, O Sevenfold, one are ye". Mr. L. W. King, the translator, comments upon it as follows: "There is no doubt that the name was applied to a group of gods who were so closely connected that, though addressed in the plural, they could in the same sentence be regarded as forming a single personality".

Like the Egyptian Osiris, the Babylonian Merodach was a highly complex deity. He was the son of Ea, god of the deep; he died to give origin to human life when he commanded that his head should be cut off so that the first human beings might be fashioned by mixing his blood with the earth; he was the wind god, who gave "the air of life"; he was the deity of thunder and the sky; he was the sun of spring in his Tammuz character; he was the daily sun, and the planets Jupiter and Mercury as well as Sharru (Regulus); he had various astral associations at various seasons.

Ishtar and Isis as Bisexual Deities

Ishtar, the goddess, was Iku (Capella), the water channel star, in January–February, and Merodach was Iku in May–June. This strange system of identifying the chief deity with different stars at different periods, or simultaneously, must not be confused with the monotheistic identification of him with other gods. Merodach changed his forms with Ishtar, and had similarly many forms. This goddess, for instance, was, even when connected with one particular heavenly body, liable to change. According to a tablet fragment she was, as the planet Venus, "a female at sunset and a male at sunrise"–that is, a bisexual deity like Nannar of Ur, the father and mother deity combined, and Isis of Egypt. Nannar is addressed in a famous hymn:

Father Nannar, Lord, God Sin, ruler among the gods....
Mother body which produceth all things....
Merciful, gracious Father, in whose hand the life of the whole land is contained.

One of the Isis chants of Egypt sets forth, addressing Osiris:

There cometh unto thee Isis, lady of the horizon, who hath
begotten herself alone in the image of the gods ...
She hath taken vengeance before Horus, the woman
who was made a male by her father Osiris.

Merodach, like Osiris-Sokar, was a "lord of many existences", and likewise "the mysterious one, he who is unknown to mankind". It was impossible for the human mind "a greater than itself to know".

The Babylonian Planetary Deities

Evidence has not yet been forthcoming to enable us to determine the period at which the chief Babylonian deities were identified with the planets, but it is clear that Merodach's ascendancy in astral form could not have occurred prior to the rise of that city god of Babylon as chief of the pantheon by displacing Enlil. At the same time it must be recognized that long before the Hammurabi age the star-gazers of the Tigro-Euphrates valley must have been acquainted with the movements of the chief planets and stars, and, no doubt, they connected them with seasonal changes as in Egypt, where Isis was identified with Sirius long before the Ptolemaic age, when Babylonian astronomy was imported. Horus was identified not only with the sun but also with Saturn, Jupiter and Mars. Even the primitive Australians, as has been indicated, have their star myths; they refer to the stars Castor and Pollux as two young men, like the ancient Greeks, while the African Bushmen assert that these stars are two girls. It would be a mistake, however, to assume that the prehistoric Sumerians were exact astronomers. Probably they were, like the Aryo-Indians of the Vedic period, "not very accurate observers".

It is of special interest to find that the stars were grouped by the Babylonians at the earliest period in companies of seven. The importance of this magical number is emphasized by the group of seven demons which rose from the deep to rage over the land. Perhaps the sanctity of Seven was suggested by Orion, the Bears and the Pleiad, one of which constellations may have been the "Sevenfold" deity addressed as "one". At any rate arbitrary groupings of other stars into companies of seven took place, for references are made to the seven Tikshi, the seven Lumashi and the seven Mashi, which are older than the signs of the Zodiac; so far as can be ascertained these groups were selected from various constellations. When the five planets were identified, they were associated with the sun and moon and connected with the chief gods of the Hammurabi pantheon. A bilingual list in the British Museum arranges the sevenfold planetary group in the following order:

The moon, Sin.
The sun, Shamash.
Jupiter, Merodach.
Venus, Ishtar.
Saturn, Ninip (Nirig).
Mercury, Nebo.
Mars, Nergal.

An ancient name of the moon was Aa, A, or Ai, which recalls the Egyptian Aah or Ah. The Sumerian moon was Aku, "the measurer", like Thoth of Egypt, who in his lunar character as a Fate measured out the lives of men, and was a god of architects, mathematicians and scribes. The moon was the parent of the sun or its spouse; and might be male, or female, or both as a bi-sexual deity.

As the "bull of light" Jupiter had solar associations; he was also the shepherd of the stars, a title shared by Tammuz as Orion; Nin-Girsu, a developed form of Tammuz, was identified with both Orion and Jupiter.

Ishtar's identification with Venus is of special interest. When that planet was at its brightest phase, its rays were referred to as "the beard" of the goddess; she was the "bearded Aphrodite" – a bisexual deity evidently. The astrologers regarded the bright Venus as lucky and the rayless Venus as unlucky.

Saturn was Nirig, who is best known as Ninip, a deity who was displaced by Enlil, the elder Bel, and afterwards regarded as his son. His story has not been recovered, but from the references made to it there is little doubt that it was a version of the widespread myth about the elder deity who was slain by his son, as Saturn was by Jupiter and Dyaus by Indra. It may have resembled the lost Egyptian myth which explained the existence of the two Horuses – Horus the elder, and Horus, the posthumous son of Osiris. At any rate, it is of interest to find in this connection that in Egypt the planet Saturn was Her-Ka, "Horus the Bull". Ninip was also identified with the bull. Both deities were also connected with the spring sun, like Tammuz, and were terrible slayers of their enemies. Ninip raged through Babylonia like a storm flood, and Horus swept down the Nile, slaying the followers of Set. As the divine sower of seed, Ninip may have developed from Tammuz as Horus did from Osiris. Each were at once the father and the son, different forms of the same deity at various seasons of the year. The elder god was displaced by the son (spring), and when the son grew old his son slew him in turn. As the planet Saturn, Ninip was the ghost of the elder god, and as the son of Bel he was the solar war god of spring, the great wild bull, the god of fertility. He was also as Ber "lord of the wild boar", an animal associated with Rimmon.

Nebo (Nabu), who was identified with Mercury, was a god of Borsippa. He was a messenger and "announcer" of the gods, as the Egyptian Horus in his connection with Jupiter was Her-ap-sheta, "Horus the opener of that which is secret". Nebo's original character is obscure.

He appears to have been a highly developed deity of a people well advanced in civilization when he was exalted as the divine patron of Borsippa. Although Hammurabi ignored him, he was subsequently invoked with Merodach, and had probably much in common with Merodach. Indeed, Merodach was also identified with the planet Mercury. Like the Greek Hermes, Nebo was a messenger of the gods and an instructor of mankind. Jastrow regards him as "a counterpart of Ea", and says: "Like Ea, he is the embodiment and source of wisdom. The art of writing – and therefore of all literature – is more particularly associated with him. A common form of his name designates him as the 'god of the stylus'". He appears also to have been a developed form of Tammuz, who was an incarnation of Ea. Professor Pinches shows that one of his names, Mermer, was also a non-Semitic name of Ramman. Tammuz resembled Ramman in his character as a spring god of war. It would seem that Merodach as Jupiter displaced at Babylon Nebo as Saturn, the elder god, as Bel Enlil displaced the elder Ninip at Nippur.

The god of Mars was Nergal, the patron deity of Cuthah, who descended into the Underworld and forced into submission Eresh-ki-gal (Persephone), with whom he was afterwards associated. His "name", says Professor Pinches, "is supposed to mean 'lord of the great habitation', which would be a parallel to that of his spouse, Eresh-ki-gal". At Erech he symbolized the destroying influence of the sun, and was accompanied by the demons of pestilence. Mars was a planet of evil, plague and death; its animal form was the wolf. In Egypt it was called Herdesher, "the Red Horus", and in Greece it was associated with Ares (the Roman Mars), the war god, who assumed his boar form to slay Adonis (Tammuz).

Nergal was also a fire god like the Aryo-Indian Agni, who, as has been shown, links with Tammuz as a demon slayer and a god of fertility. It may be that Nergal was a specialized form of Tammuz, who, in a version of the myth, was reputed to have entered the Underworld as a conqueror when claimed by Eresh-ki-gal, and to have become, like Osiris, the lord of the dead. If so, Nergal was at once the slayer and the slain.

Planets as Forms of Tammuz and Ghosts of Gods

The various Babylonian deities who were identified with the planets had their characters sharply defined as members of an organized pantheon. But before this development took place certain of the prominent heavenly bodies, perhaps all the planets, were evidently regarded as manifestations of one deity, the primeval Tammuz, who was a form of Ea, or of the twin deities Ea and Anu. Tammuz may have been the "sevenfold one" of the hymns. At a still earlier period the stars were manifestations of the Power whom the jungle dwellers of Chota Nagpur attempt to propitiate – the "world soul" of the cultured Brahmans of the post-Vedic Indian Age. As much is suggested by the resemblances which the conventionalized planetary deities bear to Tammuz, whose attributes they symbolized, and by the Egyptian conception that the sun, Jupiter, Saturn and Mars were manifestations of Horus. Tammuz and Horus may have been personifications of the Power or World Soul vaguely recognized in the stage of Naturalism.

The influence of animistic modes of thought may be traced in the idea that the planets and stars were the ghosts of gods who were superseded by their sons. These sons were identical with their fathers; they became, as in Egypt, "husbands of their mothers". This idea was perpetuated in the Aryo-Indian Laws of Manu, in which it is set forth that "the husband, after conception by his wife, becomes an embryo and is born again of her". The deities died every year, but death was simply change. Yet they remained in the separate forms they assumed in their progress round "the wide circle of necessity". Horus was remembered as various planets – as the falcon, as the elder sun god and as the son of Osiris; and Tammuz was the spring sun, the child, youth, warrior, the deity of fertility and the lord of death (Orion-Nergal), and, as has been suggested, all the planets.

The stars were also the ghosts of deities who died daily. When the sun perished as an old man at evening, it rose in the heavens as Orion, or went out and in among the stars as the shepherd of the flock, Jupiter, the planet of Merodach in Babylonia, and Attis in Asia Minor. The flock was the group of heavenly spirits invisible by day, the "host of heaven" – manifestations or ghosts of the emissaries of the controlling power or powers.

The planets presided over various months of the year. Sin (the moon) was associated with the third month; it also controlled the calendar; Ninip (Saturn) was associated with the fourth month, Ishtar (Venus) with the sixth, Shamash (the sun) with the seventh, Merodach (Jupiter) with the eighth, Nergal (Mars) with the ninth and a messenger of the gods, probably Nebo (Mercury), with the tenth.

The Signs of the Zodiac

Each month was also controlled by a zodiacal constellation. In the Creation myth of Babylon it is stated that when Merodach engaged in the work of setting the Universe in order he "set all the great gods in their several stations", and "also created their images, the stars of the Zodiac, and fixed them all".

Our signs of the Zodiac are of Babylonian origin. They were passed on to the Greeks by the Phoenicians and Hittites. "There was a time", says Professor Sayce, "when the Hittites were profoundly affected by Babylonian civilization, religion and art...". They "carried the time-worn civilizations of Babylonia and Egypt to the furthest boundary of Egypt, and there handed them over to the West in the grey dawn of European history.... Greek traditions affirmed that the rulers of Mykenae had come from Lydia, bringing with them the civilization and treasures of Asia Minor. The tradition has been confirmed by modern research. While certain elements belonging to the prehistoric culture of Greece, as revealed at Mykenae and elsewhere, were derived from Egypt and Phoenicia, there are others which point to Asia Minor as their source. And the culture of Asia Minor was Hittite".

The early Babylonian astronomers did not know, of course, that the earth revolved round the sun. They believed that the sun travelled across the heavens flying like a bird or sailing like a boat. In studying its movements they observed that it always travelled from west to east along a broad path, swinging from side to side of it in the course of the year. This path is the Zodiac – the celestial "circle of necessity". The middle line of the sun's path is the Ecliptic. The Babylonian scientists divided the Ecliptic into twelve equal parts, and grouped in each part the stars which formed their constellations; these are also called "Signs of the Zodiac". Each month had thus its sign or constellation.

The names borne at the present day by the signs of the Zodiac are easily remembered even by children, who are encouraged to repeat the following familiar lines:

The Ram, the Bull, the heavenly Twins,
And next the Crab, the Lion shines.
The Virgin and the Scales;
The Scorpion, Archer and Sea goat,

The man that holds the water pot,
And Fish with glitt'ring tails.

The "Four Quarters"

The celestial regions were also divided into three or more parts. Three "fields" were allotted to the ancient triad formed by Ea, Anu and Bel. The zodiacal "path" ran through these "fields". Ea's field was in the west, and was associated with Amurru, the land of the Amorites; Anu's field was in the south, and was associated with Elam; and Bel's central "field" was associated with the land of Akkad. When the rulers of Akkad called themselves "kings of the four quarters", the reference was to the countries associated with the three divine fields and to Gutium (east = our north-east). Was Gutium associated with demons, as in Scandinavia the north-east was associated with the giants against whom Thor waged war?

The Babylonian Creation myth states that Merodach, having fixed the stars of the Zodiac, made three stars for each month. Mr. Robert Brown, jun., who has dealt as exhaustively with the astronomical problems of Babylonia as the available data permitted him, is of opinion that the leading stars of three constellations are referred to, viz.: (1) the central or zodiacal constellations, (2) the northern constellations and (3) the southern constellations. We have thus a scheme of thirty-six constellations. The "twelve zodiacal stars were flanked on either side by twelve non-zodiacal stars". Mr. Brown quotes Diodorus, who gave a resume of Babylonian astronomico-astrology, in this connection. He said that "the five planets were called 'Interpreters'; and in subjection to these were marshalled 'Thirty Stars', which were styled 'Divinities of the Council' ... The chiefs of the Divinities are twelve in number, to each of whom they assign a month and one of the twelve signs of the Zodiac". Through these twelve signs sun, moon and planets run their courses. "And with the zodiacal circle they mark out twenty-four stars, half of which they say are arranged in the north and half in the south". Mr. Brown shows that the thirty stars referred to "constituted the original Euphratean Lunar Zodiac, the parent of the seven ancient lunar zodiacs which have come down to us, namely, the Persian, Sogdian, Khorasmian, Chinese, Indian, Arab and Coptic schemes".

The three constellations associated with each month had each a symbolic significance: they reflected the characters of their months. At the height of the rainy season, for instance, the month of Ramman, the thunder god, was presided over by the zodiacal constellation of the water urn, the northern constellation "Fish of the Canal", and the southern "the Horse". In India the black horse was sacrificed at rain-getting and fertility ceremonies. The months of growth, pestilence and scorching sun heat were in turn symbolized. The "Great Bear" was the "chariot" = "Charles's Wain", and the "Milky Way" the "river of the high cloud", the Celestial Euphrates, as in Egypt it was the Celestial Nile.

Cosmic Periods in Babylonia, India, Greece and Ireland

Of special interest among the many problems presented by Babylonian astronomical lore is the theory of Cosmic periods or Ages of the Universe. In the Indian, Greek and Irish mythologies there are four Ages – the Silvern (white), Golden (yellow), the Bronze (red) and the Iron (black). As has been already indicated, Mr. R. Brown, jun., shows that "the Indian system of Yugas, or ages of the world, presents many features which forcibly remind us of the Euphratean scheme". The Babylonians had ten antediluvian kings, who were reputed to have reigned for vast periods, the total of which amounted to 120 saroi, or 432,000 years. These figures at once recall the Indian Maha-yuga of 4,320,000 years = 432,000 X 10. Apparently the Babylonian and Indian systems of calculation were of common origin. In both countries the measurements of time and space were arrived at by utilizing the numerals 10 and 6.

When primitive man began to count he adopted a method which comes naturally to every schoolboy; he utilized his fingers. Twice five gave him ten, and from ten he progressed to twenty, and then on to 100 and beyond. In making measurements his hands, arms and feet were at his service. We are still measuring by feet and yards (standardized strides) in this country, while those who engage in the immemorial art of knitting, and, in doing so, repeat designs found on neolithic pottery, continue to measure in finger breadths, finger lengths and hand breadths as did the ancient folks who called an arm length a cubit. Nor has the span been forgotten, especially by boys in their games with marbles; the space from the end of the thumb to the end of the little finger when the hand is extended must have been an important measurement from the earliest times.

Babylonian System of Calculation

As he made progress in calculations, the primitive Babylonian appears to have been struck by other details in his anatomy besides his sets of five fingers and five toes. He observed, for instance, that his fingers were divided into three parts and his thumb into two parts only; four fingers multiplied by three gave him twelve, and multiplying 12 by 3 he reached 36. Apparently, the figure 6 attracted him. His body was divided into 6 parts – 2 arms, 2 legs, the head and the trunk; his 2 ears, 2 eyes and mouth, and nose also gave him 6. The basal 6, multiplied by his fingers, gave him 60, and 60 x 2 (for his 2 hands) gave him 120. In Babylonian arithmetic 6 and 60 are important numbers, and it is not surprising to find that in the system of numerals the signs for 1 and 10 combined represent 60.

In fixing the length of a mythical period his first great calculation of 120 came naturally to the Babylonian, and when he undertook to measure the Zodiac he equated time and space by fixing on 120 degrees. His first zodiac was the Sumerian lunar zodiac, which contained thirty moon chambers associated with the "Thirty Stars" of the tablets, and referred to by Diodorus as "Divinities of the Council". The chiefs of the Thirty numbered twelve. In this system the year began in the winter solstice. Mr. Hewitt has shown that the chief annual festival of the Indian Dravidians begins with the first full moon after the winter festival, and Mr. Brown emphasizes the fact that the list of Tamil (Dravidian) lunar and solar months are named like the Babylonian constellations. "Lunar chronology", wrote Professor Max Muller, "seems everywhere to have preceded solar chronology". The later Semitic Babylonian system had twelve solar chambers and the thirty-six constellations.

Each degree was divided into sixty minutes, and each minute into sixty seconds. The hours of the day and night each numbered twelve.

Multiplying 6 by 10 (pur), the Babylonian arrived at 60 (soss); 60 x 10 gave him 600 (ner), and 600 x 6, 3600 (sar), while 3600 x 10 gave him 36,000, and 36,000 x 12, 432,000 years, or 120 saroi, which is equal to the "sar" multiplied by the "soss" x 2. "Pur" signifies "heap"–the ten fingers closed after being counted; and "ner" signifies "foot". Mr. George Bertin suggests that when 6 x 10 fingers gave 60 this number was multiplied by the ten toes, with the result that 600 was afterwards associated with the feet (ner). The Babylonian sign for 10 resembles the impression of two feet with heels closed and toes apart. This suggests a primitive record of the first round of finger counting.

Traced in Indian Yuga System

In India this Babylonian system of calculation was developed during the Brahmanical period. The four Yugas or Ages, representing the four fingers used by the primitive mathematicians, totalled 12,000 divine years, a period which was called a Maha-yuga; it equalled the Babylonian 120 saroi, multiplied by 100. Ten times a hundred of these periods gave a "Day of Brahma". Each day of the gods, it was explained by the Brahmans, was a year to mortals. Multiplied by 360 days, 12,000 divine years equalled 4,320,000 human years. This Maha-yuga, multiplied by 1000, gave the "Day of Brahma" as 4,320,000,000 human years.

The shortest Indian Yuga is the Babylonian 120 saroi multiplied by 10 = 1200 divine years for the Kali Yuga; twice that number gives the Dvapara Yuga of 2400 divine years; then the Treta Yuga is 2400 + 1200 = 3600 divine years, and Krita Yuga 3600 + 1200=4800 divine years.

The influence of Babylonia is apparent in these calculations. During the Vedic period "Yuga" usually signified a "generation", and there are no certain references to the four Ages as such. The names "Kali", "Dvapara", "Treta" and "Krita" "occur as the designations of throws of dice". It was after the arrival of the "late corners", the post-Vedic Aryans, that the Yuga system was developed in India.

In Indian Myth and Legend it is shown that the Indian and Irish Ages have the same colour sequence: (1) White or Silvern, (2) Red or Bronze, (3) Yellow or Golden and (4) Black or Iron. The Greek order is: (1) Golden, (2) Silvern, (3) Bronze and (4) Iron.

The Babylonians coloured the seven planets as follows: the moon, silvern; the sun, golden; Mars, red; Saturn, black; Jupiter, orange; Venus, yellow; and Mercury, blue.

Astrology

As the ten antediluvian kings who reigned for 120 saroi had an astral significance, their long reigns corresponding "with the distances separating certain of the principal stars in or near the ecliptic", it seems highly probable that the planets were similarly connected with mythical ages which were equated with the "four quarters" of the celestial regions and the four regions of the earth, which in Gaelic story are called "the four red divisions of the world".

Three of the planets may have been heralds of change. Venus, as "Dilbat", was the "Proclaimer", and both Jupiter and Mercury were called "Face voices of light", and "Heroes of the rising sun" among other names. Jupiter may have been the herald of the "Golden Age" as a morning star. This planet was also associated with bronze, as "Kakkub Urud", "the star of bronze", while Mars was "Kakkub Aban Kha-urud", "the star of the bronze fish stone". Mercury, the lapis lazuli planet, may have been connected with the black Saturn, the ghost of the dead sun, the demoniac elder god; in Egypt lapis lazuli was the hair colour of Ra when he grew old, and Egyptologists translate it as black. The rare and regular appearances of Mercury may have suggested the planet's connection with a recurring Age. Venus as an evening star might be regarded as the herald of the lunar or silver age; she was propitious as a bearded deity and interchanged with Merodach as a seasonal herald.

Connecting Jupiter with the sun as a propitious planet, and with Mars as a destroying planet, Venus with the moon, and Mercury with Saturn, we have left four colour schemes which suggest the Golden, Silvern, Bronze and Iron Ages. The Greek order of mythical ages may have had a solar significance, beginning as it does with the "golden" period. On the other hand the Indian and Irish systems begin with the Silvern or white lunar period. In India the White Age (Treta Yuga) was the age of perfect men, and in Greece the Golden Age was the age of men who lived like gods. Thus the first ages in both cases were "Perfect" Ages.

The Bronze Age of Greece was the age of notorious fighters and takers of life; in Babylonia the bronze planet Mars was the symbol of the destroying Nergal, god of war and pestilence, while Jupiter was also a destroyer as Merodach, the slayer of Tiamat. In India the Black Age is the age of wickedness. The Babylonian Saturn, as we have seen, is black, and its god, Ninip, was the destroying boar, which recalls the black boar of the Egyptian demon (or elder god) Set. The Greek Cronos was a destroyer even of his own children. All the elder gods had demoniac traits like the ghosts of human beings.

As the Babylonian lunar zodiac was imported into India before solar worship and the solar zodiac were developed, so too may have been the germs of the Yuga doctrine, which appears to have a long history. Greece, on the other hand, came under the influence of Babylon at a much later period. In Egypt Ra, the sun god, was an antediluvian king, and he was followed by Osiris. Osiris was slain by Set, who was depicted sometimes red and sometimes black. There was also a Horus Age.

The Irish system of ages suggests an early cultural drift into Europe, through Asia Minor, and along the uplands occupied by the representatives of the Alpine or Armenoid peoples who have been traced from Hindu Kush to Brittany. The culture of Gaul resembles that of India in certain particulars; both the Gauls and the post-Vedic Aryans, for instance, believed in the doctrine of Transmigration of Souls, and practised "suttee". After the Roman occupation of Gaul, Ireland appears to have been the refuge of Gaulish scholars, who imported their beliefs and traditions and laid the foundations of that brilliant culture which shed lustre on the Green Isle in late Pagan and early Christian times.

The part played by the Mitanni people of Aryan speech in distributing Asiatic culture throughout Europe may have been considerable, but we know little or nothing regarding their movements and influence, nor has sufficient evidence been forthcoming to connect them with the cremating invaders of the Bronze Age, who penetrated as far as northern Scotland and Scandinavia. On the other hand it is certain that the Hittites adopted the planetary system of Babylonia and passed it on to Europeans, including the Greeks. The five planets Ninip, Merodach, Nergal, Ishtar and Nebo were called by the Greeks after their gods Kronos, Zeus, Ares, Aphrodite and Hermes, and by the Romans Saturnus, Jupiter, Mars, Venus and Mercurius.

It must be recognized, however, that these equations were somewhat arbitrary. Ninip resembled Kronos and Saturnus as a father, but he was also at the same time a son; he was the Egyptian Horus the elder and Horus the younger in one. Merodach was similarly of complex character – a combination of Ea, Aim, Enlil and Tammuz, who acquired, when exalted by the Amoritic Dynasty of Babylon, the attributes of the thunder god Adad-Ramman in the form of Amurru, "lord of the mountains". During the Hammurabi Age Amurru was significantly popular in personal names. It is as Amurru-Ramman that Merodach bears comparison with Zeus. He also links with Hercules. Too much must not be made, therefore, of the Greek and Roman identifications of alien deities with their own. Mulla, the Gaulish mule god, may have resembled Mars somewhat, but it is a "far cry" from Mars-Mulla to Mars-Nergal, as it is also from the Gaulish Moccus, the boar, called "Mercury", to Nebo, the god of culture, who was the "Mercury" of the Tigro-Euphrates valley. Similarly the differences between "Jupiter-Amon" of Egypt and "Jupiter-Merodach" of Babylon were more pronounced than the resemblances.

Beliefs of the Masses

The basal idea in Babylonian astrology appears to be the recognition of the astral bodies as spirits or fates, who exercised an influence over the gods, the world, and mankind. These were worshipped in groups when they were yet nameless. The group addressed, "Powerful, O sevenfold, one are ye", may have been a constellation consisting of seven stars. The worship of stars and planets, which were identified and named, "seems never to have spread", says Professor Sayce, "beyond the learned classes, and to have remained to the last an artificial system. The mass of the people worshipped the stars as a whole, but it was only as a whole and not individually". The masses perpetuated ancient animistic beliefs, like the pre-Hellenic inhabitants of Greece. "The Pelasgians, as I was informed at Dodona", wrote Herodotus, "formerly offered all things indiscriminately to the gods. They distinguished them by no name or surname, for they were hitherto unacquainted with either; but they called them gods, which by its etymology means disposers, from observing the orderly disposition and distribution of the various parts of the universe". The oldest deities are those which bore no individual names. They were simply "Fates" or groups called "Sevenfold". The crude giant gods of Scotland are "Fomhairean" (Fomorians), and do not have individual names as in Ireland. Families and tribes were controlled by the Fates or nameless gods, which might appear as beasts or birds, or be heard knocking or screaming.

In the Babylonian astral hymns, the star spirits are associated with the gods, and are revealers of the decrees of Fate. "Ye brilliant stars ... ye bright ones ... to destroy evil did Anu create you.... At thy command mankind was named (created)! Give thou the Word, and with thee let the great gods stand! Give thou my judgment, make my decision!"

The Indian evidence shows that the constellations, and especially the bright stars, were identified before the planets. Indeed, in Vedic literature there is no certain reference to a single planet, although constellations are named. It seems highly probable that before the Babylonian gods were associated with the astral bodies, the belief obtained that the stars exercised an influence over human lives. In one of the Indian "Forest Books", for instance, reference is made to a man who was "born under the Nakshatra Rohini". "Nakshatras" are stars in the Rigveda and later, and "lunar mansions" in Brahmanical compositions. "Rohini, 'ruddy', is the name of a conspicuously reddish star, a Tauri or Aldebaran, and denotes the group of the Hyades". This reference may be dated before 600 BCE, perhaps 800 BCE.

Greece and Babylonia

From Greece comes the evidence of Plutarch regarding the principles of Babylonian astrology. "Respecting the planets, which they call the birth-ruling divinities, the Chaldeans", he wrote, "lay down that two (Venus and Jupiter) are propitious, and two (Mars and Saturn) malign, and three (Sun, Moon, and Mercury) of a middle nature, and one common". "That is", Mr. Brown comments, "an astrologer would say, these three are propitious with the good, and may be malign with the bad".

Jastrow's views in this connection seem highly controversial. He holds that Babylonian astrology dealt simply with national affairs, and had no concern with "the conditions under which the individual was born"; it did not predict "the fate in store for him". He believes that the Greeks transformed Babylonian astrology and infused it with the spirit of individualism which is a characteristic of their religion, and that they were the first to give astrology a personal significance.

Jastrow also perpetuates the idea that astronomy began with the Greeks. "Several centuries before the days of Alexander the Great", he says, "the Greeks had begun to cultivate the study of the heavens, not for purposes of divination, but prompted by a scientific spirit as an intellectual discipline that might help them to solve the mysteries of the universe". It is possible, however, to overrate the "scientific spirit" of the Greeks, who, like the Japanese in our own day, were accomplished borrowers from other civilizations. That astronomy had humble beginnings in Greece as elsewhere is highly probable. The late Mr. Andrew Lang wrote in this connection: "The very oddest example of the survival of the notion that the stars are men and women is found in the Pax of Aristophanes. Trygaeus in that comedy has just made an expedition to heaven. A slave meets him, and asks him: 'Is not the story true, then, that we become stars when we die?' The answer is, 'Certainly'; and Trygaeus points out the star into which Ion of Chios has just been metamorphosed". Mr. Lang added: "Aristophanes is making fun of some popular Greek superstition". The Eskimos, Persians, Aryo-Indians, Germans, New Zealanders and others had a similar superstition.

Jastrow goes on to say that the Greeks "imparted their scientific view of the Universe to the East. They became the teachers of the East in astronomy as in medicine and other sciences, and the credit of having discovered the law of the precession of the equinoxes belongs to Hipparchus, the Greek astronomer, who announced this important theory about the year 130 BCE". Undoubtedly the Greeks contributed to the advancement of the science of astronomy, with which, as other authorities believe, they became acquainted after it had become well developed as a science by the Assyrians and Babylonians.

"In return for improved methods of astronomical calculation which", Jastrow says, "it may be assumed (the italics are ours), contact with Greek science gave to the Babylonian astronomers, the Greeks accepted from the Babylonians the names of the constellations of the ecliptic". This is a grudging admission; they evidently accepted more than the mere names.

Jastrow's hypothesis is certainly interesting, especially as he is an Oriental linguist of high repute. But it is not generally accepted. The sudden advance made by the Tigro-Euphratean astronomers when Assyria was at the height of its glory, may have been due to the discoveries made by great native scientists, the Newtons and the Herschels of past ages, who had studied the data accumulated by generations of astrologers, the earliest recorders of the movements of the heavenly bodies. It is hard to believe that the Greeks made much progress as scientists before they had identified the planets, and become familiar with the Babylonian constellations through the medium of the Hittites or the Phoenicians. What is known for certain is that long centuries before the Greek science was heard of, there were scientists in Babylonia. During the Sumerian period "the forms and relations of geometry", says Professor Goodspeed, "were employed for purposes of augury. The heavens were mapped out, and the courses of the heavenly bodies traced to determine the bearing of their movements upon human destinies".

Eclipses Foretold

Several centuries before Hipparchus was born, the Assyrian kings had in their palaces official astronomers who were able to foretell, with varying degrees of accuracy, when eclipses would take place. Instructions were sent to various observatories, in the king's name, to send in reports of forthcoming eclipses. A translation of one of these official documents sent from the observatory of Babylon to Nineveh, has been published by Professor Harper. The following are extracts from it: "As for the eclipse of the moon about which the king my lord has written to me, a watch was kept for it in the cities of Akkad, Borsippa and Nippur. We observed it ourselves in the city of Akkad.... And whereas the king my lord ordered me to observe also the eclipse of the sun, I watched to see whether it took place or not, and what passed before my eyes I now report to the king my lord. It was an eclipse of the moon that took place.... It was total over Syria, and the shadow fell on the land of the Amorites, the land of the Hittites and in part on the land of the Chaldees". Professor Sayce comments: "We gather from this letter that there were no less than three observatories in Northern Babylonia: one at Akkad, near Sippara; one at Nippur, now Niffer; and one at Borsippa, within sight of Babylon. As Borsippa possessed a university, it was natural that one of the three observatories should be established there".

It is evident that before the astronomers at Nineveh could foretell eclipses, they had achieved considerable progress as scientists. The data at their disposal probably covered nearly 2,000 years. Mr. Brown, junior, calculates that the signs of the Zodiac were fixed in the year 2084 BCE. These star groups do not now occupy the positions in which they were observed by the early astronomers, because the revolving earth is rocking like a top, with the result that the pole does not always keep pointing at the same spot in the heavens. Each year the meeting-place of the imaginary lines of the ecliptic and equator is moving westward at the rate of about fifty seconds. In time – ages hence – the pole will circle round to the point it spun at when the constellations were named by the Babylonians. It is by calculating the period occupied by this world-curve that the date 2084 BCE has been arrived at.

As a result of the world-rocking process, the present-day "signs of the Zodiac" do not correspond with the constellations. In March, for instance, when the sun crosses the equator it enters the sign of the Ram (Aries), but does not reach the constellation till the 20th.

When "the ecliptic was marked off into the twelve regions" and the signs of the Zodiac were designated, "the year of three hundred sixty-five and one-fourth days was known", says Goodspeed, "though the common year was reckoned according to twelve months of thirty days each, and equated with the solar year by intercalating a month at the proper times.... The month was divided into weeks of seven days.... The clepsydra and the sundial were Babylonian inventions for measuring time".

The Dial of Ahaz

The sundial of Ahaz was probably of Babylonian design. When the shadow went "ten degrees backward" (2 Kings, xx, 11) ambassadors were sent from Babylon "to enquire of the wonder that was done in the land" (2 Chron., xxxii, 31). It was believed that the king's illness was connected with the incident. According to astronomical calculation there was a partial eclipse of the sun which was visible at Jerusalem on 11th January, 689 BCE, about 11:30 a.m. When the upper part of the solar disc was obscured, the shadow on the dial was strangely affected.

Omens of Heaven and Air

The Babylonian astrologers in their official documents were more concerned regarding international omens than those which affected individuals. They made observations not only of the stars, but also the moon, which, as has been shown, was one of their planets, and took note of the clouds and the wind likewise.

As portions of the heavens were assigned to various countries, so was the moon divided into four quarters for the same purpose – the upper part for the north, Gutium, the lower for the south, Akkad or Babylonia, the eastern part for Elam, and the western for Amurru. The crescent was also divided in like manner; looking southward the astrologers assigned the right horn to the west and the left to the east. In addition, certain days and certain months were connected with the different regions. Lunar astrology was therefore of complicated character. When the moon was dim at the particular phase which was connected with Amurru, it was believed that the fortunes of that region were in decline, and if it happened to shine brightly in the Babylonian phase the time was considered auspicious to wage war in the west. Great importance was attached to eclipses, which were fortunately recorded, with the result that the ancient astronomers were ultimately enabled to forecast them.

The destinies of the various states in the four quarters were similarly influenced by the planets. When Venus, for instance, rose brightly in the field of Anu, it was a "prosperor" for Elam; if it were dim it foretold misfortune. Much importance was also attached to the positions occupied by the constellations when the planets were propitious or otherwise; no king would venture forth on an expedition under a "yoke of inauspicious stars".

Biblical References to Constellations

Biblical references to the stars make mention of well-known Babylonian constellations:

Canst thou bind the sweet influences of Pleiades, or loose the bands of Orion?
Canst thou bring forth Mazzaroth (?the Zodiac) in his season? or canst
thou guide Arcturus with his sons? Knowest thou the ordinances of heaven?
canst thou set the dominion thereof in the earth? Job, xxxviii, 31-33.

Which maketh Arcturus, Orion and Pleiades, and
the chambers of the south. Job, ix, 9.

Seek him that maketh the seven stars and Orion, and turneth the shadow of
death into the morning, and maketh the day dark with night. Amos, v, 8.

The Past in the Present

The so-called science of astrology, which had origin in ancient Babylonia and spread eastward and west, is not yet extinct, and has its believers even in our own country at the present day, although they are not nearly so numerous as when Shakespeare made Malvolio read:

In my stars I am above thee; but be not afraid of greatness:
some are born great, some achieve greatness, and some have
greatness thrust upon 'em. Thy Fates open their hands....

or when Byron wrote:

Ye stars! which are the poetry of heaven!
If in your bright leaves we would read the fate
Of men and empires–'t is to be forgiven
That in our aspirations to be great,
Our destinies o'erleap their mortal state
And claim a kindred with you....

Our grave astronomers are no longer astrologers, but they still call certain constellations by the names given them in Babylonia. Every time we look at our watches we are reminded of the ancient mathematicians who counted on their fingers and multiplied 10 by 6, to give us minutes and seconds, and divided the day and the night into twelve hours by multiplying six by the two leaden feet of Time. The past lives in the present.

Magic, Demonology & Superstition

Introduction

DONALD A. MACKENZIE describes the very tangible, literal nature of both good and bad Babylonian spirits, pointing out that in contrast to what Paul preached to the Athenians (that God "dwelleth not in temples made with hands; neither is worshipped with men's hands as though he needed anything … we ought not to think that the Godhead is like unto gold, or silver, or stone, graven by art and man's device"):

"Temples were houses of the gods in the literal sense; the gods were supposed to dwell in them, their spirits having entered into the graven images or blocks of stone. It is probable that like the Ancient Egyptians they believed a god had as many spirits as he had attributes. The gods, as we have said, appear to have evolved from early spirit groups. All the world swarmed with spirits, which inhabited stones and trees, mountains and deserts, rivers and ocean, the air, the sky, the stars and the sun and moon. The spirits controlled Nature: they brought light and darkness, sunshine and storm, summer and winter; they were manifested in the thunderstorm, the sandstorm, the glare of sunset and the wraiths of mist rising from the steaming marshes. They controlled also the lives of men and women. The good spirits were the source of luck. The bad spirits caused misfortunes, and were ever seeking to work evil against the Babylonian. Darkness was peopled by demons and ghosts of the dead. The spirits of disease were ever lying in wait to clutch him with cruel invisible hands."

The first part of this chapter derives from Mackenzie, while from 'Priestly Magicians, Wizards and Witches' is Lewis Spence's discussion of this fascinating area of Babylonian belief.

Demons, Fairies and Ghosts

Germ Theory Anticipated

SOME MODERN WRITERS, who are too prone to regard ancient peoples from a twentieth-century point of view, express grave doubts as to whether "intelligent Babylonians" really believed that spirits came down in the rain and entered the soil to rise up before men's eyes as stalks of barley or wheat. There is no reason for supposing that they thought otherwise. The early folks based their theories on the accumulated knowledge of their age. They knew nothing regarding the composition of water or the atmosphere, of the cause of thunder and lightning, or of the chemical changes effected in soils by the action of bacteria. They attributed all natural phenomena to the operations of spirits or gods.

In believing that certain demons caused certain diseases, they may be said to have achieved distinct progress, for they anticipated the germ theory. They made discoveries, too, which have been approved and elaborated in later times when they lit sacred fires, bathed in sacred waters and used oils and herbs to charm away spirits of pestilence. Indeed, many folk cures, which were originally associated with magical ceremonies, are still practised in our own day. They were found to be effective by early observers, although they were unable to explain why and how cures were accomplished, like modern scientific investigators.

In peopling the Universe with spirits, the Babylonians, like other ancient folks, betrayed that tendency to symbolize everything which has ever appealed to the human mind. Our painters and poets and sculptors are greatest when they symbolize their ideals and ideas and impressions, and by so doing make us respond to their moods. Their "beauty and their terror are sublime". But what may seem poetic to us, was invariably a grim reality to the Babylonians. The statue or picture was not merely a work of art but a manifestation of the god or demon.

As has been said, they believed that the spirit of the god inhabited the idol; the frown of the brazen image was the frown of the wicked demon. They entertained as much dread of the winged and human-headed bulls guarding the entrance to the royal palace as do some of the Arab workmen who, in our own day, assist excavators to rescue them from sandy mounds in which they have been hidden for long centuries. When an idol was carried away from a city by an invading army, it was believed that the god himself had been taken prisoner, and was therefore unable any longer to help his people.

Early Gods indistinguishable from Demons

In the early stages of Sumerian culture, the gods and goddesses who formed groups were indistinguishable from demons. They were vaguely defined, and had changing shapes. When attempts were made to depict them they were represented in many varying forms. Some were winged bulls or lions with human heads; others had even more remarkable composite forms. The "dragon of Babylon", for instance, which was portrayed on walls of temples, had a serpent's head, a body covered with scales, the fore legs of a lion, hind legs of an eagle and a long wriggling serpentine tail. Ea had several monster forms. The following description of one of these is repulsive enough:

The head is the head of a serpent,
From his nostrils mucus trickles,
His mouth is beslavered with water;
The ears are like those of a basilisk,
His horns are twisted into three curls,
He wears a veil in his head band,
The body is a suh-fish full of stars,
The base of his feet are claws,
The sole of his foot has no heel,
His name is Sassu-wunnu,
A sea monster, a form of Ea.
– R. C. Thompson's translation

Even after the gods were given beneficent attributes to reflect the growth of culture, and were humanized, they still retained many of their savage characteristics. Bel Enlil and his fierce son, Nergal, were destroyers of mankind; the storm god desolated the land; the sky god deluged it with rain; the sea raged furiously, ever hungering for human victims; the burning sun struck down its victims; and the floods played havoc with the dykes and houses of human beings. In Egypt the sun god Ra was similarly a "producer of calamity", the composite monster god Sokar was "the lord of fear". Osiris in prehistoric times had been "a dangerous god", and some of the Pharaohs sought protection against him in the charms inscribed in their tombs. The Indian Shiva, "the Destroyer", in the old religious poems has also primitive attributes of like character.

The Sumerian gods never lost their connection with the early spirit groups. These continued to be represented by their attendants, who executed a deity's stern and vengeful decrees. In one of the Babylonian charms the demons are referred to as "the spleen of the gods" – the symbols of their wrathful emotions and vengeful desires. Bel Enlil, the air and earth god, was served by the demons of disease, "the beloved sons of Bel", which issued from the Underworld to attack mankind. Nergal, the sulky and ill-tempered lord of death and destruction, who never lost his demoniac character, swept over the land, followed by the spirits of pestilence, sunstroke, weariness and destruction. Anu, the sky god, had "spawned" at creation the demons of cold and rain and darkness. Even Ea and his consort, Damkina, were served by groups of devils and giants, which preyed upon mankind in bleak and desolate places when night fell. In the ocean home of Ea were bred the "seven evil spirits" of tempest – the gaping dragon, the leopard which preyed upon children, the great Beast, the terrible serpent, etc.

Egyptian, Indian, Greek, and Germanic Parallels

In Indian mythology Indra was similarly followed by the stormy Maruts, and fierce Rudra by the tempestuous Rudras. In Teutonic mythology Odin is the "Wild Huntsman in the Raging Host". In Greek mythology the ocean furies attend upon fickle Poseidon. Other examples of this kind could be multiplied.

As we have seen, the earliest group of Babylonian deities consisted probably of four pairs of gods and goddesses as in Egypt. The first pair was Apsu-Rishtu and Tiamat, who personified the primordial deep. Now the elder deities in most mythologies – the "grandsires" and "grandmothers" and "fathers" and "mothers" – are ever the most powerful and most vengeful. They appear to represent primitive "layers" of savage thought. The Greek Cronos devours even his own children, and, as the late Andrew Lang has shown, there are many parallels to this myth among primitive peoples in various parts of the world.

Lang regarded the Greek survival as an example of "the conservatism of the religious instinct". The grandmother of the Teutonic deity Tyr was a fierce giantess with 900 heads; his father was an enemy of the gods. In Scotland the hag-mother of winter and storm and darkness is the enemy of growth and all life, and she raises storms to stop the grass growing, to slay young animals, and prevent the union of her son with his fair bride. Similarly the Babylonian chaos spirits, Apsu and Tiamat, the father and mother of the gods, resolve to destroy their offspring, because they begin to set the Universe in order. Tiamat, the female dragon, is more powerful than her husband Apsu, who is slain by his son Ea. She summons to her aid the gods of evil, and creates also a brood of monsters – serpents, dragons, vipers, fish men, raging hounds, etc. – so as to bring about universal and enduring confusion and evil. Not until she is destroyed can the beneficent gods establish law and order and make the earth habitable and beautiful.

But although Tiamat was slain, the everlasting battle between the forces of good and evil was ever waged in the Babylonian world. Certain evil spirits were let loose at certain periods, and they strove to accomplish the destruction of mankind and his works. These invisible enemies were either charmed away by performing magical ceremonies, or by invoking the gods to thwart them and bind them.

Animal Demons

Other spirits inhabited the bodies of animals and were ever hovering near. The ghosts of the dead and male and female demons were birds, like the birds of Fate which sang to Siegfried. When the owl raised its melancholy voice in the darkness the listener heard the spirit of a departed mother crying for her child. Ghosts and evil spirits wandered through the streets in darkness; they haunted empty houses; they fluttered through the evening air as bats; they hastened, moaning dismally, across barren wastes searching for food or lay in wait for travellers; they came as roaring lions and howling jackals, hungering for human flesh.

The "shedu" was a destructive bull which might slay man wantonly or as a protector of temples. Of like character was the "lamassu", depicted as a winged bull with human head, the protector of palaces; the "alu" was a bull-like demon of tempest, and there were also many composite, distorted, or formless monsters which were vaguely termed "seizers" or "overthrowers", the Semitic "labashu" and "ach-chazu", the Sumerian "dimmea" and "dimme-kur". A dialectic form of "gallu" or devil was "mulla". Professor Pinches thinks it not improbable that "mulla" may be connected with the word "mula", meaning "star", and suggests that it referred to a "will-o'-the-wisp". In these islands, according to an old rhyme,

Some call him Robin Good-fellow,
Hob-goblin, or mad Crisp,

And some againe doe tearme him oft
By name of Will the Wisp.

Other names are "Kitty", "Peg" and "Jack with a lantern". "Poor Robin" sang:

I should indeed as soon expect
That Peg-a-lantern would direct
Me straightway home on misty night
As wand'ring stars, quite out of sight.

In Shakespeare's Tempest a sailor exclaims: "Your fairy, which, you say, is a harmless fairy, has done little better than played the Jack with us". Dr. Johnson commented that the reference was to "Jack with a lantern". Milton wrote also of the "wandering fire",

Which oft, they say, some evil spirit attends,
Hovering and blazing with delusive light,
Misleads th' amaz'd night wand'rer from his way
To bogs and mires, and oft through pond or pool;
There swallowed up and lost from succour far.

"When we stick in the mire", sang Drayton, "he doth with laughter leave us". These fires were also "fallen stars", "death fires" and "fire drakes":

So have I seen a fire drake glide along
Before a dying man, to point his grave,
And in it stick and hide.

"Adam's first wife, Lilith"

Pliny referred to the wandering lights as stars. The Sumerian "mulla" was undoubtedly an evil spirit. In some countries the "fire drake" is a bird with gleaming breast: in Babylonia it assumed the form of a bull, and may have had some connection with the bull of Ishtar. Like the Indian "Dasyu" and "Dasa", Gallu was applied in the sense of "foreign devil" to human and superhuman adversaries of certain monarchs. Some of the supernatural beings resemble our elves and fairies and the Indian Rakshasas. Occasionally they appear in comely human guise; at other times they are vaguely monstrous. The best known of this class is Lilith, who, according to Hebrew tradition, preserved in the Talmud, was the demon lover of Adam. She has been immortalized by Dante Gabriel Rossetti:

Of Adam's first wife Lilith, it is told
(The witch he loved before the gift of Eve)
That, ere the snake's, her sweet tongue could deceive,
And her enchanted hair was the first gold.
And still she sits, young while the earth is old,
And, subtly of herself contemplative,
Draws men to watch the bright web she can weave,
Till heart and body and life are in its hold.

The rose and poppy are her flowers; for where
Is he not found, O Lilith, whom shed scent
And soft shed kisses and soft sleep shall snare?
Lo! as that youth's eyes burned at thine, so went
Thy spell through him, and left his straight neck bent
And round his heart one strangling golden hair.

Lilith is the Babylonian Lilithu, a feminine form of Lilu, the Sumerian Lila. She resembles Surpanakha of the Ramayana, who made love to Rama and Lakshmana, and the sister of the demon Hidimva, who became enamoured of Bhima, one of the heroes of the Mahabharata, and the various fairy lovers of Europe who lured men to eternal imprisonment inside mountains, or vanished forever when they were completely under their influence, leaving them demented. The elfin Lilu similarly wooed young women, like the Germanic Laurin of the "Wonderful Rose Garden", who carried away the fair lady Kunhild to his underground dwelling amidst the Tyrolese mountains, or left them haunting the place of their meetings, searching for him in vain:

A savage place! as holy and enchanted
As ere beneath the waning moon was haunted
By woman wailing for her demon lover . . .
His flashing eyes, his floating hair!
Weave a circle round him thrice,
And close your eyes with holy dread,
For he on honey dew hath fed
And drunk the milk of Paradise.
– Coleridge's *Kubla Khan*

Another materializing spirit of this class was Ardat Lili, who appears to have wedded human beings like the swan maidens, the mermaids and Nereids of the European folk tales, and the goddess Ganga, who for a time was the wife of King Shantanu of the Mahabharata.

The Labartu, to whom we have referred, was a female who haunted mountains and marshes; like the fairies and hags of Europe, she stole or afflicted children, who accordingly had to wear charms round their necks for protection. Seven of these supernatural beings were reputed to be daughters of Anu, the sky god.

The Demon of Nightmare

The Alu, a storm deity, was also a spirit which caused nightmares. It endeavoured to smother sleepers like the Scandinavian hag Mara, and similarly deprived them of power to move. In Babylonia this evil spirit might also cause sleeplessness or death by hovering near a bed. In shape it might be as horrible and repulsive as the Egyptian ghosts which caused children to die from fright or by sucking out the breath of life.

Ghosts as Enemies of the Living

As most representatives of the spirit world were enemies of the living, so were the ghosts of dead men and women. Death chilled all human affections; it turned love to hate; the deeper the love had been, the deeper became the enmity fostered by the ghost. Certain ghosts might also be regarded as particularly virulent and hostile if they happened to have left the body of one who was ceremonially impure.

The Vengeful Dead Mother

The most terrible ghost in Babylonia was that of a woman who had died in childbed. She was pitied and dreaded; her grief had demented her; she was doomed to wail in the darkness; her impurity clung to her like poison. No spirit was more prone to work evil against mankind, and her hostility was accompanied by the most tragic sorrow. In Northern India the Hindus, like the ancient Babylonians, regard as a fearsome demon the ghost of a woman who died while pregnant, or on the day of the child's birth. A similar belief prevailed in Mexico. In Europe there are many folk tales of dead mothers who return to avenge themselves on the cruel fathers of neglected children.

A sharp contrast is presented by the Mongolian Buriats, whose outlook on the spirit world is less gloomy than was that of the ancient Babylonians. According to Mr. Jeremiah Curtin, this interesting people are wont to perform a ceremony with purpose to entice the ghost to return to the dead body – a proceeding which is dreaded in the Scottish Highlands. The Buriats address the ghost, saying: "You shall sleep well. Come back to your natural ashes. Take pity on your friends. It is necessary to live a real life. Do not wander along the mountains. Do not be like bad spirits. Return to your peaceful home…. Come back and work for your children. How can you leave the little ones?" If it is a mother, these words have great effect; sometimes the spirit moans and sobs, and the Buriats tell that there have been instances of it returning to the body. In his Arabia Deserta Doughty relates that Arab women and children mock the cries of the owl. One explained to him: "It is a wailful woman seeking her lost child; she has become this forlorn bird". So do immemorial beliefs survive to our own day.

Fate of Childless Ghosts

The Babylonian ghosts of unmarried men and women and of those without offspring were also disconsolate night wanderers. Others who suffered similar fates were the ghosts of men who died in battle far from home and were left unburied, the ghosts of travellers who perished in the desert and were not covered over, the ghosts of drowned men which rose from the water, the ghosts of prisoners starved to death or executed, the ghosts of people who died violent deaths before their appointed time. The dead required to be cared for, to have libations poured out, to be fed, so that they might not prowl through the streets or enter houses searching for scraps of food and pure water. The duty of giving offerings to the dead was imposed apparently on near relatives. As in India, it would appear that the eldest son performed the funeral ceremony: a dreadful fate therefore awaited the spirit of the dead Babylonian man or woman without offspring. In Sanskrit literature there is a reference to a priest who was not allowed to enter Paradise, although he had performed rigid penances, because he had no children.

Hags and Giants and Composite Monsters

There were hags and giants of mountain and desert, of river and ocean. Demons might possess the pig, the goat, the horse, the lion, or the ibis, the raven or the hawk. The seven spirits of tempest, fire and destruction rose from the depths of ocean, and there were hosts of demons which could not be overcome or baffled by man without the assistance of the gods to whom they were hostile. Many were sexless; having no offspring, they were devoid of mercy and compassion. They penetrated everywhere:

The high enclosures, the broad enclosures, like a flood they pass through,
From house to house they dash along.
No door can shut them out;
No bolt can turn them back.
Through the door, like a snake, they glide,
Through the hinge, like the wind, they storm,
Tearing the wife from the embrace of the man,
Driving the freedman from his family home.

These furies did not confine their unwelcomed attentions to mankind alone:

They hunt the doves from their cotes,
And drive the birds from their nests,
And chase the marten from its hole....
Through the gloomy street by night they roam,
Smiting sheepfold and cattle pen,
Shutting up the land as with door and bolt.
– R. C. Thompson's translation

The Babylonian poet, like Burns, was filled with pity for the animals which suffered in the storm:

List'ning the doors an' winnocks rattle,
I thought me o' the ourie cattle,
Or silly sheep, wha bide this brattle
O' winter war....
Ilk happing bird, wee, helpless thing!
That in the merry months o' spring
Delighted me to hear thee sing,
What comes o' thee?
Whare wilt thou cow'r thy chittering wing,
And close thy e'e?

Tempest Fiends

According to Babylonian belief, "the great storms directed from heaven" were caused by demons. Mankind heard them "loudly roaring above, gibbering below". The south wind was raised by Shutu, a plumed storm demon resembling Hraesvelgur of the Icelandic Eddas:

Corpse-swallower sits at the end of heaven,
A Jotun in eagle form;
From his wings, they say, comes the wind which fares
Over all the dwellers of earth.

Legend of Adapa and the Storm Demon

The northern story of Thor's fishing, when he hooked and wounded the Midgard serpent, is recalled by the Babylonian legend of Adapa, son of the god Ea. This hero was engaged catching fish, when Shutu, the south wind, upset his boat. In his wrath Adapa immediately attacked the storm demon and shattered her pinions. Anu, the sky god, was moved to anger against Ea's son and summoned him to the Celestial Court. Adapa, however, appeared in garments of mourning and was forgiven.

Anu offered him the water of life and the bread of life which would have made him immortal, but Ea's son refused to eat or drink, believing, as his father had warned him, that the sky god desired him to partake of the bread of death and to drink of the water of death.

Wind Hags of Ancient Britain

Another terrible atmospheric demon was the south-west wind, which caused destructive storms and floods, and claimed many human victims like the Icelandic "corpse swallower". She was depicted with lidless staring eyes, broad flat nose, mouth gaping horribly and showing tusk-like teeth, and with high cheek bones, heavy eyebrows and low bulging forehead.

In Scotland the hag of the south-west wind is similarly a bloodthirsty and fearsome demon. She is most virulent in the springtime. At Cromarty she is quaintly called "Gentle Annie" by the fisher folks, who repeat the saying: "When Gentle Annie is skyawlan (yelling) roond the heel of Ness (a promontory) wi' a white feather on her hat (the foam of big billows) they (the spirits) will be harrying (robbing) the crook" – that is, the pot which hangs from the crook is empty during the spring storms, which prevent fishermen going to sea.

In England the wind hag is Black Annis, who dwells in a Leicestershire hill cave. She may be identical with the Irish hag Anu, associated with the "Paps of Anu". According to Gaelic lore, this wind demon of spring is the "Cailleach" (old wife). She gives her name In the Highland calendar to the stormy period of late spring; she raises gale after gale to prevent the coming of summer.

Angerboda, the Icelandic hag, is also a storm demon, but represents the east wind. A Tyrolese folk tale tells of three magic maidens who dwelt on Jochgrimm mountain, where they "brewed the winds". Their demon lovers were Ecke, "he who causes fear"; Vasolt, "he who causes dismay"; and the scornful Dietrich in his mythical character of Donar or Thunor (Thor), the thunderer.

Zu Bird Legend and Indian Garuda Myth

Another Sumerian storm demon was the Zu bird, which is represented among the stars by Pegasus and Taurus. A legend relates that this "worker of evil, who raised the head of evil", once aspired to rule the gods, and stole from Bel, "the lord" of deities, the Tablets of Destiny, which gave him his power over the Universe as controller of the fates of all. The Zu bird escaped with the Tablets and found shelter on its mountain top in Arabia. Anu called on Ramman, the thunderer, to attack the Zu bird, but he was afraid; other gods appear to have shrunk from the conflict. How the rebel was overcome is not certain, because the legend survives in fragmentary form.

There is a reference, however, to the moon god setting out towards the mountain in Arabia with purpose to outwit the Zu bird and recover the lost Tablets. How he fared it is impossible to ascertain. In another legend – that of Etana – the mother serpent, addressing the sun god, Shamash, says:

Thy net is like unto the broad earth;
Thy snare is like unto the distant heaven!
Who hath ever escaped from thy net?
Even Zu, the worker of evil, who raised the head of evil [did not escape]!
– L. W. King's translation

In Indian mythology, Garuda, half giant, half eagle, robs the Amrita (ambrosia) of the gods which gives them their power and renders them immortal. It had assumed a golden body, bright as the sun. Indra, the thunderer, flung his bolt in vain; he could not wound Garuda, and only displaced a single feather. Afterwards, however, he stole the moon goblet containing the Amrita, which Garuda had delivered to his enemies, the serpents, to free his mother from bondage. This Indian eagle giant became the vehicle of the god Vishnu, and, according to the Mahabharata, "mocked the wind with his fleetness".

It would appear that the Babylonian Zu bird symbolized the summer sandstorms from the Arabian desert. Thunder is associated with the rainy season, and it may have been assumed, therefore, that the thunder god was powerless against the sandstorm demon, who was chased, however, by the moon, and finally overcome by the triumphant sun when it broke through the darkening sand drift and brightened heaven and earth, "netting" the rebellious demon who desired to establish the rule of evil over gods and mankind.

Legend of the Eagle and the Serpent

In the "Legend of Etana" the Eagle, another demon which links with the Indian Garuda, slayer of serpents, devours the brood of the Mother Serpent. For this offence against divine law, Shamash, the sun god, pronounces the Eagle's doom. He instructs the Mother Serpent to slay a wild ox and conceal herself in its entrails. The Eagle comes to feed on the carcass, unheeding the warning of one of his children, who says, "The serpent lies in this wild ox":

He swooped down and stood upon the wild ox,
The Eagle … examined the flesh;
He looked about carefully before and behind him;
He again examined the flesh;
He looked about carefully before and behind him,
Then, moving swiftly, he made for the hidden parts.
'When he entered into the midst,
The serpent seized him by his wing.

In vain the Eagle appealed for mercy to the Mother Serpent, who was compelled to execute the decree of Shamash; she tore off the Eagle's pinions, wings and claws, and threw him into a pit where he perished from hunger and thirst. This myth may refer to the ravages of a winged demon of disease who was thwarted by the sacrifice of an ox. The Mother Serpent appears to be identical with an ancient goddess of maternity resembling the Egyptian Bast, the serpent mother of Bubastis. According to Sumerian belief, Nintu, "a form of the goddess Ma", was half a serpent. On her head there is a horn; she is "girt about the loins"; her left arm holds "a babe suckling her breast":

From her head to her loins
The body is that of a naked woman;
From the loins to the sole of the foot
Scales like those of a snake are visible.
– R. C. Thompson's translation

Demons and the Moon God

The close association of gods and demons is illustrated in an obscure myth which may refer to an eclipse of the moon or a night storm at the beginning of the rainy season. The demons go to war against the high gods, and are assisted by Adad (Ramman) the thunderer, Shamash the sun and Ishtar. They desire to wreck the heavens, the home of Anu:

They clustered angrily round the crescent of the moon god,
And won over to their aid Shamash, the mighty, and Adad, the warrior,
And Ishtar, who with Anu, the King,
Hath founded a shining dwelling.

The moon god Sin, "the seed of mankind", was darkened by the demons who raged, "rushing loose over the land" like to the wind. Bel called upon his messenger, whom he sent to Ea in the ocean depths, saying: "My son Sin … hath been grievously bedimmed". Ea lamented, and dispatched his son Merodach to net the demons by magic, using "a two-coloured cord from the hair of a virgin kid and from the wool of a virgin lamb".

Plague Deities

As in India, where Shitala, the Bengali goddess of smallpox, for instance, is worshipped when the dreaded disease she controls becomes epidemic, so in Babylonia the people sought to secure immunity from attack by worshipping spirits of disease. A tablet relates that Ura, a plague demon, once resolved to destroy all life, but ultimately consented to spare those who praised his name and exalted him in recognition of his bravery and power. This could be accomplished by reciting a formula. Indian serpent worshippers believe that their devotions "destroy all danger proceeding from snakes".

Classification of Spirits

Like the Ancient Egyptians, the Babylonians also had their kindly spirits who brought luck and the various enjoyments of life. A good "labartu" might attend on a human being like a household fairy of India or Europe: a friendly "shedu" could protect a household against the attacks of fierce demons and human enemies. Even the spirits of Fate who served Anu, god of the sky, and that "Nom" of the Underworld, Eresh-ki-gal, queen of Hades, might sometimes be propitious: if the deities were successfully invoked they could cause the Fates to smite spirits of disease and bringers of ill luck. Damu, a friendly fairy goddess, was well loved, because she inspired pleasant dreams, relieved the sufferings of the afflicted and restored to good health those patients whom she selected to favour.

In the Egyptian Book of the Dead the kindly spirits are overshadowed by the evil ones, because the various magical spells which were put on record were directed against those supernatural beings who were enemies of mankind. Similarly in Babylonia the fragments of this class of literature which survive deal mainly with wicked and vengeful demons. It appears probable, however, that the highly emotional Sumerians and Akkadians were on occasion quite as cheerful a people as the inhabitants of ancient Egypt. Although they were surrounded by bloodthirsty furies who desired to shorten their days, and their nights were filled with vague lowering phantoms which inspired fear, they no doubt shared, in their charm-protected houses, a comfortable feeling of security after performing magical ceremonies, and were happy enough when they gathered round flickering lights to listen to ancient song and story and gossip about crops and traders, the members of the royal house, and the family affairs of their acquaintances.

The Babylonian spirit world, it will be seen, was of complex character. Its inhabitants were numberless, but often vaguely defined, and one class of demons linked with another. Like the European fairies of folk belief; the Babylonian spirits were extremely hostile and irresistible at certain seasonal periods; and they were fickle and perverse and difficult to please even when inclined to be friendly. They were also similarly manifested from time to time in various forms. Sometimes they were comely and beautiful; at other times they were apparitions of horror. The Jinn of present-day Arabians are of like character; these may be giants, cloudy shapes, comely women, serpents or cats, goats or pigs.

Traces of Progress from Animism to Monotheism

Some of the composite monsters of Babylonia may suggest the vague and exaggerated recollections of terror-stricken people who have had glimpses of unfamiliar wild beasts in the dusk or amidst reedy marshes. But they cannot be wholly accounted for in this way. While animals were often identified with supernatural beings, and foreigners were called "devils", it would be misleading to assert that the spirit world reflects confused folk memories of human and bestial enemies. Even when a demon was given concrete human form it remained essentially non-human: no ordinary weapon could inflict an injury, and it was never controlled by natural laws.

The spirits of disease and tempest and darkness were creations of fancy: they symbolized moods; they were the causes which explained effects. A sculptor or storyteller who desired to convey an impression of a spirit of storm or pestilence created monstrous forms to inspire terror. Sudden and unexpected visits of fierce and devastating demons were accounted for by asserting that they had wings like eagles, were nimble footed as gazelles, cunning and watchful as serpents; that they had claws to clutch, horns to gore and powerful fore legs like a lion to smite down victims. Withal they drank blood like ravens and devoured corpses like hyaenas.

Monsters were all the more repulsive when they were partly human. The human-headed snake or the snake-headed man and the man with the horns of a wild bull and the legs of a goat were horrible in the extreme. Evil spirits might sometimes achieve success by practising deception. They might appear as beautiful girls or handsome men and seize unsuspecting victims in deathly embrace or leave them demented and full of grief, or come as birds and suddenly assume awesome shapes.

Fairies and elves, and other half-human demons, are sometimes regarded as degenerate gods. It will be seen, however, that while certain spirits developed into deities, others remained something between these two classes of supernatural beings: they might attend upon gods and goddesses, or operate independently now against mankind and now against deities even. The "namtaru", for instance, was a spirit of fate, the son of Bel-Enlil and Eresh-ki -gal, queen of Hades. "Apparently", writes Professor Pinches, "he executed the instructions given him concerning the fate of men, and could also have power over certain of the gods".

To this middle class belong the evil gods who rebelled against the beneficent deities. According to Hebridean folk belief, the fallen angels are divided into three classes – the fairies, the "nimble men" (aurora borealis) and the "blue men of the Minch". In Beowulf the "brood of Cain" includes "monsters and elves and sea-devils–giants also, who long time fought with God, for which he gave them their reward". Similarly the Babylonian spirit groups are liable to division and subdivision. The various classes may be regarded as relics of the various stages of development from crude animism to sublime monotheism: in the fragmentary legends we trace the floating material from which great mythologies have been framed.

Priestly Magicians, Wizards and Witches

THERE WERE AT LEAST TWO CLASSES OF PRIESTS who dealt in the occult – the *barû*, or seers, and the *asipû*, or wizards. The caste of the barû was a very ancient one, dating at least from the time of Hammurabi. The barû performed divination by consulting the livers of animals and also by observation of the flight of birds. We find many of the kings of Babylonia consulting this class of soothsayer. Sennacherib, for example, sought from the barû the cause of his father's violent death. The asipû, on the other hand, was the remover of taboo and bans of all sorts; he chanted the rites described in the magical texts, and performed the ceremony of atonement. It is:

He that stilleth all to rest, that pacifieth all.
By whose incantations everything is at peace.
The gods are upon his right hand and his left, they are behind and before him.

The wizard and the witch were known as *Kassapu* or *Kassaptu*. These were the sorcerers or magicians proper, and that they were considered dangerous to the community is shown by the manner in which they are treated by the code of Hammurabi, in which it is ordained that he who charges a man with sorcery and can justify the charge shall obtain the sorcerer's house, and the sorcerer shall plunge into the river. But if the sorcerer be not drowned then he who accused him shall be put to death and the wrongly accused man shall have his house.

A series of texts known as 'Maklu' provides us, among other things, with a striking picture of the Babylonian witch. It tells how she prowls the streets, searching for victims, snatching love from handsome men, and withering beauteous women. At another time she is depicted sitting in the shade of the wall making spells and fashioning images. The suppliant prays that her magic may revert upon herself, that the image of her which he has made, and doubtless rendered into the hands of the priest, shall be burnt by the fire-god, that her words may be forced back into her mouth. "May her mouth be fat, may her tongue be salt", continues the prayer. The *baltappen-plant* along with sesame is sent against her. "O, witch, like the circlet of this seal may thy face grow green and yellow!"

An Assyrian text says of a sorceress that her bounds are the whole world, that she can pass over all mountains. The writer states that near his door he has posted a servant, on the right and left of his door has he set Lugalgirra and Allamu, that they might kill the witch.

The library of Assur-bani-pal contains many cuneiform tablets dealing with magic, but there are also extant many magical tablets of the later Babylonian Empire. These were known to the Babylonians by some name or word, indicative perhaps of the special sphere of their activities. Thus we have the Maklu ('burning'), Surpu ('consuming'), Utukki limnûti ('evil spirits') and Labartu ('witch-hag') series, besides many other texts dealing with magical practices.

The Maklu series deals with spells against witches and wizards, images of whom are to be consumed by fire to the accompaniment of suitable spells and prayers. The Surpu series contains prayers and incantations against taboo. That against evil spirits provides the haunted with spells which will exorcise demons, ghosts and the powers of the air generally, and place devils under a ban. In other magical tablets the diseases to which poor humanity is prone are guarded against, and instructions are given on the manner in which they may be transferred to the dead bodies of animals, usually swine or goats.

A Toothache Myth

THE ASSYRIAN PHYSICIAN had, inevitably, to be something of a demonologist, as possession by devils was held to be the cause of divers diseases, and we find incantations sprinkled among prescriptions. Occasionally, too, we come upon the fag-end of a folktale or dip momentarily into myth, as in a prescription for the toothache, compounded of fermented drink, the plant *sakilbir* and oil – probably as efficacious in the case of that malady as most modern ones are. The story attached to the cure is as follows:

When Anu had created the heavens, the earth created the rivers, the rivers the canals, and the canals the marshes, which in turn created the worm. And the worm came weeping before Ea, saying, "What wilt thou give me for my food, what wilt thou give me for my devouring?" "I will give thee ripe figs", replied the god, "ripe figs and scented wood". "Bah", replied the worm, "what are ripe figs to me, or what is scented wood? Let me drink among the teeth and batten on the gums that I may devour the blood of the teeth and the strength thereof". This tale alludes to a Babylonian superstition that worms consume the teeth.

The Word of Power

AS IN EGYPT, the word of power was held in great reverence by the magicians of Chaldea, who believed that the name, preferably the secret name, of a god possessed sufficient force in its mere syllables to defeat and scatter the hordes of evil things that surrounded and harassed mankind.

The names of Ea and Merodach were, perhaps, most frequently used to carry destruction into the ranks of the demon army. It was also necessary to know the name of the devil or person against whom his spells were directed. If to this could be added a piece of hair, or the nail-parings in the case of a human being, then special efficacy was given to the enchantment. But just as hair or nails were part of a man so was his name, and hence the great virtue ascribed to names in art-magic, ancient and modern. The name was, as it were, the vehicle by means of which the magician established a link between himself and his victim, and the Babylonians in exorcising sickness or disease of any kind were wont to recite long catalogues of the names of evil spirits and demons in the hope that by so doing they might chance to light upon that especial individual who was the cause of the malady. Even long lists of names of persons who had died premature deaths were often recited in order to ensure that they would not return to torment the living.

Babylonian Vampires

IN ALL LANDS AND EPOCHS the grisly conception of the vampire has gained a strong hold upon the imagination of the common people, and this was no less the case in Babylonia and Assyria than elsewhere.

There have not been wanting those who believed that vampirism was confined to the Slavonic race alone, and that the peoples of Russia, Bohemia and the Balkan Peninsula were the sole possessors of the vampire legend. Recent research, however, has exposed the fallacy of this theory and has shown that, far from being the property of the Slavs or even of Aryan peoples, this horrible belief is or was the possession of practically every race, savage or civilized, that is known to anthropology. The seven evil spirits of Assyria are, among other things, vampires of no uncertain type. An ancient poem which was chanted by them commences thus (note the last lines in particular):

Seven are they! Seven are they!
In the ocean deep, seven are they!
Battening in heaven, seven are they!
Bred in the depths of the ocean;
Not male nor female are they,
But are as the roaming wind-blast.
No wife have they, no son can they beget;
Knowing neither mercy nor pity,
They hearken not to prayer, to prayer.
They are as horses reared amid the hills,
The Evil Ones of Ea;
Throne-bearers to the gods are they,
They stand in the highway to befoul the path;
Evil are they, evil are they!

Seven are they, seven are they,
Twice seven are they!

Destructive storms (and) evil winds are they,
An evil blast that heraldeth the baneful storm,
An evil blast, forerunner of the baleful storm.
They are mighty children, mighty sons,
Heralds of the Pestilence.
Throne-bearers of Ereskigal,
They are the flood which rusheth through the land.
Seven gods of the broad earth,
Seven robber(?)-gods are they,
Seven gods of might,
Seven evil demons,
Seven evil demons of oppression,
Seven in heaven and seven on earth.

Spirits that minish heaven and earth,
That minish the land,
Spirits that minish the land,
Of giant strength,
Of giant strength and giant tread,
Demons (like) raging bulls, great ghosts,
Ghosts that break through all houses,
Demons that have no shame,
Seven are they!
Knowing no care, they grind the land like corn;
Knowing no mercy, they rage against mankind,
They spill their blood like rain,
Devouring their flesh (and) sucking their veins.
Where the images of the gods are, there they quake (?)
In the Temple of Nabu, who fertilises the shoots (?) of wheat.
They are demons full of violence, ceaselessly devouring blood.

Gods Once Demons

MANY OF THE BABYLONIAN GODS retained traces of their primitive demoniacal characteristics, and this applies to the great triad, Ea, Anu and En-lil, who probably evolved into godhead from an animistic group of nature spirits. Each of these gods was accompanied by demon groups. Thus the disease-demons were 'the beloved sons of Bel', the fates were the seven daughters of Anu, and the seven storm-demons the children of Ea. In a magical incantation describing the primitive monster form of Ea it is said that his head is like a serpent's, the ears are those of a basilisk, his horns are twisted into curls, his body is a sun-fish full of stars, his feet are armed with claws and the sole of his foot has no heel.

Ea was 'the great magician of the gods'; his sway over the forces of nature was secured by the performance of magical rites, and his services were obtained by human beings who performed requisite ceremonies and repeated appropriate spells. Although he might be worshipped and propitiated in his temple at Eridu, he could also be conjured in mud huts. The latter, indeed, as in Mexico, appear to have been the oldest holy places.

The Legend of Ura

It is told that Ura, the dread demon of disease, once made up his mind to destroy mankind. But Ishnu, his counsellor, appeased him so that he abandoned his intention, and he gave humanity a chance of escape. Whoever should praise Ura and magnify his name would, he said, rule the four quarters of the world, and should have none to oppose him. He should not die in pestilence, and his speech should bring him into favour with the great ones of the earth. Wherever a tablet with the song of Ura was set up, in that house there should be immunity from the pestilence.

Purification

PURIFICATION BY WATER entered largely into Babylonian magic. The ceremony known as the 'Incantation of Eridu', so frequently alluded to in Babylonian magical texts, was probably some form of purification by water, relating as it does to the home of Ea, the sea-god.

Another ceremony prescribes the mingling of water from a pool 'that no hand hath touched', with tamarisk, *mastakal*, ginger, alkali and mixed wine. Therein must be placed a shining ring, and the mixture is then to be poured upon the patient. A root of saffron is then to be taken and pounded with pure salt and alkali and fat of the *matku*-bird brought from the mountains, and with this strange mixture the body of the patient is to be anointed.

The Chamber of the Priest-Magician

LET US ATTEMPT TO DESCRIBE the treatment of a case by a priest-physician-magician of Babylonia. The following is a rather obscure one, but by the aid of imagination as well as the assistance of Babylonian representation we may construct a tolerably clear picture.

The chamber of the sage is almost certain to be situated in some nook in one of those vast and imposing fanes which more closely resembled cities than mere temples. We draw the curtain and enter a rather darksome room. The atmosphere is pungent with chemic odours, and ranged on shelves disposed upon the tiled walls are numerous jars, great and small, containing the fearsome compounds which the practitioner applies to the sufferings of Babylonian humanity. The asipu, shaven and austere, asks us what we desire of him, and in the role of Babylonian citizens we acquaint him with the fact that our lives are made miserable for us by a witch who sends upon us misfortune after misfortune, now the blight or some equally intractable and horrible disease, now an evil wind, now unspeakable enchantments which torment us unceasingly. In his capacity of physician the asipu examines our bodies, shrunken and exhausted with fever or rheumatism, and having prescribed for us, compounds the mixture with his own hands and enjoins us to its regular application. He mixes various ingredients in a stone mortar, whispering his spells the while, with many a prayer to Ea the beneficent and Merodach the all-powerful that we may be restored to health. Then he promises to visit us at our dwelling and gravely bids us adieu, after expressing the hope that we will graciously contribute to the upkeep of the house of religion to which he is attached.

Leaving the darkened haunt of the asipu for the brilliant sunshine of a Babylonian summer afternoon, we are at first inclined to forget our fears, and to laugh away the horrible superstitions, the relics of barbarian ancestors, which weigh us down. But as night approaches we grow more fearful, we crouch with the children in the darkest corner of our clay-brick dwelling, and tremble at every sound. The rushing of the wind overhead is for us the noise of the Labartu, the hag-demon, come hither to tear from us our little ones, or perhaps a rat rustling in the straw may seem to us the Alu-demon. The ghosts of the dead gibber at the threshold, and even pale Uru, lord of disease, himself may glance in at the tiny window with ghastly countenance and eager, red eyes. The pains of rheumatism assail us. Ha, the evil witch is at work, thrusting thorns into the waxen images made in our shape that we may suffer the torment brought about by sympathetic magic, to which we would rather refer our aches than to the circumstance that we dwell hard by the river-swamps.

A loud knocking resounds at the door. We tremble anew and the children scream. At last the dread powers of evil have come to summon us to the final ordeal, or perhaps the witch herself, grown bold by reason of her immunity, has come to wreak fresh vengeance. The flimsy door of boards is thrown open, and to our unspeakable relief the stern face of the asipu appears beneath the flickering light of the taper. We shout with joy, and the children cluster around the priest, clinging to his garments and clasping his knees.

The Witch-Finding

The priest smiles at our fear, and motioning us to sit in a circle produces several waxen figures of demons which he places on the floor. It is noticeable that these figures all appear to be bound with miniature ropes. Taking one of these in the shape of a Labartu or hag-demon, the priest places before it twelve small cakes made from a peculiar kind of meal. He then pours out a libation of water, places the image of a small black dog beside that of the witch, lays a piece of the heart of a young pig on the mouth of the figure and some white bread and a box of ointment beside it. He then chants something like the following: "May a guardian spirit be present at my side when I draw near unto the sick man, when I examine his muscles, when I compose his limbs, when I sprinkle the water of Ea upon him. Avoid thee whether thou art an evil spirit or an evil demon, an evil ghost or an evil devil, an evil god or an evil fiend, hag-demon, ghoul, sprite, phantom, or wraith, or any disease, fever, headache, shivering, or any sorcery, spell, or enchantment".

Having recited some such words of power the asipu then directs us to keep the figure at the head of our bed for three nights, then to bury it beneath the earthen floor. But alas! no cure results. The witch still torments us by day and night, and once more we have recourse to the priest-doctor; the ceremony is gone through again, but still the family health does not improve. The little ones suffer from fever, and bad luck consistently dogs us. After a stormy scene between husband and wife, who differ regarding the qualifications of the asipu, another practitioner is called in. He is younger and more enterprising than the last, and he has not yet learned that half the business of the physician is to 'nurse' his patients, in the financial sense of the term. Whereas the elderly asipu had gone quietly home to bed after prescribing for us, this young physician, who has his spurs to win, after being consulted goes home to his clay surgery and hunts up a likely exorcism.

Next day, armed with this wordy weapon, he arrives at our dwelling and, placing a waxen image of the witch upon the floor, vents upon it the full force of his rhetoric. As he is on the point of leaving, screams resound from a neighbouring cabin. Bestowing upon us a look of the deepest meaning our asipu darts to the hut opposite and hales forth an ancient crone, whose appearance of age and illness give her a most sinister look. At once we recognize in her a wretch who dared to menace our children when in innocent play they cast hot ashes upon her thatch and introduced hot swamp water into her cistern. In righteous wrath we lay hands on the abandoned being who for so many months has cast a blight upon our lives. She exclaims that the pains of death have seized upon her, and we laugh in triumph, for we know that the superior magic of our asipu has taken effect. On the way to the river we are joined by neighbours, who rejoice with us that we have caught the witch. Great is the satisfaction of the party when at last the devilish crone is cast headlong into the stream.

But ere many seconds pass we begin to look incredulously upon each other, for the wicked one refuses to sink. This means that she is innocent! Then, awful moment, we find every eye directed upon us, we who were so happy and light-hearted but a moment before. We tremble, for we know how severe are the laws against the indiscriminate accusation of those suspected of witchcraft. As the ancient crone continues to float, a loud murmuring arises in the crowd, and with quaking limbs and eyes full of terror we snatch up our children and make a dash for freedom.

Luckily the asipu accompanies us so that the crowd dare not pursue, and indeed, so absurdly changeable is human nature, most of them are busied in rescuing the old woman. In a few minutes we have placed all immediate danger of pursuit behind us. The asipu has departed to his temple, richer in the experience by the lesson of a false 'prescription'. After a hurried consultation we quit the town, skirt the arable land which fringes it, and plunge into the desert. She who was opposed to the employment of a young and inexperienced asipu does not make matters any better by reiterating "I told you so". And he who favoured a 'second opinion', on paying a night visit to the city, discovers that the 'witch' has succumbed to her harsh treatment; that his house has been made over to her relatives by way of compensation, and that a legal process has been taken out against him. Returning to his wife he acquaints her with the sad news, and hand in hand with their weeping offspring they turn and face the desert.

The Magic Circle

THE MAGIC CIRCLE, as in use among the Chaldean sorcerers, bears many points of resemblance to that described in mediaeval works on magic. The Babylonian magician, when describing the circle, made seven little winged figures, which he set before an image of the god Nergal. After doing so he stated that he had covered them with a dark robe and bound them with a coloured cord, setting beside them tamarisk and the heart of the palm, that he had completed the magic circle and had surrounded them with a sprinkling of lime and flour.

That the magic circle of mediaeval times must have been evolved from the Chaldean is plain from the strong resemblance between the two. Directions for the making of a mediaeval magic circle are as follows:

In the first place the magician is supposed to fix upon a spot proper for such a purpose, which must be either in a subterranean vault, hung round with black, and lighted by a magical torch, or else in the centre of some thick wood or desert, or upon some extensive unfrequented plain, where several roads meet, or amidst the ruins of ancient castles, abbeys, or monasteries, or amongst the rocks on the seashore, in some private detached churchyard, or any other melancholy place between the hours of twelve and one in the night, either when the moon shines very bright, or else when the elements are disturbed with storms of thunder, lightning, wind and rain; for, in these places, times and seasons, it is contended that spirits can with less difficulty manifest themselves to mortal eyes, and continue visible with the least pain.

When the proper time and place are fixed upon, a magic circle is to be formed within which the master and his associates are carefully to retire. The reason assigned by magicians and others for the institution and use of the circles is, that so much ground being blessed and consecrated by holy words and ceremonies has a secret force to expel all evil spirits from the bounds thereof, and, being sprinkled with sacred water, the ground is purified from all uncleanness; beside the holy names of God being written over every part of it, its force becomes proof against all evil spirits.

More on Babylonian Demons

BABYLONIAN DEMONS WERE LEGION and most of them exceedingly malevolent. The Utukku was an evil spirit that lurked generally in the desert, where it lay in wait for unsuspecting travellers, but it did not confine its haunts to the more barren places, for it was also to be found among the mountains, in graveyards and even in the sea. An evil fate befell the man upon whom it looked.

The Rabisu is another lurking demon that secretes itself in unfrequented spots to leap upon passers-by. The Labartu, which has already been alluded to, is, strangely enough, spoken of as the daughter of Anu. She was supposed to dwell in the mountains or in marshy places, and was particularly addicted to the destruction of children. Babylonian mothers were wont to hang charms round their children's necks to guard them against this horrible hag.

The Sedu appears to have been in some senses a guardian spirit and in others a being of evil propensities. It is often appealed to at the end of invocations along with the Lamassu, a spirit of a similar type. These malign influences were probably the prototypes of the Arabian jinn, to whom they have many points of resemblance.

Many Assyrian spirits were half-human and half-supernatural, and some of them were supposed to contract unions with human beings, like the Arabian jinn. The offspring of such unions was supposed to be a spirit called Alu, which haunted ruins and deserted buildings and indeed entered the houses of men like a ghost to steal their sleep. Ghosts proper were also common enough, as has already been observed, and those who had not been buried were almost certain to return to harass mankind. It was dangerous even to look upon a corpse, lest the spirit or edimmu of the dead man should seize upon the beholder. The Assyrians seemed to be of the opinion that a ghost like a vampire might drain away the strength of the living, and long formulae were in existence containing numerous names of haunting spirits, one of which it was hoped would apply to the tormenting ghost, and these were used for the purposes of exorcism. To lay a spirit the following articles were necessary: seven small loaves of roast corn, the hoof of a dark-coloured ox, flour of roast corn and a little leaven. The ghosts were then asked why they tormented the haunted man, after which the flour and leaven were kneaded into a paste in the horn of an ox and a small libation poured into a hole in the earth. The leaven dough was then placed in the hoof of an ox, and another libation poured out with an incantation to the god Shamash. In another case figures of the dead man and the living person to whom the spirit has appeared are to be made and libations poured out before both of them, then the figure of the dead man is to be buried and that of the living man washed in pure water, the whole ceremony being typical of sympathetic magic, which thus supposed the burial of the body of the ghost and the purification of the living man. In the morning incense was to be offered up before the sun-god at his rising, when sweet woods were to be burned and a libation of sesame wine poured out.

If a human being was troubled by a ghost, it was necessary that he should be anointed with various substances in order that the result of the ghostly contact might be nullified.

An old text says, "When a ghost appeareth in the house of a man there will be a destruction of that house. When it speaketh and hearkeneth for an answer the man will die, and there will be lamentation".

Taboo

THE BELIEF IN TABOO was universal in ancient Chaldea. Amongst the Babylonians it was known as *mamit*. There were taboos on many things, but especially upon corpses and uncleanness of all kinds. We find the taboo generally alluded to in a text "as the barrier that none can pass".

Among all barbarous peoples the taboo is usually intended to hedge in the sacred thing from the profane person or the common people, but it may also be employed for sanitary reasons. Thus the flesh of certain animals, such as the pig, may not be eaten in hot countries. Food must not be prepared by those who are in the slightest degree suspected of uncleanness, and these laws are usually of the most rigorous character; but should a man violate the taboo placed upon certain foods, then he himself often became taboo. No one might have any intercourse with him. He was left to his own devices, and, in short, became a sort of pariah. In the Assyrian texts we find many instances of this kind of taboo, and numerous were the supplications that these might be removed. If one drank water from an unclean cup he had violated a taboo. Like the Arab he might not "lick the platter clean". If he were taboo he might not touch another man, he might not converse with him, he might not pray to the gods, he might not even be interceded for by anyone else. In fact he was excommunicate. If a man cast his eye upon water which another person had washed his hands in, or if he came into contact with a person who had not yet performed his ablutions, he became unclean. An entire purification ritual was incumbent on any Assyrian who touched or even looked upon a dead man.

It may be asked, wherefore was this elaborate cleanliness essential to avoid taboo? The answer undoubtedly is – because of the belief in the power of sympathetic magic. Did one come into contact with a person who was in any way unclean, or with a corpse or other unpleasant object, he was supposed to come within the radius of the evil which emanated from it.

Popular Superstitions

THE SUPERSTITION THAT THE EVIL-EYE of a witch or a wizard might bring blight upon an individual or community was as persistent in Chaldea as elsewhere. Incantations frequently allude to it as among the causes of sickness, and exorcisms were duly directed against it. Even today, on the site of the ruins of Babylon children are protected against it by fastening small blue objects to their headgear.

Just as mould from a grave was supposed by the witches of the Middle Ages to be particularly efficacious in magic, so was the dust of the temple supposed to possess hidden virtue in Assyria. If one pared one's nails or cut one's hair it was considered necessary to bury them lest a sorcerer should discover them and use them against their late owner; for a sorcery performed upon a part was by the law of sympathetic magic thought to reflect upon the whole. A like superstition attached to the discarded clothing of people, for among barbarian or uncultured folk the apparel is regarded as part and parcel of the man. Even in our own time simple and uneducated people tear a piece from their garments and hang it as an offering on the bushes around any of the numerous healing wells in the country that they may have journeyed to. This is a survival of the custom of sacrificing the part for the whole.

If one desired to get rid of a headache one had to take the hair of a young kid and give it to a wise woman, who would "spin it on the right side and double it on the left", then it was to be bound into fourteen knots and the incantation of Ea pronounced upon it, after which it was to be bound round the head and neck of the sick man. For defects in eyesight the Assyrians wove black and white threads or hairs together, muttering incantations the while, and these were placed upon the eyes. It was thought, too, that the tongues of evil spirits or sorcerers could be 'bound', and that a net because of its many knots was efficacious in keeping evilly disposed magicians away.

Omens and the Practice of Liver-reading

DIVINATION AS PRACTISED by means of augury was a rite of the first importance among the Babylonians and Assyrians. This was absolutely distinct from divination by astrology. The favourite method of augury among the Chaldeans of old was that by examination of the liver of a slaughtered animal.

It was thought that when an animal was offered up in sacrifice to a god that the deity identified himself for the time being with that animal, and that the beast thus afforded a means of indicating the wishes of the god. Now among people in a primitive state of culture the soul is almost invariably supposed to reside in the liver instead of in the heart or brain. More blood is secreted by the liver than by any other organ in the body, and upon the opening of a carcass it appears the most striking, the most central and the most sanguinary of the vital parts. The liver was, in fact, supposed by early peoples to be the fountain of the blood supply and therefore of life itself. Hepatoscopy or divination from the liver was undertaken by the Chaldeans for the purpose of determining what the gods had in mind. The soul of the animal became for the nonce the soul of the god, therefore if the signs of the liver of the sacrificed animal could be read the mind of the god became clear, and his intentions regarding the future were known. The animal usually sacrificed was a sheep, the liver of which animal is most complicated in appearance. The two lower lobes are sharply divided from one another and are separated from the upper by a narrow depression, and the whole surface is covered with markings and fissures, lines and curves which give it much the appearance of a map on which roads and valleys are outlined. This applies to the freshly excised liver only, and these markings are never the same in any two livers.

Certain priests were set apart for the practice of liver-reading, and these were exceedingly expert, being able to decipher the hepatoscopic signs with great skill. They first examined the gallbladder, which might be reduced or swollen. They inferred various circumstances from the several ducts and the shapes and sizes of the lobes and their appendices. Diseases of the liver, too, particularly common among sheep in all countries, were even more frequent among these animals in the marshy portions of the Euphrates Valley.

The literature connected with this species of augury is very extensive, and Assur-bani-pal's library contained thousands of fragments describing the omens deduced from the practice. These enumerate the chief appearances of the liver, as the shade of the colour of the gall, the length of the ducts and so forth. The lobes were divided into sections, lower, medial and higher, and the interpretation varied from the phenomena therein observed. The markings on the liver possessed various names, such as 'palaces', 'weapons', 'paths' and 'feet', which terms remind us somewhat of the bizarre nomenclature of astrology. Later in the progress of the art the various combinations of signs came to be known so well, and there were so many cuneiform texts in existence which afforded instruction in them, that a liver could be quickly 'read' by the *barû* or reader, a name which was afterward applied to the astrologists as well and to those who divined through various other natural phenomena.

One of the earliest instances on record of hepatoscopy is that regarding Naram-Sin, who consulted a sheep's liver before declaring war. The great Sargon did likewise, and we find Gudea applying to his 'liver inspectors' when attempting to discover a favourable time for laying the foundations of the temple of Nin-girsu. Throughout the whole history of the Babylonian monarchy in fact, from its early beginnings to its end, we find this system in vogue. Whether it was in force in Sumerian times we have no means of knowing, but there is every likelihood that such was the case.

The Ritual of Hepatoscopy

Quite an elaborate ritual grew up around the readings of the omens by the examination of the liver. The barû who officiated must first of all purify himself and don special apparel for the ceremony. Prayers were then offered up to Shamash and Hadad or Rammon, who were known as the 'lords of divination'. Specific questions were usually put. The sheep selected for sacrifice must be without blemish, and the manner of slaughtering it and the examination of its liver must be made with the most meticulous care. Sometimes the signs were doubtful, and upon such occasions a second sheep was sacrificed.

Nabonidus, the last King of Babylon, on one occasion desired to restore a temple to the moon-god at Harran. He wished to be certain that this step commended itself to Merodach, the chief deity of Babylonia, so he applied to the 'liver inspectors' of his day and found that the omen was favourable. We find him also desirous of making a certain symbol of the sun-god in accordance with an ancient pattern. He placed a model of this before Shamash and consulted the liver of a sheep to ascertain whether the god approved of the offering, but on three separate occasions the signs were unfavourable. Nabonidus then concluded that the model of the symbol could not have been correctly reproduced, and on replacing it by another he found the signs propitious. In order, however, that there should be no mistake he sought among the records of the past for the result of a liver inspection on a similar occasion, and by comparing the omens he became convinced that he was safe in making a symbol.

Peculiar signs, when they were found connected with events of importance, were specially noted in the literature of liver divination, and were handed down from generation to generation of diviners. Thus a number of omens are associated with Gilgamesh, the mythical hero of the Babylonian epic, and a certain condition of the gall-bladder is said to indicate "the omen of Urumush, the king, whom the men of his palace killed".

Bad signs and good signs are enumerated in the literature of the subject. Thus like most peoples the Babylonians considered the right side as lucky and the left as unlucky. Any sign on the right side of the gallbladder, ducts or lobes, was supposed to refer to the king, the country, or the army, while a similar sign on the sinister side applied to the enemy. Thus a good sign on the right side applied to Babylonia or Assyria in a favourable sense, a bad sign on the right side in an unfavourable sense. A good sign on the left side was an omen favourable to the enemy, whereas a bad sign on the left side was, of course, to the native king or forces.

It would be out of place here to give a more extended description of the liver-reading of the ancient Chaldeans. Suffice it to say that the subject is a very complicated one in its deeper significance, and has little interest for the general reader in its advanced stages. Certain well-marked conditions of the liver could only indicate certain political, religious, or personal events. It will be more interesting if we attempt to visualise the act of divination by liver reading, as it was practised in ancient Babylonia, and if our imaginations break down in the process it is not the fault of the very large material they have to work upon.

The Missing Caravan

The ages roll back as a scroll, and I see myself as one of the great banker-merchants of Babylon, one of those princes of commerce whose contracts and agreements are found stamped upon clay cylinders where once the stately palaces of barter arose from the swarming streets of the city of Merodach. I have that morning been carried in my litter by sweating slaves, from my white house in a leafy suburb lying beneath the shadow of the lofty temple-city of Borsippa. As I reach my place of business I am aware of unrest, for the financial operations in which I engage are so closely watched that I may say without self-praise that I represent the pulse of Babylonian commerce. I enter the cool chamber where I usually transact my business, and where a pair of officious Persian slaves commence to fan me as soon as I take my seat. My head clerk enters and makes obeisance with an expression on his face eloquent of important news. It is as I expected – as I feared. The caravan from the Persian Gulf due to arrive at Babylon more than a week ago has not yet made its appearance, and although I had sent scouting parties as far as Ninnur, these have returned without bringing me the least intelligence regarding it.

I feel convinced that the caravan with my spices, woven fabrics, rare woods and precious stones will never come tinkling down the great central street to deposit its wealth at the doors of my warehouses; and the thought renders me so irritable that I sharply dismiss the Persian fan-bearers, and curse again and again the black-browed sons of Elam, who have doubtless looted my goods and cut the throats of my guards and servants. I go home at an early hour full of my misfortune. I cannot eat my evening meal. My wife gently asks me what ails me, but with a growl I refuse to enlighten her upon the cause of my annoyance. Still, however, she persists, and succeeds in breaking down my surly opposition.

"Why trouble thy heart concerning this thing when thou may know what has happened to thy goods and thy servants? Get thee tomorrow to the Baru, and he will enlighten thee", she says.

I start. After all, women have sense. There can be no harm in seeing the Baru and asking him to divine what has happened to my caravan. But I bethink me that I am wealthy, and that the priests love to pluck a well-feathered pigeon. I mention my suspicions of the priestly caste in no measured terms, to the distress of my devout wife and the amusement of my soldier-son.

Restlessly I toss upon my couch, and after a sleepless night feel that I cannot resume my business with the fear of loss upon me. So without breathing a word of my intention to my wife, I direct my litter-slaves to carry me to the great temple at Borsippa.

Arrived there, I enquire for the chief Baru. He is one of the friends of my youth, but for years our paths have diverged, and it is with surprise that he now greets me. I acquaint him with the nature of my dilemma, and nodding sympathetically he assures me that he will do his utmost to assist me. Somewhat reassured, I follow him into a tiled court near the far end of which stands a large altar. At a sign from him two priests bring in a live sheep and cut its throat. They then open the carcass and extract the liver. Immediately the chief Baru bends his grey head over it. For a long time he stares at it with the keenest attention. I begin to weary, and my old doubts regarding the sacerdotal caste return. At last the grey head rises from the long inspection, and the Baru turns to me with smiling face.

"The omen is good, my son", he says, with a cheerful intonation. "The compass and the hepatic duct are short. Thy path will be protected by thy Guardian Spirit, as will the path of thy servants. Go, and fear not".

He speaks so definitely and his words are so reassuring that I seize him by the hands, and, thanking him effusively, take my leave. I go down to my warehouses in a new spirit of hopefulness and disregard the disdainful or pitying looks cast in my direction. I sit unperturbed and dictate contracts and letters of credit to my scribe.

Ha! what is that? By Merodach, it is – it is the sound of bells! Up I leap, upsetting the wretched scribe who squats at my feet, and trampling upon his still wet clay tablets, I rush to the door. Down the street slowly advances a travel-worn caravan, and at the head of it there rides my trusty brown-faced captain, Babbar. He tumbles out of the saddle and kneels before me, but I raise him in a close embrace. All my goods, he assures me, are intact, and the cause of delay was a severe sickness which broke out among his followers. But all have recovered and my credit is restored.

As I turn to re-enter my warehouse with Babbar, a detaining hand is placed on my shoulder. It is a messenger from the chief Baru.

"My brother at the temple saw thy caravan coming from afar", he says politely, "and his message to thee, my son, is that, since thou hast so happily recovered thine own, thou shouldst devote a tithe of it to the service of the gods".

Mythological Monsters & Animals

Introduction

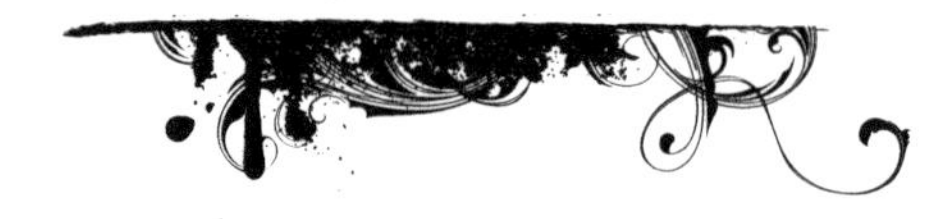

TIAWATH WAS NOT (as Lewis Spence explains) the only monster known to Babylonian mythology. But she is sometimes likened to or confounded with the serpent of darkness with which she had originally no connection whatever.

This being was, however, like Tiawath, the offspring of the great deep and the enemy of the divine powers. We are told in the second verse of Genesis that "the earth was without form and void, and darkness was upon the face of the deep", and therefore resembling the abyss of Babylonian myth. We are also informed that the serpent was esteemed as "more subtle than other beast of the field", and this, it has been pointed out by Professor Sayce, was probably because it was associated by the author or authors of Genesis with Ea, the god of waters and of wisdom. To Babylonian geographers as to the Greeks, the ocean was a coiling, snake-like thing, which was often alluded to as the great serpent, and this soon came to be considered as the source of all evil and misfortune. The serpent appears to have been called Aibu, 'the enemy'. We can see how the serpent of darkness, the offspring of chaos and confusion, became also the Hebrew symbol for mischief. He was first the source of physical and next the source of moral evil.

We will show how other animals and monsters had their place in Babylonian cult, including the gazelle, who represented Ea, and the goat, embodied in the god Uz. Adar, the sun-god of Nippur, was in the same manner connected with the pig, which may have been the totem of the city he ruled over; and many other gods had attendant animals or birds, like the sun-god of Kis, whose symbol was the eagle.

Winged Bulls

THE WINGED BULLS so closely identified with ancient Chaldean mythology were probably associated with Merodach.

These may have represented the original totemic forms of the gods in question, but we must not confound the bull forms of Merodach and Ea with those winged bulls which guarded the entrances to the temples. These, to perpetrate a double 'bull', were not bulls at all but divine beings, the gods or genii of the holy places. The human head attached to them indicated that the creature was endowed with humanity and the bull-like body symbolized strength. When the Babylonian translated the word 'bull' from the Akkadian tongue he usually rendered it 'hero' or 'strong one'. It is thought that the bull forms of Ea and Merodach must have originated at Eridu, for both of these deities were connected with the city. The Babylonians regarded the sky-country as a double of the plain in which they dwelt, and they believed that the gods as planets ploughed their way across the azure fields of air. Thus the sun was the 'Bull of Light', and Jupiter, the nearest of the planets to the ecliptic, was known as the 'Planet of the Bull of Light'.

The Dog in Babylonia

STRANGELY ENOUGH THE DOG was classed by the Babylonians as a monster animal and one to be despised and avoided. In a prayer against the powers of evil we read, "From the dog, the snake, the scorpion, the reptile and whatever is baleful ... may Merodach preserve us". We find that although the Babylonians possessed an excellent breed of dog they were not fond of depicting them either in painting or bas-relief.

Dogs are seen illustrated in a bas-relief of Assur-bani-pal, and five clay figures of dogs now in the British Museum represent hounds which belonged to that monarch. The names of these animals are very amusing, and appear to indicate that those who bestowed them must have suffered from a complete lack of the humorous sense, or else have been blessed with an overflow of it. Translated, the names are: 'He-ran-and-barked', 'The-Producer-of-Mischief', 'The-Biter-of-his-foes', 'The-Judge-of-his-companions' and 'The-Seizer-of-enemies'. How well these names would fit certain dogs we all know or have known! Here is good evidence from the buried centuries that dog nature like human nature has not changed a whit.

But why should the dog, fellow hunter with early man and the companion of civilized humanity, have been regarded as evil? Professor Sayce considers that the four dogs of Merodach "were not always sent on errands of mercy, and that originally they had been devastating winds".

A Dog Legend

The fragment of a legend exists which does not exhibit the dog in any very favourable light. Once there was a shepherd who was tormented by the constant assaults of dogs upon his flocks. He prayed to Ea for protection, and the great god of wisdom sent his son Merodach to reassure the shepherd.

"Ea has heard thee", said Merodach. "When the great dogs assault thee, then, O shepherd, seize them from behind and lay them down, hold them and overcome them. Strike their heads, pierce their breasts. They are gone; never may they return. With the wind may they go, with the storm above it! Take their road and cut off their going. Seize their mouths, seize their mouths, seize their weapons! Seize their teeth, and make them ascend, by the command of Ea, the lord of wisdom; by the command of Merodach, the lord of revelation".

Gazelle and Goat Gods

THE GAZELLE OR ANTELOPE was a mythological animal in Babylonia so far as it represented Ea, who is entitled 'the princely gazelle' and 'the gazelle who gives the earth'.

But the gazelle/antelope was also appropriated to Mul-lil, the god of Nippur, who was specially called the 'gazelle god'. It is likely, therefore, that this animal had been worshipped totemically at Nippur. Scores of early cylinders represent it being offered in sacrifice to a god, and bas-reliefs and other carvings show it reposing in the arms of various deities.

The goat, too, seems to have been peculiarly sacred, and formed one of the signs of the zodiac. A god called Uz has for his name the Akkadian word for goat. Mr. Hormuzd Rassam found a sculptured stone tablet in a temple of the sun-god at Sippara on which was an inscription to Sin, Shamash and Ishtar, as being "set as companions at the approach to the deep in sight of the god Uz". This god Uz is depicted as sitting on a throne watching the revolution of the solar disc, which is placed upon a table and made to revolve by means of a rope or string. He is clad in a robe of goatskin.

The Goat Cult

This cult of the goat appears to be of very ancient origin, and the strange thing is that it seems to have found its way into medieval and even into modern magic and pseudo-religion. There is very little doubt that it is the Baphomet of the knights-templar and the Sabbatic goat of the witchcraft of the Middle Ages.

It seems almost certain that when the Crusaders sojourned in Asia-Minor they came into contact with the remains of the old Babylonian cult. When Philip the Fair of France arraigned them on a charge of heresy a great deal of curious evidence was extorted from them regarding the worship of an idol that they kept in their lodges. The real character of this they seemed unable to explain.

It was said which the image was made in the likeness of 'Baphomet', which name was said to be a corruption of Mahomet, the general Christian name at that period for a pagan idol, although others give a Greek derivation for the word. This figure was often described as possessing a goat's head and horns. That, too, the Sabbatic goat of the Middle Ages was of Eastern and probably Babylonian origin is scarcely to be doubted. At the witch orgies in France and elsewhere those who were afterwards brought to book for their sorceries declared that Satan appeared to them in the shape of a goat and that they worshipped him in this form.

The Sabbatic meetings during the fifteenth century in the wood of Mofflaines, near Arras, had as their centre a goat-demon with a human countenance, and a like fiend was adored in Germany and in Scotland. From all this it is clear that the Sabbatic goat must have had some connection with the East. Eliphas Levi drew a picture of the Baphomet or Sabbatic goat to accompany one of his occult works, and strangely enough the symbols that he adorns it with are peculiarly Oriental – moreover the sun-disc figures in the drawing. Now Leví knew nothing of Babylonian mythology, although he was moderately versed in the mythology of modern occultism, and it would seem that if he drew his information from modern or mediaeval sources that these must have been in direct line from Babylonian lore.

The Invasion of the Monsters

THOSE MONSTERS who had composed the host of Tiawath were supposed, after the defeat and destruction of their commandress, to have been hurled like Satan and his angels into the abyss beneath. We read of their confusion in four tablets of the creation epic. This legend seems to be the original source of the belief that those who rebelled against high heaven were thrust into outer darkness. In the Book of Enoch we read of a 'great abyss' regarding which an angel said to the prophet, "This is a place of the consummation of heaven and earth", and again, in a later chapter, "These are of the stars who have transgressed the command of God, the Highest, and are bound here till 10,000 worlds, the number of the days of their sins, shall have consummated ... this is the prison of the angels, and here they are held to eternity". Eleven great monsters are spoken of by Babylonian myth as comprising the host of Tiawath, besides many lesser forms having the heads of men and the bodies of birds. Strangely enough we find these monsters figuring in a legend concerning an early Babylonian king.

The tablets upon which this legend was impressed were at first known as 'the Cuthaean legend of creation' – a misnomer, for this legend does not give an account of the creation of the world at all, but deals with the invasion of Babylonia by a race of monsters who were descended from the gods, and who waged war against the legendary king of the period for three years. The King tells the story himself. Unfortunately the first portions of both tablets containing the story are missing, and we plunge right away into a description of the dread beings who came upon the people of Babylonia in their multitudes.

We are told that they preferred muddy water to clear water. These creatures, says the King, were without moral sense, glorying in their power, and slaughtering those whom they took captives. They had the bodies of birds and some of them had the faces of ravens. They had evidently been fostered by the gods in some inaccessible region, and, multiplying greatly, they came like a storm-cloud on the land, 360,000 in number. Their king was called Benini, their mother Melili and their leader Memangab, who had six subordinates. The King, perplexed, knew not what to do. He was afraid that if he gave them battle he might in some way offend the gods, but at last through his priests he addressed the divine beings and made offerings of lambs in sacrifice to them. He received a favourable answer and decided to give battle to the invaders, against whom he sent an army of 120,000 men, but not one of these returned alive. Again he sent 90,000 warriors to meet them, but the same fate overtook these, and in the third year he dispatched an army of nearly 70,000 troops, all of whom perished to a man. Then the unfortunate monarch broke down, and, groaning aloud, cried out that he had brought misfortune and destruction upon his realm. Nevertheless, rising from his lethargy of despair, he stated his intention to go forth against the enemy in his own person, saying, "The pride of this people of the night I will curse with death and destruction, with fear, terror and famine, and with misery of every kind".

Before setting out to meet the foe he made offerings to the gods. The manner in which he overcame the invaders is by no means clear from the text, but it would seem that he annihilated them by means of a deluge. In the last portion of the legend the King exhorts his successors not to lose heart when in great peril but to take courage from his example.

He inscribed a tablet with his advice, which he placed in the shrine of Nergal in the city of Cuthah. "Strengthen thy wall", he said, "fill thy cisterns with water, bring in thy treasure-chests and thy corn and thy silver and all thy possessions". He also advises those of his descendants who are faced by similar conditions not to expose themselves needlessly to the enemy.

It was thought at one time that this legend applied to the circumstances of the creation, and that the speaker was the god Nergal, who was waging war against the brood of Tiawath. It was believed that, according to local conditions at Cuthah, Nergal would have taken the place of Merodach, but it has now been made clear that although the tablet was intended to be placed in the shrine of Nergal, the speaker was in reality an early Babylonian king.

The Eagle

AS WE HAVE SEEN, the eagle was perhaps regarded as a symbol of the sun-god. A Babylonian fable tells how he quarrelled with the serpent and incurred the reptile's hatred. Feeling hungry he resolved to eat the serpent's young, and communicated his intention to his own family. One of his children advised him not to devour the serpent's brood, because if he did so he would incur the enmity of the god Shamash. But the eagle did not hearken to his offspring, and swooping down from heaven sought out the serpent's nest and devoured his young. On his arrival at home the serpent discovered his loss, and at once repaired in great indignation to Shamash, to whom he appealed for justice. His nest, he told the god, was set in a tree, and the eagle had swooped upon it, destroying it with his mighty wings and devouring the little serpents as they fell from it.

"Help, O Shamash!" cried the serpent. "Thy net is like unto the broad earth, thy snare is like unto the distant heaven in wideness. Who can escape thee?"

Shamash hearkening to his appeal, described to him how he might succeed in obtaining vengeance upon the eagle.

"Take the road", said he, "and go into the mountain and hide thyself in the dead body of a wild ox. Tear open its body, and all the birds of heaven shall swoop down upon it. The eagle shall come with the rest, and when he seeks for the best parts of the carcass, do thou seize him by his wing, tear off his wings, his pinions and his claws, pull him in pieces and cast him into a pit. There may he die a death from hunger and thirst".

The serpent did as Shamash had bidden him. He soon came upon the body of a wild ox, into which he glided after opening up the carcass. Shortly afterwards he heard the beating of the wings of numberless birds, all of which swooped down and ate of the flesh. But the eagle suspected the purpose of the serpent and did not come with the rest, until greed and hunger prompted him to share in the feast.

"Come", said he to his children, "let us swoop down and let us also eat of the flesh of this wild ox".

Now the young eagle who had before dissuaded his father from devouring the serpent's young, again begged him to desist from his purpose.

"Have a care, O my father", he said, "for I am certain that the serpent lurks in yonder carcass for the purpose of destroying you".

But the eagle did not hearken to the warning of his child, but swooped on to the carcass of the wild ox. He so far obeyed the injunctions of his offspring, however, as closely to examine the dead ox for the purpose of discovering whether any trap lurked near it. Satisfied that all was well he commenced to feed upon it, when suddenly the serpent seized upon him and held him fast. The eagle at once began to plead for mercy, but the enraged reptile told him that an appeal to Shamash was irrevocable, and that if he did not punish the king of birds he himself would be punished by the god, and despite the eagle's further protests he tore off his wings and pinions, pulled him to pieces, and finally cast him into a pit, where he perished miserably as the god had decreed.

Etana and the Eagle

In one fragmentary legend which was preserved in the tablet-library of Assur-bani-pal, the Assyrian monarch, Etana (a legendary ancient Sumerian king of the city of Kish) obtained the assistance of the Eagle to go in quest of the Plant of Birth. His wife was about to become a mother, and was accordingly in need of magical aid. A similar belief caused birth girdles of straw or serpent skins, and eagle stones found in eagles' nests, to be used in ancient Britain and elsewhere throughout Europe apparently from the earliest times.

On this or another occasion Etana desired to ascend to highest heaven. He asked the Eagle to assist him, and the bird assented, saying: "Be glad, my friend. Let me bear thee to the highest heaven. Lay thy breast on mine and thine arms on my wings, and let my body be as thy body". Etana did as the great bird requested him, and together they ascended towards the firmament. After a flight which extended over two hours, the Eagle asked Etana to gaze downwards. He did so, and beheld the ocean surrounding the earth, and the earth seemed like a mountainous island. The Eagle resumed its flight, and when another two hours had elapsed, it again asked Etana to look downwards. Then the hero saw that the sea resembled a girdle which clasped the land. Two hours later Etana found that he had been raised to a height from which the sea appeared to be no larger than a pond. By this time he had reached the heaven of Anu, Bel and Ea, and found there rest and shelter.

Here the text becomes fragmentary. Further on it is gathered from the narrative that Etana is being carried still higher by the Eagle towards the heaven of Ishtar, "Queen of Heaven", the supreme mother goddess. Three times, at intervals of two hours, the Eagle asks Etana to look downwards towards the shrinking earth. Then some disaster happens, for further onwards the broken tablet narrates that the Eagle is falling. Down and down eagle and man fall together until they strike the earth, and the Eagle's body is shattered.

Istar of Babylon: A Phantasy

Extracts from Book II: The Great City

Introduction

THIS 1902 NOVEL by American writer Margaret Horton Potter tells the story of Charmides, a young Greek rhapsode, who, hearing the story of the living goddess, Istar (Ishtar) of Babylon, becomes inspired with the desire to see and worship her. Charmides sets out from the Greek city of Selinous for the long journey to the Orient. Book I of the novel relates Charmides' travels to Babylon, the people he meets and adventures he endures to get to his destination.

Book II picks up once Charmides has reached his destination. He not only finds a way to meet Istar, but eventually uses his musical talents to ingratiate himself into her court. This is where the story of Istar comes into focus: Istar was the greatest and most powerful goddess of the Babylonians who came down to Earth and dwelt among men. She uses her magical abilities to protect her city from enemies and to maintain her position of authority. As the story unfolds, Istar becomes embroiled in a complex political plot that threatens to destroy her and her city. She must use all of her cunning and magical abilities to outsmart her enemies and protect her people.

Specific chapters from Book II have been selected here for their vivid descriptions of ancient Babylon and its inhabitants. This tale is set in the Great City under the rule of Nabonidus, the grandson of Nebuchadrezzar and last native king. Potter interweaves Babylonian mythology and Biblical history into a stunning historical narrative of the drama of the mortality of a goddess and the inevitable fall of Babylon.

Chapter 1

The Â-Ibur-Sabû

AS THE FIRST YELLOW STREAKS of the false dawn paled in the east on this morning of the eleventh of June, the city of Babylon awoke. And by the time that Shamash had come forth from the world beyond the Euphrates, the city streets were alive with men, women and animals. An hour later these were fixed in two long phalanxes, twenty rows deep, on either side of the Â-Ibur-Sabû – King Nebuchadrezzar's sacred way, that stretched, from the gate of Bel on the south side of the city, northward as far as the sanctuary of Istar. Half-way along its course this street, or boulevard, ran through the great square of the gods, that was today the centre of interest; for here, upon the right hand and upon the left, were the temples of Nebo and Nergal, whose feast-day this was. The great religious procession of gods and men was to pass from the second monastery of Zicarî southward across the canal of the Ukhatû to the temple of Istar, where they would enter upon the Â-Ibur-Sabû, and so pass directly down to the temples where the sacrifice was to be conducted by the high-priests of the temples of Bel, of Marduk, of Nebo and of Nergal, in the presence of the Lady Istar, the gods her brothers, the king of Babylon and the king's son. The day was an annual holiday in the city, whose three million inhabitants were now, apparently, every one of them struggling to obtain the best position on the Â-Ibur-Sabû, just at the entrance of the square of the gods.

The noise in this part of the city was such as only a vast, good-natured crowd can make. They pushed and elbowed, and indulged in guttural altercations that commanded too speedy mirth from bystanders ever to result in an actual quarrel. Frequently a commoner, driving his bullock cart down some side street towards the main thoroughfare, would be hauled from his place to see his vehicle led back to a distant point. Men and women on donkeys, however, were permitted to trot on unmolested; for the little, mouse-coloured creatures found a passage where their riders would have been wholly at fault. Now and then a drove of goats passed down the sacred way in a cloud of dust, their owner doing a thriving business in the way of selling milk from his animals to the thirsty throng. Venders of eggs, ready-cooked grain, fresh water, fruits and sweetmeats added their long-drawn, half-incomprehensible cries to the general clamour; while at frequent intervals a squad of cavalry or the chariot of a nobleman clattered along the Â-Ibur, causing the people to scurry from beneath their hoofs, but never making the slightest move to draw up for unfortunates.

The sun rose higher, and the heat grew stifling. Water-sellers emptied their skins so rapidly that the liquid had no time to cool by evaporation before it was taken, in its tepid, nauseous state. The morning was well advanced. Children began to cry with fatigue, and men and women alike became impatient for the procession. But by the time Charmides reached the temple of Nebo there was still no sign of its approach.

The Greek had slept late, under the shadow of the great wall; and when he awoke the sun was well up, Hodo [A Babylonian trader with whom Charmides had travelled from Tyre to the Great City] was nowhere to be seen, and the rébit was empty of those that had passed the night there. Charmides arose with a very hasty prayer to Apollo, performed some ablutions at the public well, and then, his heart beating high with long-delayed curiosity, passed the gate and went into the Great City.

He entered directly upon the Â-Ibur-Sabû; and the distance from the gate to the square of the gods was not great. Plenty of people were moving in the direction of the temples, and presently the rhapsode, a little bewildered with their number, wholly interested in their appearance, halted on the right hand of the street, beside a building, to watch those around him for a little while. He remained at his vantage-point for some time, regarding with interested eyes all that passed. Finally, however, the sight of a young girl, tall, lithe, straight, with brilliant eyes and dark skin, brought him back with a start to his great object, the quest of Istar. In passing, the girl flashed an impudent little smile at him, and on impulse he ran forward, to ask her in his own way how to reach the temple of the goddess. Whether by instinct, intuition, or divine Providence, the girl understood what he said; but her quick answer was unintelligible to him, and he had only her gesture to go by. That, however, commanded him to keep to the north, and he started eagerly forward in that direction.

Fifteen minutes' rapid walking brought him to the edge of the dense crowd that bordered the square of the gods. Here the people bewildered him. He felt the heat intensely, and, incidentally, had become both thirsty and hungry. There was food and drink enough on all sides of him for sale; but the youth felt disinclined to offer a piece of his Sicilian money in exchange for a breakfast; not on account of any penurious notions, but because, utterly ignorant as he was of Babylonish coinage, he dreaded Babylonish curiosity or the ridicule that might be expressed on presentation of such foreign coins as he had. Therefore he wavered on the outer edge of the crowd, chafing with impatience, extremely uncomfortable, and still afraid to make known his needs. The throng was dense, and the Greek by no means tall enough to see over the many heads in front of him. Therefore whatever might be going on in the square beyond was quite hidden from his view. Presently he trod, by mistake, upon the fringed tunic of a man beside him. Turning to offer an apology, his eyes suddenly fell upon a face that seemed familiar – so familiar that he made an effort to remember where he had seen it before.

After all, it proved to be only the little goat-girl who had been in the rébit on the previous evening. This time, however, the child saw him; and she seemed to find something in his face that kept her eyes riveted on his for a long moment, and then sent them drooping, till he could see the pretty, olive lids and the long, black lashes; while at the same time a wave of crimson swept up and over her face. Then Charmides discovered that, after all, he knew something of women. He felt at once that from this girl there would be no ridicule for him. The goat was still with her; and, as he went quickly to her side, he perceived, round the creature's neck, a metal cup on a string, the purpose of which vessel he was not slow to guess.

The girl waited for Charmides, and pushed her goat away for him with evident pleasure. As he halted, her big eyes were upraised, and her look travelled ingenuously from his sunlit hair over his burned face down to his roughly sandalled feet. Then she watched him open the little money bag that he had drawn from his bundle. From it he extracted a silver piece, stamped with the parsley sprig of Selinous, and, holding it out to her, he pointed from the cup on the goat to his own lips and then back to the animal again. The business was done. Baba, disregarding the proffered money, knelt down beside the docile animal and obtained Charmides' belated breakfast with a practised hand.

Charmides drank the warm milk with relish, and, the cup emptied, placed his coin inside it and returned it to the girl. She took it with a shy smile, that suddenly vanished when she perceived the silver. Picking up the coin, she examined it for some seconds. Then, while

Charmides looked on uneasily, Baba opened a pouch at her side, extracted therefrom a handful of small, copper disks, and held them out to the Greek, saying something to him at the same time. He shook his head and smiled at her as he accepted them. They were all alike: little scraps of stamped copper, which he afterwards learned to be *se*, the smallest of the Babylonish coins.

The chief matter of the moment thus satisfactorily concluded, the Greek lingered still at Baba's side, debating on the advisability of questioning her further. She seemed not disinclined to conversation, and as he glanced at her furtively he found her eyes again fixed upon his face. He answered the look, and then, with the usual effort, said, in the thick way of the Babylonians, the one word:

"Ishtar".

Baba appeared to understand him at once. "Belit will come to the square of the gods and the temples there in the sacred procession", she said, pointing at the same time to the north along the Â-Ibur-Sabû.

Charmides understood the gesture, not the words; and, thanking her in his own language, he left her, not without a vague hope that he might find her again sometime. As he strode away he did not know how longingly Baba's eyes followed him; how for a few steps she crept after him, this new god with the hair of gold, and how at length, abashed by the thought of her own boldness, she sat down beside her goat and addressed a fervent prayer to Lady Istar to send peace to her thoughts.

Meantime the object of this homage was hurrying down a narrow street that ran westward; and, having a good notion of localities and distance, he succeeded in skirting the crowd on the square without much difficulty, and in reaching the Â-Ibur-Sabû again a little farther to the north. Here, indeed, the throng seemed denser than ever; and here, as Charmides now guessed, Istar herself would come in procession with the gods and priests this very morning – nay, within the hour. With the thought his heart beat furiously, his throat grew dry, and his eyes were dim. His head swam with emotion as he started to edge a way through the mass of people. Not a little to his surprise, he found this easy to do. The people voluntarily gave place to him, staring in wonder at his beauty, his bright hair and the shining lyre that he carried in his hand. Ignorant as he was of the gigantic system of superstition that formed the foundation of the Chaldaic religious life, he still concluded, vaguely, that they were regarding him as something more than human, all these people that inclined a little as he usurped their room. As a matter of fact, he had been identified by some as one of the Annunâki, or earth-spirits; by others as one of the band of Îgigî, or heavenly beings, come among them today to do honour to his lords and theirs, the great gods of civil administration and of learning, Father Nebo and his son Nergal.

Here was Charmides at last at his journey's end, standing in the heart of the Great City, upon the Â-Ibur-Sabû, the ziggurat of Nebo on his right hand, the house of the high-priest of Bel opposite, the broad Euphrates winding through the sunshine far in front, and, somewhere to the north, moving towards him from her holy temple, Istar, the living goddess of the city of kings. It all seemed a dream to him now. The miles that lay between him and his home had put him into another life, still unreal, but always more and more tangible as he looked around and moved and breathed. The great multitude hardly caught his attention. He wished himself free to think under the spell of the new world. But now, far up the street, could be seen a whirling cloud of dust, in which low-moving forms were all but hidden. These presently resolved into three droves of animals – goats, bullocks and sheep for the sacrifice, driven by eunuchs of the temple. The horns of the bullocks were gilded, and the necks of the smaller beasts were twined with wreaths of flowers – just as the hecatombs of Zeus were ornamented at home. Charmides watched the flocks pass with joy at his heart. The familiar sight made Babylon homelike to him. His fingers sought the strings of his lyre, and he hummed to himself a genial little tune, that ceased when there rose about him a murmur of exclamations, followed by a quick silence. Charmides turned his eyes to the north. There again was dust; this time gleaming with brass work and glinting with trappings of horses. Into the silence came a distant sound of cymbals and wooden flutes. The great procession was moving – was coming. *She* was coming – Istar – the Lady of Babylon – the Divine One.

The crowd on either side of the street voluntarily pressed back to allow a wider space for the passage of the gods. No one was speaking now, and Charmides himself was breathless with expectation. The wavering dust cloud advanced towards the square, and the blare of trumpets grew louder, yet the procession seemed barely to move. Distant shouts of praise and acclamation could be heard, and there was a short, silent struggle for place. That was all. Everything waited.

Presently a phalanx of men, marching in excellent order and at a rapid pace, resolved from the dust and passed the house of the high priest. These wore the regulation priest's tunic of white muslin; but they had no goat skins on the shoulder, and the knives in their girdles proclaimed them slayers of the sacrifice. They were, in fact, Zicarû, or under-priests, from the monastery below the temple of Nebo. Behind them came a chariot, in which stood one man, a tall, muscular fellow, dark and bearded, with the goat skin over his left arm, a golden girdle about his waist, and a rosetted tiara on his head – Vul-Ramân of the great Bit-Yakin, high-priest of Nebo, and, next to Amraphel of Bel, the most powerful official of the priesthood. Behind him, borne on the shoulders of six Enû, or elders, and surrounded by a group of sixteen anointers (Pasisû), and officials of the libation (Ramkû), was the great bronze statue of Bel-Marduk, the father-god of the city, before whose passage the people bent their heads and prayed. After this idol came his priest Amraphel, ruler of the Babylonish orders, in his dazzling chariot, wearing a leopard skin over his cloudy tunic. Charmides looked into the face of this man, and in the one glance experienced a curious sensation – a sense of evil that he never quite forgot.

Now there came an apparently endless string of temple servants, priests in chariots and little gods carried by their worshippers. Also there were groups of prophets (Asipû), dream interpreters (Makhatû) and the great seer Nâbu-bani-âkhi. Charmides watched them all go by without great interest, for his expectation was becoming keener. Each moment he thought to perceive, in the distance, *her*; and by the heartthrob that followed the thought he knew that he should recognize her presence from afar. As time passed, however, he began to grow fearful lest, after all, she was not; lest Kabir [A Phoenician trader with whom Charmides had travelled to Tyre], first, and afterwards Hodo and the rest, had spoken falsely, had deceived him, had brought him to this great, lonely place, out of his world, with no hope of return, and no prospect in life. The thought brought a spasm of fear to his heart. Yet – yet – there, up the line, was a great burst of music from a band of musicians that surrounded a new, dazzling chariot, in which stood a solitary figure, clad – Charmides turned faint and shut his eyes. Then, hearing shouts of acclamation, he opened them again, fearfully, and looked up to behold – a man.

The first feeling was wholly of bewilderment. Then, as the rhapsode's eyes saw more, they forgot to fall. If Istar of Babylon was a man, at least he was one to look upon with wonder. Never before had Charmides beheld so imperial a face. Never had he imagined such features. The skin, as compared with his own, was very dark; yet it was whiter than that of any other Chaldee. Black hair, cut almost short, clustered about the head. The face was smooth-shaven, after the custom of the royal house; and, though Charmides could not see it from where he stood, the eyes were blue – the deep, purplish blue of a storm cloud. The man wore the dress of the priesthood, yet it went incongruously with his bearing. Power and the habit of command stood out in every line of his figure, in the Zeus-like poise of the head, in the hand that controlled the two powerful black horses which drew the chariot along. If this were Istar – well, Charmides could hardly regret. So much he muttered aloud, in Phoenician. To his amazement, the words were answered from behind him:

"That is no Istar, fool! That is Belshazzar, the prince royal, the tyrant of Babylon".

"And Istar – the goddess!" cried the Greek, turning to the man that spoke.

"The creature Istar? She comes", was the frowning reply made by the hook-nosed, ill-kempt man at his shoulder.

Charmides said no more. His pulses were throbbing violently. At a little distance he perceived a new vehicle, a triumphal car, at the approach of which the great masses of people to the right and left sank, as a man, to their knees, bowing to the dust. Charmides raised his eyes and beheld her sitting upon the broad platform of the car. And as he looked, as he knelt, even as his brow touched the ground, Charmides knew that he had not been deceived, that rumour had spoken truth, because more than truth could not here be spoken. Yet when she had passed, the Greek did not know her. He had not seen so much as a line of her figure. She swam in a glory of light that radiated from herself. Her head had been crowned, yet with what he did not know. His heart and head were afire, and he heeded nothing more of the procession. Most of all, he did not hear the words of the man behind him, who had knelt with the rest at the approach of the car, because fear of death is a great leveller; but had the words that he muttered been heard and understood by the populace, it is doubtful whether all his influence had saved his life from them.

"Asha confound this instrument of evil! Yahveh's wrath light upon her soul! God of Judea visit her with the fires of Sheol!" And then the former servant of Nebuchadrezzar the Great rose and turned away through the crowd. Charmides later sought vainly for his Phoenician-tongued informant, whom men today call Daniel the prophet.

While the Greek still stood, dazed and stupid, his head swimming with the delight of knowing her actually to be, the procession passed, and a great multitude of people swept along at its heels towards the temple square. Any attempt to force a passage through that packed throng would have been useless. This Charmides perceived at once, and presently, as the crowd melted away from where he stood, he turned and began to walk slowly towards the north, along the Â-Ibur-Sabû. In the street there were not a few people who, like himself, had felt it useless to try for a place to see the sacrifice, and, the procession over, were on the way home, perhaps to some family festival. But Charmides saw little enough of those around him. His feet moved mechanically while his thoughts soared.

He had seen her – he had seen Istar. The object of his journey was over; and yet – to leave Babylon now, without knowing more of her, was impossible. He felt that while Babylon was the shrine of such a being, in Babylon he must worship. Sicily, his friends, his mother, were now become things of another life – things fair and dear to think upon, but for which he no longer yearned. Istar, far above his reach as she was, yet made his interest, his religion – in fine, his home – in this new land.

It was while such thoughts as these were mingling in his heart that the Greek found himself brought to a halt. He had come to the end of the famous street that terminated in a square nearly two miles north of the temples of Nebo and his son and the square of the gods. On the edge of the new square Charmides paused and looked around him. Beside him, to the right and to the left, were two large buildings of the usual brick, low-roofed, and surrounded by walls in which the great wrought bronze gates were shut. Through their bars he caught glimpses of fair gardens filled with flowers of brilliant hues and shaded by flowering bushes and tall date palms. But in these places there was no sign of life; nor was any living creature to be seen on the flat roofs that served, in Babylon, the purpose of summer living rooms. On the right-hand side of the square stood what was unmistakably a temple. Here, on the top of the broad platform, and again on the steps ascending it, and about the open doors of the holy house, several people moved, while others were dotted on the broad incline that ran around the outside of the ziggurat, or tower, without which no holy building was complete, and which stood, campanile-like, to the left of the temple itself.

Glad of company, even that of total strangers, and seeing that the platform stair offered opportunity for a much-needed rest, Charmides moved wearily across the square, mounted a step or two, and sat down with a long sigh of relief. Near him were three or four people – venders of various commodities suited to the place. An old man held between his knees a basket of small, clay bricks, inscribed with Accadian prayers. Close to him was a scribe of a semi-religious order, ready provided with cuneiform iron and a supply of kneaded clay. A little beyond, a street watercarrier had stopped to rest, with his heavy pigskin beside him. Nearest of all was a young girl, holding on her lap a basket of nosegays. The picture in itself was pleasing; but Charmides soon discovered about it something that interested him much more. This was the sight of half a wheaten loaf and a handful of dates that lay, nearly covered with a bit of cloth, in a corner of the flower basket.

The nourishment in Charmides' early breakfast of goat's milk had not served to keep up his strength so long as this, and now the sight of solid food made him faint for it. He hesitated a little what to do; for he could not be sure whether what he saw were the girl's noonday meal or the remains of it. Having gazed long and eagerly, however, at the loaf, he suddenly lifted his eyes to encounter her own – very pretty ones they were – fixed on him with a mixture of curiosity and admiration. Thereupon courage born of hunger came upon the rhapsode with a mighty rush. He rose and went over to the side of the flower girl, and, taking from his bag the coppers given him by Baba, he proffered them all to the flower seller. Smiling till she showed a very pretty set of small, white teeth, she picked up all her remaining bouquets and held them up to him in both hands. Charmides looked at them lovingly, but shook his head. With surprise written in her face, the girl put them down again and seemed to wait for him to speak. Thereupon Charmides seated himself carefully on the other side of the basket, put one finger on the wheaten loaf, pointed to his mouth, and looked inquiringly at his new friend. She understood instantly, and, laughing, took up the food and set it before the Greek.

While he ate they talked – in the universal language of primitive sounds and gestures. And so skilful at this occupation did the two of them find themselves, that Charmides shortly learned how the girl had partaken of her noon meal some time before, and that he was quite welcome to what was left of it. Hereupon the rhapsode spread out all his *se*, nine of them, in a neat row, and suggested that she take as many as the bread and fruit were worth. The maiden hesitated over this part of the affair, but, as Charmides was quite firm, she finally picked out three of the coppers and put them in a little pouch hanging from her girdle; and Charmides perceived, without much thinking about it, that this pouch was the counterpart of that from which Baba had that morning extracted his change.

During his meal, which Charmides caused to last for some time, his eyes were much employed. He was making a careful scrutiny of his new companion – one so very careful that, in the interest of it, the awe and fiery enthusiasm excited in him by the sight of Istar was gradually dispelled. Thus he came gracefully down to human interests, and discovered that this Babylonian maid was rather more to his taste than any Doric Sicilian he could remember.

In very truth, Ramûa of Beltani's house, the flower girl of the temple of the great goddess, was a goodly sight for tired eyes. Young and fresh of colour, sweet of voice and modest of demeanour she always was. To be sure, her long tunic was colourless, old, and much patched. Her pretty feet were bare, and her only head covering the long, silken hair that was plaited and coiled round and round her shapely head. But it had been a pity to hide those glossy locks under the rarest of coronets. No jewels that she could have worn would have rivalled her eyes in brilliancy; and as for the small, brown feet – Charmides surveyed them covertly with unique enjoyment, and could not remember to have seen a sandal fit to grace them.

Musing in this profitable fashion, the rhapsode finished his meal, and invested another *se* in the purchase of a cup of water from the water seller. This he proffered first to the girl, who refused it with exceeding grace, and a very definite hope in her eyes that the sunny Greek would not yet depart. Evidently he had ideas of so doing, for, returning to her side, but not sitting down, he once more pronounced his pass-word:

"Istar?"

"This is her temple", was the quick reply, as Ramûa pointed to the top of the platform.

Charmides caught hopefully at the gesture. "This is the temple of Istar? The goddess will return here?" he asked, uselessly, in Greek.

Ramûa smiled at him.

Charmides felt irritated and helpless. He looked from the girl to the temple, and back again. Then he paused, wavered, might perhaps have cursed in his own tongue, and finally sat down again where he had been before. Silence ensued. Ramûa played in a very unbusiness-like way with a flower, till she had spoiled it. Charmides, more stolid and less concerned, stared out upon the sunny square and down the far stretch of the Â-Ibur-Sabû, from which far-distant sounds of music came faintly to his ears. Gradually he fell into a noonday reverie, from which he was roused by Ramûa, who, hoping perhaps to attract his attention, had lifted his lyre and was running her hand over its strings. Charmides looked up at her in surprise, and at once she held the instrument out to him, motioning him to play. Nothing loath, he took it, stood up and turned to her. For a moment his hand wandered among the strings. Then he found the melody he sought, and sang it to her in full-throated, mellifluous Greek – the myth of the Syracusan nymph, Arethuse, and Alpheus, the river-god.

The flower girl listened spellbound to such sounds as she had never heard before; and, on stopping, Charmides found a group of pedestrians, attracted by his song, standing near at hand behind him. One of them, a stiff-robed, high-crowned nobleman, tossed him a piece of money at the conclusion of the poem. Charmides took it up with a momentary impulse to throw it back at the man. Prudence, however, came to his aid, and, after a moment of inward rebellion, he accepted the coin, realizing that chance had just shown him a way for a future livelihood. He might, perhaps, have sung again, but for an interruption that claimed the attention of everyone around the temple.

The noise of distant trumpets had become much louder, and two specks afar down the Â-Ibur-Sabû had by now resolved themselves into a two-horse chariot and the car of Istar – both of them coming towards the temple.

Charmides' heart bounded as he distinguished the radiant figure that sat upon the golden platform of the divine vehicle. So he was to see her again – now – so soon. This time, if she passed him closely, she might even see him. And if her eyes should fall upon him – *had* she eyes? Had she features and organs? Was she, in fact, anything but a mystic vision that people saw dizzily and turned from, half blinded? He glanced down at the flower girl by his side, and it came over him with a rush of pleasure that she was human and susceptible to human emotions.

Istar's car approached the platform steps. It was followed by the attendant chariot, in which Charmides once more beheld Belshazzar, the "tyrant of Babylon", whom at first sight he had reckoned as a demi-god. As the car stopped, the prince leaped from his place and went to stand near the goddess as she alighted. The little company of people that had assembled to watch Istar's arrival, bent the knee. Charmides alone remained upright – why, he could not have told. Certainly it was not from lack of reverence. His eyes were fixed upon the form of Istar, while with all the strength of his mind he strove to pierce the veil of impenetrable, dazzling light that hung about her like a garment. As she rose from her sitting posture, Charmides looked to see her slaves offer assistance in her descent from the high place. But the eunuchs at her horses' heads did not move, and Belshazzar stood motionless on the first step, his head slightly bowed, but his strange eyes fixed as eagerly as Charmides' own.

Presently the goddess was beside the prince. How she had descended, Charmides did not know. He seemed to have seen her float down a shaft of light to the ground.

After performing the proper obeisance to their lady, the people rose, as Istar, with Belshazzar at her elbow, began to ascend the platform steps. Charmides could see that her feet moved, yet they barely touched the bricks. He did not know, however, that a year ago she had had no need for steps. As yet, it had never even been whispered by any man that she was more than formerly of earth.

One, two, three stairs Istar mounted. The young Greek was choking with excitement. In another moment she would be abreast of him – nay, was abreast of him, had ceased to move, had turned her head. Belshazzar, on the other side, halted in astonishment. Charmides' heart stopped. He found himself looking into a pair of great, unfathomable eyes that gazed into his own with the light of all knowledge. At the look, courage, confidence and an unspeakable joy took possession of him. Without amazement he heard her speak to him in his own tongue.

"Welcome, thou Charmides, to Babylon! I had word of your coming when Allaraine [the archetype of song] banished thy desert fever, in order that the Great City, and I in it, should know thy voice".

"Istar!"

"The journey has been long, and has taken patience and fortitude".

"The way has been but a dream of my goddess. Long ago, through Lord Apollo, I beheld thee".

"Yes – in the temple of Selinous – that dedicated to Apollo, who is Allaraine to me. Charmides, you have no home in Babylon. Will you take up an abode in that of the flower girl beside you?"

Charmides made no answer in words. Turning a little towards the young girl, who stood, pale and wide-eyed, on his right hand, he smiled at her.

Then Istar also turned to Ramûa, and spoke in Chaldaic: "Thou, maiden, take you at evening time this stranger home to the house of your mother, Beltani, and keep him there as he were one of you; and in return he will bring you great happiness. This is my wish".

Ramûa fell again upon her knees and bowed her head upon the clay bricks. She was incapable of speech; but the flush of crimson that had overspread her face told Istar that the command would not be unwillingly obeyed. Then the goddess turned again to the Greek.

"Charmides, go thou home tonight with the maiden here. Her name is called Ramûa, and she is of her mother Beltani, that is a widow. At sunset, when her flowers are gone, follow you after her. And again you shall come to me in my temple and play to me the music of your lyre. You have heard the chords of Allaraine of the skies. They shall come again to you to fill your heart with peace, and you shall be the most wonderful of all musicians in the Great City. Let, then, far Sicily, vanish forever from your mind".

Charmides bowed low. His tongue was tied with awe. He knew not what reply to make to her. When he lifted his eyes again she had passed, and was floating like a silver cloud across the great platform towards the open portals of the temple. Thereupon the Greek turned his face to Ramûa, and, as he clasped her hand in his and saw her black eyes lifted up, he laughed in his heart with joy of the Great City, and what he had found it to hold for him.

Chapter 2

The Sanctuary of Istar

THE TEMPLE OF THE LADY OF ERECH [Istar], in Babylon, was the smallest of the eight temples consecrated to the worship of the twelve great gods. This temple contained but three parts – the entrance hall, the great hall of the sacrifice, and, at the farthest end of this room, the inmost shrine, or holy of holies, where the statue of the god was generally kept. Besides these, there were half a dozen little places, hardly more than niches, where the priestesses and hierodules could don sacrificial garments. At the end of the great hall, in front of the rich curtain that hid the door of the inmost shrine, and behind the sacrificial altar and the table for shew-bread, was the Parakhû, or mercy-seat, from which the god, generally in spirit, it was thought, was accustomed to hear and answer the prayers of his worshippers, to perform miracles of healing, and to accept offerings. Here, each day, Istar was accustomed to sit for an hour, hearing many plaints, listening to many woes, learning much of the piteous side of the lives of men and women of the world. And from this place Istar had delivered many an oracle. Here, too, she cogitated painfully over the sins of mankind, which were all incomprehensible to her. She, who was alone of her race on earth, sorrowed most over the loneliness of others – those that mourned a friend dead, a lover lost, a child in far-off lands – because this grief she could in some measure understand. But though the face of the goddess was always sad when she left the mercy-seat, the brilliance of her aureole was more bewildering than ever, for pity quickened her divinity continually to fresh life.

Behind the temple of worship was the building in which Istar dwelt. It was a little labyrinth of small, open courts and narrow, dimly lighted rooms. Nearer to the dwelling-place than to the temple, on the same platform with them both, was the ziggurat – that most characteristic feature of Babylonian architecture. On top of it, in the centre of the space used by astronomers and astrologers attached to the temple, was the little room devoted to the person of the goddess. It was here that she was supposed to sleep by night when wearied with the labours of the long day. Istar's chamber on her ziggurat was rendered almost unapproachably sacred by the fact that here she had first been found; here she was supposed to have undergone her incarnation; and probably here she would resume intangibility, when her period of life on earth was over. In point of fact, Istar was devoted to this little place. During the hot summer months she generally stayed within it from sunset to dawn, perhaps asleep, perhaps fled in spirit to other regions. The place had been fitted up with incredible costliness, and was kept in scrupulous order by servants consecrated especially for the work, who entered it only at stated periods when its mistress was absent.

On her return from the long ceremonials attendant on the sacrifice to Nebo and Nergal, Istar went to the mercy-seat at once, for it was past her accustomed hour. There were few suppliants for pity today. Babylon had just propitiated two of its great gods with a wholesale slaughter of animals, and the people doubtless felt that for a day, at least, they might rest from the continual round of religious duties, relying meantime on the newly invigorated power of Nebo and Nergal to protect them from the legions of hellish and earthly demons that beset life with such innumerable ills.

Istar's hour was not long to her. Her thoughts were centred on Charmides, his young, sunny presence, and the light of wonder and worship in his face when she had spoken to him. She had seen that he carried his lyre with him; and she dreamed of the day when he should come before her and sing as none other but Allaraine could sing. Meantime his face was before her and would not be banished, although in the shadows before the altar stood another man whose presence had long been part of her surroundings, towards whom she felt – if indeed she felt at all – as towards no other human being; whose whole presence was as perfect a contrast to that of Charmides as could well be imagined. It was Belshazzar, who, since matters of government did not much hold him, had, in the last months become Istar's shadow. He lingered about the temple whenever she was there; he followed her over the city in his chariot when she went abroad; at sunset he ascended the ziggurat, to stand outside the curtained door of her sanctuary, unable to see her, but feeling her presence. When she was near him his eyes were not always upon her, yet her slightest movement never escaped him. And at such times a kind of divinity – a reflection, perhaps, from her – was thrown about him, till it had once or twice been said that the prince, like his goddess, moved in a silver cloud. Whether or not it was possible that Belshazzar – Belshazzar the tyrannical, the dissolute, the fierce-tempered – had by dint of will-power and persistence been able to pierce the veil that hid Istar secure from all mortal eyes, it would be impossible to tell. Istar herself did not know. But now, as many times before, she wondered vaguely if her unearthly powers would or would not hold her from the understanding of this unholy man.

The mercy hour over, two attendant ûkhatû approached her with the purifying water and her white garment for the evening. Istar washed away from her own person the sins and sorrows of her suppliants, suffered the robe to be laid over her shoulders, and then sent away the women, forbidding the temple to be lighted till she was gone from it, and commanding the dismissal of the two that prayed near the basin of the sea. So, presently, she was alone in the vast, shadowy room with Belshazzar, who still stood, silent, immovable, arms folded, head slightly bent, beside the shew-table, his storm-blue eyes fixed in a side glance on her face.

Istar rose and descended from the high place, and then moved slowly in her floating way to Belshazzar's side. There, a few inches from him, she halted, and, putting forth her hand, laid it lightly on his arm.

A tremor of intense feeling shot through him. He shook for a moment as with palsy. Then, raising both hands in the attitude of prayer, he uttered the one word – "Belit!"

Istar regarded him with a kind of curiosity. "Bel-shar-utsur", she said, lingeringly, with a suggestion of hesitation. Again the prince trembled. "Bel-shar-utsur – wilt thou follow me?"

"To the kingdom of Lillât, if my goddess asks", he answered, quickly, in a maze of confused delight.

The light of her divinity burned brighter round the figure of the goddess, and she made a slight gesture for the man to walk beside her. He obeyed with an eagerness that was tempered by a peculiar, half-resisted reluctance which Istar perceived but did not understand; for the soul of this majestic body was unknown, utterly unknown to her.

Together, however, they left the temple and passed across the deserted platform, which was still flooded with sunlight, till they reached the foot of the ziggurat. Here Belshazzar halted with a quick breath and an inaudible exclamation. Istar, turning a little towards him, gave him a wondering glance.

"You fear?" she asked, hardly knowing how to voice her idea.

And Belshazzar, he who had in his youth, in pursuance of amusement, swum the Euphrates lashed to the back of a wounded crocodile, now raised his hands again, saying imploringly: "O Belit! – I fear!"

"And what? Is it I?"

He bent his head.

"Belshazzar – come thou and teach me".

"Teach – you!"

"Yea, for there is much that I must know. There, on the ziggurat, where the air is sweet, where we shall be nearer the silver sky, thou shalt learn the purpose of my earth-life, and shalt tell me how to attain it; for I of myself know not the way. Come".

This time Belshazzar obeyed the command without hesitation, silently. Together they made the ascent of the broad, inclined plane that wound round and round up the tower. The man's steps were swinging and vigorous; yet, walk as rapidly as he would, the goddess kept always a little ahead of him though she made neither effort nor motion, except that now and then she touched her feet lightly to the bricks. At the top, opening from the broad gallery that ran round the building of the tower, was the low doorway that gave entrance to the holy of holies, Istar's shrine. There was no one on the height today, though ordinarily at this hour several ascended the ziggurat to watch the ascent of the goddess. Rejoicing in the solitude, Istar leaned over the south parapet of the wall, and looked out upon the light-flooded city, while Belshazzar, in a dream, waited at her shoulder. After a little while she turned, and, pushing aside the leathern curtain that hung across the door, conducted the prince over the threshold of the sacred place.

It was a wonderful room. At the time of the coming of Istar, indeed, all Babylon had contributed to its adorning. Not more than ten feet square was the little place, yet so did it glisten and shine with the lustre of clear gems and burnished gold, that it seemed to contain unfathomable depths, and to be imbued with something of the divine radiance of its mistress. The couch in it, like the walls, was covered with plates of beaten gold, and piled high with the softest and costliest stuffs from the famous Babylonian looms. The throne and the two chairs, or tabourets, were of Indian ebony, inlaid with ivory; and the table and deep basin for water were of chased silver, worked with crystals and emeralds. All the daylight that could enter this room must come through the arched doorway; but a swinging-lamp of wrought gold, hanging in the centre of the little place, burned continually, night and day, and shed a dim effulgence over everything.

When this interior was first revealed to him, Belshazzar halted where he stood, gazing around with self-contained pleasure till Istar, seating herself on the great chair that was her throne, motioned him to one of the lower seats. Belshazzar sat in her presence, and a silence fell between them: a silence that the prince could not have broken had his life been at stake. Istar, looking from her place out through the doorway into the tower-tipped sky, seeming not to feel in the slightest the great discomfort of her guest, finally said, softly:

"Belshazzar, from thy heart, tell me, what are thy gods?"

The man looked at her in quick amazement. For an instant he was about to speak on impulse. Then he resisted; and when he did make answer the reply was conventional. "Thou, Istar, art my goddess. Babylon is mine only god".

"That last thou hast said well. Yet it, too, is a false god".

"But thou, O Istar, I know – "

"I am no goddess, Belti-shar-utsur".

The prince started nervously to his feet. "You are not mortal?"

"No. I think, indeed, that I am not. Yet I am not sure. You came to earth a baby, born of woman – is it not so?"

"Like all men".

"And I descended from the highest void through space, till I touched earth almost upon this spot, a woman as I am now, clothed in my silver garment. It was by the command of god, the great Bel, the One, the True, that I came hither from the upper realms of the great kingdom. I was what they call archetype. I was decreed to pass through the fire of the world and return not to my home till the hearts of men were bare before my eyes, till I learned the secret of the creation. Yet how these things are to be shown to me I do not know. Thy heart, O Belshazzar – what is it?"

"It is thine, Lady of All".

"Open it to me that I may read".

The pleading simplicity of the tone made Belshazzar look at her sharply, and in a new way. Still his eyes failed to pierce the wave of baffling light that flowed about her; and still her purpose was enigmatical to him. She had become more incomprehensible than ever.

"The hearts of men, Istar, are not always known to themselves. Mine I could not show you".

Istar thought for a little while in troubled silence. Then she asked once more, not hopefully: "Your loves and hates, your joys and sorrows, your hopes and fears – knowing these, could I not understand them and you?"

"It may be. I do not know".

"Then let me hear, that I may judge".

"All of them, Istar – love, hate, hope, fear, joy, sorrow – are woven around my city, Babylon, the gate of god. My love is for her and my fear for her enemies. As she is the greatest of all cities, so is she the most loved and the most hated. In her lie all my joy and sorrow. In her dwell many that I love, some that I hate, one that I fear. But this – "

"This will not open to me your secret heart, Belshazzar. It is an affectation".

"By the power of the twelve great gods – it is not!"

"Then there are two lives in you: this one, and another that is hidden".

Belshazzar looked at her again strangely. "It is true", he said, at length, a curious smile curving his lips.

"It is of this second life that you must tell me".

"I cannot!" he said, quickly.

"Wherefore?"

"It is too ignoble for your ears".

"Too ignoble? What should be that for me? Nay, prince of the city, my earth-life is weary and long, because that I am kept away from life. I am set apart, worshipped as one afar off, and true life is not laid before me. To teach your race the secret of the one god is forbidden. It is I that come hither to learn; yet I am given no way of learning. What am I? Whither am I to go, that I may learn truth from the hearts of men?"

"Hearts, Divine One, may read each other. But no immortal that cannot feel the world may understand them".

"Let me, then, become mortal, O God!"

The cry rang out louder than it had been spoken, and seemed to echo forth, to vibrate through the room, to flow out and away into the distant sky. The two in the sanctuary listened to it in silence, wondering. Then Istar, tremulous, and wavering with light, arose.

"Leave me, Belshazzar!" she cried, suddenly. "Leave me alone here! I fear you!"

"Fear me?" He spoke softly, taking the attitude of prayer. "You are the goddess of Babylon. It is I that fear. I beseech thee, lady, spare me thy wrath. As a reed shalt thou bend me. As a twig shall I be broken before the strength of thy will. Divine One, grant me favour! Lady Belit, have pity upon my mortality!"

As he spoke she stood looking at him, shrinkingly, uncertainly, trying to fathom the false ring of the conventional phrases. His attitude, his expression, his demeanour, were perfectly sincere; yet, whether he himself were conscious of it or not, the words were not honest. She perceived it instantly. After the little pause of thought she repeated, faintly:

"Depart from me!" adding, afterwards, "You mock at me".

The prince drew a quick breath that sounded like a gasp. Then, coming forward, he sank to his knees, took the hem of her fiery garment, and held it for a moment to his lips. Its flame did not harm. Rather, it sent through his whole being a shock of vitality. Rising hurriedly after the obeisance, he inclined himself again before her and swept away, as she had commanded, leaving her alone in her sanctuary.

Istar remained where he left her, lying back in the chair, one hand supporting her cheek, her thoughts chaotic and troubled as never before. For many months past she had felt, vaguely, that which had just definitely come home to her. Her time on earth was passing uselessly away. She was now no closer to mankind than she had been before her descent. She was treated with such reverent awe as utterly precluded anything like familiar intercourse with anyone. The very prayers were addressed to her in terms as florid and as general as possible. Her personal attendants performed their duties in silent reverence. The priesthood treated her with the impenetrable respect that they showed towards the graven images of the gods. And now, for the first time, the significance of all these things came to her definitely. She perceived how they were baffling her purpose, and the thought caused her deep disquiet. There seemed to be but one way of opening life to her immortal vision. It was through the person of Belshazzar, who dared, before her, to keep his individuality. This way, however, as she had told him, she feared. What the fear was, when it had come or why, who could tell? Not Istar. Now, for so long a time the prince had been part of her wearisome, objective existence that, up to tonight, she had been more inclined to regard him as something spiritual than as a man. Mentally she reviewed him and his personality, and she found therein much that was beyond her undeveloped powers of appreciation and analysis. His deep eyes – how was it that they looked on her? She had not seemed to him so awe-inspiring a thing as others found her. Why? His continual presence before her – was it all from a sense of pure religion? Yet, if it were not, what was the motive? Istar did not, could not, know. He did not pray to her – quite. His attitude was peculiar – distant – reverent – yet at times there was something other than reverence in his face. What it was – the look that seemed to burn through her veil – Istar could not tell. Yet it was that look that had made her fear.

How long she sat, passive and quiet-browed within her sanctuary, thinking of these many things, she did not know. But when finally she straightened, the clouds in the east were pink with the reflected light of the setting sun.

The sky was singularly beautiful to her. It held in its far depths the mystery of her birth. She regarded it sometimes with yearning, sometimes with an unfathomable wisdom held in her inmost being. Now the curtain hid it from her gaze, and, with an oppressive sadness in her heart, she crossed to the doorway and lifted the curtain folds, to encounter the piercing gaze of a man who stood more than halfway across the sanctuary threshold. Thin, pallid, hook-nosed, bearded and wretchedly clothed, he stood over her radiant person and seemed to peer into her very soul – this child of the West, Beltishazzar the Jew [also called Daniel].

Istar gasped and shrank quickly back into the room, without letting go her hold on the curtain. Daniel pressed his advantage and intruded farther, till he also was inside. Her face was indistinguishable to him, for the light waves had quickened protectively round her whole body, till she swam in glory. Seemingly unabashed, [he] addressed her:

"Istar of Babylon, grant me an hour wherein I may hold speech with you – here, or without – upon the ziggurat".

There was less of entreaty than of command in the tone; and Istar, unduly affected by the fanatical appearance of the man, put his presence on a level with her own personality, and, replying to his speech in Hebrew, his language, said:

"Then enter here, O Daniel, and I will listen to you".

"You know me!" he said, quickly.

"I know men's names".

"And their hearts?"

"Their hearts! You have said it! Their hearts! Oh, thou man of Jerusalem, canst thou give me knowledge as to them?"

He looked at her closely, as if to make sure of her meaning. Then, taking courage, he replied: "Men's hearts! Who, in truth, but Yaveh, the one God, shall know them?"

Istar made no answer to the question, but once more motioned [Daniel] to enter the faintly lighted room. This he did without hesitation. Thereupon she covered the doorway with its curtain, turned without any sign of haste, and seated herself once more on the high throne, but left [Daniel] to stand before her. Finally, before the words he had framed could leave his lips, she swayed forward slightly and asked:

"What have you, the child of Yaveh, to gain from me?"

"Much – or nothing".

"It is no answer, Daniel".

Beltishazzar bent his head and folded his arms over his breast. So he stood for many minutes, silent and motionless, while Istar waited serenely for him to speak; and, when he spoke, she was not startled by his words and their blunt directness.

"Istar of Babylon, what are you – who are you? child of God, or instrument of the devil? – archangel, as some say, or archfiend, as many think? What is your mission in Babylon? Whence came you? Whither do you go?"

Istar smiled. "Neither angel nor fiend am I, Beltishazzar, but archetype of God's creation. I came from space. Into it, in time, I shall return again. My mission I have told you. I come to learn the hearts of men, their relationship to God".

As she ceased to speak she found Beltishazzar's eyes fixed upon her in a look so penetrating that it seemed impossible it should not pierce her veil. Presently, in the silence that followed, [he] began to pace up and down the little room. He walked nervously. His brows were knitted, his shoulders drawn up, his head sunk between them in an abstraction that Istar never thought of disturbing. When, at length, he looked up at her again, she found in him a new enthusiasm, a spirituality, an exaltation even, that gleamed like fire from his sunken eyes and increased his unhealthy pallor till his skin was like that of a dead man.

"Istar", he began, in a voice low and tremulous with incipient passion – "Istar, you have said it was from God that you came hither from space – you, a heavenly being, an archangel. God dispatched you to earth for an unknown purpose, a purpose that, in its fulness, hath not been confided to you, but is revealed unto me, the prophet of Nebuchadrezzar, the great king. Listen, and thou shalt feel the response of truth throb within thee at my words.

"Forty-and-seven years ago the holy city of Judah fell before the onslaught of the Babylonian king. Zedekiah and his race were taken captive by the hands of the wicked, and were carried away into exile to the city abhorred of God – Babylon, the queen of evil. Since then, in sickness and sorrow, in captivity and death, our people have dwelt here, a piteous hunger for the promised land gnawing at their hearts, while Babylon waxed great and strong in her wickedness off the fat of many captive lands and peoples. Long have we been without hope of salvation. But now Nebuchadrezzar, the fierce ruler, is dead many years since. In his kingdom are sown the seeds of dissension and strife, and, in the weakness of her strength, she shall reap bitter fruit. For Babylon, even as Nineveh before her, must fall. At the hands of her captives shall the great city suffer destruction and death. Again in their strength the Jews shall rise up and smite the tyrant down. And now, O Istar, hear thou the word of the Lord! In this great retribution it is thou that shalt lead us, the chosen ones; thou that shalt win glory and honour among us; thou that, as Moses from Egypt, shalt lead us out of Babylonia through the wilderness, back to the land of our fathers!"

He paused for an instant in the midst of his delight, to note the effect of his words on the woman – or angel. She sat before him radiant, wavering with light, motionless, unmoved, inscrutable, showing no desire to interrupt the flow of his words; rather, in her silence, urging him to greater heights. So he continued:

"For forty-and-seven years have we, the captives, dwelt in the land of bondage; and in that time, even with the hand of God heavy upon us, have acquired honour and riches in the country of our woe. Is it not a sign that God is with us – that he holds sacred that spot in which we dwell? Thou also art from Him! The end of our trial approaches! By night I hear the voice of the Lord crying from the high places that thou art here as a sign of His protection. And I and thou are destined to lead the children of Jerusalem out of bondage. Mine is the hand that will strike down the weak and faltering king of Babylon – Nabu-Nahid, the foolish one. At our hands priest and noble, citizen and soldier, yea, mother and infant of this unholy people, shall be made to drink of their own blood. And for thee, O Istar, shall be reserved the triumph, the deed of danger and of glory! For by thy hand, in stealth, when he shall come to worship idolatrously at thy shrine, shalt thou strike to earth the monster tyrant of the city, Nabu-Nahid's son, the child of sin, Belshazzar! Now behold – "

"Thou infamous one!"

Daniel's rush of words suddenly ceased. He paused long enough, fully enough, this time, to perceive and to understand the situation. Istar, trembling with anger and disgust, had risen from her place and towered above him like an archangel indeed. Through the blaze of light her two eyes glowed like burning coals upon the insignificant creature cowering below her. Beyond her exclamation, Istar found no words to say. The two confronted each other in palpitating stillness, and as they stood, Daniel, inch by inch, began to regain his stature, and gradually to move away, backward, towards the door. When finally he had his shoulders against the leathern curtain, and knew his ability to effect a quick escape should it become necessary, he delivered himself of a final oracle:

"Thou thing of evil, the Lord hath stripped from mine eyes the veil! I behold thee nourishing the serpent in thy bosom. Thy master, Satan, stands at thy right shoulder. Upon the other hand is Belshazzar, thy paramour. But I say unto you that the streets of Babylon shall run with the tyrant's blood. There shall come a night when Babylon shall burst into flames; when Nabonidus will be no more; when Belshazzar's life shall be taken by the hands of his own people; when thou, in mortal terror, shalt flee the city of thy wickedness; when the Jew shall triumph over Bel, and the God of Judea lift up his sword in the heavens! Thus, in mine ear, sounds the mighty voice of the Lord!"

Then, with one baleful gesture, and a fiery glance of hatred from his bright, black eyes, Daniel flung back the curtain of the sanctuary and slunk away, with his usual gait, out into the twilight and down the winding plane of the ziggurat.

For many minutes Istar remained as she had stood while listening to the last words of the leader of the captive race. Her limbs trembled. Her eyes were dim. When presently she felt the cool breath of the evening envelop her, her senses swam. In the midst of it all, in the midst of that terrible vision that [Daniel] had conjured up before her, there was one thing that stood out before all else, till the rest had lost all significance. Kill Belshazzar! *She* kill Belshazzar! Over and over she repeated it to herself, unable to understand why the horror of the mere thought should be so great.

The swinging lamp in the sanctuary mingled its dim, steady light with that of the rosy evening. From far below, over the Great City, came the faint hum of weary millions that had ceased from toil – a drowsy, restful murmur, suggestive of approaching sleep. The sound came gratefully to Istar's ears. Here were no battle cries, no shouts of attack, no wails of the dying. Beltishazzar surely lied. Nay, over her senses began to steal a sensation of subtle delight, of exquisite content, of freedom from earth-weariness. The hum of the city was gradually replaced by a long-drawn celestial chord, spun out and out with fainter, increasing vibrations, till it died away in the glow of unearthly light that was gradually suffusing the room.

Istar gave one low cry of love and relief, and, moving from her strained position, lay down upon the soft couch in an attitude of expectancy and happiness. Minute by minute the glow increased in brilliance till the little shrine palpitated with the fires of a midsummer sunset. Vapours of gold, in hot, whirling eddies, floated from ceiling to floor. The objects in the room became indistinguishable, and the light was such as must have struck mortal eyes blind. Gradually, in the meeting-point of the radiating light-streams, there became visible a darkly opaque shape upon which Istar fixed her eyes. It became more and more definable. Suddenly, from the head, there flashed forth five points of diamond light; and at the same instant Allaraine, star-crowned, emerged in mortal semblance from the melting glory. The moon-daughter rose from her couch, and silently the two greeted each other, looking eye into eye with all the companionship of divinity. While they stood thus, Allaraine touched his lyre, and the chords of the night-song of stillness and peace spread through the room and out into the darkness beyond. To mortal senses it was the essence of the summer day, with its fragrance and its passion, hanging still, by early night, over the land and the drowsy city. But to immortal ears it was as the voice of God. Istar drank it in as a thirsty field receives the rivulets of irrigation. And, little by little, as the spell was woven to its close, the star-crowned one drew her towards the throne, on which he caused her to sit, himself floating at a little distance.

"Allaraine! Allaraine! You bring again the breath of space, my home!"

"Yea, Istar!"

"And a half-mortal sadness looks upon me from your incarnate eyes".

"Beloved of the skies, I am troubled – troubled for you. It is as a messenger knowing little that I come to you from the great throne".

"What message? What message?"

"This: 'As immortal men are yet mortal, so shalt thou be. And by means of pain, of sin, of death and of love, shalt thou in the end know mankind through thyself; and for thee will there be freedom of choice'."

Measuredly, clearly, but unintelligently, Allaraine pronounced the words that were to him a mystery; and Istar listened, wondering, a dim foreboding at her heart. After a long pause she spoke mechanically the two words:

"*Mortal! I!*"

"Mortal. Thou. Istar, the heavens mourn!"

"And why, Allaraine?"

"To see thee in pain, in sin, in death – "

Istar raised her hand. "Have peace! These are in the world, but they are not all. There is something besides, that I have seen, yet that neither I, nor thou, nor any of our kind can understand. Sweeter than all the rest are hard, higher than sin is low, more joyful than death is sad, love reigns over men. Love is from the central fire of God, as we are but its outer rays. Love walks through all the earth, passing to and fro among men, making them to forswear sin, to forget suffering, to overcome death. Those that love are happy in spite of all things. This much have I learned on earth. And if mortality is decreed for me, I shall find love with the rest. Fear not for me, for willingly I bow down in acceptance of suffering, of pain, of wandering in the maze of ignorance, for the sake of this thing that men know and that I cannot understand".

"And thou wilt gladly forget us?"

"Nay, Allaraine. In the long nights and troubled days, thou, as ever, wilt bring me comfort".

"Ah, Istar – that may not be".

"May not? I shall lose the music – the communion – "

"All things divine will be lost. You enter into the wilderness of the world".

Istar bent her head and was silent. She who had seemed to understand so much, realized nothing. At last, lifting her head heavily, she asked: "When does it come, this farewell to – my home?"

"Not until you, of your own will, renounce divinity".

"Not till I seek it? Nay, this very night I asked it of the Almighty".

"Yea, and the cry was heard. Mortality shall be yours whenever of your own free will you renounce us all for that which mortality will give".

"Ah, then – then, immortal one – I shall remain the Narahmouna [Her archetypal name, Istar being only a cognomen, the name. given her by the people]"

Allaraine shook his head thoughtfully and said: "Of that I do not know. I have brought the message. Sleep, celestial woman. I go".

Obediently Istar lay down upon her couch, and the white eyelids closed over the unfathomable eyes. Allaraine, standing over her, looking down upon her mortal form with infinite pity, infinite ignorance, lifted up his lyre once more, and, by the magic of his power, Istar's spirit quickly fled to the land of dreams. There Allaraine left her to await the dawn of the new day, with its monotonous, wearying duties, and its weight of dim, indefinable foreboding, that as yet was all of the earth-life of Narahmouna the divine.

Chapter 3

A Babylonish Household

BABYLON, THE LARGEST, richest and most powerful city in the world, and of Oriental cities probably the most beautiful, presented, to the discerning eye, not a few glaring incongruities. Though its population had always been large, and was at the present time greater than ever before or after, the actual area of the city was, nevertheless, much too great for the number of people that dwelt in it. There have been kingdoms of fewer acres than those over which the monster city spread. Between the two walls, Imgur and Nimitti-Bel, were grain fields of sufficient extent to supply the entire population with sesame, barley and wheat in the event of a prolonged siege. This part of Babylon, therefore, called city by courtesy, was really more in the nature of farmlands than anything else. While within the inner wall, indeed almost in the heart of the city, were many bare and unsightly acres, used for nothing better than dumping-grounds, or for encampments of the troops of dogs that wandered freely through the streets as scavengers. In some quarters, however, and especially along the banks of the five canals cut from the Euphrates, and winding out towards Borsip on the west and Cutha on the east, every available inch of soil was occupied. Houses jutted over the streets and were crowded together, side by side and back-to-back, without any attempt at system: tenement districts such as the worst cities of later times never dreamed of. Here the three-story, flat-roofed buildings would be rented out, room by room, to as many people as poverty obliged to live in them. And these were myriad. For as Babylon was the wealthiest of cities, so she concealed in her depths nests of filthy, swarming life, of suffering and of privation such as only human beings could see and still tolerate.

On the edge of one of these districts, between the square of Nisân and the square of the gods, on the north bank of the canal of the New Year, in two tiny rooms, with a little space also on the roof, lived the widow Beltani, her daughters and their male slave. The slave was Beltani's sole inheritance from her husband. He was her luxury, her delight, the outlet of her not unfrequent tempers, and one of the three sources of a very limited income. Her daughters were the other two means of livelihood, but to them – though as girls go they were pretty – she was indifferent. Beltani herself was not, like so many of the Babylonish women, in trade. She did the work of the household; cooked – what there was to cook; washed – also what there was to wash; kept the rooms clean, as was consistent with tradition; and, hardest of hard tasks, managed the general income so that, in the two years of their unprotected life, none of the four had starved outright, and none of them had gone naked, while the rent was also paid as regularly as it could not be avoided. Besides this, Beltani held the patronage of two of the great gods; and by their help, together with frequent incantations, had kept the devils of the under-world from inflicting upon her any particularly direful misfortune. Images of the god Sin, of Bel-Marduk, and of the demons of Headache and the West Wind, were the only ornaments of her rooms. Each of these, however, had its shrine, and was regularly addressed three times a day; and it is to be hoped that if any demon had a due sense of proportion, he would refrain from inflicting any further ill of life upon these poor and pious creatures.

Neither chair nor rug had Beltani. Four pallets, such as they were, three in an inner room, one in a corner of the living-room; a wooden movable table and a brick stationary one; some vessels of clay, two iron pots, three knives and a two-pronged fork, together with an iron brazier that was kept upon the roof, and lastly, three or four rough, wooden stools, formed the furniture of the house. Nevertheless laughter, and that from very pretty throats, was a thing not unheard in this poverty-stricken place; and as many human sensations, from joy of life to pain of death, had run their course in these rooms as in the magnificent abode of Lord Ribâta Bit-Shumukin, just across the canal.

At sunset on the day of the great sacrifice to Nebo and Nergal, Beltani stood in the doorway of her living room, watching the gory light burn over the city, and, fist on hip, shouting gossip to neighbour Noubta of the next tenement.

"Have you been on the Â-Ibur today, Beltani?" called the Bee, when one of their intimates had been pretty well demolished at that distance.

"No. Few enough holidays are mine to take. From morning to night the girls run about the city, and someone must be at home to manage".

"Ay, there's your slave. What good is he if he can't take the rooms in charge once in a month? We have no slave, and my man's at work on the reservoir all day; but I slipped out this morning and went off to see the sights. Such crowds! All the city was out. I've a rent in my fresh tunic".

"Well, I couldn't go. One's slave may do much, but he isn't to be trusted with everything. Bazuzu, is the sesame ground?" This last ostentatiously; for Noubta was busily pounding her own barley.

Bazuzu made some reply from within, and after a moment came out of the room, bowl in hand. Jet-black, high-shouldered and slightly lame, for all that as powerful as an ox was Bazuzu. His appearance was startlingly uncouth as he limped out in answer to Beltani's question. But a gentler light never shone from mortal eyes than from his; and a gentler nature never lurked in so ugly a body.

Beltani took the bowl from his hand, and, calling a goodnight to her neighbour, proceeded leisurely to the stairway that ran up the outside of the building to the roof. It was on the roof that every family in the tenement did its cooking, except, indeed, in the rainy season. In all these districts the roof was the one luxury, the one comfortable, light, shaded spot, cool and airy in the summer evenings, protected through the day by an awning hung each morning and taken down at sunset. Roof-space was portioned off to tenants according to the number of their rooms; and up here, for them, life was sometimes really worth the living.

While Beltani was upstairs beginning the preparations for supper, Bazuzu remained in the doorway, shading his eyes from the light of the west, and looking with some interest out towards the canal. Noubta the Bee, still pounding barley, looked also, and presently called to him:

"Baba is coming, there, with the goat, Bazuzu".

And Baba presently appeared. She walked slowly, with a limp, for her feet were sore and inflamed from contact with the burning pavements. Beside her the silky goat, Zor, trotted along with gentle friendliness. Over her left shoulder hung a long string of pinecones, gathered in a grove by the river and brought home for firewood. As she reached the doorway the slave took these from her and carried them up to Beltani. Baba, meantime, entered the house, passed into the second room, where she, her mother and sister slept, and threw herself wearily down upon her bed. She lay here quite still, eyes wide open, one thin, brown fist thrown above her head, the other hand on her breast, an expression of intense, never-ending weariness upon her peaked little face. Over her, lying thus as usual after the long day of wandering, Zor stood, looking at her with half-human disturbance. Presently she ran her tongue sympathetically over Baba's hand, and then, with a goat-sigh, settled down on the floor beside her, her white, silken coat close to Baba's coarse, cotton garment. It was a peaceful half-hour that they spent before Bazuzu came to relieve Zor of her burden of milk. Then Baba opened her eyes, realizing that it approached suppertime. Rising with an effort, she passed into the other room to wash at the big, open jar of water standing there. Her head, arms and hair were just dripping refreshingly, when there came an incursion from without. First arrived Beltani, flushed with astonishment and anger; after her followed Ramûa, in company with a golden-haired youth bearing a silver lyre. At sight of him Baba gave a spasmodic gurgle of amazement, and then stood wet and staring, while her sister gave an explanation of the coming of Charmides.

"Istar hath bidden it, O my mother", she said, pleadingly, while Beltani still glared. "He is come from over the desert. He is weary, and he is poor".

This last explanation was the worst mistake that Ramûa could have made. "Poor!" burst forth Beltani, angrily. "*Poor!* And is it thy thought that our wealth is so great that we must house here another one – we who have not the wherewithal to exist except in misery? Why is the great goddess wroth with us? Wherein have I offended her, that she sends me another mouth to feed? What can he do, this pale-eyed, white-headed thing? Who is he that you bring him home with you? What have you done, Ramûa? How speak you to men that you do not know – men of his class? I will – "

She suddenly stopped; for Charmides' "pale" eyes were fastened on her intently, as if he would have read her words from her expression. And indeed, if this was his idea, the success of it was unique. For when the gaze that caused Beltani to stop speaking, Baba to shake with cold, confusion and hysterical laughter, and Ramûa to turn fiery red with shame, had lasted as long as Beltani could endure it, Charmides, with business-like precision, brought forth his money bag, drew therefrom a piece of silver, and quietly proffered it to the mistress of the house.

Beltani accepted the money without the grace of an instant's hesitation. Moreover, she advanced into the light, where she could examine it more closely to make sure that it was good. "It is not our money. Has it any value?" she asked, looking squarely at the Greek.

Baba went white, Ramûa blushed crimson, and only Charmides kept his countenance unchanged. It was to Ramûa that he looked, this time, for some guidance as to Beltani's meaning; and, looking at her, he presently forgot to wonder why the old woman still held his leafy coin suspiciously up in the light, after a moment repeating, sharply:

"Is the money of real silver, I say?"

"Yes, yes, yes!" cried Baba, disrespectfully. "This very morning I changed one of them for twenty *se*".

"*You* changed one?" asked Ramûa, wonderingly. "How?"

"He bought of me a cup of Zor's milk this morning as we stood near the square of the gods in the Â-Ibur".

Ramûa laughed merrily. "Then it was your *se* that he paid me for bread and dates at noon".

"He pays, then?" queried Beltani.

Ramûa had begun her reply when, to the surprise of all three of them, Charmides himself, who at last had understood a whole phrase, and thus grasped the situation, came out with a stammering and broken, "I pay". And forthwith he took from his bag another piece of silver and held it out to Beltani, who received it shamelessly, while both girls, indignant and helpless, looked on. Fortunately, at this juncture, Bazuzu came downstairs to say that the sesame boiled, the dates were cooled and the jar of beer had been set out on the roof.

Baba returned to her neglected toilet; while Beltani, turning to Ramûa with a very agreeable "Bring the stranger up-stairs", departed in haste to see that enough had been cooked to include Charmides in the meal, and yet leave something for Bazuzu afterwards.

Ramûa waited till Baba had retired to the sleeping room to bind up her hair; and then, rather apologetically, indicated to Charmides the water jar. He proceeded, not without a little qualm of distaste, to plunge his head and arms into the same water used ten minutes before by Baba. How Ramûa managed Charmides never learned; for, while he shook the water from his hair, and wiped his face and hands with a garment of his own taken from his bundle, his companion followed her sister to the inner room, from which they presently emerged together, glowing, demure, smooth-haired and ragged only as to tunics. The three together then mounted the brick staircase in the deepening twilight, to find the whole tenement on the roof at supper.

Beltani, who had waited impatiently for their appearance, was shouting across to a friend certain pieces of information in a way that terrified Ramûa. Charmides might again display that unlooked-for comprehension; and if he did! – Ramûa flushed in the semi-darkness. But the rhapsode, though he did not understand one word in twenty of those that were spoken about him, had already formed a very fair opinion of Ramûa's mother; and nothing that she could have said would much have amazed him. But, disagreeable as she was, he felt that more than she might be endured for the sake of sitting, at each meal, so close to that delightful bit of humanity, Ramûa. As to Baba, with her big eyes and pinched face, and the wonderfully beautiful little body concealed by her hopelessly insolvent garments, she meant nothing to him now, one way or the other. It was all Ramûa – Ramûa, who, with her pretty, quiet helpfulness, her modesty and also, in no small measure, her very apparent satisfaction in his presence, made the impressionable Sicilian at home in Babylon.

Before supper was begun Bazuzu came up to the roof again, bearing in his hand a lighted dish-lamp. Chaldean twilights were very short. Day and night were too fond to be kept at arm's length, and almost before a sunset had time to reach the height of its glory, grey shadows, the loving arms of darkness, were encircling the glow, and presently – lo! – from the east a string of stars was shining forth, and day had fallen to the night's caress.

The hour of the meal was as a dream to Charmides; a dream so vivid that, long years after, when he approached old age, he found himself able to recall with ease every look, every gesture, every shadow that passed before his eyes. The taste of boiled sesame and garlic never failed to bring back the impression of this meal; and time came to be when the master-singer, of his own accord, would go forth to purchase the coarse food that should conjure up again before him Beltani's masculine face watching him out of the shadows; Baba's big eyes fixed unwinkingly upon him; the ungainly figure of Bazuzu, standing in the background beside Zor, the goat; lastly, delight of all delights, Ramûa again beside him, at his shoulder, her head turned just a little away, her eyes refusing, out of shyness, to meet his, her pure profile all that was to be seen of her face, a little of her smooth shoulder just visible through a sudden rent in the tunic. And at this point Charmides would cover his eyes with his hands to hold the memory, and laugh a little out of pure joy that it had all been so.

At the time of its happening, however, one could not have called Charmides joyful. He was weary, he was hungry, he was conscious that the object of his journey had been fulfilled, and that, now that all was done, his home was at a measureless distance, and there seemed no immediate prospect of returning to it. Onion-flavoured grain, eaten with an awkward wooden spoon out of the same dish from which three others were also eating, might be poetic to think of, but was not delightful in actuality. To eat with Ramûa – well and good in its way; with Beltani, however – no! and as for Baba, he regarded her already with displeasure. Her eyes were too big and her body too meagre.

There was not much conversation at supper. The uncertainty as to the actual powers of Charmides in the way of understanding the Babylonish tongue was dampening to the general spirit. Beltani could only dream of the morrow, when she should have an hour's rest, at any cost, for chatter with Noubta; at which time the estate and importance of the fair-haired one would be definitely settled. Meantime supper must be got over as rapidly as possible. The sesame duly finished, what remained in the dish was handed over to Bazuzu; and bread, dates and cheese being portioned out, the women rose from their stiff postures and took up less constrained positions in various spots on the roof. Ramûa carried her fruit over to the edge of the roof and sat there in the starlight, her feet hanging over the unrailed edge, munching comfortably. Charmides finished his second course where he sat at table. Baba had thrown herself down by Zor, who was eating a hearty supper of refuse; and Beltani went to the other end of the roof to visit a friend. Now the Greek, scenting an opportunity, finished his dates, and darted down the stairway, to return after a few minutes' search in the darkness with his lyre. Ramûa did not notice his return, for she had not seen him go. But Baba's little hand tightened on Zor's silken hair, when she felt that he had come back to the roof. Without moving or making any sound, without even a change in expression, she saw him hesitate for the fraction of a second, and then pass quietly over and seat himself at Ramûa's side.

Charmides was disappointed, perhaps, that the maiden made no sign of satisfaction at his coming. She sat staring up into the high, star-spangled heavens, oblivious, apparently, of everything below them. He also remained silent, looking off towards the dark canal that wound, black and smooth, between the high buildings jutting over it on either side. After all, Babylon, the city of which he had dreamed so long, held nothing that was strange to him. It had been so long his heart-home that he loved it now. As he thought of all that he had done for the sake of being within its giant walls, and as he reflected upon the success of his great purpose, he forgot Ramûa beside him. He had not come for her. She was only a part of the city, the city that he had discovered out of the mighty west. How far above him he had thought all Babylon must be! Yet here it was, at his right hand; and he might touch it where he would, it would welcome him.

Pleased with his thoughts, Charmides ran his fingers over the silver strings of his lyre; and, because he was accustomed to express his emotions in that way, he lifted up his voice and sang, in a gentle tone, some rippling Grecian verses in a melody so delightful that Ramûa turned to marvel, and little Baba laid her head down upon Zor's warm coat in rapturous delight.

Presently, however, Charmides stopped short. Beltani, drawn by the sound of his voice, returned to her corner of the roof, and in the darkness stumbled over Baba's prostrate body. There was a harshly angry exclamation, a sharp blow, a stifled cry of distress and then her mother was at Ramûa's side, commanding her downstairs. The girl obeyed without protest, and Charmides followed her, distressed and helpless. In the rooms below, a torch and a lamp gave forth a dim and greasy light. In the first room, against the wall, sat Bazuzu, who had just finished arranging a bed for the stranger. It was but a heap of rags and mats, covered over with a torn rug; and Charmides was soon made to understand that upon this he was expected to pass the night.

The whole room was utterly uninviting. However, he was tired enough genuinely to welcome the thought of rest, and he looked for the women to retreat to their own room at once. He soon discovered, however, that there was no hope of their immediate retirement. Baba, having driven her goat into its corner, where it obediently lay down, went back to the doorway and stood looking out upon the night. Ramûa was busy making a little fire on the brick table, out of two pinecones. Beltani held a bit of wood, which she was laboriously shaping with a knife into a crude imitation of a human figure. Charmides watched her with no little curiosity. Her whittling finished, she carefully gathered up all the shavings and threw them into the fire. Then, with a word, she summoned Baba and Bazuzu to her side, and, with an imperious gesture, brought the Greek also into the circle around the little fire. Very solemnly she placed in the centre of the flame the wooden image that she had carved; and, while the fire caught it up, the four Babylonians lifted their voices dolefully, in the old Accadian incantation against demons:

"O witch, whosoever thou art, whose heart conceiveth my misfortune, whose tongue uttereth spells against me, whose lips poison me, and in whose footsteps death standeth, I ban thy mouth, I ban thy tongue, I ban thy glittering eyes, I ban thy swift feet, I ban thy toiling knees, I ban thy laden hands, I ban thy hands behind. And may the moon-god, our god, destroy thy body; and may he cast thee abroad into the lake of water and of fire. Amanû".

This prayer, of which Charmides understood not a word, but the import of which he pretty clearly guessed, was the regular conclusion of the day. No Babylonian of the lower class could have passed the night in peace having omitted this exorcism. When it was over Bazuzu filled a dish with the ashes and carried it outside the door, setting it just over the threshold, where no thing of evil could enter the house without passing it. This done, Beltani, with a gesture of good night to the stranger, retreated into her bedroom, with Baba on the one side of her and Ramûa on the other.

Now at last Charmides was free to rest. Bazuzu, of course, was in the room; but he, having extinguished the lamp, and making signs that when Charmides was ready to sleep he should put out the torch, laid himself down upon his pallet, and, turning his face to the wall, fell soundly asleep. Charmides did not follow immediately. In the flickering light he knelt down and prayed to his lord, Apollo of the Silver Bow, rendering thanks for the safe accomplishment of his journey, and acknowledging the god-head of Istar, whom, in his heart, he regarded as Artemis incarnate.

His devotions over, he rose, extinguished the torch and felt his way to the bed. He sank upon it with a sensation of delight. His weary limbs relaxed, and for a moment his head swam with the relief of the reclining position. Nevertheless, it was some time before he slept. Through the open doorway the cool, sweet breath of the summer night stole in upon him. In the square, black patch of sky visible where he lay came two or three stars: the same stars that had looked on him in Sicily. A sudden spasm of longing and of fear – fear of his strangeness, his helplessness in this vast city, came over him then. From out of the night he heard his mother's voice calling him from the shore of the sea; and he answered her with a moan. For a little time her form stood out before his eyes, clear and luminous against the black background. Then, gradually, the blinding rays of Istar's aureole replaced her, and Istar herself was before him, in all her surpassing beauty. After a time she flashed out of his sight, but not before the thought had come to him, unsummoned, that he had not yet finished with Istar of Babylon in her city; that she, the great, the unapproachable goddess, would need him at some future time to succour her. He smiled at the idea, thinking it a dream. And with the thought of dreams he entered the land of them, nor came forth again till morning dawned.

The night wore along, and there came to be but one sleeper in the room. Black Bazuzu was awake, sitting – no, standing up. He moved noiselessly to the doorway, and picked up there one of the baskets of his own making. With this he crossed the threshold of the door, stepping carefully over the witch's plate, and presently disappeared into the blackness beyond. An hour later he came quietly in again, put his basket into its place, and stopped to listen carefully to the sound of his companion's breathing. It had not changed. With a satisfied nod the slave returned to his couch, laid him gladly down and slept.

Sunlight streaming over his face, the sound of a quick exclamation, and a little ripple of laughter, brought the Greek to his senses next morning. Ramûa, bright-eyed and smiling, sat in the doorway, a heap of fresh and dewy flowers in her lap, a basket-tray beside her. She was fastening up little bouquets of roses, lilies, heliotrope, nasturtiums, iris, narcissi and the beautiful lotus. Baba, as usual, was playing with Zor, who had just made another rent in her much-tattered garments; and Bazuzu lay upon his pallet, still asleep. Presumably Beltani was on the roof. Charmides hoped so. He had already come to prefer her at a distance. But at present the rather unusual arrangements of this household puzzled him; and he could not tell, from precedent, where any of its members would ordinarily be at this hour.

Charmides rose, not a little embarrassed at having been asleep in the presence of Ramûa and her sister. He became in time accustomed to the very free manners current among Babylonians of the lower class; but at present he was mightily relieved when Ramûa, with a tact hardly to be hoped for, jumped up from her place, and, calling to Baba to follow her, departed towards the roof with her fragrant burden. Charmides at once began his toilet, which he happily finished without interruption. Then, leaving Bazuzu still asleep, he sought his hosts in the upper air. Breakfast was ready, and it proved to be a gala meal. There was meat – goat's flesh from the yesterday's sacrifice. For on days that followed great religious festivals the flesh from the sacrificial hecatombs was sold at a minimum price to the poor, so that the greater part of Babylon had meat to eat. Besides this, there were milk and bread; and Charmides, in a sunny mood, felt that the king himself could have desired nothing more.

The meal was quickly over, and, a few minutes afterwards, Charmides could scarcely have told how, he found himself walking, lyre in hand, at Ramûa's side, along the bank of the canal, on the way to the temple of Istar. On her head Ramûa carried her basket of fresh flowers. The Greek watched her closely and with delight as she moved, lithe, straight and graceful as a young tiger, her bare feet making delicate marks in the dust of the way, her hair, today unbound, swinging behind her in long, silken masses. And Charmides' beauty-loving eyes brought joy to his soul as he regarded her. Yet his walk was not wholly a light-hearted one. His mind was troubled with thinking, as other men thought, as he had not thought before, of a means of livelihood. Here he was, thrown utterly on his own resources. If he would live he must work – must gain enough to keep him, however simply, when his father's money was used up. This conviction was not an easy one to face. There was but one thing that he knew how to do well, and at all times liked to do, and that thing held forth small promise of earning him money. His poor lyre! In any province of Greece, or Lydia, there had been small cause for worry. Rhapsodists were of a class apart, and were reverenced by an art-loving people as on an equality with their priests. Zeus might be the greatest Olympian; but Apollo had a shrine in every heart. Babylonia, however, was not Greece; and what the Babylonian fancy for music might be, Charmides did not know. Thus when the long walk was ended, and Ramûa had taken her place on the platform steps below the temple of Istar, she looked up into his face to find the usually bright countenance as solemn as that of an ibis. Nor could any word or look of hers bring more than the shadow of a smile to his lips.

Charmides stood beside her for a few moments, looking across the thinly peopled square. Then his shoulders straightened. He gave a little outward manifestation of his mental state, looked at Ramûa with a farewell smile, and left her, walking swiftly away towards the Â-Ibur-Sabû.

Ramûa, confounded, cried after him impulsively: "You will return! You will return to me at noon?"

Charmides looked round, nodding reassuringly, but whether in response to her words or merely in answer to her voice, the maiden could not tell. She sat quite still where he had left her, her head drooping a little, utterly forgetful of her business, paying not the least attention to possible buyers. The sun poured its bright, scorching heat down upon the grey bricks. Water-sellers were to be heard crying their ever-welcome refreshment. Chariots, carts and litters passed through the square. The city's voice rose murmurously through the heat, and one by one the usual beggars and venders made their appearance on the platform steps.

Through the hours Ramûa sat spiritless, watching those that passed up the temple steps, selling her flowers unsmilingly, half unwillingly, to those that offered to buy. At early noon she felt a first qualm of hunger, and looked up to find the sun at its zenith. With a start she came to herself. It was past her usual luncheon hour. All around her little meals of bread, sesame and dates were being brought forth by the habitués of the steps. The cripple on Ramûa's left hand, thinking perhaps that she must go hungry today, proffered her half of his loaf with a compassionate, misshapen grin. Ramûa refused him with a forced smile, and, heavy-hearted, took out her food and showed it to him. There was enough for two in her package today; and she regarded it unhappily, still hesitating to eat, while the hope that Charmides might return died within her. Once again she looked over the deserted square, and then, resolutely turning her face to the temple, took one dry mouthful of bread. Charmides was gone for evermore. She should not see him again. Another bite: Charmides had been killed. A third: his body was floating, face downward, in the black, hurrying waters of the cruel Euphrates. A fourth, a fifth, a sixth and there appeared a tear, that rolled uncontrollably down her pretty nose. She put her bread away – when before had she not been hungry at noon? – and then sat with her head bent, trying to conceal her grief from the sympathetic beggar.

Presently someone came up the steps and sat down close beside her. She felt the presence, but did not look round. Suddenly a big, ripe melon was placed before her, by a hand too white for Babylon. Ramûa started up, with a spasmodic breath, and her face glowed like the sun after a summer storm. Charmides, the morning trouble all gone from his face, was at her side. In one hand he held a number of ripe figs. The other had borne the melon. Ramûa retired at once within herself, too shy to do more than smile faintly and then try to hide her face, with its unconcealable joy. But such a welcome pleased the Greek more than anything else; for, as he was beginning to realize, his instincts regarding woman nature were quite unexpectedly reliable.

Luncheon was now eaten in earnest; and the cripple could not but be amazed at the change in Ramûa's appetite. With a little laugh she broke the melon on the steps, and proffered a large piece of it, together with his bread and dates, to the Greek. She herself ate slowly but willingly, answering the looks of the rhapsode, and even talking to him in the tongue that he could not understand.

There came a time, however, after the last fig was gone and the cup of water had been bought and drunk, when embarrassment fell between the two. Ramûa feared, dreaded and then half hoped that Charmides would rise and go away again, this time to stay. She felt that she could make no effort to keep him at her side. She would have given half her life to be able to treat him with natural gayety; and yet, had she been able to do so, the essence of delight in all this would be gone. Charmides himself was suffering from the inability to talk to her. But after an unbearable period of awkward silence he strove to solve their difficulty. Leaning over from where he sat, and touching the girl's tunic, he said to her, by means of signs and looks, and a word or two:

"What is the name of this?"

Ramûa smiled with delight. "*Kadesh*" she replied; and in this way Charmides' course of study was begun. The first lesson lasted for an hour, and at the end of it the Greek knew not a few words that promised to stick in his memory. When he felt that he could retain no more, he stopped her, and sat conning his lesson on the steps in the sunshine, while she, tardily recalled to duty, took her flower basket and went forth into the square to proffer her somewhat drooping bouquets to the passersby. By the time she returned to her companion the sun was midway down the heavens, and Charmides, lyre in hand, stood, evidently waiting for her. By means of signs he made her understand that he must leave her till after sunset, when he would return again to the square to go home with her.

Ramûa did not ask his destination. Very probably he could not have made her understand it had she done so. She watched him pass down a narrow street that led to the southwest, out of the square of Istar, in the direction of the temple of Sin. It was to the holy house of the moon-god that Charmides went; for his single morning in Babylon had found him a means of livelihood.

Though he himself was unaware of the exact position that he held, he was attached to the temple as an oracle. That morning, as he had hummed himself through the square of Sin, one of the Zicarû, or monks in service at the temple, had chanced to hear his voice, and, perceiving that the singer was of foreign race, and being himself a highly educated man, as were all of his order, addressed the fair-haired one in the westernmost language that he knew – Phoenician. Charmides had come near to falling at his feet and worshipping in the delight of finding someone to speak to. But the Zicarî led him gravely into one of the inner rooms of the temple and there asked him sing and speak and play upon his instrument, and after a time made him an offer to join the temple service, unordered as he was, and to do exactly what he was told for about three hours in the day. The pay was high, and to Charmides it seemed that a miracle of fortune had befallen him. Such being the case, it was, perhaps, just as well that he did not understand the full significance of his duties. For an hour in the morning he was to stand inside of the heroic statue of the god, and to speak through the half-open mouth words whispered in his ear by an attendant priest. He was not told that his peculiar pronunciation of the Babylonian syllables and the melodious softness of his voice were invaluable adjuncts to the oracle of Sin; and that, furthermore, the fact that he understood not a word of what he said made him more desirable for the place than any member of the under-priesthood would have been. Besides this curious work, he was supposed to assist at sacrifices by playing on the flute or lyre; and by means of these light duties his livelihood became an assured thing, and his place in Babylon was secure. He asked no questions, either of himself or of the priest, his master. He accepted everything with childlike faith; and, verily, it seemed that, brush as he would against the world, the bloom of his pristine innocence would never be rubbed from Charmides' unstained soul.

So, having found a home and an occupation, within forty-eight hours after his arrival in the Great City, Charmides' life in Babylon began.

Chapter 4

Belshazzar

CHARMIDES FOUND no loneliness in his Babylonish life. In an unaccountable way he felt it to be the home of his spirit. The dirty, narrow, barely furnished rooms of the tenement of Ut; the vast temple of Sin, where he performed the light tasks that gave him his livelihood; the platform of the temple of the goddess, where, with Ramûa close at hand, the hours were wont to fly on rosy wings; the long streets, the myriads of people, the hum of the city, the curious, solemn, ceremonious bearing of its inhabitants, all these welded themselves into such a life that sometimes, in dead of night, he cried out in the fear that it was all a dream: a dream from which he could only pray not to wake.

In the second week there happened something that gave him a great thrill of exalted pride. It was eight days after his arrival; in fact, the noon after the third Sabbatû of the month of Duzu (June). He was sitting with Ramûa on the steps of the temple of Istar, munching dates and struggling with new phrases in the apparently hopeless Chaldean tongue, when a veiled hierodule came out of the temple and down the platform stairs with the request that Charmides follow her to the presence of Belit Istar, who longed for the sound of his voice.

The Greek felt a quiver, half of fear, half of delight; and, rising at once, and leaving Ramûa and his meal behind, followed the attendant, not into the temple, but behind it, towards the entrance court of Istar's dwelling. Here, upon a heap of rugs, beneath a canopy of Egyptian embroidery, the goddess reclined. Charmides, however, did not see her till after he had encountered the gaze of one who stood just inside the arch of the door in the wall. This was he who had followed Istar in his chariot home from the procession of the gods, he at whose remarkable appearance Charmides had so marvelled: Belshazzar, the king's son. Still was he godlike, imperial enough to look upon; but the Greek forgot his presence while Istar was again before him. When his gaze fell on her he started slightly, turned his eyes away for an instant, and looked again. Yes – it was true. Through the shimmering veil her form was clearly visible. She was not now only a cloud of dazzling, palpitating light. Immortal still, and radiant she was, but – Charmides let his thoughts break off quickly. Istar was commanding him, in Greek, to play to her. He lifted his lyre at once, and, under the spell of music, he forgot himself, half forgot her before whom he played, in contemplation of the ideal created by the harmonies. When, after half an hour, he was stopped and dismissed, he left the divine presence in a state of exaltation. Belshazzar was but a blur beside the doorway, and Ramûa, when he returned to her, seemed a trifle less beautiful than usual.

After this, every day, Charmides gave half of his noon hour to this new form of worship. It was Ramûa's pride as well as his. She never grudged the time; and, on his return to her side, never failed to ask of his success, nor to beam with delight when he confessed it. At each of these visits Charmides realized that Belshazzar was present; but the fact made little impression on him. He saw her whom he worshipped quicken to new life, to new radiance, at sound of his voice and the chords of his lyre; and, when he left the court, the storm in the eyes of the king's son went unnoticed. Yet the storm was there, daily increasing in fury; and there came a time when it passed control and burst forth in the very presence of her whom both men worshipped.

It was noon on the seventh of Abû (July), a day on which Babylon lay quivering under a fiercer sun than before. The city was exhausted with the recent end of the annual three-day feast of Tammuz; and Charmides himself was weary and a little faint when he entered Istar's presence. Belshazzar, with what seemed a scarce pardonable liberty, had thrown himself face downward on a rug near the portal of the court. At the first note of Charmides' song a slight twitching of the muscles in the prince's back betrayed his hearing of the song. But as the voice went on, as Charmides, even in his weariness, sang with a depth of feeling that he had never before exhibited, the other man lifted his head to look at Istar. Under the spell of the music that was a divine gift, she was becoming more and more the old-time unapproachable goddess. The rays of the aureole, which, half an hour before, had vibrated so slowly as scarcely to disturb the eye, were quickened to a new life. Blinding streams of light poured about her now. And Istar herself was quivering with a strength, with a delight, that was apart from earthly things. Charmides' voice showed its power, its beauty, its clear heights, its mellow depths, as never before. He had begun with a most delicate pianissimo, in tones of exquisite restraint and purity, the old myth of Alpheus and Arethuse – a thing that he had sung a hundred times before, yet never as now. The tones blended with the rippling harmonies of his lyre in a stream as pure and limpid as the current of the sacred river. The Greek syllables, music in themselves, fitted so perfectly to the melody, that Allaraine himself, afar off, listened with surprise and pleasure. Belshazzar alone, perceiving how Istar's divinity increased with each sweep of the instrument, trembled with anger. The song rose towards its climax. Istar had become oblivious to everything but the sound of that voice. Charmides, inspired, had lost himself in the heaven of his own making. Suddenly, from beside him, came a hoarse, choked cry, the sound of hurried running, and the lyre was struck furiously from his hands down to the brick pavement.

... The song stopped. Panting with broken emotion, Charmides faced about. His face was pale and his lips drawn with displeasure – with something more than that. Before him, shaking with jealous wrath, towered Belshazzar, his hand uplifted, his eyes flaming.

There was silence. Charmides waited immovably for the blow to fall. But Belshazzar did not strike him. Istar lay back, trembling. Under the influence of these human and gross emotions, the vibrations of light around her diminished so rapidly that one could see them melt away; and soon she was left almost without divine protection – a woman, in woman's garb. Finally, however, with no trace of weakness in her manner, she rose, confronting the two men. For a moment her gaze travelled from one to the other. Then, passing to Charmides, she halted by his side, touched his shoulder lightly with her hand, and pointed to the doorway.

"Go, thou disciple of Apollo. Fear not. I will send to thee a lyre that is not dishonoured. Tomorrow come to me again – as always".

Then, while the Greek still quivered with the thrill of her touch, she walked with him, two or three steps, towards the open arch.

In the meantime Belshazzar, broken now, waited before her place. When the light trailing of her garments passed near his feet again, he suddenly lifted his head and looked at her. They were face to face, and their eyes met. Istar's glance shone clear and baffling upon the man, yet before it Belshazzar would not lower his. He was making an almost inhuman effort, mental and physical, to overcome the perfect poise that proclaimed her more than human. But Belshazzar could not cope with a thing divine. His strength, to the last drop, was gone. She was superior to him. He knew it. Goddess she was – must be! He must acknowledge it – must submit. Slowly he lifted his arms and crossed them on his breast. Slowly his dark head was lowered. With bitter humiliation he gave the signal of defeat. Istar moved slightly.

"Give me the broken lyre", she said, softly.

Belshazzar sought it where it lay, bright and shattered on the pavement. He proffered it to her humbly, and saw her, receiving it, touch it to her breast. He shut his eyes that he might not see the hated thing made whole; but, looking up again, he saw the instrument still splintered, still unstrung. She had not, then, performed the miracle.

He had but a moment more with her. Presently she raised her hand, and, with the slightest of gestures, dismissed him from her presence. Belshazzar could not disobey the command. Blindly, weakly, without a glance behind, he moved towards the portal. Thus he did not see the goddess, as he left the court, suddenly reel, and an instant afterwards fall back upon the pile of rugs, covering her face with her hands, and exhibiting every sign of human distress. On the contrary, humiliated, hopeless and disturbed by the temerity of his thoughts, yet as rebellious as before, the prince of Babylon crossed the platform and descended the steps where Charmides sat with Ramûa. The prince scarcely saw the Greek as he passed him; and Charmides only lifted his eyes in time to behold Belshazzar's back, and to watch him cross the square to the spot where his chariot waited. The driver, at his master's approach, leaped to his place, drawing up the heads of the powerful black animals. The prince entered the vehicle. Nebo-Ailû gave a quavering cry. The horses plunged forward, and the shining chariot clattered after them down the Â-Ibur-Sabû.

[Belshazzar travelled to the house of Amraphel, the high priest of Babylon, and brings the high priest to see the king. When the high priest seeks to get Istar out of the city and moved away, Belshazzar convinces the kind otherwise. Amraphel, the high priest, and Daniel, leader and prophet of the Jews, conspire to assassinate Istar. Amraphel recruits three priests to do the deed during the dedication to the newly rebuilt the temple of Istar. During the journey to Erech, Istar gives in to love and lust to Belshazzar and becomes human, losing her divinity. She can't enter the temple because she is mortal and afraid. Because of this, she escapes her planned murder. Meanwhile, Ramua's slave is caught stealing flowers from Ribata's garden – the flowers Ramua sells every day on the steps of the temple. He gives up his mistress's identity and brings her to the garden where Ribata demands that she marry him. Baba sacrifices herself for her sister, and her love for Charmides, by offering to become Ribata's wife/slave in place of Ramua.]

Chapter 9

Babylon by Night

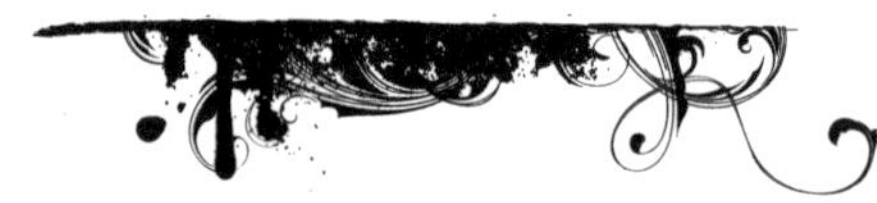

BABA'S DEPARTURE into her new life left an unexpectedly large gap in the household of the tenement. The child's personality had been very strong; and though she had been little heard, little seen even, she had been much felt. Charmides especially found this true. He had always believed, when he played and sang for himself at home, that Ramûa's presence had given him the support of understanding and sympathy. He was scarcely willing to admit, even to himself, that, in the absence of Baba, the pleasure of improvisation had materially lessened. Baba's action in going to Ribâta he still misunderstood. But as time passed and the want of her was as strong as ever, she came gradually to assume in his mind a place that she had dreamed of filling but had never hoped to attain.

Though Baba was at liberty to visit her home, if she chose, during the four or five hours at mid-day, when her lord would never demand her presence, she had the strength to withstand the temptation, knowing that by such visits her unhappiness would be greater than ever. Her homesickness was pitiable enough. She managed to conceal it from the eyes of the curious very well. Her tears would never flow when anyone was near. But by day and by night the iron entered into her soul; and as day followed day, the weight of the hours past, and yet more the presage of those to come, crushed her spirit with a merciless slowness. Baba was too young to realize the healing power of time, how it bears forgetfulness on its kindly wings, how its shadow becomes finally a shield by which the keen daggers of remembrance are blunted and turned aside. She did not know that the human soul can suffer only so far. Her capacity seemed infinite. She appeared to have entered into an eternally dreary land, the boundless valley of shadow. She wept till tears were gone. Day renewed the misery that night confirmed. Finally, when she had come to dream wildly of death as the one desirable thing, the limit of her unhappiness was reached and the tide turned. The beginning of the change for the better was made by the appearance of Zor, her beloved goat, who had mourned for her mistress so continually that life in the neighbourhood with her became impossible, and finally Bazuzu carried the creature to the gates of Ribâta's palace, and commanded the magnificent slaves of the portal to carry it instantly to the Lady Baba. The Lady Baba being, at the moment, an unconscious but none the less real power in my lord's household, Bazuzu was obeyed with alacrity, and the eunuch that led the animal into the court-yard, where Baba lay alone upon her cushions, could only stand in open-mouthed astonishment to see that lady run forward, screaming with delight, throw her arms about the animal's neck, and clasp it to her heart with a warmth that my lord had never discovered in her.

Zor herself baaed with joy; and, having completely forgotten the anything but affectionate parting of two weeks before, put her nose to her mistress' cheek and loudly sounded her pleasure.

Baba always remembered this meeting as the first ray of light in her gloomy existence. Little by little, now, the luxury of her new home began to grow more worthy in her eyes, when she contrasted it with the squalor of her childhood's home. Little by little, as the feeling of silken garments became more familiar, she lost the craving for her rags, and the hair that could fall in unrebuked tangles round her face. The courts, the halls and the rooms of Ribâta's beautiful abode, no longer looked vast, barren and tomblike to her eyes. Ribâta himself was not an object of terror now. He had always been gentle, always kind, with her. This, long ago, she had begun to realize. And now, at length, a visit to the tenement began to seem possible – desirable. Bazuzu, indeed, had come to see her more than once, to bring her her mother's love, and to say that she and Ramûa would see her as soon as she could come. Ramûa was very busy and very happy. Her wedding with Charmides was to be celebrated before the first rains of Tasritû (September), and it was now well along in Ulûlu, the last of summer. Baba heard the news without surprise, but determined to wait till the knot was tied before she went back to see her home.

The time came soon enough. It was not quite three months after the Greek's first sight of the Great City that he took up that city as his abode for life, bound to it by every tie that can bind a man to his home. Throughout his wedding-day, with its quaint ceremonies and its high feasting, Charmides' mind was upon his mother and her distant land. Could she only know his wife, see her for an hour, behold her pretty gentleness and read her great love for him, Charmides felt that Heraia would rejoice with him. But, as it was, through this, the most important day of his life, the youth was rather silent and grave, save when Ramûa looked at him with her shy, inquiring smile.

The wedding ceremony was long and fatiguing. It meant prayer and purification in the morning before the assembled images of the gods. Then there was the procession to the nearest temple, the signing of contracts, the giving of Ramûa's hard-won dower by Beltani, and Charmides' reverent pledge to support, protect, and cherish his wife so long as she should remain faithful to him. Then his wrist and hers were bound together with a woollen cord, a prayer was chanted, there was a great blare of trumpets and clashing of cymbals, a public proclamation that Charmides had taken unto himself Ramûa, the daughter of Beltani of the tenement of Ut, and then, at last, the sacrifice. The chief portion of the animals slaughtered was carried to the house of the bride for the wedding feast, which lasted as long as the food held out.

Not till early evening did Charmides find himself alone. The guests had departed, and Ramûa and her mother were upstairs in the little room that Charmides had taken for Ramûa and himself on the top floor of the tenement. The Greek seated himself on a stool in the doorway of the living-room, watching the sunset, that poured, a river of living gold, over the lane and square before him. The thought of Sicily and his family there was with him still; and he tried, for a little while, to be alone by the sea with his parents and his brother. With all his soul he prayed to Apollo for happiness in the new life, for forgiveness of any past wrong, for a blessing for his wife, and a continuous renewal of their love for each other. Then between him and Ramûa came the thought of little Baba. Her life was dishonourable, despicable, in his eyes; yet it was she that had saved him either from a great crime or the loss of that that was dearest to him. Did she know of her sister's wedding? If she knew, why had she not come to it? There was no telling. But, in any case, he thought of her very kindly tonight, as he sat alone with the gathering dusk.

Charmides' head was bent with abstraction and he was no longer looking at the square before him. Presently a four-footed creature ran against his knee and laid its head there. He looked up quickly, to find Zor at his side and Baba in the square. She came towards him through the twilight like a wraith, in her trailing, silken garments, with her hair piled up on her small head in a crown of black braids fastened with wrought golden pins. Beneath the dark hair her face looked very pale and pointed. It was infinitely different from the face he had known. There was no longer anything of the child in it. The elf-look was gone. In its place was an expression of gentle weariness, of patience, of long-suffering that affected the Greek strangely. As she came closer he looked her full in the eyes, and, with one of his old, shining smiles, held out both hands to her.

Baba had steeled herself to meet any greeting, but this was the one that came nearest to breaking down her self-control. She managed to answer the look steadily; and no one, least of all Charmides, could have dreamed how her heart was bleeding. She gave him her hands, and he saw what she carried in one of them.

"For Ramûa's bridal", she said, placing on his knee a long, golden chain of Phoenician workmanship. It was far more valuable than anything Ramûa had dreamed of possessing; and Charmides, examining the fine work on the metal links, said so to her.

Baba dropped her eyes. "It was from my lord to me", she said. "But it is my hand that brings it to Ramûa. Thou wilt let her wear it – for me – Charmides?" The tone was doubtful.

Much as he might not have desired it, the Greek could not refuse her. "Ramûa is above. Go thou and make thy costly gift to her thyself, Baba".

Baba bent her head, accepting the dismissal with the unquestioning obedience that she had had instilled into her all her life through. While she mounted to her sister, to hear the tale of that sister's perfect happiness, Charmides sat him down again, the current of his thoughts quite changed; his dreams all of the new life, no longer of the old....

[One week later, Charmides was walking home after a night out with a friend.] Pausing for a moment or two to gather a little warmth for his chilled body from the dying embers of the nearest fire, preparatory to setting forth into the city, he saw, coming towards him out of the gloom of the opposite side of the square, two well-robed men, one of whom he recognized as an under-priest in the temple of Sin. They were going in his direction, and as they passed he moved after them, that he might keep himself awake by listening to snatches of their conversation. Both of them were oblivious of his presence, wholly absorbed in themselves. They did not talk at first; but a sensitive person would have realized that they were indulging in that species of mental intercourse that exists only for those whose hearts are bare to each other. Charmides, even in his irresponsible condition, recognized the sympathy, but could not, of course, partake of it. At the first spoken word, however, he pricked up his ears and listened with all his mind. Oddly enough, he found their topic one of peculiar interest to himself. It was the priest of Charmides' temple who spoke.

"From Siatû-Sin I heard all the tale – all that anyone knows. It is incredible, thrice incredible, that she was cried 'mortal' by the people".

"The people! The cattle, rather!" rejoined his companion, scornfully.

"Howbeit – howbeit – there is something strange in the story. Divine, she knew that death was intended. *Human*, she feared it. That we know".

Kaiya shook his head impatiently. "Since Babylon knew her again, neither Amraphel nor Beltishazzar has dared go to her".

"Amraphel, nor Daniel – nor any man. Her very priestesses, we are told, do not see her face. The silver glory is gone from around her, they say. Now walks she veiled in black and gold from Babylonish looms. Veiled she sits in the mercy-seat. Veiled she receives her food. Veiled she ascends to the ziggurat, and there passes whole days alone in meditation".

"And it is said that one standing on the ziggurat, by the door of the sanctuary, may hear the sound of human weeping in that room".

"Istar weeping! Ho, Kaiya – thou laughest!"

"No. I say what I am told", repeated the other, seriously.

"A goddess – does not weep".

There was a little pause. The conversation had reached a point whence it could not proceed. Neither man would make the inference implied. It was preposterous – also unnecessary.

Presently, however, when the reverence had been strained a little, Bel-Dur, the priest of Sin, broke into a laugh. "Love we the woman, Kaiya?" he asked, in amusement.

Kaiya was no laggard. He whipped off his religious mood like a garment, and went a step further than his companion. "Let us love her!" said he.

Bel-Dur turned his head to stare at his companion, and once more began to laugh. "Why not? Is it forbidden? Let us carry comfort to the weeping one. Let us banish her loneliness. Let us – "

"Nay, be silent, Bel-Dur, and listen to me. If she be proved a woman, and hath thus deceived all in the Great City, let her – let her, for punishment or reward, be removed – from one temple of Istar into the other".

Kaiya looked swiftly over his companion's face, and then let his eyes move farther afield. Charmides, behind the two men, listening intently, but slow, from weariness, to understand, waited stupidly for the next speech. Kaiya continued:

"Too long we have worshipped her as Istar to banish her now from Istar's place. Let her be carried to the greater temple, and placed there in the inner shrine on the golden couch of the false goddess. Eh? Say you that I speak well?"

At these ruthless words, spoken in jest though they were, Charmides halted. The blood poured into his brain. He clenched his hands. There was a moment of wild impulse to rush forward and throw himself bodily on the Zicarî that spoke. But the two figures moved on through the darkness, and he lost the next words. Much as the priests had shocked him, Charmides felt the greatest anxiety to hear more of their talk. He stumbled forward again as fast as he could, and presently caught up with them, realizing their nearness by the distinctness of their voices; for the moon was now under a cloud, and the night was black and thick. When he was again able to distinguish words, Bel-Dur was speaking; and the topic had evidently shifted a long way from its previous point. Charmides was puzzled at the first sentences.

"I do not know. Amraphel only admits the Patêsû, Sangû and Enû to their councils; these, and, of course, the three Jewish leaders: Daniel and the sons of Êgibi. The men of Judea – captives, they call themselves – will be a strong force in the uprising".

"Will this come in winter?"

"I do not know. Nothing is commonly known. Yet, in the rainy season, the army of the Elamite could not move northward without great difficulty. It is whispered through the temple that there are to be two armies – one that of Kurush himself; another that of Gobryas, the governor of Gutium. Have you heard it?"

"Whispered, yes. But nothing is sure. If this uprising were to be a matter of three months hence, surely more would be known of it than is known now. Everything is rumoured; nothing is definite – "

"Save that Amraphel covets Nabonidus' high place – and will have it. Belshazzar, look you, will never sit upon the golden throne of his fathers".

"Istar being no woman – maybe Belshazzar will be proved no man".

"Then is he a demon. Nabonidus, indeed, may be a woman in man's garb, O Kaiya. But thou wilt find Belshazzar no sluggard in war".

"Verily I believe it. Here is my house. Wilt come in to us, Bel-Dur?"

"Nay, I keep my way to the temple. There is but a short time for purification before the auguries of dawn".

"Farewell. Amraphel be with you!"

Bel-Dur laughed at the bold sacrilege and departed towards the temple of Sin, while the Zicarî entered into the little house of which he was a member. Charmides was left alone in the narrow street, too weary to go as far as the tenement, undecided as to where to turn his lagging steps for a sorely needed shelter.

Even while he stood, fagged and drooping with sleep, at the door of the monastery, the dawn broke. Night melted and swam before his eyes in rivulets of misty grey. Shadowy buildings reared out of the dim light. From the far-away came the faint howls of waking dogs. There was the gay crow of a cock from some distant field. Then the world was still again. The sky grew eerily clear. Charmides saw the white stars and the fallen moon sink away into the bright heavens. Still the morning was not one of sunlight. It was only a luminous fog that poured down from the sky in swirls. In the midst of it the Greek shuddered with cold, and longed for his lost cloak. Somewhere – somewhere he must go, and quickly. Somewhere he must find shelter from the coming rain. His head throbbed. He was wretchedly nauseated. The night that was past stretched behind him hideously, like the tail of a loathsome reptile. All things were distorted in his mind. He cursed Hodo for making possible for him the night that he had secretly desired. Finally, he put away every thought save that of physical distress, and moved forward at a crawling pace down the narrow street, till he came to the square of the true Istar, whose temple loomed up before him like a cloud-shadow.

The temple gates were open. As Charmides entered the grateful refuge he found more than one wanderer asleep in the silent twilight of the holy house, where sacrificial lights burned by day and by night. Here Charmides also should have laid him down; but, for some inexplicable reason, he was not satisfied with the place. His mind groped for something else. Istar was not here; and he wished to be near her, to feel her presence closer than it was. Following his instinct, he hurried out of the temple and crossed the platform to the foot of the ziggurat, on top of which, in her shrine, Istar had begun to pass her nights; though of this fact the Greek, in his right mind, was quite unaware. He made his way upward, round and round the thick tower, along the inclined plane, till he had reached the top. There was the door to the sanctuary. Across it the leathern curtain was closely pulled. Charmides went to stand beside it, listening intently for the sound of weeping. Had not Bel-Dur said that she wept? No sound came from within. Still, Charmides was quite sure that his goddess was there. With a long, shivering sigh he laid himself down protectively across the doorway, pillowed his bare head upon the bricks, and then, all numb and drowsy with fatigue and cold, he sank into a heavy sleep.

Chapter 10

The Anger of Bel

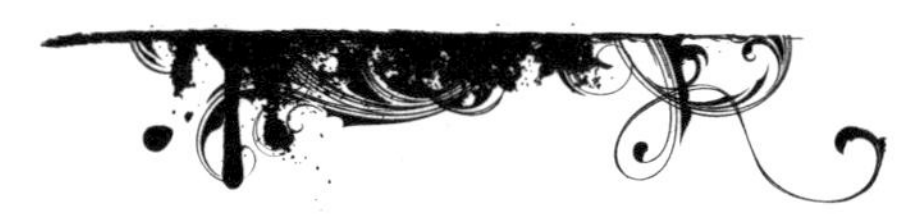

CHARMIDES WAS ROUSED by an exclamation. His eyes fell open, and he found himself gazing up into a face that for months had baffled alike his dreams and his actual vision, and that now stood out clearly above him. He sat hastily up, and immediately a pair of gentle hands were laid upon his shoulders, and the most wonderful of voices said to him, sorrowfully and in amazement:

"Rhapsode! Rhapsode! How came you here? Rise quickly from that place!"

The Greek obediently tried to scramble to his feet, but relinquishing the attempt, he put his hands to his burning head and dizzily closed his eyes.

"'Tis the cold!" he gasped, wretchedly.

Istar looked around her. Far below, in the square, many people moved. But the things that took place on the ziggurat were invisible to them.

"Come thou within – into the shrine. Here wilt thou find warmth", she said, drawing him with her own strength to his feet, and pushing back the curtain before the door.

Charmides went with her blindly, and blindly obeyed her whispered behests. He lay down upon her own couch, was covered over with the costly rugs that she herself had used, and felt the human warmth of the little place with a sense of peace and comfort.

"Oh, goddess – forgive – this profanation – of – thy – high – pla –" The murmur ceased, and before the last word had been completed he had sunk away to sleep, this time in a manner to recuperate his strength.

Istar of Babylon drew a stool to the side of the couch and seated herself thereon, almost without moving her look from the face of the youth before her. Again and again her great eyes traversed his features, the delicate, straight brows, the white eyelids, the long, golden-brown lashes, the short, straight nose and that perfect mouth which, on a woman, might well have caused another Trojan war. A face as beautiful as ever man possessed was this, and as she watched it a great sigh, that was like a sob, broke from her lips.

"Thou, too – thou, too, perhaps, hast been immortal!" she whispered over him.

Charmides did not hear her. He lay like a statue, his sleep made dreamless and perfect by the presence of her whom he worshipped. And the face of the Greek bore the marks of a peace and content that were not on hers. Istar the goddess, the superb, the omniscient, was no more. Instead – Ah! There was a question that lay eternally at Istar's heart, that she could not answer, that burned her with its insistence. Now she bent closely and more close over her charge, seeking to forget herself in contemplation of his beauty. The eager suppression of herself was pitiable, for the power of her self-control showed how great was its necessity. It was while her lashes almost touched the cheek of the Sicilian that from beyond the curtain came the voice of a ministering eunuch, raised in his regular morning formula:

"Belit Istar, the sacrifice is made: the meats have known the fire. A sweet savour ascends from the consecrated flesh, inviting the goddess to her morning repast. Let Belit Istar command her slave".

"Bring to me goat's flesh, and milk and cakes of sesame. Let these things be placed outside my sanctuary door. Let no one enter my shrine this day, on penalty of my wrath".

"Belit Istar is obeyed".

Istar sat up, straight and stiff, for full five minutes after this dialogue had taken place. She was pale with the momentary danger, the remote possibility that the slave, contrary to custom, might have lifted the curtain of the shrine, and, looking in, have beheld Charmides there. And now that the eunuch had safely gone, a trembling seized her, and she leaned forward, burying her face in her hands. The rumours that had spread through the city concerning her were in so much true, that she was in a state of great suffering. The world had become her wilderness. It enclosed her now as a prison from which she could not escape, yet in which her liberty was appalling. Her sense of omniscience, of companionship with the infinite, was quite gone. Nothing was left except – except what she feared as a woman, except what, as a goddess, she cried aloud to the high God and his archetypes mercifully to spare her. Things to which she would give no definite place in her thoughts crushed her by day and by night with their indeterminate weight. That the worst had not come, that a great and terrifying cataclysm, which would rend her spirit in twain, drew day by day nearer to her, she knew too well. And as these days, these miserable, pain-filled days, crawled one by one away, she would fain have held them to her forever; for, wretched as they were, they were almost happy in comparison to that that must finally come upon her. At this moment as she leaned again over the young rhapsode, Istar scanned his face carefully, minutely, to find a trace of human unhappiness. And, finding none, a great envy of him and of the life that he had found in Babylon came over her. Was it possible that so much of joy might belong to any of God's creatures? And was she, then, utterly forgotten? She pulled herself up with a start. *This* was human, this question of hers. For a moment or two she saw truly what she had become, and a fresh wave of fear swept over her. It passed, however. The supernatural perception was rarely with her now, and then only in quick, reminiscent flashes. She was indeed one of those whom she had so profoundly pitied from her dim abode; for whom she had broken the law of her order; in whose name God had driven her forth from the realm of high indifference into the sentient world, the world of pain.

This vague and unhappy reverie was broken in upon by the return of the eunuch with food, which he set down outside her door. The proceeding was unusual, and after the man's departure Istar was seized with a new fear. What would the slave think, that she had bidden him not enter the shrine? Would he suspect? Of all things now, she dreaded suspicion; she dreaded being watched; she dreaded beyond measure the exposure that must inevitably come – but not yet! Not yet for a little while! Stealthily now she drew aside the curtain and looked out upon the narrow platform of the ziggurat. No one was there. Upon the doorsill were two dishes of chased gold, the one filled with steaming goat's flesh and roasted pigeons, the other heaped with barley cakes; and the two of them were flanked by a tall silver jar of warm goat's milk. These Istar lifted one by one, carried them into the shrine, and set them upon the table where her shew-bread was usually placed. Then, when the meal was safe within and ready, she went over to where Charmides still lay motionless, and laid her hand gently upon his forehead.

"Rise thou, Charmides", she said.

"Ramûa!" muttered the Greek. He stirred slightly. His eyes opened. Then, suddenly realizing where he was, he leaped to his feet, stared about him irresponsibly for an instant, and finally threw himself on his face before Istar.

"Forgive me, my goddess! I knew not what I did!" he whispered, terror-stricken.

Istar smiled mournfully. "You ask forgiveness for that that I bade you do. Rise, my Greek. Eat of the food that is here. I command it".

Charmides looked quickly up. He could not deny that he was ravenously hungry. The smell of the meats caused his nostrils to quiver, and the sight of them did away with his reverent wish to refuse. Istar watched him closely as he sat down to her morning meal. She herself could have taken not one mouthful of food, but she had already had a draught of milk; and now, urging the Greek to eat his fill, she turned aside and sat down near the door-way, waiting in silence till the young fellow, after a final cup of the mild beverage, wiped his dagger on his tunic, muttered a line of grace to the gods of Greece, and rose a little shamefacedly.

"Thou hast eaten and art filled, Charmides?" Istar asked, turning to him quietly, with the shadow of a smile.

For answer the Greek bent his knee and bowed his head.

"And now thou goest forth again into the city?"

Charmides looked at her to read the answer that she wished him to make. But the words on his lips were never spoken.

Istar was standing before him a little to the left of the doorway, from which the curtain was half pulled aside. The daylight fell relentlessly over her face and her form. It was upon her face that the Greek's eyes rested: rested in wonder, in amazement, finally with something more than either of those things. Was this last expression one of horror? Istar saw the look and read it; and before its piercing inquiry she quivered. Involuntarily she began to shrink away from him, but escape him now she could not. Knowledge was his. There was no concealment. Then, at length, she accepted the situation, as it was necessary that she should.

"I am a woman", she said, with a gentleness and an unconscious dignity that nonplussed him anew. "Thou mayst not kneel to a woman, Greek. Rise up".

"I kneel to thee, O Istar!" was his reply.

Then, indeed, her lips quivered, but with a little effort she regained her self-control. "Go then, Charmides. Thou knowest me – now".

Charmides got to his feet, but he made no move towards departure. Instead, after an instant's hesitation, he went a little closer to her, and spoke as he might have spoken to Baba – Baba as she was now.

"Istar – art thou indeed the Istar whom first I beheld in Babylon?"

"Yea, Charmides. I am that Istar; yet I am not the same. Then was I more than human. Now – less".

"Who decreed it? Who defiled thee?" he asked, as much of the air around him as of her.

"That thou must not ask. It is what none shall ever know. Depart from me and go thy way. Tell whom thou wilt what I am become. Not long – Ah! It is not long when all the world must know me – as I am".

"Not from the words of my mouth, Belit", Charmides said, sadly. Then, for a little, silence fell between them. He knew that she waited for him to go, and yet, before he went, he felt that he must warn her of the danger that she ran – that danger that he had learned by night. Twist it as he might, the facts were too brutal to be made plain to her. He flushed as he connected, even in thought, the scene of the past night with the grave and grandly beautiful creature before him. Woman she might be, but the mark of her godhead was on her still, could never leave her; for no living woman, of his race or of any other, was comparable to her. And while he thought these things she also stood regarding him, and finally, having read half his mind, opened her mouth and spake:

"Charmides, tell me thy thoughts. I will bear with them".

He grasped the opportunity eagerly: "O Belit, I must warn thee – warn thee against all the priesthood, those of every temple and house in the city. They threaten thee with untellable disaster. Watch them, lady, and take heed to thyself. Beware whither thy steps lead thee, what things thou turnest thy hands unto. They watch thee with numberless and unholy eyes. They mean great wrong".

"If they will bring me death, I welcome it gladly".

He shot a glance at her that caused her suddenly to drop her eyes. Then he said, quietly: "It is not death. Ah, Istar, do not ask its horror. I myself would deal thee death with my right hand to save thee from it".

Istar shuddered.

"Belit, know this. When comes the day of thy trial, if thou wouldst seek shelter from the pursuers, ask to be taken to the palace of Lord Ribâta Bit-Shumukin, on the canal of the New Year. There, at the gate, demand the presence of the Lady Baba. Baba will conduct thee to the home I live in. It is very lowly, but in it thou shalt find safety. Thou wilt remember this?"

"Truly, Charmides, thou deservest all happiness!" she said, impulsively, coming nearer to him.

He bowed his head. "For thee I came to Babylon. Through thee my heart has found its home. Therefore, when thou shalt ask it of me, my life it is thine".

With this, then, and a last puzzled look at her, he went forth to his much-belated temple duties.

Istar, once more left alone, turned slowly back into her shrine. The little interlude that had broken in upon her loneliness made her shrink from the pall that waited to overwhelm her again. Thereafter the one hour of Charmides' presence remained like a little golden disk in the memory of her solitary months. But now the momentary sense of companionship was too terribly contrasted with the melancholy of her solitude. Hurriedly covering herself with a great, silver-woven, heavy-meshed veil, she left her retreat in the upper morning and left the ziggurat for her dwelling-place behind the temple.

She did not see her sanctuary again for seven months. It was not that she felt any reluctance about entering it. Simply, her apathy had become such that she was incapable of the physical effort necessary for the ascent of the tower. Once a day she took her place in the mercy-seat in the temple. All the remaining time she spent in the inmost court of her particular suite of rooms, or in the miniature apartment where she was accustomed to sleep. She reclined generally at full length, doing no work of any kind, her eyes shut, the heavy veil shrouding her figure but thrown back from her face, her body perfectly motionless, her very thoughts apparently at rest. Her attendants watched her, wondering at the great change that was working upon that formerly magnificent personality. And through these same temple-slaves, eunuchs and hierodules, strange rumours concerning the once universally worshipped goddess continued to fly abroad through the city. Certainly there appeared to be little enough of the divine about this weak, ill woman; though why the change had come none of those connected with her had the faintest idea.

These were the days of Istar's wandering in the wilderness. Pain, mental and physical, she learned in every stage, from slight discomfort to nerveless agony. Each morning she woke with the prayer in her heart that night might bring the end of it all, yet knowing well that her end was far away. Her old, archetypal world became gradually more and more indistinct to her memory, till she had all but forgotten it. Her one wish, that she dared not utter, was for annihilation. Yet this would involve a sin that she could not but recognize as unpardonable; for Istar of Babylon bore within her another life, a life that was, as yet, part of her, that by natural law was hers to cherish, that she could not love, that she dared not hate. And it was the day when this new life should take unto itself individuality that she lay dreading through all those dreary months, from the death of summer to Airû, when the new spring came to Babylon.

The fall of Istar was accomplished. This, by day and by night, she cried to herself, in her agony of self-mortification. It seemed to her that the wheel of the law was the most merciless of all ordained things. The former dead-alive existence of her godhead seemed holy, now that she could know it no more. The very present, indeed, unendurable as it was, was infinitely better than what was to come. As a matter of fact, her extreme dread of the future was very near to turning her brain, for at every hour she lived the moment of discovery, till, at times, she was like to go mad with it, and to disclose it all, then and there, and so have done with it.

There were two or three of her priestesses who realized, through many of her symptoms, her mortal state; and these were very tender to her in this time of her trial. From their lips no word of her condition reached the outside world. The underlings, only, talked; and it was from underling to Zicarî, Zicarî to Pasîsû, Pasîsû to Sângî, and so to the Patêsi at last, that distorted accounts of Istar's life and suffering passed rapidly in the late autumn. And these rumours quickly reached the ears of the three people who had the strongest personal interest in Istar of Babylon. Two of them were her enemies, bitter, unscrupulous and powerful. These two were also closely connected. But, while one knew perfectly the mind of the other, and each knew that the greatest desire of the other's political life was Istar's ruin, yet, while matters slowly ripened and daily grew more absorbing, the subject of the approaching disgrace of the whilom goddess was never once opened between them. Amraphel of Bel, from his palace on the Â-Ibur-Sabû, and Daniel of Judea, from his humble house south of the canal of the Prophet, in the Jews' quarter, watched, planned, listened, read each other's hearts, and bided their time, in the way peculiar to those that know well their world. The time for action would come, and without any planning on the part of either of them. But when it did arrive there must be no bungling of the affair.

Only one little thing in the case, as these two considered it, failed to assume its proper proportion in the perspective of their reasoning. The cause of Istar's undoing was as much a mystery to them as it was to the lowliest kalî in Istar's temple. Both Amraphel and Daniel had long ago ceased to reckon Belshazzar as a factor in this affair. The old suspicion had been a mistake – an incomprehensible mistake. The prince royal went no more to the temple of the goddess, never spoke of or to her, gave rather all his time to affairs of state; which at this moment sorely needed the firm will and the strong hand that he alone, of all his house, possessed.

It was well enough that Amraphel could not read Belshazzar's heart. There was indelibly written what would have startled that reverent man out of all his omniscient composure. For if Istar mourned unceasingly the loss of her godhead, Belshazzar, of the house of the Sun, mourned the loss of her to his life as he would hardly have mourned the fall of that kingdom that was dearer to him than his life. After the strange return from Erech, he had gone daily for two months to Istar's temple, and had sought by entreaty, threat, prayer and imprecation, to be admitted to her. And again and again, and yet again, had he been refused, till finally he turned his thoughts to the life of his city. But by this means she was not taken from his heart. By night he dreamed of her, and by day, when she was as far from him as the sun, as near as his children, as unapproachable as the silver sky, she was forever a subconsciousness in his thoughts.

Thus passed, unhappily and uneventfully, the long winter months of the last year of Nebuchadrezzar's Babylon. In the first week of Airû (April), Belshazzar determined finally to reach Istar's presence. The stories of her condition had of late become alarming, and in the depths of his heart he had begun to dread what had never occurred to him before – the possibility of her death. The mere thought left him agonized, and he felt himself unable to keep away from her longer.

It was late in the morning – a glowing morning in Babylon's fairest month – when he left the palace on foot, clad in a dark mantle that completely covered his head and his figure, rendering him unrecognizable to any but his closest companions. He chose this hour for going because he knew that now Istar's vitality would be strongest, and he dared not give her the shock of seeing him at a time when she would be especially weak. The matter of his admission to her dwelling had been arranged by Ribâta the week before, through hirelings whom he had kept in the temple precincts for some months past. Unnoticed by anyone, then, the prince arrived at the bronze door of the building behind the temple. It was instantly opened, wide enough to permit of his passing through; and inside stood a veiled woman, who, after a silent acknowledgment of his rank, led the way through the succession of courts and passages to a closely curtained doorway.

"Belit Istar is within", she whispered. Then on the instant she turned and glided swiftly away.

For the moment Belshazzar stood trembling upon the threshold. His dread was evenly matched with his fever. The throbbing of his heart sent the blood pounding through all his arteries. His hands grew cold and useless. The effect on him of the mere thought of beholding this woman again was something that he did not pretend to understand. Women, ordinarily, were little enough to him. But *this* woman – she who was hidden from him by the single fold of an embroidered curtain – this woman made his earth and his heaven, his soul, his brain, his body and his blood. Go to her it seemed he could not, for very desire. Once his hand moved forth to lift the curtain, but it fell again to his side. His head whirled. Long as it was since he had seen Istar, yet the picture of her as she had lain unconscious in his arms on the morning of the fall at Erech, came again before him to the smallest detail – perfect, finished, immutable. He felt her weight, he beheld the living pallor of her flesh, he saw the heavy-fringed eyelids close over the eyes that lighted his world. She would live so in his mind forever. Now – he was about to turn away, to leave her alone in peace.

So far there had been no sound in the room beyond. But just as he was about to depart there came to his ears some words spoken in her voice – her low, exquisite voice, now so weary and so much weaker than it had been of old. The words reached him distinctly; and instantly they caught his attention. The spell of his reluctance was broken, and all the fire of his eagerness blazed up at the first syllable spoken by her. Quickly he lifted the curtain and stepped out of the sun-flooded court over the threshold of the dimly lighted room. Istar was on her knees before him, her back turned to the door, her head bowed, her long, black veil trailing on the floor around her. Her voice was lifted in prayer, the first words of which had caught his attention, and held him spellbound by means of the sweet, forlorn monotony of her tone, the ring of yearning, of pathos, of utter hopelessness indescribably felt through all the rhythmical cadences, till Belshazzar bent his head in helpless pity over her incomprehensible plight....

With a gasp that resembled a sob, Istar faced about, still on her knees. In turning, she drew the heavy veil that had hung around her close over her face, so that, to anyone but him who looked at her, she would have been unrecognizable. Belshazzar, indeed, confronted by the black mask, felt his speech suddenly suppressed within him. His cloak had fallen to his feet, and he stood revealed in all the splendour of his strength and royal beauty. But before her he was powerless to act. He left the situation helplessly to her.

Istar herself, for the moment, was stunned. In that first minute that she looked upon him again, the world around her grew grey and indistinct. Her cold body trembled. In her dry throat a sob struggled to come forth. But in her heart – ah, who would have believed it! – was rising a great, overweening joy. God had heard her! God sent the answer to her prayer – such an answer as she had not dreamed of. Yet she knew that the Comforter was come. In this thought Istar loosened the veil again and took it from her head, so that her face, white, thin, great-eyed, mournful and still divinely perfect, was revealed to him.

"Istar!" he cried, half in sudden woe at her too apparent illness, half still in passionate admiration. He had seen her before with the silver aureole gone, but now her very face, in its shining purity, was of refined silver. "Istar!" He spoke the word tenderly, and went a little nearer to her.

She had fixed her eyes upon his, and the painfully strained look in her face showed him that she strove to read his mind: his purpose in coming to her. As he approached nearer still she rose suddenly to her feet, for one instant held the protecting veil close around her figure, and then, still without taking her fear-stricken eyes from his face, let it drop, and stood there revealed before him, clothed from head to heel in a scant, straight tunic of white wool.

For an instant Belshazzar saw her stupidly. His eyes travelled over her and suddenly he saw, and his self-control broke down. With a great, hoarse cry of pity and of love, he rushed to her and caught her close in both of his strong, protecting arms.

"Istar! Istar! Thou untrusting one! My beloved! Thou hast suffered alone and told me nothing! Where was thy faith? Hast thou for an hour doubted my love? Know you not how, in my heart, I have mourned thee, have yearned for thee, day by day? Yea, the anger of Bel alone has kept us apart one from the other. The very gods are jealous that I should have thee, thou lotus-flower of the world! Speak to me, O my beloved!"

"Belshazzar! Belshazzar!" she whispered, once, twice, thrice. Then, seeming to gain courage from the syllables of his name, she went on, half fearfully still: "I have hardly loved thee until now. God hath heard me, I think. But, oh! the long, rainy months! The endless days! The eternal nights! How have I prayed to die in them, prayed with my heart and with my lips to die".

He caught her the more convulsively in his arms. "And now?" he asked.

"Ah, now! Now is my strength restored within me! I have new courage. I shall bear my trial now. Thou needst not fear. Suffering will be sweet, for I no longer dread the anger of Bel – of the one God".

"Istar, are we not now as God? Together shall we not defy all? The eleven great gods, and – high Istar herself?"

Istar of Babylon looked dazedly into his eyes. "Do you not believe on me?" she asked, faintly.

"I believe in thy love. That is all my belief".

"But the divinity that was mine?"

He caught her a little closer. "Istar, art thou not a woman?" he asked, gently, but inexorably.

There was a silence. Istar was making her last struggle against fate. At the defeat her head fell heavily forward upon his breast. "Yea, I am a woman", she muttered, faintly.

Belshazzar's lips were pressed upon her forehead. Then suddenly he lifted her in his arms and carried her over to the couch that stood at one end of the room. On this he laid her, and covered her over with one of the heavy, silken shawls used for that purpose. Then he stood off and inspected her, to see that she was comfortable.

"Lie thou there", he said, "till I return within the hour with a litter borne by my household slaves. In thy trial I will be beside thee; thou shalt be in my house, protected by my name, lodged as my princess. But one hour more, and then, for all time, we shall be together!"

He spoke with perfect confidence, and, having finished his explanation, would have departed had not Istar risen quickly from her couch and moved towards him again.

"Gratitude be to my lord!" she said, with a faint smile. "Yet I may not leave this temple till the hour comes. There will be a day when Bel shall cast me forth alone into the city. But, of myself, I may not leave the house to which the All-Father entrusted me. Nor shall mine eyes again behold thee here. Go forth in peace, Belshazzar. My great love is thine; and before many days I think that I must come to thee. But we must patiently abide apart until the time. Now must thou leave me. Farewell!"

"Istar! What is this folly that you speak! You are mine – mine to care for, to cherish. Your suffering is also mine. I go now, but to return again for you. Or shall I dispatch one of your eunuchs to the palace with my message? Yea, that will I do, and remain at your side till the litter comes".

The impatient tone was such as he might have used to one of his wives, to Khamma, to any woman who by law belonged to him. Istar heard him, but felt no anger at the words. Her manner showed only dispassionate self-possession.

"Belshazzar, I have spoken. Shall I say the words again? Go thou forth in peace. When my hour comes I will turn to thee. But we must wait that hour, for it is the will of the great Bel".

The prince royal was taken aback. This was not a woman's way, yet neither was it after the manner of men. He tried her again, this time more gently, with reason, with persuasion, finally with undisguised entreaty. She did not change. The dependent Istar, Istar the supplicator, the woman, was gone. In her place was come the oracle of the mercy-seat. Belshazzar dared not be angered by her unchanging assurance. In the end he acknowledged himself defeated. He could only kneel and implore that the hour of her homecoming be soon. Then, having held her for one moment more in his arms, he left her, wrapping the mantle closely about him as he stepped forth again into the hot sunshine of his new and mysterious world.

As for Istar, with the answering of her prayer she entered the land of heart's peace. God in high heaven had not forgotten her. Belshazzar, on earth below, waited her coming. She could feel that the day of her suffering was close at hand, and she was fortifying herself to endure it. Thus ten days – ten days of the fair spring – passed by. Istar's black-veiled form was seen morning and evening on the temple platform, and she sat in the temple regularly at the mercy-hour, but did not ascend the ziggurat. During this time she knew but ten uneasy moments. These were when, once each day, always, as it were, by chance, she encountered the lean and bent figure of Daniel ..., who lurked, morning and evening, about this spot. His thin, vulture-like face, with its scrawny, gray-streaked beard and his small, beady, piercing eyes, haunted Istar's thoughts and remained with her as an omen of evil; and she shrank from him even less for herself than for some unreasonable ill that he seemed to promise to Belshazzar, her earth-lover. Daniel never addressed her, never failed profoundly to salute her, never remained longer than a bare second within her sight. And she strove to put him from her mind, and to give all of her days and nights to careful preparation for the approaching hours of her trial.

On the morning of April 21st her attendants found her lying in a swoon on her bed. She was quickly revived, and awoke to the world with a look of such happiness in her face that her women wondered silently, and went back to their duties rejoicing. Istar attended the morning sacrifice – a thing that she had not done for three months past. She drank a cupful of milk, watched the goat's flesh roasted on the altar, heard the prayers for the morning, and extended the mercy-hour far into the afternoon. The sun hung just above the horizon when she re-entered the courtyard of her dwelling and called for her evening meal. With unquestioning surprise it was brought her, and she ate of it. Then, in the mellow evening, she said her farewell to the consecrated home where she had dwelt so long.

As Istar left her dwelling and walked slowly towards the foot of the ziggurat, she saw that the whole city lay in a flood of gold. Her steps were slow and fraught with pain. As she halted at the foot of the high tower to look upward, wondering how she should reach its top, a voice from another sphere spoke to her and bade her hasten her steps. It was almost seven months ago that her feet had last touched this pavement. Then she had not been physically weak, but mentally – ! She sighed as she remembered her terror of herself and of all her surroundings. At last, with a deep breath, she began her ascent. Up, up and up, step by step, while the glorified light of day's death swam before her vision and the evening wind fanned her cheeks, while the sweet scent of the flowers that covered the desert was borne to her by the breeze, she went, a prayer in her heart, a resolute determination to endure bravely holding her thoughts. Up and up she mounted, till at last the empty summit of the tower was gained, and she stood again at the door of the room that had seen her incarnation.

Here, on the height, Istar stopped to look out over Babylon. It stretched around and below her like a mirage, like the vision of a holier city, wrapped all in clouds of blinding fire. A little to the east, near enough so that the white designs on the shining turquoise groundwork were fairly distinct, rose, from the tufty green of the surrounding park, the new palace built by Nabonidus, in which Belshazzar lived. Along the east side of this building ran the bright Euphrates, passing here the most imposing point in all its mighty course. Opposite the new palace, on the other bank, were the two huge structures once inhabited by Nabopollassar and his son, that greatest of Babylonish rulers. Across from Nebuchadrezzar's former home, connected with it by the great bridge, itself a triumph of engineering, was the palace-crowned mound of the great one's Median queen, called by subsequent generations "the hanging gardens". This alone of all the unused royal dwellings was kept in repair by the present ruler. And now, at the time of the day's highest glory, Istar's eyes eagerly sought its fresh verdure, the tier on tier of leafy foliage that hid such fragrances and such blossoms as she rarely saw. And while she gazed upon the monument of a king's devotion, the lonely woman found it in her heart to wish that she might have been that queen whose sorrows and whose earthly joys were now so comfortably ended, whose mortality had come to dust, whose soul enjoyed its just rewards.

Istar's eyes moved on down the river to the lower part of the city, which consisted of acre upon acre of low, brick buildings, hardly relieved by a single tower or raised roof, stretching in grey monotony off to where Imgur-Bel suddenly reared its gigantic height skyward. Over this wall and the top of its still loftier brother, Nimitti-Bel, Istar, high as she stood, could not see. Her brick-weary eyes yearned for some glimpse of the quiet palm-groves that lined the riverbank beyond Babylon. Indeed, their fragrant freshness was borne up to her by the evening wind. Closing her eyes, she saw them as, nine months before, she had watched them from her barge on the way to Erech. And thus, while she contemplated many things, the sunset light began to fade, the shadows mingled together over the grey roofs and bright towers of the city. Twilight deepened; and the moon was not yet risen. So at last Istar turned from the far-stretching scene and lifted up the curtain of her long-unused shrine.

She was greeted by darkness. Evidently it was many weeks since anyone had entered the little room. A fine, white dust lay sifted over the rugs, the table, the golden chair, the couch where Charmides last had lain. Istar looked round with a sob in her heart – a sob of pitiable weakness and pain. It was impossible now for her to summon any attendant. Neither had she strength to descend the ziggurat again. Leaving the curtain pulled wide open, that she might feel some communication with the world beyond, she went to the couch, removed the top rug with all its dust, then let fall her veil, and offered up one last prayer for pity and for strength before she lay down resignedly in the night.

Twilight slowly passed across the earth and trailed away into the beyond. Thereupon came terror of the dark, together with the first stabs of sharp pain. She had one swift, torturing moment, and a low cry at the strangeness of it escaped her. Then calmness returned. She was prepared, she thought, for the rest. One moment, two, three, passed, in strained expectation. The darkness hung around her like a covering, but the suffering did not return. Her lips moved continually, but her brain refused to work. It seemed to her that the night must be passing. Soon, perhaps, she might sleep. Her eyes were closed; her mind was slipping away into freedom, when – she started up again. It was once more upon her, this dreaded thing; and now she knew that there was no escape. When it had passed this time she waited, stiff and strong, hands clenched, breath coming and going rapidly, for the return.

It came once again, and yet again, more and more swiftly, more and more terribly. She made no sound now. Her eyes stared straight into the blackness with the gaze of one that does not see. Here was something that, with all her months of preparation, she was not prepared for. No imagination could have painted this; and her loneliness but added to her terror. From the night 1,000 malignant eyes seemed fixed upon her with the look of Daniel.... Yet presently she discovered that these eyes were stars – fair, silver stars that shone, far away, through the open doorway. A little later the night grew luminous, and the hideous darkness was softened and smoothed away. Pale, yellow rays shot up the sky, dimming the stars' white radiance, banishing their gaze. It was the moon, the blessed moon, Istar's father, who, entering the heavens, put her tormentors to flight. The woman's thoughts were growing incoherent. She was a little delirious. Her body was racked and torn and bruised. The agony, too great to be realized and endured, drove her into numb unconsciousness – an unconsciousness that was hideous with subconscious understanding. The one thought to which she clung through all the hours of anguish was of the morning – the merciless daylight, when the searching sun, the discerning, prying sun, must come upon her here, must see, must know – must disclose all to the wondering world.

The fair moonlight sickened her now. Her eyes swam and her head reeled with its bluish light. She prayed for clouds – and rain. Rain! Water! The thought reached her suddenly, out of the aching void. If there were only someone – one only creature, to put water to her dying lips! She burned, she parched, she scorched with thirst. Ah, if someone were at hand! She tried to think of a name to call. And presently one recurred to her. She did not stop to think over it. The syllables hung ready on her lips – were said in a voice so faint and weak that one standing in the doorway could not have heard them. It was a liquid word, one easy to hear, and the only one that her mind, in its strange plight, retained.

"Allaraine!" she whispered.

A breath of cool air poured into the little room, and borne upon it was a rosy beam that gradually suffused the bed in a delicate radiance. With the first shedding of this light, Istar's pain suddenly ceased. Her spirit was uplifted with the mighty relief. Her fast-shut eyes opened again. Above and about her was open space. The roof of the shrine was gone, and its walls also. All around there floated a vast concourse of dimly outlined forms – millions of archetypes, borne on their outspread wings. A chord of distant music rang down the shaft of light, and Istar knew from whom it came. Gravely the goddess greeted her companions; yet none returned the greeting, or seemed to recognize her presence. She tried to go to them, but the bed remained beneath her. She was still a prisoner. After some moments of waiting in the midst of this familiar scene, the rainbow path into her room palpitated with fresh, living light. The bells rang louder in her ears. One form had separated itself from the confused mass, and became distinct to her eyes. Allaraine dropped out of the high space, and was presently standing at her bedside. The room closed in again. The pink light disappeared. Once more the moonlight stole upon her. The night was sweet with the perfume of the lotus, and Istar wept with delight. She was there alone with Allaraine, her brother of the skies.

Through the long hours he ministered to her, holding the cup of water to her lips, plaiting up the heavy masses of hair that swept the floor at her side. And when the last agony came upon her, his voice held her fast to the thread of her strange existence. Finally, at the night's end, it was he who put into her arms the living one whom she had brought into the world.

Bending over them both, the god blessed the child and kissed the mother's brows before he went his way out into space, leaving behind him a trail of song that was sweeter than the perfume of the jasmine. There, from the spot into which he flew, the day broke, and the moon fainted on the western horizon. Istar's heart throbbed with a great, new peace and a human love. Life was no longer strange to her. The bringing of it forth brought her understanding of its richness. And, as the child on her breast lay sleeping, so at last her own eyes closed, until, while the light brightened and the great city woke again, the soul of Istar was at peace.

At sunrise a flood of yellow beams poured into the little room, illuminating everything in it, throwing a halo over the motionless figures of the mother and child on their well-ordered couch. Suddenly the smooth light was broken by a shadow that darkened the doorway. A man stood there on the threshold, peering into the room. His bright, black eyes travelled swiftly over the scene, resting last on the bed. He gave then a sudden, swift start. Glancing quickly behind him to make sure that he was alone, he took a single noiseless step inside, and, inch by inch, moved to the couch, bending over it till the end of his grizzled beard all but touched the cheek of Istar.

As if the glance of the intruder could be felt through the unconsciousness of sleep, Istar stirred restlessly. The infant on her breast gave forth a faint cry and opened its deep eyes upon the morning world. Thereat [Daniel], in timely fright, turned and scurried hastily from the room, escaping Istar's glance by no more than three seconds. And as Istar, deeply disturbed, looked out upon the world, she suddenly caught her little one close to her in her protecting arms, murmuring gently:

"O God! O God! I give Thee praise! Spare me this inestimable gift! Leave me for my joy this little life of mine – and take all that Thou hast given else, great Father!"

Chapter 11

From the House of Heaven

WHEN DANIEL WAS far beyond the range of Istar's vision he did not lessen the rapidity of his gait. Rather, he increased it, till the last five yards of his descent of the ziggurat were done in a quick run; and the few people already abroad in the square of Istar looked up in amazement to see the unkempt figure of the slinking [man] advancing at an eager trot across the open space and into the Â-Ibur-Sabû.

Beltishazzar, however, had at that time little thought for the opinions of the people whom he passed. The one thing that he desired above all others, the thing that had assumed a place paramount to his disinterested historical desires – the downfall of Babylon and the freeing of his race – had come to pass. Moreover, the accomplishment of it was, apparently, by the will of God alone. Surely no man earnestly wishful of attaining to a certain end ever arrived at it by simpler or more thorough process. It was a miracle. It required no explanation, no twisting of facts, no blustering denunciations. Who would ask stronger proof of the mortality of this impostor than the sight of her child, and her own weakness? Reverence for the motherlove, for its beauty, for heart's peace, did not occur to the prophet. He felt that Istar's great sin, her tremendous fraud, her immense daring, were things that a statesman might secretly marvel at, possibly admire, in a way. But naturally these feelings would never be expressed.

In such a course wound Daniel's triumphant thoughts as he hurried with them down the wide street towards the palace of the high priest of Bel. It was unusually early in the day for an interview with Amraphel; and of this [Daniel] had scarcely stopped to think when he halted before the outer gate of the ecclesiastical dwelling. The night-guards had not yet made way for the more gorgeously attired eunuchs of the day; but [Daniel] was too familiar a figure to all Amraphel's household to be denied admittance by any of his servants. There was some little doubt expressed as to their lord's having risen. But the doubts were couched in reverent terms, and shortly the lean and ill-kempt [man] was ushered through the vast, empty courts and halls, to the little dining-room of the high-priest's private suite.

Only two slaves, servitors, were in this room when the visitor entered it; and these were busy preparing for the arrival of the master. The wrought ivory and ebony couch had already been drawn up before the table on which various fruits were laid out. And shortly after Daniel made his appearance; a place was added to the table and an armchair drawn to it, evidently for him. He would have seated himself, when there came a sound of steps in the passageway, and Amraphel, white-robed and whiter-bearded, came in, followed by two cringing slaves bearing the long-handled feather fans in use even at this early season. Beltishazzar read the priestly mood at sight. It bore small relation to that benign and fatherly manner assumed for the morning sacrifice, and coming on naturally of an evening, after the long day of adulation and worship. Daniel almost prostrated himself on the old man's entrance, and got in return a slight acknowledgment of his presence, and the words:

"Is your visit early, … or the last of your night?"

"The last. – May it please you, lord of Bel, to see me alone. My news is not such as should grow cold. Over it, all Babylon will laugh for joy".

Amraphel looked at this companion of many schemes a little sourly as he sank back on his couch, and took up an orange from its dish of gold. "What is the nature of this laughing news that you should impart it by stealth?"

Suddenly Daniel lost his patience – a thing not usual with him. "My lord receives it thus" – he snapped his fingers – "and behold, I take it to Vul-Ramân of Bit-Yakin, who, hearing it, will not scoff". And [he] actually made as if to get up from his chair.

"Stop!" cried the high priest, sharply. "There is no cause for anger. Sit you, and we will speak of it".

Daniel shrugged his indifference, but slipped into his chair again, without, however, offering to touch food.

My lord looked round upon his slaves, indicating each of them with a little glance, and designating those that fanned him with a gesture. "Depart and leave us", he said, shortly.

His command was obeyed with decided alacrity, and when the bare feet had patted their noiseless way far down the adjoining corridor, Daniel straightened up in his chair with a little rustle and said, in a low tone: "My news, Amraphel, is, shortly, this: Istar of Babylon, whom we have feared, is a woman – a woman, weak, powerless, full of sin".

Daniel paused, and Amraphel looked at him with a little curl of the lip. "Is that all?" he said, after a pause. "Is that all? Art thou drunk … ?"

Daniel did not lose his temper now. He smiled, contemplatively, and went on: "Nay, I am not drunk, lord high-priest, neither is that all my news – yet, in a way, it is all told. If all Babylon knew too well that Istar were a woman – and weak – and sinful? *Hein?* Would it not be enough?"

"If the *people* knew – the people – yea, it might be".

Thereupon Daniel told without more ado all that he had seen, and how Istar lay at this moment in her sanctuary with the infant in her arms.

Then, indeed, Amraphel was touched to the quick. Verily, here was news! Here was such news as caused the most unemotional man in the Great City to start up from his couch and pace the floor with hurried and uneven steps, his eyes alight, his pale face tinged with red excitement, his hands busily twisting his robe. It was some moments before he spoke, but, once begun, Daniel sat silent and amazed.

"Ah, Beltishazzar, wisely mayst thou rejoice now. Babylon – Babylon, the city of Nabopolassar, my father, shall at last stand free before me! Listen, listen, all ye people! Istar of Babylon is fallen. She is fallen who reigned as a goddess – over me. Mark me … time was when Istar of Babylon was divine. The glory of the unknown God flowed around her. Her lips spoke truth. In her heart was hidden all knowledge. The life that she lived was unapproachable by mortal man. And while she remained thus, I dared not try my full power in the city.

"But now – now! Ah, Beltishazzar, now the fear is gone! The goddess has tasted the bitterness of human love and is become mortal. Her sin has found her out. Today, even today, she shall be driven from that temple that her presence defiles. Her downfall shall be cried aloud to them that have worshipped her. Her disgrace shall be proclaimed throughout the kingdom. Let her invoke what aid she may, human or divine! I defy her now to deny me omnipotence in Babylon.

"And thou, Daniel – thou that broughtest this word – have no fear that thy people shall lack favour in my sight, and in the sight of the mighty lord of Elam. Let us henceforth work together for that end which, in the name of our gods and of the God of Judah, shall be accomplished within the year!"

He paused in his speech and in his walk, and his head fell upon his breast. He descended quickly, did Amraphel, from heroics to practicality; and this, perhaps, was one reason of his great success in life. Daniel eyed him in silence till the echoes of the tirade had died away and there had been time for thought. Then he said, shortly:

"You will drive her from the temple, Amraphel? How?"

"By Nebo, with an ox-goad, that is used for cattle!"

Daniel shrugged incredulously. "And whither drive you her?"

"She may go, if she will, to her proper abode – the temple of false Istar, near the gate of the setting sun".

Daniel drew a sharp breath. "Father Abraham!" he muttered, himself amazed at Amraphel's pitiless joy in triumph. Then, a moment later, he added: "It is a just ending. Well, my lord, I take my departure now".

"Thy departure! By Marduk, thou shalt come with me to the temple! Thou must be at my side when I enter her shrine".

Daniel cringed quickly, and proffered a swift excuse. Keen he might be; bold in his way; master of diplomacy, of deceit and cunning; but discreet, cautious, nay, cowardly, when it came to his personal safety, he was always. It was true that Istar was no more and no less than a weak and unfortunate woman; but enough of divinity still clung to the thought of her to keep [him] far from any desire to stand before the people as her accuser. Amraphel might be angry, might persuade or command. In the present matter Beltishazzar was immovable. Amraphel recognized it presently, and saw that nothing was to be done but to summon Vul-Ramân, with all possible speed, from the neighbouring temple, and to command a chariot to be prepared at once and brought into the outer court of the palace.

These things were quickly done; and Daniel had been gone for many minutes by the time Vul-Ramân answered the peremptory summons and stood before his superior. The priest of Nebo was in a temper, and greeted Amraphel in an undisguisedly irritable tone.

"My lord, it is the hour for sacrifice. My place was at the altar. By your message hath Nebo lost his morning savour, and the temple the flesh of three goats. What is needed of me here?"

"And has the freeing of Babylon cost the price of three goats, O Bit-Yakin? Pray thou for strength to endure the loss!"

Vul-Ramân looked at him in displeasure. "Are thy words oracles?" he said, sourly.

"Within the hour their light will illume thy understanding. Now thou art to drive with me up to the temple of Istar. They bring my cloak".

Vul-Ramân looked on with sudden interest as two slaves entered the room where he stood. One of them carried a long, woollen garment of Tyrian weave, heavily embroidered in golden threads in a pattern containing the various symbols of the different gods. It was a mantle worn only upon the greatest occasions. This being fastened upon Amraphel's shoulders with well-wrought pins of gold, the second slave crowned the high-priest with his golden-feathered tiara, sandalled him with sandals embroidered in the same rich metal, and finally put into his hand something that caused Vul-Ramân to exclaim:

"What, in the name of Nergal's holiness, do you with the bullock's goad, Amraphel!"

"Come you with me, Vul-Ramân. Our way lies to the north, to the temple of Istar. From it I shall drive forth the false woman that dwells there receiving worship. For – "

"Amraphel!" Vul-Ramân stopped short. "Art thou raving? What canst thou do against Istar? Because by her mercy we are spared punishment for our last sin against her, darest thou again attempt her downfall? Attempt it by such means as this? If thy mind has not left thy body, then thine arrogance leads thee to death!"

The high priest waited till the other had finished his protest. Then he said, calmly: "Istar of Babylon is a woman with child. Her divinity is gone. I go to drive her from the heavenly house".

In silence the two men proceeded to the courtyard, where, surrounded by a group of slaves, stood the golden chariot with its white horses and flashing harness. The driver stood holding the reins in his hands. On the arrival of the two priests there was a general obeisance. Amraphel entered the vehicle first. Vul-Ramân, not without a perceptible hesitation, followed him. The master raised his hand, the driver shouted to his steeds, and the powerful animals, with one spring, shot forward, drawing the whirring chariot after them through the bronze gate way, out into the Â-Ibur-Sabû.

"The temple of Istar!" said Amraphel.

The flashing wheels turned to the north, and in brave silence they proceeded towards the square at the end of the broad street. Not a word was spoken during the drive. The two priests, one on either side of the driver, stood like statues – Vul-Ramân with a face as white as a summer cloud, Amraphel in immovable calm. The right hand of the high priest rested on the rim of the chariot in front of him. His left, the one with which he clasped the short, black goad, with its two cruel leathern thongs, hung at his side. As they went along, the people in the street stopped to stare in curiosity as to the wherefore of Amraphel's state magnificence, and Vul-Ramân's appearance so far from his temple at the hour of morning sacrifice. When finally they entered the square of Istar, it was wholly deserted; for service was going on in the temple, and a respectable throng was assembled to witness the weekly slaughter of doves and the broiling of their flesh over the cone-fire on the altar.

"Istar will be there at the sacrifice, doubtless", whispered Vul-Ramân, hurriedly, as they alighted together at the steps of the platform.

"Let us seek her", was all the reply he got. Amraphel exhibited not a trace of uneasiness, and yet, to a certain extent, the fear of the priest of Nebo had its effect on him. Mentally he cursed the prudent cowardice of Daniel, who, having arranged this situation, had left him to run the chance of disgrace and defeat alone.

As they came to the door of the temple the two priests found themselves confronting the throng of men and women who were just emerging into daylight. The sacrifice was over. But as Amraphel, in all his magnificence halted before them in the doorway, the people also came to a stand-still, lowered their heads and waited silently to learn if there was a reason for his coming. For some seconds, however, Amraphel stood passive. He perceived the officiating priestess coming towards him from the altar, and he waited for her to reach his side. Then she, and Bit-Yakin, and finally the high-priest, performed the ceremonious greetings of the religious code; and only after these were over did Amraphel say:

"We seek the lady – Istar of Babylon. Is she in the temple, O servant of the great goddess?"

"The spirit of the goddess hath attended on the sacrifice. So spake the omens, most high lord", was the disturbed reply.

"Belit Istar, then, is not here?"

"Nay, Lord Amraphel. She is in her shrine at the top of the ziggurat, to which she retired at sunset yesterday".

"We will ascend into her presence".

The priestess started. "Nay – nay! Let my lord remain here below. The goddess is alone with her brothers. She commands that none shall ascend to her today".

"Begone, woman!" shouted Amraphel, suddenly breaking out into a very well-arranged burst of anger. "Begone, thou deceived and deceiving servant of a false goddess! Hear ye, ye people!" And he turned to the astonished multitude. "Hear ye who, for many months – nay, years – have worshipped at an altar of evil! Istar of Babylon, whom, unknowing, ye have called Belit, spouse of the great Bel, is no goddess. As the great gods have revealed to me by night, she is but a woman, sacrilegiously dwelling in the house of heaven, accepting the homage of the multitude, delivering oracles from the mercy-seat, receiving offerings and the sacrifice day by day throughout the months, deceiving you and them that dwell with you. Now I come to expose her and to deliver her up to you to do with as ye will. Come ye forth and assemble about the foot of the ziggurat while I ascend, that ye may behold her when she comes forth from the holy shrine of the outraged goddess that dwells afar from us in the silver sky".

Amraphel made this speech with such an air of mingled sorrow and outraged dignity that Vul-Ramân, for all his amazement, could not but applaud it. The crowd showed less indignation than bewilderment and curiosity. But as the old man turned from them to cross the platform, the people followed him like sheep, leaving only the wailing hierodules behind them in the temple.

Bit-Yakin and the high-priest arrived at the foot of the ziggurat side by side, with the foremost of the company ten feet behind. Here, once more, Amraphel turned to them, raising his right hand majestically as he spoke: "Wait here for her whom I shall drive unto you; but see that, on penalty of the wrath of the gods, ye ascend not to the shrine".

Then, hearing the low murmur that told the acquiescence of the obedient flock, Amraphel and his shadow began their ascent. From below, the people watched them in growing wonder, in growing uneasiness. They had seen the ox-goad in the high-priest's hand, and they were thrilled with strange terrors as they considered what its use might be. Istar – their Istar – Istar, the great goddess – flogged! Impossible! Yet – yet – the curiosity was upon them, and they waited to see.

And now the two priests stood at the doorway of the shrine. The leathern curtain was closed before them. Nothing could be seen. There was a little pause, and, for the shadow of an instant, Amraphel wavered. Vul-Ramân, closely watching him, felt his heart sink.

"Shall I lift the curtain?" he whispered, devoutly hoping for a negative reply.

But Amraphel had gone too far now to falter. He nodded.

The heart of the priest of Nebo gave a throb of fear. He made no move to obey the command. Amraphel glanced at him sharply, took one step forward, and dragged the curtain from the door.

There was a low, frightened cry, supplemented by a weak wail from a faint and tender voice. The high priest shaded his eyes with his hand till he could see into the interior of the room; and then, indeed, his heart beat high.

In that room, sitting now upon the great golden chair, was Istar of Babylon. She was clothed in the long, white, woollen tunic, that was scarcely so pale as her face. She was unveiled, and her silken hair, unbound and tangled, fell over her whole form and down to the floor on either side. Upon her knees, wrapped in a square of sacrificial muslin, its little form bathed in a dim, effulgent light that radiated from its body, lay the babe – her child.

Upon the entrance of the two priests, after the one startled cry, Istar sat perfectly quiet, her drawn face no whiter than before, her great, dark eyes staring wonderingly at the intruders, her breath coming and going rapidly between her parted lips.

Amraphel, whose self-composure had returned to him doubled in strength now that he was sure of his position, stood surveying her leisurely, with undisguised triumph. Vul-Ramân, on the other side, had also lost his fear. His delight at the turn of affairs was hardly less than his amazement; for, since the morning at Erech, Istar had had, in all Babylonia, no firmer believer in her divinity than Vul-Ramân of Bit-Yakin. Yet now, human, mortal, weak, she certainly was. Fitting, indeed, was it that she should leave the temple of the great goddess. And as he thought upon the manner of her expulsion, his lips curled in an involuntary smile.

At that moment Istar's eyes were resting on his face. She saw his expression, and she read all the cruelty of it; for suddenly, raising the infant in her arms, she rose to her feet.

"Why have you come hither?" she whispered, hoarsely, her eyes moving from one to the other.

"Thou deceiver! Thou blasphemer! Thou thing of evil, of unholiness! We are come in the name of her whose abode thou hast so long profaned, to drive thee forth from Ê-Âna to thy true dwelling – the temple of the false Istar!"

Istar's nostrils quivered with scorn. She lifted her head in a final proud defiance of the words of the high priest. At the same instant Amraphel's left hand was raised. The goad whirred through the air, and the thongs came stinging across the face of the woman.

A sharp scream, that could be heard by the multitude below, rang out from the shrine on the ziggurat. The woman caught her baby close to her breast, shielding it as well as she could with both arms. The cut of the whip had left a bright crimson weal across both cheeks and just over her mouth. The goad was lifted over her again, and this time she shrank backward from it.

"Get you forth, false creature, from the heavenly house!" cried Vul-Ramân, in raucous tones.

Amraphel moved out of her path, and Istar, blind and dumb with terror and amazement, started towards the door. As she went the whip fell again, this time on her shoulders, and again the scream followed it. Hugging the babe yet closer to her breast, she ran out upon the ziggurat platform in the blaze of the sunlight, and, with Amraphel and Vul-Ramân close at her heels, began an ever-hastening descent, round and round the tower, towards the square below. Up to her ears, from that square, came a long-drawn, minor groan. The people below were waiting for her, waiting for her as vultures wait. Behind her, driving her on to them, were their priests. She herself, helpless, bewildered, numb with the pain of exertion, beside herself with a desperate, fierce sense of mother-protection, knew scarcely what she did, was unmindful of what must come to her.

Since the priests had left them, the numbers of the crowd were considerably swelled. Istar's temple-servants, eunuchs and women both, had come pouring from the temple and the dwelling to witness the issue of this undreamed-of struggle. Also everyone that entered the square of Istar, whether on foot or in chariot, had either been directly summoned by the mob or had joined it voluntarily from curiosity. These people, by now 200 strong, were awaiting the development of the affair in an undecisive humour. More of them believed in the divinity of Istar than in the word of Amraphel, powerful as he was. But now, suddenly, there was to be seen, circling towards them from above, a woman's figure, utterly dishevelled, with long hair flying about her and straight woollen tunic impeding her progress, clasping in both arms a tiny bundle, and fleeing, in very evident terror, from those that followed her, one of whom held the goad uplifted in his hand. And as her weakness, her mortality, her too evident confusion, became apparent, the people felt all the old, inherent savagery of their race rise over the lately acquired civilization, and they watched with delight the approach of their helpless prey.

Istar, as she came nearer the ground, could see the crowd there close up its ranks and draw nearer the foot of the tower. She realized its attitude instantly, and her heart palpitated fast with excitement. Go back she could not. Keep on she must. And soon she reached the last few feet of the inclined plane, and felt the very breath, hot and hostile, of her one-time worshippers rise about her. She stopped, faltering. Her shoulders quivered in expectation of a blow; for Amraphel was close upon her. The blow was struck – fiercely – and it cut through her garment like a knife, blackening the white skin beneath it. At the same time Amraphel's voice thundered out to all the crowd:

"I bring ye the false witch out of the holy temple of Istar. Do with her as ye think fitting and meet, in reverence to the outraged goddess".

There was a deep, universal cry, a cry of hatred, of triumph, of the purest brutality, from the throng. Istar, looking down upon the massed faces before her, reeled slightly. Then, for her child's sake, with a mighty effort she straightened up again. Knowing not what else to do, she stepped forward to the crowd. A great hand was quickly thrust into her face. Another struck her on the shoulder – but not so cruelly as the whip could strike. A dozen men seized her about the body. Then she lost every feeling save only one, that was more an instinct than a definite idea. She must protect her child. She must save it, while she lived, from the hands of her assailants. She was in the very midst of the mob. Heads, arms, hands, all struggled around and towards her, striking, bumping, pushing her. Her hair and her tunic were torn. No one as yet had threatened her with a weapon; but this, she felt, was only a matter of time; and then vaguely she commended herself to the God whose will had been hers also.

All at once, however, she felt more room around her. She was in the middle of a small, empty space, about which her own eunuchs stood in a circle, their backs to her, fighting with the men of the mob that sought to reach her. With a gleam of hope, she saw that all were not hostile. Her head swam and the world grew misty around her, yet still she clung to her shred of consciousness, that she might keep the baby safe. And, while she still controlled herself, someone appeared out of the tangle of struggling forms. Someone came close to her side, saying to her, in a once familiar voice:

"Belit Istar, keep to my side, and I will make a way for you through these men".

Istar turned her half-blinded eyes upon the defender, and smiled at him – the golden-haired, the silver-voiced, whom long ago she had sheltered in her shrine.

"I will keep to thy side – Charmides. Or – I die here. Yet I fear not death. Life – only – is – terrible", she muttered, faintly.

The Greek did not answer her. Seeing an opening in the throng, he threw one arm around her, and, holding his right hand out in front of them both, hurried quickly forward. Istar never remembered how it happened. She saw her eunuchs all around her. She knew little of the angry people beyond. Presently she and her rescuer stood together beyond the mob on the edge of the platform steps.

"Thy eunuchs, I think, will keep the crowd from pursuit. They have been bravely true to thee. Now, canst reach my dwelling, lady? The way is far".

"To thy dwelling I cannot go. May the Almighty God make thee forever happy! Leave me now. I follow my path alone".

Charmides regarded her as slightly crazy. As she started quickly forward he kept close at her side. "Come with me – a little to the right", he suggested, gently.

She shook her head. "Nay, Charmides, I know the way. It is to the house of my lord that I go. Haste! Haste! They follow me!"

She started forward as she spoke, running in terror down the steps into the square, and turning unhesitatingly into the Â-Ibur-Sabû. Charmides kept to her and supported her as she went, knowing not what else to do, not daring to take the child, to which she clung with such a mother-clasp that none could have presumed to ask her to relinquish it. And in this wise they proceeded together up the great road, finally turning into the street of Palaces leading towards the river. As they passed, no man or woman failed to turn and stare at the couple, for surely such a sight as this had never before been seen in Babylon. How long the walk lasted, minutes, hours, or days, or how it was that Istar kept from losing consciousness after the terrible hour she had been through, Charmides never knew. Some of the agony, mental and physical, that the woman was enduring he could read in her face. The greater part of it no mortal could have known or borne, for it was the death of her immortal existence and the beginning of her real earth-life, her life as a human being, a woman without power, without strength, without knowledge of what was to come.

Noon glared over the city as the two of them reached the border of the hunting-park that surrounded Nabu-Nahid's palace. A little farther along was the palace gateway, with its group of guards in their magnificent liveries. Charmides looked at them in despair, for surely the poor woman at his side would meet with no courtesy here. Such fears did not trouble Istar. Advancing to the first soldier, she said at once:

"Admit me, now, to" – she faltered over the name – "to my Lord Belshazzar".

For a moment the man stared into her haggard and colourless face, crossed with the red weal of the whip, looked into the wild eyes, saw the burden that she bore, and laughed.

Istar heard him, saw him, was still and silent for a moment, and then turned dully to Charmides. The Greek's eyes brimmed with tears – tears of rage at his helplessness and unutterable pity for Istar.

"Belit, come away with me. I will keep you till my lord receives you here", he whispered to her imploringly.

Istar shook her head and turned hurriedly to the second man. "I will be taken to my Lord Belshazzar! Admit me to him!" she cried, querulously.

"There is he, then, if you would speak to him", was the jeering answer, as the man, with a grin, swept his thumb in the direction of the first court, just inside the gate.

Istar darted forward to look.

"Thou fool! Now she will scream!" said the first soldier to his comrade.

Truly enough, Belshazzar was in the court, walking slowly towards the gate of his wing of the palace. Istar's eyes fell on him instantly. She smiled a little. Then – she called:

"Belshazzar! Belshazzar – my lord!"

At the first syllable Belshazzar stopped, lifted his bowed head, and listened. At the repetition of the cry he turned towards the gate and came running – running as never before, towards it. The guards, watching him in something like consternation, opened the gate at his approach.

"Istar! Istar! Thou – here!" came in a great cry of love, of anger, of ineffable pity, from the lips of the prince royal.

Istar tremulously smiled, and held out her infant to her husband. "I – have – come", she whispered, vaguely. Then, as Belshazzar took the child from her, she gave a gasping sob, and fell forward upon the hot bricks at his feet.

Chapter 12

Êgibi & Sons

BY NOON THAT DAY Babylon was ringing with the story of Istar's fall and her miraculous escape from the hands of the mob of priests and the people. The tale, from the first appearance of Amraphel and Vul-Ramân in their chariot on the Â-Ibur-Sabû at so early an hour, down to the arrival of Charmides and Istar at the edge of the royal park on the street of Palaces, was in the mouth of every man. But, strangely enough, the beginning and the end of it all, Beltishazzar the Jew and Belshazzar the prince, were never once mentioned by anyone. Amraphel in the temple and Daniel in the street listened, each with his own ears, in his own way, to learn how much was known; and possibly both were relieved that the beginning was unguessed; but certainly both were annoyed to find that they could learn no more of the close of the drama than anyone. Istar had simply disappeared. Her Greek guide was known, had even been seen in the afternoon walking from the temple of Sin towards the canal of the New Year. But no move was made towards his apprehension, for he was highly valued by the priesthood of his temple, and no amount of questioning on the part of anyone drew from him a single satisfactory reply as to the final disposal of Istar and her child.

Nevertheless, Charmides' mind and heart were full. Not until the afternoon had he an opportunity, or, indeed, the wish, to review the great event in which he had played so important a part that morning. All the circumstances had been shoved into the background and forced to lie still in his subconsciousness throughout the morning, while he performed his regular duties at the temple. And only now was he free to let them come once more to the surface and quietly consider them in his homeward walk. First, there was the errand that had taken him to the temple of Istar at that hour of the morning – a message concerning two oracles that must be identical, to be delivered at the same hour at two temples. Charmides had been more likely than any of the priests to win Istar's consent to the arrangement and to the deceit that it involved. And it was thus that he arrived at the temple of the goddess at the hour of the close of sacrifice, to find an unusual and excited throng assembled round the foot of the ziggurat, upon which, Charmides learned, Istar had slept on the previous night. Entirely ignorant of the portent of this mob, the Greek had joined them – hearing only that Istar was still above. From there, in such wise, he watched her expulsion from the sanctuary; saw her struck by the whip of the high priest; perceived the burden that she bore; and, finally, knew that she was swallowed up in the mob that had been threatening her life. Then, at last, a furious desire for action came over the Greek. He looked around eagerly. On his right hand stood a company of men that were taking no part in the turmoil, regarding it rather with an expression of anxiety in their faces. These were the eunuchs of Istar's household, wearing her livery: servitors that had been willing slaves. Charmides saw that in them lay his goddess' only chance. He rallied them and brought them together by means of a few sharp words of encouragement and explanation; and with them close-pressed around him, he made an onslaught on the disordered throng.

It was thus that Istar's rescue had been affected. There was little in it that was remarkable; but Istar's endurance in the long walk that followed was certainly little less than miraculous. It was, however, the scene at the end of this walk that had affected Charmides most powerfully. In Belshazzar's reception of her, Charmides had not failed to read something of the history that had made that reception possible. Love for her, this wonderfully fallen woman, helpless, weary and persecuted as she was, the prince unquestionably bore. She had come to him in her hour of sorest need, and he had not failed her. Could she then, always, in her former glory, have rejected him? It seemed impossible. And at this thought Charmides grew troubled. He could not bear that Istar should be tainted by contact with any mortal. Yet now, alas! he knew that she must be so tainted. With this thought the world grew human again, and Charmides turned his mind to Ramûa, his wife, her who had first made Babylon beautiful to him. In another two or three minutes now he would be with her, for he had nearly finished his homeward walk. Directly opposite him were the palace and gardens of Lord Ribâta, behind whose walls dwelt Baba, that other being whose life had for a moment touched his, and had then flown off again at a tangent that could not but separate them more and more as time went on. For Baba, Charmides felt a lurking tenderness, that had developed since he won his happiness through her; and as he rounded the corner of the tenement of Ut and hastened his pace towards his own doorway, he was not sorry to find three women watching for him in that space – Ramûa, Beltani and, lastly, Baba herself.

It was evident that news of the great happening of the morning had already reached this remote corner of the city; for the instant that he was within speaking distance of his family, the Greek was assailed with such a volley of questions as only women could have marshalled under a single breath. It must be confessed that Charmides heard them with something like despair. Yet he knew also that he would do best to submit to the inevitable without protest. Therefore, seating himself upon a new stool in the living room, he proceeded to utilize the moments unoccupied by women's voices in explaining as lucidly as possible the morning's adventure. Baba alone was silent during his recital. She stood perfectly still, her hands folded in front of her, her large eyes fixed solemnly on his face, listening, with an eagerness that he could not but perceive, to his every syllable. Immediately upon the end she turned, with a rustle of silk and a jingle of golden chains, towards the door. Then, beckoning Charmides to come with her, she led him along for a few yards, and, fixing her gaze upon him, said, seriously:

"Charmides, you must know that you have incurred danger by this act. The eyes of all the priesthood, of Amraphel, of Vul-Ramân, of Beltishazzar …, will from this time forth be upon you. Take care that, though you have won the love of every woman in Babylon by your act, you do not also receive some mortal injury from these others. I warn you as one that loves you. Remember it".

And with these words, and a nod to her sister behind, Baba let Charmides go, and went on alone towards her pleasant prison-house.

There was no reluctance in Baba's gait as she approached the palace of Ribâta; for the unhappiness of the first months of her new life was gone. In its place had come a contentment that was as near akin to happiness as anything she had ever known. By her own tact and wisdom she had made for herself an enviable place in Lord Ribâta's household. Everyone in it, from the first wife to the newest dancing girl and the humblest slave, liked her. She had never been known to do one of them an unkindness; and none of them had ever borne a complaint of her to their lord. For this, if for nothing else, Bit-Shumukin would have regarded her as a paragon. But my lord had other cause for keeping a close companionship with her after her novelty had worn off. Baba was no fool; and, young as she was, began, under

Ribâta's experimental tuition, to develop no mean abilities in the way of politics and political diplomacy. She had begun by having explained to her the unimportant things – dark secrets known to everybody in the state world, and to anybody else that cared to go into them. Finding from these that she possessed that unheard-of thing in woman, a bridled tongue, Ribâta trusted her further, began to make some little use of her in a statesman's way, and found that she had unusual talent in that unusual line. Finally, she had ended by becoming an unfailing necessity to him in his broad outer life. Baba went to houses, knew people, heard things repeated, received confidences that no other woman in Babylon dreamed of. In many cases she was able to save her lord's dignity in a pleasant way. She formed friendships with certain people whom he suggested to her, and obtained from them a world of amusement for herself, and an unfathomable fund of information for her master. She found Babylon to be a seething mass of plots and counterplots, little and great, honorable, ignoble, loyal and traitorous. The government was fighting its enemies with their own weapons, and intrigued vigorously, sometimes in the light of knowledge, far more often in hopeless darkness. Ribâta, as Belshazzar's closest friend, dwelt in the very midst of this world of craft, and how valuable to him and to his prince so versatile and so truthful an agent as Baba was, none but Ribâta himself knew. But it was in this way that life had grown interesting again to the little creature; and it was in this way that she gained a satisfaction in her existence, knowing that she was worthy, that she was serving a great cause well. Indeed, from her heart, in the light of all her knowledge, Baba was body and soul loyal to the king and to the prince-governor of the city. Autocratic as they were and wished to be, it took little understanding to perceive how infinitely more selfish, how infinitely more tyrannical would be the other side, that great opposing element of which Amraphel was the recognized head, and Daniel … the unrecognized but not less important right hand.

Knowing this religious body as she did, Baba's warning to Charmides had been no idle one; and on her way home she was occupied in reviewing the position of the man whom she revered as well as loved. It caused her no little anxiety, this plight of his; for, though no definite result of his generous action could be foretold, that there would be some result the little diplomatist was very sure. It was her intention, on reaching the palace, to demand audience of Ribâta at once. But when she came to the outer gate of the zenana she found a eunuch watching for her coming, and he hurried forward to her with the command that she repair instantly to the presence of her lord.

Ribâta was alone at table when Baba came to him. He greeted her arrival with extreme satisfaction, and, before dismissing the slaves, had a place made for her beside him, and food and wine brought for her refreshment. Baba watched the arrangements placidly. She was accustomed to such consideration, though no other woman of Ribâta's household had ever been treated in this way. And when the two of them were finally left alone, she began quietly to eat, asking no questions, forbearing to introduce the topic near her own heart, waiting, without the least appearance of curiosity, for Ribâta to begin the conversation.

On the instant of their being left alone, Ribâta's face lost its expression of cheerful nonchalance and took on the look of one that labours wearily in a hopeless cause. He ceased to eat and drink, and lay back on his couch with a deep sigh. It was many minutes before he spoke, and during that time Baba played steadily at eating, never once noticing his languor or commenting on his mood; for she knew her lord, and she took the only possible method of pleasing him.

"Baba", he said at last, "we have lost what should be reckoned as an army this day".

Baba slowly lifted her eyes to his. "Istar?" she said, quietly.

Ribâta nodded. There was a little pause, and then he asked again: "You know, do you not, the man that saved her from the mob?"

"Why – thou knowest, my lord, he is – "

"Charmides, thy Greek. Say it, Baba".

"He is the husband of my sister".

"But once beloved of thee?"

Baba looked at him.

"Warn thy Greek, then, that Amraphel and [Daniel] will not again let any act of his pass unnoticed. His life is endangered, I think".

Still Baba was silent. At Ribâta's words she merely bowed her head.

"And now, my Baba, now hear the rest of the day's happenings. The Great City is coming into the evening of her day. That thing that was Nabu-Nahid's greatest safeguard, because it alone was feared by the priesthood, is taken from us. In the days when Istar of Babylon shone like Shamash in her temple, Amraphel himself laid his face in the dust before her. But now, for many months, yea, since that journey to Erech, her glory has departed from her. I have looked on her long and despairingly of late weeks. This is the end that from the first I have feared. She is become no more than any woman; and with her going our power fails. Yet, Baba, this Istar is wonderfully beloved. This day, in the palace of the king, she was united in marriage with Belshazzar by word of the priest of Sin, who thereby, to all Babylonia, proclaimed her a woman".

"Wife of Belshazzar!" gasped Baba.

"Yes, verily. And I have not marvelled less than thou. Yet Belshazzar loves her with a love that is beyond approach: holding her dearer than half the kingdom – nay, then, than the whole, I think. I spake out before him of the danger of her fall to our cause, and his answer frightened me; and after that, through the whole day, he spoke to me no more.

"But by the blood of my father that flows in my veins, neither for Istar nor for any other shall Belshazzar lose his kingdom to Amraphel, Beltishazzar and Kurush the Elamite, till my spirit is fled to Ninkigal, and my blood waters the streets of the city. And till the time when the madness of the prince my brother shall be ended, I alone will uphold the state against her enemies".

He came to an abrupt and thoughtful pause, which Baba softly filled.

"My lord knows that his will is also mine".

Ribâta drew a quick sigh and then smiled at her words. Afterwards he rose from his couch and seated himself on the great pile of rugs and cushions in a corner, at the same time motioning Baba to join him. She went, obediently, and seated herself at his feet, her eyes resting inquiringly on his face, her chin on her hands. Before he began to speak, he placed one hand caressingly on her hair, much as one would have patted the head of a little child, for, in spite of her precocious discretion and level-headedness, Baba always impressed one first with her childlike personality.

"Now, Baba, there is something for thee to do, whereby we may gain much for our king. Thou knowest the woman Bunanitû, and the great house of Êgibi, of which she is mistress?"

Baba smiled. "Hast thou not many times bidden me go to her? And hath she not come here to visit me? Ugh! My lord knows that I do not love her and her race".

Ribâta smiled. "My Baba, the king's treasury has never in its richest time held half the wealth of the house of Êgibi. With them is that power of gold without which Amraphel himself would soon be helpless. There, Baba, in that house of Jews, is where more than half the secret meetings of the traitors are held. It is from there, and from the house of Zicarû, near the temple of Marduk, that Babylon may look for its doom to come forth. Listen, then, to me. If any meeting ever hath been held by our enemies – and, by thy goat, there have been a hundred of them! – there will be one tomorrow, either in the monastery or in this house of Êgibi: and I think 'twill be in the last. Their best time is noon, after sacrifice and before mercy, when business ceases and the city dines. Now, there will be a eunuch temple servant that is in my pay in the house of Zicarû, waiting, at the same hour that I would have you go to the house of Êgibi. You must enter it, Baba, as a female visitor to Bunanitû, veiled and on foot, carrying embroidery, or a lute, or something that womankind fancies, creating no suspicion that you come from me or my house. Only greet Bunanitû, and tell her you are come to pay a visit and to gossip with her for an hour. Then, being in that house, keep thou watch. Tell me the men that are to be seen about the place, or, if there is none to see, look for any chance event that may befall to give a clew to the traitors' workings. If you be shut away from the men's rooms, cry out for faintness or with heat, and so run out into the shop where moneys are changed. Or make you any excuse to look and learn – I care not what it may be, or what you do. But, my Baba, for every fact you bring me, there shall be a golden hairpin for your hair on your return".

Baba looked up at him quickly. "My lord will learn in time that I love not gold. I do my lord's bidding for love of his work. Let him not pay me like a servant".

Ribâta smiled and took up her two hands. "Baba is good, and also wise. Let her bear always in mind that the Achaemenian threatens the Great City; and that before him, if there works treachery inside the walls, I and thou, Belshazzar and the king, Istar of Babylon and thy pale-eyed Greek, must surely fall. I shall not see thee again ere thou go; but the household is at thy command, to do with as thou wilt in preparation for thy adventure".

Then Ribâta tapped her forehead in token of dismissal, and watched her as she jumped to her feet, made her reverence and went away with her hands folded on her breast.

Though the evening was young, Baba retired straightway, but without any intention of sleeping. Once in her bed she was not liable to interruptions of women or children, who clamoured lustily round her in her waking hours. Now she was eager to think out her plans for the morrow, and how best to accomplish the most important mission ever entrusted to her. It was full three hours, and the whole zenana had grown sleepy-still, before at last she turned upon her side and closed her eyes in the satisfaction of knowing that, of all the plans she could think of, the one she had finally decided on held out the greatest chance of success.

Next morning, the twenty-second of the fair month, found the city still wrought up over the strange happenings of the day before. Istar's fall was not a matter of rejoicing to Babylon in general. Many a woman had wept, and many a workman turned silent and solemn on hearing of her expulsion from the temple. In one quarter of the city only was there a universal sense of delight. This was in the extreme southwest, south of the canal of the Prophet, and accessible from the outside only by the gate of the Maskim. This little spot was a settlement of an alien race, and its inhabitants enjoyed a mode of life peculiarly their own. It was the quarter that had been assigned, fifty years before, to the Jewish people, when Nebuchadrezzar had brought them, 10,000 strong, from their far, barren country, to be a menace and a curse unto his descendant.

So entirely distinctive a life did these captives live, that their quarter was not greatly frequented by Babylonians. But there was one house, standing near the traders' square, covering a large plot of ground, and much more richly tiled than any of its neighbours, that had been and was frequented by the greatest men in Babylon – prince and priest, judge and minister – and the business of which was on a greater scale than that of any similar native house, and which was in the end destined to become famous in the annals of Babylonish history. This was the great banking-firm of Êgibi & Sons; and it was managed at the present time by three generations of the family: Bunanitû, a remarkable old woman of more than sixty years of age; Kalnea, her son, a man something over forty; and Kabtiya, her grandson, a youth in his twentieth year and still unmarried. The establishment that was run by these three to tremendous advantage to themselves, and not a little to that of some others, had become, through the influence of Daniel, the rendezvous for the priestly traitors of the city. Both Kalnea and his son were dangerously implicated in the schemes of Amraphel; and, though Bunanitû had always shrunk a little from the councils held within her walls, her racial prejudices against the reigning family were too strong for her not to be wholly in sympathy with their enemies.

An hour after its accomplishment the news of the fall of Istar had reached this household, through a message from Amraphel himself, who commanded them to prepare for a meeting at noon on the following day – the very obvious consequence that Ribâta had foreseen. The message made no difference in the usual business of the morning; and at noon, as a matter of course, trade was relaxed for the dinner-hour. Few people were in the streets, and no customers haunted the various small shops in the quarter. The house of Êgibi, however, was more fortunate than its neighbours. Between twelve and half-past no fewer than seven men passed in the door of the bank; and, more unusual still, when the last one of them went in, the first had not yet come out. A little peculiar, certainly; but to the single person who witnessed the arrivals from a safe retreat behind a great pile of porous water-jars displayed for sale in the street nearby, the event appeared to have less of the strange than of the satisfactory in it. This watcher was a small, half-robed letter-carrier, who had loitered about the neighbourhood for half an hour, unseen by a single soul. He waited for five or ten minutes after the entrance of the last of the seven, made his way round the corner behind the house, and was presently to be seen dashing round it at breakneck speed, up to the open door of the establishment.

Bunanitû was alone in the large room, and she came to the door, looking out with some anxiety at the small, black creature that stood panting before her.

"Thy business, boy?" she demanded, sharply.

The boy peered up at her, giving her eye for eye suspiciously. "Who are you?" he croaked.

"Bunanitûm Bit-Êgibi".

"Mother of Kalnea?"

"Yea".

"Oho! Then I give thee this, to be" – the boy put a mysterious finger to one side of his nose and whispered so softly that the woman bent over to catch his words – "to be delivered to Amraphel, my lord, in council – if thou knowest the place". And he held up a neat little brick, covered with exquisitely minute writing and elaborately sealed.

Bunanitûm, growing rather large over the affair, took the epistle with a nod. "I know", she whispered, in return, and the boy, with an answering look, turned as if to go away.

The woman, hasty with her new importance, did not stay to watch his departure. She turned about and started for the back part of the house, leaving the outer room quite empty for the space of three minutes. And during that three minutes Baba brought her plan to a successful issue.

No one saw the little letter-carrier enter the shop. Still less did anyone know when he darted out of it and back into the maze of corridors and rooms behind. Here, in a well-chosen corner, very dimly lighted, Baba huddled herself up, to await the return of Bunanitû to her post of duty, which would leave the whole rear of the house open to inspection. Shortly [Bunanitû] could be seen passing quickly along an adjoining hallway, on her way back to the shop, whither she had been hastily sent by her son. And when she was gone, Baba, with a long breath, left her hiding place. The most uncertain and perhaps the most dangerous part of her work was over; but the important half of it remained still to be done. She was confident of the efficacy of her disguise; and she was free to move rapidly in her scant tunic with her black-stained, bare limbs, and her flowing hair crammed under a woolly, black wig. Nevertheless her heart beat violently as she left her corner and began to search for the room where the secret council would sit, or for some hiding place where the sound of voices would come to her ears. She had proceeded nearly to the back wall of the house, and was beginning to fear that the council-room was too well concealed for discovery, when a faint murmur of talking reached her ears. It came, apparently, from somewhere below, and, with the first murmurous sound, Baba stopped short to look about.

The room where she stood was large, almost dark and scantily furnished. Its walls, however, were hung with elaborate draperies, and its floors covered with costly rugs. Save for two or three inlaid chairs, with embroidered cushions and carven feet, the room was empty of furniture. But from somewhere, and somewhere below, came that unceasing murmur of conversation. The intruder examined her surroundings from floor to ceiling. Then she looked all round the walls, and finally back again to the floor. Here, on a certain spot, her eyes stopped. It was where the corner of a great crimson rug was turned up, as if it had been hastily laid. And by this upturned corner was a black spot that was not shadow. In the dim light Baba could distinguish nothing very clearly; but she moved noiselessly across to this place, and found when she came to it that the voices had become definite, and she could hear what was being said. There was a square opening in the floor, all but four or five inches of which was quite concealed by the rug.

Without any hesitation Baba threw herself flat down, and then, realizing to the full the risk that she ran, pushed the rug yet farther away from the opening, put her face close to it, and looked down.

Below was a good-sized vault, made, probably, in the brick platform on which the house stood. It was well lighted with torches and lamps, hung with richly embroidered tapestry, and sealed with glazed bricks of bright colours. Its furniture consisted of piles of rugs and cushions on which, seated in an orderly circle, sat, not nine, but fourteen men, all but four of whom wore the goatskin. Baba did not know them all, even by sight; but half were familiar figures, and the other half – well, Ribâta should tell her their names tonight, after her description. Those that she knew were Amraphel, Vul-Ramân of Nebo and Nergal, Larissib-Sin of Marduk, Zir-Iddin of Shamash at Sippar, Siatû-Sin, Itti-Bel, and Gûla-Zir, together with [Daniel] and his fellows Kalnea and young Kabtiya of the house of Êgibi; and the rest were one more hawk-eyed fellow of the tribe of Judah, and five priests, none of them above the rank of elder.

In her first downward glance Baba perceived that Amraphel had in his hand the brick letter that she herself had sent him; and evidently its contents had been surprising enough to displace the former topic of discussion and to raise a storm of talk. Amraphel and Beltishazzar were silent, waiting, with more or less patience, for a chance of being heard. After a little time this opportunity came, for the majority of those present were too ignorant of their subject to be particularly instructive; and at last they quieted, one by one, and turned to the place where their leaders sat.

Amraphel spoke the first words that Baba was able to catch definitely, and from that time on there was nothing that she did not hear and remember.

"Now that ye take council with silence, men of emptiness, learn of me that there is little enough danger in the fact, even if it be true, that Belshazzar has taken the woman of Babylon to wife. Answer me severally one by one, if there has been in any of your temples a rumour of such a marriage made by any of its priests. Siatû-Sin – dost thou remember?"

"Nay, Lord Amraphel".

This answer was repeated by every priest present. Then, in the little pause that followed before Amraphel went on, Daniel, with a faint smile, observed:

"Yesterday, at four hours after noon, Kasmani, second sacrificial priest of the temple of Sin, entered the gates of Nabu-Nahid's palace, and drove away again in an hour in the golden chariot of Prince Belshazzar".

Everyone looked to Amraphel for his idea of this information. The high priest only smiled, in slow indifference, and continued: "The woman of Babylon desires, then, to be queen in the Great City. A queen is not a goddess; and yet I say unto you that she shall never be queen. She whom I drove forth yesterday from the temple is fallen ill under her disgrace. This morning at dawn came to me Nergal-Yukin, rab-mag of the king's household, for a charm to ward off a fever from a divine lady".

Here Amraphel hesitated for the fraction of a second, while a thin smile spread over Daniel's keen face. "That charm – "he urged.

"That charm", said Amraphel, carefully, "was what the great Elamite would have desired".

"The sword?" demanded Vul-Ramân, bluntly.

"Ten drops of the liquor from an adder's fang, to be rubbed upon a prick in the left wrist at sunset today".

Baba gasped; but from the men assembled below there was only a quick round of applause.

"By dawn tomorrow there will be no more of 'Istar of Babylon'", observed Daniel, satisfaction oiling his tone.

"And the Great City is open to its saviour", concluded Siatû-Sin.

Now Baba was in a sudden agony to escape, for she felt that the life of Istar rested in her hands. Yet sunset was still many hours away, and the talk that was beginning gave signs of proving exactly what Ribâta had told her to hear. Therefore from minute to minute she lingered on in her place, while the story of treachery and blood-guiltiness was made clear to her, and it seemed as if, with the evidence in her hands, it must soon be possible to have these men put to death without imprisonment and with a mere form of trial. And had it been two centuries earlier this might perhaps have been arranged. But Babylon was not Nineveh, and the power of Nabonidus was not that of the old monarchs of Chaldea; neither was the king by nature a tyrant, or even a strict ruler. And possibly because of these things, and only because of them, these councils were ventured at all.

"What is the last word from Kurush?" demanded Salathiel ... of Amraphel.

There was a general little murmur of interest, and a settling down upon the cushions as if for a lengthy talk.

"Kurush", said Amraphel, with all the authority of Cyrus himself, "is now in the marsh country south of Teredou, and from there he dispatches a letter to us. Ye shall hear it".

Amraphel drew from the pocket of his broad girdle a clay tablet, slightly larger than those in general use for letters, and covered with neatly pressed cuneiform characters. This, with the aid of a small, round magnifying-glass, always used in correspondence, he read aloud to those assembled – and to Baba above:

"'Unto Amraphel, high servant of the ancient gods of Babylon, and to those that are with him, thus saith Kurush the Achaemenian: With me it is well. With thee and thy houses may it be exceeding well. Now I, the king, lie secretly in the country to the south of the city of Teredou, not far from the gulf of the setting sun. And here, from the east and from the north, the army will assemble about me. The people in the land are poor and ill-content. Little grain have they to eat, and short measure of milk to drink. The king their lord knows them not. To me they turn, in their extremity. Soon shall ye learn of revolts among the dwellers in the lowlands:

know, then, that it will be by my hand. After this we will march northward, towards the gates of the Great City.

"'Gobryas, my general, the governor of Gutium, is in the north. Before him, in the month of Duzu (June), Sippar and its works shall fall.

"'Look to it only that ye hold Babylon estranged from its king. She whom we have feared – doth she bear herself yet divinely? The captive Jews that are in the city, greet them well for me. Tell them that, after my coming, those that open to me the Great City shall know again the land of their fathers and their fathers' fathers. And those of the Babylonians that shall acclaim me master, to each of these shall be given out of the public moneys thirty shekels of silver; but to the great that bow before shall be given high offices, honour and much wealth. And in the month of Ab, Queen of the Bow, shall Babylon know me'."

The seal of Cyrus was affixed to the end of the epistle; and the brick was passed round the circle, that each man present might be sure that it was genuine.

Now began a discussion that proved tedious and scarcely comprehensible to Baba. It was about numbers and divisions of men, and was accompanied by the reading of endless lists of names, and the checking of each as true or untrue to the cause of rebellion. And after listening to this talk until she found that it would be utterly hopeless for her to attempt to remember anything valuable in it, Baba rose, pulled the rug carefully back to its original place, listened for a moment to make sure that she was undiscovered, and then, with the utmost caution, made her way to the rear door of the house, which she unfastened, and through which she safely passed. Once outside, in the glare of day, her heart afire with anxiety for Istar, she started away, in a light-running pace, up through the city that she knew so well. Through the Traders' square, across the canal of the Prophet, along the riverbank for an endless distance she ran, till she came to the great bridge, across which loomed the high, blue walls of the new palace.

The sun was swinging down towards the horizon now, and the life of Istar swung with it in its balance, when the dishevelled figure of Ribâta's slave halted at the palace gates and demanded the admission that her disguise gained for her.

Chapter 13

The Rab-Mag

THROUGH THE WHOLE of the day following her expulsion from the temple, Istar, wife of Belshazzar the prince royal, lay in her newly assigned bedroom in the far wing of the palace, in a profound stupor. She was unconscious, apparently, of everything around her – of Belshazzar, sitting at her bedside; of the child that lay wailing on her arm; of the peace and the orderly quiet of this new home. The spell of her mighty shame and woe was over her. She had broken under it like the reed in the storm. Everything that had passed since she was driven by the blows of the ox-goad out into the day-glare on top of the ziggurat, had been but a dim vision to her. Physically, she was very ill. This was not wonderful. But Belshazzar, mad with rage at the whole of the priesthood, and overwhelmed with pity for the woman he loved as only he would have dared to love, was beside himself with anxiety. All night the rab-mag of his father's household, the most renowned charm-doctor in Babylonia, had watched beside him in her room; had repeated prayers and formula without number; and had burned beans, leeks, barley, cakes, butter, frankincense and liquor, till the room smelled indescribably, and Belshazzar himself, resorting to common-sense, ordered a dozen slaves to clear the atmosphere with fans and with pungent strong-waters. In the new air Istar seemed to breathe more easily, and had even moved her lips, though no sound issued from them. Then Belshazzar commanded the rab-mag to depart until daylight, when he should return with new wisdom.

Thereupon Nergal-Yukin, half angry, half ashamed, wholly chagrined, went forth through the silent streets to the house of Amraphel. Here he was made to undergo a change of feeling. The priest recognized an opportunity in the first three sentences that the doctor spoke, and instantly took advantage of it. He set to work to play upon the alchemist's feelings, and such was his success that presently, by means of sympathy for the insults he had endured and promises of dazzling wealth, coupled with righteous denunciations of Istar as the queen of darkness, of wickedness, of all the vices, the learned man found his price, bent the knee before his preceptor and hied him back to his den of charms, where, kept in a convenient cage, was an adder, dwelling effectively among the other insignia of this awe-inspiring profession.

Nergal-Yukin did not re-enter Belshazzar's presence that morning; but he sent a slave to say that he was preparing a new and infallible charm, that could not, to be most efficacious, be applied before the hour of sunset. Belshazzar was pleased with the message; perhaps not less pleased because it gave him the chance of being alone at Istar's side all through the day. Not for one moment did he leave or even turn his thoughts from her. Councillors and courtiers, officials and judges, tax-collectors, officers of his regiment, treasurer and usurers, were kept from his presence by peremptory command. He refused food for himself; but he made an effort to force something between Istar's pallid lips – and in the attempt succeeded in rousing her for a moment from her stupor. As he knelt by her side, supporting her head upon his arm, his hand, unsteady with an emotion that none would have believed possible to him, holding the cup of warm milk to her mouth, Istar's great eyes opened and she looked at him. There was a fulness in Belshazzar's throat that presently broke into a sob. Blindly he groped in the realm of prayer for some words into which he could put his heart. And his will rose up in him, till he would have pitted himself against all the powers of hell for the sake of saving the life of this woman who was lawfully and spiritually his own.

"You shall not die – you shall not die – not die!" he muttered, over and over again.

Then Istar sank back upon her many pillows. The heavy lids once more shut off her wonderful eyes from his sight. Her face was colorless and drawn. He could trace with ease the course of each tiny blue vein in her fair temples. He looked at her hands – so white, so transparent, so frailly beautiful; and over them he bent his head, touching them with his lips. As he kissed them there came a wail from the baby. Instinctively, half conscious as she was, Istar gathered the child to her side, while he, the man, looked on, wondering and helpless.

Noon, with its breathless, stifling heat, came and went again. An hour after it a slave tiptoed into the room and whispered a name to Belshazzar. The prince's expression brightened a little. "Let him come in to me", he said, softly.

A moment or two afterwards Ribâta noiselessly entered the room.

Belshazzar held out both hands, greeting his friend with such an air of weary helplessness that Ribâta stared at him uncomfortably.

"Name of the great Marduk, Belshazzar, what is come to thee?" he asked, holding his friend at arm's-length and looking into his face with a mixture of sympathy and perplexity.

"Hush! Curb thy voice! She will be disturbed".

Ribâta looked about him with intense curiosity. "Belshazzar, art thou gone mad? What is this thing that absents thee from thy duties? Thou art needed today – in council – at the review – "

"Nay – let others look to these things; let my father look to his own", whispered Belshazzar, in reply, drawing his friend down on the cushions beside him.

Ribâta found no answer to the words. Here was a Belshazzar whom he did not know. He ventured no further remarks, but remained sitting quietly beside his friend – waiting. By degrees, as the silence continued without much prospect of abating, Bit-Shumukin's eyes began to study the passive face of Istar. The nobleman had never before been so near her; and never before, even in the old days when he had seen her, towering in a cloud of silver above the multitude in her triumphal car, had he been so impressed with her divine purity. There was that in her face, marked and mortalized by suffering as it was, that put mortal things far away from her. His wonder at Belshazzar's boldness grew greater. The spirit which could have moved any man to look upon that face with a feeling of equality, daring the hope of making her his own, was enough, in Ribâta's eyes, to raise that man above the level of humanity. He turned to look upon the prince. Belshazzar lay back on the divan, lost in some unfathomable reverie. Ribâta hesitated to bring him back into the present, yet felt a kind of discomfort in the presence of these two strange beings. Unable to contain himself, he suddenly started up, with the idea of leaving the apartment. Belshazzar, however, was instantly roused by his move.

"Ribâta", he said, quietly, "do not go from us".

The friend turned to him, answering: "My lord knows there is much to be done. I go to thy work".

Belshazzar rose and laid both hands tenderly on the shoulders of his friend. "My brother", he said, "for my father, and for the sake of the crown that will one day be mine, I have laboured long; and for them I will labor again, even unto the end. But now, for a little while, I tarry here, beside the bed of my beloved, for whose coming I have waited many weary months. Then wilt thou not watch here with me through one little hour? I ask it for the love I bear thee, Bit-Shumukin; and be sure that there is no other in Babylon, nay, or in all the world, that could hold thy place in my heart".

A wave of emotion that was half wonder swept over Ribâta. Never before had Belshazzar spoken like this to him – never before like it to any man or to any woman. Bit-Shumukin made no reply in words, but he yielded instantly to the gentle pressure of the prince's hand and sank back again on the cushions. Once more he turned his gaze upon the white, passive features of Istar, and, without looking away from her, he asked:

"Dost thou leave her like this, with neither medicines nor prayers? Where is the rab-mag, that he attends not on her sickness?"

"All through the night he has worked over her with charms and incantations. At sunset today he will come again, bringing with him a new charm more powerful than any ever used before. The hour of sunset is not far away. Then if she – "

The speech was interrupted by the appearance of a eunuch, who, making his prostration in the doorway, stood silently waiting permission to speak.

"What is thy business? Say it softly", whispered the prince, with a frown.

"May the ears of my lord incline themselves kindly! There is at the gate a letter-carrier that bears a message for the Lady Istar. He bade me seek thee, saying: 'For divine Istar my word bears life. If she heed me not, death seizes her in his arms'."

"Bring the fellow here, guarded by two eunuchs and bound about the arms that he may make no dangerous move".

The slave bowed and disappeared. When he was gone, Ribâta observed, thoughtfully: "It is well that he be bound. Day by day thy life is growing more precious to Babylon, more desired by the priesthood. By day and night, if thou wert mine to care for, I would have thee guarded".

Belshazzar smiled a little, shaking his head; and they spoke no more till Baba, fast bound and also gagged, was thrust into the room by two soldiers that moved behind her. The little creature was dizzy with the heat, covered from head to foot with dust and half fainting from weariness. At sight of Ribâta she gave a gurgling, choked cry behind her gag, and, twisting herself suddenly from the soldiers' grasp, fell in a little heap at the feet of her lord.

"Baba!" he cried, gazing in bewilderment at the unrecognizable figure, but knowing her posture and her smothered voice.

"Thou knowest this fellow, Ribâta?" queried Belshazzar, curiously.

"'Tis a woman, lord prince, though her name is a man's. I will answer with my life for her fidelity to thee and to the Lady Istar. Let thy soldiers depart – then she will speak", he said, imperatively, beginning to unloose the rope that bound her arms.

Belshazzar, as always, accepted his friend's word, dismissed the guardsmen with a nod, and turned to examine, with some interest, the panting heap of humanity at Ribâta's feet. Bit-Shumukin had removed the gag, and was still struggling with the stiff knots in the cactus-rope. Belshazzar finally cut them with his knife and set Baba free. She rose uncertainly to her feet, stretching her arms above her head. Then, suddenly, she grasped her hair, gave a great tug and pulled the wig from her head, leaving her own long, black locks to float freely around her shoulders.

"Where didst thou get the stain for thy skin? Thou'rt black as a Nubian", said her lord, smiling at her uncouth appearance. Then he added, hastily: "Nay, child, let us not play. What hast thou learned in the house of Êgibi; and what is thy matter of life or death with the divine Istar?"

Before she had uttered the first word of her answer, Baba's eyes fell on the form that lay stretched out on the bed. She gave a little cry of astonishment and reverent admiration. Then she cast herself on her knees before Belshazzar.

"May it please the prince my lord to heed my words, for I speak those that fell an hour agone from the lips of Amraphel of Bel. At sunset of this day will come Nergal-Yukin, rab-mag of the great king, to the side of the Lady Istar. He will bring with him a new charm that shall purport to be for Istar to make her well, and that will bring her to her death. Amraphel hath promised the man honour and riches when he shall make a cut upon the Lady Istar's wrist, rubbing into it ten drops of the poison drawn from an adder's fangs".

"By all the gods – !" Belshazzar leaped to his feet. "Nergal-Yukin dies this day!"

"Where hast thou heard this story, Baba?"

"At the council of priests, in the house of Êgibi".

"Say on – all thou hast heard!" commanded Belshazzar, sharply.

Thereupon Baba, seating herself on the floor, recounted to the two men her adventure of the afternoon. The whole council, as she had overheard it, the names or the faces of the men that took part in it, and the letter from Cyrus the Elamite, word for word, she unravelled from the warp and woof of her memory. Her auditors listened in silence, staring into each other's faces, neither of them wholly amazed, yet both strongly moved by this confirmation of their worst suspicions – the suspicions that Nabonidus would not entertain. Baba gave the story in detail, and took some time over it. She had barely finished, and there had been no time for question or comment, when the attendant eunuch reappeared at the door, saying:

"It is the hour of sunset. Nergal-Yukin craves admittance to my lord and to the divine Lady Istar".

"Come thou hither", said Belshazzar, beckoning the eunuch to his side. "Let Nergal-Yukin come hither to this room", he said, softly, "and as soon as he shall be within, summon thou six soldiers of the guard and command them to wait my call outside in the hall. Let them bring ropes of stout cactus and a gag of wood, and cause them to keep silence there without until I shall summon them. Now, behold, I have spoken. Go thy way and obey my word".

The eunuch departed obediently, and a moment later Nergal-Yukin entered the bedchamber of the lady of Babylon. He was a tall fellow, this rab-mag of the king; lean and withered in body, black-robed and wearing the peaked hat that belonged to the livery of the royal household. Around his waist was a golden cord, at the end of which dangled a narrow-bladed knife of Indian steel, its handle inlaid with lapis-lazuli and gold. In his hand he bore a golden phial of rare workmanship. His salute to the prince was markedly obsequious, but he regarded the two others in the room with great disfavour.

"Let the prince my lord command everyone to be dismissed from his presence. Otherwise my spell must lose its potency".

"These are my friends. Let them remain here", returned Belshazzar, shortly.

"Then let my lord give me leave to depart out of his presence. The work will be useless", said the old man, with something like a sneer, beginning to back towards the door.

But Belshazzar was master of himself and of the situation. He lifted his hand, and the physician halted. "Nergal-Yukin, on pain of death, get thee to thy work. Pronounce the spell; and may the gods take heed of it".

The words were spoken quietly enough; and yet there could be no disobeying that tone. Nergal-Yukin's face darkened; but, however unwillingly, he advanced to Istar's side. Lifting over her both his long, withered hands, he began to pray in the Accadian tongue to Nergal, the god of health. Belshazzar, Ribâta and Baba stood listening stolidly, while the high-pitched voice went on and on, from prayers to exorcisms, and finally into mystic exclamations and phrases. Here the man's manner changed, and he gave symptoms of a working into religious frenzy. His auditors, however, remained painfully unresponsive, and the final "Amanû" was succeeded by a biting silence. It was then, with a resentful satisfaction, that the rab-mag began the consummation of his work. He commanded a basin of water and a fine towel. These provided, he lifted Istar's right hand from the coverlet, and proceeded to wash and dry it during the repetition of further prayers. Then he turned to Belshazzar.

"May it please the prince my lord to learn that this remedy which I am about to apply to the lady of Babylon is the most powerful and the most dangerous of any known to mankind, or to the gods above. To them that are pure in heart it cannot fail to restore perfect health. By it, indeed, the very dead may sometimes be lifted up from Ninkigal and given once more to the light of Shamash. But if the person to whom the magic liquid be applied is guilty of great sin, then is it true that death may perhaps come upon that one. Now wills the prince my lord that I finish the spell?"

"How shall it be finished?" inquired Belshazzar, phlegmatically.

Nergal-Yukin grinned with displeasure and disappointment at having failed to arouse any feeling by his words. "O high and powerful one, with this knife that hangs at my girdle I cut the flesh of the right wrist till a drop of red blood flows therefrom. Then into the wound I pour the dazzling stream from this precious phial; and when they have mingled well with the blood of the lady, you shall behold her rise up and call thee to her arms". He concluded this explanatory speech with an obeisance, and had already turned to the couch again when Belshazzar gave a low call.

Instantly there was an influx of armed men into the apartment. Nergal-Yukin turned in time to see the entrance of the last one. The next instant he was violently seized by two stalwart men. His cries of amazement were stifled with a gag; he was bound about from head to foot with the unbreakable cactus-rope, and then, at a nod from Belshazzar, borne out of the unconscious presence of Istar into the hall beyond. Thither Belshazzar and Ribâta followed him; but Baba, at a sign from her lord, remained where she was.

Belshazzar's face was a thing to fear as he bade the guardsmen stand the rab-mag up before him. Nergal-Yukin could speak only with his eyes, but these were eloquent indeed. Terror and agonized pleading were the dominant expressions on the face of the wretched creature. Belshazzar heeded neither one. In three words he commanded his men to free the right arm of the magician. Then, while Ribâta and the soldiers were clustered round, watching the scene in silent fascination, and a scream of terror was about to break through the gag, Belshazzar took the doctor's right hand in his own, holding it in an iron grasp; and with the other he seized the knife that still hung at Nergal-Yukin's side. The eyes of the doomed man were starting from their sockets. Ribâta came forward a little, that he might obtain a better view of the affair. The soldiers crowded close around. Belshazzar lifted the knife and made a long, delicate slit in the back of the physician's wrist. Then, when the blood had begun to flow thinly forth, Ribâta handed his master the golden bottle that had been left on the foot of Istar's couch. Belshazzar nodded his thanks, and, without a second's hesitation, opened it. The liquid that rolled out was thick and rather brown in colour. The prince did his work deftly. With one finger he rubbed the stuff all about and around the wound, mixing it with the fresh blood, and allowing none of it to drip off the wrist. With the other hand he helped two of his soldiers to hold the rab-mag still; for the fellow was now struggling so violently that this was not a task for a single arm. There was no escape, however. When the poison had been made to enter the wound thoroughly, Belshazzar tore a strip of embroidered linen from the bottom of his tunic and bound it round the arm, fastening it with a pin from Ribâta's apparel. Then he stood back from his victim.

"Take this man away, and bring me only the message of his death".

Obediently the soldiers lifted their burden, now rigid and stiff with terror, and bore him like a log of wood out of the presence of the prince and across the courtyard, back into some little-known rooms used only for the most obscure servants of the palace.

Belshazzar drew a long breath of relief. His rage had passed. Only, as he turned to smile at Ribâta, he was slightly pale. Ribâta nodded at him in approval.

"That was well done", he said. "Those that live like dogs, like dogs let them die".

"And now, Ribâta – "

"Now, O prince, I return with Baba to my house. Thou hast heard all that my slave learned of the treachery lurking in the Great City. It is to you that Babylon looks for her defence. Her people are yours. Do with us all as you will. We are in your hands". Ribâta made the lowest obeisance, something not due from his rank to anyone except a god; and Belshazzar hastily raised him up.

"It is to thy loyalty, O faithful one, that Babylon will owe her freedom. Baba likewise shall receive her reward. She hath saved Istar's life – that is more to me than Babylon, than myself, than all the earth. Command a litter for her now, and take thou my chariot for thy return. The council of lords sits tomorrow after sacrifice. Then we will speak of the invader. Till then – Bel keep you safely!"

Smiling, Ribâta turned back into the other apartment. He found Baba on her knees, beside Istar's couch, gazing in ecstasy into Istar's open eyes. On the other side the baby, haloed round with a soft and luminous light, slept quietly. Ribâta was reluctant to draw Baba from the scene; but the child was faint with fatigue, and so, leading her gently away, he lifted her, when they were outside the door, in both his arms, and carried her, all black and dishevelled as she was, out to the gate, where, in the face of a dozen astonished men, he placed her in a litter, himself mounted Belshazzar's chariot, and drove away in it in the direction of the canal of the Four Seasons.

If Baba's day of labour had just ended, that of Belshazzar only now began. The affair of the rab-mag had left him intensely uneasy, and this, coupled with his great anxiety over the sedition in the city, promised a sleepless night. Still, till further news of Nergal-Yukin's state should be brought him, he was powerless to act, and therefore he returned to Istar's room and seated himself there, with his head resting on his hands. The minutes passed unheeded, for his mind was full. He knew that his wife lay near him, and, though her eyes had been open when he entered the room, he believed her still incapable of sight or hearing. Presently, when his head had sunk lower still, he felt the lightest touch on his arm, and he started to his feet, to cry out in amazement as he beheld Istar, tall and white, swaying beside him.

"*Thou!*" he said, gasping.

"The heart of Belshazzar is troubled. From far away come I to bring thee consolation in thine hours of woe", she said, quietly, as one speaking from a great distance. "Be comforted, O my lord! That that is ordained for the Great City must come to pass. Neither thou nor any other can prevent it. But be not troubled in thy heart, my prince. In the end this world shall grow dim before thine eyes, for there will be opened before them another kingdom where there shall be no time, neither any evil doing. Until the coming of that day, my lord, be comforted – take heart – and be comforted!"

In that one moment Istar shone forth in all her radiant glory, like some spirit from a divine sunset. And the prince fell down before her on his knees, worshipping silently. But after she ceased to speak the radiance went, and she fainted before him in her weakness of the flesh. So he caught her in his arms and brought her once more to her couch. When she woke again, only Belshazzar remembered the words that she had spoken to him. Yet he knew that the message had come from out of the silver sky, and with this knowledge peace came to him, and he went and lay down upon the divan in the room.

He had lain there for some minutes, his mind filled less with foreboding than with wonder, when, for the third time, the eunuch appeared at the door, this time wearing on his carefully trained face an untoward expression of interest.

"Speak, Âpla", whispered Belshazzar, anxiously.

"May it please my lord – Nergal-Yukin is dead".

"How? How?"

"In great anguish. Being ungagged, he cried mightily, and screamed aloud to the gods and demons, uttering curses on Amraphel the priest of Bel, and upon Belshazzar my lord, and upon the king Nabu-Nahid. Thus is Nergal-Yukin dead".

"It is well that all dogs should die. Listen, then, Âpla, and do my bidding. Let forty of my runners, attired in their liveries, go forth into the city with trumpets and cymbals, and let them cry aloud through all Babylon the story of the rab-mag's treachery and his end. The name of Amraphel must not be spoken; but the criers shall so word their story that no man can be ignorant of the fact that Amraphel himself prompted this deed out of hatred to me. Listen, then, while I tell thee the story of the sin of the rab-mag, and thou must repeat it as I say it to you, to all my criers".

Then Belshazzar proceeded to recount, tersely and truthfully, the tale of the attempted assassination of Istar. When he had finished, and Âpla, big-eyed and eager, had repeated the words after him, he dismissed the eunuch to assemble the runners, and then the prince, his work beginning to assume definite proportions in his mind, summoned two women to watch over the goddess, and, leaving them with her, went his way to the apartments of the king his father.

Nabonidus sat in his coolest room, comfortably partaking of his supper. A dancing-girl had just finished her postures before him, and he had dismissed her, while his favourite poet was summoned to take her place. Nabonidus' gentle, sheep-like face wore an air of benign content as his hand moved regularly from mouth to plate, and his head swayed to the rhythm of the tune that had been played. The poet was just mounting his dais and unrolling his strip of Egyptian papyrus when the prince reached the door of his father's apartment. It was really pitiable that all this pleasant twilight delight should be so roughly disturbed. But disturbed it was, as a lake's calm by the east wind, as soon as Belshazzar entered his father's presence and made his obeisance. Nabonidus' expression was more that of resignation than of displeasure as he said, courteously:

"Let there be a couch brought in for thee, Bel-shar-utsur, and partake with me of this flesh of the whirring-bird, and barley, while Kibâ recites to us the tale of Izdubar and Êa-bani full of wisdom". Nabonidus made his suggestion with an air of hopefulness that belied his real feeling; and he was not surprised, however much disappointed, when Belshazzar replied:

"May it please the king my lord to grant me a private audience. There are matters of great import to be laid before him. I beg that my lord be moved to grant this wish".

These words, couched as they were in the form of supplication, were spoken in such a tone of command as Nabu-Nahid dared not refuse. But in justice to the son be it said that this manner only ever gained for anyone, save poets and architects, a moment's consideration with the king. By this method, however, Belshazzar succeeded; and presently he and his father were alone.

Nabu-Nahid had ceased to eat, and sat regarding his son with an air of petulant displeasure. "Now speak to me quickly", he said, in his mildly injured fashion. "The season is too late for lion-hunting; your command over the treasury equals mine; I have at present not one dancer that would please you; and for the matter of soldiers – go to Nânâ-Babilû at Sippar. I am not the commanding general. What, then, seeing these things, canst thou ask of me?"

Belshazzar snapped his fingers and frowned mightily. The fears in his mind might be vague and ill-defined as yet; but when he did consider, in some presentient fashion, the scenes of terror that were soon to be enacted in the Great City, and when he imagined his father, weak, gentle, yielding as he was, swept into that furious vortex of blood and of death, what could there be but pity for the old man and dread for his inevitable end? Now, for a moment, indeed, Belshazzar wondered how it was that his father had held his throne even one little twelvemonth, after the strife that had preceded his coronation. Yet for seventeen prosperous years this one ruler had held city and state together peaceably; and there were few Chaldean kings that had done as much.

"My father", said Bit-Shamash at last, "it is for no matter of pleasure or mine own affluence that I seek thee tonight. It is for thee, for thy throne, for the sake of thy kingdom, of ancient Babylonia, that I would take council with thee here".

Hearing these words, Nabu-Nahid's face assumed an expression that was unexpectedly complex – a little inscrutable, indeed. "Since what time, O my son, have thy thoughts turned towards the welfare of the throne? Since when hath thy mind been more engaged with affairs of the state than with wines and with feasting, dancing-girls and hunters – thou and thy companion, Ribâta of Shumukin?"

Belshazzar flushed slightly. "My father hath judged me", was his only answer.

Nabu-Nahid merely nodded his head a trifle, and then sat looking at his son with a stupid expression, waiting for him to depart, as at this stage he usually did. In point of fact, Belshazzar had a strong impulse to turn on the instant and leave his father to his supper and his poetry. But for once his anxiety was stronger than his pride, and he fought back the angry taunt that had risen to his lips, and asked, bluntly:

"Know you, O king, that letters of invitation pass from our city to Kurush, king of Elam, to come and take his place on the throne of Babylon?"

"Letters from the hands of Amraphel of Bel and [Daniel]? Ay, Bit-Shamash. Think you I do not know my city?"

Belshazzar was first astonished, then inexpressibly relieved. Was it possible that he had so long misjudged his father? Was it possible that this shambling and vacant manner concealed a sound mind and a great understanding? Had he for so long kept his own best self from the king to find out his grave mistake when it was almost too late? He bent his head more humbly than he had ever bent it before to any man. "I crave pardon of my lord", he said. "Behold, I go my way".

But Belshazzar had not all the magnanimity of the family. Nabu-Nahid suddenly straightened up, and commanded a couch to be moved to the table. Wines of Lebanon and Helbon were brought from the cellars, and Belshazzar was waved into his place with a gesture that admitted of no refusal. The prince obeyed the invitation rather reluctantly. He dreaded the return of the poet, and had no desire now to discuss affairs of state with his father. However, Nabonidus opened such a discussion in a very tactful way.

"Tell me, Belshazzar, how many days is it since this conspiracy of the priests hath been known to you?"

"For more than three months I have suspected it. It is but today that it hath become a certainty".

"And the matter frightens thee?"

"Yea, truly, my father. When I came to thee tonight my heart was sick with the thought of Babylon's great danger. But since thou, the king, knowest all and fearest naught, my fears are also laid at rest. The king my father is very great. May he live forever!" and Belshazzar smiled filially into his father's eyes.

"You do me honour to trust in me, Belshazzar", said the king, gently. "Yet do you well, also; for to whom save their king can a people look for their safety? I will tell you how the Great City is to be protected against the plots of her enemies. Priest and lord alike may prove false, and men and soldiers turn against me. I have put my strength and my trust in those that are above princes. Hark you, Belshazzar. When, a month past, I learned from certain watchers whom I employ, of the great plot against the crown, I bethought me long and earnestly of my course. Finally I sent out secret messengers to every temple-city in Babylonia, and from every heavenly house that my hand hath restored from ancient decay I caused to be sent hither to me the oldest and holiest god-image. These, to the number of twenty-one, are now in a little temple by the riverbank, where I daily visit them and perform sacrifice before them till the time when they shall move in procession through the city, and go each to his special shrine. And that day approaches; for the city grows uneasy under the seditions of the priests and their oracles. But when my new gods are set up in their golden houses to be worshipped by the multitude in the city, think you not that the first care of these heavenly ones will be the safety and preservation of me and of my line?"

Belshazzar said nothing for some time. It seemed impossible for him to speak. This sudden revelation of his father's incomprehensible childishness, following, as it did, the equally unexpected evidence of his understanding of the situation of the state, had completely overcome him. It was well that the dim, bluish lamplight made all faces look pale; for at this moment the prince's skin was destitute of colour. All his first fears came back to him, added to a new one, that increased the horror of the first a thousandfold. With what frightful disaster was Babylon not threatened? And what hope had she of fighting against devastation under the leadership of a half-crazy old man that had placed an unalterable and inhuman faith in the power of certain blocks of grey and crumbling stone, shaped into images that a child would hardly believe in? Faugh! Belshazzar turned sick with disgust.

"Speak, Belshazzar! What think you of this hope of mine?"

"The king is great. May he live forever!" was the response, given in a tone of soothing calmness. With the words the prince royal also rose from his couch. "Now, father, I go. I must depart from thee", he said, hurriedly. "There is a matter to be attended to. Give me leave to quit thy presence".

"As you entered it of your own will, so depart", returned his father, in a subdued and disappointed manner.

But Belshazzar, whose feeling was more of grief and pity than anything else, went to his father, took his hand and laid it upon his brow in token of devotion and obedience.

"Thy head is hot", observed the king.

Belshazzar smiled faintly. "Grant me leave to depart", he urged again.

"Yea, in peace depart!"

Somewhat relieved at the old man's tone, a little quieted by the silence and the dim light around him, the prince moved to the door and was all but gone when the king turned and spoke to him again in a way that revealed another phase of his curious character. "Belshazzar", he said, "look well to this [man], Daniel. He was a member of the court of the mighty Nebuchadrezzar, thy grandfather. A traitor and a dangerous man is he; but he is a prophet also; and gold will buy him. If, after my death, the city should be threatened with destruction, look to him, if it is possible, for help".

Belshazzar, dully amazed again, yet too weary of the changes of his father's moods to pay very much attention to him, answered this advice with an obeisance only, and then went his way towards his own rooms. But, even as he went, his father's last words rang again through his ears. "A traitor and a dangerous man, but a prophet also; and gold will buy him – gold will buy him!" Thus Belshazzar pondered still.

In his private room the prince found his evening meal laid out and waiting his coming. Food, however, was not his desire; and, letting it remain where it stood, he began slowly to pace his room, up and down, up and down the cool, tiled floor. His fan-slaves watched him curiously. They had never seen quite such an expression on their lord's face. In truth, Belshazzar's brain throbbed when he thought of what a way lay before him to be traversed. Babylon tottered before his weary mental vision; and finally, inexpressibly heavy-hearted with it all, he sat down to eat his chilled supper, at the same time dispatching a slave for Khamma.

The dancing girl, with her gauze draperies and tinkling ankle-bells, came in to him, followed by her fellow-slaves with drum and lute. The maid had lost neither her grace of movement nor her love for her Lord, and therefore Belshazzar, successfully diverted for the moment, finished his meal more pleasantly than he had begun it. When finally he rose from his couch it was late. The moon hung in the heavens, and the courtyard was flooded with silver light. A group of guardsmen, clustering round a fire, sat chanting charms in chorus. Belshazzar heard their voices with a vague longing for shouts of men, for the shrill neighs of horses, for the rattle of chariot wheels, the clash of arms, the thunderous murmur of battle as he had known it in his youth. If only war, open and honourable, lay between him and Kurush of Elam – well enough. In that he stood his fair chance of winning; and if he lost, it was death at his own hands. The game that he feared and that he hated was the one of underhandedness, of lies, of treachery, of bribery. When a man could be bought for gold there was none to trust, none to feel sure of. And upon these things the prince wearily pondered as he gazed out into the night, wondering, half consciously, whether to go to Ribâta or to seek rest from his mental burden in sleep.

While he debated this point with himself there came a commotion at the palace gate, the arrival of a fast chariot, a peremptory call for admittance and his own name spoken in a familiar voice. An instant later a slave ran to him with the word:

"May it be pleasing to the prince my lord, Lord Amraphel, the high priest of Bel, asks conduct to the presence of the Prince Belshazzar".

"Bring him here to my side", was the quick reply.

The slave left him obediently, and Belshazzar prepared to receive his visitor. Retreating a little towards the centre of his dining-room, he stood with the torchlight at his back and the glow of the lamp too far in front to shine upon his face. Here he awaited the coming of his father's enemy.

Amraphel entered the presence of the prince royal with his usual unruffled dignity. He was followed by two slaves, who stood behind him during the performance of the elaborate salutations. Then they were dismissed, and bidden to await the return of their master to his chariot.

Belshazzar was unattended. Thus the departure of these slaves left the two men quite alone, out of the sight and out of the hearing of the rest of the world. However much the prince was on his guard, his manner betrayed nothing but cold courtesy. This sudden incident had come as a relief to him. Action of any sort was welcome. He was perfectly at his ease, barely polite, little respectful of the age and station of the priest.

With Amraphel it was different. The instant that his attendants departed his air of unbending dignity dropped off him like a cloak, and into his face there came so marked an expression of hatred and of suppressed fury that Belshazzar's eyes, meeting by chance those of his adversary, forgot their course, and remained fascinated and fixed on that other gaze. Simultaneously both stepped forward.

"My lord Amraphel honours me unexpectedly", said the prince, giving the other a free opening.

"It is not to thy honour, but rather on account of thy infamy, that I come", was the reply.

Belshazzar's lips straightened themselves out haughtily. "Let me summon a seer to interpret thy words", he said.

"My words shall interpret themselves to you. What answer make you to the charge of murdering Nergal-Yukin?"

For a moment Belshazzar was silent. Then he laughed – a clear, ringing laugh.

Instantly Amraphel lost his self-control. Reaching Belshazzar's side in two strides, he lifted his right hand in the face of the prince. Before the blow fell Belshazzar had seized the priest's arm fast in his grip, and with all his giant strength thrust from him the figure of the old man.

"Beware, Amraphel", he said, so softly that the priest just caught the words.

"Hark you, son of the sheep-king, hark you! If within the hour your slaves, the criers of Nergal-Yukin's death, be not recalled from the city streets, not one of them shall be left alive by morning".

"If that is thy thought, Amraphel of Bel, at daybreak tomorrow not a priest in the city shall dare openly to wear the goatskin and still live".

"You defy the gods?"

"I defy their ministers".

"Then, by all that is holy in heaven and earth, be thou and thine foully cursed forevermore!"

Belshazzar's lips curled again; and again, desecrating all the traditions of his race, he laughed – loud, and long, but not mirthfully.

Amraphel, as he gathered his scarlet robe close about his meagre frame, grew white – very white. His head was held high, and his eyes flashed with a fire that age could not quell, as he spoke his final word: "Be *thou* ware, Belshazzar of Babylon, lest the curse of the gods be given for fulfilment into the hands of men!"

As he turned on his heel Belshazzar's answer came, and by it the priest learned how surely the governor of the city was of his mother's loins, and not of his father's blood. "Thy hand and that of Daniel ..., yea, and of him ye call the Achaemenian, will find space enough on my body whereon to strike and strike again, O Amraphel. But see that ye fight as men, and not as dogs. Else, by my faith, as dogs ye shall surely die!"

Belshazzar hurled the last word after the priest into the courtyard, for Amraphel was now well on his way back to his chariot. The echo of the prince's voice rolled off into silence; and after a little time Belshazzar found himself still standing beside the table, his head bent, his eyes moving vacantly over the floor, while his thoughts were as empty as he felt his words to have been. A little after the interview he sought his rest. And when morning dawned again and he called his slaves to his side, the criers of Nergal-Yukin's death had not been slain; though perhaps in the end that consummation had been better for the royal house of Babylon.

Chapter 14

Strange Gods

NERGAL-YUKIN'S DEATH, the circumstances of it, and the blatant proclamation of these things by Belshazzar's slaves, facts skilfully manipulated by Amraphel and his order, threw all Babylon into an uproar. Naturally, the city was divided into factions. The priests and their satellites formed a sufficiently attractive nucleus to draw around it a great body of the common people whose lives at best were only a round of prayers and exorcisms; while all the army, that feared and followed Belshazzar as it feared and followed no god, drew to itself the other faction of citizens loyal to the crown. From the first, however, the priests, who counted also the Jews to a man in their party, were stronger than their opponents. And Amraphel, moved as he was by the two great forces of hate and overweening ambition, worked early and late to increase his majority. He seized every slightest advantage, manipulated it dauntlessly, and expanded it incredibly. His final interview with the prince was regarded by both sides as a declaration of open hostility; and while the royal party was now apparently quiescent, the things that Amraphel would not do to win over to his side a single man, were scarce worth considering.

While Cyrus and Gobryas with their invading armies were still far away in the south and in the north of the country, nothing that would precipitate matters could be done in Babylon. Indeed, a premature rebellion was the one thing that could save the Great City to her lawful rulers; and no one in the city knew this better than its high-priest. It was for this reason only that Amraphel had failed to carry out his threat with regard to Belshazzar's criers. And it was also for this reason that Belshazzar had so openly and so recklessly defied his enemy at their last meeting. Could Amraphel have been irritated past his self-control and so forced into some rash act that would precipitate the rebellion before Cyrus was at hand, the contest would at least be an equal one. But with Beltishazzar at his elbow, and the funds of the house of Êgibi at Daniel's command and Daniel's command only, there was no chance of matters coming to a crisis before their appointed time. For Daniel's whole soul and mind were in this plot; and, whatever doubt there might be about the soul, it was quite certain that his mind was no ordinary one.

Amraphel's most telling means of influencing the common people was by temple harangues. Every day, after the early sacrifice, a priest would come before the throng of assembled people and talk to them, not of their duty towards the gods and the priests of the gods, but of the falseness and the iniquity of the royal house. These preachments began almost immediately after the death of the rab-mag, the tale of which, with its accompanying moral, was worn threadbare in order that Belshazzar's brutal instincts might be made sufficiently plain to the dense minds of the listening commoners. The fact that Belshazzar held priestly office and a priestly title was of no consequence. Indeed, it became a subject for further revilings. Certainly it could not be denied that the heir-apparent was extremely lax in his religious duties. Scarcely one day out of ten did he appear in the precincts of the temple, much less officiate at sacrifice. Without doubt, the gods were angry with him. How could it be otherwise?

It was not long before Belshazzar began to feel the breath of unpopularity. When he drove forth into the city few people took notice of him, none did him reverence, a few eyed him askance, and once or twice he was assailed by some opprobrious phrase. He felt rather keenly the disfavour of the people, but made no attempt to remedy the matter. He knew very well the direction that affairs were taking; but he could do nothing but bide his time, and at night keep his eyes from the future, since sleeplessness brings back to no man his wealth. One thing, however, the prince, as governor of the city, could do, under the general directorship of Nânâ-Babilû at Sippar. He could keep the guards of the city in form, and this he did well. There were at this time about 10,000 of the regular army in Babylon, and of these the finest were Belshazzar's own regiment, under command of Shâpik-Zeri, all of them men of Gutium – the province of which Gobryas had once been governor. These, the best-trained soldiers in Babylonia, were loyal to their last drop of blood to their lord. Belshazzar was a fine soldier, iron-clad in his rules, and known to be himself fearless on the field. His men worshipped his physique, feared his strength and delighted in paying him the honour and obedience that he would otherwise have exacted by force of arms. Thus Belshazzar was seen no longer in the goat-skin, but he made up for the deficiency by appearing at every hour of the day in helmet and shield, on his way either to or from the great parade-ground where the daily reviews of the various regiments were held.

It was about this time, the middle of the month of May, that Charmides the Greek experienced a sudden disgust for his position in the temple and left it, pleading that the illness of his wife demanded his continued presence at her side. Unworldly, improvident, sentimental as his move was, he nevertheless experienced a great relief when he turned his back for an indefinite period on the great House of Lies. For things had been done there that the young Greek could not think of without furious gusts of anger and rebellion. Besides this, Ramûa was ill, wretchedly ill, as the result of a fall that had caused a series of complications over which both Charmides and Beltani were exceedingly anxious. Still, she was in no real danger, and in spite of his statement, Charmides did not spend all of his hours at her side.

About ten days after his leaving the temple, Charmides had cause of rather a curious nature for regretting that he was no longer in a situation to know the inner aspects of certain things. A proclamation had gone through the city striking astonishment to every heart, and to none more than those of the priesthood. It was to the effect that, on the first day of the month of Duzu, twenty new gods would take up their residence in the Great City.

Poor Nabu-Nahid, reading aright the threatening signs of his own and his son's unpopularity, believed that the time had come for his great act. As a priest of the highest order he was empowered to command the high-priest of every temple, with the exception of Amraphel alone, that he, together with two Enû, two Asipû and two Barû, should form part of the great procession of strange gods when these entered the city. Moreover, each temple was to be especially purified and prepared for the reception of a new statue, and henceforth double services must take place in each temple, that both the old god and the new one might be properly honoured. The date for the procession was set for the last of Sivân. A document explanatory of the whole matter, and signed and sealed by the house of Shamash, was sent to each of the priests, and to every monastery of Zicarû; and these were also read aloud in the temples by eunuchs, till all Babylon was informed of the king's act, and all Babylon prepared for the holy day.

That morning dawned like every other morning of the season, in a flush of fierce crimson, gradually melting into the living gold that flooded the sky with a furnace heat and poured a shower of burning light upon the river with its clinging city, and over the yellow desert far beyond. Holiday had been proclaimed, and at an early hour every street leading to a temple was packed on either side with gayly dressed men and women and their children. Charmides went alone. Ramûa could not walk, and Beltani had preferred remaining with her to standing for hours in the glare of the sun, waiting for the procession. Both women, however, had begged Charmides to go and see it, that he might describe it to them on his return. Therefore the Greek took up his position on the edge of the square of Istar, into the deserted temple of which the old and sacred statue of the goddess of Erech was to be carried first of all.

The crowd here was especially thick. Only by vigorous pushing and squeezing, and some very rapid talking, could Charmides find a place for himself. Having reached a vantage-point, however, he proceeded to fall into a reverie – a reverie of a year ago, when he had stood waiting for a pageant, an utter stranger to the city, hungry, friendless and homesick. He could recall every trivial incident of the day with ease, from Baba and the goat's milk she gave him, to the long afternoon with Ramûa, now for nine months his wife. He had got to a philosophical stage in his dreams when a light hand was laid on his arm, and he looked up to find Baba at his elbow. He was glad to see her, glad of a companion to talk to; and so they two watched the procession together, bent to the dust before the little black images dotting the line in twenty places, and borne each on its golden platform on the shoulders of six eunuchs.

Nabu-Nahid, in white, drove first of all. Behind him, frowning and stiff, and in anything but a pleasant frame of mind, was Vul-Ramân in his car. Belshazzar came farther along the line, standing unconcernedly in his place, his white muslin robe falling to his feet, the goatskin fastened over his left shoulder. Everywhere he was greeted with murmurs of disapproval; but though he could hardly have failed to hear some of them, his face gave no sign of it. Quiet, immovable, slightly scornful in his expression, he endured the mental and physical discomforts of the day with a nonchalance that would have deceived Amraphel himself.

The procession left the little temple by the riverbank at ten o'clock in the morning and broke ranks in the square of the temple of Marduk just at sunset, with the last ceremony concluded – Nabonidus' last card played. Twenty new gods would watch over the city that night, and twenty extra sacrifices would take place in their honour on the morrow. Perhaps it was as well that Nabonidus, in his pathetic faith, should not have heard the comments of the tired temple-servants as they worked through the night, preparing for the next day's services. Twenty new gods asleep in Babylon – twice twenty demons at work in the minds of men. Could the outcome of the fast-approaching struggle still look doubtful to any reasonable thinker whose heart was on neither side?

Belshazzar and his father drove home together from the square of Marduk. Weary as he was, Nabu-Nahid was in a joyous frame of mind. He talked incessantly about the success of his great experiment. Secure in the favour of Heaven, he could easily cast aside all fears of earthly disfavour, and his whole person so radiated delight that Belshazzar's mood passed unnoticed, his expression of unhappiness was transfigured by the sunset glare into one as rapt and as joyous as his father's own.

When at last they two dismounted together before the palace gates, Belshazzar's heart gave a great throb of relief. He had that day felt against him all the hostility of that Great City, and though they were his own, and he should be called upon someday perhaps to die for them, yet he felt a sensation akin to hatred for all the people whose superstitious and pitifully cringing hearts could be moved by the priesthood to moods and beliefs inimical in every particular to the hopes and plans of their temporal lords.

Belshazzar made his way straight to his private apartments and there doffed his priest's dress, commanding it to be carried out of his sight, and vowing that never again would he put it on. Then he donned a tunic of grey cotton cloth and took his way to the seraglio, into the presence of Istar. He found her sitting on the broad pile of rugs and cushions that filled half her living-room, holding the child in her arms, crooning over it as only a mother can. She welcomed her husband with eagerness, however, showing by the light in her face her delight in his coming.

"And do these new gods hold not their high places in Babylon, my lord?" she asked, when, having called for food and wine, he threw himself down beside her.

Belshazzar's answer was a bitter little smile.

"And they were received in silence? Tell me of the image that was put up into the shrine of Istar. Did the people honour it – did they praise it and bow down before it?"

"More than any other they showed it honour. Ah, my beloved, for my sake the people hate thee! Knowest thou how they hate me? My name is taught to be reviled in every temple. I am an enemy of the priests, therefore am I mocked in the high places. Istar – Istar – I sometimes dream that not much longer shall I and my father dwell in our Great City". He spoke the words lingeringly, with his eyes fixed on her face.

Istar answered the look well. Not a suggestion of fear, not a hint of dread was to be found in her smile. And while her hand caressed the tiny palm of the sleeping child, she said, quietly:

"Whither thou goest, dear lord, there I will go. Unto the ends of the earth – and beyond – I will follow thee".

"Istar! Thou art happy in me?" he cried, impulsively, leaning over and putting his hand to her lips.

The smile still lingered as she kissed the hand; and then, taking it gently away, she answered and said: "Happy – Yea, Belshazzar, so happy that I, too, believe that our earth-time nears its end. I believe that I have found what I sought. It is the love for his fellows lying in the heart of every man that binds him to the greater love of the All-Father. The love of one for another sanctifies every life. Thee and this – my little child – I love".

Belshazzar looked wistfully upon his wife. There were times when she was too far above him for his own content. Yet in her words there was always something that, vaguely understood, stirred his brain to a painful effort to follow her to her height. Now, as if he would hold her back with him, he took both her hands, leaving the child to lie in her lap unheeded, and asked, with a change of tone: "Hast thou been alone through all the weary day, beloved?"

"Nay, Baba of Ribâta's house and Charmides the Greek came here together to me, after noon. Thou knowest the Greek – him whose lyre once you broke before me".

"Ay. He is a temple-servant".

"He serves no longer in the temple. Out of loyalty to us – to thee and to me – he works no more in the statue of oracles, nor does he play at sacrifice".

"Loyalty to me!" Belshazzar laughed slightly.

Istar gave him a quiet look, and her half-open lips closed again.

"Art thou angered with me, O my beloved, for being forever jealous? Istar! Couldst thou but know half of my love! If thou couldst read the terror in my heart – the terror of losing thee and thy love – "

He broke off quickly as the eunuchs brought in a table covered with meat and wine. It was placed before the prince, and Belshazzar, faint with his long fast, applied himself to the food and drink, and the intimate little passage with his wife was finished.

The following twelve days passed quietly in the palace. Belshazzar withdrew himself absolutely from city affairs, and, beyond going daily to the reviews and drills of his regiment of Guti and the city guards, he never passed the palace gates. Nabu-Nahid, on the other hand, worked feverishly. The state of public affairs was beginning to trouble him. Five days after the procession of his gods he was obliged to acknowledge to himself that his great hopes for their intercession were not to be fulfilled. Just how far Nabonidus' blind faith went, no one, not even himself, really knew. That which was artistic in his nature – and he was no mean artist at heart – had led him into the pursuit of architecture for the love of it. A passion for things of antiquity had caused him to explore the deserted ruins of many a crumbling temple, with results that made the soul of the seeker after knowledge tremble with delight. Many a long-buried library had been brought by his efforts into the light of day; and the religion of Accad of old, with its heroic tales, its prayer-poems, its chronicles of war and the chase, had been opened to his eyes and to those of the scholars that worked with him. The gods of other days had been brought forth from their ruinous shrines and placed in newer, brighter homes. And after these things, it somehow seemed to him that a reward should be forthcoming from his country.

But when Nabonidus came to know that, at the instigation of Amraphel, the new gods were left unworshipped in their shrines, that sacrifices were no longer offered up in the temples, that people were turned away out of the holy places with the word that the great gods were angered by the intrusion of these others, that none of them would heed prayers and burnt-offerings till the strangers were removed from the Sun-built House, then the heart of the king grew sick within him, and suddenly he came to a realizing sense of the power of the priesthood. Councils were held in the palace. Lords, chancellors, judges and officers from every department, together with deputies from the provinces, met in the palace and were presided over by the king. Plans were brought up, discussed and discarded. There was only one thing, apparently, to be done; yet the doing of it would involve such political cataclysms that, dangerous as was the position of the crown, Nabu-Nahid still hesitated to force Amraphel from his place.

At this time, when Adar's month was a third gone, came news of a great battle fought in the south country around Larsam, between the troops of Cyrus and the defending army, resulting in the victory of the invader and the utter rout and defeat of the Chaldees. Before the news of this could have reached the north country, another army – the Persian, in command of the traitor-governor Gobryas of Gutium, Cyrus' ablest general – had gathered about Hit to begin a rapid southward march towards Sippar, by way of Agade. The meaning of this movement was only too plain. Cyrus and Gobryas, between them sweeping Babylonia from south to north, would come together for their final siege before the walls of the Great City.

This plan unfolded itself slowly before the eyes of the king and his council, and Gobryas was within two days' march of Sippar before Nabonidus was fully aware of the danger. Well might Amraphel and Daniel ... laugh together and rejoice at the success of their allies. At a time like this, what reproof for neglect of the gods could be given them by a king threatened with such certain disaster? A month now, at the outside, and Cyrus would be at the gates of Babylon. By then the long labour of plotting and of treachery would be over. There remained only the final stroke, now preparing, and then the swift, clean end.

During this time, while Nabu-Nahid seemed to be aging a year a day under the pressure of difficulties that he was too weak to avert or to overcome, Belshazzar was living a life of careless idleness with Istar and his child. The two of them knew that the time of their joy of love was nearly over. Both were unwilling that anything should come between them before the inevitable end. How it was that Belshazzar could put away all trouble, all apprehension of the future from his mind, he himself did not know. Perhaps he had been under the spell of apprehension for so long that now, when the dread of it had reached his father, he was empowered to straighten up and put down his load, till he must pick it up again increased in weight a thousandfold. But during the days that followed he could remember his first two weeks of summer as a foretaste of the peace eternal of the silver sky. From dawn to dawn, barring those two noon hours when Istar slept and he rode out to the parade, Belshazzar was at his wife's side. Their thoughts, their dreams, their desires, were alike. There was no need to talk one to the other. The mind of each was to the other as a written tablet; and they read in silence, clasped each in the other's arms. Istar had become very tender, very clinging, very feminine now. Those periods of divinity when her personality became elusive and her mind attained to unfathomable heights were gone. She was of earth, human in her beauty and in her frailty of physique, radiant only with an earthly love. It was Belshazzar that was becoming transfigured – transfigured through his love for her; for his passion had broadened into a power of renunciation; and he showed the woman a glorified reverence, which, beyond her to conceive, had been beyond her to command.

It was in this wise that their twelve days passed; and on the night of the twelfth of June Nabu-Nahid entered unannounced into the presence of his son, with the decree that ended Belshazzar's dream lying written in his face.

Istar, dressed in robes of deep crimson silk, girdled and sandalled with gold, lay back upon her divan, softly singing to a lute that she played herself. The light from a hanging-lamp fell over her figure and left the rest of the room in shadow. In this shadow, seated upon an ivory chair, was the prince, holding the murmuring child fast in his gentle arms. They had been thus for an hour when the interruption came and Nabu-Nahid entered, bringing with him the atmosphere in which he had been living of doubts and fears, hates and quarrels, intrigues and treacheries and dispelling instantly the love-dreams of youth.

Nabonidus was not yet an old man in years; but few would have been able to make out whether it had taken fourscore years, or five, to produce his peculiar appearance. He was a vision of white. Hair, skin, hands, robes, sandals, all were white; and which the whitest one could not have told. His face was bloodless, and resembled a piece of bleached papyrus which, having lain in a damp place, had curled up into 1,000 minute wrinkles, from the midst of which a pair of dark, dull eyes looked wearily forth. These eyes were the only feature that one much regarded. The others sloped insignificantly into the pallid plain of the cheeks. And Nabonidus' whole mood was apparent in his walk. So dragging, so weary, so despondent was every step, that, as he entered Istar's room, Belshazzar shrank back from his presence in involuntary despair.

Just inside the doorway the king stopped and looked about him. Istar laid down her lute and rose, regarding the intruder with quiet apprehension. Seeing her, Belshazzar, too, came forward out of the gloom, holding the child still in his arms. And his voice first broke the silence.

"Enter thou, my father, and sit down with us!"

Istar supplemented the words with a little gesture.

Nabu-Nahid listened, looked closely at his son and the burden in his arms, and then turned slowly to the woman, gazing at her for a long time before he spoke. "And thou art she – whom we worshipped", he murmured, musingly.

Istar drew back a little, and Belshazzar took two rapid strides forward. "Dost thou desire speech with me, my father? Let us then retire to my apartments. There we will talk".

"Twelve days hast thou been sought in thy apartment; twelve days hath this been thy abode. Let it then be mine for an hour. After that I will go forth again – alone". There was a kind of strength in this last word that sounded strange from the lips of the king, and to which neither Belshazzar nor Istar could find any reply.

Istar went to her husband and took the child from him, saying, softly: "I will leave thee here and go into another room. Cause thy father to sit and talk with thee. And – if there is need of thee, I pray that my lord will come to bid me farewell before he goes". Her voice trembled slightly, and as she lifted her eyes to Belshazzar's he found them shining with tears.

Her husband gave her the child and would have let her go; but Nabonidus raised his hand.

"Let her take the child, Belshazzar, for it is not meet that thou shouldst sit as a nurse of infants. But as Istar is thy wife and beloved of thee, let her remain here, that ye may both hear my last words concerning Babylon".

"*Thy last words!*" cried the prince, quickly.

"Yea, for I am come to bid ye both farewell. Tomorrow I go up to Sippar, which is threatened with destruction".

"Gobryas is there?"

"Tonight he lies six kasbi north of the city".

"But Nânâ-Babilû and all the army are there. There will be a siege. We will send reinforcements from Babylon. Sippar cannot fall".

For the first time in many years Nabonidus regarded his son with something akin to scorn. "In the twelve days that thou hast lain hidden here many things have come to pass. Sippar is in revolt. The priests of the sun-college have incited the people to rebel against my rule; and they threaten to open the gates to Gobryas. Nânâ-Babilû sends me messengers to say that half his army will fail him when it comes to the battle. It is for this reason that I go to Sippar".

Belshazzar rose, his face alight with eagerness. "Not thou, O king, not thou, but I, will go up tomorrow into the city of the north. My regiment of Gutium shall follow me. There, with those men alone, I will hold Sippar against Gobryas – ay, and Kurush, too, if – "

"Many things I have known thee do, Bel-shar-utsur; yet boaster wert thou never before. If thou know it not, my son, then I tell thee now, for it is well that thou shouldst learn it from my lips, Babylonia hates thee – for thy arrogance, for thy strength, for thy will, for sacrilege committed often against the gods; above all, for thy tyranny over the priests. If thou shouldst set forth to Sippar, thy life would not endure a single day. And the regiment of Gutium must stay in Babylon. It is in them that the Great City puts her trust. Thou, also, as governor of the city, must be here to lead them. I came not to thy presence to be taught, but rather to talk with thee upon thy position here".

Belshazzar stood silent, flushed with chagrin, yet in his heart acknowledging the truth of his father's words. Moreover, there was in his father's manner something that had not been there before. Beset as he was on every side, Nabu-Nahid had suddenly become a king. Istar perceived it and marvelled; and, though she did not speak, the old man found sympathy in her presence. Belshazzar forced himself at last to ask, in a subdued tone:

"Where wilt thou go in Sippar, O my father? Into the household of Nânâ, or to the river-palace?"

"Neither of these places. I shall go to the priests' college. It was there that my youth was spent. Five years ago I dwelt there through the summer. When Nitocris died, I went there after the month of wailing. It hath long been a refuge to me. I will seek it again. If I have yet any power in the world, it is there that I shall find it".

Belshazzar nodded thoughtfully. He recognized the truth of his father's words; yet he was only beginning to realize the danger of this desperate journey. It came over him again, in a vast wave, how great were the straits in which his city lay. There seemed to be nothing for him to say, so completely was his father master of the situation. And presently Nabonidus, with a faint sigh, lifted up his voice again:

"Belshazzar, thou seest surely the danger that all are in. Of my own free will I go forth to Sippar; yet I have little thought that I shall return thence again. All things are in the hands of the great gods. If it is decreed that I perish at the hands of my enemies, I pray only that Ânû will hold for me a place in the silver sky. Through seventeen years I have ruled over the Great City, and in that time I have never willingly wronged any man. Why it should be that men wrong me, I know not; and I ask not.

"Thou, my son, art trained to the thought of ruling over the mighty kingdom of the Chaldees. I charge thee only that if word of my death reach thine ears, rule over thy people and mine as a brave king and not a cruel one. In the years to come let thy people look to thee confidently and in love. Be just with all; and let none know thee in hate.

"Thou, Istar of the skies, who hast dwelt as a goddess in the holy temple of Ê-Âna, and art now become a princess of the king's house, if in time thou art made queen of Babylon, let not thy heart beat with pride. Love thy king. Bear his children and rear them in temperance and peace. Open thy lips to no words of folly. Unveil thy face before no man. Be the faithful servant and companion of him who holds thee dearer than all others. And, having heard my bidding, hold also my memory in reverence.

"Behold, I have said my say, and I go forth. On the morrow, Belshazzar, thou wilt be master in the palace. Take up thy duties, and leave the child to its mother's arms. Now Ânû, Ea and Bel, the three lords of the gods, keep our fortunes, our lives and our hearts in safety evermore!"

Nabu-Nahid held out a thin, white hand to each of them, Belshazzar and Istar, his children, and each of them pressed it reverently to brow and breast. Then the old man threw the corner of his white mantle once more over his shoulder, and, with a stateliness born of his newly royal spirit, departed from the room.

Istar and Belshazzar saw him go in silence. Their own days of happiness were at an end; but he who had ended them had given them both the desire to meet the veiled future in a manner worthy of their God and of the king that went before....

[*King Nabonidas flees to the city of Sippar, which gets conquered by Gobryas of Kurush, and the king becomes a prisoner.*]

Chapter 16

Belti-Shar-Uzzur

EIGHT DAYS AFTER the fall of Sippar, the army of the Elamite king lay encamped before Babylon. Not so vast an army, after all, this that had come out of lower Chaldea, after a series of astounding victories, to take the Great City from her king. Less than half a mile from where the gigantic height of Nimitti-Bel shut off the northeast horizon, the tents of Cyrus' army lay scattered over the parched plain. The largest of these, over which hung the royal standard, stood in the centre of the first line of the encampment, where it was most prominent to the eye from the city walls, and in the place of greatest danger in case of a sortie from the city.

Inside of Cyrus' tent, on this third day of the inactive siege, sat the royal commander himself, hard at work. The weather, even to a Babylonian born and bred, was nearly unendurable. To one who had been reared in the hills and had ruled over mountain-built Susa, with her fresh northerly winds and cold torrent streams, the temperature of a Chaldean summer was something to be marvelled at. Today the conqueror half sat, half lay upon the couch in his tent, dictating letters to three scribes, who bent over their bricks in a steaming row in the door of the tent. Both the manner and the voice of the Achaemenian betrayed his intense fatigue. Nevertheless he kept steadily on, formulating various curious plans for the prosecution of his siege.

A short, rather stocky man, this Cyrus, with thick, curling hair, a beard more golden-brown than black and eyes so piercingly brilliant that it was difficult to determine their shade. His face had been tanned to a leathery brown by years of exposure in various climes; but his hands were smooth, shapely and well-kept. In dress, there was no hint of either soldier or ruler. His head was bound round with a red fillet embroidered in black and gold. His body was clothed in the lightest and simplest of yellowish cotton tunics, narrowly bordered with red. On his feet he wore sandals, and his ankles and calves were bare. Only by his eyes and by the quick decisiveness of his manner could one have guessed that his station was high. And yet, with these two things to go by, few would have failed to select this man out of a hundred others as being indeed Kurush, the king.

Besides the king and his three scribes, there was one other person in the royal tent on this blazing afternoon of the twenty-second of the month Duzu. This was a young man, tall and meagre in body, with a peculiarly long head, a face not wholly devoid of beauty, but with an expression lurking about the lips and eyes that one who loved him would not have cared to analyse. Richly dressed was this youth, much belted, chained and braceleted with silver and gold, his tunic elaborately embroidered, the very thongs of his sandals wrought with lapis-lazuli and crystals. It was Cambyses, eldest son and heir of the great Cyrus, who thus lay in the presence of his father, sighing out his weariness with the heat, with the campaign, with the lack of fighting, with the length of days – with anything and everything that it came into his head to say, and with that everything twisted into a complaint.

Cyrus, long accustomed to this monotone as an accompaniment to his afternoons of labour, listened to it abstractedly as he continued his letters. The train of thought that could not be disturbed by words, however, was presently broken by a shadow passing the doorway of the tent; and he suddenly looked up, staring at the second scribe, trying to return to his sentence, but able to think of nothing but the last imprecation uttered by his son.

"In the name of Ahura the blessed, Cambyses, get you from my presence till these labours are at an end! Follow Bardiya into the camp, go where you will, but leave me to the letters that must be dispatched tonight if there be no word from Gobryas this afternoon".

"May he soon come!" muttered the first scribe; and the second and third, hearing, sighed in unison and wiped the sweat from their dripping brows.

Cambyses had risen and was doubtfully contemplating the prospect of the camp. Cyrus had come back to the subject of his epistle, and the scribe sat with his cuneiform iron poised in the air, when the scene was broken up. A horse, carrying a rider who clung to its bare back like a monkey, one hand twisted in the mane for guidance, came dashing up over the plain from the northwest and stopped at the tent door. The rider leaped to the ground, bending his head slightly before the king, and shouting, in a clear, fresh voice:

"News, my father! News at last! Gobryas with his army is three miles away. He will reach us by nightfall!"

Cyrus sprang to his feet. "How know you this, Bardiya?"

"I have seen them all, spoken with the general, and return to thee as his messenger".

Cyrus quickly waved his hand to the scribes. "Get you to your tents. Do not return to me till I shall command".

He waited while the three men picked up their stools in sober joy, and, saluting the royal master with a single accord, departed in an orderly file. When they were out of hearing, and Cyrus and his two sons were quite alone, the king let fall the crimson flap over the tent door, and then turned to Bardiya with his face very eager. "The king, Bar – "

"Gobryas brings with him Nabu-Nahid, the king of Babylon, a prisoner, to deliver him up to you".

Cyrus nodded, with less satisfaction than the boy had expected, and then thoughtfully bent his head. There was a short silence, which neither of the sons dared break. They saw an expression of trouble creep into their father's face. They saw him frown, and they heard him sigh. Then suddenly he crossed to a small coffer in the lent, and drew from it a long, white streamer.

"Bardiya, fasten this to the head of the spear on top of the tent. Put it there thyself, and at once".

The boy, in extreme surprise, received the pennant from his father's hand and went outside with it. Fifteen minutes later it was floating in the hot afternoon wind from the top of the royal tent; and ten minutes after that a white-robed acolyte had left the summit of Nimitti-Bel and was speeding through the fields on his way to a certain house in the centre of the city.

The afternoon passed. It came to be the hour of day's death, and in that hour the final junction of the two invading armies was to be affected. Seven months before, in the hills of Elam, they had separated, Gobryas marching to the north, Cyrus to the south. And now, each of them having fulfilled to the letter his plan of campaign, there remained only one thing more to do, the taking of that city which, six years ago, Cyrus had found impregnable to arms, and which he was now to assault in a less honourable and surer way.

The lamps in the royal tent were already swinging from their chains in a glow of fire, and the full moon was rising from the east over the city, though the sky was still too white for stars, when Cyrus, with Cambyses on his right hand and Bardiya on his left, stood in the doorway of his tent, waiting. Over the plain, at no great distance, could be seen a slow-moving line of horses and men. In front of this line, advancing at full gallop, came a single chariot, drawn by three white horses harnessed abreast, and carrying three men – the driver and two others. This vehicle hurried along straight in the direction of the royal tent, until presently Cyrus stepped eagerly forward, while his sons cried in one voice, "Gobryas!"

The chariot came to a halt, and from it leaped a tall, bearded fellow, whom Cyrus seized in his arms and clasped delightedly. "Welcome, lord of Sippar. Welcome, O conqueror!" he cried, in the Aramaic language, generally used in his camp, and understood by Babylonian, Jew and Elamite alike.

Having been embraced, Gobryas saw fit to bend the knee before his master, saying: "I bring the king my lord his royal prisoner. He is full of years and weary with the length of day. Let him, I pray, be removed to some tent that befits his rank, where refreshment may be given him".

Three pairs of eyes looked quickly up to the chariot, but Nabonidus' back was turned to them. He stood there alone, his chained arms at his sides, looking off upon the walls of Babylon. His face was invisible; but Cyrus, seeing it, would not have known the expression. As it was, when the conqueror stepped up to the chariot and spoke a word of courteous greeting, the old man turned to him a dull and gentle countenance.

"O king, Nabu-Nahid of the Great City, let thy body find rest and refreshment here in my frail dwelling-place! In the name of the blessed Ahura-Mazda, I, Kurush, bid thee welcome. Descend from the hot chariot and enter my tent".

Nabonidus acknowledged the courtesy with old-accustomed graciousness. In alighting from the vehicle he stumbled a little in his great exhaustion. Instantly Bardiya and Gobryas started to his side, and, each taking an arm, assisted the fallen king gently inside the tent, prepared for him the couch on which Cambyses had spent the afternoon, and made him comfortable upon it while Cyrus called to a slave to bring food and wine to all.

The five of them partook together of the evening meal, while conversation ran upon general topics. Nabonidus did not speak; nor, though the others did not guess it, did he listen to what was said. Cyrus and his general might have discussed their most secret plans without risk of being overheard or understood, for Nabonidus' heart was beyond them, in Babylon, and his thoughts were of his world, not of theirs.

After the meal was over, however, Gobryas leaned across to the king and whispered, just audibly: "I must go forth now, for a time, to oversee the encampment that you have commanded. While I am gone, were it not well that Nabonidus be put in a tent of his own, under guard, that when I return we may talk freely of many things?"

"Nabu-Nahid –" Cyrus hesitated a little in his reply. "Nabu-Nahid will, I think, not sleep in this camp tonight. He is to be delivered into other hands, to which, many weeks ago, I promised to entrust him".

"Whose are they?" demanded Gobryas, roughly, without any of the respect due to his lord.

Cyrus failed to resent the breach. His expression betokened regret as he opened his lips to reply. But before a word left his mouth two figures appeared suddenly in the doorway – two white-robed figures, only one of whom wore the goatskin on his shoulder. Before Cyrus could turn to them, the prisoner on the couch sprang suddenly to his feet, and a cry rang out into the night:

"Amraphel – thou dog!"

Then silence ensued. Gobryas, whose back had turned to the door, moved slowly round. Catching sight of the newcomers, he suddenly realized what Cyrus had meant: suddenly knew why Nabonidus would not sleep that night safely guarded in the camp. The high-priest of Babylon, and the leader of the Jews, in response to a prearranged signal, had come to claim their own – part of their payment for the betrayal of the city.

As he looked and understood yet more, Gobryas' face darkened with disgust. He could imagine well enough what was to follow, and his spirit revolted against taking any part in it.

"Let my lord give me permission to retire!" he demanded gruffly of Cyrus.

The king nodded to him, and the general forthwith, with a curl of the lip and a flash of disdain at the Babylonians, brushed his way by them and hurriedly left the tent. His departure removed the single disinterested element in the scene – and those that remained to enact it drew mental breath. For a moment or two no one moved. Priest and Jew stood facing the conqueror, the three of them eying one another in full understanding of this consummation of their plot. The conqueror's sons, more than half cognizant of the whole significance of the affair, shifted their glances from one figure to another with a vague sense of foreboding. Lastly, Nabonidus, the central figure in the scene, stiff and faint in his unutterable desertion, hair and face far whiter than his stained garments, confronted, with an air of supreme accusation, the two betrayers of his people. The silence was long, and nearly unendurable. Amraphel would not speak; Cyrus could not; the young men did not dare. It remained for Belti-shar-uzzur, evading that burning glance of Nabu-Nahid's, to address himself to the conqueror:

"We have seen the signal, Kurush, and have answered it. We are come to receive our own".

For the shadow of an instant Cyrus dropped his eyes. He said, anxiously: "Leave the prisoner here. I swear to his safety. He shall come to no harm!"

Amraphel stepped forward with menace in his eyes. "The promise! Remember the promise! Remember, or we fail you. Babylon to thee – Nabu-Nahid to us!"

At these words two cries rang out through the tent. The one was from Nabu-Nahid, the other from Cyrus' youngest son. The boy stepped forward quickly, his feeling plainly written in his young face. "My father!" was all he said; but before the words, and the unutterable things they told, the head of the great warrior fell and his heart smote him.

"Give us our tribute, Kurush!" sneered the [man], scorning the scene.

"Take what was promised you", answered the conqueror, slowly.

Belti-shar-uzzur stepped forward exultantly and would have put out his hand to touch Nabonidus' arm, when the old man quickly turned from him and cast himself at Cyrus' feet.

"Thou wearest, there at thy waist, a knife, O conqueror! Let it by thy hand rest in my heart!" he cried out. "Send me not forth, great king, in the power of these two, or I die terribly! I die alone, in the night, with none to close my eyes!"

Cyrus turned his head away. "Take the prisoner from my sight, ye dogs, or I will hold ye both here also! Take him from me!"

At this Daniel, starting forward, threw himself on the kneeling king, caught him about the meagre body, swung him up to shoulder, and would have started out of the tent when Amraphel stopped him.

"The gag", he muttered, sharply.

Bardiya started forward, his hand on his sword; but his father, catching him by the girdle, held him in a grasp of iron till the operation was over and the piece of wood lay in Nabu-Nahid's mouth, fastened there with a white bandage. His hands and feet were also bound with leathern thongs, and after this the body, now as helpless as a log, was borne out into the night.... Then Cyrus and his sons were left alone, nor, during the remainder of that unhappy night, did they speak one to another.

In the meantime Daniel had carried the king to where, some yards from the entrance of the royal tent, there stood a closed litter, such as was used by women of rank. Beside it, as it rested on the ground, were its four bearers, stalwart men, muffled from head to foot in white – slaves of the house of Amraphel. None of these mute, dark-faced creatures stirred as their master returned to them with his companion and his companion's burden. Only, as they came close, the foremost fellow silently threw back the curtain from one side of the basket-like couch. Daniel stooped and laid the body of the king on his back on the cushions inside. The king closed his eyes. The curtain was lowered and Amraphel gave the signal. The four slaves seized the poles and, softly singing their working-chorus, raised their burden waist-high and began their walk back to the gate of Sand.

It was a twenty-minute walk, and was accomplished without adventure. When they came to a halt outside the gate, Nabonidus, anxiously listening, could hear nothing but a suggestion of whispering between Amraphel and someone whom he believed to be the captain of the gate. Presently their way was resumed, and the company passed into the city. A little distance inside, the litter stopped again and was set down on the ground. The curtains were thrown back, Daniel bent again over the king, took him about the body, and, lifting him, laid him in one of two chariots that stood waiting. In his single fleeting glance Nabonidus recognized both of these as belonging to Amraphel's house. The king lay in the one that Daniel entered. From the other, where Amraphel stood, came presently the long, peculiar cry for the starting of the horses. Daniel's driver echoed it. The animals sprang forward, and the long drive through the city began.

In spite of the jolting misery of that ride, Nabonidus preferred it to the litter. Air came freely to his lips, and now he could see a little of what they passed. The moon was well up in the unclouded sky, lighting the fields and streets of the Great City for the last passage of her last native king. Nabonidus' heart was full, but he did not weep. The end to which he was going was unknown. Yet this, for him, was, as he knew well, the last sight of his beloved city. Still, even as he went, the moonlight fell athwart the sapphire charm that hung upon his neck, and sent forth a thin gleam of the blue light of hope – a hope that could not be brought to fulfilment by anything short of a miracle.

The horses on both the chariots were swift, and it took scarcely a half-hour to reach the second gate of Sand in Imgur-Bel. Through this they passed without parley, and the journey across the inner city was begun. They had entered Babylon at the extreme west, a little to the north of the canal of the New Year, which, as they drove, could be seen in the distance, shining clear as silver frost in the moonlight, reflecting in its placid surface the shadowy black buildings near it on either side. Ribâta's house was too far distant to be seen; and the tenement of Ut rose tall and gaunt a long way to the south. Ten minutes later the hurrying vehicles clattered into the Â-Ibur-Sabû. They continued along the famous way for little more than a quarter of a mile, and then turned to the east again, till, at something near eleven o'clock, they came to a halt beside a small, neglected building on the bank of the river Euphrates: mighty Euphrates whose Chaldaic waves were of tears tonight. Here, evidently, was their destination. Nabonidus, aching in every joint, groaning wretchedly in his heart, was lifted again in Daniel's arms. He had one glance at the river and the group of royal buildings clustered thereon but a little distance away. For one instant the three famous palaces and the mound of the hanging gardens met his eyes. Then they were lost to him, for the world swam and grew black, and he fainted.

Two minutes later, when he returned into a dim consciousness, he was in a place that he soon came to recognize. It was the temporary abode of his strange gods. The interior, lighted by two torches, that burned blue and ghostlike on the bare brick walls, was utterly forlorn. The walls, floors, and ceiling were of crumbling grey brick, unrelieved by a single colour or attempt at ornament; and the usually open doorway was now closed by a black curtain. So much he saw in the first moment of arrival. In the next he realized that the gag had been taken from his mouth and that his arms were being unbound. In the third the voice of Amraphel was heard, bidding him rise. Obediently he made the attempt, got, with much effort, to his feet, reeled blindly, and was saved from falling again by Daniel. Amraphel's lip curled. Nevertheless he helped the old man to sit down with his back to the wall. Then, when Nabonidus had blinked a little and grown steadier as to his head, the high priest stood over him and spoke:

"Thou, O weak one, hast been king of the Great City. King of her shalt thou be nevermore. Here thou art, alone, unheard, unseen, in my power and the power of the captive Jew. Death hangs over thy head; yet by one means thou mayst save thyself. Wilt thou hear?"

Nabonidus, looking at him steadily, nodded.

Amraphel continued: "No man, Nabonidus, either fears or loves thee. Thy power over the people of the Great City does not by one-twentieth equal mine. But at thy passing there are two – two whom I hate – and, I say it, fear – that will struggle for the crown thou hast borne. One of these thou hast seen tonight – the Achaemenian. The other is the child of thy flesh, not of thy spirit – Belshazzar the prince. Nabu-Nahid, if thou tonight wilt swear, on penalty of the curse of all the gods, to remove thy son and thy son's wives, and thyself and thy wives and all thy household, from the royal palace, and wilt swear that thou and he will go forth in peace out of the Great City, to return no more to it forever, if thou wilt do this – "

"Thou fool!"

Amraphel faced round. "What sayest thou...?"

"Thou fool! Wilt thou put faith in the word of a man in the death fear? Wilt thou play me false? There was to be no choice here tonight. Mine eyes were to behold the blood of the enemy of my race. He shall find no mercy – or, if he finds it, then thou shalt not!"

Amraphel grew white with anger; but, before he spoke again, Nabonidus had struggled to his feet and stood supporting himself against the wall, gazing with fiery eyes at his enemy.

"I also say it: – thou fool!" he said. "Think you, indeed, that because I am old and feeble, and in the power of traitors, I would sell the birthright of my son? Thou fool!"

At these words Daniel turned to the old man and looked thoughtfully at him. But Amraphel, with a sneer, advanced a step or two, and said, in a soft and menacing voice: "The hour is come, Nabu-Nahid. Prepare thyself!"

"O Bel! Receive my spirit into the silver sky!"

Slowly Daniel drew his knife, but Amraphel was before him. Nabonidus saw the weapon of his enemy flash in the torchlight. The gleam of it passed over his deathly face. Just at the moment of the blow, a faint cry left his lips. Then a long spurt of heart's blood shot from the body. There was a sickening gasp – a fall – and the flesh only was there with the murderers. Nabu-Nahid had gone. Belshazzar was king in Babylon.

[Daniel] had gone rather sick, and Amraphel himself was white to the lips. "Let us go forth", he muttered, unsteadily.

"Fool!" said Daniel, for the second time. "Wilt thou leave here the body of the king, that all Babylon may look on it at dawn? Shall thy charioteer and mine say who it was that brought Nabonidus here? Thou hast struck the blow. Hast thou lost strength to finish the work?"

Amraphel caught at his nerves and said: "What is there to be done?"

Daniel's lip curled, but he did not reply in words. Passing into a far corner of the temple, he took up two fallen bricks that lay there and brought them over to the body. At the sight Amraphel came to his senses.

"I will make fast this one to his feet if thou takest the hands", he said, quietly.

Accordingly Daniel drew from his girdle two more leathern thongs, and with them the weights were bound upon the body. Then the two stood back and looked at their work. Amraphel was satisfied. Not so [Daniel]. One more brick he fetched from the little heap in the corner and fastened it on Nabonidus' neck, never noticing that in the operation he loosened and dislodged something that had been around the throat of the king. The last task finished, he stood back once more, carefully examining the bloody corpse.

"Take out thy dagger", he said, finally, to his companion.

Amraphel shrank back. "I cannot!" he whispered.

Beltishazzar bent over and drew it from the wound. Blood followed it in a thick stream. [He]wiped the weapon off on the skirt of Nabonidus' robe and silently handed it to his companion. "Now – take thou the feet", he commanded, himself lifting the shoulders of the light body.

Revolting as it all was, Amraphel could not but obey the word.... Together they bore the body out of the temple, into the still moonlight, down to the edge of the quietly flowing river. For an instant they held it over the brink. Then, at a whisper from [Daniel], they let go together. There was a splash, an eddy in the water, a little red stain on the clear stream, and then only a widening circle of ripples remained to mark the resting-place of Babylon's last king.

* * *

Late on the afternoon of the next day, Belitsum, the low-born second wife of Nabonidus, sat, as usual, in the courtyard of her part of the seraglio, in her usual canopied idleness. Morning prayers and exorcisms had been said; the daily omens looked to; all the endless details of superstition finished; and now the queen of Babylon was free to dream away the rest of the day in comparative quiet. Beside her lay a piece of unfinished embroidery, badly done; for her plebeian fingers had never taken kindly to this work of the gentle born. Two eunuchs waved over her huge feather fans, of which the extreme size denoted her rank. Beside her sat a pretty slave with a lute in her hand, though Belitsum was paying no attention to the sweet monotony of the tune she played. The queen was lost in one of those vacant reveries in which long years of idleness and neglect had taught her to remain for hours.

Suddenly there came an interruption upon this quiet scene. A eunuch of the outer palace hurriedly entered the court, and, prostrating himself profoundly before Belitsum, asked permission to speak.

The queen was a moment or two coming out of her dreams, but she presently recovered enough to find her curiosity, and to say with some eagerness: "Speak, slave! Deliver thy message. Is it from the king?"

"May it be pleasing to the queen my lady! No word hath come from Nabu-Nahid. It is a soothsayer that comes in royal state, beseeching the ears of the queen to incline to him".

"A soothsayer?" Belitsum relapsed into tranquillity. "Let him be taken into the shrine. But also cause him to know that for this day the gods have been propitiated".

As the eunuch departed, Belitsum, who had long since lost claim to youth and the slenderness thereof, rose with an effort to her feet. "Kudûa", she said to the slave, who had also scrambled up, "wait thou my return. I am going to the shrine".

Kudûa fell back willingly enough, while the queen, followed by her fan-bearers, waddled slowly across the courtyard towards the specially consecrated room in which any member of the royal harem might hold conference with men of the outer world. In spite of her slow pace, the queen reached the dimly lighted apartment in advance of the soothsayer; and she occupied her time till his arrival in offering up a quick prayer to Nindar, her especial deity. The Amanû had hardly been reached when two figures appeared in the doorway, one the attendant eunuch, the other a magnificently robed and coroneted man, in whom one accustomed to his usual slovenly appearance would have had great difficulty in recognizing Beltishazzar....

Belitsum, entirely ignorant of his race and station, judging him only by his dress and bearing, came forward with hasty respect, leaving her fan-bearers on either side of the small altar. At the same time Daniel, accustomed of old to the rigorous etiquette of the court, made a proper and graceful obeisance.

"Art thou indeed but a soothsayer?" inquired Belitsum, admiringly.

"No soothsayer I, lady queen of Babylon, but a prophet and a dreamer of dreams. And it is by reason of a dream sent me by the Lord of my race that I come to you, seeking audience. Open my lips, O queen, that I may tell this dream!"

"Wilt thou have gold? Wilt thou have gems and silver? How shall I open thy lips?"

"Bid me only to speak. Grant me the favour. Let me tell the dream, and restrain thy tears till its truth be known".

At these last words Belitsum nervously clasped and unclasped her hands. "Speak!" she said, quickly. "Tell thy dream! Speak!"

"In the evening of yesterday I lay down and slept. And in my sleep the Lord appeared to me in a vision, saying: 'Go thou down to the temple of strange gods by the side of the river, and there shalt thou find him who was king in Babylon'. And thereat, in my dream, I arose and went down through the city to the riverbank and the deserted temple thereon. And there I beheld Nabu-Nahid, the king, in mortal combat with two men that sought to kill him. And in my sleep I was withheld from giving him aid. I saw him fall by the blow from a golden dagger, and when he was dead the assassins, whose faces remained black to me, lifted him in their arms and cast him into the river, and he sank from my sight. Then said the Lord unto me again: 'Having beheld this thing, hasten to her who was the wife of him that is dead and relate it to her'. And behold, when I awoke I obeyed the word of the Lord; and, obeying, I now go forth from thy presence". Whereupon Daniel, with a delightfully dramatic effect, turned short on his heel, leaving the shrine, and in three minutes was outside the palace gates.

Through his recital Belitsum and her eunuchs had remained open-mouthed, rooted where they stood. It was not till [Daniel] had actually disappeared from her sight that the queen's amazement was overcome by her dismay, and, with a long-drawn, preliminary howl, she fell flat upon the floor in an agony of despair. Nabonidus, her husband, was dead. Never for one instant did her devout soul doubt the word of the prophet. Nabonidus was dead, and she was a widow. The shrine echoed to the sounds of shrieks, of groans, of wailing, finally of hysterical laughter. Now and then an attendant, drawn thither by the sounds of woe, appeared in the doorway, looked at her, at the bewildered eunuchs behind her, and scurried away again in empty-headed wonder. Finally one, wiser than the rest, went to the room where Belshazzar sat in council, and informed him that his step-mother was dying in the harem shrine. The prince was forced to believe the frightened and excited manner of the slave, and, hastily excusing himself to his lords, he strode through the palace to the shrine. In the doorway he halted. Belitsum was kneeling on the floor, beating her breast and wailing out prayers for the dead. She did not even notice the appearance of the prince.

"Belitsum – lady – what is thy grief?" he asked, gently.

No response. Ejaculations and redoubled wails.

Then Belshazzar, perceiving that she was bordering on frenzy, went forward and took her by the shoulders. "Art thou stricken with a sickness?" he demanded, loudly.

"Thy father – Nabu-Nahid – the king!" was all the answer he could get.

Belshazzar grew a shade paler. "My father!" He looked about him, and caught the eye of one of the eunuchs in the corner. This man he addressed. "What is the cause of this weeping? Knowest thou wherefore she cries?"

The man nodded solemnly.

"Speak, then!"

Forthwith the slave began an intelligent recital of the occurrences of the last half-hour, including a repetition of the dream in Daniel's own words. Belitsum quieted enough during this speech to listen again to the dream; but, after it was finished, the look on Belshazzar's face somehow withheld her from recommencing her lamentations.

"Who was this man? Didst thou know him?" demanded the prince of the slave.

"O prince, live forever! He was a strange prophet. Never before have mine eyes beheld him".

Belshazzar bit his lip. His face was very grave. After a short pause he took Belitsum by the arm and lifted her up. Then, turning again to the eunuch, he said, quietly:

"Go thou and command my chariot to be brought, and let the driver be alone in it".

Then, having almost tenderly returned Belitsum to the harem, and bidding her restrain her weeping till his return, Belshazzar went forth to dismiss his council for the morning, retaining Ribâta alone out of all the councillors. Fifteen minutes later he and Bit-Shumukin together mounted the chariot and set forth for the little temple of strange gods on the bank of the Euphrates. During the drive Belshazzar related to Ribâta the substance of what he knew; and, like himself, Ribâta's first question was as to the identity of the prophet.

"There is one whom it might be", suggested the nobleman, when Belshazzar had confessed himself at fault. "It may, perhaps, be Daniel…".

"So at first I thought. Yet when has any man ever beheld Daniel in such raiment as this prophet wore? [He] is poor".

Ribâta demurred a little, yet could not but admit that Belshazzar had all the evidence on his side. Then, as they neared the temple, silence fell between them.

The little building stood before them utterly deserted. Not a human being was in sight. It was a lonely spot – too far south of the bridge and too far north of the ferry to be frequented by anyone. The prince dismounted from the chariot first, but in the curtained doorway of the temple he paused.

"Ribâta", said he, softly, "I am afraid".

Bit-Shumukin's reply was to lay a brother's hand on his shoulder. Then Belshazzar lifted back the curtain and entered the room. There came a great cry from his lips, and the hideous sight was once more veiled in gloom.

"There is blood, Ribâta! It is blood!" whispered the prince, hoarsely.

"I saw it, Belshazzar. Yet it may be the blood of an animal, or of some other man. I cannot think that thy father was yester-night in Babylon. Come, let us look, my prince. Within we may find some trace – some evidence of what has happened".

The prince shrank. "Wilt thou do it, Ribâta?" he asked.

Accordingly, while Belshazzar held aside the curtain that some light might enter by the doorway, Ribâta, sick at heart, hunted over the blood-splashed floor for some clew to the identity of what it was that had died here. Belshazzar presently turned his back and stood staring into the street, refusing to look, yet listening with every sense for a dreaded exclamation from his friend. It came. As Bit-Shumukin bent over the corner where Nabonidus had fallen, he found something that wrung from him a low cry.

Belshazzar turned deathly white. "What is it?" he said, quietly.

Ribâta came to him with something in his hand. It was a small, shining, blue stone, that showed itself in the sunshine to be an Egyptian-cut sapphire of great value, attached to a wire of twisted gold.

Belshazzar took it dully from his hand. "My father wore it always on his neck. Let us return to the palace", he said.

"But the body – it may surely be found!"

"The river hath it. Let her keep her own".

And so the two remounted the vehicle and started on their way back through the city of which Belshazzar was king.

Chapter 17

The Woman's Woe

ON THAT FATEFUL MORNING Belshazzar was away from the palace less than one hour; yet when he re-entered it he was aged ten years at heart, and one, at least, in appearance. He neither saw nor heard anyone as he hurried through the great courtyard to his own room, whither Ribâta accompanied him and remained with him till late afternoon, while they two took council together. Belshazzar was unnaturally calm. Through all their talk neither he nor Ribâta once hinted that either knew or cared to know the identity of the murderers. For, whatever they suspected, whatever was all but a certainty, both of them were too painfully aware of Babylon's present situation not to know that any accusation they might make of those whose power was now supreme, would do infinitely more harm than good: would merely precipitate that frightful climax that both of them dreaded and neither spoke of. Therefore, after a careful debate, it was decided to keep the murder of Nabonidus a profound secret until such time as the disclosure might be safely made.

"I charge thee as my brother, Ribâta", were Belshazzar's parting words to his friend that day, "that thou let no man or woman, of whatever station, know from thy lips who is king of Babylon. And save for Istar, who is as myself, none shall know it from my lips. But also, as I live and reign, there shall come a day, not too distant, when justice shall be done – when this foul crime shall be avenged, as never crime before, on them that have accomplished it".

Ribâta gave his promise in all devotion, and, embracing his king, bade him farewell and set off to his own abode, his mind unstrung by the fearful discovery of the morning.

Long hours before, Belshazzar had sent a message of reassurance to Belitsum; and now, with a weary sigh of relief, he turned his steps towards the distant apartments of his wife and child. With Istar, as he knew, was peace and sympathy. Never yet had she failed to understand him, and to offer him in his trials the comfort that he needed. His mind, like his heart, was absolutely hers. Arrived at the threshold of the room where, at this hour, she was always to be found, he stopped, his hand upon the curtain. Someone within had been singing. Now, noiseless as was his approach, the voice was silent. The curtain was pushed aside. Istar stood before him with a smile in her eyes.

"I felt thy presence, lord", she said, in such a tone that his face kindled with love-light. "Thou – Belshazzar! Art thou ill?"

"Yea, at heart", he answered. "Not in body. Be not afraid. Let me come in to thee, that I may tell thee Babylon's new woe".

Istar took him gently by the hand and led him into the apartment. Inside stood Baba, holding the baby to her breast. It was she whose voice Belshazzar had heard. Belshazzar greeted the little slave, and then Istar, knowing how he wished to be alone with her, whispered a word to Baba, who a moment later went quietly away.

When they were alone Belshazzar sank back on the divan in the corner, and Istar, laying her baby upon the bed, seated herself at her lord's feet, laid her hands in his, and anxiously scanned his care-worn face.

"Kurush hath stormed the walls, Belshazzar? The city is taken?" she asked.

"Nay, my beloved. My father hath been murdered in the city – in the temple of the strange gods, by the riverbank".

"Thy father!" Istar gasped with horror. "Thy father! Oh, my lord – my lord – save thyself! If they should do this with – "Istar's head sank forward. She brought both Belshazzar's hands to her lips and held them there in an agony of love and terror. So they remained for a long time, sorrowing together silently: Istar for her lord, Belshazzar for the city. But Istar's presence brought comfort to the heart of the king, and her touch filled him with that high sense of protectiveness that generates the truest courage. In this woman life had given him enough. He had neither desire nor need for further blessings. His father had not been to him all that a stronger man might have been. It was the horror of that father's lonely death that now so completely overwhelmed him. But Istar, feminine, weak even, as she had come to be, brought him his full meed of consolation. The two of them wore the night away in council for Babylon; for Istar's fears for her king had now become abnormal. Belshazzar listened in surprise to her desperate prayers that he surround himself with every protection, that he beware against venturing out at night, that he wear armour under his tunic, and that he carry weapons of defence always around with him.

"They that sought thy father's life seek also thine", she insisted, till in the end Belshazzar left her with the promise that he would care for himself as he would have cared for her.

If this promise were not to the letter kept, it was hardly to be laid at Belshazzar's door as a fault. For at such a time as this, when the city was in such peril, an example of cowardly fear from its ruler would have resulted badly. After the death of Nânâ-Babilû at Sippar, and in the face of the continued absence of Nabonidus, Belshazzar had taken on himself the duties of absolute monarch – lord of the people and general of the army. And certainly it never could be charged to him that he neglected these duties. Early and late, sometimes from dawn until dawn again, he worked on those endless details of civil and military life that he alone could attend to. The city was in a state of siege. All the gates in Nimitti-Bel were closed, and those in Imgur-Bel doubly guarded. Also, in consideration of the fact that the food supplies coming from the country were cut off, the great fields between the outer and inner walls were under cultivation. A census was taken of every soul in the city, and preparations made for the regular daily grain allotments to come now from the granaries, and later from the new crops when they should be ready for harvest. For, by careful management, no one in Babylon need ever suffer from hunger, no matter how long a siege should last. This Cyrus had learned once before, six years ago; and the question now in the mind of every man was: Could he be made to cover it again?

Certainly the siege was conducted on an extraordinary plan. For ten days the besieging army had lain in camp before the walls of the city, yet not an arrow had as yet been shot on either side, not a javelin hurled nor a stone slung. The handful of soldiers inside the walls were hardly more than enough to man the watchtowers and guard the gates; and they were under orders from Belshazzar to await developments passively. Meantime they were kept in excellent form. Every day Belshazzar reviewed them in the great field between the walls, and daily he examined a certain number of men from his own regiment of Guti as to their intelligence and ability. Also, late in the afternoon, it had become his custom to drive on top of Nimitti-Bel in his chariot, showing himself to the enemy and to the city also. There was little danger in this drive, since the range from Cyrus' camp was too long for any known weapon, and the height of the wall was an excellent safeguard against shots from nearer at hand. At this time quite an extensive stable was maintained on the giant wall. Chariots had been wheeled up the inclined plane that led to the top of it, and orders were carried from gate to gate on horseback along the top. Belshazzar's wild drives on that dizzy height became one of the favourite sights of the citizens; and it grew to be the fashion for numbers of people of all classes to drive out to Nimitti-Bel in the afternoon, to witness the spectacle of the storm-prince in his golden chariot lashing his four white horses madly along that smooth way, 250 feet above the ground.

On the afternoon of the twelfth day of the siege, one of the last days in the month of Duzu, Charmides walked out beyond Imgur-Bel to see this much-talked-of sight. At this time the Greek presented rather a different appearance from that of six months ago. His resignation from the temple of Sin had proved disastrous; and there were now times when the meanest of food was not to be found in the house of Beltani. Charmides had no work to do, would not beg, hated the thought of the temple, grew gaunt and big-eyed, went unkempt as to dress and mourned over Ramûa, who in turn wept over him, both of them, and Beltani, too, concealing their state from Baba with the utmost care. Today, after a troubled hour at home, where Ramûa's efforts at cheerfulness were like blows to him, the Greek went out, in the face of a prostrating heat, to seek by rapid walking an escape from the thoughts that pursued him, and to evade the admission to himself of the inevitable end: that he must go back to the profession of lies and of deceit; of treachery, of crimes, of death. He made his way quickly across the city and out beyond the first wall to a spot where green, well-watered fields stretched before his eyes, putting him suddenly back into his youth. He halted in his walk at a distance of thirty yards from the great wall, just behind a group of people come evidently for the same purpose as his – that of watching Belshazzar's drive. Rather absent-mindedly the Greek noticed the man immediately in front of him, who had been in a measure connected with his old life of the temple; and he watched the movements of that lean, ill-kempt figure with the same keen subconsciousness that one sometimes exercises when the thoughts are very intent on something else. It was in this way that he noted the sling in the right hand of [Daniel].

There was not long to wait for the coming of Belshazzar. At a little murmur from the men in front, Charmides turned his head and saw, far down the wall, a black speck that gradually increased in size, and finally resolved itself into four flying horses, harness and crests flashing in the light of approaching sunset, that raced neck and neck under the long, black lash wielded by him who stood alone in the rattling vehicle – a figure the poise of which was beyond question royal. Charmides looked on it with undisguised admiration – the superb head with its golden coronet, the broad shoulders, to which was fastened a fluttering, crimson cloak, and the hands flashing with jewels the least of which would have kept the Greek's stricken household well fed for months.

Absorbed as were Charmides' eyes in the sight of the approaching figure, he nevertheless felt his gaze suddenly withdrawn to the man in front of him, who was now busily fumbling with the weapon in his right hand. Suddenly a stone had been fitted into the sling and aim taken, and at the same time Charmides' slow thoughts resolved themselves. Leaning forward, he twitched the sleeve on [Daniel]'s right arm at the moment in which the stone flew forth, wide of its mark, while the chariot passed safely by. Beltishazzar, with a Hebrew exclamation, wheeled sharply about. Charmides faced him in silence. A look only passed between them, but it was enough. In that little time they knew each other. Charmides had made an enemy, and the all-powerful [man] felt a twinge of fear.

An hour after this incident Charmides and the king met, face to face, in the middle of the Â-Ibur-Sabû. Belshazzar was in his ordinary chariot, slowly returning from the walls. Charmides was on foot, going his weary way back to the tenement of Ut. It occurred to the Greek to speak to the lord of the city on the subject of his personal safety. He therefore stopped in the road, directly in front of the royal horses. With a sharp exclamation Belshazzar drew up his reins. Catching sight of the Greek's face, however, and recognizing it, he paused to listen when Charmides spoke.

"Lord prince of the Great City – live forever!" he began, formally. "There was today an attempt upon the most royal life of the prince my lord".

Belshazzar stared a little. "How, Greek?"

"As the royal chariot drove along the top of Nimitti-Bel, a man, one of the subjects of my lord, made endeavour to fell him by a shot from a sling. I, pulling his sleeve at the moment, caused the stone to fly wide of the mark. When next my lord drives it may be that I shall not be at hand".

Belshazzar looked quizzically into the face of him who spoke these laconic words. But he found no guile in the emaciated face. Instead, there was something there that roused his interest. "Mount beside me, Greek. I have not forgotten thee. Thou shalt return with me to the palace".

Charmides refused. He had no desire for a cross-examination on the subject that he had detailed as fully as he intended to the prince. All efforts on Belshazzar's part to induce him to come were in vain. Therefore, seeing that Charmides would have his way, Belshazzar did what he could for the very apparent signs of pecuniary distress in the youth's appearance. Detaching from his neck a golden chain wrought with well-cut gems, he silently held it out to the Greek.

Charmides was much displeased. It was the first time that he had ever needed a gift, and therefore the thought of taking this one shamed him. "My words, O prince, were not a suit for gifts".

"Thy wife", suggested Belshazzar, inconsequently.

A flicker passed through the Greek's eyes, but he did not waver. "My lord, I shall probably re-enter the priesthood".

"I think thee no such enemy to me. Come into my regiment of Gutium".

"Nay. I cannot fight. I will have no blood on my hands. I follow music alone; and music forbids murder".

Belshazzar laughed slightly at the fellow's incomprehensible attitude. "Go back, then, to temple service. I will trust thee there", he said, good-naturedly. "And now, the name of him that would have had my life?"

Charmides opened his lips to speak, and then closed them again. "Ask me not. Only beware and guard thyself".

The king bent his brows. "Greek, hast thou lied to me?"

"No, lord prince".

Belshazzar shrugged. "Out of my way, then!" he cried. And Charmides stepped quickly out of the road while the king brought his whip over the haunches of his steeds and started forward, tossing, as he went, the chain of gold at the feet of the Greek. Nor was he ungenerous enough to cast a single backward glance to see whether or no the hungry fellow picked it up.

So Belshazzar proceeded on his way back to the palace, musing rather on the incident of his little talk with Charmides than upon its subject – the attempt on his life. More than this one time, and in more dangerous ways than a slingshot at 100 yards, he had been threatened with death. Those very drives round the walls carried with them the possibility of a far more frightful end. But Belshazzar's was an adventurous nature. And danger was his life, a life that the city's state of quiescence had once led him to seek by other than reputable paths.

On his arrival at the palace he went immediately to Istar's rooms, determined to tell her nothing of the event of the afternoon, for her fears for his personal safety would be thereby enormously increased. But when he came to her he found another subject ready to occupy all his thoughts. Istar was not watching for him at the door, as was her invariable custom. Instead, he found her hanging over the bed on which her baby lay ill – so ill that Belshazzar, on first seeing it, turned pale for Istar's sake. And the look that he found in her face, when, with a glad cry that he had come, she turned it to him, sent a pang to his heart.

Istar's child, the fruit of her earth-love, had cost her her godhead, but had returned her joy a thousandfold dearer than divinity had been. Only now, as she stood bending over the helpless little form, racked as it was with mortal pain, did the greatest world-horror, the horror of death, first lay its hold upon her. The thought that this little being whom she had brought into the world – whom, day and night since its coming she had cherished with an all-powerful love and joy – *could* die, could cease to live for her forever, rushed over her as the waters close over the head of a drowning woman.

Until an hour before the coming of Belshazzar, Istar had been alone with the child, believing it to be suffering from some infantine ailment. But finally the little creature's fever was so manifestly high, and its distress so great, that she had commanded the attendance of the new rab-mag, a man widely celebrated for the potency of his charms. He came at once, examined the baby from head to foot, and noted certain things that caused him to turn to the mother with a look of deep anxiety.

"Great lady", he said to her, "thou wilt do well to leave this child alone, though before dawn it die. I, Kidish-Nindar, say it. Accept my words, and put the child from thee for the sake of the Great City over which thy husband rules!"

Then Istar, in fear and amazement – quickly and sharply dismissed the man from her presence and turned again to the infant, that lay now in a quiet stupor. It was so that Belshazzar found her, wetting the child's forehead with her tears, pouring forth mingled prayers and the incoherent, birdlike talk of a mother, while her own face took on the colour of chalk, and her eyes were bright with a dread to which she would not, even to herself, give form.

The king, for a moment, took her place over the infant, and stood regarding him while Istar told the story of the rab-mag's desertion. Belshazzar would have commanded his return had not the mother forbidden it. But when his displeasure had cooled a little, the king began to ponder over the evident fear of Kidish-Nindar; and finally, bidding Istar remain where she was, he took the child in his arms, carried it across the room, and seated himself with it upon his knees directly under a light. His back was turned to the divan, and Istar did not see what he did. When he had finished his examination and carried the faintly moaning child back to its place, he went over to her, and she could not but start with dismay at the ghastly pallor that had come upon him. Rising, she laid both hands upon his arm, looking silently, wistfully, into his sad eyes.

"My lord!" she whispered, fear unlocking her lips.

Belshazzar, knowing the ineffable tenderness of her motherhood, could not tell her what he knew. He said only: "Beloved, we will watch together through the night".

But before that watch began Belshazzar left Istar's rooms for the space of half an hour while he sought the apartment of Kidish-Nindar. The rab-mag was frantically purifying his body and repeating mingled prayers and exorcisms, in the hope of warding off that which he so unspeakably dreaded. The king, by means of threats and bribes adroitly alternated, extorted from the man an oath of silence, and then left him grovelling on his knees before an image of Sin, while he, the king of Babylon, returned to the vigil of his child.

Through the long night they sat together, man and wife, by the bedside of the child. Together they watched the progress of that terrible disease of which Istar was so happily ignorant. Together they saw the flame of life struggle with the suffocating darkness in which it burned. And they saw the little light grow feebler, and the flame flutter in the wind that came across the dark valley of the beyond. Istar's brain reeled and her heart grew sick. Still, as she sat with her gaze fixed on the drawn face of the child, unconscious that Belshazzar's eyes were always upon her, she refused to believe what was too apparent.

And there came a time in the early dawn when the mother could hold away no longer. Lifting the baby from its place, she clasped it close to her breast, carried it across to the soft divan and lay down with the little, fever-flushed body pressed warm over her heart. In this position her eyes, weary with the long vigil, closed; and while she slept the day broke. Belshazzar remained close at her side to watch the end alone. He could not have told what it was that caused him to lift up his hands there in the faint light, groping for something to which to cling, for some higher power that should ease the terrible aching of his heart. Suddenly the world had become a vast waste, and he was in it alone, helpless and unutterably weary. And it was still without the hand of God to help him that he saw the end come – the death of Istar's happiness and of his own. It was while Istar still quietly slept that the white shadow passed into space. And the woman awoke to find Belshazzar's hand in hers, and the little body lying stiff and rigid across her bosom.

When Istar realized what had happened she made no outcry. She sat clasping the lifeless form tighter to her own. Tearless, speechless, motionless, she sat alone with that unbearable thing that mortals know as the death-sorrow. Pitilessly it ate its way into her vitals. She forgot everything that had been in her heart before. She was unconscious of any living presence.

She was bereft – bereft – and of her offspring. It was in her mind to curse the God that had conceived such suffering and put it upon man. And then there came a touch upon her arm that stilled all her rebellion. Belshazzar's tears fell hot upon her cheek. Without a word she lifted up to him the baby that was also his: and, when he took it in his arms, she crept again over to the pillows, and as she laid her face among them, the blessed tears came forth, and she could weep.

How long she lay there no one knew. Belshazzar had carried away the body – the little body that had been hers; and when he returned to her he brought a cup of wine. The child was gone. As he lifted her up in his arms she asked a mute question with her eyes, and he answered her softly:

"The baby, most beloved, is gone. Our eyes may not again behold him. Some day – someday – "he got no further. For an instant Istar had looked at him in a dull, meaningless sort of way. Then, no longer knowing what she did, her nerves suddenly giving way, she threw herself upon him in blind anger, struggling like one gone mad, crying that he had stolen her child from her, screaming till her voice was gone and her strength gave way, and she fell into his arms a helpless, lifeless form.

Later in the day, when, with invincible patience and tenderness, he had soothed her into quietude and had gone forth to his inevitable duties, Baba came – Baba, who, since her day in the house of Êgibi, had been Istar's constant companion.

Baba had come to love Istar's child almost as Istar herself loved it. When, therefore, the little slave first came to the mother, she could speak no words of comfort. Her tears flowed faster than Istar's own, and she could only grieve beside the queen. Yet in some way this human woe brought to Istar's lonely heart its first breath of comfort and of hope. In the evening she began to speak to Baba of many half-forgotten things – of her own mysterious birth, of her dim remembrances of a great preceding existence, of those beings that had sometimes come to her on earth from space. In the last few weeks Istar had become almost utterly oblivious of her one-time divinity. Natural life and natural love had so blunted her former faculties of perception that the past remained only as a misty background to her life. Yet as her mind struggled to pierce the mists that hid from her the glory of bygone days, a longing was born within her heart – a longing ill-defined, yet so strong that she made, perforce, painful efforts to formulate it.

"I have beheld the glory of the setting sun – the pale light of the newly risen moon. The murmur of waters came to me as I slept. I beheld great lakes and white palaces, and high towers shining in the morning light. The scent of the lotus filled the air, and the rustle of the wind was in the palm-trees. Tell me, my Baba – tell me that for which I thirst! Tell me the great desire of my heart! Tell me, oh my Baba, where, in the same hour, have I known all these perfect things?"

Baba, gazing at her with the big, wondering eyes that had never in all her little life shone with the light of complete happiness, understood the words of her golden lady. "I will bring the great comfort to thee", she said. "Wait till I come again". And, rising, she left the palace.

Through two still hours Istar waited there with her heart-sorrow, trusting in Baba to bring that for which she thirsted. And at last, when she had grown weary with waiting, Baba came again, and with her someone else – Charmides, with his burnished hair and his pale, gaunt face, carrying his lyre in his hand. With a silent obeisance to Istar, he stood off at a little distance, and, opening his lips, began to sing.

Then, indeed, came the glory of the setting sun, the pale light of the newly risen moon, with the whisper of waters and the shining gold of great lakes. And around fair white towers and palaces hung the scent of lotus flowers, and the murmur of the evening wind was in the palm-trees. All things far and beautiful came home in the same hour to Istar's senses. And as he sang again, the tears of mingled joy and woe flowed from her eyes. Once more, and music, which is divine, opened divinity again before her vision, and she rose up transfigured, crying:

"Allaraine! Allaraine! Mine eyes behold thee once again!"

Then the moment of fire faded, and she was alone with only Charmides and his careworn, ethereal face, singing on in the fragrant accents of his Sicilian land, till Istar's passion faded gently away, and she smiled a little, and her eyelids grew heavy with sleep. Presently her flower-like head drooped forward. The frail, white hands fell from where they had been clasped upon her breast. Baba drew her down upon the divan, and when Charmides' voice died at length away, a great silence was in the room. Baba and the Greek were alone together. Charmides stood transfixed, his eyes fastened upon the sleeping figure of her whom he had once worshipped. He was roused from the look by a touch on his hand. Baba was kneeling at his side, and her lips were pressed to the fingers that had touched the magic lyre-strings, bringing peace to the soul of Istar of Babylon.

And thereafter ten days passed away, and it was the time of the great yearly feast of Tammuz, the beautiful god of spring....

[*It was during the feast at the temple that Amrphel, the high priest, and his lower priests revealed their treachery by betraying the king and siding with Cyrus in his conquering of Babylon.*]

The two doors of the temple were burst apart, and those within found themselves face to face with the army of Cyrus and a vast Babylonish mob.

Chapter 19

The Regiment of Guti

THE TERRIBLE SPELL of silence that had spread over the feasters at the temple was broken by a woman's scream. That scream brought men and women alike back to life. With a loud shout Belshazzar the king leaped down the steps of the shrine and ran forward, crying lustily to his guard to form into line. Old as he was, Amraphel, Cyrus' tool, was an instant before the king; and he, with Daniel the prophet close beside him, made his way through the band of soldiers that had gathered near the door, to the ranks of the enemy, in the vast throng of whom priest and Jew were presently lost to sight.

Meantime Belshazzar hurriedly rallied his men around him, had them quickly in order, and lined them before the opening, from which by this time doors and gates had been entirely torn away. The men of Guti were armoured and armed. The scent of battle came to their nostrils. They were at home with it. Their blood tingled with joy, and Belshazzar saw how they would fight for him, every man to the end.

Now came the first sharp volley of arrows and sling-stones from the multitude at the doors. Two or three of the guards fell. The ranks were quickly closed up and the volley answered.

Then the range became too short for bows. Men of Elam and Babylonish traitors were hand-to-hand with the defenders of the temple. In the semi-darkness it was hard to distinguish between friend and foe; and the struggle became as man to man. Shouts and cries ascended from the indivisible mass. In the midst of everything rose the trumpet tones of Belshazzar, crying encouragement to his men. But the rich and mellow voice of Cyrus was not to be heard giving commands to the other side. Cyrus was not here tonight. Only the open field and honourable combat were his. And he had left the dishonour of such a victory to Amraphel the high-priest, and Cambyses, his own son, who had asked for it.

In the temple, behind the ranks of the regiment of Guti, the royal eunuchs, creatures of silent courage and loyalty, had gathered together all the women into one group, round which, for protection, they and the lords of the council were piling the temple furniture into a barricade. Istar alone was not here. Since the first battle-cry no one had seen her; and now, in the excitement of the moment, she, being unseen, was also forgotten.

Baba, in her silks and chains, was with the women of Ribâta's household, all of whom their lord had placed carefully in one corner of the protecting barricade, behind a pile of divans and stone tables laid beside the sacrificial altar. In the rush of the moment Ribâta had but a word with his favourite slave. For an instant, however, he bent over her, to see that she was well protected, and in that time he pressed his lips as a seal against her forehead, muttering hurriedly, at the same time: "Courage, little one! Be not afraid. Our lives are in the hands of the great Bel. Pray to him, but do not weep".

And Baba answered readily, without any sign of fear: "My lord is my lord. I obey his word".

Then, as he left her side, the young girl lay back on the floor close against a couch that had been tipped beside her, and stayed there, silent and open-eyed, listening to the tumult of the battle round the door. The chorus of shouts and yells was deafening. Babylonish battle-cries mingled with Median phrases of triumph. And closer at hand, all around her, in fact, the women of high station lay wailing out their fright. Ribâta's two wives were near, crazed with terror for themselves, for their lord, for Babylon, for the king. Now and then, high above the general tumult, came the shrill, fierce voice of Belitsum, crying her anguish. Nabonidus was the name that continually left her lips, till Belshazzar himself, from the thickest of the fight, caught the syllables, and fought the more fiercely for the memory of his father.

While the men of Gutium held the door, there appeared to be nothing to fear for the women in the temple. Ribâta, before joining in the conflict, passed among his friends of the council, bidding them hold back a little from the thick of the fight, that, should it prove necessary, they might be unhurt to defend the women. The holders of the temple were in bad enough straits, to be sure, yet there was no immediate danger. Belshazzar's men, flanked by two bands of eunuchs and noblemen, who fought with sacrificial knives and axes, were for the moment holding all Babylon and the army of Cyrus at bay. Baba knew this, as she lay, quiet and silent, gazing up into the shadowy spaces of the roof. Presently, while all that terrible din sounded in her ears, with that throng of writhing, struggling, bleeding men twenty yards away, a little smile stretched itself over her lips, and her eyes fell shut. She lay wrapped in a vision of her own: a vision of fair fields and broad, blue water, where, on the shore, stood a man; a man whose hair shone like the sun, and who bore in his hands a five-stringed lyre. And presently, from out of the racket, she could hear the pure tones of Charmides' voice, singing, as he had always sung throughout his life, for love.

Baba was lying unconscious of her surroundings in this little ecstasy, when suddenly the low wailing of the women was heightened into loud cries of well-warranted horror. The little slave felt a new presence at hand. She lifted up her eyes, and saw something that caused her heart to rise into her throat. The barricade was breaking down before a band of armed temple-servants that were advancing to the murder of the women. A cold stream poured round Baba's heart, and for the first time tonight she screamed aloud. Her cry was answered by Ribâta, who was trying desperately to gather the lords out of the conflict at the door. But the fight there was going badly. More than half the defenders of the temple had fallen, and each of those that remained was pressed by half a dozen of the enemy. Many of the guards had been drawn out into the square and were keeping up the battle there while they lived. But it seemed all at once that the defence could not last many minutes more. Not a man could come to the rescue of the women caught in so terrible a trap. And in the faces of the inhuman creatures that threatened them, there was no hope for their lives. The murderers were nearly all of them Zicarû from the third college, which was Amraphel's own; and into their hearts hatred for the upper classes had been instilled for years. Now, as they looked upon their helpless prey, all the animal savagery of their race rose up in them, and their eyes sparkled and their lips twitched in the lust for blood. The wife of Nabû-Mashetic-Urrâ, one of the old councillors of Nabonidus, received the first blow. The knife of a seer struck her to the heart; and with that first gush of blood the general carnage began. Defenceless as they were, the women were roused to action. With their hands, their limbs, their teeth, the pins that fastened their hair, they fought uselessly for life. From the place where she lay half concealed, Baba watched the scenes of murder around her. The woman next her had been dodging the knife that continually pursued her, till, stabbed in a dozen places, hair and body dripping with her blood, she proffered her heart to the assassin, who mercifully plunged his dripping blade up to its hilt in her breast.

Baba gave a hoarse shriek, threw up her hands, and fell, face down, upon the floor. A second after a streak of fire ran deep into her right shoulder. Then, immediately, all the noise died away. The world reeled with her and became black; and for her this scene of incredible brutality was at an end.

Not so Belshazzar's desperate task. At the moment when the Zicarû, appearing from the back rooms of the temple, had set about the slaughter of the women, the king, in the midst of a little band of five soldiers, had pressed through the front ranks of the enemy, out into the temple square. This was packed with the city mob that had gathered from the feast in the temples of Nebo, Nergal, Istar and Sin, and come hither under the leadership of their officiating priests. In the darkness it was impossible to tell friend from foe. Belshazzar's self-constituted bodyguard fought madly to preserve his life; but, fifteen minutes after they had passed the temple doors, the last of them, wounded in twenty places, had fallen at the feet of his king, and Belshazzar of Babylon was alone with the darkness and with besetting death. Many set upon him where he stood on the eastern edge of the square; but perhaps none of his assailants knew him. He was armed only with a short sword taken from the hand of a dying Elamite; but with this weapon his execution was terrible. As man after man went down before his tigerish strength, the attention of many was drawn to him, and presently he found himself backing down a narrow and crooked street running out of the square, engaged with three men, variously armed, that vainly strove to fell him. An arrow stuck in the flesh of his right forearm, and there was a great gash upon one of his knees. He left behind him a trail of blood; but, in the heat of contest, he felt not a twinge of pain. The noise of the battle perceptibly diminished. He heard it vaguely, caring at this time very little how the fight was going. His adversaries pressed him hard; yet he smiled, as continually he beat them back. The brute, the tiger in him, was uppermost now. He had not a thought for anything but fighting. In his slow and certain way he had retreated perhaps 200 yards, and was approaching the house of one of the under-priests of Bel. From its open doorway a flood of light poured into the street, and as Belshazzar moved into the luminous spot a cry of recognition broke from the lips of his oppressors. At the same moment a white-robed figure came quickly out of the house, and, unseen by him, moved behind Belshazzar. In the moment that followed, a knife gleamed in the light behind the king. The blow fell. With a great cry Belshazzar reeled, sank to his knee, straightened up again with a superhuman effort, thrust weakly in the direction of the men in front, and sank back on the ground with a faint moan. At the same time his assassin, motioning the three soldiers to go back, stepped in front of his victim and bent over him.

"Amraphel!" muttered the king.

"Ay, Amraphel, thou dog! Amraphel, thou tyrant of the city! Amraphel, thou last ruler of a hated line! Amraphel, that stands at last alone in the land of his desire! Hear thou, then, the name of Amraphel. Know his everlasting hatred for thee and thine, and knowing – die!" Then, with his sandalled foot, the old man spurned the face of him that was fallen, hoping to bring some craven word to the lips of the king.

But Belshazzar was himself in death as in life. Gazing steadily into the face of the high-priest, he permitted himself to smile – a slight, scornful smile, such as he had sometimes worn during the sacrifice. Seeing it, the high-priest was goaded into a hot fury. With what strength he had he kicked the face of the dying man. Then, drawing his bloody skirts about him, he turned and passed once more into the house of the priest, out of Belshazzar's sight forever.

So at last the king lay alone, unmolested, with the night and with his thoughts. Babylon was fallen – was fallen the Great City, before the hand of no invader, but by treachery and stealth, by means of murder and of outrage. All this the king knew; yet no regret for the inevitable disturbed these final moments. Rather he turned his mind to that that was his alone, to that which constituted his true, his inner life, that made his great happiness, that had redeemed him from all mental pain – his supreme love for Istar the woman.

In that dim dream into which all surrounding things were fading, her name floated to his lips. Once, twice, thrice he repeated it to himself, lingeringly, adoringly, loving each syllable as he spoke it. He had no thought, no hope of seeing her again. She was somewhere, far away, in the midst of those direful scenes beyond him. He commended her to his gods as best he could. Then he thought of himself as at her side, the mist of her hair hiding the world from his eyes, the perfume of her breath causing his head to swim. He thought of her as she had been to him in the last months. And then – suddenly – she was with him.

Out of the gloom of the narrow street she came, searching after him, calling his name. The veil had fallen back from her pallid face. Her eyes were staring wide with fear and with the horror of blood. Her movement was slow, indeterminate, vague. Not till after he had watched her for a full minute did she come upon his figure in its pools of blood. Then, with a faint, fluttering cry she ran to him, only half-believing her poor vision. Their meeting was ineffable. She lay upon his body, eye on eye, lip on lip to him, her cries stifled by his gasping breath, her wandering hands caressing his hair, his brow, his neck, his bloody vestment. Not knowing what she did, she pulled the broken arrow from his arm, and then screamed to think of where it had been. Of the two, Belshazzar's state of mind was infinitely clearer, infinitely stronger than hers. It was with a supreme effort that he took his lips from hers that he might speak, might try to make her understand what this moment must be to them.

"Oh, thou art wounded, my king, my beloved! Look – here upon thee is blood – blood on the white of thy robe. Why art thou red?" she repeated, once and again, anxiously examining the wet, dark stains that flowed ever freshly from his body.

Belshazzar saw that her brain was turned, and his anguish became terrible. Was she to bid him good-bye like this? Must he leave her forever with the infinite unsaid? How could he bring her mind back to him, if but for one moment? He could not think. All that he could do was to say, thickly, with the blood in his mouth:

"Istar, beloved, I die! Dost thou hear?"

"Yea, Belshazzar, and I also. Allaraine hath written it upon the wall. Didst thou not see? 'Hast thou found man's relation to God? The silver sky waits for thy soul'. I also die".

"Thou!" he murmured, quickly. "Art thou wounded, Istar?" His feeble hands searched over her body, but felt no sign of blood. She had been untouched by any weapon. And now his eyes grew dull with suffering, and he said, faintly, and with reluctance: "Fare thee far and well, my Istar – Istar of my city. I go".

"Belshazzar!"

What it had been, tone or word of his, that roused her at last, the dying man could not tell. But that name rang through the night in a scream of living agony. Now she knew what it meant – that her Babylon was fallen around her – that the world was empty – that the lord of her life was passing – that henceforward her way lay through the valley of loneliness. What mattered now the writing on the wall, hopeless prophecy of her own death? Belshazzar was here, beneath her, dying; while she – Istar – his wife – had received no wound.

She raised him in her arms and their eyes met for the last time. How much passed in the look cannot be told, for it was a final mingling of souls. All their love, their infinite happiness, their sorrow, their tears unshed, the humanity of their two lives, was embodied in that look. Grief of parting was not there, for the two were striving to make parting endurable, each to each, by the look. It was finished at last, with Belshazzar's whispered words:

"In the silver sky, O my glorious one, I wait for thee!"

"O my beloved, wait for me! Wait for me!"

Then the body dropped inert in her arms. Belshazzar was gone. Istar was left alone in the world.

How long afterwards she rose from that place she did not know. Many people – soldiers of the invading army and men of the mob, with blood-dripping swords – had passed her as she lay along the ground, face down, beside the body. And none of these offered to molest her, for they thought that two dead lay there in the semi-darkness. The light in the house of the priest of Bel had gone out, and the shouts of conflict had long since been hushed. Still, through all the city, there was the murmur of uneasiness, of many men awake and stirring. The night was filled with stars, and with that curious white glow that comes in midsummer to the Orient. But it seemed strange that the skies did not turn from the hideous spectacle of Babylon that night.

Forth into the city, from the body that she loved, Istar went. Guided and protected by some divine spirit, she passed unhurt among groups of strange, uncouth warriors that laughed and talked in an unknown tongue. She crossed streets where dead lay piled together. For those that were loyal to the city had not been spared by the men of Amraphel. She passed houses in which sat women wailing out their terror through the long hours before the dawn; and came finally to the open doors of a small temple in which the feast of Tammuz had been celebrated through the day. Before this Istar paused. Inside she could see the glowing of the sacrificial lights and the disorderly desertion of the room – the long, empty tables covered with half-filled cups and plates, and the altar whence, from the smouldering fire, a thin stream of blue incense still poured upward. The woman's weary eyes saw these long, soft divans with a sense of desire and of relief. She entered the room and went quickly towards the nearest resting-place. She was about to lay herself down. Her eyes were all but closed under their weight of weariness, when suddenly, from the shadowy spaces beyond her, came a sound that caused her to start back from the couch, and hasten in nervous terror towards the door. It had been only the bleating of a little group of hungry sheep in their pen near the temple kitchen; yet the unexpected noise had shattered Istar's nerves, and she fared forth again out of the holy house into the long, winding streets of the city.

Whither she went, how far, with what purpose, no one knew, no one cared. She saw the river winding its tranquil way between well-stoned banks, with the shadows of vast buildings mirrored in its depths, while the glittering stars from their high dome shone like pale, white eyes in the glassy, lazily moving stream. Wandering Euphrates! Took it any heed of the deeds of good or evil performed upon its banks? God had bequeathed to it eternal calm, had made the sight of it an eternal balm for weary eyes. This night it brought peace on its waves and a promise of rest to the soul of the woman. As she stood gazing down into its baffling green, there came to her again the message from the kingdom, written in golden letters on the surface of the water. Again Istar read and again she wondered, yet in her soul understood the words:

"Hast thou found man's relation to God? The silver sky waits for thy soul".

Istar, in her great woe, stood looking upon the fiery words, that seemed to have burned themselves into her brain; and her whole heart rebelled against them. Those that she loved had been taken from her. With Belshazzar, the light of her life was extinguished. Man was bound to God only by great suffering, by grief, by heart-sorrow! A sob came into her throat, and there was anger in her mind as she would have turned away from the mystical words. But at that instant they flashed out into darkness, and the gleam was gone. For a moment the night grew thickly black, and Istar reeled where she stood. Afterwards she found herself walking on the bank of the river, only a little distance west of the spot where the huge temple of Marduk reared its bulk into the air. It was now in Istar's mind to go back to the place where Belshazzar's body lay, and to remain there at his side till dawn should banish the horrors of the night. But just as she would have left the river for the second time, there came out upon the path that ran along its bank a group of white-robed men, whom Istar knew for priests, bearing with them a heavy burden covered over with a purple cloth. At sight of them Istar turned suddenly dizzy and crouched on the bricks of the pavement.

Arrived at the edge of the river, the five priests of Amraphel's temple laid their burden on the ground and removed the cloth that covered it. Belshazzar's body was exposed to view. Istar, with a little moan, pressed both hands tightly across her breast. But neither sound nor movement attracted any attention from the priests. These now indulged in a short parley, that ended in their taking from the corpse the royal ornaments that covered it and dividing them evenly among the five.

"Now, Bel-shar-utsur, tyrant of the city, go down by river to plead with the Lady Mulge in Ninkigal for a drink from the spring of life; for thou shalt drink no more, in the Great City, of the wines of Helbon and Izalla!"

With this only farewell, three of them lifted the body up, swung it thrice in the air by the feet and by the head, and at the third swing let it fly out into the waters of the river that had so short a time before received the worn frame of the dead man's father.

As the body left their hands the priests were startled to hear a long, low cry that came from a few yards to the right. Looking, they saw a woman's figure run to the riverbank and peer into the waters below, where the body of the king, as on a funeral barge, went floating down towards the city of the dead that lay south of Babylon.

Without any attempt at accosting her who mourned, the men of Amraphel presently turned away and began their return to the temple, carrying with them the new wealth of jewels. Istar also rose, half consciously, and knowing neither any abiding-place where to lay her head, nor anyone to seek who could give her help, she moved away aimlessly down the bank of the stream. A few yards to the south there was a great ferry station, where, by day, a dozen boats were wont to ply back and forth across the stream. By night only one barge went its way backward and forward; and as Istar came down to the little quay the broad scow was just ready to start to the western shore with its load of men and soldiers. She ran quickly down the steps and on to this moving bridge. The west bank of the river was home to her. She knew its streets and its people. There, to the north, was the palace of Belshazzar, and the temple in which she had once dwelt. There, somewhere, she would find shelter.

When the barge finally touched the landing at the western shore and Istar, last of anyone, was about to leave it, she was stopped by one of the ferrymen.

"Lady, it is two *se* for the passage".

"Two *se*! Money? I have none", said Istar, slowly.

"Thou shalt not leave the barge till the price is paid", retorted the boatman, angrily.

But vaguely understanding what he meant, Istar pulled the veil from her face and fixed her great eyes upon him, the better to comprehend what it was he told her. The man gave a great start, for in the semi-darkness her marvellous beauty shone like a star. Then the rough fellow bent his head before her.

"It is the lady of Babylon! Great Istar, forgive our fault! Let it please thee to leave the barge!" he exclaimed, reverently.

Istar did not pause to wonder that he knew her. She saw that her way was open, and she went forth, up the steps, across the path at the top, and into the lower city. Too weary, too stricken for either rest or sleep, she felt her brain burn and her limbs grow cold as she walked. Now there was a fire in her veins; now they grew chill as the snows of Elam. In the pale grey of the dawn she trembled with sickness. The coming of day was not beautiful to her eyes. In the first pink flush from the east she found herself standing before a miserable hut on the border of a canal, and from the dark door-way came a voice crying in great fear:

"The plague! The plague! It is come upon us! Behold the gods visit their wrath upon men! Woe, woe to them that see light in Babylon today!"

Istar shuddered at the cry. From another place farther to the north the words of horror and grief were repeated. The reign of death was thus proclaimed in the city. Now there was a great ringing in Istar's ears. Lights shot up before her eyes. It seemed to her that over all the city, from the five millions of human tongues, rose that cry of woe: "The plague! The plague!"

The memory of her dead child was with her. A few more paces she staggered through, half consciously. Then, of a sudden, someone appeared beside her – someone whom she knew and had forgotten. At sight of the well-known face the woman's brain gave way. With a long, heartbroken sob, she fell helpless, lifeless, into the reverent arms of Charmides, her bard.

It was thus that, on the night of July 3d, in the year 538 BCE, Persian rule began in Babylon, and native rule in the Great City was ended forever....

Biographies & Sources

Fiona Collins
Foreword
Fiona Collins is a storyteller and author. She has been a professional storyteller of myths and legends for over 30 years. She has a special interest in the stories of ancient Sumer, and was a member of Zipang, a storytelling company specializing in stories from Mesopotamia, told in English for modern audiences. Zipang worked closely with Professor Jeremy Black's Electronic Text Corpus of Sumerian Literature. Fiona's version of 'Inana' can be heard on Zipang's CD 'Asag: Stories from Ancient Sumer' (Purple Patch Records). Now living in Wales, she has published eight collections of folktales in both languages of Wales.

Margaret Potter Horton
Istar of Babylon: A Phantasy
Margaret Potter Horton (1881–1911) was an American novelist who specialized in historical fiction. Her first novel, *A Social Lion*, was published while she was still a teenager. The book, modelled on actual people and events of Chicago, Illinois, was so scandalous that her family tried to prevent its publication. During her short writing career, Horton published ten novels, as well as numerous articles, short stories and poems. Horton married in 1902 and in about 1905 became addicted to morphine. In 1910 she was declared mentally incompetent due to chronic alcoholism and morphine addiction and institutionalized. In 1911 she was released from the hospital, but her husband divorced her and, shortly thereafter, she died from an accidental morphine overdose at age 30. Parts of her novel *Istar of Babylon: A Phantasy* (1902) are used in the present volume.

Samuel Noah Kramer
Myths of Creation, Myths of Kur
Samuel Noah Kramer (1897–1990) was one of the world's leading Assyriologists, an expert in Sumerian history and Sumerian language. Born in Russia, Kramer was taken to the United States in 1906. His early years were spent in Philadelphia. He studied at Dropsie College (1926–27) and the University of Pennsylvania in 1929. In 1930–31 he was in the field in Iraq and excavated at Tell Billah, Tepe Gawra and Fara. From 1932 to 1942 he was on the staff of the Oriental Institute, University of Chicago, specializing in the Sumerian language. From 1942 to 1968 he was associated with the University of Pennsylvania, as research associate in the Babylonian collection of the University Museum in 1942–43, associate curator of the tablet collection from 1943 to 1947, and curator of the tablet collection and Clark Research Professor of Assyriology from 1948 to 1968. In 1968–69 Kramer was at the University of Indiana where he gave the Patton Lectures. In 1970 he was appointed to the department of religious sciences at the Ecole Pratique des Hautes Etudes in Paris. Kramer's research and extensive travels in search of Sumerian literary texts have been fundamental in the reconstruction of Sumerian literature. Among scholars, his work is considered transformative for the field of Sumerian history. His popular book *History Begins at Sumer* made Sumerian literature accessible to the general public. He is the author of *Sumerian Mythology* (1946), selections from which are used in the present volume.

Donald A. Mackenzie

The Land of Rivers and the God of the Deep, Rival Pantheons and Representative Deities, Ashur the National god of Assyria, Demons, Fairies and Ghosts, Creation Legend: Merodach the Dragon Slayer, Astrology and Astronomy

Donald Alexander Mackenzie (1873–1936) was a Scottish journalist and folklorist and a prolific writer on religion, mythology and anthropology in the early twentieth century. Born in Cromarty, he became a journalist in Glasgow, later moving to be editor and/or owner of publications in Dingwall, Dundee and Edinburgh. He wrote nearly fifty books, mostly on ancient history and mythology, as well as articles and poems. He often gave lectures, and also broadcast talks on Celtic mythology. He is the author of *Myths of Babylonia and Assyria* (1915), selections of which are used in the present volume.

Robert W. Rogers

Adapa and the Food of Life

Robert William Rogers (1864–1930) was a fellow of the Royal Geographical Society and a renowned Semitist. He was Professor of Exegetical Theology at Drew Theological Seminary and author of multiple books, including *A History of Babylonia and Assyria*, *The Religion of Babylonia and Assyria*, *A History of Ancient Persia* and *Outlines of History in Early Babylonia*. He is the translator and editor of *Cuneiform Parallels to the Old Testament* (1912), which is used in the present volume.

Lewis Spence

From *Priestly Magicians, Wizards and Witches* to *Omens and the Practice of Liver-reading; Mythological Monsters & Animals; Tales of Kings*

James Lewis Thomas Chalmers Spence (1874–1955) was a Scottish journalist, poet, author, folklorist and occult scholar. After graduating from Edinburgh University he pursued a career in journalism, during which time his interest was sparked in the myth and folklore of Mexico and Central America. Spence was a Fellow of the Royal Anthropological Institute of Great Britain and Ireland, and vice-president of the Scottish Anthropological and Folklore Society. He also founded the Scottish National Movement. Over his long career, Spence published more than forty books of history and mythology. He was also a published poet. He is the author of *Myths and Legends of Babylonia and Assyria* (1916), selections of which are used in the present volume.

R. Campbell Thompson

The Epic of Gilgamesh

Reginald Campbell Thompson (1876–1941) was a British archaeologist, Assyriologist and cuneiformist. He entered Caius College Cambridge in 1895 where he read Oriental (Hebrew and Aramaic) Languages; in 1897 he won the Stewart of Rannoch Hebrew Scholarship and was put in the First Class in the Oriental Tripos the following year. In 1899 he was appointed an assistant in the Egyptian and Assyrian Department of The British Museum where he worked until his resignation in December 1905. He subsequently held the post of Assistant Professor of Semitic Languages in the University of Chicago (1907–09). He travelled the world in search of antiquities, and excavated at Nineveh, Ur, Nebo and Carchemish among numerous sites. In addition to over a dozen books on Assyrian history, he also wrote fiction and poetry. His translation of the epic of Gilgamesh (1928, originally spelt 'Gilgamish' in his version) is used in the present volume.

The Electronic Text Corpus of Sumerian Literature (ETCSL)
Lugalbanda and Enmerkar, Other Stories, City Laments, Ninguszida's Journey to the Nether World, How Grain Came to Sumer, The Sumunda Grass
Edited by J.A. Black, G. Cunningham, J. Ebeling, E. Flückiger-Hawker, E. Robson, J. Taylor and G. Zólyomi, The Electronic Text Corpus of Sumerian Literature (http://etcsl.orinst.ox.ac.uk/), Oxford 1998–2006, is a project of the University of Oxford. It comprises a selection of nearly 400 literary compositions recorded on sources which come from ancient Mesopotamia (modern Iraq) and date to the late third and early second millennia BCE. The corpus contains Sumerian texts in transliteration, English prose translations and bibliographical information for each composition. Nineteen texts from the ETCSL are featured, with permission, in the present volume.

GOTHIC FANTASY